The Editor

ALBERT J. RIVERO is Professor of English at Marquette University. He is author of *The Plays of Henry Fielding: A Critical Study of His Dramatic Career* and editor of *New Essays on Samuel Richardson*, *Augustan Subjects: Essays in Honor of Martin C. Battestin*, and *Critical Essays on Henry Fielding*. He is the editor of the Norton Critical Edition of *Gulliver's Travels*.

W. W. NORTON & COMPANY, INC.
Also Publishes

ENGLISH RENAISSANCE DRAMA: A NORTON ANTHOLOGY
edited by David Bevington et al.

THE NORTON ANTHOLOGY OF AFRICAN AMERICAN LITERATURE
edited by Henry Louis Gates Jr. and Nellie Y. McKay et al.

THE NORTON ANTHOLOGY OF AMERICAN LITERATURE
edited by Nina Baym et al.

THE NORTON ANTHOLOGY OF CHILDREN'S LITERATURE
edited by Jack Zipes et al.

THE NORTON ANTHOLOGY OF DRAMA
edited by J. Ellen Gainor, Stanton B. Garner Jr., and Martin Puchner

THE NORTON ANTHOLOGY OF ENGLISH LITERATURE
edited by M. H. Abrams and Stephen Greenblatt et al.

THE NORTON ANTHOLOGY OF LITERATURE BY WOMEN
edited by Sandra M. Gilbert and Susan Gubar

THE NORTON ANTHOLOGY OF MODERN AND CONTEMPORARY POETRY
edited by Jahan Ramazani, Richard Ellmann, and Robert O'Clair

THE NORTON ANTHOLOGY OF POETRY
edited by Margaret Ferguson, Mary Jo Salter, and Jon Stallworthy

THE NORTON ANTHOLOGY OF SHORT FICTION
edited by R. V. Cassill and Richard Bausch

THE NORTON ANTHOLOGY OF THEORY AND CRITICISM
edited by Vincent B. Leitch et al.

THE NORTON ANTHOLOGY OF WORLD LITERATURE
edited by Sarah Lawall et al.

THE NORTON FACSIMILE OF THE FIRST FOLIO OF SHAKESPEARE
prepared by Charlton Hinman

THE NORTON INTRODUCTION TO LITERATURE
edited by Alison Booth and Kelly J. Mays

THE NORTON READER
edited by Linda H. Peterson and John C. Brereton

THE NORTON SAMPLER
edited by Thomas Cooley

THE NORTON SHAKESPEARE, BASED ON THE OXFORD EDITION
edited by Stephen Greenblatt et al.

For a complete list of Norton Critical Editions, visit
www.wwnorton.com/college/English/nce_home.htm

A NORTON CRITICAL EDITION

Daniel Defoe

MOLL FLANDERS

AN AUTHORITATIVE TEXT

CONTEXTS

CRITICISM

Edited by

ALBERT J. RIVERO
MARQUETTE UNIVERSITY

W • W • NORTON & COMPANY • *New York* • *London*

W. W. Norton & Company has been independent since its founding in 1923, when William Warder and Mary D. Herter Norton first published lectures delivered at the People's Institute, the adult education division of New York City's Cooper Union. The Nortons soon expanded their program beyond the Institute, publishing books by celebrated academics from America and abroad. By mid-century, the two major pillars of Norton's publishing program—trade books and college texts—were firmly established. In the 1950s, the Norton family transferred control of the company to its employees, and today—with a staff of four hundred and a comparable number of trade, college, and professional titles published each year—W. W. Norton & Company stands as the largest and oldest publishing house owned wholly by its employees.

This title is printed on permanent paper containing
30 percent post-consumer waste recycled fiber.

Printed in the United States of America.
First Edition.

The text of this book is composed in Fairfield Medium
with the display set in Bernhard Modern.
Composition by Binghamton Valley Composition, Inc.
Manufacturing by the Courier Companies—Westford division.
Book design by Antonina Krass.
Production manager: Ben Reynolds.

Library of Congress Cataloging-in-Publication Data

Defoe, Daniel, 1661?–1731.
Moll Flanders: an authoritative text, contexts, criticism / Daniel Defoe;
edited by Albert J. Rivero.
p. cm.—(Norton critical edition)
Includes bibliographical references (p.).

ISBN 0-393-97862-1 (pbk.)

1. Defoe, Daniel, 1661?–1731. Fortunes and misfortunes of the famous Moll Flanders. 2. Children of prisoners—Fiction. 3. British—Virginia—Fiction. 4. Women—England—Fiction. 5. London (England)—Fiction. 6. Prostitutes—Fiction. 7. Repentance—Fiction. 8. Criminals—Fiction. 9. Virginia—Fiction. I. Rivero, Albert J., 1953– II. Title. III. Series.

PR3404.M6 2003

823'.5—dc22 2003060948

W. W. Norton & Company, Inc., 500 Fifth Avenue, New York, N.Y. 10110
www.wwnorton.com

W. W. Norton & Company Ltd., Castle House,
75/76 Wells Street, London W1T 3QT

6 7 8 9 0

Contents

Preface

Published in London on January 27, 1722, by W. Chetwood and T. Edlin (misspelled "Edling" on the title page), *The Fortunes and Misfortunes of the Famous Moll Flanders* was famous enough to warrant a "second edition corrected" in July, "printed for, and sold by" T. Edlin, W. Chetwood, W. Mears, J. Brotherton, C. King, and J. Stagg (misspelled "Stags"), as well as another "second edition, corrected," this one "printed for John Brotherton" alone. Near the end of the year two issues of the "third edition, corrected" appeared, one "printed for John Brotherton," the other "printed for, and sold by" the same six publishers who had collaborated on the second edition. Except for different title pages and minor textual variations, the second and third editions offer essentially the same text, an abridgement of the first edition which, while sometimes correcting errors, introduces others, the publishers' main goal apparently being the reduction of the length of the book to save paper and decrease other printing costs. It is thus more proper to speak, as previous editors have argued, of a first edition and four issues of the second, though, until such modern editors of the novel as Herbert Davis and J. Paul Hunter began to cast doubts on Defoe's involvement in its publication, the "third" edition was thought to be the most authoritative. Therefore, most readers of *Moll Flanders*, from the eighteenth century through the first six decades of the twentieth, read the novel either in its reduced "third" edition or in abridgements or chapbook versions not by Defoe. In agreement with current critical consensus, the text of the new Norton Critical Edition of *Moll Flanders* is based on that of the first edition. Although I have silently corrected some obvious typographical errors, I have tried to reproduce the original text as closely as possible, including its original punctuation, altered only (and very rarely) to avoid confusion, and adopting readings from the second edition only in those cases where they improve the sense. I have also changed all instances of "whether" to "whither" and substituted "then" for "than" and "than" for "then" when the immediate context calls for such correction. In a more radical move, explained more fully below (pp. 269–72), I have amended the text to eliminate the muddle caused by the contradictory passages appearing near the end of the narrative—a textual problem first identified by J. Paul

Hunter in his edition of the novel in 1970—by implementing the solution persuasively advanced by Rodney M. Baine in 1972 (see bibliography) that, since the second passage was very likely meant to supplant the first, the first passage should be deleted and replaced with the second.

The varied textual history of *Moll Flanders* in the first two decades or so after its publication suggests that, beginning with its original publishers, the work was marketed to appeal to as many segments of the public as possible, from those whose attention spans would hold through over four hundred pages of text (in the first edition) to those whose reading skills needed the aid of woodcuts (in chapbooks). Though not approaching the huge popularity of *Robinson Crusoe* (1719), Defoe's first work of prose fiction and one of the best-sellers of all time, *Moll Flanders* succeeded in a marketplace of readers, of varying degrees of literacy, eager to consume all kinds of printed matter, especially "histories" purporting to tell the true yet surprising adventures of men and women who, though usually of humble if not obscure origins, find themselves in extraordinary circumstances that test both their mettle and (at times) their readers' credulity. The variety of Moll's life, as advertised on the title page, suggests several potential audiences, ranging from readers of spiritual biographies and autobiographies (tempted by the word "penitent"), to readers of amatory fiction (seduced by the word "wife" and the hint of incest), to readers of criminal biographies (enticed by those inevitably conjoined words "whore" and "thief"). But the "low" cast of Moll's story, coupled with its dissemination in emphatically downmarket formats like chapbooks and ballads, ensured that the reading of it would be identified primarily with the lower classes. Thus, an anonymous couplet appearing on March 1, 1729, in *The Flying Post; or Weekly Medley*—a periodical long hostile to Defoe and, therefore, more likely interested in political point-scoring than cultural criticism—scoffs that "Down in the kitchen, honest Dick and Doll / Are studying Colonel Jack and Flanders Moll." In a similar vein, in the first plate of *Industry and Idleness* (1747), William Hogarth shows the idle apprentice asleep at his loom under the ballad of *Moll Flanders*—the initial fatal step, it turns out, on his way to the gallows. It would not be until after the publication of Samuel Richardson's *Pamela* (1740) that upper-class readers would be willing to come out of their reading closets to declare their predilection for "low" reading material. It would be at that point, in a story frequently told by literary historians, that the elevation and legimitization of the English novel would begin, as Richardson and Henry Fielding, occluding their debts to those who came before them—women novelists like Aphra Behn, Delarivier Manley, and Eliza Haywood, not to mention Daniel Defoe—staked their rival claims to have founded a new species of writing.

Defoe's major contribution to the making of the English novel has long been recognized, though at times his fictional works have been all too easily dismissed as little more than artless reportage. As Ian Watt argued in *The Rise of the Novel* (1957), the hallmark of Defoe's fiction—and of the novel in general—is "formal realism," a term one may roughly define as the author's concern with depicting physical objects or other aspects of his characters' world in their fullness. In Watt's view, the fictions of Defoe and Richardson exhibit formal realism while Fielding's show "realism of assessment," a more abstract concept referring to ways of structuring narrative that takes into account techniques beyond the representational. For Watt, moreover, the "rise" of the novel is tied to the emergence of the middle class and to the increase in literacy in eighteenth-century Britain. As many readers of Watt's book have noted, his argument is at times circular and based on little if any historical evidence, not to mention that his use of the term "realism" is not very precise. Moreover, his focus on three male writers and virtual exclusion of women authors make his story of the rise of the novel historically untenable. Yet, as an explanation of what happens in Defoe's fiction, Watt's thesis is difficult to best. Whether transcribing Crusoe's account of his building of his fortifications or describing the mechanics of Moll's stealing of a watch and her subsequent ramble through London streets his readers would have been familiar with, Defoe focuses our attention on details that, in the aggregate, give us an illusion of reality, of life lived in the world as we know it. We occasionally catch glimpses of this kind of realism in previous English fiction, but it is Defoe who first manages to sustain this illusion for whole narratives. Defoe's remarkable recreations of the worlds of a stranded mariner in *Robinson Crusoe*, of a man trying to hold on to his sense of self as the city of London collapses around him in *A Journal of the Plague Year* (1722), and of women struggling to survive by the sheer force of their wills and wits in *Moll Flanders* and *Roxana* (1724) appear so artless precisely because they are so artful.

Fortunately for Defoe, his artistic achievement has been recognized and celebrated, even if, at times, reluctantly. The last half of the twentieth century, for example, saw the publication of many important books and articles examining his fictional works in such wide-ranging contexts as criminal biography, economics, the Puritan tradition of spiritual biography and autobiography, and British social and political history. *Moll Flanders*, in particular, became the object of intense critical scrutiny in the 1960s and 1970s, when the extent of Defoe's control over the novel's irony was fiercely debated. Is the novel, critics asked, consciously ironic or is its irony a function of something else—perhaps, given its rough grammar and syntax, of the author's hasty and careless writing? Framed in those terms, the controversy generated more heat than light, as Defoe gained or lost ground depending on the critic's assessment of his presumed command over the work's irony. With the advent of feminist criticism, the degree to which *Moll Flanders* is a feminist or antifeminist novel became the topic of critical discussion. Is Defoe, in impersonating a woman, advancing the cause of women's liberation from the restraints imposed by a patriarchal society? Or should we question the motives of a male author who, like Defoe and Richardson, engages in literary transvestism? Should we suspect that, rather than liberating his heroines, Defoe is actually coopting them? After all, Moll repents of her acts of transgression and is punished for them, while Roxana, as her narrative breaks off, is racked with guilt over her crimes and terrified of the horrible retribution yet to come. As with the contention over its irony, the controversy over its feminism, while of necessity inconclusive, proved that *Moll Flanders* remained culturally relevant even as critical trends changed, a situation still true today, as the novel continues to generate passionate conversations among critics of varied methodologies and political orientations. Whether interpreted as ironic, feminist or antifeminist, based on criminal biographies, or the product of its author's dissenting background, Defoe's enigmatic text continues to fascinate, challenge, and, as most readers can testify, entertain us.

While I am indebted to previous editors of *Moll Flanders*, I have based my annotations on my own research into primary and secondary sources. I have derived my definitions primarily from the *Oxford English Dictionary*, though I have also consulted the first edition of Johnson's *Dictionary* (1755) and Eric Partridge's *A Dictionary of Slang and Unconventional English*. From the seemingly inexhaustible archive of contextual materials, I have selected a few items—excerpts from sequels, criminal biographies, and the legal codes of Maryland and Virginia—that will help twenty-first-century students situate the novel in its historical milieu. Of the many excellent critical assessments of *Moll Flanders*, I have reprinted a representative sampling, reflecting various critical methodologies, of the best recent work done on the novel; I have also chosen these critical pieces because of their accessibility to undergraduates.

This edition of *Moll Flanders* would not have been possible without the help and encouragement of many friends and colleagues. Carol Bemis invited me to undertake the project and, whenever called upon, offered her usual expert guidance. Having published a groundbreaking edition of the novel thirty years ago and at work on another, J. Paul Hunter generously shared his editorial discoveries and knowledge of a text few know as well as he does. Paula Backscheider not only agreed to take time out from her busy schedule to rewrite a section of her biography of Defoe for this edition, but also, from the very beginning, provided excellent advice on textual and contextual matters. Ian Bell, Max Novak, and John Richetti gave good counsel and (as Moll would phrase it) kept money in my pocket by making publishers' fees considerably dwindle or completely disappear. Scott Simpkins and Hans Turley were equally bountiful in granting the permissions they controlled. Ellen Pollak alerted me to a revised version of her essay and was instrumental in securing permission to reprint it. Jonathan Arac, Alison Conway, Claudia L. Johnson, George Justice, Linda Zionkowski, and Lisa Zunshine intervened at crucial points. I am grateful to many people at the Marquette University Library, especially the indefatigable Christopher Daniel, who, by ordering microfilms and photocopies of primary sources, greatly expedited my research; similar thanks are due to Carla Zecher and her assistants at the Newberry Library. I am also indebted to the staffs of the British Library and the University of Chicago Library for their assistance. Finally, as always, I owe my most heartfelt gratitude to my wife, Lisa, and my son, Albert Harley, for their love, support, and bemused tolerance of my obsession with all things Moll.

The Text of
MOLL FLANDERS

THE
FORTUNES
AND
MISFORTUNES

Of the FAMOUS

Moll Flanders, &c.

Who was Born in NEWGATE, and during a Life of continu'd Variety for Threescore Years, besides her Childhood, was Twelve Year a *Whore*, five times a *Wife* (whereof once to her own Brother) Twelve Year a *Thief*, Eight Year a Transported *Felon* in *Virginia*, at last grew *Rich*, liv'd *Honest*, and died a *Penitent*.

Written from her own MEMORANDUMS.

LONDON: Printed for, and Sold by W. CHETWOOD, at *Cato's-Head*, in *Russel-street*, *Covent-Garden*; and T. EDLING, at the *Prince's-Arms*, over-against *Exerter-Change* in the *Strand*. MDDCXXI.

THE PREFACE.

THE World is so taken up of late with Novels and Romances, that it will be hard for a private History[1] to be taken for Genuine, where the Names and other Circumstances of the Person are concealed, and on this Account we must be content to leave the Reader to pass his own Opinion upon the ensuing Sheets, and take it just as he pleases.

THE Author is here suppos'd to be writing her own History, and in the very beginning of her Account, she gives the Reasons why she thinks fit to conceal her true Name, after which there is no Occasion to say any more about that.

IT is true, that the original of this Story is put into new Words, and the Stile of the famous Lady we here speak of is a little alter'd, particularly she is made to tell her own Tale in modester Words than she told it at first; the Copy which came first to Hand, having been written in Language more like one still in *Newgate*,[2] than one grown Penitent and Humble, as she afterwards pretends[3] to be.

THE Pen employ'd in finishing her Story, and making it what you now see it to be, has had no little difficulty to put it into a Dress fit to be seen, and to make it speak Language fit to be read: When a Woman debauch'd from her Youth, nay, even being the Off-spring of Debauchery and Vice, comes to give an Account of all her vicious Practises, and even to descend to the particular Occasions and Circumstances, by which she first became wicked; and of all the progression of Crime which she run through in threescore Year, an

1. Echoing a commonplace of the period, Defoe argues for the historical authenticity of his work; in the preface to *Roxana* (1724), for example, he claims that, since "*the* Foundation *of This is laid in Truth of* Fact . . . *the Work is not a Story, but a History*." He thus distinguishes his "private History" from such fictional narratives as Eliza Haywood's lubricious *Love in Excess* (1719), also published by William Chetwood (the publisher of *Moll Flanders*) and identified as "a novel" on its title page, and from such scandalous romances or "secret histories" as Delariviere Manley's politically charged *The New Atalantis* (1709).
2. London's most famous (and infamous) prison for serious offenders. Defoe was imprisoned there in 1703 (May–November) on the charge of publishing a "seditious pamphlet," *The Shortest Way with the Dissenters* (1702).
3. Asserts or alleges, not necessarily with intent to deceive.

Author must be hard put to it to wrap it up so clean, as not to give room, especially for vitious Readers to turn it to his Disadvantage.

ALL possible Care however has been taken to give no leud[4] Ideas, no immodest Turns in the new dressing up this Story, no not to the worst parts of her Expressions; to this Purpose some of the vicious part of her Life, which cou'd not be modestly told, is quite left out, and several other Parts are very much shortn'd; what is left 'tis hop'd will not offend the chastest Reader, or the modestest Hearer: and as the best use is made even of the worst Story, the Moral 'tis hop'd will keep the Reader serious, even where the Story might incline him to be otherwise: To give the History of a wicked Life repented of, necessarily requires that the wick'd Part should be made as wicked, as the real History of it will bear; to illustrate and give a Beauty to the Penitent part, which is certainly the best and brightest, if related with equal Spirit and Life.

IT is suggested there cannot be the same Life, the same Brightness and Beauty, in relating the penitent Part, as is in the criminal Part: If there is any Truth in that Suggestion, I must be allow'd to say, 'tis because there is not the same taste and relish in the Reading, and indeed it is too true that the difference lyes not in the real worth of the Subject; so much as in the Gust[5] and Palate of the Reader.

BUT as this Work is chiefly recommended to those who know how to Read it, and how to make the good Uses of it, which the Story all along recommends to them; so it is to be hop'd that such Readers will be much more pleas'd with the Moral, than the Fable, with the Application,[6] than with the Relation; and with the End of the Writer, than with the Life of the Person written of.

THERE is in this Story abundance of delightful Incidents, and all of them usefully apply'd. There is an agreeable turn Artfully given them in the relating, that naturally Instructs the Reader, either one way, or other. The first part of her leud Life with the young Gentleman at *Colchester*, has so many happy Turns given it to expose the Crime, and warn all whose Circumstances are adapted to it, of the ruinous End of such things, and the foolish Thoughtless and abhorr'd Conduct of both the Parties, that it abundantly attones for all the lively Discription she gives of her Folly and Wickedness.

THE Repentance of her Lover at the *Bath*, and how brought by the just alarm of his fit of Sickness to abandon her; the just Caution given there against even the lawful Intimacies of the dearest Friends, and how unable they are to preserve the most solemn Resolutions

4. Lewd.
5. Individual taste, liking, or inclination.
6. Practical lesson derived from a general statement. As appears below, Defoe is borrowing the word from homiletics, to signify the "religious Uses" to which a preacher "applies" a "doctrine" after "opening" (i.e., interpreting) a biblical text.

of Vertue without divine Assistance; these are Parts, which to a just Discernment will appear to have more real Beauty in them, than all the amorous Chain of Story, which introduces it.

IN a Word, as the whole Relation is carefully garbl'd[7] of all the Levity, and Looseness that was in it: So it is all applied, and with the utmost care to vertuous and religious Uses. None can without being guilty of manifest Injustice, cast any Reproach upon it, or upon our Design in publishing it.

THE Advocates for the Stage, have in all Ages made this the great Argument to persuade People that their Plays are useful, and that they ought to be allow'd in the most civiliz'd, and in the most religious Government; Namely, That they are applyed to vertuous Purposes, and that by the most lively Representations, they fail not to recommend Vertue and generous Principles, and to discourage and expose all sorts of Vice and Corruption of Manners; and were it true that they did so, and that they constantly adhered to that Rule, as the Test of their acting on the *Theatre*, much might be said in their Favour.

THROUGHOUT the infinite variety of this Book, this Fundamental[8] is most strictly adhered to; there is not a wicked Action in any Part of it, but is first or last rendered Unhappy and Unfortunate: There is not a superlative Villain brought upon the Stage, but either he is brought to an unhappy End, or brought to be a Penitent: There is not an ill thing mention'd, but it is condemn'd, even in the Relation, nor a vertuous just Thing, but it carries its Praise along with it: What can more exactly answer the Rule laid down, to recommend, even those Representations of things which have so many other just Objections lying against them? Namely, of Example, of bad Company, obscene Language, and the like.

UPON this Foundation this Book is recommended to the Reader, as a Work from every part of which something may be learned, and some just and religious Inference is drawn, by which the Reader will have something of Instruction, if he pleases to make use of it.

ALL the Exploits of this Lady of Fame, in her Depredations upon Mankind stand as so many warnings to honest People to beware of them, intimating to them by what Methods innocent People are drawn in, plunder'd and robb'd, and by Consequence how to avoid them. Her robbing a little innocent Child, dress'd fine by the vanity of the Mother, to go to the Dancing-School, is a good Memento to such People hereafter; as is likewise her picking the Gold-Watch from the young Ladies side in the *Park*.

HER getting a parcel from a hair-brained Wench at the Coaches

7. Cleansed.
8. I.e., fundamental principle.

in St. *John-street*; her Booty made at the Fire, and again at *Harwich*; all give us excellent Warnings in such Cases to be more present to ourselves in sudden Surprizes of every Sort.

HER application to a sober Life, and industrious Management at last in *Virginia*, with her Transported Spouse, is a Story fruitful of Instruction, to all the unfortunate Creatures who are oblig'd to seek their Re-establishment abroad; whether by the Misery of Transportation,[9] or other Disaster; letting them know, that Diligence and Application have their due Encouragement, even in the remotest Parts of the World, and that no Case can be so low, so despicable, or so empty of Prospect, but that an unwearied Industry will go a great way to deliver us from it, will in time raise the meanest Creature to appear again in the World, and give him a new Cast[1] for his Life.

THESE are a few of the serious Inferences which we are led by the Hand to in this Book, and these are fully sufficient to Justifie any Man in recommending it to the World, and much more to Justifie the Publication of it.

THERE are two of the most beautiful Parts still behind,[2] which this Story gives some idea of, and lets us into the Parts of them, but they are either of them too long to be brought into the same Volume; and indeed are, *as I may call them* whole Volumes of themselves, (*viz.*) I. The Life of her Governess, as she calls her, who had run thro', it seems in a few Years all the eminent degrees of a Gentlewoman, a Whore, and a Bawd; a Midwife, and a Midwife-keeper, as *they are call'd*, a Pawn-broker, a Child-taker, a Receiver of Thieves, and of Thieves purchase, that is to say, of stolen Goods; and in a Word, her self a Thief, a Breeder up of Thieves, and the like, and yet at last a Penitent.

THE second is the Life of her Transported Husband, a Highwayman; who it seems liv'd a twelve Years Life of successful Villany upon the Road, and even at last came off so well, as to be a Voluntier Transport, not a Convict; and in whose Life there is an incredible Variety.

BUT as I have said, these are things too long to bring in here, so neither can I make a Promise of their coming out by themselves.[3]

WE cannot say indeed, that this History is carried on quite to the End of the Life of this famous *Moll Flanders*, as she calls her self,

9. Since the middle of the seventeenth century, to relieve prison overcrowding and sometimes in lieu of execution, convicted criminals were transported to the English colonies in America to work off their sentences under conditions often resembling slavery.
1. Roll of the dice, chance. *Appear again in the World*: Make a fresh start in society.
2. Yet to come.
3. Always alert to future marketing possibilities, Defoe here sets up expectations for sequels or spinoffs. Although several such publications appeared, none can be attributed to him. For example, *Fortune's Fickle Distribution* (1730) offers the reader, in three parts, a condensed version of the life and death of Moll Flanders; the life of Jane Hackabout, her governess; and the life of James Mac-Faul, her Lancashire husband.

for no Body can write their own Life to the full End of it, unless they can write it after they are dead; but her Husband's Life being written by a third Hand, gives a full Account of them both, how long they liv'd together in that Country, and how they came both to *England* again, after about eight Year, in which time they were grown very Rich, and where she liv'd it seems, to be very old; but was not so extraordinary a Penitent, as she was at first; it seems only that indeed she always spoke with abhorence of her former Life, and of every Part of it.

In her last Scene at *Maryland*, and *Virginia*, many pleasant things happen'd, which makes that part of her Life very agreeable, but they are not told with the same Elegancy as those accounted for by her-self; so it is still to the more Advantage that we break off here.

THE HISTORY AND MISFORTUNES Of the FAMOUS *Moll Flanders*, &c.

My True Name is so well known in the Records, or Registers at *Newgate*, and in the *Old-Baily*,[1] and there are some things of such Consequence still depending there, relating to my particular Conduct, that it is not to be expected I should set my Name, or the Account of my Family to this Work; perhaps, after my Death it may be better known, at present it would not be proper, no, not tho' a general Pardon should be issued, even without Exceptions and reserve of Persons or Crimes.

It is enough to tell you, that as some of my worst Comrades, who are out of the Way of doing me Harm, having gone out of the World by the Steps and the String[2] as I often expected to go, know[3] me by the Name of *Moll Flanders*; so you may give me leave to speak of myself, under that Name till I dare own who I have been, as well as who I am.

I Have been told, that in one of our Neighbour Nations, whether it be in *France*, or where else, I know not; they have an Order from the King, that when any Criminal is condemn'd, either to Die, or to the Gallies,[4] or to be Transported, if they leave any Children, as such

1. A criminal court, located next to Newgate prison.
2. The ladder (steps) leading up to the hangman's noose (string).
3. Changed to "knew" in the second edition.
4. I.e., Galleys. Moll is referring to the punishment whereby a convict was forced to man an oar in a galley ship.

are generally unprovided for, by the Poverty or Forfeiture of their Parents; so they are immediately taken into the Care of the Government, and put into an Hospital call'd the *House* of *Orphans*, where they are Bred up, Cloath'd, Fed, Taught, and when fit to go out, are plac'd out to Trades, or to Services, so as to be well able to provide for themselves by an honest industrious Behaviour.

HAD this been the Custom in our Country, I had not been left a poor desolate Girl without Friends, without Cloaths, without Help or Helper in the World, as was my Fate; and by which, I was not only expos'd to very great Distress, even before I was capable, either of Understanding my Case, or how to Amend it, nor brought into a Course of Life, which was not only scandalous in itself, but which in its ordinary Course, tended to the swift Destruction both of Soul and Body.

BUT the Case was otherwise here, my Mother was convicted of Felony for a certain petty Theft, scarce worth naming, (*viz.*) Having an opportunity of borrowing three Pieces of fine *Holland*,[5] of a certain Draper in *Cheapside*: The Circumstances are too long to repeat, and I have heard them related so many Ways, that I can scarce be certain, which is the right Account.

HOWEVER it was, this they all agree in, that my Mother pleaded her Belly,[6] and being found quick with Child; she was respited for about seven Months, in which time having brought me into the World, and being about again, she was call'd Down, as they term it, to her former Judgment, but obtain'd the Favour of being Transported to the Plantations, and left me about Half a Year old; and in bad Hands you may be sure.

THIS is too near the first Hours of my Life, for me to relate any-thing of myself, but by hear say, 'tis enough to mention, that as I was born in such an unhappy Place, I had no Parish[7] to have Recourse to for my Nourishment in my Infancy, nor can I give the least Account how I was kept alive; other, than that as I have been told, some Relation of my Mothers took me away for a while as a Nurse, but at whose Expence, or by whose Direction I know nothing at all of it.

THE first account that I can Recollect, or could ever learn of myself, was, that I had wandred among a Crew of those People they

5. Linen fabric, from the province of Holland in the Netherlands.
6. Claimed to be pregnant, since pregnant women could not be executed. Unless pardoned or (as in the case of Moll's mother) transported to the American plantations, they would be put to death after delivery.
7. Under the provisions of the Act of Settlement of the Poor (1662), a parish was obligated to care for its destitute and for orphans or abandoned children born within its boundaries. If Moll's claim is correct, those born in Newgate were apparently excluded from parish assistance.

call *Gypsies*,[8] or *Egyptians*; but I believe it was but a very little while that I had been among them, for I had not had my Skin discolour'd, or blacken'd, as they do very young to all the Children they carry about with them, nor can I tell how I came among them, or how I got from them.

IT was at *Colchester* in *Essex*, that those People left me; and I have a Notion in my Head, that I left them there, (that is, that I hid myself and wou'd not go any farther with them) but I am not able to be particular in that Account; only this I remember, that being taken up by some of the Parish Officers of *Colchester*, I gave an Account, that I came into the Town with the *Gypsies*, but that I would not go any farther with them, and that so they had left me, but whither they were gone that I knew not, nor could they expect it of me; for tho' they sent round the Country to enquire after them, it seems they could not be found.

I WAS now in a Way to be provided for; for tho' I was not a Parish Charge upon this, or that part of the Town by Law; yet as my Case came to be known, and that I was too young to do any Work, being not above three Years old, Compassion mov'd the Magistrates of the Town to order some Care to be taken of me, and I became one of their own, as much as if I had been born in the Place.

IN the Provision they made for me, it was my good hap[9] to be put to Nurse, as they call it, to a Woman who was indeed Poor, but had been in better Circumstances, and who got a little Livelihood by taking such as I was suppos'd to be; and keeping them with all Necessaries, till they were at a certain Age, in which it might be suppos'd they might go to Service, or get their own Bread.

THIS Woman had also a little School, which she kept to teach Children to Read and to Work; and having, as I have said, liv'd before that in good Fashion, she bred up the Children she took with a great deal of Art, as well as with a great deal of Care.

BUT that which was worth all the rest, she bred them up very Religiously, being herself a very sober pious Woman. (2.) Very Housewifly and Clean, and, (3.) Very Mannerly, and with good Behaviour: So that in a Word, excepting a plain Diet, course[1] Lodging, and mean Cloths, we were brought up as Mannerly and as Genteely, as if we had been at the Dancing School.

I WAS continu'd here till I was eight years Old, when I was terrified

8. Though believed to have come from Egypt because of their dark skin, gypsies were of Hindu origin; they began to appear in England about the beginning of the sixteenth century. In *Joseph Andrews* (1742), Henry Fielding uses abduction by gypsies as a major plot device: both Joseph and his beloved Fanny, while infants, are stolen—and switched—by gypsies.

9. Fortune.

1. Spelling of "coarse" throughout the text.

with News, that the Magistrates, as I think they call'd them, had order'd that I should go to Service; I was able to do but very little Service where ever I was to go, except it was to run of Errands, and be a Drudge to some Cook-Maid, and this they told me of often, which put me into a great Fright; for I had a thorough Aversion to going to Service, as they call'd it, that is to be a Servant, tho' I was so young; and I told my Nurse, as we call'd her, that I believ'd I could get my Living without going to Service if she pleas'd to let me; for she had Taught me to Work with my Needle, and Spin Worsted,[2] which is the chief Trade of that City, and I told her that if she wou'd keep me, I wou'd Work for her, and I would Work very hard.

I talk'd to her almost every Day of Working hard; And in short, I did nothing but Work and Cry all Day, which griev'd the good kind Woman so much, that at last she began to be concern'd for me, for she lov'd me very well.

ONE Day after this, as she came into the Room, where all we poor Children were at Work, she sat down just over against me, not in her usual Place as Mistress, but as if she set herself on purpose to observe me, and see me Work: I was doing something she had set me to, as I remember, it was Marking some Shirts, which she had taken to Make, and after a while she began to Talk to me: Thou foolish Child, says she, thou art always Crying; (for I was Crying then) Prethee, What doest Cry for? because they will take me away, *says I*, and put me to Service, and I can't Work House-Work; well Child, says she, but tho' you can't Work House-Work, as you call it, you will learn it in time, and they won't put you to hard Things at first; yes they will, says I, and if I can't do it, they will Beat me, and the Maids will Beat me to make me do great Work, and I am but a little Girl, and I can't do it, and then I cry'd again, till I could not speak any more to her.

THIS mov'd my good Motherly Nurse, so that she from that time resolv'd I should not go to Service yet, so she bid me not Cry, and she wou'd speak to Mr. *Mayor*, and I should not go to Service till I was bigger.

WELL this did not Satisfie me, for to think of going to Service, was such a frightful Thing to me, that if she had assur'd me I should not have gone till I was 20 years old, it wou'd have been the same to me, I shou'd have cry'd, I believe all the time, with the very Apprehension of its being to be so at last.

WHEN she saw that I was not pacify'd yet, she began to be angry with me, and what wou'd you have? *says she*, don't I tell you that you shall not go to Service till you are bigger? Ay, says I, but then I

2. Woolen yarn.

must go at last, why, what? said she, is the Girl mad? what, would you be a Gentlewoman? Yes *says I*, and cry'd heartily, till I roar'd out again.

THIS set the old Gentlewoman a Laughing at me, as you may be sure it would: Well, Madam forsooth, says she, *Gibing at me*, you would be a Gentlewoman, and pray how will you come to be a Gentlewoman? what, will you do it by your Fingers Ends?

YES, *says I again*, very innocently.

WHY, what can you Earn, *says she*, what can you get at your Work?

THREE Pence, *said I*, when I Spin, and 4*d*. when I Work plain Work.

ALAS! poor Gentlewoman, *said she again*, Laughing, what will that do for thee?

IT will keep me, *says I*, if you will let me live with you; and this *I said*, in such a poor petitioning Tone, that it made the poor Womans Heart yearn to me, as she told me afterwards.

BUT, *says she*, that will not keep you, and buy you Cloths too; and who must buy the little Gentlewoman Cloths, *says she*, and smil'd all the while at me.

I will Work Harder then, *says I*, and you shall have it all.

POOR Child! it won't keep you, *says she*, it will hardly keep you in Victuals.

THEN I will have no Victuals? *says I*, again very Innocently, let me but live with you.

WHY, can you live without Victuals? *says she, yes, again says I*, very much like a Child, you may be sure, and still I cry'd heartily.

I HAD no Policy in all this, you may easily see it was all Nature, but it was joyn'd with so much Innocence, and so much Passion, That in short, it set the good Motherly Creature a weeping too, and she cry'd at last as fast as I did, and then took me, and led me out of the teaching Room; come *says she*, you shan't go to Service, you shall live with me, and this pacify'd me for the present.

SOMETIME after this, she going to wait on the *Mayor*, and talking of such things as belong'd to her Business, at last my Story came up, and my good Nurse told Mr. *Mayor* the whole Tale: He was so pleas'd with it, that he would call his Lady, and his two Daughters to hear it, and it made Mirth enough among them, you may be sure.

HOWEVER, not a Week had pass'd over, but on a suddain comes Mrs. *Mayoress*, and her two Daughters to the House to see my old Nurse, and to see her School and the Children: When they had look'd about them a little: Well, Mrs.——— says the *Mayoress* to my Nurse; and pray which is the little Lass that intends to be a Gentlewoman? I heard her, and I was terrible frighted at first, tho' I did not know why neither; but Mrs. *Mayoress* comes up to me, Well Miss says she, And what are you at Work upon? The Word Miss[3] was a Language that had hardly been heard of in our School, and I wondred what sad Name it was she call'd me; However, I stood up, made a Curtsy, and she took my Work out of my Hand, look'd on it, and said it was very well; then she took up one of my Hands, nay, says she, the Child may come to be a Gentlewoman for ought any body knows, she has a Gentlewoman's Hand, says she; this pleas'd me mightily you may be sure, but Mrs. *Mayoress* did not stop there, but giving me my Work again, she put her Hand in her Pocket, gave me a Shilling, and bid me mind my Work, and learn to Work well, and I might be a Gentlewoman for ought she knew.

Now all this while, my good old Nurse, Mrs. *Mayoress*, and all the rest of them did not understand me at all, for they meant one Sort of thing, by the Word Gentlewoman, and I meant quite another; for alas, all I understood by being a Gentlewoman, was to be able to Work for myself, and get enough to keep me without that terrible Bug-bear *going to Service*, whereas they meant to live Great, Rich, and High, and I know not what.

WELL, after Mrs. *Mayoress* was gone, her two Daughters came in, and they call'd for the Gentlewoman too, and they talk'd a long while to me, and I answer'd them in my Innocent way; but always if they ask'd me whether I resolv'd to be a Gentlewoman, I answer'd YES: At last one of them ask'd me, what a Gentlewoman was? that puzzel'd me much; but however, I explain'd myself negatively, that it was one that did not go to Service, to do House-Work; they were pleas'd to be familiar [with] me, and lik'd my little Prattle to them, which it seems was agreeable enough to them, and they gave me Money too.

As for my Money I gave it all to my Mistress Nurse, as I call'd her, and told her she should have all I got for myself when I was a Gentlewoman, as well as now; by this and some other of my talk, my old Tutress began to understand me, about what I meant by being a Gentlewoman; and that I understood by it no more, than to be able to get my Bread by my own Work, and at last, she ask'd me whether it was not so.

I told her *yes*, and insisted on it, that to do so, was to be a Gentlewoman; for says I, there is such a one, naming a Woman that mended Lace, and wash'd the Ladies Lac'd-heads,[4] she, *says I*, is a Gentlewoman, and they call her Madam.

POOR Child, says my good old Nurse, you may soon be such a

3. A young, unmarried girl, but perhaps used here by Mrs. Mayoress to poke fun at little Moll's aspirations to gentility. The word also referred to a kept mistress or concubine—thus, ironically, "a sad Name," given Moll's later sexual adventures.
4. Headdresses or caps edged with lace.

Gentlewoman as that, for she is a Person of ill Fame, and has had two or three Bastards.

I DID not understand any thing of that; but I answer'd, I am sure they call her Madam, and she does not go to Service nor do House-Work, and therefore I insisted that she was a Gentlewoman, and I would be such a Gentlewoman as that.

THE Ladies were told all this again to be sure, and they made themselves Merry with it, and every now and then the young Ladies, Mr. *Mayor's* Daughters would come and see me, and ask where the little Gentlewoman was, which made me not a little Proud of myself.

THIS held a great while, and I was often visited by these young Ladies, and sometimes they brought others with them; so that I was known by it, almost all over the Town.

I WAS now about ten Years old, and began to look a little Womanish, for I was mighty Grave and Humble; very Mannerly, and as I had often heard the Ladies say I was Pretty, and would be a very handsome Woman, so you may be sure, that hearing them say so, made me not a little Proud; however, that Pride had no ill effect upon me yet, only as they often gave me Money, and I gave it my old Nurse, she *honest Woman*, was so just to me, as to lay it all out again for me, and gave me Head-Dresses, and Linnen, and Gloves and Ribbons, and I went very Neat, and always Clean; for that I would do, and if I had Rags on, I would always be Clean, or else I would dabble them in Water myself; but I *say*, my good Nurse, when I had Money given me, very honestly laid it out for me, and would always tell the Ladies, this, or that, was bought with their Money; and this made them oftentimes give me more; Till at last, I was indeed call'd upon by the Magistrates as I understood it, to go out to Service; but then I was come to be so good a Workwoman myself, and the Ladies were so kind to me, that it was plain I could maintain myself, that is to say, I could Earn as much for my Nurse as she was able by it to keep me; so she told them, that if they would give her leave, she would keep the Gentlewoman as she call'd me, to be her Assistant, and teach the Children, which I was very well able to do; for I was very nimble at my Work, and had a good Hand with my Needle, though I was yet very young.

BUT the kindness of the Ladies of the Town did not End here, for when they came to understand that I was no more maintain'd by the publick Allowance, as before, they gave me Money oftner than formerly; and as I grew up, they brought me Work to do for them; such as Linnen to Make, and Laces to Mend, and Heads to Dress up, and not only paid me for doing them, but even taught me how to do them; so that now I was a Gentlewoman indeed, as I understood that Word, and as I desir'd to be, for by that time, I was twelve Years old,

I not only found myself Cloaths, and paid my Nurse for my keeping, but got Money in my Pocket too before-hand.

THE Ladies also gave me Cloaths frequently of their own, or their Childrens, some Stockings, some Petticoats, some Gowns, some one thing, some another, and these my old Woman Managed for me like a meer[5] Mother, and kept them for me, oblig'd me to Mend them, and turn them and twist them to the best Advantage, for she was a rare House-Wife.

AT last one of the Ladies took so much Fancy to me, that she would have me Home to her House, for a Month she said, to be among her Daughters.

NOW tho' this was exceeding kind in her, yet as my old good Woman said to her, unless she resolv'd to keep me for good and all, she would do the little Gentlewoman more harm than good: Well, says the Lady, that's true, and therefore I'll only take her Home for a Week then, that I may see how my Daughters and she agree together, and how I like her Temper, and then I'll tell you more; and in the mean time, if any Body comes to see her as they us'd to do, you may only tell them, you have sent her out to my House.

THIS was prudently manag'd enough, and I went to the Ladies House, but I was so pleas'd there with the young Ladies, and they so pleas'd with me, that I had enough to do to come away, and they were as unwilling to part with me.

HOWEVER I did come away, and liv'd almost a Year more with my honest old Woman, and began now to be very helpful to her; for I was almost fourteen Years old, was tall of my Age, and look'd a little Womanish; but I had such a Taste of Genteel living at the Ladies House, that I was not so easie in my old Quarters as I us'd to be, and I thought it was fine to be a Gentlewoman indeed, for I had quite other Notions of a Gentlewoman now, than I had before; and as I thought, I say, that it was fine to be a Gentlewoman, so I lov'd to be among Gentlewomen, and therefore I long'd to be there again.

ABOUT the Time that I was fourteen Years and a quarter Old, my good old Nurse, Mother I ought rather to call her, fell Sick and Dyed; I was then in a sad Condition indeed, for as there is no great Bustle in putting an end to a Poor bodies Family, when once they are carried to the Grave; so the poor good Woman being Buried, the Parish Children she kept were immediately remov'd by the Church-Wardens; the School was at an End, and the Children of it had no more to do but just stay at Home, till they were sent some where else; and as for what she left, her Daughter a married Woman with six or seven Children, came and swept it all away at once, and removing the Goods, they had no more to say to me, than to Jest with me,

5. Perfect.

and tell me, that the little Gentlewoman might set up for her self if she pleas'd.

I was frighted out of my Wits almost, and knew not what to do, for I was, as it were turn'd out of Doors to the wide World, and that which was still worse, the old honest Woman had two and twenty Shillings of mine in her Hand, which was all the Estate the little Gentlewoman had in the World; and when I ask'd the Daughter for it, she huft[6] me and laught at me, and told me, she had nothing to do with it.

IT was true, the good poor Woman had told her Daughter of it, and that it lay in such a Place, that it was the Child's Money, and had call'd once or twice for me, to give it me, but I was unhappily out of the way, some where or other; and when I came back she was past being in a Condition to speak of it: However, the Daughter was so Honest afterward as to give it me, tho' at first she us'd me Cruelly about it.

Now was I a poor Gentlewoman indeed, and I was just that very Night to be turn'd into the wide World; for the Daughter remov'd all the Goods, and I had not so much as a Lodging to go to, or a bit of Bread to Eat: But it seems some of the Neighbours who had known my Circumstances, took so much Compassion of me, as to acquaint the Lady in whose Family I had been a Week, as I mention'd above; and immediately she sent her Maid to fetch me away, and two of her Daughters came with the Maid tho' unsent; so I went with them Bag and Baggage, and with a glad Heart you may be sure: The fright of my Condition had made such an Impression upon me, that I did not want now to be a Gentlewoman, but was very willing to be a Servant, and that any kind of Servant they thought fit to have me be.

BUT my new generous Mistress,[7] for she exceeded the good Woman I was with before, in every Thing, as well as in the matter of Estate; I say in every Thing except Honesty; and for that, tho' this was a Lady most exactly Just, yet I must not forget to say on all Occasions, that the First tho' Poor, was as uprightly Honest as it was possible for any One to be.

I was no sooner carried away as I have said by this good Gentlewoman, but the first Lady, *that is to say*, the *Mayoress* that was, sent her two Daughters to take Care of me; and another Family which had taken Notice of me, when I was the little Gentlewoman, and had given me Work to do, sent for me after her, so that I was mightily made of, as we say; nay, and they were not a little Angry, especially, Madam the *Mayoress*, that her Friend had taken me away from her as she call'd it; for as she said, I was Hers by Right, she having been

6. Scolded.
7. At this point, two clauses are inserted in the second edition, which, while probably not by Defoe, improve the sense: " . . . had better Thoughts for me, I call her generous,. . . ."

the first that took any Notice of me, but they that had me wou'd not part with me; and as for me, tho' I shou'd have been very well Treated with any of the other, yet I could not be better than where I was.

HERE I continu'd till I was between 17 and 18 Years old, and here I had all the Advantages for my Education that could be imagin'd; the Lady had Masters home to the House to teach her Daughters to Dance, and to speak *French*, and to Write, and others to teach them Musick; and as I was always with them, I learn'd as fast as they; and tho' the Masters were not appointed to teach me, yet I learn'd by Imitation and enquiry, all that they learn'd by Instruction and Direction. So that in short, I learn'd to Dance and speak *French* as well as any of them, and to Sing much better, for I had a better Voice than any of them; I could not so readily come at playing on the Harpsicord or Spinnet, because I had no Instrument of my own to Practice on, and could only come at theirs in the intervals, when they left it, which was uncertain, but yet I learn'd tollerably well too, and the young Ladies at length got two Instruments, that is to say, a Harpsicord, and a Spinnet too, and then they Taught me themselves; But as to Dancing they could hardly help my learning Country Dances, because they always wanted me to make up even Number; and on the other Hand, they were as heartily willing to learn me every thing that they had been Taught themselves, as I could be to take the Learning.

BY this Means I had, as I have said above, all the Advantages of Education that I could have had, if I had been as much a Gentlewoman as they were, with whom I liv'd, and in some things, I had the Advantage of my Ladies, tho' they were my Superiors; but they were all the Gifts of Nature, and which all their Fortunes could not furnish. First, I was apparently Handsomer than any of them. Secondly, I was better shap'd, and Thirdly, I Sung better, by which I mean, I had a better Voice; in all which you will I hope allow me to say, I do not speak my own Conceit of myself, but the Opinion of all that knew the Family.

I HAD with all these the common Vanity of my Sex (*viz.*) That being really taken for very Handsome, or if you please for a great Beauty, I very well knew it, and had as good an Opinion of myself, as any body else could have of me; and particularly I lov'd to hear any body speak of it, which could not but happen to me sometimes, and was a great Satisfaction to me.

THUS far I have had a smooth Story to tell of myself, and in all this Part of my Life, I not only had the Reputation of living in a very good Family, and a Family Noted and Respected every where, for Vertue and Sobriety, and for every valluable Thing; but I had the Character too of a very sober, modest, and vertuous young Woman, and such

I had always been; neither had I yet any occasion to think of any thing else, or to know what a Temptation to Wickedness meant.

BUT that which I was too vain of, was my Ruin, or rather my vanity was the Cause of it. The Lady in the House where I was, had two Sons, young Gentlemen of very promising Parts,[8] and of extraordinary Behaviour; and it was my Misfortune to be very well with them both, but they manag'd themselves with me in a quite different Manner.

THE eldest a gay[9] Gentleman that knew the Town, as well as the Country, and tho' he had Levity enough to do an ill natur'd thing, yet had too much Judgment of things to pay too dear for his Pleasures; he began with that unhappy Snare to all Women, (*viz.*) taking Notice upon all Occasions how pretty I was, as he call'd it; how agreeable, how well Carriaged, and the like; and this he contriv'd so subtilly, as if he had known as well, how to catch a Woman in his Net, as a Partridge when he went a Setting; for he wou'd contrive to be talking this to his Sisters when tho' I was not by, yet when he knew I was not so far off, but that I should be sure to hear him: His Sisters would return softly to him, Hush Brother, she will hear you, she is but in the next Room; then he would put it off, and Talk softlier, as if he had not known it, and begun to acknowledge he was Wrong; and then as if he had forgot himself, he would speak aloud again, and I that was so well pleas'd to hear it, was sure to Lissen for it upon all Occasions.

AFTER he had thus baited his Hook, and found easily enough the Method how to lay it in my Way, he play'd an opener Game; and one Day going by his Sister's Chamber when I was there, doing something about Dressing her, he comes in with an Air of gayty, O! Mrs. *Betty*,[1] said he to me, How do you do Mrs. *Betty*? don't your Cheeks burn, Mrs. *Betty*? I made a Curtsy and blush'd, but said nothing; What makes you talk so Brother, *says the Lady*; Why, says he, we have been talking of her below Stairs this half Hour; *Well says his Sister*, you can say no Harm of her, that I am sure; so 'tis no matter what you have been talking about; nay, *says he*, 'tis so far from talking Harm of her, that we have been talking a great deal of good, and a great many fine Things have been said of Mrs. *Betty*, I assure you; and particularly, that she is the Handsomest young Woman in *Colchester*; and, in short, they begin to Toast her Health in the Town.

I wonder at you Brother, *says the Sister; Betty* wants but one Thing, but she had as good want every Thing, for the Market is against our

8. Talents, abilities.
9. Light-hearted, playful, exuberantly cheerful.
1. Traditionally glossed as a generic name for a female servant or chambermaid, but it is also possible that no such connotation is present here. *Mrs.*: Both married and unmarried women were referred to as "Mrs." or "Mistress" in Defoe's time.

Sex just now; and if a young Woman have Beauty, Birth, Breeding, Wit, Sense, Manners, Modesty, and all these to an Extream; yet if she have not Money,[2] she's no Body, she had as good want them all, for nothing but Money now recommends a Woman; the Men play the Game all into their own Hands.

HER younger Brother, who was by, cry'd *Hold Sister*, you run too fast, I am an Exception to your Rule; I assure you, if I find a Woman so Accomplish'd as you Talk of, *I say*, I assure you, I would not trouble myself about the Money.

O, says the Sister, but you will take Care not to Fancy one then, without the Money.

YOU don't know that neither, *says the Brother*.

BUT why Sister, (*says the elder Brother*) why do you exclaim so at the Men, for aiming so much at the Fortune? you are none of them that want a Fortune, what ever else you want.

I understand you Brother, (*replies the Lady very smartly*,) you suppose I have the Money, and want the Beauty; but as Times go now, the first will do without the last, so I have the better of my Neighbours.

WELL, *says the younger Brother*, but your Neighbours, as you call them may be even with you; for Beauty will steal a Husband sometimes in spite of Money; and when the Maid chances to be Handsomer than the Mistress, she oftentimes makes as good a Market, and rides in a Coach before her.

I thought it was time for me to withdraw, and leave them, and I did so; but not so far, but that I heard all their Discourse, in which I heard abundance of fine things said of myself, which serv'd to prompt my Vanity; but as I soon found, was not the way to encrease my Interest in the Family; for the Sister, and the younger Brother fell grievously out about it; and as he said some very dissobliging things to her, upon my Account, so I could easily see that she Resented them, by her future Conduct to me; which indeed was very unjust to me, for I had never had the least thought of what she suspected, as to her youngest Brother: Indeed the elder Brother in his distant remote Way, had said a great many things, as in Jest, which I had the folly to believe were in earnest, or to flatter myself, with the hopes of what I ought to have suppos'd he never intended, and perhaps never thought of.

IT happen'd one Day that he came running up Stairs, towards the Room where his Sisters us'd to sit and Work, as he often us'd to do; and calling to them before he came in, as was his way too, I being

2. The importance of money in the marriage "market" was widely debated and usually deplored; becoming a major theme in the emergent English novel, it would find one of its most trenchant explorations in Jane Austen's fiction. Identifying it as one of the principal "abuses" of the marriage bed, Defoe called marrying for money "matrimonial whoredom" in *Conjugal Lewdness; or, Matrimonial Whoredom* (1727).

there alone, step'd to the Door, and said, Sir, the Ladies are not here, they are Walk'd down the Garden; as I step'd forward, to say this towards the Door, he was just got to the Door, and clasping me in his Arms, as if it had been by Chance, O! Mrs. *Betty, says he*, are you here? that's better still; I want to speak with you, more than I do with them, and then having me in his Arms he Kiss'd me three or four times.

I struggl'd to get away, and yet did it but faintly neither, and he held me fast, and still Kiss'd me, till he was almost out of Breath, and then sitting down, says, *dear Betty* I am in Love with you.

His Words I must confess fir'd my Blood; all my Spirits flew about my Heart, and put me into Disorder enough, which he might easily have seen in my Face: He repeated it afterwards several times, that he was in Love with me, and my Heart spoke as plain as a Voice, that I lik'd it; nay, when ever he said, I am in Love with you, my Blushes plainly reply'd, *wou'd you were* Sir.

However nothing else pass'd at that time; it was but a Surprise, and when he was gone, I soon recover'd myself again. He had stay'd longer with me, but he happen'd to look out at the Window, and see his Sisters coming up the Garden, so he took his leave, Kiss'd me again, told me he was very serious, and I should hear more of him very quickly, and away he went leaving me infinitely pleas'd tho' surpris'd, and had there not been one Misfortune in it, I had been in the Right, but the Mistake lay here, that Mrs. *Betty* was in Earnest, and the Gentleman was not.

From this time my Head run upon strange Things, and I may truly say, I was not myself; to have such a Gentleman talk to me of being in Love with me, and of my being such a charming Creature, as he told me I was, these were things I knew not how to bear, my vanity was elevated to the last Degree: It is true, I had my Head full of Pride, but knowing nothing of the Wickedness of the times, I had not one Thought of my own Safety, or of my Vertue about me; and had my young Master offer'd it at first Sight, he might have taken any Liberty he thought fit with me; but he did not see his Advantage, which was my happiness for that time.

After this Attack, it was not long, but he found an opportunity to catch me again, and almost in the same Posture, indeed it had more of Design in it on his Part, tho' not on my Part; *it was thus*; the young Ladies were all gone a Visiting with their Mother; his Brother was out of Town; and as for his Father, he had been at *London* for a Week before; he had so well watched me, that he knew where I was, tho' I did not so much as know that he was in the House; and he briskly comes up the Stairs, and seeing me at Work comes into the Room to me directly, and began just as he did before with taking me in his Arms, and Kissing me for almost a quarter of an Hour together.

IT was his younger Sisters Chamber, that I was in, and as there was no Body in the House, but the Maids below Stairs, he was it may be the ruder: In short, he began to be in Earnest with me indeed; perhaps he found me a little too easie, for God knows I made no Resistance to him while he only held me in his Arms and Kiss'd me, indeed I was too well pleas'd with it, to resist him much.

HOWEVER as it were, tir'd with that kind of Work, we sat down, and there he talk'd with me a great while; *he said*, he was charm'd with me, and that he could not rest Night, or Day till he had told me how he was in Love with me; and if I was able to Love him again, and would make him happy, I should be the saving of his Life; and many such fine things. I said little to him again, but easily discover'd[3] that I was a Fool, and that I did not in the least perceive what he meant.

THEN he walk'd about the Room, and taking me by the Hand, I walk'd with him; and by and by, taking his Advantage, he threw me down upon the Bed, and Kiss'd me there most violently; but to give him his Due, offer'd no manner of Rudeness to me, only Kiss'd me a great while; after this he thought he had heard some Body come up Stairs, so he got off from the Bed, lifted me up, professing a great deal of Love for me, but told me it was all an honest Affection, and that he meant no ill to me; and with that he put five Guineas[4] into my Hand, and went away down Stairs.

I WAS more confounded with the Money than I was before with the Love, and began to be so elevated, that I scarce knew the Ground I stood on: I am the more particular in this part, that if my Story comes to be read by any innocent young Body, they may learn from it to Guard themselves against the Mischiefs which attend an early Knowledge of their own Beauty; if a young Woman once thinks herself Handsome, she never doubts the Truth of any Man, that tells her he is in Love with her; for if she believes herself Charming enough to Captivate him, tis natural to expect the Effects of it.

THIS young Gentleman had fir'd his Inclinations, as much as he had my vanity, and as if he had found that he had an opportunity, and was sorry he did not take hold of it, he comes up again in half an Hour, or thereabouts, and falls to Work with me again as before, only with a little less Introduction.

AND First, when he enter'd the Room, he turn'd about, and shut the Door. Mrs. *Betty*, said he, I fancy'd before, some Body was coming up Stairs, but it was not so; however, *adds he*, if they find me in the Room with you, they shan't catch me a Kissing of you; I told him I did not know who should be coming up Stairs, for I believ'd there

3. Betrayed, revealed.
4. English gold coins, originally minted for the Africa trade and worth 20 shillings (the equivalent of an English pound); after 1717, their value rose to 21 shillings.

was no Body in the House, but the Cook, and the other Maid, and they never came up those Stairs; well my Dear, *says he*, 'tis good to be sure however; and so he sits down and we began to Talk; and now, tho' I was still all on fire with his first visit, and said little, he did as it were put Words in my Mouth, telling me how passionately he lov'd me, and that tho' he could not mention such a thing, till he came to his Estate, yet he was resolv'd to make me happy then, and himself too; *that is to say, to Marry me*, and abundance of such fine things, which I poor Fool did not understand the drift of, but acted as if there was no such thing as any kind of Love but that which tended to Matrimony; and if he had spoke of that, I had no Room, as well as no Power to have said No; but we were not come that length yet.

WE had not sat long, but he got up, and stoping my very Breath with Kisses, threw me upon the Bed again; but then being both well warm'd, he went farther with me than Decency permits me to mention, nor had it been in my power to have deny'd him at that Moment, had he offer'd much more than he did.

HOWEVER, tho' he took these Freedoms with me, it did not go to that, which they call the last Favour, which, to do him Justice, he did not attempt; and he made that self denyal of his a Plea for all his Freedoms with me upon other Occasions after this: When this was over, he stay'd but a little while, but he put almost a Handful of Gold in my Hand, and left me; making a thousand Protestations of his Passion for me, and of his loving me above all the Women in the World.

IT will not be strange, if I now began to think, but alas! it was but with very little solid Reflection: I had a most unbounded Stock of Vanity and Pride, and but a very little Stock of Vertue; I did indeed cast[5] sometimes with myself what my young Master aim'd at, but thought of nothing, but the fine Words, and the Gold; whether he intended to Marry me, or not to Marry me, seem'd a Matter of no great Consequence to me; nor did my Thoughts so much as suggest to me the Necessity of making any Capitulation for myself, till he came to make a kind of formal Proposal to me, as you shall hear presently.

THUS I gave up myself to a readiness of being ruined without the least concern, and am a fair *Memento* to all young Women, whose Vanity prevails over their Vertue: Nothing was ever so stupid on both Sides, had I acted as became me, and resisted as Vertue and Honour requir'd, this Gentleman, had either Desisted his Attacks, finding no room to expect the Accomplishment of his Design, or had made fair, and honourable Proposals of Marriage; in which Case, whoever had

5. Debate.

blam'd him, no Body could have blam'd me. In short, if he had known me, and how easy the Trifle he aim'd at, was to be had, he would have troubled his Head no farther, but have given me four or five Guineas, and have lain with me the next time he had come at me; and if I had known his Thoughts, and how hard he thought I would be to be gain'd, I might have made my own Terms with him; and if I had not Capitulated for an immediate Marriage, I might for a Maintenance till Marriage, and might have had what I would; for he was already Rich to Excess, besides what he had in Expectation; but I seem'd wholly to have abandoned all such Thoughts as these, and was taken up Onely with the Pride of my Beauty, and of being belov'd by such a Gentleman; as for the Gold I spent whole Hours in looking upon it; I told[6] the Guineas over and over a thousand times a Day: Never poor vain Creature was so wrapt up with every part of the Story, as I was, not Considering what was before me, and how near my Ruin was at the Door; indeed I think, I rather wish'd for that Ruin, than studyed to avoid it.

IN the mean time however, I was cunning enough, not to give the least room to any in the Family to suspect me, or to imagine that I had the least Correspondence[7] with this young Gentleman; I scarce ever look'd towards him in publick, or Answer'd if he spoke to me, if any Body was near us; but for all that, we had every now and then a little Encounter, where we had room for a Word or two, and now and then a Kiss; but no fair opportunity for the Mischief intended; and especially considering that he made more Circumlocution, than if he had known my Thoughts he had occasion for, and the Work appearing Difficult to him, he really made it so.

BUT as the Devil is an unwearied Tempter, so he never fails to find opportunity for that Wickedness he invites to: It was one Evening that I was in the Garden[8] with his two younger Sisters, and himself, and all very innocently Merry, when he found Means to convey a Note into my Hand, by which he Directed me to understand, that he would to Morrow desire me publickly to go of an Errand for him into the Town, and that I should see him somewhere by the Way.

ACCORDINGLY after Dinner, he very gravely says to me, his Sisters being all by, Mrs. *Betty*, I must ask a Favour of you: What's that? *says his second Sister*; nay, Sister *says he*, very gravely, if you can't spare Mrs. *Betty* to Day, any other time will do; *yes they said*, they could spare her well enough, and the Sister beg'd Pardon for asking; which she did but of meer Course, without any Meaning; Well, but Brother? says the eldest Sister, you must tell Mrs. *Betty* what it is; if

6. Counted.
7. Communication, with a punning glance at sexual intercourse, as in a man's "correspondence" with his wife.
8. Traditional place of seduction in love stories, recalling Eve's temptation and the Fall in the Garden of Eden.

it be any private Business that we must not hear. You may call her out, there she is, Why Sister, says the Gentleman, very gravely, What do you mean? I only desire her to go into the *High-street*, (and then he pulls out a Turn-Over)[9] to such a Shop, and then he tells them a long Story of two fine Neckcloths he had bid Money for, and he wanted to have me go and make an Errand to buy a Neck to the Turn-Over that he showed, to see if they would take my Money for the Neckcloths; to bid a Shilling more, and Haggle with them; and then he made more Errands, and so continued to have such petty Business to do, that *I* should be sure to stay a good while.

WHEN he had given me my Errands, he told them a long Story of a Visit he was going to make to a Family they all knew, and where was to be such and such Gentlemen, and how Merry they were to be; and very formally asks his Sisters to go with him, and they as formally excus'd themselves, because of Company that they had Notice was to come and Visit them that Afternoon, which by the Way he had contriv'd on purpose.

HE had scarce done speaking to them, and giving me my Errand, but his Man came up to tell him that Sir *W*——*H*——s Coach stop'd at the Door; so he runs down, and comes up again immediately, alas! *says he*, aloud, there's all my Mirth spoil'd at once; Sir *W*—— has sent his Coach for me, and desires to speak with me, upon some earnest Business: It seems this Sir *W*—— was a Gentleman, who liv'd about three Miles out of Town, to whom he had spoken on purpose the Day before, to lend him his Charriot for a particular occasion; and had appointed it to call for him, as it did about three a-Clock.

IMMEDIATELY he calls for his best Wig, Hat and Sword, and ordering his Man to go to the other Place to make his Excuse, that was to say, he made an Excuse to send his Man away; he prepares to go into the Coach: As he was going, he stop'd a while, and speaks mighty earnestly to me about his Business, and finds an Opportunity to say very softly to me, *come away my Dear as soon as ever you can*. I said nothing, but made a Curtsy, as if I had done so to what he said in publick; in about a Quarter of an Hour I went out too, I had no Dress, other than before, except that I had a Hood, a Mask,[1] a Fan and a pair of Gloves in my Pocket; so that there was not the least Suspicion in the House: He waited for me in the Coach in a back *Lane*, which he knew *I* must pass by; and had directed the Coachman whither to go, which was to a certain Place, call'd *Mile-End*, where lived a Confident[2] of his, where we went in, and where was all the Convenience in the World to be as Wicked as we pleas'd.

9. Linen band or the like worn round the neck and turned down; a turn-down collar or neck-band.
1. A covering, with apertures for seeing, worn to protect the face against the sun and wind; it could also be used for disguise in love assignations, balls, masquerades, etc.
2. Confidant.

WHEN we were together, he began to Talk very Gravely to me; and to tell me, he did not bring me there to betray me; that his Passion for me, would not suffer him to Abuse me; that he resolv'd to Marry me as soon as he came to his Estate, that in the mean time, if *I* would grant his Request, he would Maintain me very Honourably, and made me a thousand Protestations of his Sincerity, and of his Affection to me; and That he would never abandon me, and as *I* may say, made a thousand more Preambles than he need to have done.

HOWEVER as he press'd me to speak, I told him, I had no Reason to question the Sincerity of his Love to me, after so many Protestations, But——and there I stopp'd, as if I left him to Guess the rest; BUT WHAT my Dear? *says he*, I guess what you mean; what if you should be with Child, is not that it? Why then, *says he*, I'll take Care of you, and Provide for you, and the Child too, and that you may see I am not in Jest, *says he*, here's an Earnest for you; and with that he pulls out a silk Purse, with an Hundred Guineas in it, and gave it me; and I'll give you such another, *says he*, every Year till I Marry you.

MY Colour came, and went, at the Sight of the Purse, and with the fire of his Proposal together; so that I could not say a Word, and he easily perceiv'd it; so putting the Purse into my Bosom, I made no more Resistance to him, but let him do just what he pleas'd; and as often as he pleas'd; and thus I finish'd my own Destruction at once, for from this Day, being forsaken of my Vertue, and my Modesty, I had nothing of Value left to recommend me, either to God's Blessing, or Man's Assistance.

BUT things did not End here, I went back to the Town, did the Business he publickly directed me to, and was at Home before any Body thought me long; as for my Gentleman, he staid out as he told me he would, till late at Night, and there was not the least Suspicion in the Family, either on his Account or on mine.

WE had after this, frequent Opportunities to repeat our Crime; chiefly by his contrivance; especially at home; when his Mother and the young Ladies went Abroad a Visiting, which he watch'd so narrowly, as never to miss; knowing always before-hand when they went out; and then fail'd not to catch me all alone, and securely enough; so that we took our fill of our wicked Pleasure for near half a Year; and yet, which was the most to my Satisfaction, I was not with Child.

BUT before this half Year was expir'd, his younger Brother, of whom I have made some mention in the beginning of the Story, falls to work with me; and he finding me alone in the Garden one Evening, begins a Story of the same Kind to me, made good honest Professions of being in Love with me; and in short, proposes fairly and Honourably to Marry me, and that before he made any other Offer to me at all.

I was now confounded and driven to such an Extremity, as the like was never known; at least not to me; I resisted the Proposal with Obstinancy; and now I began to Arm myself with Arguments: I laid before him the inequallity of the Match, the Treatment I should meet with in the Family; the Ingratitude it wou'd be to his good Father and Mother, who had taken me into their House upon such generous Principles, and when I was in such a low Condition; and in short, I said every thing to dissuade him from his Design that I could imagine, except telling him the Truth, which wou'd indeed have put an end to it all, but that I durst not think of mentioning.

BUT here happen'd a Circumstance that I did not expect indeed, which put me to my Shifts;[3] for this young Gentleman as he was plain and Honest, so he pretended to nothing with me, but what was so too; and knowing his own Innocence, he was not so careful to make his having a Kindness for Mrs. *Betty*, a Secret in the House, as his Brother was; and tho' he did not let them know that he had talk'd to me about it, yet he said enough to let his Sisters perceive he Lov'd me, and his Mother saw it too, which tho' they took no Notice of it to me, yet they did to him, and immediately I found their Carriage[4] to me alter'd, more than ever before.

I saw the Cloud, tho' I did not foresee the Storm; it was easie, *I say*, to see that their Carriage to me was alter'd, and that it grew worse and worse every Day; till at last I got Information among the Servants, that I shou'd, in a very little while, be desir'd to remove.

I was not alarm'd at the News, having a full Satisfaction that I should be otherwise provided for; and especially, considering that I had Reason every Day to expect I should be with Child, and that then I should be oblig'd to remove without any Pretences for it.

AFTER some time, the younger Gentleman took an Opportunity to tell me, that the Kindness he had for me, had got vent[5] in the Family; he did not Charge me with it, *he said*, for he knew well enough which way it came out; he told me his plain way of Talking had been the Occasion of it, for that he did not make his respect for me so much a Secret as he might have done, and the Reason was, that he was at a Point;[6] that if I would consent to have him, he would tell them all openly that he lov'd me, and that he intended to Marry me: That it was true his Father and Mother might Resent it, and be unkind, but that he was now in a Way to live, being bred to[7] the Law, and he did not fear Maintaining me, agreeable to what I should expect; and that in short, as he believed I would not be asham'd of him, so he was resolv'd not to be asham'd of me, and that he scorn'd to be afraid to

3. I.e., led me to resort to my own contrivances or stratagems.
4. Behavior.
5. Had been let out or divulged, had become known.
6. I.e., he was resolved, determined.
7. Trained in.

own me now, who he resolv'd to own after I was his Wife, and therefore I had nothing to do but to give him my Hand, and he would Answer for all the rest.

I was now in a dreadful Condition indeed, and now I repented heartily my easiness with the eldest Brother, not from any Reflection of Conscience, but from a View of the Happiness I might have enjoy'd, and had now made impossible; for tho' I had no great Scruples of Conscience *as I have said* to struggle with, yet I could not think of being a Whore to one Brother, and a Wife to the other; but then it came into my Thoughts, that the first Brother had promis'd to make me his Wife, when he came to his Estate; but I presently remember'd what I had often thought of, that he had never spoken a Word of having me for a Wife, after he had Conquer'd me for a Mistress; and indeed till now, tho' I said I thought of it often, yet it gave me no Disturbance at all, for as he did not seem in the least to lessen his Affection to me, so neither did he lessen his Bounty, tho' he had the Discretion himself to desire me not to lay out a Penny of what he gave me in Cloaths, or to make the least show Extraordinary, because it would necessarily give Jealousie[8] in the Family, since every Body knew I could come at such things no manner of ordinary Way; but by some private Friendship, which they would presently have suspected.

BUT I was now in a great strait, and really knew not what to do, the main Difficulty was this; the younger Brother not only laid close Siege to me, but suffered it to be seen; he would come into his Sisters Room, and his Mothers Room, and sit down, and Talk a Thousand kind things of me, and to me, even before their Faces, and when they were all there: This grew so Publick, that the whole House talk'd of it, and his Mother reprov'd him for it, and their Carriage to me appear'd quite Altered: In short, his Mother had let fall some Speeches, as if she intended to put me out of the Family, that is in *English*, to turn me out of Doors. Now, I was sure this could not be a Secret to his Brother, only, that he might not think as indeed no Body else yet did, that the youngest Brother had made any Proposal to me about it; But as I easily cou'd see that it would go farther, so I saw likewise there was an absolute Necessity to speak of it to him, or that he would speak of it to me, and which to do first I knew not; that is, whether I should break it to him, or let it alone till he should break it to me.

UPON serious Consideration, for indeed now I began to Consider things very seriously, and never till now: I say, upon serious Consideration, I resolv'd to tell him of it first, and it was not long before I had an Opportunity, for the very next Day his Brother went to *Lon-*

8. Raise suspicion.

don upon some Business, and the Family being out a Visiting, just as it had happen'd before, and as indeed was often the Case, he came according to his Custom to spend an Hour or Two with Mrs. *Betty*.

WHEN he came and had sate down a while, he easily perceiv'd there was an alteration in my Countenance, that I was not so free and pleasant with him, as I us'd to be, and particularly, that I had been a Crying; he was not long before he took notice of it, and ask'd me in very kind Terms what was the Matter, and if any thing Troubl'd me: I wou'd have put it off if I could, but it was not to be Conceal'd; so after suffering many Importunities to draw that out of me, which I long'd as much as possible to Disclose; I told him that it was true, something did Trouble me, and something of such a Nature, that I could not Conceal from him, and yet, that I could not tell how to tell him of it neither; that it was a thing that not only Surpriz'd me, but greatly perplex'd me, and that I knew not what Course to take, unless he would Direct me: He told me with great Tenderness, that let it be what it wou'd, I should not let it Trouble me, for he would Protect me from all the World.

I then begun at a Distance, and told him I was afraid the Ladies had got some secret Information of our Correspondence; for that it was easie to see, that their Conduct was very much chang'd towards me for a great while, and that now it was come to that pass, that they frequently found Fault with me, and sometimes fell quite out with me, tho' I never gave them the least Occasion: That whereas, I us'd always to lye with the Eldest Sister, I was lately put to lye by my self, or with one of the Maids; and that I had over-heard them several times talking very Unkindly about me; but that which confirm'd it all, was, that one of the Servants had told me, that she had heard I was to be Turn'd out, and that it was not safe for the Family, that I should be any longer in the House.

HE smil'd when he heard all this, and I ask'd him, how he could make so light of it, when he must needs know, that if there was any Discovery, I was Undone for ever? and that even it would hurt him, tho' not Ruin him, as it would me: I upbraided him, that he was like all the rest of the Sex, that when they had the Character and Honour of a Woman at their Mercy, often times made it their Jest, and at least look'd upon it as a Trifle, and counted the Ruin of those, they had had their Will of, as a thing of no value.

HE saw me Warm and Serious, and he chang'd his Stile immediately; *he told me*, he was sorry I should have such a thought of him; that he had never given me the least Occasion for it, but had been as tender of my Reputation, as he could be of his own; that he was sure our Correspondence had been manag'd with so much Address, that not one Creature in the Family had so much as a Suspicion of it; that if he smil'd when I told him my Thoughts, it was at the

Assurance he lately receiv'd, that our understanding one another, was not so much as known or guess'd at; and that when he had told me, how much Reason he had to be Easie, I should Smile as he did, for he was very certain, it would give me a full Satisfaction.

THIS is a Mystery I cannot understand, *says I*, or how it should be to my Satisfaction, that I am to be turn'd out of Doors; for if our Correspondence is not discover'd, I know not what else I have done to change the Countenances of the whole Family to me, or to have them Treat me as they do now, who formerly used me with so much Tenderness, as if I had been one of their own Children.

WHY look you Child, *says he*, that they are Uneasie about you, that is true; but that they have the least Suspicion of the Case as it is, and as it respects you and I, is so far from being True, that they suspect my Brother *Robin*; and in short, they are fully persuaded he makes Love to you: Nay, the Fool has put it into their Heads too himself, for he is continually Bantring them about it, and making a Jest of himself; I confess, I think he is wrong to do so, because he can not but see it vexes them, and makes them Unkind to you; but 'tis a Satisfaction to me, because of the Assurance it gives me, that they do not suspect me in the least, and I hope this will be to your Satisfaction too.

So it is, *says I*, one way, but this does not reach my Case at all, nor is this the chief Thing that Troubles me, tho' I have been concern'd about that too: What is it then, *says he*? With which, I fell into Tears, and could say nothing to him at all: He strove to pacifie me all he could, but began at last to be very pressing upon me, to tell what it was; at last *I answer'd*, that I thought I ought to tell him too, and that he had some right to know it, besides, that I wanted his Direction in the Case, for I was in such Perplexity, that I knew not what Course to take, and then I related the whole Affair to him: *I told him*, how imprudently his Brother had manag'd himself, in making himself so Publick; for that if he had kept it a Secret, as such a Thing ought to have been, I could but have Denied him Positively, without giving any Reason for it, and he would in Time have ceas'd his Sollicitations; but that he had the Vanity, first, to depend upon it that I would not Deny him, and then had taken the Freedom to tell his Resolution of having me, to the whole House.

I *told him* how far I had resisted him, and *told him* how Sincere and Honourable his Offers were, but *says I*, my Case will be doubly hard; for as they carry it Ill to me now, because he desires to have me, they'll carry it worse when they shall find I have Deny'd him; and they will presently say, there's something else in it, and then out it comes, that I am Marry'd already to somebody else, or else that I would never refuse a Match so much above me as this was.

THIS Discourse surpriz'd him indeed very much: He *told me*, that it was a critical Point indeed for me to Manage, and he did not see which way I should get out of it; but he would consider of it, and let me know next time we met, what Resolution he was come to about it; and in the mean time, desir'd I would not give my Consent to his Brother, nor yet give him a flat Denial, but that I would hold him in Suspence a while.

I seem'd to start at his saying I should not give him my Consent; I *told him*, he knew very well, I had no Consent to give; that he had Engag'd himself to Marry me, and that my Consent was at the same time Engag'd to him; that he had all along told me, I was his Wife, and I look'd upon my self as effectually so, as if the Ceremony had pass'd;[9] and that it was from his own Mouth that I did so, he having all along persuaded me to call myself his Wife.

WELL my Dear *says he*, don't be Concern'd at that now, if I am not your Husband, I'll be as good as a Husband to you, and do not let those things Trouble you now, but let me look a little farther into this Affair, and I shall be able to say more next time we meet.

HE pacify'd me as well as he could with this, but I found he was very Thoughtful, and that tho' he was very kind to me, and kiss'd me a thousand Times, and more I believe, and gave me Money too, yet he offer'd no more all the while we were together, which was above two Hours, and which I much wonder'd at, indeed at that Time, considering how it us'd to be, and what Opportunity we had.

HIS Brother did not come from *London*, for five or six Days, and it was two Days more, before he got an Opportunity to talk with him; but then getting him by himself, he began to talk very Close to him about it; and the same Evening got an Opportunity, (for we had a long Conference together) to repeat all their Discourse to me, which as near as I can remember, was to the purpose following. He *told him* he heard strange News of him since he went, (*viz.*) that he made Love to Mrs. *Betty*: Well, *says his* Brother, a little Angrily, and so *I do*, And what then? What has any body to do with that? Nay, *says his* Brother, don't be Angry *Robin*, I don't pretend to have any thing to do with it; nor do I pretend to be Angry with you about it: But I find they do concern themselves about it, and that they have used the poor Girl Ill about it, which I should take as done to my self; Who do you mean by THEY? *says* Robin, I mean my Mother, and the Girls, *says the* elder Brother.

9. Before the Hardwicke Marriage Act of 1753, whose avowed intent was to prevent clandestine marriages, a man and a woman were considered legally married if they had exchanged promises to live with each other as husband and wife, even if privately and without ecclesiastical sanction. As Defoe states in the *Review*, "Marriage being nothing but a Promise, the Ceremony is no Addition to the Contract" (Supplement for November 1704), "the Essence of Matrimony consisting in the mutual Consent of Parties" (Supplement for January 1705).

BUT hark ye, *says* his Brother, are you in Earnest, do you really Love the Girl? you may be free with me you know, Why then *says* Robin, I will be free with you, I do Love her above all the Women in the World, and I will have Her, let *them say*, and do what they will, I believe the Girl will not Deny me.

IT stuck me to the Heart when he *told me* this, for tho' it was most rational to think I would not Deny him, yet I knew in my own Conscience, I must Deny him, and I saw my Ruin in my being oblig'd to do so; but I knew it was my business to Talk otherwise then, so I interrupted him in his Story thus,

AY! *said* I, does he think I can not Deny him? but he shall find I can Deny him, for all that.

WELL my dear *says he*, but let me give you the whole Story as it went on between us, and then say what you will.

THEN he went on and *told me*, that he reply'd thus: But Brother, you know She has nothing, and you may have several Ladies with good Fortunes: 'Tis no matter for that, *said* Robin, I Love the Girl; and I will never please my Pocket in Marrying, and not please my Fancy; and so my Dear *adds he*, there is no Opposing him.

YES, yes, *says I*, you shall see I can Oppose him, I have learnt to say NO now, tho' I had not learnt it before; if the best Lord in the Land offer'd me Marriage now, I could very cheerfully say NO to him.

WELL, but my Dear *says he*, What can you say to him? You know, as you said when we talk'd of it before, he will ask you many Questions about it, and all the House will wonder what the meaning of it should be.

WHY *says I* smiling, I can stop all their Mouths at one Clap, by telling him and them too, that I am Married already to his elder Brother.

HE smil'd a little too at the Word, but I could see it Startled him, and he could not hide the disorder it put him into; however, he return'd, Why tho' that may be true in some Sense, yet I suppose you are but in Jest, when you talk of giving such an Answer as that, it may not be Convenient on many Accounts.

No, no, *says I* pleasantly, I am not so fond of letting that Secret come out, without your Consent.

BUT what then can you say to him, or to them, *says he*, when they find you positive against a Match, which would be apparently so much to your Advantage?

WHY, *says I*, should I be at a loss? First of all, I am not oblig'd to give them any Reason at all, on the other hand, I may tell them I am Married already, and stop there, and that will be a full Stop too to him, for he can have no Reason to ask one Question after it.

AY *says he*, but the whole House will teize you about that, even to

Father and Mother, and if you deny them positively, they will be Disoblig'd at you, and Suspicious besides.

Why *says I*, What can I do? What would you have me do? I was in strait enough before, and as I *told you*, I was in Perplexity before, and acquainted you with the Circumstances, that I might have your Advice.

My dear *says he*, I have been considering very much upon it, you may be sure, and tho' it is a piece of Advice, that has a great many Mortifications in it to me, and may at first seem Strange to you, yet all Things consider'd, I see no better way for you, than to let him go on; and if you find him hearty and in Earnest, Marry him.

I gave him a look full of Horror at those Words, and turning Pale as Death, was at the very point of sinking down out of the Chair I sat in: When giving a start, my Dear, *says he* aloud, What's the matter with you? Where are you a going? and a great many such things; and with joging and calling to me, fetch'd me a little to my self, tho' it was a good while before I fully recover'd my Senses, and was not able to speak for several Minutes more.

When I was fully recover'd he began again; My dear *says he*, What made you so Surpriz'd at what I said, I would have you consider Seriously of it? you may see plainly how the Family stand in this Case, and they would be stark Mad if it was my Case, as it is my Brothers, and for ought I see, it would be my Ruin and yours too.

Ay! *says I*, still speaking angrily; are all your Protestations and Vows to be shaken by the dislike of the Family? Did I not always object that to you, and you made a light thing of it, as what you were above, and would not Value; and is it come to this now? *Said I*, is this your Faith and Honour, your Love, and the Solidity of your Promises?

He continued perfectly Calm, notwithstanding all my Reproaches, and I was not sparing of them at all; but *he reply'd* at last, My Dear, I have not broken one Promise with you yet; I did tell you I would Marry you when I was come to my Estate; but you see My Father is a hail healthy Man, and may live these thirty Years still, and not be Older than several are round us in the Town; and you never propos'd my Marrying you sooner, because you know it might be my Ruin; and as to all the rest, I have not fail'd you in any thing, you have wanted for nothing.

I could not deny a Word of this, and had nothing to say to it in general; but why then, *says I*, can you perswade me to such a horrid stop, as leaving you, since you have not left me? Will you allow no Affection, no Love on my Side, where there has been so much on your Side? Have I made you no Returns? Have I given no Testimony of my Sincerity, and of my Passion? are the Sacrifices I have made of Honour and Modesty to you, no Proof of my being ty'd to you in Bonds too strong to be broken?

BUT here my Dear, *says he*, you may come into a safe Station, and appear with Honour, and with splendor at once, and the Remembrance of what we have done, may be wrapt up in an eternal Silence, as if it had never happen'd; you shall always have my Respect, and my sincere Affection, only then it shall be Honest, and perfectly Just to my Brother, you shall be my Dear Sister, as now you are my Dear——and there he stop'd.

YOUR Dear whore, *says I*, you would have said, if you had gone on; and you might as well have said it; but I understand you: However, I desire you to remember the long Discourses you have had with me, and the many Hours pains you have taken to perswade me to believe myself an honest Woman; that I was your Wife intentionally, tho' not in the Eye of the World; and that it was as effectual a Marriage that had pass'd between us, as if we had been publickly Wedded by the Parson of the Parish; you know and cannot but remember, that these have been your own Words to me.

I found this was a little too close upon him, but I made it up in what follows; he stood stock still for a while, and said nothing, and I went on thus, you cannot, *says I*, without the highest injustice believe that I yielded upon all these Perswasions without a Love not to be questioned, not to be shaken again by any thing that could happen afterward: If you have such dishonourable Thoughts of me, I must ask you what Foundation in any of my Behaviour have I given for such a Suggestion.

IF then I have yielded to the Importunities of my Affection; and if I have been perswaded to believe that I am really, and in the Essence of the Thing your Wife, shall I now give the Lye to all those Arguments, and call myself your Whore, or Mistress, which is the same thing? And will you Transfer me to your Brother? Can you Transfer my Affection? Can you bid me cease loving you, and bid me love him? is it in my Power think you to make such a Change at Demand? No Sir, *said I*, depend upon it 'tis impossible, and whatever the Change of your Side may be, I will ever be True; and I had much rather, since it is come that unhappy Length, be your Whore than your Brothers Wife.

HE appear'd pleas'd, and touch'd with the impression of this last Discourse, and told me that he stood where he did before; that he had not been Unfaithful to me in any one Promise he had ever made yet, but that there were so many terrible things presented themselves to his View in the Affair before me, and that on my Account in particular, that he had thought of the other as a Remedy so effectual, as nothing could come up to it: That he thought this would not be an entire parting us, but we might love as Friends all our Days, and perhaps with more Satisfaction, than we should in the Station we were now in, as things might happen: That he durst say, I could not apprehend any thing from him, as to betraying a Secret, which could not but be the Destruction of us both, if it came out: That he had but one Question to ask of me, that could lye in the way of it, and if that Question was answer'd in the Negative, he could not but think still it was the only Step I could take.

I guess'd at his Question presently, namely, Whether I was sure I was not with Child? As to that, *I told him*, he need not be concern'd about it, for I was not with Child; why then my Dear, *says he*, we have no time to Talk farther now; consider of it, and think closely about it, I cannot but be of the Opinion still, that it will be the best Course you can take; and with this, he took his Leave, and the more hastily too, his Mother and Sisters Ringing at the Gate, just at the Moment that he had risen up to go.

HE left me in the utmost Confusion of Thought; and he easily perceiv'd it the next Day, and all the rest of the Week, for it was but *Tuesday* Evening when we talked; but he had no Opportunity to come at me all that Week, till the *Sunday* after, when I being indispos'd did not go to Church, and he making some Excuse for the like, stay'd at Home.

AND now he had me an Hour and a Half again by myself, and we fell into the same Arguments all over again, or at least so near the same, as it would be to no purpose to repeat them; at last, *I ask'd him* warmly what Opinion he must have of my Modesty, that he could suppose, I should so much as Entertain a thought of lying with two Brothers? And assur'd him it could never be: *I added* if he was to tell me that he would never see me more, than which nothing but Death could be more Terrible, yet I could never entertain a thought so Dishonourable to my self, and so Base to him; and therefore, I entreated him if he had one Grain of Respect or Affection left for me, that he would speak no more of it to me, or that he would pull his Sword out and Kill me. He appear'd surpriz'd at my Obstinancy as he call'd it, *told me* I was unkind to my self, and unkind to him in it; that it was a Crisis unlook'd for upon us both, and impossible for either of us to foresee; but that he did not see any other way to save us both from Ruin, and therefore he thought it the more Unkind; but that if he must say no more of it to me, he added with an unusual Coldness, that he did not know any thing else we had to talk of; and so he rose up to take his leave; I rose up too, as if with the same Indifference, but when he came to give me as it were a parting Kiss, I burst out into such a Passion of Crying, that tho' I would have spoke, I could not, and only pressing his Hand, seem'd to give him the Adieu, but cry'd vehemently.

HE was sensibly mov'd with this; so he sat down again, and said a great many kind things to me, to abate the excess of my Passion; but still urg'd the necessity of what he had proposed; all the while insisting, that if I did refuse, he would notwithstanding provide for me; but letting me plainly see, that he would decline me in the main Point; nay, even as a Mistress; making it a point of Honour not to lye with the Woman, that for ought he knew, might come to be his Brothers Wife.

THE bare loss of him as a Gallant was not so much my Affliction, as the loss of his Person, whom indeed I Lov'd to Distraction; and the loss of all the Expectations I had, and which I always had built my Hopes upon, of having him one Day for my Husband: These things oppress'd my Mind so much, that in short, I fell very ill, the agonies of my Mind, in a word, threw me into a high Feaver, and long it was, that none in the Family expected my Life.

I was reduc'd very low indeed, and was often Delirious and light Headed; but nothing lay so near me, as the fear, that when I was light Headed, I should say something or other to his Prejudice; I was distress'd in my Mind also to see him, and so he was to see me, for he really Lov'd me most passionately; but it could not be; there was not the least Room to desire it, on one side, or other, or so much as to make it Decent.

IT was near five Weeks that I kept my Bed, and tho' the violence of my Feaver abated in three Weeks, yet it several times Return'd; and the Physicians said two or three times, they could do no more for me, but that they must leave Nature and the Distemper to fight it Out; only strengthening the first with Cordials[1] to maintain the Strugle: After the end of five Weeks I grew better, but was so Weak, so Alter'd, so Melancholly, and recover'd so Slowly, that the Physicians apprehended I should go into a Consumption; and which vex'd me most, they gave it as their Opinion, that my Mind was Oppress'd, that something Troubl'd me, and in short, that I was IN LOVE; upon this, the whole House was set upon me to Examine me, and to press me to tell, whether I was in Love or not, and with who? but as I well might, I deny'd my being in Love at all.

THEY had on this Occasion a Squable one Day about me at Table, that had like to have put the whole Family in an Uproar, and for sometime did so; they happen'd to be all at Table, but the Father; as for me I was Ill, and in my Chamber: At the beginning of the Talk, which was just as they had finish'd their Dinner, the old Gentlewoman who had sent me somewhat to Eat, call'd her Maid to go up, and ask me if I would have any more; but the Maid brought down Word, I had not Eaten half what she had sent me already.

ALAS, *says the* old Lady, that poor Girl; I am afraid she will never be well.

1. Medicines for invigorating the heart.

WELL *says the* elder Brother, How should Mrs. *Betty* be well, *they say* she is in Love?

I believe nothing of it *says the old* Gentlewoman.

I don't know *says the* eldest Sister, what to say to it, they have made such a rout about her being so Handsome, and so Charming, and I know not what, and that in her hearing too, that has turn'd the Creatures Head I believe, and who knows what possessions[2] may follow such Doings? for my Part I don't know what to make of it.

WHY Sister, you must acknowledge she is very Handsome, *says the* elder Brother.

AY, and a great deal Handsomer than you Sister, *says* Robin, and that's your Mortification.

WELL, well, that is not the Question, *says his* Sister, the Girl is well enough, and she knows it well enough; she need not be told of it to make her Vain.

WE are not a talking of her being Vain, *says the* elder Brother, but of her being in Love; it may be she is in Love with herself, it seems my Sisters think so.

I would she was in Love with me, *says* Robin, I'd quickly put her out of her Pain.

WHAT d' ye mean by that Son, *says the* old Lady, How can you talk so?

WHY Madam, *says* Robin again, very honestly, Do you think I'd let the poor Girl Die for Love, and of one that is near at hand to be had too?

FYE Brother, *says the* second Sister, how can you talk so? would you take a Creature that has not a Groat[3] in the World?

PRETHEE Child *says* Robin, Beauties a Portion,[4] and good Humour with it, is a double Portion; I wish thou hadst half her Stock of both for thy Portion: So there was her Mouth stopp'd.

I find, *says the* eldest Sister, if *Betty* is not in Love, my Brother is; I wonder he has not broke his Mind to *Betty*, I warrant she won't say NO.

THEY that yield when they're ask'd *says* Robin, are one step before them that were never ask'd to yield, Sister, and two Steps before them that yield before they are ask'd: And that's an Answer to you Sister.

THIS fir'd the Sister, and she flew into a Passion, and said, things were come to that pass, that it was time the Wench, *meaning me*, was out of the Family; and but that she was not fit to be turn'd out,

2. Ideas, or delusions taking possession of the mind. *Rout:* Clamor, fuss.
3. I.e., does not have any money. Coined in 1351–52, the English groat was worth 4 pence; it ceased to be issued for circulation in 1662.
4. Robin is punning on "portion" as inheritance from an estate or what Moll is allotted by providence as a natural endowment, and "portion" as dowry.

she hop'd her Father and Mother would consider of it, as soon as she could be remov'd.

Robin reply'd, That was business for the Master and Mistress of the Family, who were not to be taught by One, that had so little Judgment as his eldest Sister.

IT run up a great deal farther; the Sister Scolded, *Robin* Rally'd[5] and Banter'd, but poor *Betty* loss'd Ground by it extreamly in the Family: I heard of it, and I cry'd heartily, and the old Lady came up to me, some body having told her that I was so much concern'd about it: I complain'd to her, that it was very hard the Doctors should pass such a Censure[6] upon me, for which they had no Ground; and that it was still harder, considering the Circumstances I was under in the Family; that I hop'd I had done nothing to lessen her Esteem for me, or given any Occasion for the Bickering between her Sons and Daughters; and I had more need to think of a Coffin, than of being in Love, and beg'd she would not let me suffer in her Opinion for any bodies Mistakes, but my own.

SHE was sensible of the Justice of what I said, but *told me*, since there had been such a Clamour among them, and that her younger Son Talk'd after such a rattling[7] way as he did; she desir'd I would be so Faithful to her, as to Answer her but one Question sincerely; I told her I would with all my heart, and with the utmost plainess and Sincerity: Why then the Question was, Whether there was any thing between her Son *Robert* and me? I told her with all the Protestations of Sincerity that I was able to make, and as I might well do, that there was not, nor ever had been; *I told her* that Mr. *Robert* had rattled and jested, as she knew it was his way, and that I took it always as I suppos'd he meant it, to be a wild airy way of Discourse that had no Signification in it: And again assured her, that there was not the least tittle of what she understood by it between us; and that those who had Suggested it, had done me a great deal of Wrong, and Mr. *Robert* no Service at all.

THE old Lady was fully satisfy'd, and kiss'd me, spoke chearfully to me, and bid me take care of my Health, and want for nothing, and so took her leave: But when she came down, she found the Brother and all his Sisters together by the Ears; they were Angry even to Passion, at his upbraiding them with their being Homely, and having never had any Sweet-heart, never having been ask'd the Question, and their being so forward as almost to ask first: He rallied them upon the Subject of Mrs. *Betty*; how Pretty, how good Humour'd, how she Sung better than they did, and Danc'd better, and how much Handsomer she was; and in doing this, he omitted

5. Teased, ridiculed.
6. Judgment, criticism.
7. Thoughtless, noisy.

no Ill-natur'd Thing that could vex them, and indeed, push'd too hard upon them: The old Lady came down in the height of it, and to put a stop to it, told them all the Discourse she had had with me, and how I answer'd, that there was nothing between Mr. *Robert* and I.

SHE's wrong there, *says* Robin, for if there was not a great deal between us, we should be closer together than we are: I told her I Lov'd her hugely, *says he*, but I could never make the Jade believe I was in Earnest; I do not know how you should *says his* Mother, no body in their Senses could believe you were in Earnest, to Talk so to a poor Girl, whose Circumstances you know so well.

BUT prethee Son *adds she*, since you tell me that you could not make her believe you were in Earnest, what must we believe about it? for you ramble so in your Discourse, that no body knows whether you are in Earnest or in Jest: But as I find the Girl by your own Confession has answer'd truely, I wish you would do so too, and tell me seriously, so that I may depend upon it; Is there any thing in it or no? Are you in Earnest or no? Are you Distracted indeed, or are you not? 'Tis a weighty Question, and I wish you would make us easie about it.

BY my Faith Madam, *says* Robin, 'tis in vain to mince[8] the Matter, or tell any more Lyes about it, I am in Earnest, as much as a Man is, that's going to be Hang'd. If Mrs. *Betty* would say she Lov'd me, and that she would Marry me, I'd have her to morrow Morning fasting; and say, *To have, and to hold*, instead of eating my Breakfast.

WELL, *says the Mother*, then there's one Son lost; and she said it in a very mournful Tone, as one greatly concern'd at it.

I hope not Madam, *says* Robin, no Man is lost, when a good Wife has found him.

WHY but Child, *says the* old Lady, she is a Beggar.

WHY then Madam, she has the more need of Charity *says* Robin; I'll take her off of the hands of the Parish, and she and I'll Beg together.

ITS bad Jesting with such things, *says the Mother*.

I don't Jest Madam, *says* Robin: We'll come and beg your Pardon Madam; and your Blessing Madam, and my Fathers.

THIS is all out of the way Son, *says the Mother*, if you are in Earnest you are Undone.

I am afraid not *says he*, for I am really afraid she won't have me, after all my Sisters huffing and blustring; I believe I shall never be able to persuade her to it.

THAT's a fine Tale indeed, she is not so far out of her Senses neither; Mrs. *Betty* is no Fool, *says the youngest Sister*, Do you think she has learnt to say NO, any more than other People?

8. Extenuate, make light of.

NO Mrs. *Mirth-Wit* says Robin, Mrs. *Betty's* no Fool; but Mrs. *Betty* may be Engag'd some other way, And what then?

NAY, *says the eldest Sister*, we can say nothing to that, Who must it be to then? She is never out of the Doors, it must be between you.

I have nothing to say to that *says* Robin, I have been Examin'd enough; there's my Brother, if it must be *between us*, go to Work with him.

THIS stung *the elder Brother* to the Quick, and he concluded that *Robin* had discover'd something: However, he kept himself from appearing disturb'd; Prethee *says he*, don't go to sham your Stories off upon me, I tell you, I deal in no such Ware; I have nothing to say to Mrs. *Betty*, nor to any of the *Miss Betty*'s in the Parish; and with that he rose up and brush'd off.

NO, *says the eldest Sister*, I dare answer for my Brother, he knows the World better.

THUS the Discourse ended; but it left *the elder Brother* quite confounded: He concluded his Brother had made a full Discovery, and he began to doubt, whether I had been concern'd in it, or not; but with all his Management, he could not bring it about to get at me; at last, he was so perplex'd, that he was quite Desperate, and resolv'd he wou'd come into my Chamber and see me, whatever came of it: In order to this, he contriv'd it so; that one Day after Dinner, watching *his eldest Sister*, till he could see her go up Stairs, he runs after her, *Hark ye Sister, says he*, Where is this sick Woman? may not a body see her? YES, *says the Sister*, I believe you may, but let me go first a little, and I'll tell you; so she run up to the Door, and gave me notice; and presently call'd to him again: BROTHER, *says she*, you may come if you please; so in he came, just in the same kind of Rant: Well, *says he*, at the Door *as he came in*, Where is this sick Body that's in Love? How do ye do Mrs. *Betty*? I would have got up out of my Chair, but was so Weak I could not for a good while; and he saw it and his Sister too, and she said, *Come do not strive to stand up*, my Brother desires no Ceremony, especially, now you are so Weak. No, No, No, Mrs. *Betty*, pray sit still *says he*, and so sits himself down in a Chair over-against me, and appear'd as if he was mighty Merry.

HE talk'd a deal of rambling Stuff to his Sister, and to me; sometimes of one thing, sometimes of another, on purpose to Amuse[9] his Sister; and every now and then, would turn it upon the old Story, directing it to me: Poor Mrs. *Betty, says he*, it is a sad thing to be in Love, why it has reduced you sadly; at last I spoke a little; I am glad to see you so Merry: Sir *says I*, but I think the Doctor might have found some thing better to do, than to make his Game at his Patients:

9. Beguile, delude.

If I had been Ill of no other Distemper, I know the Proverb too well to have let him come to me: What Proverb *says he*? O! I remember it now: What,

> *"Where Love is the Case,*
> *"The* Doctor's *an Ass.*[1]

Is not that it Mrs. *Betty*? I smil'd, and said nothing: Nay, *says he*, I think the effect has prov'd it to be Love; for it seems the Doctor has been able to do you but little Service, you mend very slowly they say, I doubt there's somewhat in it Mrs. *Betty*, I doubt you are Sick of the Incureables, and that is Love; I smil'd and said, No, *indeed Sir*, that's none of my Distemper.

WE had a deal of such Discourse, and sometimes others that signify'd as little; by and by He ask'd me to Sing them a Song; at which I smil'd, and said, my singing Days were over: At last he ask'd me, if he should Play upon his Flute to me; his Sister said, she believ'd it wou'd hurt me, and that my Head could not bear it; I bow'd and said, No, it would not hurt me: And pray Madam, *said I*, do not hinder it, I love the Musick of the Flute very much; then his Sister said, well do then Brother; with that he pull'd out the Key of his Closet, Dear Sister, *says he*, I am very Lazy, do step to my Closet and fetch my Flute, it lies in *such a Drawer*, naming a Place where he was sure it was not, that she might be a little while a looking for it.

As soon as she was gone, he related the whole Story to me, of the Discourse his Brother had about me, and of his pushing it at him, and his concern about it, which was the Reason of his contriving this Visit to me: I assur'd him, I had never open'd my Mouth either to his Brother, or to any Body else: I told him the dreadful Exigence I was in; that my Love to him, and his offering to have me forget that Affection, and remove it to another, had thrown me down; and that I had a thousand Times wish'd I might Die, rather than Recover, and to have the same Circumstances to strugle with as I had before; and that this backwardness to Life, had been the great Reason of the slowness of my Recovering: I added, that I foresaw, that as soon as I was well, I must quit the Family; and that as for Marrying his *Brother*, I abhor'd the thoughts of it, after what had been my Case with him, and that he might depend upon it, I would never see his Brother again upon that Subject: That if he would break all his Vows and Oaths, and Engagements with me, be that between his Conscience and his Honour, and himself: But he should never be able

1. Previous editors have identified several possible sources for this aphorism: Roger L'Estrange's translation of Francisco de Quevedo's *Visions* (1667); John Ray's *A Collection of English Proverbs*, 2nd ed. (1678); and John Taylor's *A Shilling or, The Trauailes of a Twelue-pence* (1621).

to say, that I who he had persuaded to call my self his Wife, and who had given him the Liberty to use me as a Wife, was not as Faithful to him as a Wife ought to be, what ever he might be to me.

HE was going to reply, and had said, That he was sorry I could not be persuaded, and was a going to say more, but he heard his Sister a coming, and so did I; and yet I forc'd out these few Words as a reply, That I could never be persuaded to Love one Brother, and Marry another: He shook his Head and said, *Then I am Ruin'd*, meaning himself; and that Moment his Sister enter'd the Room, and told him she could not find the Flute; Well, *says he* merrily, this Laziness won't do, so he gets up, and goes himself to go to look for it, but comes back without too; not but that he could have found it, but because his Mind was a little Disturb'd, and he had no mind to Play; and besides, the Errand he sent his Sister of, was answer'd another way; for he only wanted an Opportunity to speak to me, which he gain'd, tho' not much to his Satisfaction.

I had however, a great deal of Satisfaction in having spoken my Mind to him with Freedom, and with such an honest Plainess, as I have related; and tho' it did not at all Work that way, I desir'd, *that is to say*, to oblige the Person to me the more; yet it took from him all possibility of quiting me but by a down right breach of Honour, and giving up all the Faith of a Gentleman to me, which he had so often engaged by, never to abandon me, but to make me his Wife as soon as he came to his Estate.

IT was not many Weeks after this, before I was about the House again, and began to grow well; but I continu'd Melancholly, silent, dull, and retir'd, which amaz'd the whole Family, except he that knew the Reason of it; yet it was a great while before he took any Notice of it, and I *as backward to speak, as he*, carried respectfully to him, but never offer'd to speak a Word to him, that was particular of any kind whatsoever; and this continu'd for sixteen or seventeen Weeks, so that as I expected every Day to be dismiss'd the Family, on Account of what Distaste they had taken another Way, in which I had no Guilt; so I expected to hear no more of this Gentleman, after all his solemn Vows, and Protestations, but to be ruin'd and abandon'd.

AT last I broke the way myself in the Family, for my Removing; for being talking seriously with the old Lady one Day, about my own Circumstances in the World, and how my Distemper had left a heaviness upon my Spirits, that I was not the same thing I was before: The old Lady said, I am afraid *Betty*, what I have said to you, about my Son, has had some Influence upon you, and that you are Melancholly on his Account; Pray will you let me know how the Matter stands with you both? if it may not be improper, for as for *Robin*, he does nothing but Rally and Banter when I speak of it to him: Why truly Madam, *said I*, that Matter stands as I wish it did not, and I shall be very sincere with you in it, what ever befalls me for it, Mr. *Robert* has several times propos'd Marriage to me, which is what I had no Reason to expect, my poor Circumstances consider'd; but I have always resisted him, and that perhaps in Terms more positive than became me, considering the Regard that I ought to have for every Branch of your Family: But *said I*, Madam, I could never so far forget my Obligations to you, and all your House, to offer to Consent to a Thing, which I know must needs be Disobliging to you, and this I have made my Argument to him, and have possitively told him, that I would never entertain a Thought of that kind, unless I had your Consent, and his Fathers also, to whom I was bound by so many invincible Obligations.

AND is this possible Mrs. *Betty*, says the old Lady? then you have been much Justier to us, than we have been to you; for we have all look'd upon you as a kind of a Snare to my Son; and I had a Proposal to make to you, for your Removing, for fear of it; but I had not yet mention'd it to you, because I thought you were not thorough Well, and I was afraid of grieving you too much, least it should thro' you down again, for we have all a Respect for you still, tho' not so much, as to have it be the Ruin of my Son; but if it be as you say, we have all wrong'd you very much.

As to the Truth of what I say, Madam, *said I*, I refer you to your Son himself; if he will do me any Justice, he must tell you the Story just as I have told it.

AWAY goes the old Lady to her Daughters, and tells them, the whole Story, just as I had told it her, and they were surpris'd at it, you may be sure, as I believ'd they would be; one *said*, she could never have thought it; another said, *Robin* was a Fool, a *Third* said, she would not believe a Word of it, and she would warrant that *Robin* would tell the Story another way; but the old Gentlewoman, who was resolv'd to go to the bottom of it, before I could have the least Opportunity of Acquainting her Son, with what had pass'd, resolv'd too, that she would Talk with her Son immediately, and to that purpose sent for him, for he was gone but to a Lawyers House in the Town, upon some petty Business of his own, and upon her sending, he return'd immediately.

UPON his coming up to them, for they were all still together; sit down *Robin, says the old Lady*, I must have some talk with you; with all my Heart, Madam, *says* Robin *looking very Merry*; I hope it is about a good Wife, for I am at a great loss in that Affair: How can that be, *says his Mother*, did not you say, you resolved to have Mrs. *Betty*? Ay Madam, says *Robin*; but there is one has *forbid the Banns*: Forbid the Banns! *says his Mother*, who can that be? Even Mrs. *Betty* herself, says *Robin*. How so, *says his Mother*; Have you ask'd her the

Question then? *Yes, indeed Madam, says* Robin; I have attack'd her in Form,[2] five times since she was Sick, and am beaten off; the Jade is so stout, she won't Capitulate, nor yield upon any Terms, except such as I cannot effectually Grant: Explain your self, *says the Mother*, for I am surpris'd, I do not understand you, I hope you are not in Earnest.

WHY Madam, *says he*, the Case is plain enough upon me, it explains itself; she wont have me, *she says*; is not that plain enough? I think 'tis plain, and pretty rough too; well but *says the Mother*, you talk of Conditions, that you cannot Grant, what, does she want a Settlement? her Jointure[3] ought to be according to her Portion; but what Fortune does she bring you? Nay, as to Fortune, *says* Robin, she is rich enough; I am satisfy'd in that Point; but *'tis I* that am not able to come up to her Terms, and she is positive she will not have me without.

HERE the Sisters put in, Madam, *says the second Sister*, 'tis impossible to be serious with him; he will never give a direct Answer to any thing; you had better let him alone, and talk no more of it to him; you know how to dispose of her out of his way, if you thought there was any thing in it; *Robin* was a little warm'd with his Sisters rudeness, but he was even with her; and yet with good Manners too: There are two sorts of People, Madam, *says he, turning to his Mother*, that there is no contending with, that is a wise Body and a Fool, 'tis a little hard I should engage with both of them together.

THE younger Sister then put in, we must be Fools indeed, *says she*, in my Brother's Opinion, that he should think we can believe, he has seriously ask'd Mrs. *Betty* to Marry him, and that she has refus'd him.

Answer, and *Answer not*, says *Solomon*,[4] *replyed her Brother*: When your Brother had said to your Mother, that he had ask'd her no less than five Times, and that it was so, that she positively Denied him; methinks a younger Sister need not question the Truth of it, when her Mother did not: My Mother you see did not understand it, *says the second Sister*: There's some difference *says* Robin, between desiring me to Explain it, and telling me she did not believe it.

WELL but Son, *says the old Lady*, if you are dispos'd to let us into the Mystery of it, What were these hard Conditions? Yes Madam *says* Robin, I had done it before now, if the *Teazers* here had not worried me by way of Interruption: The Conditions are, that I bring my Father and you to Consent to it, and without that, she protests she

2. According to the rules or prescribed methods, formally.
3. Estate settled on a wife to provide for her in widowhood, usually proportionate to her dowry.
4. Proverbs 26:4–5: "Answer not a fool according to his folly, lest thou also be like unto him. Answer a fool according to his folly, lest he be wise in his conceit."

will never see me more upon that Head; and these Conditions *as I said*, I suppose I shall never be able to Grant; I hope my warm Sisters will be Answer'd now, and Blush a little; if not, I have no more to say till I hear farther.

THIS Answer was surprizing to them all, tho' less to the Mother, because of what I had said to her; as to the Daughters they stood Mute a great while; but the Mother said with some Passion, WELL, I had heard this before, *but I cou'd not believe it*; but if it is so, then we have all done BETTY wrong, and she has behav'd better than I ever expected: Nay, *says the eldest Sister*, if it is so, she has acted Handsomely indeed: I confess *says the Mother*, it was none of her Fault, if he was Fool enough to take a Fancy to her; but to give such an Answer to him, shews more Respect to your Father and me, than I can tell how to Express; I shall value the Girl the better for it, as long as I know her. But I shall not *says* Robin, unless you will give your Consent: I'll consider of that a while *says the Mother*; I assure you, if there were not some other Objections in the way, this Conduct of hers would go a great way to bring me to Consent: I wish it would go quite thro' with it, *says* Robin; if you had as much thought about making me Easie,[5] as you have about making me Rich, you would soon Consent to it.

WHY *Robin, says the Mother again*, Are you really in Earnest? Would you so fain have her as you pretend? Really Madam *says* Robin, I think 'tis hard you should Question me upon that Head,[6] after all I have said: I won't say that I will have her, how can I resolve that point, when you see I cannot have her without your Consent? besides I am not bound to Marry at all: But this I will say, I am in Earnest in, that I will never have any body else, if I can help it; so you may Determine for me, *Betty*, or no Body, is the Word; and the Question which of the Two shall be in your Breast to decide Madam; provided only, that *my good humour'd Sisters here, may have no Vote in it*.

ALL this was dreadful to me, for the Mother began to yield, and *Robin* press'd her Home in it: On the other hand, she advised with the eldest Son, and he used all the Arguments in the World to persuade her to Consent; alledging his Brothers passionate Love for me, and my generous Regard to the Family, in refusing my own Advantages, upon such a nice point of Honour, and a thousand such Things: And as to the Father, he was a Man in a hurry of publick Affairs, and getting Money, seldom at Home, thoughtful of the main Chance;[7] but left all those Things to his Wife.

5. Free from mental anxiety, care, or apprehension.
6. Heading or topic.
7. Concerned with social position and acquiring wealth.

YOU may easily believe, that when the Plot was thus, as *they thought* broke out,[8] and that every one thought they knew how Things were carried: It was not so Difficult, or so Dangerous, for the elder Brother, who no body suspected of any thing, to have a freer Access to me than before: Nay the Mother, *which was just as he wish'd*, Propos'd it to him to Talk with Mrs. *Betty*; for it may be Son *said she*, you may see farther into the Thing than I; and see if you think she has been so Positive as Robin says she has been, or no. This was as well as he could wish, and he as it were yielding to Talk with me at his Mother's Request, She brought me to him into her own Chamber; told me her Son had some Business with me at her Request, and desir'd me to be very Sincere with him; and then she left us together, and he went and shut the Door after her.

HE came back to me, and took me in his Arms and kiss'd me very Tenderly; but told me, he had a long Discourse to hold with me, and it was now come to that Crisis, that I should make my self Happy or Miserable, as long as I Liv'd: That the Thing was now gone so far, that if I could not comply with his Desire, we should be both Ruin'd: Then he told me the whole Story between *Robin*, as he call'd him, and his Mother, and Sisters, and himself; as it is above: And now dear Child, *says he*, consider what it will be to Marry a Gentleman of a good Family, in good Circumstances, and with the Consent of the whole House, and to enjoy all that the World can give you: And what on the other Hand, to be sunk into the dark Circumstances of a Woman that has lost her Reputation; and that tho' I shall be a private Friend to you while I live, yet as I shall be suspected always; so you will be afraid to see me, and I shall be afraid to own you.

HE gave me no time to Reply, but went on with me thus: What has happen'd between us Child, so long as we both agree to do so, may be buried and forgotten: I shall always be your sincere Friend, without any Inclination to nearer Intimacy, when you become my Sister; and we shall have all the honest part of Conversation[9] without any Reproaches between us, of having done amiss: I beg of you to consider it, and do not stand in the way of your own Safety and Prosperity; and to satisfie you that I am Sincere, *added he*, I here offer you 500 *l.* in Money, to make you some Amends for the Freedoms I have taken with you, which we shall look upon as some of the Follies of our Lives, which 'tis hop'd we may Repent of.

HE spoke this in so much more moving Terms than it is possible for me to Express, and with so much greater force of Argument than I can repeat: That I only recommend it to those who Read the Story,

8. Completely uncovered.
9. Not necessarily limited to discourse but including social exchange or contact in general. The word also had sexual connotations—hence the elder brother's emphasis on "the honest part."

to suppose, that as he held me above an Hour and Half in that Discourse, so he answer'd all my Objections, and fortified his Discourse with all the Arguments, that humane[1] Wit and Art could Devise.

I cannot say however, that any thing he said, made Impression enough upon me, so as to give me any thought of the Matter; till he told me at last very plainly, that if I refus'd, he was sorry to add, that he could never go on with me in that Station as we stood before; that tho' he Lov'd me as well as ever, and that I was as agreeable to him, as ever; yet, Sense of Vertue had not so far forsaken him, as to suffer him to lye with a Woman, that his Brother Courted to make his Wife; and if he took his leave of me, with a denial in this Affair; whatever he might do for me in the Point of support, grounded on his first Engagement of maintaining me, yet he would not have me be surpriz'd, that he was oblig'd to tell me, he could not allow himself to see me any more; and that indeed I could not expect it of him.

I receiv'd this last part with some tokens of Surprize and Disorder, and had much ado, to avoid sinking down, for indeed I lov'd him to an Extravagance, not easie to imagine; but he perceiv'd my Disorder, he entreated me to consider seriously of it, assur'd me that it was the only way to Preserve our mutual Affection, that in this Station we might love as Friends, with the utmost Passion, and with a love of Relation untainted, free from our just Reproaches, and free from other Peoples Suspicions; that he should ever acknowledge his happiness owing to me; that he would be Debtor to me as long as he liv'd, and would be paying that Debt as long as he had Breath; Thus he wrought me up, in short, to a kind of Hesitation in the Matter; having the Dangers on one Side represented in lively Figures, and indeed heightn'd by my Imagination of being turn'd out to the wide World, a meer cast off Whore, *for it was no less*, and perhaps expos'd as such; with little to provide for myself; with no Friend, no Acquaintance in the whole World; *out of that Town*, and there I could not pretend to Stay; all this terrify'd me to the last Degree, and he took care upon all Occasions to lay it home to me, in the worst Colours that it could be possible to be drawn in; on the other Hand, he fail'd not to set forth the easy prosperous Life, which I was going to live.

HE answer'd all that I could object from Affection, and from former Engagements, with telling me the Necessity that was before us of taking other Measures now; and as to his Promises of Marriage, the nature of things *he said*, had put an End to that, by the probability of my being his Brothers Wife, before the time to which his Promises all referr'd.

THUS in a Word, I may say, he Reason'd me out of my Reason; he conquer'd all my Arguments, and I began to see a Danger that I was

1. Human.

in, which I had not consider'd of before, and that was of being drop'd by both of them, and left alone in the World to shift for myself.

THIS and his perswasion, at length Prevail'd with me to Consent, tho' with so much Reluctance, that it was easie to see I should go to Church, like a Bear to the Stake;[2] I had some little Apprehensions about me too, least my new Spouse, who by the way, I had not the least Affection for; should be skilful enough to Challenge me on another Account, upon our first coming to Bed together; but whether he did it with Design, or not, I know not; but his elder Brother took care to make him very much Fuddled before he went to Bed; so that I had the Satisfaction of a drunken Bedfellow the first Night: How he did it I know not, but I concluded that he certainly contriv'd it that his Brother might be able to make no Judgment of the difference between a Maid and a married Woman; nor did he ever Entertain any Notions of it, or disturb his Thoughts about it.

I should go back a little here, to where I left off; the elder Brother, having thus manag'd me, his next business was to Manage his Mother, and he never left till he had brought her to acquiesce, and be passive in the thing; Even without acquainting the Father, other than by Post Letters: So that she consented to our Marrying privately, and leaving her to manage the Father afterwards.

THEN he Cajol'd with his Brother, and perswaded him what Service he had done him, and how he had brought his Mother to Consent, which *tho' True*, was not indeed done to serve him, but to serve himself; but thus diligently did he cheat him, and had the Thanks of a faithful Friend for shifting off his Whore into his Brothers Arms for a Wife. So certainly does Interest banish all manner of Affection, and so naturally do Men give up Honour and Justice, Humanity, and even Christianity, to secure themselves.

I must now come back to Brother *Robin*, as we always call'd him; who having got his Mother's Consent *as above*, came big[3] with the News to me, and told me the whole Story of it; with a Sincerity so visible; that I must confess it griev'd me, that I must be the Instrument to abuse so honest a Gentleman; but there was no Remedy, he would have me, and I was not oblig'd to tell him, that I was his Brother's Whore, tho' I had no other way to put him off; so I came gradually into it, to his Satisfaction, and behold, we were Married.

MODESTY forbids me to reveal the Secrets of the Marriage Bed, but nothing could have happen'd more suitable to my Circumstances than that, *as above*, my Husband was so Fuddled when he came to Bed, that he could not remember in the Morning, whether he had

2. Proverbial expression for reluctance, drawn from bear-baiting, the "sport" of setting dogs to attack a bear chained to a stake.
3. Bursting ("big with" is also a colloquial expression for "pregnant").

had any Conversation[4] with me or no, and I was oblig'd to tell him *he had*, tho' in reallity *he had not*, that I might be sure he could make no enquiry about any thing else.

IT concerns the Story in hand very little, to enter into the farther particulars of the Family, or of myself, for the five Years that I liv'd with this Husband; only to observe that I had two Children by him, and that at the end of five Year he Died: He had been really a very good Husband to me, and we liv'd very agreeably together; But as he had not receiv'd much from them, and had in the little time he liv'd acquir'd no great Matters, so my Circumstances were not great; nor was I much mended[5] by the Match: Indeed I had preserv'd the elder Brother's Bonds to me, to pay me 500 *l.* which he offer'd me for my Consent to Marry his Brother; and this with what I had saved of the Money he formerly gave me, and about as much more by my Husband, left me a Widow with about 1200 *l.* in my Pocket.

MY two Children were indeed taken happily off of my Hands, by my Husband's Father and Mother, and that by the way was all they got by Mrs. *Betty*.

I confess I was not suitably affected with the loss of my Husband; nor indeed can I say, that I ever Lov'd him as I ought to have done, or as was proportionable to the good Usage I had from him, for he was a tender, kind, good humour'd Man as any Woman could desire; but his Brother being so always in my sight, *at least*, while we were in the Country, was a continual Snare to me; and I never was in Bed with my Husband, but I wish'd my self in the Arms of his Brother; and tho' his Brother never offer'd me the least Kindness that way, after our Marriage, but carried it just as a Brother ought to do; yet, it was impossible for me to do so to him: In short, I committed Adultery and Incest with him every Day in my Desires, which without doubt, was as effectually Criminal in the Nature of the Guilt, as if I had actually done it.

BEFORE my Husband Died, his elder Brother was Married, and we being then remov'd to *London*, were written to by the old Lady to come, and be at the Wedding; my Husband went, but I pretended Indisposition, and that I could not possibly Travel, so I staid behind; for in short, I could not bear the sight of his being given to another Woman, tho' I knew I was never to have him my self.

I was now *as above*, left loose to the World, and being still Young and Handsome, as every body said of me, *and I assure you, I thought my self so*, and with a tollerable Fortune in my Pocket, I put no small value upon my self: I was Courted by several very considerable Tradesmen; and particularly, very warmly by one, a *Linnen-Draper*,

4. Sexual intercourse (see n. 9, p. 46).
5. Financially improved.

at whose House after my Husband's Death I took a Lodging, his Sister being my Acquaintance; here I had all the Liberty, and all the Opportunity to be Gay, and appear in Company that I could desire; my Landlord's Sister being one of the Madest, Gayest things alive, and not so much Mistress of her Vertue, as I thought at first she had been: She brought me into a World of wild Company, and even brought home several Persons, *such as she lik'd well enough to Gratifie*, to see her pretty Widow, *so she was pleas'd to call me*, and that Name I got in a little time in Publick; now as Fame and Fools make an Assembly, I was here wonderfully Caress'd; had abundance of Admirers, and such as call'd themselves *Lovers*; but I found not one fair Proposal among them all; as for their common Design, that I understood too well to be drawn into any more Snares of that Kind: The Case was alter'd with me, I had Money in my Pocket, and had nothing to say to them: I had been trick'd once by *that Cheat* call'd, LOVE, but the Game was over; I was resolv'd now to be Married, or Nothing, and to be well Married, or not at all.

I lov'd the Company indeed of Men of Mirth and Wit, Men of Gallantry and Figure, and was often entertain'd with such, as I was also with others; but I found by just Observation, that the brightest Men came upon the dullest Errand, *that is to say*, the Dullest, as to what I aim'd at; on the other Hand, those who came with the best Proposals, were the Dullest and most disagreeable Part of the World: I was not averse to a Tradesman, but then I would have a Tradesman forsooth, that was something of a Gentleman too; that when my Husband had a mind to carry me to the Court, or to the Play, he might become a Sword,[6] and look as like a Gentleman, as another Man; and not be one that had the mark of his Apron-strings upon his Coat, or the mark of his Hat upon his Perriwig; that should look as if he was set on to his Sword, when his Sword was put on to him, and that carried his Trade in his Countenance.

WELL, at last I found this amphibious Creature, this *Land-water-thing*, call'd, *a Gentleman-Tradesman*; and as a just Plague upon my Folly, I was catch'd in the very Snare, which *as I might say*, I laid for my self; *I say laid for my self*, for I was not Trepan'd[7] I confess, but I betray'd my self.

THIS was a *Draper* too, for tho' my Comrade would have brought me to a Bargain with her Brother, yet when it came to the Point, it was it seems for a Mistress, not a Wife, and I kept true to this Notion, that a Woman should never be kept for a Mistress, that had Money to keep her self.

THUS my Pride, not my Principle, my Money, not my Vertue, kept me Honest; tho' as it prov'd, I found I had much better have been

6. I.e., wear a sword becomingly or with graceful fitness.
7. Caught in a trap.

Sold by my *She Comrade* to her Brother, than have Sold my self as I did to a Tradesman, that was Rake, Gentleman, Shop keeper, and Beggar all together.

BUT I was hurried on (by my Fancy to a Gentleman) to Ruin my self in the grossest Manner that ever Woman did; for my new Husband coming to a lump of Money at once, fell into such a profusion of Expence, that all I had, and all he had before, if he had any thing worth mentioning, would not have held it out above one Year.

HE was very fond of me for about a quarter of a Year, and what I got by that, was, that I had the pleasure of seeing a great deal of my Money spent upon my self, and as I may say, had some of the spending it too: Come, my dear, *says he to me one Day*, Shall we go and take a turn into the Country for about a Week? Ay, my Dear, *says I*, Whither would you go? I care not whither *says he*, but I have a mind to look like Quality for a Week; we'll go to OXFORD *says he*: How *says I*, shall we go, I am no Horse Woman, and 'tis too far for a Coach; too far *says he*, no Place is too far for a Coach and Six: If I carry you out, you shall Travel like a Dutchess; hum *says I*, my Dear 'tis a Frolick, but if you have a mind to it I don't care. Well the time was appointed, we had a rich Coach, very good Horses, a Coachman, Postilion, and two Footmen in very good Liveries; a Gentleman on Horseback, and a Page with a Feather in his Hat upon another Horse; The Servants all call'd him my Lord, and the Inn-Keepers you may be sure did the like, and I was *her Honour*, the Countess; and thus we Travel'd to OXFORD, and a very pleasant Journey we had; for, give him his due, not a Beggar alive knew better how to be a Lord than my Husband: We saw all the Rareties at OXFORD, talk'd with two or three Fellows of Colleges, about putting out a young Nephew, that was left to his Lordship's Care to the University, and of their being his Tutors; we diverted our selves with bantering several other poor Scholars, with hopes of being at least his Lordship's Chaplains and putting on a Scarf;[8] and thus having liv'd like Quality indeed, as to Expence; we went away for *Northampton*, and in a word, in about twelve Days ramble came Home again, to the Tune of about 93 *l.* Expence.

VANITY is the perfection of a Fop; my Husband had this Excellence, that he valued nothing of Expence, and as his History you may be sure, has very little weight in it; 'tis enough to tell you, that in about two Years and a Quarter he Broke, and was not so happy to get over into the *Mint*, but got into a *Spunging-House*,[9] being Arrested in an

8. Part of clerical attire, usually made of silk, worn by a nobleman's chaplain.
9. A house kept by a bailiff or sheriff's officer as a place of preliminary confinement for debtors. *Broke*: Went bankrupt. *Mint*: Debtors' sanctuary located in Southwark.

Action too heavy for him to give Bail to, so he sent for me to come to him.

It was no surprize to me, for I had foreseen *sometime*, that all was going to Wreck, and had been taking care to reserve something if I could, *tho' it was not much* for myself: But when he sent for me, he behav'd much better than I expected, and told me plainly, he had plaid the Fool and suffer'd himself to be Surpriz'd which he might have prevented; that now he foresaw he could not stand it, and therefore he would have me go Home, and in the Night take away every thing I had in the House of any Value and secure it; and after that, he told me, that if I could get away 100 *l.* or 200 *l.* in Goods out of the Shop, I should do it, only *says he*, let me know nothing of it, neither what you take, or whither you carry it; for as for me *says he*, I am resolv'd to get out of this House and be gone; and if you never hear of me more, my Dear, *says he*, I wish you well; I am only sorry for the Injury I have done you: He said some very handsome Things to me indeed at Parting; for *I told you* he was a *Gentleman*, and that was all the benefit I had of his being so; that he used me very handsomely, and with good Manners upon all Occasions, even to the last, only spent all I had, and left me to Rob the Creditors for something to Subsist on.

However I did as he bad me, *that you may be sure*, and having thus taken my leave of him, I never saw him more; for he found means to break out of the Bailiff's House that Night, or the next, and got over into *France*; and for the rest, the Creditors scrambl'd for it as well as they could: How I knew not, for I could come at no Knowledge of any thing, more than this; that he came Home about three a Clock in the Morning, caus'd the rest of his Goods to be remov'd into the *Mint*, and the Shop to be shut up; and having rais'd what Money he could get together, he got over as I said to *France*, from whence I had one or two Letters from him, and no more.

I did not see him when he came Home, for he having given me such Instructions as above, and I having made the best of my Time; I had no more Business back again at the House, not knowing but I might have been stop'd there by the Creditors; for a *Commission of Bankrupt*, being soon after Issued, they might have stop'd me by Orders from the *Commissioners*: But my Husband having so dextrously got out of the Bailiff's House by letting himself down in a most desperate Manner, from almost the top of the House, to the top of another Building, and leaping from thence which was almost two Stories, and which was enough indeed to have broken his Neck: He came home and got away his Goods, before the Creditors could come to Seize, *that is to say*, before they could get out the Commission, and be ready to send their Officers to take Possession.

My Husband was so civil to me, *for still I say, he was much of a*

Gentleman, that in the first Letter he wrote me from *France*, he let me know where he had Pawn'd 20 Pieces of fine *Holland* for 30 *l.* which were really worth above 90 *l.* and enclos'd me the Token, and an order for the taking them up, paying the Money, which I did, and made in time above 100 *l.* of them, having Leisure to cut them and sell them, some and some,[1] to private Families, as opportunity offer'd.

HOWEVER with all this, and all that I had secur'd before, I found upon casting things up, my Case was very much alter'd, and my Fortune much lessen'd, for including the Hollands, and a parcel of fine Muslins, which I carry'd off before, and some Plate, and other things; I found I could hardly muster up 500 *l.* and my Condition was very odd, for tho' I had no Child, (*I had had one by my Gentleman* Draper, *but it was buried*,) yet I was a Widow bewitch'd, I had a Husband, and no Husband, and I could not pretend to Marry again, tho' I knew well enough my Husband would never see *England* any more, if he liv'd fifty Years: *Thus I say*, I was limitted from Marriage, what Offer soever might be made me: and I had not one Friend to advise with, in the Condition I was in, at least not one I durst Trust the Secret of my Circumstances to, for if the Commissioners were to have been inform'd where I was, I should have been fetch'd up, and examin'd upon Oath, and all I had sav'd be taken away from me.

UPON these Apprehensions the first thing I did, was to go quite out of my Knowledge,[2] and go by another Name: This I did effectually, for I went into the *Mint* too, took Lodgings in a very private Place, drest me up in the Habit of a Widow, and call'd myself Mrs. *Flanders*.

HERE, however I conceal'd myself, and tho' my new Acquaintances knew nothing of me, yet I soon got a great deal of Company about me; and whether it be that Women are scarce among the Sorts of People that generally are to be found there; or that some Consolation in the Miseries of the Place, are more Requisite than on other Occasions; I soon found an agreeable Woman was exceedingly valuable among the Sons of Affliction there; and that those that wanted Money to pay Half a Crown in the Pound to their Creditors, and that run in Debt at the Sign of the *Bull* for their Dinners, would yet find Money for a Supper, if they lik'd the Woman.

HOWEVER, I kept myself Safe yet, tho' I began like my Lord *Rochester's* Mistress,[3] that lov'd his Company, but would not admit him

1. Little by little, gradually.
2. I.e., leave the area she was familiar with and where she was known.
3. John Wilmot, second earl of Rochester (1647–80), was one of Defoe's favorite poets, whom he ranked among the "Giants" of "Wit and Sense." Moll is remembering the concluding lines of the "song" to "*Phillis*," in which the poet admonishes his mistress, "Then if to make your ruin more, / You'll peevishly be coy, / *Dye* with the scandal of a *Whore*, / And never know the joy." In *An Essay at a Plain Exposition of That Difficult Phrase A Good*

farther, to have the Scandal of a Whore, without the Joy; and upon this score tir'd with the Place, and indeed with the Company too, I began to think of Removing.

IT was indeed a Subject of strange Reflection to me, to see Men who were overwhelm'd in perplex'd Circumstances; who were reduc'd some Degrees below being Ruin'd; whose Families were Objects of their own Terror and other Peoples Charity; yet while a Penny lasted, nay, even beyond it, endeavouring to drown their Sorrow in their Wickedness; heaping up more Guilt upon themselves, labouring to forget former things, which now it was the proper time to remember, making more Work for Repentance, and Sinning on, as a Remedy for Sin past.

BUT it is none of my Talent to preach; these Men were too wicked, even for me; there was something horrid and absurd in their way of Sinning, for it was all a Force even upon themselves; they did not only act against Conscience, but against Nature; they put a Rape upon their Temper to drown the Reflections, which their Circumstances continually gave them; and nothing was more easie than to see how Sighs would interrupt their Songs, and paleness, and anguish sit upon their Brows, in spite of the forc'd Smiles they put on; nay, sometimes it would break out at their very Mouths, when they had parted with their Money for a lewd Treat, or a wicked Embrace; I have heard them, turning about, fetch a deep Sigh, and cry *what a Dog am I*! Well *Betty*, my Dear, I'll drink thy Health tho', *meaning the Honest Wife*, that perhaps had not a Half a Crown for herself, and three or four Children: The next Morning they are at their Penitentials again, and perhaps the poor weeping Wife comes over to him, either brings him some Account of what his Creditors are doing, and how she and the Children are turn'd out of Doors, or some other dreadful News; and this adds to his self Reproaches; but when he has Thought and Por'd on it till he is almost Mad, having no Principles to Support him, nothing within him or above him, to Comfort him; but finding it all Darkness on every Side, he flyes to the same Relief again, (*viz.*) to Drink it away, Debauch it away, and falling into Company of Men in just the same Condition with himself, he repeats the Crime, and thus he goes every Day one Step onward of his way to Destruction.

I was not wicked enough for such Fellows as these *yet*; on the contrary, I began to consider here *very seriously* what I had to do; how things stood with me, and what Course I ought to take: I knew

---

Peace (1711), while complaining of having anonymous works attributed to him, Defoe adapts Rochester's lines to his own case: "I have the Scandal without the Joy, the Reproach without the Profit of the Charge."

I had no Friends, no not one Friend or Relation in the World; and that little I had left apparently wasted, which when it was gone, I saw nothing but Misery and Starving was before me: Upon these Considerations, I say, and fill'd with Horror at the Place I was in, and the dreadful Objects, which I had always before me, *I resolv'd to be gone*.

I had made an Acquaintance with a very sober good sort of a Woman, who was a Widow too like me, but in better Circumstances; her Husband had been a Captain of a Merchant Ship, and having had the Misfortune to be Cast away coming Home on a Voyage from the *West-Indies*, which would have been very profitable, if he had come safe, was so reduc'd by the Loss, that tho' he had saved his Life then, it broke his Heart, and kill'd him afterwards, and his Widow being persued by the Creditors was forc'd to take Shelter in the *Mint*: She soon made things up with the help of Friends, and was at Liberty again; and finding that I rather was there to be conceal'd, than by any particular Prosecutions, and finding also that I agreed with her, *or rather she with me* in a just Abhorrence of the Place, and of the Company; she invited me to go Home with her, till I could put myself in some posture of settling in the World to my Mind; withal telling me, that it was ten to one, but some good Captain of a Ship might take a Fancy to me, and Court me, in that part of the Town where she liv'd.

I accepted her Offer, and was with her Half a Year, and should have been longer; but in that interval what she propos'd to me happen'd to herself, and she marry'd very much to her Advantage; but whose Fortune soever was upon the Encrease, mine seem'd to be upon the Wane, and I found nothing present, except two or three Boatswains, or such Fellows, but as for the Commanders they were generally of two Sorts. 1. Such as having good Business, *that is to say*, a good Ship, resolv'd not to Marry, but with Advantage, that is, with a good Fortune. 2. Such as being out of Employ, wanted a Wife to help them to a Ship, I mean. (1). A Wife, who having some Money could enable them to hold, as they call it, a good part of a Ship themselves, so to encourage Owners to come in; Or. (2.) A Wife who if she had not Money, had Friends who were concern'd in Shipping, and so could help to put the young Man into a good Ship, which to them is as good as a Portion, and neither of these was my Case; so I look'd like one that was to *lye on Hand*.[4]

This Knowledge I soon learnt by Experience, (*viz.*) That the State of things was altered, as to Matrimony, and that I was not to expect at *London*, what I had found in the Country; that Marriages were

4. Remain in stock (as in a shop) until bought or sold.

here the Consequences of politick Schemes, for forming Interests, and carrying on Business, and that LOVE had no Share, or but very little in the Matter.

THAT, as my Sister in Law, at *Colchester* had said, Beauty, Wit, Manners, Sence, good Humour, good Behaviour, Education, Vertue, Piety, or any other Qualification, whether of Body or Mind, had no power to recommend: That Money only made a Woman agreeable: That Men chose Mistresses indeed by the gust of their Affection, and it was requisite to a Whore to be Handsome, well shap'd, have a good Mien, and a graceful Behaviour; but that for a Wife, no Deformity would shock the Fancy, no ill Qualities, the Judgement; the Money was the thing; the Portion was neither crooked, or Monstrous, but the Money was always agreeable, whatever the Wife was.

ON the other Hand, as the Market run very Unhappily on the Mens side, I found the Women had lost the Privilege of saying No, that it was a Favour now for a Woman to have THE QUESTION ask'd, and if any young Lady had so much Arrogance as to Counterfeit a Negative, she never had the Opportunity given her of denying twice; much less of Recovering that false Step, and accepting what she had, but seem'd to decline: The Men had such Choice every where, that the Case of the Women was very unhappy; for they seem'd to Plie at every Door, and if the Man was by great Chance refus'd at one House, he was sure to be receiv'd at the next.

BESIDES this, I observ'd that the Men made no scruple to set themselves out, and to go a Fortune Hunting, *as they call it*, when they had really no Fortune themselves to Demand it, or Merit to deserve it; and That they carry'd it so high, that a Woman was scarce allow'd to enquire after the Character, or Estate of the Person that pretended to her: This, I had an Example of, in a young Lady at the next House to me, and with whom I had Contracted an intimacy; she was Courted by a young Captain, and though she had near 2000 *l.* to her Fortune, she did but enquire of some of his Neighbours about his Character, his Morals, or Substance; and he took Occasion at the next Visit to let her know, truly, that he took it very ill, and that he should not give her the Trouble of his Visits any more: I heard of it, and as I had begun my Acquaintance with her, I went to see her upon it: She enter'd into a close Conversation with me about it, and unbosom'd herself very freely; I perceiv'd presently that tho' she thought herself very ill us'd, yet she had no power to resent it, and was exceedingly Piqu'd that she had lost him, and particularly that another of less Fortune had gain'd him.

I fortify'd her Mind against such a Meanness, *as I call'd it*; I told her, that as low as I was in the World, I would have despis'd a Man that should think I ought to take him upon his own Recommendation only, without having the liberty to inform myself of his Fortune, and of his Character; also *I told her*, that as she had a good Fortune, she had no need to stoop to the Dissaster of the times; that it was enough that the Men could insult us that had but little Money to recommend us; but if she suffer'd such an Affront to pass upon her without Resenting it, she would be render'd low-priz'd upon all Occasions, and would be the Contempt of all the Women in that part of the Town; that a Woman can never want an Opportunity to be Reveng'd of a Man that has us'd her ill, and that there were ways enough to humble such a Fellow as that, or else certainly Women were the most unhappy Creatures in the World.

I found she was very well pleas'd with the Discourse, and she told me seriously that she would be very glad to make him sensible of her just Resentment, and either to bring him on again, or have the Satisfaction of her Revenge being as publick as possible.

I told her, that if she would take my Advice, I would tell her how she should obtain her Wishes in both those things; and that I would engage I would bring the Man to her Door again, and make him beg to be let in: *She smil'd at that*, and soon let me see, that if he came to her Door, her Resentment was not so great as to give her leave to let him stand long there.

HOWEVER, she lissened very willingly to my offer of Advice; so *I told her*, that the first thing she ought to do, was a piece of Justice to herself; namely, that whereas she had been told by several People, that he had reported among the Ladies, that he had left her, and pretended to give the Advantage of the Negative to himself; she should take care to have it well spread among the Women, which she could not fail of an Opportunity to do in a Neighbourhood, so addicted to Family News, as that she liv'd in was; that she had enquired into his Circumstances, and found he was not the Man as to Estate he pretended to be: Let them be told Madam, *said I*, that you had been well inform'd that he was not the Man that you expected, and that you thought it was not safe to meddle with him, that you heard he was of an ill Temper, and that he boasted how he had us'd the Women ill upon many Occasions, and that particularly he was Debauch'd in his Morals, *&c*. The last of which indeed had some Truth in it; but at the same time, I did not find that she seem'd to like him much the worse for that part.

As I had put this into her Head, she came most readily into it; immediately she went to Work to find Instruments, and she had very little difficulty in the Search; for telling her Story in general to a Couple of Gossips in the Neighbourhood, it was the Chat of the Tea Table all over that part of the Town, and I met with it where ever I visited: Also, as it was known that I was Acquainted with the young Lady herself, my Opinion was ask'd very often; and I confirm'd it with all the necessary Aggravations, and set out his Character in the blackest Colours; but then as a piece of secret Intelligence, I added, as what the other Gossips knew nothing of (*viz.*) That I had heard he was in very bad Circumstances; that he was under a Necessity of a Fortune to support his Interest with the Owners of the Ship he Commanded: That his own Part was not paid for, and if it was not paid quickly his Owners would put him out of the Ship, and his Chief Mate was likely to Command it, who offer'd to buy that Part which the Captain had promis'd to take.

I added, for I confess I was heartily piqu'd at the Rogue, *as I call'd him*, that I had heard a Rumour too, that he had a Wife alive at *Plymouth*, and another in the *West Indies*, a thing which they all knew was not very uncommon for such kind of Gentlemen.

THIS work'd as we both desir'd it, for presently the young Lady at next Door, *who had a Father and Mother that Govern'd, both her, and her Fortune*, was shut up, and her Father forbid him the House: Also in one Place more where he went, the Woman had the Courage, *however strange it was*, to say No, and he could try no where but he was Reproached with his Pride, and that he pretended not to give the Women leave to enquire into his Character, *and the like*.

WELL by this time he began to be sensible of his mistake, and having allarm'd all the Women on that side the Water, he went over to *Ratcliff*,[5] and got access to some of the Ladies there; but tho' the young Women there too, were according to the Fate of the Day, pretty willing to be ask'd, yet such was his ill luck, that his Character follow'd him over the Water, and his good Name was much the same there, as it was on our side; so that tho' he might have had Wives enough, yet it did not happen among the Women that had good Fortunes, which was what he wanted.

BUT this was not all, she very ingeniously manag'd another thing her self, for she got a young Gentleman, who was a Relation, and was indeed a marry'd Man, to come and visit her Two or Three times a Week in a very fine Chariot and good Liveries, and her Two Agents and I also, presently spread a Report all over, that this Gentleman came to Court her; that he was a Gentleman of a Thousand Pounds a Year, and that he was fallen in Love with her, and that she was going to her Aunt's in the City, because it was inconvenient for the Gentleman to come to her with his Coach in *Redriff*,[6] the Streets being so narrow and difficult.

THIS took immediately, the Captain was laugh'd at in all Companies, and was ready to hang himself; he tryed all the ways possible

5. Area east of the Tower of London, north of the Thames. *Allarm'd*: Put on the alert.
6. Colloquial name for Rotherhithe, a London dock district on the south side of the Thames. Like Ratcliff, it was home to sailors and their families.

to come at her again, and wrote the most passionate Letters to her in the World, excusing his former Rashness, and in short, by great Application, obtained leave to wait on her again, *as he said*, to clear his Reputation.

AT this meeting she had her full Revenge of him; for *she told him* she wondred what he took her to be, that she should admit any Man to a Treaty of so much Consequence, as that of Marriage, without enquiring very well into his Circumstances; that if he thought she was to be huff'd into Wedlock, and that she was in the same Circumstances which her Neighbours might be in, (*viz.*) to take up with the first good Christian that came, he was mistaken; that in a word his Character was really bad, or he was very ill beholding to his Neighbours; and that unless he could clear up some Points, in which she had justly been Prejudiced, she had no more to say to him, but to do herself Justice, and give him the Satisfaction of knowing, that she was not afraid to say NO, either to him, or any Man else.

WITH that she told him what she had heard, *or rather rais'd*[7] *herself by my means, of his Character*; his not having paid for the Part he pretended to Own of the Ship he Commanded; of the Resolution of his Owners to put him out of the Command, and to put his Mate in his stead; and of the Scandal rais'd on his Morals; his having been reproach'd with such and such Women; and his having a Wife at *Plymouth* and in the *West-Indies, and the like*; and she ask'd him, whether he could deny that she had good Reason, if these things were not clear'd up, to refuse him, and in the mean time to insist upon having Satisfaction in Points so significant as they were?

HE was so confounded at her Discourse that he could not answer a word, and she almost began to believe that all was true, by his disorder, tho' at the same time she knew that she had been the raiser of all those Reports herself.

AFTER some time he recover'd himself a little, and from that time became the most humble, the most modest, and the most importunate Man alive in his Courtship.

SHE carried her jest on a great way, she ask'd him, if he thought she was so at her last shift, that she could or ought to bear such Treatment, and if he did not see that she did not want[8] those who thought it worth their while to come farther to her than he did, meaning the Gentleman who she had brought to visit her by way of sham.

SHE brought him by these tricks to submit to all possible measures to satisfie her, as well of his Circumstances, as of his Behaviour. He brought her undeniable Evidence of his having paid for his part of the Ship; he brought her Certificates from his Owners, that the

7. Originated.
8. Lack. *Shift*: Resource.

Report of their intending to remove him from the Command of the Ship, and put his chief Mate in, was false and groundless; in short, he was quite the reverse of what he was before.

THUS I convinc'd her, that if the Men made their Advantage of our Sex in the Affair of Marriage, upon the supposition of there being such Choice to be had, and of the Women being so easie; it was only owing to this, that the Women wanted Courage to maintain their Ground, and to play their Part; and that according to my Lord *Rochester*,

> *"A Woman's ne'er so ruin'd but she can*
> *"Revenge herself on her undoer, Man.*[9]

AFTER these things, this young Lady plaid her part so well, that tho' she resolved to have him, and that indeed having him was the main bent of her design, yet she made his obtaining her be TO HIM the most difficult thing in the World; and this she did, not by a haughty Reserv'd Carriage, but by a just Policy, turning the Tables upon him, and playing back upon him his own Game; for as he pretended by a kind of lofty Carriage, to place himself above the occasion of a Character,[1] and to make enquiring into his Character a kind of an affront to him; she broke with him upon that Subject; and at the same time that she made him submit to all possible enquiry after his Affairs, she apparently shut the Door against his looking into her own.

IT was enough to him to obtain her for a Wife, as to what she had, she told him plainly, that as he knew her Circumstances, it was but just she should know his; and tho' at the same time he had only known her Circumstances by common Fame, yet he had made so many Protestations of his Passion for her, that he could ask no more but her Hand to his grand Request, *and the like ramble*[2] *according to the Custom of Lovers*: In short, he left himself no room to ask any more questions about her Estate, and she took the advantage of it like a prudent Woman, for she plac'd part of her Fortune so in Trustees, without letting him know any thing of it, that it was quite out of his reach, and made him be very well content with the rest.

IT is true she was pretty well besides, that is to say, she had about 1400 *l.* in Money, which she gave him, and the other, after some time, she brought to light, as a perquisite to her self; which he was to accept as a mighty Favour, seeing though it was not to be his, it might ease him in the Article of her particular Expences; and I must

9. Slight misquotation of Rochester's "A Letter from *Artemiza* in the Town, to *Chloë* in the Country" (1679?), ll. 185–86: "A Woman's ne'r so wretched but she can / Be still revenged on her undoer, Man." Later editions of the poem change "wretched" to "ruyn'd" or "ruin'd," as Defoe spells it.
1. Detailed report of his personal qualities.
2. Wandering, meaningless discourse.

add, that by this Conduct the Gentleman himself became not only the more humble in his Applications to her to obtain her, but also was much the more an obliging Husband to her when he had her: I cannot but remind the Ladies here how much they place themselves below the common Station of a Wife, which if I may be allow'd not to be Partial is low enough already; *I say* they place themselves below their common Station, and prepare their own Mortifications, by their submitting so to be insulted by the Men before-hand, which I confess I see no Necessity of.

THIS Relation may serve therefore to let the Ladies see, that the Advantage is not so much on the other Side, as the Men think it is; and tho' it may be true, that the Men have but too much Choice among us, and that some Women may be found, who will dishonour themselves, be Cheap, and Easy to come at, and will scarce wait to be ask'd; yet if they will have Women, *as I may say*, worth having, they may find them as uncomatable[3] as ever; and that those that are otherwise, are a Sort of People that have such Defficiencies, *when had*, as rather recommend the Ladies that are Difficult than encourage the Men to go on with their easie Courtship, and expect Wives equally valluable that will come at first call.

NOTHING is more certain, than that the Ladies always gain of the Men, by keeping their Ground, and letting their pretended Lovers see they can Resent being slighted, and that they are not affraid of saying No. They, I observe insult us mightily, with telling us of the Number of Women; that the Wars and the Sea, and Trade, and other Incidents have carried the Men so much away, that there is no Proportion between the Numbers of the Sexes; and therefore the Women have the Disadvantage; but I am far from Granting that the Number of the Women is so great, or the Number of the Men so small; but if they will have me tell the Truth, the Disadvantage of the Women, is a terrible Scandal upon the Men, and it lyes here, and here only; *Namely*, that the Age is so Wicked, and the Sex so Debauch'd, that in short the Number of such Men, as an honest Woman ought to meddle with, is small indeed, and it is but here and there that a Man is to be found who is fit for a Woman to venture upon.

BUT the Consequence even of that too amounts to no more than this; that Women ought to be the more Nice;[4] For how do we know the just Character of the Man that makes the offer? To say, that the Woman should be the more easie on this Occasion, is to say, we should be the forwarder to venture, because of the greatness of the Danger; which in my way of Reasoning is very absurd.

ON the contrary, the Women have ten Thousand times the more

3. Unattainable.
4. Fastidious, finely discriminative.

Reason to be wary, and backward, by how much the hazard of being betray'd is the greater; and would the Ladies consider this, and act the wary Part, they would discover every Cheat that offer'd; for, *in short*, the Lives of very few Men now a-Days will bear a Character; and if the Ladies do but make a little Enquiry, they will soon be able to distinguish the Men, and deliver themselves: As for Women that do not think their own Safety worth their Thought, that impatient of their present State, resolve *as they call it* to take the first good Christian that comes; that run into Matrimony, as a Horse rushes into the Battle;[5] I can say nothing to them, but this, that they are a Sort of Ladies that are to be pray'd for among the rest of distemper'd People; and to me they look like People that venture their whole Estates in a Lottery[6] where there is a Hundred Thousand Blanks to one Prize.

No Man of common Sense will value a Woman the less, for not giving up herself at the first Attack, or for not accepting his Proposal without enquiring into his Person or Character; on the contrary, he must think her the weakest of all Creatures in the World, as the Rate of Men now goes; In short, he must have a very contemptible Opinion of her Capacities, nay, even of her Understanding, that having but one Cast for her Life, shall cast that Life away at once, and make Matrimony like Death, be a *Leap in the Dark*.[7]

I would fain have the Conduct of my Sex a little Regulated in this particular, which is the Thing, in which of all the parts of Life, I think at this Time we suffer most in: 'Tis nothing but lack of Courage, the fear of not being Marry'd at all, and of that frightful State of Life, call'd *an old Maid*; of which I have a Story to tell by itself: This I say, is the Woman's Snare; but would the Ladies once but get above that Fear, and manage rightly, they would more certainly avoid it by standing their Ground, in a Case so absolutely Necessary to their Felicity, than by exposing themselves as they do; and if they did not Marry so soon as they may do otherwise, they would make themselves amends by Marrying safer; she is always Married too soon, who gets a bad Husband, and she is never Married too late, who gets a good one: In a Word, there is no Woman, *Deformity, or lost Reputation excepted*, but if she manages well, may be Marry'd

5. This simile also appears in Defoe's *Religious Courtship* (1722) and *Conjugal Lewdness*.
6. Annual lotteries were sanctioned by Parliament to raise funds for public projects and to alleviate an ever-increasing national debt. As Moll asserts, the odds of winning were indeed long and made even longer, it was alleged, by fraud and corruption. Henry Fielding satirizes the false hopes of wealth and gentility roused by this scheme in his play, *The Lottery: A Farce* (1732).
7. A hazardous action undertaken in uncertainty as to the consequences; the *OED* cites this passage from *Moll Flanders* as illustration. The phrase was widely accepted as Thomas Hobbes's dying words and cited as such by Defoe in connection with marriage in *Religious Courtship*. It was also contemporary criminal slang for execution by hanging. *Cast*: See n. 1, p. 6.

safely one time or other; but if she Precipitates herself, it is ten Thousand to one but she is undone.

BUT I come now to my own Case, in which there was at this time no little Nicety. The Circumstances I was in, made the offer of a good Husband, the most necessary Thing in the World to me; but I found soon that to be made Cheap, and Easy, was not the way: It soon began to be found that the Widow had no Fortune, and to say this, was to say all that was Ill of me; for I began to be dropt in all the Discourses of Matrimony: Being well Bred, Handsome, Witty, Modest and agreeable; all which I had allowed to my Character, whether justly or no, is not to the Purpose; I say, all these would not do without the Dross,[8] which was now become more valuable than Virtue itself. In short, *the Widow*, they said, *had no Money*.

I resolv'd therefore, as to the State of my present Circumstances; that it was absolutely Necessary to change my Station, and make a new Appearance in some other Place where I was not known, and even to pass by another Name if I found Occasion.

I Communicated my Thoughts to my intimate Friend the Captain's Lady; who I had so faithfully serv'd in her Case with the Captain; and who was as ready to serve me in the same kind as I could desire: I made no scruple to lay my Circumstances open to her, my Stock was but low, for I had made but about 540 *l.* at the Close of my last Affair, and I had wasted some of that; However, I had about 460 *l.* left, a great many very rich Cloaths, a gold Watch, and some Jewels, tho' of no extraordinary value, and about 30 or 40 *l.* left in Linnen not dispos'd of.

MY Dear and faithful Friend, the Captain's Wife was so sensible of the Service I had done her in the Affair above, that she was not only a steddy Friend to me, but knowing my Circumstances, she frequently made me Presents as Money came into her Hands; such as fully amounted to a Maintenance; so that I spent none of my own; and at last she made this unhappy Proposal to me (*viz.*) that as we had observ'd, *as above*, how the Men made no scruple to set themselves out as Persons meriting a Woman of Fortune, when they had really no Fortune of their own; it was but just to deal with them in their own way, and if it was possible, to Deceive the Deceiver.[9]

THE Captain's Lady, in short put this Project into my Head, and told me if I would be rul'd by her I should certainly get a Husband of Fortune, without leaving him any room to Reproach me with want of my own; I told her as I had Reason to do, That I would give up myself wholly to her Directions, and that I would have neither

8. Foreign matter extracted from a substance to achieve purity. Money, the "dross" that ought to be discarded, has become, in Moll's mercenary world, the object most prized.
9. Defoe quotes this "old Latin Proverb, *Fallere fallentem non est fraus*," in *The Political History of the Devil* (1726).

Tongue to speak, or Feet to step in that Affair, but as she should direct me, depending that she would Extricate one out of every Difficulty that she brought me into, which she said she would Answer for.

THE first step she put me upon, was to call her Cousin, and go to a Relations House of hers in the Country, where she directed me; and where she brought her Husband to visit me; and calling me Cousin, she work'd Matters so about, that her Husband and she together Invited me most passionately to come to Town and be with them, for they now liv'd in a quite different Place from where they were before. In the next Place she tells her Husband, that I had at least 1500 *l.* Fortune, and that after some of my Relations I was like to have a great deal more.

IT was enough to tell her Husband this, there needed nothing on my Side; I was but to sit still and wait the Event, for it presently went all over the Neighbourhood that the young Widow at Captain——s was a Fortune, that she had at least 1500 *l.* and perhaps a great deal more, and *that the Captain said so*; and if the Captain was ask'd at any time about me, he made no scruple to affirm it, tho' he knew not one Word of the Matter, other than that his Wife had told him so; and in this he thought no Harm, for he really believ'd it to be so, because he had it from his Wife; so slender a Foundation will those Fellows build upon, if they do but think there is a Fortune in the Game: With the Reputation of this Fortune, I presently found myself bless'd with admirers enough, and that I had my Choice of Men, as scarce as they said they were, *which by the way confirms what I was saying before*: This being my Case, I who had a subtile Game to play, had nothing now to do but to single out from them all, the properest Man that might be for my Purpose; *that is to say*, the Man who was most likely to depend upon the *hear say* of a Fortune, and not enquire too far into the particulars; and unless I did this, *I did nothing*, for my Case would not bare[1] much Enquiry.

I Pick'd out my Man without much difficulty, by the judgment I made of his way of Courting me; I had let him run on with his Protestations and Oaths that he lov'd me above all the World; that if I would make him happy, that was enough; all which I knew was upon Supposition, nay, it was upon a full Satisfaction,[2] that I was very Rich, tho' I never told him a Word of it myself.

THIS was my Man, but I was to try him to the bottom, and indeed in that consisted my Safety; for if he baulk'd, I knew I was undone, as surely as he was undone if he took me; and if I did not make some scruple about his Fortune, it was the way to lead him to raise some about mine; and first therefore, I pretended on all occasions to doubt

1. Changed to "bear" in the second edition.
2. Satisfying proof, conviction.

his Sincerity, and told him, perhaps he only courted me for my Fortune, he stop'd my Mouth in that part, with the Thunder of his Protestations, *as above*, but still I pretended to doubt.

ONE Morning he pulls off his Diamond Ring, and writes upon the Glass[3] of the Sash in my Chamber this Line,

You I Love, and you alone.

I read it, and ask'd him to lend me his Ring, with which I wrote under it thus,

And so in Love says every one.

He takes his Ring again, and writes another Line thus,

Virtue alone is an Estate.

I borrow'd it again, and I wrote under it,

But Money's Vertue; Gold is Fate.

He colour'd as red as Fire to see me turn so quick upon him, and in a kind of a Rage told me he would Conquer me, and writes again *thus*,

I scorn your Gold, and yet I Love.

I ventur'd all upon the last cast of Poetry, as you'll see, for I wrote boldly under his last,

I'm Poor: Let's see how kind you'll prove.

This was a sad Truth to me, whether he believ'd me or no I cou'd not tell; I supposed then that he did not. However he flew to me, took me in his Arms, and kissing me very eagerly, and with the greatest Passion imaginable he held me fast till he call'd for a Pen and Ink, and then *told me* he could not wait the tedious writing on the Glass, but pulling out a piece of Paper, he began and wrote again,

Be mine, with all your Poverty.

I took his Pen and follow'd him immediately thus,

Yet secretly you hope I lie.

HE told me that was unkind, because it was not just, and that I put him upon contradicting me, which did not consist with good Manners, any more than with his Affection; and therefore since I had insensibly drawn him into this poetical scribble, he beg'd I would not oblige him to break it off, so he writes again,

Let Love alone be our Debate.

I wrote again,

She Loves enough, that does not hate.

This he took for a favour, and so laid down the Cudgels,[4] that is to say the Pen; I say he took it for a favour, and a mighty one it was, if he had known all: However he took it as I meant it, that is, to let

3. Writing on windows was a custom of the period. Moll and her lover engage in a version of the game of topping verses; the scene is also reminiscent, in a debased and parodic form, of the witty exchanges between the upper-class heroes and heroines of Restoration comedy (e.g., the "proviso" scene between Mirabell and Millamant in the fourth act of William Congreve's *The Way of the World*).
4. Stopped the contest (a cudgel is a short stick or club used as a weapon).

him think I was inclin'd to go on with him, as indeed I had all the Reason in the World to do, for he was the best humoured merry sort of a Fellow that I ever met with; and I often reflected on my self, how doubly criminal it was to deceive such a Man; but that Necessity,[5] which press'd me to a Settlement suitable to my Condition, was my Authority for it, and certainly his Affection to me, and the Goodness of his Temper, however they might argue against using him ill, yet they strongly argued to me, that he would better take the Disappointment, than some fiery tempered Wretch, who might have nothing to recommend him but those Passions which would serve only to make a Woman miserable all her Days.

BESIDES, tho' I had jested with him, as he suppos'd it, so often about my Poverty, yet, when he found it to be true, he had foreclosed all manner of objection, seeing whether he was in jest or in earnest, he had declar'd he took me without any regard to my Portion, and whether I was in jest or in earnest, I had declar'd my self to be very Poor, so that *in a word*, I had him fast both ways; and tho' he might say afterwards he was cheated, yet he could never say that I had cheated him.

HE persued me close after this, and as I saw there was no need to fear losing him, I play'd the indifferent part with him longer than Prudence might otherwise have dictated to me: But I considered how much this caution and indifference would give me the advantage over him, when I should come to be under the Necessity of owning my own Circumstances to him; and I manag'd it the more warily, because I found he inferr'd from thence, as indeed he ought to do, that I either had the more Money, or the more Judgment, and would not venture at all.

I TOOK the freedom one Day, after we had talk'd pretty close to the Subject, to tell him, that it was true I had receiv'd the Compliment of a Lover from him; namely, that he would take me without enquiring into my Fortune, and I would make him a suitable return in this, (*viz.*) that I would make as little enquiry into his as consisted with Reason, but I hoped he would allow me to ask a few Questions, which he should answer or not as he thought fit; and that I would not be offended if he did not answer me at all; one of these Questions related to our manner of living, and the place where, because I had heard he had a great Plantation in *Virginia*, and that he had talk'd

5. In the *Review* (15 September 1711), Defoe asserts that "Men rob for Bread, Women whore for Bread: Necessity is the Parent of Crime"—a sentiment Robinson Crusoe echoes in the second chapter of his *Serious Reflections* (1720) when he writes, "Necessity makes an honest man a knave." The plea of "necessity"—roughly, destitution (or the threat of destitution) as justification for morally reprehensible action—recurs throughout Defoe's works; it is a key concept in his fiction, as he represents and examines the ethical complexities of human behavior.

of going to live there, and I told him I did not care to be Transported.

HE began from this Discourse to let me voluntarily into all his Affairs, and to tell me in a frank open way, all his Circumstances, by which I found he was very well to pass in the World; but that great part of his Estate consisted of three Plantations, which he had in *Virginia*, which brought him in a very good Income, generally speaking, to the tune of 300 *l.* a Year; but that if he was to live upon them, would bring him in four times as much very well; thought I, you shall carry me thither as soon as you please, tho' I won't tell you so before-hand.

I JESTED with him extremely about the Figure he would make in *Virginia*; but I found he would do any thing I desired, tho' he did not seem glad to have me undervalue his Plantations, so I turn'd my Tale; I told him I had good reason not to desire to go there to live, because if his Plantations were worth so much there, I had not a Fortune suitable to a Gentleman of 1200 *l.* a Year, as he said his Estate would be.

HE reply'd generously, he did not ask what my Fortune was, he had told me from the beginning he would not, and he would be as good as his word; But whatever it was, he assur'd me he would never desire me to go to *Virginia* with him, or go thither himself without me, unless I was perfectly willing, and made it my Choice.

ALL this, you may be sure, was as I wish'd, and indeed nothing could have happen'd more perfectly agreeable; I carried it on as far as this with a sort of indifferency, that he often wondred at, more than at first, But which was the only support of his Courtship; and I mention it the rather to intimate again to the Ladies, that nothing but want of Courage for such an Indifferency, makes our Sex so cheap, and prepares them to be ill us'd as they are; would they venture the loss of a pretending Fop now and then, who carries it high upon the point of his own Merit, they would certainly be slighted less, and courted more; had I discovered really and truly what my great Fortune was, and that in all I had not full 500 *l.* when he expected 1500 *l.* yet I had hook'd him so fast, and play'd him so long, that I was satisfied he would have had me in my worst Circumstances; and indeed it was less a surprize to him when he learnt the Truth, than it would have been, because having not the least blame to lay on me, who had carried it with an air of indifference to the last, he could not say one word, except that indeed he thought it had been more, but that if it had been less he did not repent his bargain; only that he should not be able to maintain me so well as he intended.

IN short, we were married, and very happily married on my side I assure you, *as to the Man*; for he was the best humour'd Man that ever Woman had, but his Circumstances were not so good as I imagined, as on the other hand he had not bettered himself by marrying so much as he expected.

WHEN we were married I was shrewdly put to it to bring him that little Stock I had, and to let him see it was no more; but there was a necessity for it, so I took my opportunity one Day when we were alone, to enter into a short Dialogue with him about it; MY DEAR, *said* I, we have been married a Fortnight, is it not time to let you know whether you have got a Wife with something, or with nothing; your own time for that, my Dear, *says he*, I am satisfied that I have got the Wife I love, I have not troubled you much, *says he*, with my enquiry after it.

THAT'S true, *said I*, but I have a great difficulty upon me about it, which I scarce know how to manage.

WHAT'S that, my Dear, *says he*?

WHY *says I*, 'tis a little hard upon me, and 'tis harder upon you; I am told that Captain——(meaning my Friend's Husband) has told you I had a great deal more Money than I ever pretended to have, and I am sure I never employ'd him to do so.

WELL, *says he*, Captain——may have told me so, but what then, if you have not so much that may lye at his Door, but you never told me what you had, so I have no reason to blame you if you have nothing at all.

THAT is so just, *said I*, and so generous, that it makes my having but a little a double Affliction to me.

THE less you have, *my Dear, says he*, the worse for us both; but I hope your Affliction you speak of, is not caus'd for fear I should be unkind to you, for want of a Portion, No No, if you have nothing tell me plainly, and at once; I may perhaps tell the Captain he has cheated me, but I can never say you have cheated me, for did you not give it under your Hand that you were Poor, and so I ought to expect you to be.

WELL, said I, *my Dear*, I am glad I have not been concern'd in deceiving you before Marriage, if I deceive you since, 'tis ne'er the worse; *that I am Poor* is too true, but not so Poor as to have nothing neither; so I pull'd out some Bank Bills, and gave him about a Hundred and Sixty Pounds, there's something, my Dear, *says I*, and not quite all neither.

I HAD brought him so near to expecting nothing, by what I had said before, that the Money, tho' the Sum was small in it self, was doubly welcome to him; he own'd it was more than he look'd for, and that he did not question by my Discourse to him, but that my fine Cloths, Gold Watch, and a Diamond Ring or two had been all my Fortune.

I LET him please himself with that 160 *l.* two or three Days, and then having been abroad that Day, and as if I had been to fetch it,

I brought him a Hundred Pounds more home in Gold, and told him there was a little more Portion for him; and in short, in about a Week more I brought him 180 *l.* more, and about 60 *l.* in Linnen, which I made him believe I had been oblig'd to take with the 100 *l.* which I gave him in Gold, as a Composition[6] for a Debt of 600 *l.* being little more than Five Shilling in the Pound, and overvalued too.

AND now, MY DEAR, *says I to him*, I am very sorry to tell you, that there is all, and that I have given you my whole Fortune; I added, that if the Person who had my 600 *l.* had not abus'd me, I had been worth a Thousand Pound to him, but that as it was, I had been faithful to him, and reserv'd nothing to my self, but if it had been more he should have had it.

HE was so oblig'd by the Manner, and so pleas'd with the Sum, for he had been in a terrible fright least it had been nothing at all, that he accepted it very thankfully: And thus I got over the Fraud of *passing for a Fortune without Money*, and cheating a Man into Marrying me on pretence of a Fortune; which, *by the way*, I take to be one of the most dangerous Steps a Woman can take, and in which she runs the most hazard of being ill us'd afterwards.

MY Husband, *to give him his due*, was a Man of infinite good Nature, but he was no Fool; and finding his Income not suited to the manner of Living which he had intended, if I had brought him what he expected, and being under a Disappointment in his return of his Plantations in *Virginia*, he discover'd many times his inclination of going over to *Virginia* to live upon his own; and often would be magnifying the way of living there, how cheap, how plentiful, how pleasant, *and the like*.

I BEGAN presently to understand his meaning, and I took him up very plainly one Morning, and told him that I did so; that I found his Estate turn'd to no account at this distance, compar'd to what it would do if he liv'd upon the spot, and that I found he had a mind to go and live there; and I added, that I was sensible he had been disappointed in a Wife, and that finding his Expectations not answer'd that way, I could do no less to make him amends than tell him, that I was very willing to go over to *Virginia* with him and live there.

HE said a thousand kind things to me upon the subject of my making such a Proposal to him: He told me, that however he was disappointed in his Expectations of a Fortune, he was not disappointed in a Wife; and that I was all to him that a Wife could be, and he was more than satisfied in the whole when the particulars were put together; but that this offer was so kind, that it was more than he could express.

6. A contract or agreement to cancel a debt by taking partial payment in lieu of the whole amount.

To bring the story short, we agreed to go; *he told me*, that he had a very good House there, that it was well Furnish'd, that his Mother was alive and liv'd in it, and one Sister, which was all the Relations he had; that as soon as he came there, his Mother would remove to another House which was her own for life, and his after her Decease; so that I should have all the House to my self; and I found all this to be exactly as he had said.

To make this part of the story short, we put on board the Ship *which we went in*, a large quantity of good Furniture for our House, with stores of Linnen and other Necessaries, and a good Cargoe for Sale, and away we went.

To give an account of the manner of our Voyage, which was long and full of Dangers, is out of my way, I kept no Journal, neither did my Husband; all that I can say is, that after a terrible passage, frighted twice with dreadful Storms, and once with what was still more terrible, I mean a Pyrate, who came on board and took away almost all our Provisions; and which would have been beyond all to me, they had once taken my Husband to go along with them, but by entreaties were prevail'd with to leave him: I say, after all these terrible things, we arriv'd in *York River* in *Virginia*, and coming to our Plantation, we were receiv'd with all the Demonstrations of Tenderness and Affection (by my Husband's Mother) that were possible to be express'd.

WE liv'd here all together, my Mother-in-law, *at my entreaty*, continuing in the House, for she was too kind a Mother to be parted with; my Husband likewise continued the same as at first, and I thought my self the happiest Creature alive; when an odd and surprizing Event put an end to all that Felicity in a moment, and rendred my Condition the most uncomfortable, if not the most miserable, in the World.

MY Mother was a mighty chearful good humour'd old Woman, I may call her old Woman, for her Son was above Thirty; I say she was very pleasant, good Company, and us'd to entertain *me, in particular*, with abundance of Stories to divert me, as well of the Country we were in, as of the People.

AMONG the rest, she often told me how the greatest part of the Inhabitants of the Colony came thither in very indifferent Circumstances from *England*; that, generally speaking, they were of two sorts, either (1.) such as were brought over by Masters of Ships to be sold as Servants, *such as we call them*, my Dear, *says she*, but they are more properly call'd *Slaves*.[7] Or, (2.) Such as are Transported from *Newgate* and other Prisons, after having been found guilty of Felony and other Crimes punishable with Death.

7. In the sense that, having been "sold," indentured servants were in effect "slaves," not free agents, during the period of their service (usually five to seven years).

WHEN they come here, *says she*, we make no difference, the Planters buy them, and they work together in the Field till their time is out; when 'tis expir'd, *said she*, they have Encouragement given them to Plant for themselves; for they have a certain number of Acres of Land allotted them by the Country, and they go to work to Clear and Cure the Land, and then to Plant it with Tobacco and Corn[8] for their own use; and as the Tradesmen and Merchants will trust them with Tools, and Cloaths, and other Necessaries, upon the Credit of their Crop before it is grown, so they again Plant every Year a little more than the Year before, and so buy whatever they want with the Crop that is before them.

HENCE Child, *says she*, many a *Newgate* Bird becomes a great Man, and we have, *continued she*, several Justices of the Peace, Officers of the Train Bands, and Magistrates of the Towns they live in, that have been burnt in the Hand.[9]

SHE was going on with that part of the Story, when her own part in it interrupted her, and with a great deal of good-humour'd Confidence she told me, she was one of the second sort of Inhabitants herself; that she came away openly, having ventur'd too far in a particular Case, so that she was become a Criminal, and here's the Mark of it, CHILD, *says she*, and pulling off her Glove, look ye here, *says she*, turning up the Palm of her Hand, and shewed me a very fine white Arm and Hand, but branded in the inside of the Hand, as in such cases it must be.

THIS Story was very moving to me, but my Mother (smiling) said, you need not think such a thing strange, *Daughter*, for as I told you, some of the best Men in this Country are burnt in the Hand, and they are not asham'd to own it; there's Major ——— *says she*, he was an Eminent Pickpocket; there's Justice *Ba——r* was a Shoplifter, and both of them were burnt in the Hand, and I could name you several, such as they are.

WE had frequent Discourses of this kind, and abundance of instances she gave me of the like; after some time, as she was telling some Stories of one that was Transported but a few Weeks ago, I began in an intimate kind of way to ask her to tell me something of her own Story, which she did with the utmost plainness and Sincerity; how she had fallen into very ill Company in *London* in her young Days, occasion'd by her Mother sending her frequently to carry Victuals and other Relief to a Kinswoman of hers who was a Prisoner in *Newgate*, and who lay in a miserable starving Condition, was after-

8. Not maize, but the grain or seed of cereals like wheat, rye, barley, or oats. *Cure*: Free from timber.
9. Branded in the hand, not only as a form of punishment but also as a mark or notification to authorities, should a future arrest occur, of a prior felony conviction. *Train Bands*: A trained company of citizen-soldiers, organized in London and other parts in the sixteenth, seventeenth, and eighteenth centuries.

wards Condemned to be Hang'd, but having got Respite by pleading her Belly, dyed afterwards in the Prison.

HERE my Mother-in-Law ran out in a long account of the wicked practices in that dreadful Place, and how it ruin'd more young People than all the Town besides; and Child, *says my Mother*, perhaps you may know little of it, or it may be have heard nothing about it, but depend upon it, *says she*, we all know here, that there are more Thieves and Rogues made by that one Prison of *Newgate*, than by all the Clubs and Societies of Villains in the Nation; 'tis that cursed Place, *says my Mother*, that half Peoples this Colony.

HERE she went on with her own Story so long, and in so particular a manner, that I began to be very uneasy, but coming to one Particular that requir'd telling her Name, I thought I should have sunk down in the place; she perceived I was out of order, and asked me if I was not well, and what ail'd me? I told her I was so affected with the melancholy Story she had told, and the terrible things she had gone thro', that it had overcome me; and I beg'd of her to talk no more of it: *Why*, my Dear, *says she, very kindly*, what need these things trouble you? These Passages were long before your time, and they give me no trouble at all now, nay I look back on them with a particular Satisfaction, as they have been a means to bring me to this place. Then she went on to tell me how she very luckily fell into a good Family, where behaving herself well, and her Mistress dying, her Master married her, by whom she had my Husband and his Sister, and that by her Diligence and good Management after her Husband's Death, she had improv'd the Plantations to such a degree as they then were, so that most of the Estate was of her getting, not her Husband's, for she had been a Widow upwards of sixteen Year.

I HEARD this part of the Story with very little attention, because I wanted much to retire and give vent to my Passions, which I did soon after; and let any one judge what must be the Anguish of my Mind, when I came to reflect, that this was certainly no more or less *than my own Mother*, and I had now had two Children, and was big with another by my own Brother, and lay with him still every Night.

I WAS now the most unhappy of all Women in the World: O had the Story never been told me, all had been well; it had been no Crime to have lain with my Husband, since as to his being my Relation, I had known nothing of it.

I HAD now such a load on my Mind that it kept me perpetually waking; to reveal it, *which would have been some ease to me*, I cou'd not find wou'd be to any purpose, and yet to conceal it wou'd be next to impossible; nay, I did not doubt but I should talk of it in my sleep, and tell my Husband of it whether I would or no: If I discover'd it, the least thing I could expect was to lose my Husband, for he was too nice and too honest a Man to have continued my Husband after he had known I had been his Sister, so that I was perplex'd to the last degree.

I LEAVE it to any Man to judge what Difficulties presented to my view, I was away from my native Country at a distance prodigious, and the return to me unpassable; I liv'd very well, but in a Circumstance unsufferable in it self; if I had discover'd my self to my Mother, it might be difficult to convince her of the Particulars, and I had no way to prove them: *On the other hand*, if she had question'd or doubted me, I had been undone, for the bare Suggestion would have immediately separated me from my Husband, without gaining[1] my Mother or him, who would have been neither a Husband or a Brother; so that between the surprise on one hand, and the uncertainty on the other, I had been sure to be undone.

IN the mean time, as I was but too sure of the Fact, I liv'd therefore in open avowed Incest and Whoredom, and all under the appearance of an honest Wife; and tho' I was not much touched with the Crime of it, yet the Action had something in it shocking to Nature, and made my Husband, *as he thought himself*, even nauseous to me.

HOWEVER, upon the most sedate Consideration, I resolv'd, that it was absolutely necessary to conceal it all, and not make the least Discovery of it either to Mother or Husband; and thus I liv'd with the greatest Pressure imaginable for three Year more, but had no more Children.

DURING this time my Mother used to be frequently telling me old Stories of her former Adventures, which however were no ways pleasant to me; for by it, tho' she did not tell it me in plain terms, yet I could easily understand joyn'd with what I had heard my self, of my first Tutors, that in her younger Days she had been both WHORE and THIEF; but I verily believe she had lived to repent sincerely of both, and that she was then a very Pious sober and religious Woman.

WELL, let her Life have been what it would then, it was certain that my Life was very uneasie to me; for I liv'd, as I have said, but in the worst sort of Whoredom, and as I cou'd expect no Good of it, so really no good Issue came of it, and all my seeming Prosperity wore off and ended in Misery and Destruction; it was some time indeed before it came to this, for, but I know not by what ill Fate guided, every thing went wrong with us afterwards, and that which was worse, my Husband grew strangely alter'd; froward,[2] jealous, and unkind, and I was as impatient of bearing his Carriage, as the Carriage was unreasonable and unjust: These things proceeded so far, that we came at last to be in such ill Terms with one another, that I claim'd a promise of him which he entered willingly into with me, when I consented to come from *England* with him (*viz.*) that if I

1. Benefiting.
2. Hard to please, difficult to deal with.

found the Country not to agree with me, or that I did not like to live there, I should come away to *England* again when I pleas'd, giving him a Year's warning to settle his Affairs.

I SAY *I now claim'd this promise of him*, and I must confess I did it not in the most obliging Terms that could be in the World neither; but I insisted that he treated me ill, that I was remote from my Friends, and could do my self no justice, and that he was Jealous without cause, my Conversation having been unblameable, and he having no pretence for it, and that to remove to *England*, would take away all Occasion from him.

I INSISTED so peremptorily upon it, that he could not avoid coming to a point, either to keep his word with me or to break it; and this notwithstanding he used all the skill he was master of, and employ'd his Mother and other Agents to prevail with me to alter my Resolutions; indeed the bottom of the thing lay at my Heart, and that made all his Endeavours fruitless, for my Heart was alienated from him, *as a Husband*; I loathed the Thoughts of Bedding with him, and used a thousand Pretences of Illness and Humour to prevent his touching me, fearing nothing more than to be with Child again by him, which to be sure would have prevented, or at least delay'd my going over to *England*.

HOWEVER at last I put him so out of Humour, that he took up a rash and fatal Resolution. In short I should not go to *England*; and tho' he had promis'd me, yet it was an unreasonable thing for me to desire it, that it would be ruinous to his Affairs, would Unhinge his whole Family, and be next to an Undoing him in the World; That therefore I ought not to desire it of him, and that no Wife in the World that valu'd her Family and her Husbands prosperity would insist upon such a thing.

THIS plung'd[3] me again, for when I considered the thing calmly, and took my Husband as he really was, a diligent careful Man in the main Work of laying up an Estate for his Children, and that he knew nothing of the dreadful Circumstances that he was in; I could not but confess to myself that my Proposal was very unreasonable, and what no Wife that had the good of her Family at Heart wou'd have desir'd.

BUT my Discontents were of an another Nature; I look'd upon him no longer as a Husband, but as a near Relation the Son of my own Mother, and I resolv'd some how or other to be clear of him, but which way I did not know, nor did it seem possible.

IT is said *by the ill-natured World* of our Sex, that if we are set on a thing, it is impossible to turn us from our Resolutions: *In short*, I never ceas'd poreing upon the Means to bring to pass my Voyage,

3. Overpowered (with trouble or difficulty).

and came that length with my Husband at last, as to propose going without him. This provok'd him to the last degree, and he call'd me not only an unkind Wife, but an unnatural Mother, and ask'd me how I could entertain such a Thought without horror as that of leaving my two Children (for one was dead) without a Mother, and to be brought up by Strangers, and never to see them more? *It was true*, had things been right, I should not have done it, but now, *it was* my real desire never to see them, or him either any more; and as to the Charge of unnatural I could easily answer it to myself, while I knew that the whole Relation was Unnatural in the highest degree in the World.

HOWEVER, it was plain there was no bringing my Husband to any thing; he would neither go with me, or let me go without him, and it was quite out of my Power to stir without his Consent, as any one that knows the Constitution of the Country I was in, knows very well.

WE had many Family quarrels about it, and they began (in time) to grow up to a dangerous Height, for as I was quite Estrang'd from my Husband (*as he was call'd*) in Affection, so I took no heed to my Words, but sometimes gave him Language that was provoking: And, *in short*, strove all I could to bring him to a parting with me, which was what above all things in the World I desir'd most.

HE took my Carriage very ill, and indeed he might well do so, for at last I refus'd to Bed with him, and carrying on the Breach upon all occasions to extremity he told me once he thought I was Mad, and if I did not alter my Conduct, he would put me under Cure; *that is to say, into a Mad-House*: I told him he should find I was far enough from Mad, and that it was not in his power, or any other Villians to Murther me; I confess at the same time I was heartily frighted at his Thoughts of putting me into a *Mad-House*, which would at once have destroy'd all the possibility of breaking the Truth out, whatever the occasion might be; for that then, no one would have given Credit to a word of it.

THIS therefore brought me to a Resolution, *whatever came of it* to lay open my whole Case; but which way to do it, or to whom, was an inextricable Difficulty, and took me up many Months to Resolve; *in the mean time*, another Quarrel with my Husband happen'd, which came up to such a mad Extream as almost push'd me on to tell it him all to his Face; but tho' I kept it in so as not to come to the particulars, I spoke so much as put him into the utmost Confusion, and in the End brought out the whole Story.

HE began with a calm Expostulation upon my being so resolute to go to *England*; I defended it; and one hard Word bringing on another as is usual in all Family strife, *he told me*; I did not Treat him as if he was my Husband, or talk of my Children, as if I was a Mother;

and *in short*, that I did not deserve to be us'd as a Wife: That he had us'd all the fair Means possible with me; that he had Argu'd with all the kindness and calmness, that a Husband or a Christian ought to do, and that I made him such a vile return, that I Treated him rather like a Dog than a Man, and rather like the most contemptible Stranger than a Husband: That he was very loth to use Violence with me, but that *in short*, he saw a Necessity of it now, and that for the future he should be oblig'd to take such Measures as should reduce me to my Duty.

MY blood was now fir'd to the utmost, *tho' I knew what he had said was very true*, and nothing could appear more provok'd; I told him for his fair means and his foul they were equally contemn'd by me; that for my going to *England*, I was resolv'd on it, come what would; and that as to treating him not like a Husband, and not showing my self a Mother to my Children, there might be something more in it than he understood at present; but, for his farther consideration, I thought fit to tell him thus much, that he neither was my lawful Husband, nor they lawful Children, and that I had reason to regard neither of them more than I did.

I CONFESS I was mov'd to pity him when I spoke it, for he turn'd pale as Death, and stood mute as one Thunder struck, and once or twice I thought he would have fainted; *in short*, it put him in a Fit something like an Apoplex; he trembl'd, a Sweat or Dew ran off his Face, and yet he was cold as a Clod, so that I was forced to run and fetch something for him to keep Life in him; when he recover'd of that, he grew sick and vomited, and in a little after was put to Bed, and in the next Morning was, as he had been indeed all Night, in a violent Fever.

HOWEVER it went off again, and he recovered tho' but slowly, and when he came to be a little better, he told me, I had given him a mortal Wound with my Tongue, and he had only one thing to ask before he desir'd an Explanation; I interrupted him, and told him I was sorry I had gone so far, since I saw what disorder it put him into, but I desir'd him not to talk to me of Explanations, for that would but make things worse.

THIS heighten'd his impatience, and indeed perplex'd him beyond all beating; for now he began to suspect that there was some Mystery yet unfolded, but could not make the least guess at the real Particulars of it; all that run in his Brain was, that I had another Husband alive, which I could not say in fact might not be true; but I assur'd him however, there was not the least of that in it; and indeed as to my other Husband he was effectually dead in Law to me, and had told me I should look on him as such, so I had not the least uneasiness on that score.

BUT now I found the thing too far gone to conceal it much longer, and my Husband himself gave me an opportunity to ease my self of the Secret much to my Satisfaction; he had laboured with me three or four Weeks, *but to no purpose*, only to tell him, whether I had spoken those words only as the effect of my Passion, to put him in a Passion? Or whether there was any thing of Truth in the bottom of them? But I continued inflexible, and would explain nothing, unless he would first consent to my going to *England*, which he would never do, *he said*, while he liv'd; on the other hand I said it was in my power to make him willing when I pleas'd, NAY to make him entreat me to go; and this increased his Curiosity, and made him importunate to the highest degree, *but it was all to no purpose*.

AT length he tells all this Story to his Mother, and sets her upon me to get the main Secret out of me, and she us'd her utmost Skill with me indeed; but I put her to a full stop at once, *by telling her* that the Reason and Mystery of the whole matter lay in herself; and that it was my Respect to her that had made me conceal it, and that in short I could go no farther, and therefore conjur'd her not to insist upon it.

SHE was struck dumb at this Suggestion, and could not tell what to say or to think; but laying aside the supposition as a Policy[4] of mine, continued her importunity on account of her Son, and if possible to make up the breach between us two; as to that, *I told her*, that it was indeed a good design in her, but that it was impossible to be done; and that if I should reveal to her the Truth of what she desir'd, she would grant it to be impossible, and cease to desire it: At last I seem'd to be prevail'd on by her importunity, and told her I dar'd trust her with a Secret of the greatest Importance, and she would soon see that this was so, and that I would consent to lodge it in her Breast, if she would engage solemnly not to acquaint her Son with it without my consent.

SHE was long in promising this part, but rather than not come at the main Secret she agreed to that too, and after a great many other Preliminaries, I began and told her the whole Story: First I told her how much she was concern'd in all the unhappy breach which had happen'd between her Son and me, by telling me her own Story, and her *London* Name; and that the surprize she see I was in, was upon that Occasion: Then I told her my own Story and my Name, and assur'd her by such other Tokens as she could not deny that I was no other, nor more or less than her own Child, *her Daughter* born of her Body in *Newgate*; the same that had sav'd her from the Gallows by being in her Belly, and the same that she left in such and such Hands when she was Transported.

IT is impossible to express the Astonishment she was in; she was

4. Contrivance, expedient, with the sense of cunning or craftiness.

not inclin'd to believe the Story, or to remember the Particulars; for she immediately foresaw the Confusions that must follow in the Family upon it; but every thing concurr'd so exactly with the Stories she had told me of her self, and which if she had not told me, she would perhaps have been content to have denied, that she had stop'd her own Mouth, and she had nothing to do but to take me about the Neck and kiss me, and cry most vehemently over me, without speaking one word for a long time together; at last she broke out, *Unhappy Child! says she*, what miserable chance could bring thee hither? And in the Arms of my own Son too! *Dreadful Girl*! says she, *why we are all undone*! Married to thy own Brother! Three Children, and two alive, all of the same Flesh and Blood! My Son and my Daughter lying together as Husband and Wife! All Confusion and Destraction for ever! *miserable Family*! what will become of us? what is to be said? what is to be done? and thus she run on for a great while, nor had I any power to speak, or if I had, did I know what to say, for every word wounded me to the Soul: With this kind of Amasement on our Thoughts we parted for the first time, tho' my Mother was more surpriz'd than I was, because it was more News to her than to me: However, she promis'd again to me at parting, that she would say nothing of it to her Son, till we had talk'd of it again.

It was not long, you may be sure, before we had a second Conference upon the same Subject; when, as if she had been willing to forget the Story she had told me of herself, or to suppose that I had forgot some of the Particulars, she began to tell them with Alterations and Omissions; but I refresh'd her Memory, and set her to rights in many things which I supposed she had forgot, and then came in so opportunely with the whole History, that it was impossible for her to go from it; and then she fell into her Rhapsodies[5] again, and Exclamations at the Severity of her Misfortunes: When these things were a little over with her we fell into a close Debate about what should be first done before we gave an account of the matter to my Husband, but to what purpose could be all our Consultations? we could neither of us see our way thro' it, nor see how it could be safe to open such a Scene to him; it was impossible to make any judgment, or give any guess at what Temper he would receive it in, or what Measures he would take upon it; and if he should have so little Government of himself, as to make it publick, we easily foresaw that it would be the ruin of the whole Family, and expose my Mother and me to the last degree; and if at last he should take the Advantage the Law would give him, he might put me away with disdain, and leave me to Sue for the little Portion that I had, and perhaps wast it all in the Suit, and then be a Beggar; the Children would be ruin'd

5. Extravagant, unconnected effusions of feeling.

too, having no legal Claim to any of his Effects; and thus I should see him perhaps in the Arms of another Wife in a few Months, and be my self the most miserable Creature alive.

MY Mother was as sensible of this as I; and upon the whole, we knew not what to do; after some time, we came to more sober Resolutions, but then it was with this Misfortune too, that my Mother's Opinion and mine were quite different from one another, and indeed inconsistent with one another; for my Mother's Opinion was, that I should bury the whole thing entirely, and continue to live with him as my Husband, till some other Event should make the discovery of it more convenient; and that in the mean time she would endeavour to reconcile us together again, and restore our mutual Comfort and Family Peace; that we might lie as we us'd to do together, and so let the whole matter remain a secret as close as Death, for Child, *says she*, we are both undone if it comes out.

To encourage me to this, she promis'd to make me easy in my Circumstances as far as she was able, and to leave me what she could at her Death, secur'd for me separately from my Husband; so that if it should come out afterwards, I should not be left destitute, but be able to stand on my own Feet, and procure Justice from him.

THIS Proposal did not agree at all with my Judgment of the thing, tho' it was very fair and kind in my Mother, but my Thoughts run quite another way.

As to keeping the thing in our own Breasts, and letting it all remain as it was, I told her it was impossible; and I ask'd her how she cou'd think I cou'd bear the thoughts of lying with my own Brother? In the next place I told her that her being alive was the only support of the Discovery, and that while she own'd me for her Child, and saw reason to be satisfyed that I was so, no body else would doubt it; but that if she should die before the Discovery, I should be taken for an impudent Creature that had forg'd such a thing to go away from my Husband, or should be counted Craz'd and Distracted: Then I told her how he had threaten'd already to put me into a Mad-house, and what concern I had been in about it, and how that was the thing that drove me to the necessity of discovering it to her as I had done.

FROM all which I told her, that I had on the most serious Reflections I was able to make in the Case, come to this Resolution, which I hop'd she would like, as a medium between both, (*viz.*) that she should use her endeavours with her Son to give me leave to go for *England*, as I had desired, and to furnish me with a sufficient Sum of Money, either in Goods along with me, or in Bills for my Support there, all along suggesting, that he might one time or other think it proper to come over to me.

THAT when I was gone she should then in cold Blood, and after first obliging him in the solemnest manner possible to Secresie, discover the Case to him; doing it gradually, and as her own Discretion should guide her, so that he might not be surpriz'd with it, and fly out into any Passions and Excesses on my account, or on hers; and that she should concern herself to prevent his slighting the Children, or Marrying again, unless he had a certain account of my being Dead.

THIS was my Scheme, and my Reasons were good; I was really alienated from him in the Consequence of these things; indeed I mortally hated him as a Husband, and it was impossible to remove that riveted Aversion I had to him; *at the same time* it being an unlawful incestuous living added to that Aversion; and tho' I had no great concern about it in point of Conscience, yet every thing added to make Cohabiting with him the most nauseous thing to me in the World; and I think verily it was come to such a height, that I could almost as willingly have embrac'd a Dog, as have let him offer any thing of that kind to me, for which Reason I could not bear the thoughts of coming between the Sheets with him; I cannot say that I was right in point of Policy in carrying it such a length, while at the same time I did not resolve to discover the thing to him; but I am giving an account of what was, not of what ought or ought not to be.

IN this directly opposite Opinion to one another my Mother and I continued a long time, and it was impossible to reconcile our Judgments; many Disputes we had about it, but we could never either of us yield our own, or bring over the other.

I INSISTED on my Aversion to lying with my own Brother; and she insisted upon its being impossible to bring him to consent to my going from him to *England*; and in this uncertainty we continued, not differing so as to quarrel, or any thing like it; but so as not to be able to resolve what we should do to make up that terrible breach that was before us.

AT last I resolv'd on a desperate course, and *told my Mother* my Resolution, (*viz.*) that in short, I would tell him of it my self; my Mother was frighted to the last degree at the very thoughts of it; but *I bid her be easie*, told her I would do it gradually and softly, and with all the Art and good Humour I was Mistress of, and time it also as well as I could, taking him in good Humour too: *I told her* I did not question but if I cou'd be Hypocrite enough to feign more Affection to him than I really had, I should succeed in all my Design, and we might part by Consent, and with a good Agreement, for I might love him well enough for a Brother, tho' I could not for a Husband.

ALL this while he lay at my Mother to find out, if possible, what was the meaning of that dreadful Expression of mine, as he call'd it, which I mention'd before; namely, *That I was not his lawful Wife, nor my Children his legal Children*: My Mother put him off, told him she could bring me to no Explanations, but found there was something that disturb'd me very much, and she hop'd she should get it out of me in time, and in the mean time recommended to him earnestly to use me more tenderly, and win me with his usual good Carriage; *told him* of his terrifying and affrighting me with his Threats of sending me to a Mad-house, and the like, and advis'd him not to make a Woman Desperate on any account whatever.

HE promis'd her to soften his Behaviour, and bid her assure me that he lov'd me as well as ever, and that he had no such design as that of sending me to a Mad-house, whatever he might say in his Passion; also he desir'd my Mother to use the same Perswasions to me too, that our Affections might be renew'd, and we might live together in a good understanding as we us'd to do.

I FOUND the Effects of this Treaty presently; my Husband's Conduct was immediately alter'd, and he was quite another Man to me; nothing could be kinder and more obliging than he was to me upon all Occasions; and I could do no less than make some return to it, *which I did as well as I could*; but it was but in an awkward manner at best, for nothing was more frightful to me than his Caresses, and the Apprehensions of being with Child again by him, was ready to throw me into Fits; and this made me see that there was an absolute necessity of breaking the Case to him without any more delay, which however I did with all the caution and reserve imaginable.

HE had continued his alter'd Carriage to me near a Month, and we began to live a new kind of Life with one another; and could I have satisfied my self to have gone on with it, I believe it might have continued as long as we had continued alive together. One Evening as we were sitting and talking very friendly together under a little Auning, which serv'd as an Arbour at the entrance from our House into the Garden, he was in a very pleasant agreeable Humour, and said abundance of kind things to me, relating to the Pleasure of our present good Agreement, and the Disorders of our past breach, and what a Satisfaction it was to him, that we had room to hope we should never have any more of it.

I FETCH'D a deep Sigh, and told him there was no Body in the World could be more delighted than I was, in the good Agreement we had always kept up, or more afflicted with the Breach of it, and should be so still, but I was sorry to tell him that there was an unhappy Circumstance in our Case, which lay too close to my Heart, and which I knew not how to break to him, that rendred my part of it very miserable, and took from me all the Comfort of the rest.

HE importun'd me to tell him what it was; I told him I could not tell how to do it, that while it was conceal'd from him, I alone was unhappy; but if he knew it also, we should be both so, and that therefore to keep him in the dark about it was the kindest thing that I could do, and it was on that account alone that I kept a secret from him, the very keeping of which I thought would first or last be my Destruction.

IT is impossible to express his Surprize at this Relation, and the double importunity which he used with me to discover it to him: He told me I could not be call'd kind to him, nay, I could not be faithful to him if I conceal'd it from him; I told him I thought so too, and yet I could not do it. He went back to what I had said before to him, and told me he hoped it did not relate to what I had said in my Passion; and that he had resolv'd to forget all that, as the Effect of a rash provok'd Spirit; I told him I wish'd I could forget it all too, but that it was not to be done, the Impression was too deep, and I could not do it, it was impossible.

HE then told me he was resolved not to differ with me in any thing, and that therefore he would importune me no more about it, resolving to acquiesce in whatever I did or said; only begg'd I would then agree, that whatever it was, it should no more interrupt our quiet and our mutual kindness.

THIS was the most provoking thing he could have said to me, for I really wanted his farther importunities, that I might be prevail'd with to bring out that which indeed it was like Death to me to conceal; so I answer'd him plainly, that I could not say I was glad not to be importuned, tho' I could not tell how to comply; but come, *my Dear, said I*, what Conditions will you make with me upon the opening this Affair to you?

ANY Conditions in the World, *said he*, that you can in reason desire of me; well, *said I*, come, give it me under your Hand,[6] that if you do not find I am in any fault, or that I am willingly concern'd in the Causes of the Misfortune that is to follow, you will not blame me, use me the worse, do me any Injury, or make me be the Sufferer for that which is not my fault.

THAT *says he*, is the most reasonable demand in the World; not to blame you for that which is not your fault; give me a Pen and Ink, *says he*, so I ran in and fetch'd a Pen, Ink, and Paper, and he wrote the Condition down in the very words I had proposed it, and sign'd it with his Name; well, says he, *what is next*, my Dear?

WHY *says I*, the next is, that you will not blame me for not discovering the Secret of it to you before I knew it.

VERY just again, *says he*, with all my Heart; so he wrote down that also and sign'd it.

WELL, *my Dear*, says I, then I have but one Condition more to make with you, and that is, that as there is no body concern'd in it but you and I, you shall not discover it to any Person in the World, except your own Mother; and that in all the Measures you shall take

6. With your signature.

upon the discovery, as I am equally concern'd in it with you, *tho' as innocent as your self*, you shall do nothing in a Passion, nothing to my Prejudice, or to your Mother's Prejudice, without my knowledge and consent.

THIS a little amaz'd him, and he wrote down the words distinctly, but read them over and over before he Sign'd them, hesitating at them several times, and repeating them; *my Mother*'s Prejudice! *and your Prejudice*! what mysterious thing can this be? however, at last he Sign'd it.

WELL, *says I*, my Dear, I'll ask you no more under your Hand, but as you are to bear the most unexpected and surprizing thing that perhaps ever befel any Family in the World, I beg you to promise me you will receive it with Composure and a Presence of Mind suitable to a Man of Sense.

I'LL do my utmost, *says he*, upon Condition you will keep me no longer in suspence, for you Terrify me with all these Preliminaries.

WELL, then, *says I*, it is this; as I told you before in a Heat, that I was not your lawful Wife, and that our Children were not legal Children; so I must let you know now in calmness, and in kindness, but with Affliction enough that *I am* your own Sister, *and you* my own Brother, and that we are both the Children of our Mother now alive, and in the House, who is convinc'd of the Truth of it, in a manner not to be denied or contradicted.

I SAW him turn pale, and look wild, and I said, now remember your Promise, and receive it with Presence of mind; for who cou'd have said more to prepare you for it, than I have done? However I call'd a Servant, and got him a little Glass of Rum, which is the usual Dram[7] of the Country, for he was just fainting away.

WHEN he was a little recover'd, *I said to him*, this Story you may be sure requires a long Explanation, and therefore have patience and compose your Mind to hear it out, and I'll make it as short as I can, and with this, I told him what I thought was needful of the Fact, and particularly how my Mother came to discover it to me, as above; and now my Dear, *says I*, you will see Reason for my Capitulations, and that I neither have been the Cause of this Matter, nor could be so, and that I could know nothing of it before now.

I AM fully satisfy'd of that, *says he*, but 'tis a dreadful Surprize to me; however, I know a Remedy for it all, and a Remedy that shall put an End to all your Difficulties, without your going to *England*; That would be strange, *said I*, as all the rest; No, No, *says he*, I'll make it easie, there's no Body in the way of it all, but myself: He look'd a little disorder'd, when he said this, but I did not apprehend any thing from it at that time, believing as it us'd to be said, that they

7. Liquor taken in small quantity as a cordial or stimulant.

who do those things never talk of them; or that they who talk of such things never do them.

BUT things were not come their height with him, and I observ'd he became Pensive and Melancholly; and in a Word, as *I* thought a little Distemper'd in his Head; I endeavour'd to talk him into Temper, and to Reason him into a kind of Scheme for our Government in the Affair, and sometimes he would be well, and talk with some Courage about it; but the Weight of it lay too heavy upon his Thoughts, and in short, it went so far that he made two attempts upon himself, and in one of them had actually strangled[8] himself, and had not his Mother come into the Room in the very Moment, he had died; but with the help of a *Negro* Servant, she cut him down and recover'd him.

THINGS were now come to a lamentable height in the Family: My pity for him now began to revive that Affection, which at first I really had for him, and I endeavour'd sincerely by all the kind Carriage I could to make up the Breach; but in short, it had gotten too great a Head, it prey'd upon his Spirits, and it threw him into a long ling'ring Consumption, tho' it happen'd not to be Mortal. In this Distress I did not know what to do, as his Life was apparently declining, and I might perhaps have Marry'd again there, very much to my Advantage, it had been certainly my Business to have staid in the Country; but my Mind was restless too, and uneasie; I hanker'd after coming to *England*, and nothing would satisfie me without it.

IN short, by an unwearied importunity my Husband who was apparently decaying, as I observ'd, was at last prevail'd with, and so *my own Fate pushing me on*,[9] the way was made clear for me, and *my Mother concurring*, I obtain'd a very good Cargo for my coming to *England*.

WHEN I parted with my Brother, for such I am now to call him; we agreed that after I arriv'd he should pretend to have an Account that I was Dead in *England*, and so might Marry again when he would; he promis'd, and engag'd me to Correspond with me as a Sister, and to Assist and Support me as long as I liv'd; and that if he dy'd before me, he would leave sufficient to his Mother to take Care of me still, in the Name of a Sister, and he was in some respect Careful of me, when he heard of me; but it was so oddly mannag'd that I felt the Disappointments very sensibly afterwards, as you shall hear in its time.

I CAME away for *England* in the Month of *August*, after I had been

8. Hanged.
9. Early in his narrative, after surviving two storms at sea and thinking about returning home, Robinson Crusoe laments, "But my ill Fate push'd me on now with an Obstinacy that nothing could resist. . . ."

Eight Years in that Country, and now a new Scene of Misfortunes attended me, which perhaps few Women have gone thro' the like of.

WE had an indifferent good Voyage, till we came just upon the Coast of *England*, and where we arriv'd in two and thirty Days, but were then Ruffled with two or three Storms, one of which drove us away to the Coast of *Ireland*, and we put in at *Kinsale*: We remain'd there about thirteen Days, got some Refreshment on Shore, and put to Sea again, tho' we met with very bad Weather again in which the Ship sprung[1] her Main-mast, *as they call'd it, for I knew not what they meant*: But we got at last into *Milford Haven* in *Wales*, where tho' it was remote from our Port; yet having my Foot safe upon the firm Ground of my Native Country the Isle of *Britain*, I resolv'd to venture it no more upon the Waters, which had been so terrible to me; so getting my Cloths, and Money on Shore with my Bills of Loading, and other Papers, I resolv'd to come for *London*, and leave the Ship to get to her Port as she could; the Port whither she was bound, was to *Bristol*, where my Brothers chief Correspondent[2] liv'd.

I GOT to *London*, in about three Weeks, where I heard a little while after that the Ship was arriv'd in *Bristol*; but at the same time had the Misfortune to know that by the violent Weather she had been in, and the breaking of her Mainmast; she had great damage on board, and that a great part of her Cargo was spoil'd.

I HAD now a new Scene of Life upon my Hands, and a dreadful Appearance it had; I was come away with a kind of final Farewel; what I brought with me, was indeed considerable, had it come safe, and by the help of it I might have married again tollerably well; but as it was, I was reduc'd to between two or three Hundred Pounds in the whole, and this without any hope of Recruit:[3] I was entirely without Friends, nay, even so much as without Acquaintance, for I found it was absolutely necessary not to revive former Acquaintances; and as for my subtle Friend that set me up formerly for a Fortune she was Dead, and her Husband also; as I was inform'd upon sending a Person unknown to enquire.

THE looking after my Cargo of Goods soon after oblig'd me to take a Journey to *Bristol*, and during my attendance upon that Affair, I took the Diversion of going to the *Bath*,[4] for as I was still far from

1. Cracked. Cf. Robinson Crusoe's not knowing what the sailors mean by "founder" during his second sea storm, before the ship's sinking makes him understand the word.
2. Business associate or contact. The word appears in this sense several times in *Colonel Jack*, published the same year as *Moll Flanders* (e.g., as he makes plans to return to England from Virginia, Colonel Jack sends "five Hundred Hogsheads of Tobbacco in several Ships . . . giving Notice to my Correspondent in *London*. . . .").
3. I.e., of "recruiting" more money.
4. So called from its hot springs, this city in the west of England was the site of the age's most celebrated and fashionable spa. Defoe was among its detractors, alleging that, beneath its glitter and formal manners, Bath teemed with moral depravity.

being old, so my Humour, which was always Gay, continu'd so to an Extream; and being now, *as it were*, a Woman of Fortune, tho' I was a Woman without a Fortune, I expected something, or other might happen in my way, that might mend my Circumstances as had been my Case before.

THE *Bath* is a Place of Gallantry enough; Expensive, and full of Snares; I went thither indeed in the view of taking any thing that might offer; but I must do myself that Justice, as to protest I knew nothing amiss, I meant nothing but in an honest way; nor had I any Thoughts about me at first that look'd the way, which afterwards I suffered them to be guided.

HERE I stay'd the whole latter Season,[5] *as it is call'd there*, and Contracted some unhappy Acquaintance, which rather prompted the Follies, I fell afterwards into, than fortify'd me against them: I liv'd pleasantly enough, kept good Company, *that is to say*, gay fine Company; but had the Discouragement to find this way of Living sunk me exceedingly, and that as I had no settl'd Income, so spending upon the main Stock was but a certain kind of *bleeding to Death*; and this gave me many sad Reflections in the Intervals of my other Thoughts: However I shook them off, and still flatter'd myself that something or other might offer for my Advantage.

BUT I was in the wrong Place for it; I was not now at *Redriff*, where If I had set myself tollerably up, some honest Sea Captain or other might have talk'd with me upon the honourable terms of Matrimony; but I was at the *Bath* where Men find a Mistress sometimes, but very rarely look for a Wife; and Consequently all the particular Acquaintances a Woman can Expect to make there, must have some Tendency that way.

I HAD spent the first Season well enough, for tho' I had Contracted some Acquaintance with a Gentleman, who came to the *Bath* for his Diversion, yet I had enter'd into no *felonious Treaty*, as it might be call'd: I had resisted some Casual offers of Gallantry, and had manag'd that way well enough; I was not wicked enough to come into the Crime for the meer Vice of it, and I had no extraordinary Offers made me that tempted me with the main thing which I wanted.

HOWEVER I went this length the first Season, (*viz.*) I contracted an Acquaintance with a Woman in whose House I Lodg'd, who tho' she did not keep an ill House,[6] *as we call it*, yet had none of the best Principles in herself: I had on all Occasions behav'd myself so well as not to get the least Slur upon my Reputation on any Account whatever, and all the Men that I had Convers'd with, were of so good

5. In late autumn, after the heavy tourist traffic of the summer had ended.
6. A house of ill repute, where amorous intrigues are carried out; a bawdy house.

Reputation that I had not given the least Reflection[7] by Conversing with them; nor did any of them seem to think there was room for a wicked Correspondence, if they had any of them offered it; yet there was one Gentleman, *as above*, who always singl'd me out for the Diversion of my Company, as he call'd it, which *as he was pleas'd to say* was very agreeable to him, but at that time there was no more in it.

I HAD many melancholly Hours at the *Bath* after all the Company was gone, for tho' I went to *Bristol* sometimes for the disposing my Effects, and for Recruits of Money, yet I chose to come back to *Bath* for my Residence, because being on good Terms with the Woman in whose House I lodg'd in the Summer, I found that during the Winter I liv'd rather cheaper there than I could do any where else; here, *I say*, I pass'd the Winter as heavily as I had pass'd the Autumn chearfully; But having contracted a nearer intimacy with the said Woman, in whose House I Lodg'd, I could not avoid communicating to her something of what lay hardest upon my Mind, and particularly the narrowness of my Circumstances, and the loss of my Fortune by the Damage of my Goods by Sea: I told her also that I had a Mother and a Brother in *Virginia* in good Circumstances, and as I had really written back to my Mother in particular to represent my Condition, and the great Loss I had receiv'd, which indeed came to almost 500 *l.* so I did not fail to let my new Friend know, that I expected a Supply from thence, and so indeed I did; and as the Ships went from *Bristol* to *York* River in *Virginia*, and back again generally in less time than from *London*, and that my Brother Corresponded chiefly at *Bristol*, I thought it was much better for me to wait here for my Returns, than to go to *London*, where also I had not the least Acquaintance.

MY new Friend appear'd sensibly affected with my Condition, and indeed was so very kind, as to reduce the Rate of my living with her to so low a Price during the Winter, that she convinced me she got nothing by me; and as for Lodging during the Winter, I paid nothing at all.

WHEN the Spring Season came on, she continu'd to be as kind to me as she could, and I lodg'd with her for a time, till it was found necessary to do otherwise ; she had some Persons of Character that frequently lodg'd in her House, and in particular the Gentleman who, as I said, singl'd me out for his Companion the Winter before; and he came down again with another Gentleman in his Company and two Servants, and lodg'd in the same House: I suspected that my Landlady had invited him thither, letting him know that I was still with her, but she deny'd it, and protested to me that she did not, and he said the same.

7. I.e., given cause or occasion for any censure or reproof.

In a Word, this Gentleman came down and continu'd to single me out for his peculiar Confidence as well as Conversation; he was a compleat Gentleman, *that must be confess'd*, and his Company was very agreeable to me, as mine, *if I might believe him*, was to him; he made no Professions to me but of an extraordinary Respect, and he had such an Opinion of my Virtue, that *as he often profess'd*, he believ'd if he should offer any thing else, I should reject him with Contempt; he soon understood from me that I was a Widow, that I had arriv'd at *Bristol* from *Virginia* by the last Ships; and that I waited at *Bath* till the next *Virginia Fleet* should arrive, by which I expected considerable Effects; I understood by him, and by others of him, that he had a Wife, but that the Lady was distemper'd in her Head, and was under the Conduct of her own Relations, which he consented to, to avoid any Reflections that might, *as was not unusual in such Cases*, be cast on him for mismanaging her Cure; and in the mean time he came to the *Bath* to divert his Thoughts from the Disturbance of such a melancholy Circumstance as that was.

My Landlady, who of her own accord encourag'd the Correspondence on all Occasions, gave me an advantageous Character of him, as of a Man of Honour and of Virtue, as well as of a great Estate; and indeed I had a great deal of Reason to say so of him too; for tho' we lodg'd both on a Floor, and he had frequently come into my Chamber, even when I was in Bed; and I also into his when he was in Bed,[8] yet he never offered any thing to me farther than a kiss, or so much as solicited me to any thing till long after, as you shall hear.

I Frequently took notice to my Landlady of his exceeding Modesty, and she again used to tell me, she believ'd it was so from the beginning; however she used to tell me that she thought I ought to expect some Gratification from him for my Company, for indeed he did, as it were, engross me, and I was seldom from him; *I told her* I had not given him the least occasion to think I wanted it, or that I would accept of it from him; *she told me* she would take that part upon her, and she did so, and manag'd it so dextrously, that the first time we were together alone, after she had talk'd with him, he began to enquire a little into my Circumstances, as how I had subsisted my self since I came on shore? and whether I did not want Money? I stood off very boldly, I told him that tho' my Cargo of Tobacco was damag'd, yet that it was not quite lost; that the Merchant I had been consign'd to, had so honestly manag'd for me that I had not wanted; and that I hop'd, with frugal Management, I should make it hold out till more would come, which I expected by the next Fleet; that in the mean time I had retrench'd my Expences, and whereas I kept a Maid last Season, now I liv'd without; and whereas I had a Chamber and

8. Intimate morning visits, such as Moll describes here, were not viewed as improper in polite circles in Defoe's day.

a Dining-room then on the first Floor, *as he knew*, I now had but one Room two pair of Stairs,[9] *and the like*; but I live *said I*, as well satisfy'd now as I did then; *adding*, that his Company had been a means to make me live much more chearfully than otherwise I should have done, for which I was much oblig'd to him; and so I put off all room for any offer for the present: However, it was not long before he attack'd me again, and told me he found that I was backward to trust him with the Secret of my Circumstances, *which he was sorry for*; assuring me that he enquir'd into it with no design to satisfie his own Curiosity, but meerly to assist me, if there was any occasion; but since I would not own my self to stand in need of any assistance, he had but one thing more to desire of me, and that was, that I would promise him that when I was any way streighten'd, or like to be so, I would frankly tell him of it, and that I would make use of him with the same freedom that he made the offer, *adding*, that I should always find I had a true Friend, tho' perhaps I was afraid to trust him.

I OMITTED nothing *that was fit to be said by one infinitely oblig'd*, to let him know, that I had a due Sense of his Kindness; and indeed from that time, I did not appear so much reserv'd to him as I had done before, tho' still within the Bounds of the strictest Virtue on both sides; but how free soever our Conversation was, I cou'd not arrive to that sort of Freedom which he desir'd, (*viz.*) to tell him I wanted Money, tho' I was secretly very glad of his offer.

SOME Weeks pass'd after this, and still I never ask'd him for Money; when my Landlady, a cunning Creature, who had often press'd me to it, but found that I cou'd not do it, makes a Story of her own inventing, and comes in bluntly to me when we were together, O Widow, *says she*, I have bad News to tell you this Morning; What is that, said I, are the *Virginia* Ships taken by the *French? for that was my fear*. No, no, *says she*, but the Man you sent to *Bristol* Yesterday for Money is come back, and says he has brought none.

Now I could by no means like her Project; I thought it look'd too much like prompting him, which indeed he did not want, and I saw clearly that I should lose nothing by being backward to ask, so I took her up short; I can't imagine why he should say so to you, *said I*, for I assure you he brought me all the Money I sent him for, and here it is *said I*, (pulling out my Purse with about 12 Guineas in it) and added, I intend you shall have most of it by and by.

HE seem'd distasted[1] a little at her talking as she did at first, as well as I, taking it as I fancied he would as something forward of her; but when he saw me give such an Answer, he came immediately to himself again: The next Morning we talk'd of it again, when I found

9. A single room, up two flights of stairs, on the third floor.
1. Disgusted.

he was fully satisfy'd; and smiling said, he hop'd I would not want Money and not tell him of it, and that I had promis'd him otherwise: I told him I had been very much dissatisfy'd at my Landladies talking so publicly the Day before of what she had nothing to do with; but I suppos'd she wanted what I ow'd her, which was about Eight Guineas, which I had resolv'd to give her, and had accordingly given it her the same Night she talk'd so foolishly.

HE was in a mighty good Humour, when he heard me say, *I had paid her*, and it went off into some other Discourse at that time; but the next Morning he having heard me up about my Room before him, he call'd to me, *and I answering*, he ask'd me to come into his Chamber; he was in bed when I came in, and he made me come and sit down on his Bed side, *for he said*, he had something to say to me, which was of some Moment: After some very kind Expressions he ask'd me, if I would be very honest to him, and give a sincere Answer to one thing he would desire of me? after some little Cavil with him at the word *Sincere*, and asking him if I had ever given him any Answers which were not Sincere, I promis'd him I would; why then his Request was, *he said*, to let him see my Purse; I immediately put my Hand into my Pocket, *and Laughing at him*, pull'd it out, and there was in it three Guineas and a Half; *then he ask'd me*, if there was all the Money I had? I told him no, *Laughing again*, not by a great deal.

WELL then, *he said*, he would have me promise to go and fetch him all the Money I had every Farthing: *I told him I would*, and I went into my Chamber, and fetch'd him a little private Drawer, where I had about six Guineas more, and some Silver, and threw it all down upon the Bed, and told him there was all my Wealth, honestly to a Shilling: He look'd a little at it, but did not tell it, and Huddled it all into the Drawer again, and reaching his Pocket, pull'd out a Key, and bad then me open a little Walnuttree box, he had upon the Table, and bring him such a Drawer, which I did, in which Drawer, there was a great deal of Money in Gold, I believe near 200 Guineas, but I knew not how much: He took the Drawer, and taking my Hand, made me put it in, and take a whole handful; I was backward at that, but he held my Hand hard in his Hand, and put it into the Drawer, and made me take out as many Guineas almost as I could well take up at once.

WHEN I had done so, he made me put them into my Lap, and took my little Drawer, and pour'd out all my own Money among his, and bad me get me gone, and carry it all Home into my own Chamber.

I RELATE this Story the more particularly because of the good Humour there was in it, and to show the temper with which we Convers'd: It was not long after this, but he began every Day to find fault with my Cloths, with my Laces, and Head-dresses; and in a

Word, press'd me to buy better, which by the way I was willing enough to do, tho' I did not seem to be so; for I lov'd nothing in the World better than fine Clothes; I told him I must Housewife the Money he had lent me, or else I should not be able to pay him again. He then told me in a few Words, that as he had a sincere Respect for me, and knew my Circumstances, he had not Lent me that Money, but given it me, and that he thought I had merited it from him, by giving him my Company so intirely as I had done: After this, he made me take a Maid, and keep House, and his Friend that came with him to *Bath*, being gone, he oblig'd me to Dyet[2] him, which I did very willingly, believing as *it appear'd*, that I should lose nothing by it, nor did the Woman of the House fail to find her Account in it too.

WE had liv'd thus near three Months, when the Company beginning to wear away at the *Bath*, he talk'd of going away, and fain he would have me to go to *London* with him: I was not very easie in that Proposal, not knowing what Posture I was to live in there, or how he might use me: But while this was in Debate he fell very Sick; he had gone out to a place in *Somersetshire* called *Shepton*, where he had some Business, and was there taken very ill, and so ill that he could not Travel, so he sent his Man back to *Bath* to beg me that I would hire a Coach and come over to him. Before he went, he had left all his Money and other things of Value with me, and what to do with them I did not know, but I secur'd them as well as I could, and Lock'd up the Lodgings and went to him, where I found him very ill indeed; however, I perswaded him to be carry'd in a Litter to the *Bath*, where there was more help and better advice to be had.

HE consented, and I brought him to the *Bath*, which was about fifteen Miles, *as I remember*: here he continued very ill of a Fever, and kept his Bed five Weeks, all which time I nurs'd him and tended him my self, as much and as carefully as if I had been his Wife; indeed if I had been his Wife I could not have done more; I sat up with him so much and so often, that at last indeed he would not let me sit up any longer, and then I got a Pallate Bed[3] into his Room, and lay in it just at his Bed's Feet.

I WAS indeed sensibly affected with his Condition, and with the Apprehension of losing such a Friend as he was, and was like to be to me, and I us'd to sit and Cry by him many Hours together: However at last he grew Better, and gave hopes that he would recover, as indeed he did, tho' very slowly.

WERE it otherwise than what I am going to say, I should not be backward to disclose it, as it is apparent I have done in other Cases in this Account; but I affirm, that thro' all this Conversation, abating

2. Feed.
3. A small, mean bed, couch, or mattress, usually filled with straw.

the freedom of coming into the Chamber when I or he was in Bed, and abating the necessary Offices of attending him Night and Day when he was Sick, there had not pass'd the least immodest Word or Action between us. O! that it had been so to the last.

AFTER some time he gathered Strength, and grew well apace, and I would have remov'd my Pallate Bed, but he would not let me till he was able to venture himself without any Body to sit up with him, and then I remov'd to my own Chamber.

HE took many Occasions to express his Sense of my Tenderness and Concern for him; and when he grew quite well, he made me a Present of Fifty Guineas for my Care, and, as he call'd it, for hazarding my Life to save his.

AND now he made deep Protestations of a sincere inviolable Affection for me, but all along attested it to be with the utmost reserve for my Virtue, and his own: I told him I was fully satisfyed of it; he carried it that length that he protested to me, that if he was naked in Bed with me, he would as sacredly preserve my Virtue, as he would defend it if I was assaulted by a Ravisher; I believ'd him, and told him I did so; but this did not satisfie him, he would, *he said*, wait for some opportunity to give me an undoubted Testimony of it.

IT was a great while after this that I had Occasion, on my own Business, to go to *Bristol*, upon which he hir'd me a Coach, and would go with me, and did so; and now indeed our intimacy increas'd: From *Bristol* he carry'd me to *Gloucester*, which was meerly a Journey of Pleasure to take the Air; and here it was our hap to have no Lodging in the Inn but in one large Chamber with two Beds in it: The Master of the House going up with us to show his Rooms, and coming into that Room, said very frankly to him, Sir, *It is none of my business to enquire whether the Lady be your Spouse or no*, but if not, *you may lie as honestly in these two Beds as if you were in two Chambers*, and with that he pulls a great Curtain which drew quite cross the Room, and effectually divided the Beds; well, *says my Friend*, very readily, these Beds will do, and as for the rest, we are too near a kin to lye together, tho' we may Lodge near one another; and this put an honest Face on the thing too. When we came to go to Bed he decently went out of the Room till I was in Bed, and then went to Bed in the Bed on his own side of the Room, but lay there talking to me a great while.

AT last repeating his usual saying, that he could lye in the naked Bed[4] with me and not offer me the least Injury, he starts out of his Bed, and now, *my Dear, says he*, you shall see how just I will be to you, and that I can keep my word, and away he comes to my Bed.

I resisted a little, but I must confess I should not have resisted

4. Changed to "lye naked in Bed" in the second edition.

him much, if he had not made those Promises at all; so after a little struggle, *as I said*, I lay still and let him come to Bed; when he was there he took me in his Arms, and so I lay all Night with him, but he had no more to do with me, or offer'd any thing to me other than embracing me, as I say, in his Arms, no not the whole Night, but rose up and dress'd him in the Morning, and left me as innocent for him as I was the Day I was born.

THIS was a surprizing thing to me, and perhaps may be so to others who know how the Laws of Nature work; for he was a strong vigorous brisk Person; nor did he act thus on a principle of Religion at all, *but of meer Affection*; insisting on it, that tho' I was to him the most agreeable Woman in the World, yet because he lov'd me he cou'd not injure me.

I OWN it was a noble Principle, but as it was what I never understood before, so it was to me perfectly amazing. We Travel'd the rest of the Journey as we did before, and came back to the *Bath*, where, as he had opportunity to come to me when he would, he often repeated the Moderation, and I frequently lay with him, and he with me, and altho' all the familiarities between Man and Wife were common to us, yet he never once offered to go any farther, and he valued himself much upon it; I do not say that I was so wholly pleas'd with it as he thought I was: For I own I was much wickeder than he, *as you shall hear presently*.

WE liv'd thus near two Year, only with this exception, that he went three times to *London* in that time, and once he continued there four Months, but, to do him Justice, he always supply'd me with Money to subsist me very handsomly.

HAD we continued thus, I confess we had had much to boast of; but as wise Men say, it is ill venturing too near the brink of a Command,[5] so we found it; and here again I must do him the Justice to own, that the first Breach was not on his part: It was one Night that we were in Bed together warm and merry, and having drank, I think, a little more Wine that Night, both of us, than usual, tho' not in the least to disorder either of us, when after some other follies which I cannot name, and being clasp'd close in his Arms, *I told him, (I repeat it with shame and horror of Soul)* that I cou'd find in my Heart to discharge him of his Engagement for one Night and no more.

HE took me at my word immediately, and after that, there was no resisting him; neither indeed had I any mind to resist him any more, let what would come of it.

THUS the Government of our Virtue was broken, and I exchang'd the Place of Friend, for that unmusical harsh-sounding Title of WHORE. In the Morning we were both at our Penitentials, I cried

5. Commandment. The *OED* cites this passage from *Moll Flanders* as illustration.

very heartily, he express'd himself very sorry; but that was all either of us could do at that time; and the way being thus clear'd, and the bars of Virtue and Conscience thus removed, we had the less difficulty afterwards to struggle with.

IT was but a dull kind of Conversation that we had together for all the rest of that Week, I look'd on him with Blushes; and every now and then started that melancholy Objection, *what if I should be with Child now? What will become of me then*? He encourag'd me by telling me, that as long as I was true to him he would be so to me; and since it was gone such a length, (which indeed he never intended) yet if I was with Child, he would take care of that, and of me too: This harden'd us both; I assur'd him if I was with Child, I would die for want of a Midwife rather than Name him as the Father of it; and he assur'd me I should never want if I should be with Child: These mutual assurances harden'd us in the thing; and after this we repeated the Crime as often as we pleas'd, till at length, as I had fear'd, so it came to pass, and I was indeed with Child.

AFTER I was sure it was so, and I had satisfied him of it too, we began to think of taking measures for the managing it, and I propos'd trusting the Secret to my Landlady, and asking her Advice, which he agreed to: My Landlady, a Woman (as I found) us'd to such things, made light of it; she said she knew it would come to that at last, and made us very merry about it: As I said above, we found her an Experienc'd old Lady at such Work; she undertook every thing, engag'd to procure a Midwife and a Nurse, to satisfie all Enquiries, and bring us off with Reputation, and she did so very dexterously indeed.

WHEN I grew near my time, she desir'd my Gentleman to go away to *London*, or make as if he did so; when he was gone, she acquainted the Parish Officers[6] that there was a Lady ready to lye in at her House, but that she knew her Husband very well, and gave them, as she pretended, an account of his Name, which she called Sir *Walter Cleave*; telling them, he was a very worthy Gentleman, and that she would answer for all Enquiries, and the like: This satisfied the Parish Officers presently, and I lay INN with as much Credit as I could have done if I had really been my Lady *Cleave*; and was assisted in my Travel[7] by three or four of the best Citizens Wives of *Bath*, who liv'd in the Neighbourhood, which however made me a little the more expensive to him, I often expressed my concern to him about it, but he bid me not be concern'd at it.

As he had furnish'd me very sufficiently with Money for the

6. See n. 7, p. 10.
7. Changed to "Travail" in the second edition. *Cleave*: Contemporary slang for "wanton woman," this word also appears in Genesis 2:24 when, after the creation of Eve from Adam's rib, God founds the institution of marriage: "Therefore shall a man leave his father and his mother, and shall cleave unto his wife: and they shall be one flesh." This biblical verse is one of the suggested readings in the Anglican marriage ceremony.

extraordinary Expences of my Lying Inn, I had every thing very handsome about me; but did not affect to be Gay or Extravagant neither; besides, knowing my own Circumstances, and knowing the World as I had done, and that such kind of things do not often last long, I took care to lay up as much Money as I could for a wet Day, as I call'd it; making him believe it was all spent upon the extraordinary appearance of things in my Lying Inn.

BY this means, and including what he had given me as above, I had at the end of my Lying Inn about 200 Guineas by me, including also what was left of my own.

I WAS brought to Bed of a fine Boy indeed, and a charming Child it was; and when he heard of it he wrote me a very kind obliging Letter about it, and then told me, he thought it would look better for me to come away for *London* as soon as I was up and well, that he had provided Appartments for me at *Hammersmith* as if I came thither only from *London*, and that after a little while I should go back to the *Bath*, and he would go with me.

I LIK'D this offer very well, and accordingly hir'd a Coach on purpose, and taking my Child and a Wet-Nurse to Tend and Suckle it, and a Maid Servant with me, away I went for *London*.

HE met me at *Reading* in his own Chariot, and taking me into that, left the Servant and the Child in the hir'd Coach, and so he brought me to my new Lodgings at *Hammersmith*; with which I had abundance of Reason to be very well pleas'd, for they were very handsome Rooms, and I was very well accommodated.

AND now I was indeed in the height of what I might call my Prosperity, and I wanted nothing but to be a Wife, which however could not be in this Case, there was no room for it; and therefore on all Occasions I study'd to save what I could, as I have said above, against a time of scarcity; knowing well enough that such things as these do not always continue, that Men that keep Mistresses often change them, grow weary of them, or Jealous of them, or something or other happens to make them withdraw their Bounty; and sometimes the Ladies that are thus well us'd, are not careful by a prudent Conduct to preserve the Esteem of their Persons, or the nice Article of their Fidelity, and then they are justly cast off with Contempt.

BUT I was secur'd in this Point, for as I had no Inclination to change, so I had no manner of Acquaintance in the whole House, and so no Temptation to look any farther; I kept no Company but in the Family where I Lodg'd, and with a Clergyman's Lady at next Door; so that when he was absent I visited no Body, nor did he ever find me out of my Chamber or Parlor whenever he came down, if I went any where to take the Air it was always with him.

THE living in this manner with him, and his with me, was certainly the most undesigned thing in the World; he often protested to me, that when he became first acquainted with me, and even to the very Night when we first broke in upon our Rules, he never had the least Design of lying with me; that he always had a sincere Affection for me, but not the least real inclination to do what he had done; I assur'd him I never suspected him, that if I had, I should not so easily have yielded to the freedoms which brought it on, but that it was all a surprize, and was owing to the Accident of our having yielded too far to our mutual Inclinations that Night; and indeed I have often observ'd since, and leave it as a caution to the Readers of this Story; that we ought to be cautious of gratifying our Inclinations in loose and lewd Freedoms, least we find our Resolutions of Virtue fail us in the juncture when their Assistance should be most necessary.

IT is true, *and I have confess'd it before*, that from the first hour I began to converse with him, I resolv'd to let him lye with me, if he offer'd it; but it was because I wanted his help and assistance, and I knew no other way of securing him than that: But when we were that Night together, and, as I have said, had gone such a length, I found my Weakness, the Inclination was not to be resisted, but I was oblig'd to yield up all even before he ask'd it.

HOWEVER he was so just to me that he never upbraided me with that; nor did he ever express the least dislike of my Conduct on any other Occasion, but always protested he was as much delighted with my Company as he was the first Hour we came together, I mean came together as Bedfellows.

IT is true that he had no Wife, that is to say, she was as no Wife to him, and so I was in no Danger that way, but the just Reflections of Conscience oftentimes snatch a Man, especially a Man of Sense, from the Arms of a Mistress, as it did him at last, tho' on another Occasion.

ON the other hand, tho' I was not without secret Reproaches of my own Conscience for the Life I led, and that even in the greatest height of the Satisfaction I ever took, yet I had the terrible prospect of Poverty and Starving which lay on me as a frightful Spectre, so that there was no looking behind me: But as Poverty brought me into it, so fear of Poverty kept me in it, and I frequently resolv'd to leave it quite off, if I could but come to lay up Money enough to maintain me: But these were Thoughts of no weight, and whenever he came to me they vanish'd; for his Company was so delightful, that there was no being melancholly when he was there, the Reflections were all the Subject of those Hours when I was alone.

I LIV'D six Year in this happy but unhappy Condition, in which time I brought him three Children, but only the first of them liv'd; and tho' I remov'd twice in those six Years, yet I came back the sixth

Year to my first Lodgings at *Hammersmith*: Here it was that I was one Morning surpriz'd with a kind, but melancholy Letter from my Gentleman; intimating, that he was very ill, and was afraid he should have another fit of Sickness, but that his Wife's Relations being in the House with him, it would not be practicable to have me with him, which however he express'd his great Dissatisfaction in, and that he wish'd I cou'd be allowed to Tend and Nurse him as I did before.

I WAS very much concern'd at this Account, and was very impatient to know how it was with him; I waited a Fortnight or thereabouts, and heard nothing, which surpriz'd me, and I began to be very uneasy indeed; I think I may say, that for the next Fortnight I was near to distracted: It was my particular difficulty, that I did not know directly where he was; for I understood at first he was in the Lodgings of his Wive's Mother; but having remov'd my self to *London*, I soon found by the help of the Direction I had for writing my Letters to him, how to enquire after him, and there I found that he was at a House in *Bloomsbury*, whither he had, a little before he fell Sick, remov'd his whole Family; and that his Wife and Wives Mother were in the same House, tho' the Wife was not suffered to know that she was in the same House with her Husband.

HERE I also soon understood that he was at the last Extremity, which made me almost at the last Extremity too, to have a true account: One Night I had the Curiosity to disguise my self like a Servant Maid in a Round Cap and Straw Hat, and went to the Door, as sent by a Lady of his Neighbourhood, where he liv'd before, and giving Master and Mistresses Service, I said I was sent to know how Mr.——— did, and how he had rested that Night; in delivering this Message I got the opportunity I desir'd, for speaking with one of the Maids, I held a long Gossips Tale with her, and had all the Particulars of his Illness, which I found was a Pleurisie attended with a Cough and a Fever; she told me also who was in the House, and how his Wife was, who, by her Relation, they were in some hopes might Recover her Understanding; but as to the Gentleman himself, *in short* she told me the Doctors said there was very little hopes of him, that in the Morning they thought he had been dying, and that he was but little better then, for they did not expect that he could live over the next Night.

THIS was heavy News for me, and I began now to see an end of my Prosperity, and to see also that it was very well I had play'd the good Housewife, and secur'd or saved something while he was alive, for that now I had no view of *my own living* before me.

IT lay very heavy upon my Mind too, that I had a Son, a fine lovely Boy, above five Years old, and no Provision made for it, at least that

I knew of; with these Considerations, and a sad Heart, I went home that Evening, and began to cast with my self how I should live, and in what manner to bestow[8] my self, for the residue of my Life.

YOU may be sure I could not rest without enquiring again very quickly what was become of him; and not venturing to go my self, I sent several sham Messengers, till after a Fortnights waiting longer, I found that there was hopes of his Life, tho' he was still very ill; then I abated my sending any more to the House, and in some time after I learnt in the Neighbourhood that he was about House, and then that he was Abroad[9] again.

I MADE no doubt then but that I shou'd soon hear of him, and began to comfort my self with my Circumstances being, as I thought, recovered; I waited a Week, and two Weeks, and with much surprize and amazement I waited near two Months and heard nothing, but that being recover'd he was gone into the Country for the Air, and for the better Recovery after his Distemper; after this it was yet two Months more, and then I understood he was come to his City-House again, but still I heard nothing from him.

I HAD written several Letters for him, and Directed them as usual, and found two or three of them had been call'd for, *but not the rest*: I wrote again in a more pressing manner than ever, and in one of them let him know, that I must be forc'd to wait on him myself, Representing my Circumstances, the Rent of Lodgings to pay, and the Provision for the Child wanting, and my own deplorable Condition, destitute of Subsistence after his most solemn Engagement, to take Care of, and Provide for me; I took a Copy of this Letter, and finding it lay at the House, near a Month, and was not call'd for, I found means to have the Copy of it, put into his own Hands at a Coffee-House, where I had by Enquiry found he us'd to go.

THIS Letter forc'd an Answer from him, by which, tho' I found I was to be abandon'd, yet I found he had sent a Letter to me sometime before, desiring me to go down *to the Bath again*, its Contents I shall come to presently.

IT is True that Sick Beds are the times, when such Correspondences as this are look'd on with different Countenance, and seen with other Eyes than we saw them with, or than they appear'd with before: My Lover had been at the Gates of Death, and at the very brink of Eternity; and it seems had been strook with a due remorse, and with sad Reflections upon his past Life of Gallantry, and Levity; and among the rest, this criminal Correspondence with me, which was neither more or less, than a long continu'd Life of Adultery had represented it self, as it really was, not as it had been formerly

8. Dispose of, employ.
9. Out of his house.

thought by him to be, and he look'd upon it now with a just, and a religious Ab[h]orrence.

I cannot but observe also, and leave it for the Direction of my Sex in such Cases of Pleasure, that when ever sincere Repentance succeeds such a Crime as this, there never fails to attend a Hatred of the Object; and the more the Affection might seem to be before, the Hatred will be the more in Proportion: It will always be so, indeed it can be no otherwise; for there cannot be a true and sincere Abhorrence of the Offence, and the Love to the Cause of it remain, there will with an Abhorrence of the Sin be found a detestation of the fellow Sinner; you can expect no other.

I found it so here, tho' good Manners, and Justice in this Gentleman, kept him from carrying it on to any extream; but the short History of his Part in this Affair, was thus; he perceiv'd by my last Letter, and by all the rest, which he went for after, that I was not gone to the *Bath*, that his first Letter had not come to my Hand, upon which he writes me this following.

Madam

"I AM surpriz'd that my Letter Dated the 8th of last Month did not "come to your Hand, I give you my Word it was deliver'd at your "Lodgings, and to the Hands of your Maid.

"I NEED not acquaint you with what has been my condition for "sometime past; and how having been at the Edge of the Grave, I "am by the unexpected and undeserv'd Mercy of Heaven restor'd "again: In the Condition I have been in, it cannot be strange to you "that our unhappy Correspondence has not been the least of the "Burthens which lay upon my Conscience; I need say no more, those "things that must be repented of, must be also reform'd.

"I WISH you would think of going back to the *Bath*, I enclose you "here a Bill for 50 *l.* for clearing your self at your Lodgings, and "carrying you down, and hope it will be no surprize to you to add, "that on this account only, and not for any Offence given me on "your side, I can SEE YOU NO MORE; I will take due care of the Child, "leave him where he is, or take him with you, as you please; I wish "you the like Reflections, and that they may be to your Advantage. "I am, *&c*.

I WAS struck with this Letter as with a thousand Wounds, such as I cannot describe; the Reproaches of my own Conscience were such as I cannot express, for I was not blind to my own Crime: and I reflected that I might with less Offence have continued with my Brother, and liv'd with him as a Wife, since there was no Crime in our Marriage on that score, neither of us knowing it.

BUT I never once reflected that I was all this while a marry'd

Woman, a Wife to Mr.——— the Linnen Draper, who tho' he had left me by the Necessity of his Circumstances, had no power to Discharge me from the Marriage Contract which was between us, or to give me a legal liberty to marry again; so that I had been no less than a Whore and an Adultress all this while: I then reproach'd my self with the Liberties I had taken, and how I had been a Snare to this Gentleman, and that indeed I was principal in the Crime; that now he was mercifully snatch'd out of the Gulph by a convincing[1] Work upon his Mind, but that I was left as if I was forsaken of God's Grace, and abandon'd by Heaven to a continuing in my wickedness.

UNDER these Reflections I continu'd very pensive and sad for near a Month, and did not go down to the *Bath*, having no inclination to be with the Woman who I was with before; least, as I thought, she should prompt me to some wicked course of Life again, as she had done; and besides, I was very loth she should know I was cast off as above.

AND now I was greatly perplex'd about my little Boy; it was Death to me to part with the Child, and yet when I consider'd the Danger of being one time or other left with him to keep without a Maintenance to support him, I then resolv'd to leave him where he was; but then I concluded also to be near him my self too, that I might have the satisfaction of seeing him, without the Care of providing for him.

I sent my Gentleman a short Letter therefore, that I had obey'd his Orders in all things, but that of going back to the *Bath*, which I cou'd not think of for many Reasons; that however parting from him was a Wound to me that I could never recover, yet that I was fully satisfied his Reflections were just, and would be very far from desiring to obstruct his Reformation or Repentance.

THEN I represented my own Circumstances to him in the most moving Terms that I was able: I told him that those unhappy Distresses which first mov'd him to a generous and an honest Friendship for me, would, I hope, move him to a little concern for me now; tho' the Criminal part of our Correspondence, which I believed neither of us intended to fall into at that time, was broken off; that I desir'd to Repent as sincerely as he had done, but entreated him to put me in some Condition, that I might not be expos'd to the Temptations which the Devil never fails to excite us to from the frightful prospect of Poverty and Distress; and if he had the least Apprehensions of my being troublesome to him, I beg'd he would put me in a Posture to go back to my Mother in *Virginia*, from whence he knew I came, and that would put an end to all his Fears on that account; I concluded, that if he would send me 50 *l.* more to facilitate my going away, I would send him back a general Release, and would promise never to

1. Convicting (in the sense of proving guilty), the first step toward repentance of sin. *Gulph*: Gulf or abyss (i.e., of damnation).

disturb him more with any Importunities; unless it was to hear of the well-doing of the Child, who if I found my Mother living, and my Circumstances able, I would send for to come over to me, and take him also effectually off of his Hands.

THIS was indeed all a Cheat thus far, *viz.* that I had no intention to go to *Virginia*, as the Account of my former Affairs there may convince any Body of; but the business was to get this last Fifty Pounds of him, if possible, knowing well enough it would be the last Penny I was ever to expect.

HOWEVER the Argument I us'd, namely, of giving him a general Release, and never troubling him any more, prevail'd effectually with him, and he sent me a Bill for the Money by a Person who brought with him a general Release for me to sign, and which I frankly sign'd, and receiv'd the Money; and thus, tho' full sore against my will, a final End was put to this Affair.

AND here I cannot but reflect upon the unhappy Consequence of too great Freedoms between Persons stated[2] as we were, upon the pretence of innocent intentions, Love of Friendship, *and the like*; for the Flesh has generally so great a share in those Friendships, that it is great odds but inclination prevails at last over the most solemn Resolutions; and that Vice breaks in at the breaches of Decency, which really innocent Friendship ought to preserve with the greatest strictness; but I leave the Readers of these things to their own just Reflections; which they will be more able to make effectual than I, who so soon forgot my self, and am therefore but a very indifferent Monitor.[3]

I WAS now a single Person again, *as I may call my self*, I was loos'd from all the Obligations either of Wedlock or Mistressship in the World; except my Husband the Linnen Draper, who I having not now heard from in almost Fifteen Year, no Body could blame me for thinking my self entirely freed from; seeing also he had at his going away told me, that if I did not hear frequently from him, I should conclude he was dead, and I might freely marry again to whom I pleas'd.

I NOW began to cast up my Accounts; I had by many Letters, and much Importunity, and with the Intercession of my Mother too, had a second return of some Goods from my Brother, *as I now call him*, in *Virginia*, to make up the Damage of the Cargo I brought away with me, and this too was upon the Condition of my sealing a general Release to him, and to send it him by his Correspondent at *Bristol*, which though I thought hard of, yet I was oblig'd to promise to do: However, I manag'd so well in this case, that I got my Goods away before the Release was sign'd, and then I always found something or

2. Situated.
3. Someone who gives advice or warning to others regarding their conduct.

other to say to evade the thing, and to put off the signing it at all; till *at length* I pretended I must write to my Brother, and have his Answer, before I could do it.

INCLUDING this Recruit, and before I got the last 50 *l.* I found my strength to amount, put all together, to about 400 *l.* so that with that I had above 450 *l.* I had sav'd above 100 *l.* more, but I met with a Disaster with that, which was this; that a Goldsmith in whose Hands I had trusted it, broke, so I lost 70 *l.* of my Money, the Man's Composition not making above 30 *l.* out of his 100 *l.* I had a little Plate,[4] but not much, and was well enough stock'd with Cloaths and Linnen.

WITH this Stock I had the World to begin again; but you are to consider, that I was not now the same Woman as when I liv'd at *Redriff*; for first of all I was near 20 Years older, and did not look the better for my Age, nor for my Rambles to *Virginia* and back again; and tho' I omitted nothing that might set me out to Advantage, except Painting,[5] for that I never stoop'd to, and had Pride enough to think I did not want it, yet there would always be some difference seen between Five and Twenty, and Two and Forty.

I cast about innumerable ways for my future State of Life and began to consider very seriously what I should do, *but nothing offer'd*; I took care to make the World take me for something more than I was, and had it given out that I was a Fortune, and that my Estate was in my own Hands, the last of which was very true, the first of it was as above: I had no Acquaintance, which was one of my worst Misfortunes, and the Consequence of that was, I had no adviser, at least who cou'd advise and assist together; and above all, I had no Body to whom I could in confidence commit the Secret of any Circumstances to, and could depend upon for their Secresie and Fidelity; and I found by experience, that to be Friendless is the worst Condition, next to being in want, that a Woman can be reduc'd to: *I say a Woman*, because 'tis evident Men can be their own Advisers, and their own Directors, and know how to work themselves out of Difficulties and into Business better than Women; but if a Woman has no Friend to Communicate her Affairs to, and to advise and assist her, 'tis ten to one but she is undone; nay, and the more Money she has, the more Danger she is in of being wrong'd and deceiv'd; and this was my Case in the Affair of the Hundred Pound which I left in the Hand of the Goldsmith, *as above*, whose Credit, it seems, was upon the Ebb before, but I that had no knowledge of things, and no Body to consult with, knew nothing of it, and so lost my Money.

IN the next place, when a Woman is thus left desolate and void of Council,[6] she is just like a Bag of Money, or a Jewel dropt on the

4. Silver utensils for table and domestic use, ornaments, etc.
5. Coloring the face with paint.
6. Counsel.

Highway, which is a Prey to the next Comer; if a Man of Virtue and upright Principles happens to find it, he will have it cried,[7] and the Owner may come to hear of it again; but how many times shall such a thing fall into Hands that will make no scruple of siezing it for their own, to once that it shall come into good Hands.

THIS was evidently my Case, for I was now a loose unguided Creature, and had no Help, no Assistance, no Guide for my Conduct: I knew what I aim'd at, and what I wanted, but knew nothing how to pursue the End by direct means; I wanted to be plac'd in a settled State of Living, and had I happen'd to meet with a sober good Husband, I should have been as faithful and true a Wife to him as Virtue it self could have form'd: If I had been otherwise, the Vice came in always at the Door of Necessity, not at the Door of Inclination; and I understood too well, by the want of it, what the value of a settl'd Life was, to do any thing to forfeit the felicity of it; nay, I should have made the better Wife for all the Difficulties I had pass'd thro', by a great deal; nor did I in any of the Times that I had been a Wife, give my Husbands the least uneasiness on account of my Behaviour.

BUT all this was nothing; I found no encouraging Prospect; I waited, I liv'd regularly, and with as much frugality as became my Circumstances, but nothing offer'd; nothing presented, and the main Stock wasted apace; what to do I knew not, the Terror of approaching Poverty lay hard upon my Spirits: I had some Money, but where to place it I knew not, nor would the Interest of it maintain me, at least not in *London*.

AT length a new Scene open'd: There was in the House where I Lodg'd, a North Country Woman that went[8] for a Gentlewoman, and nothing was more frequent in her Discourse, than her account of the cheapness of Provisions, and the easie way of living in her County; how plentiful and how cheap every thing was, what good Company they kept, and the like; till at last I told her she almost tempted me to go and live in her County; for I that was a Widow, tho' I had sufficient to live on, yet had no way of encreasing it, and that *London* was an expensive and extravagant Place; that I found I could not live here under a Hundred Pound a Year, unless I kept no Company, no Servant, made no Appearance, and buried my self in Privacy, as if I was oblig'd to it by Necessity.

I SHOULD have observ'd, that she was always made to believe, as every Body else was, that I was a great Fortune, or at least that I had Three or Four Thousand Pounds, if not more, and all in my own Hands; and she was mighty sweet upon me when she thought me inclin'd in the least to go into her Country; she said she had a Sister liv'd near *Liverpool*, that her Brother was a considerable Gentleman

7. Publicly announced or advertised.
8. Passed.

there, and had a great Estate also in *Ireland*; that she would go down there in about two Months, and if I would give her my Company thither, I should be as welcome as her self for a Month or more as I pleas'd, till I should see how I lik'd the Country; and if I thought fit to live there, she would undertake they would take care, tho' they did not entertain Lodgers themselves, they would recommend me to some agreeable Family, where I shou'd be plac'd to my content.

IF this Woman had known my real Circumstances, she would never have laid so many Snares, and taken so many weary steps to catch a poor desolate Creature that was good for little when it was caught; and indeed I, whose case was almost desperate, and thought I cou'd not be much worse, was not very anxious about what might befall me, provided they did me no personal Injury; so I suffered my self, tho' not without a great deal of Invitation and great Professions of sincere Friendship and real Kindness, I *say* I suffer'd my self to be prevail'd upon to go with her, and accordingly I pack'd up my Baggage, and put my self in a Posture for a Journey, tho' I did not absolutely know whither I was to go.

AND now I found my self in great Distress; what little I had in the World was all in Money, except as before, a little Plate, some Linnen, and my Cloaths; as for Household stuff I had little or none, for I had liv'd always in Lodgings; but I had not one Friend in the World with whom to trust that little I had, or to direct me how to dispose of it, and this perplex'd me Night and Day; I thought of the Bank, and of the other Companies in *London*, but I had no Friend to commit the Management of it to, and to keep and carry about with me Bank Bills, Talleys, Orders, and such things, I look'd upon it as unsafe; that if they were lost my Money was lost, and then I was undone; and on the other hand I might be robb'd, and perhaps murder'd in a strange place for them; this perplex'd me strangely, and what to do I knew not.

IT came in my Thoughts one Morning that I would go to the *Bank* my self, where I had often been to receive the Interest of some Bills I had, which had Interest payable on them, and where I had found the Clark,[9] to whom I applyed my self, very Honest and Just to me, and particularly so fair one time, that when I had miss-told my Money, and taken less than my due, and was coming away, he set me to rights and gave me the rest, which he might have put into his own Pocket.

I WENT to him, and represented my Case very plainly, *and ask'd if he would trouble himself to be my Adviser, who was a poor friendless Widow, and knew not what to do: He told me*, if I desir'd his Opinion of any thing within the reach of his Business, he would do his

9. Clerk.

Endeavour that I should not be wrong'd, but that he would also help me to a good sober Person who was a grave Man of his Acquaintance, who was a Clark in such business too, tho' not in their House, whose Judgment was good, and whose Honesty I might depend upon, *for*, added he, *I will answer for him, and for every step he takes; if he wrongs you*, Madam, *of one Farthing, it shall lye at my door, I will make it good*; and he delights to assist People in such Cases, he does it as an act of Charity.

I WAS a little at a stand at this Discourse, but after some pause I told him, I had rather have depended upon him because I had found him honest, but if that cou'd not be, I would take his Recommendation sooner than any ones else; *I dare say*, Madam, *says he, that you will be as well satisfied with my Friend as with me, and he is thoroughly able to assist you, which I am not*; it seems he had his Hands full of the Business of the Bank, and had engag'd to meddle with no other Business than that of his Office, which I heard afterwards, but did not understand then: He added, that his Friend should take nothing of me for his Advice or Assistance, and this indeed encourag'd me very much.

HE appointed the same Evening after the Bank was shut, and Business over, for me to meet him and his Friend; and indeed as soon as I saw his Friend, and he began but to talk of the Affair; I was fully satisfied that I had a very honest Man to deal with, his Countenance spoke it, and his Character, as I heard afterwards, was every where so good, that I had no room for any more doubts upon me.

AFTER the first meeting, in which I only said what I had said before, we parted, and he appointed me to come the next Day to him, *telling me*, I might in the mean time satisfie my self of him by enquiry, which however I knew not how well to do, having no Acquaintance my self.

ACCORDINGLY I met him the next Day, when I entered more freely with him into my Case, *I told him* my Circumstances at large, that *I was a Widow* come over from *America*, perfectly desolate and friendless; that I had a little Money, and but a little, and was almost distracted for fear of losing it, having no Friend in the World to trust with the management of it; that I was going into the North of *England* to live cheap, that my stock might not waste; that I would willingly Lodge my Money in the Bank, but that I durst not carry the Bills about me, and the like, as above; and how to Correspond about it, or with who, I knew not.

HE told me I might lodge the Money in the Bank as an Account, and its being entred in the Books would entitle me to the Money at any time, and if I was in the North might draw Bills on the Cashire and receive it when I would; but that then it would be esteem'd as running Cash, and the Bank would give no Interest for it; that I might buy Stock with it, and so it would lye in store for me, but that then if I wanted to dispose of it, I must come up to Town on purpose to Transfer it, and even it would be with some difficulty I should receive the half yearly Dividend, unless I was here in Person, or had some Friend I could trust with having the Stock in his Name to do it for me, and that would have the same difficulty in it as before; and with that he look'd hard at me and *smil'd a little*; at last, *says he*, why do you not get a head Steward,[1] Madam, that may take you and your Money together into keeping, and then you would have the trouble taken off of your Hands? Ay, Sir, and the Money too it may be, *said I*, for truly *I find the hazard that way is as much as 'tis t'other way*; but I remember, I *said*, secretly to my self, I wish you would ask me the Question fairly, I would consider very seriously on it before I said NO.

HE went on a good way with me, and I thought once or twice he was in earnest, but to my real Affliction, I found at last he had a Wife; but when he own'd he had a Wife he shook his Head, and said with some concern, that indeed he had a *Wife*, and *no Wife*: I began to think he had been in the Condition of my late Lover, and that his Wife had been Distemper'd or Lunatick, or some such thing: However, we had not much more Discourse at that time, but he told me he was in too much hurry of business then, but that if I would come home to his House after their Business was over, he would by that time consider what might be done for me, to put my Affairs in a Posture of Security: I told him I would come, and desir'd to know where he liv'd: He gave me a Direction in Writing, and when he gave it me he read it to me, and said, there 'tis, Madam, if you dare trust your self with me: Yes, Sir, *said I*, I believe I may venture to trust you with my self, for you have a Wife you say, and I don't want a Husband; besides, I dare trust you with my Money, which is all I have in the World, and if that were gone, I may trust my self any where.

HE said some things in Jest that were very handsome and mannerly, and would have pleas'd me very well if they had been in earnest; *but that pass'd over*, I took the Directions, and appointed to attend him at his House at seven a Clock the same Evening.

WHEN I came he made several Proposals for my placing my Money in the Bank, in order to my having Interest for it; but still some difficulty or other came in the way, which he objected as not safe; and I found such a sincere disinterested Honesty in him, that I began to muse with my self, that I had certainly found the honest Man I wanted; and that I could never put my self into better Hands; so I told him with a great deal of frankness that I had never met with

1. An overseer or administrator, to serve as both husband and money-manager.

Man or Woman yet that I could trust, or in whom I cou'd think my self safe, but that I saw he was so disinterestedly concern'd for my safety, that *I said* I would freely trust him with the management of that little I had, if he would accept to be Steward for a poor Widow that could give him no Salary.

HE smil'd, and standing up with great Respect saluted me; he told me he could not but take it very kindly that I had so good an Opinion of him; that he would not deceive me, that he would do any thing in his Power to serve me and expect no Sallary; but that he cou'd not by any means accept of a Trust, that it might bring him to be suspected of Self-interest, and that if I should die he might have Disputes with my Executors, which he should be very loth to encumber himself with.

I TOLD him if those were all his Objections I would soon remove them, and convince him, that there was not the least room for any difficulty; for that *first* as for suspecting him, if ever I should do it now was the time to suspect him, and not put the Trust into his Hands, and whenever I did suspect him, he could but throw it up then and refuse to go any farther; *Then* as to Executors, I assur'd him I had no Heirs, nor any Relations in *England*, and I would have neither Heirs or Executors but himself, unless I should alter my Condition before I died, and then his Trust and Trouble should cease together, which however I had no prospect of yet; but I told him if I died as I was, it should be all his own, and he would deserve it by being so faithful to me as I was satisfied he would be.

HE chang'd his Countenance at this Discourse, and ask'd me, how I came to have so much good will for him? and looking very much pleas'd, said, he might very lawfully wish he was a single Man for my sake; I smil'd and told him, that as he was not, my offer could have no design upon him in it, and to wish, as he did, was not to be allow'd, 'twas Criminal to his Wife.

HE told me I was wrong; for, *says he*, Madam, as I said before, I have a Wife and no Wife, and 'twould be no Sin to me to wish her hang'd, if that were all; I know nothing of your Circumstances that way, Sir, *said I*; but it cannot be innocent to wish your Wife dead; I tell you, *says he again*, she is a Wife and no Wife; you don't know what I am, or what she is.

THAT's true, *said I*, Sir, I do not know what you are, but I believe you to be an honest Man, and that's the cause of all my Confidence in you.

WELL well, *says he*, and so I am, *I hope*, too, but I am something else too, Madam; for, *says he*, to be plain with you, I am a *Cuckold*, and she is a *Whore*; he spoke it in a kind of Jest, but it was with such an awkward smile, that I perceiv'd it was what stuck very close to him, and he look'd dismally when he said it.

THAT alters the case indeed, Sir, *said I*, as to that part you were speaking of; but a *Cuckold* you know may be an honest Man, it does not alter that Case at all; besides I think, *said I*, since your Wife is so dishonest to you, you are too honest to her, to own her for your Wife; but that, *said I*, is what I have nothing to do with.

NAY, *says he*, I do think to clear my Hands of her, for to be plain with you, Madam, *added he*, I am no contented Cuckold neither: *On the other hand*, I assure you it provokes me to the highest degree, but I can't help my self, she that will be a *Whore*, will be a *Whore*.

I WAV'D the Discourse, and began to talk of my Business, but I found he could not have done with it, so I let him alone, and he went on to tell me all the Circumstances of his Case, too long to relate here, particularly, that having been out of *England* some time before he came to the Post he was in, she had had two Children in the mean time by an Officer of the Army; and that when he came to *England*, and, upon her Submission, took her again, and maintain'd her very well, yet she run away from him with a Linnen-Draper's Apprentice; robb'd him of what she could come at, and continued to live from him still; so that, Madam, *says he*, she is a Whore not by Necessity, which is the common Bait of your Sex, but by Inclination, and for the sake of the Vice.

WELL, I pitied him and wish'd him well rid of her, and still would have talk'd of my Business, but it would not do; at last he looks steadily at me, *look you*, Madam, *says he*, you came to ask Advice of me, and I will serve you as faithfully as if you were my own Sister; but I must turn the Tables, since you oblige me to do it, and are so friendly to me, and I think I must ask advice of you; *tell me what must a poor abus'd Fellow do with a Whore? what can I do to do my self Justice upon her*?

ALAS, *Sir, says I*, 'tis a Case too nice for me to advise in, but it seems she has run away from you, so you are rid of her fairly; what can you desire more? Ay, she is gone indeed, *said he*, but I am not clear of her for all that.

THAT'S true, *says I*, she may indeed run you into Debt, but the Law has furnish'd you with Methods to prevent that also, you may Cry her down,[2] *as they call it*.

No no, *says he*, that is not the Case neither, I have taken care of all that; 'tis not that part that I speak of, but I would be rid of her so that I might marry again.

WELL Sir, *says I*, then you must Divorce her; if you can prove what you say, you may certainly get that done, and then, I suppose, you are free.

THAT'S very tedious and expensive,[3] *says he*.

2. Publicly announce (e.g., in a newspaper notice or advertisement) that he is not accountable for his wife's debts.
3. Divorce could be granted only by an act of Parliament and depended largely on the peti-

WHY, *says I*, if you can get any Woman you like to take your word, I suppose your Wife would not dispute the Liberty with you that she takes herself.

AY, *says he*, but 'twou'd be hard to bring an honest Woman to do that; and for the other sort, *says he*, I have had enough of her to meddle with any more Whores.

IT occurr'd to me presently, I would have taken your word with all my Heart, if you had but ask'd me the Question, but that was to my self; *to him I reply'd*, why you shut the Door against any honest Woman accepting you, for you condemn all that should venture upon you at once, and conclude, that really a Woman that takes you now, can't be honest.

WHY, *says he*, I wish you would satisfie me that an honest Woman would take me, I'd venture it, and then turns short upon me, *will you take me*, Madam?

THAT's not a fair Question, *says I*, after what you have said; however, least you should think I wait only for a Recantation of it, I shall answer you plainly NO *not I*; my Business is of another kind with you, and I did not expect you would have turn'd my serious Application to you in my own distracted Case, into a Comedy.

WHY, Madam, *says he*, my Case is as distracted as yours can be, and I stand in as much need of Advice as you do, for I think if I have not Relief some where, I shall be mad my self, and I know not what course to take, I protest to you.

WHY, Sir, *says* I, 'tis easie to give Advice in your Case, much easier than it is in mine; speak then, *says he*, I beg of you, for now you encourage me.

WHY, *says I*, if your Case is so plain as you say it is, you may be legally Divorc'd, and then you may find honest Women enough to ask the Question of fairly, the Sex is not so scarce that you can want a Wife.

WELL then, *said he*, I am in earnest, I'll take your Advice, but shall I ask you one Question seriously before hand.

ANY Question, *said I*, but that you did before.

No, that Answer will not do, *said he*, for, in short, that is the Question I shall ask.

YOU may ask what Questions you please, but you have my Answer to that already, *said I*; besides Sir, *said I*, can you think so Ill of me as that I would give any Answer to such a Question beforehand? Can any Woman alive believe you in earnest, or think you design any thing but to banter her?

---

tioner's ability to buy political influence. The difficulty of proving adultery, virtually the only grounds for seeking a divorce, added to the time and expense.

WELL, well, *says he*, I do not banter you, I am in earnest, consider of it.

But, SIR, *says I, a little gravely*, I came to you about my own Business, I beg of you let me know, what you will advise me to do?

I WILL be prepar'd, *says he*, against you come again.

NAY, *says I*, you have forbid my coming any more.

WHY so, *said he*, and look'd a little surpriz'd?

BECAUSE, *said I*, you can't expect I should visit you on the account you talk of.

WELL, *says he*, you shall promise me to come again however, and I will not say any more of it till I have gotten the Divorce, but I desire you will prepare to be better condition'd when that's done, for you shall be the Woman, or I will not be Divorc'd at all: Why I owe it to your unlooked for kindness, if it were to nothing else, but I have other Reasons too.

HE could not have said any thing in the World that pleas'd me better; however, I knew that the way to secure him was to stand off while the thing was so remote, as it appear'd to be, and that it was time enough to accept of it when he was able to perform it; so I said very respectfully to him, it was time enough to consider of these things, when he was in a Condition to talk of them; in the mean time I told him, I was going a great way from him, and he would find Objects enough to please him better: We broke off here for the present, and he made me promise him to come again the next Day, for his Resolutions upon my own Business, which after some pressing I did; tho' had he seen farther into me, I wanted no pressing on that Account.

I CAME the next Evening accordingly, and brought my Maid with me, to *let him see* that I kept a Maid, but I sent her away, as soon as I was gone in: He would have had me let the Maid have staid, but I would not, but order'd her aloud to come for me again about Nine a Clock, but he forbid that, and told me he would see me safe Home, which by the way I was not very well pleas'd with, supposing he might do that to know where I liv'd, and enquire into my Character, and Circumstances: However, I ventur'd that, for all that the People there, or thereabout knew of me, was to my Advantage; and all the Character he had of me, after he had enquir'd, was *that I was a Woman of Fortune*, and that I was a very modest sober Body; which whether true or not in the Main, yet you may see how necessary it is, for all Women who expect any thing in the World, to preserve the Character of their Virtue, even when perhaps they may have sacrific'd the Thing itself.

I FOUND *and was not a little pleas'd with it*, that he had provided a Supper for me: I found also he liv'd very handsomely, and had a

House very handsomely furnish'd, all which I was rejoyc'd at indeed, for I look'd upon it as all my own.

WE had now a second Conference upon the Subject matter of the last Conference: He laid his business very Home indeed; he protested his Affection to me, and indeed I had no room to doubt it; he declar'd that it began from the first Moment I talk'd with him, and long before I had mention'd leaving my Effects with him; 'tis no matter when it begun, *thought I*, if it will but hold, 'twill be well enough: *He then told me*, how much the offer I had made of trusting him with my Effects, and leaving them to him, had engag'd him; so I intended it should, *thought I*, but then I thought you had been a single Man too: After we had Supp'd, I observ'd he press'd me very hard to drink two or three Glasses of Wine, which however I declin'd; but Drank one Glass or two: He then told he had a Proposal to make to me, which I should promise him I would not take ill, if I should not grant it: I told him I hop'd he would make no dishonourable Proposal to me, especially in his own House, and that if it was such, I desir'd he would not propose it, that I might not be oblig'd to offer any Resentment to him, that did not become the respect I profess'd for him, and the Trust I had plac'd in him, in coming to his House; and beg'd of him he would give me leave to go away, and accordingly began to put on my Gloves, and prepare to be gone, tho' at the same time I no more intended it, than he intended to let me.

WELL, he importun'd me not to talk of going, he assur'd me he had no dishonourable thing in his Thoughts about me, and was very far from offering any thing to me that was dishonourable and if I thought so, he would chuse to say no more of it.

THAT part I did not relish at all; I told him, I was ready to hear any thing that he had to say, depending that he would say nothing unworthy of himself, or unfit for me to hear; upon this, he told me his Proposal was this, That I would Marry him, tho' he had not yet obtain'd the Divorce from the Whore his Wife; and to satisfie me that he meant honourably, he would promise not to desire me to live with him, or go to Bed to him till the Divorce was obtain'd: My Heart said yes to this offer at first Word, but it was necessary to Play the Hypocrite a little more with him; so I seem'd to decline the Motion with some warmth, and besides a little Condemning the thing as unfair, told him, that such a Proposal could be of no Signification, but to entangle us both in great Difficulties; for if he should not at last obtain the Divorce, yet we could not dissolve the Marriage, neither could we proceed in it; so that if he was disappointed in the Divorce, I left him to consider what a Condition we should both be in.

IN SHORT, I carried on the Argument against this so far, that I convinc'd him, it was not a Proposal that had any Sense in it: WELL then he went from it to another, and that was, that I would Sign and Seal a Contract with him, Conditioning to Marry him as soon as the Divorce was obtain'd, and to be void if he could not obtain it.

I TOLD him such a thing was more Rational than the other; but as this was the first time that ever I could imagine him weak enough to be in earnest in this Affair, I did not use to say YES at first asking, I would consider of it.

I PLAY'D with this Lover, as an Angler does with a Trout: I found I had him fast on the Hook, so I jested with his new Proposal; and put him off: I told him he knew little of me, and bad him enquire about me; I let him also go Home with me to my Lodging, tho' I would not ask him to go in, for I told him it was not Decent.

IN SHORT, I ventur'd to avoid Signing a Contract of Marriage, and the Reason why I did it, was because the Lady that had invited me so earnestly to go with her into *Lancashire* insisted so possitively upon it, and promised me such great Fortunes, and such fine things there, that I was tempted to go and try; perhaps, *said I*, I may mend myself very much, and then I made no scruple in my Thoughts, of quitting my honest Citizen, who I was not so much in Love with, as not to leave him for a Richer.

IN a Word I avoided a Contract; but told him I would go into the *North*, that he should know where to write to me by the Consequence of the Business I had entrusted with him, that I would give him a sufficient Pledge of My Respect for him; for I would leave almost all I had in the World in his Hands; and I would thus far give him my Word, that as soon as he had su'd out a Divorce from his first Wife, if he would send me an Account of it, I would come up to *London*, and that then we would talk seriously of the Matter.

IT was a base Design I went with, *that I must confess*, tho' I was invited thither with a Design much worse than mine was, as the Sequel will discover; well I went with my Friend, *as I call'd her*, into *Lancashire*; all the way we went she Caressed me with the utmost appearance of a sincere undissembled Affection; treated me, except my Coach hire all the way; and her Brother brought a Gentleman's Coach to *Warrington*, to receive us, and we were carried from thence to *Liverpool* with as much Ceremony as I could desire: We were also entertain'd at a Merchant's House in *Liverpool* three or four Days very handsomely: I forbear to tell his Name, because of what follow'd; then she told me she would carry me to an Uncles House of hers, where we should be nobly entertain'd; she did so, her Uncle as she call'd him, sent a Coach and four Horses for us, and we were carried near forty Miles, I know not whither.

WE came however to a Gentleman's Seat, where was a numerous Family, a large Park, extraordin[a]ry Company indeed, and where she was call'd Cousin; I told her if she had resolv'd to bring me into such Company as this, she should have let me have prepar'd my self, and have furnish'd my self with better Cloths; the Ladies took notice of that, and told me very genteely, they did not value People in their Country so much by their Cloths, as they did in *London*; that their Cousin had fully inform'd them of my Quality, and that I did not want Cloths to set me off; in short, they entertain'd me not like what I was, but like what they thought I had been, Namely, a Widow Lady of a great Fortune.

THE first Discovery I made here was, that the Family were all *Roman Catholicks*,[4] and the Cousin too, who I call'd my Friend; however, *I must say*, that nothing in the World could behave better to me; and I had all the Civility shown me that I could have had, if I had been of their Opinion: The Truth is, I had not so much Principle of any kind, as to be Nice in Point of Religion; and I presently learn'd to speak favourably of the *Romish Church*; particularly I told them I saw little, but the prejudice of Education in all the Differences that were among Christians about Religion, and if it had so happen'd that my Father had been a *Roman Catholick*, I doubted not but I should have been as well pleas'd with their Religion as my own.

THIS oblig'd them in the highest Degree, and as I was besieg'd Day and Night with good Company, and pleasant Discourse, so I had two or three old Ladies that lay at me upon the Subject of Religion too; I was so Complaisant[5] that tho' I would not compleatly engage, yet I made no scruple to be present at their Mass, and to conform to all their Gestures as they shew'd me the Pattern, but I would not come too cheap; so that I only in the main encourag'd them to expect that I would turn *Roman Catholick*, if I was instructed in the *Catholick Doctrine* as they call'd it, and so the matter rested.

I STAY'D here about six Weeks; and then my Conducter led me back to a Country Village, about six Miles from *Liverpool*, where her Brother, (as she call'd him) came to Visit me in his own Chariot, and in a very good Figure, with two Footmen in a good Livery; and the next thing was to make Love to me: As it had happen'd to me, one would think I could not have been cheated, and indeed I thought so myself, having a safe Card at home, which I resolv'd not to quit, unless, I could mend myself very much: However in all appearance this Brother was a Match worth my lissening to, and the least his Estate was valued at, was a 1000 *l.* a Year, but the Sister said it was worth 1500 *l.* a Year, and lay most of it in *Ireland*.

I THAT was a great Fortune, and pass'd for such, was above being

4. Lancashire was well known for its large number of Roman Catholics and, consequently, viewed with fear and suspicion as a potential hotbed of Jacobitism; support there for the Jacobite rebellion of 1715 had done little to dispel that view.
5. Disposed to please.

ask'd how much my Estate was; and my false Friend taking it upon a foolish hearsay had rais'd it from 500 *l.* to 5000 *l.* and by the time she came into the Country she call'd it 15000 *l.* The *Irishman*, for such I understood him to be, was stark Mad at this Bait: In short, he Courted me, made me Presents, and run in Debt like a mad Man for the Expences of his Equipage, and of his Courtship: He had to give him his due, the Appearance of an extraordinary fine Gentleman; he was Tall, well Shap'd, and had an extraordinary Address; talk'd as naturally of his Park, and his Stables; of his Horses, his Game-Keepers, his Woods, his Tenants, and his Servants, as if we had been in the Mansion-House, and I had seen them all about me.

HE never so much as ask'd me about my Fortune, or Estate, but assur'd me that when we came to *Dublin* he would Joynture[6] me in 600 *l.* a Year good Land; and that he would enter into a Deed of Settlement, or Contract here, for the performance of it.

THIS was such Language indeed as I had not been us'd to, and I was here beaten out of all my Measures;[7] I had a she Devil in my Bosom, every Hour telling me how great her Brother liv'd: One time she would come for my Orders, how I would have my Coaches painted, and how lin'd; and another time what Cloths my Page should wear: In short, my Eyes were dazl'd, I had now lost my Power of saying No, and to cut the Story short, I consented to be married; but to be the more private we were carried farther into the Country, and married by a Romish Clergyman,[8] which I was assur'd would marry us as effectually as a Church of *England* Parson.

I CANNOT say, but I had some Reflections in this Affair, upon the dishonourable forsaking my faithful Citizen; who lov'd me sincerely, and who was endeavouring to quit himself of a scandalous Whore, by whom he had been indeed barbarously us'd, and promis'd himself infinite Happiness in his new choice; which choice was now giving up her self to another in a manner almost as scandalous as hers could be.

BUT the glittering show of a great Estate, and of fine Things, which the deceived Creature that was now my Deceiver represented every Hour to my Imagination, hurried me away, and gave me no time to think of *London*, or of any thing there, much less of the Obligation I had to a Person of infinitely more real Merit than what was now before me.

BUT the thing was done, I was now in the Arms of my new Spouse, who appear'd still the same as before; great even to Magnificence, and nothing less than a Thousand Pound a Year could support the ordinary Equipage he appear'd in.

6. See n. 3, p. 44.
7. Notions, rules, or standards of judgment.
8. Marriages performed by Roman Catholic priests were recognized as legally valid.

AFTER we had been marry'd about a Month, he began to talk of my going to *West-chester* in order to embark for *Ireland*. However, he did not hurry me, for we staid near three Weeks longer, and then he sent to *Chester* for a Coach to meet us at the *Black Rock*, as they call it, over-against *Liverpool*:[9] Thither we went in a fine Boat they call a Pinnace with Six Oars, his Servants, and Horses, and Baggage going in the Ferry Boat. He made his excuse to me, that he had no Acquaintance at *Chester*, but he would go before and get some handsome Apartment for me at a private House; I ask'd him how long we should stay at *Chester*? he said not at all, any longer than one Night or two, but he would immediately hire a Coach to go to *Holyhead*; then I told him he should by no means give himself the trouble to get private Lodgings for one Night or two, for that *Chester* being a great Place, I made no doubt but there would be very good Inns and Accommodation enough; so we lodg'd at an Inn in the West Street, not far from the Cathedral, I forget what Sign it was at.

HERE my Spouse talking of my going to *Ireland*, ask'd me if I had no Affairs to settle at *London* before we went off; I told him no not of any great Consequence, but what might be done as well by Letter from *Dublin*: Madam, says he very respectfully, I suppose the greatest part of your Estate, which my Sister tells me is most of it in Money in the Bank of *England*, lies secure enough, but in case it requir'd Transferring, or any way altering its Property, it might be necessary to go up to *London*, and settle those things before we went over.

I SEEMED to look strange at it, and told him I knew not what he meant; that I had no Effects in the Bank of *England* that I knew of; and I hoped he could not say that I had ever told him I had: No, he said, I had not told him so, but his Sister had said the greatest part of my Estate lay there, and *I only mention'd it my Dear*, said he, *that if there was any occasion to settle it, or order any thing about it, we might not be oblig'd to the hazard and trouble of another Voyage back again*, for he added, that he did not care to venture me too much upon the Sea.

I WAS surpriz'd at this talk, and began to consider very seriously, what the meaning of it must be? and it presently occurr'd to me that my Friend, who call'd him Brother, had represented me in Colours which were not my due; and I thought, since it was come to that pitch, that I would know the bottom of it before I went out of *England*, and before I should put my self into I knew not whose Hands, in a strange Country.

UPON this I call'd his Sister into my Chamber the next Morning, and letting her know the Discourse her Brother and I had been upon,

9. I.e., across the River Mersey from Liverpool.

the Evening before, I conjur'd her to tell me, what she had said to him, and upon what Foot[1] it was that she had made this Marriage? She own'd that she had told him that I was a great Fortune, and said, that she was told so at *London: Told so*, says I warmly, *did I ever tell you so*? No, she said, it was true I did not tell her so, but I had said several times, that what I had, was in my own disposal: I did so, *return'd I very quickly and hastily*, but I never told you I had any thing call'd a Fortune; no not that I had one Hundred Pounds, or the value of an Hundred Pounds in the World; and how did it consist with my being a Fortune, *said I*, that I should come here into the North of *England* with you, only upon the account of living cheap? At these words which I spoke warm and sigh'd,[2] my Husband, and her Brother, as she call'd him, came into the Room; and I desir'd him to come and sit down, for I had something of moment to say before them both, which it was absolutely necessary he should hear.

HE look'd a little disturb'd at the assurance with which I seem'd to speak it, and came and sat down by me, having first shut the Door; upon which I began, for I was very much provok'd, and turning my self to him, I am afraid, says I, *my Dear*, for I spoke with kindness on his side, that you have a very great abuse put upon you, and an Injury done you never to be repair'd in your marrying me, which however as I have had no hand in it, I desire I may be fairly acquitted of it; and that the blame may lie where it ought to lie, and no where else, for I wash my Hands of every part of it.

WHAT Injury can be done me, *my Dear*, says he, in marrying you? I hope it is to my Honour and Advantage every way; I will soon explain it to you, says I, and I fear you will have no reason to think your self well us'd, but I will convince you, *my Dear, says I again*, that I have had no hand in it, and there I stop'd a while.

HE look'd now scar'd and wild, and began, I believ'd, to suspect what follow'd; however, looking towards me, and saying only *go on*, he sat silent, as if to hear what I had more to say; so I went on; I ask'd you last Night, said I, speaking to him, if ever I made any boast to you of my Estate, or ever told you I had any Estate in the Bank of *England*, or any where else, and you own'd I had not, as is most true; and I desire you will tell me here, before your Sister, if ever I gave you any Reason from me to think so, or that ever we had any Discourse about it, and he own'd again I had not; *but said*, I had appeared always as a Woman of Fortune, and he depended on it that I was so, and hoped he was not deceived. I am not enquiring yet whether you have been deceived or not, *said I*, I fear you have, *and I too*; but I am clearing my self from the unjust Charge of being concern'd in deceiving you.

1. Footing, basis.
2. Changed to "high" in the second edition.

I have been now asking your Sister if ever I told her of any Fortune or Estate I had, or gave her any Particulars of it; and she owns I never did: And pray, Madam, *said I, turning my self to her*, be so just to me, before your Brother, to charge me, if you can, if ever I pretended to you that I had an Estate; and why, if I had, should I come down into this Country with you on purpose to spare *that little I had*, and live cheap? She could not deny one word, but said she had been told in *London* that I had a very great Fortune, and that it lay in the Bank of *England*.

AND now, *Dear Sir*, said I, *turning my self to my new Spouse again*, be so just to me as to tell me who has abus'd both you and me so much, as to make you believe I was a Fortune, and prompt you to court me to this Marriage? He cou'd not speak a word, but pointed to her; and after some more pause, flew out in the most furious Passion that ever I saw a Man in my Life; cursing her, and calling her all the Whores and hard Names he could think of; and that she had ruin'd him, declaring that she had told him I had Fifteen Thousand Pounds, and that she was to have Five Hundred Pounds of him for procuring this Match for him: He then added, directing his Speech to me, that she was none of his Sister, but had been his Whore for two Years before, that she had had One Hundred Pound of him in part of this Bargain, and that he was utterly undone if things were as I said; and in his raving *he swore* he would let her Heart's Blood out immediately, which frighted her and me too; *she cried*, said she had been told so in the House where I Lodg'd; but this aggravated him more than before, that she should put so far upon him, and run things such a length upon no other Authority than *a hear-say*; and then turning to me again, said very honestly, he was afraid we were both undone; for to be plain, *my Dear*, I have no Estate, *says he*, what little I had, this Devil has made me run out in waiting on you, and putting me into this Equipage; she took the opportunity of his being earnest in talking with me, and got out of the Room, and I never saw her more.

I WAS confounded now as much as he, and knew not what to say: I thought many ways that I had the worst of it, but his saying he was undone, and that he had no Estate neither, put me into a meer distraction; why, *says I to him*, this has been a hellish Juggle,[3] for we are married here upon the foot of a double Fraud, you are undone by the Disappointment it seems, and if I had had a Fortune I had been cheated too, for you say you have nothing.

YOU would indeed have been cheated, my Dear, *says he*, but you would not have been undone, for Fifteen Thousand Pound would have maintain'd us both very handsomly in this Country; and I assure

3. Imposture, cheat.

you, *added he*, I had resolv'd to have dedicated every Groat of it to you; I would not have wrong'd you of a Shilling, and the rest I would have made up in my Affection to you, and Tenderness of you as long as I liv'd.

THIS was very honest indeed, and I really believe he spoke as he intended, and that he was a Man that was as well qualified to make me happy, as to his Temper and Behaviour, as any Man ever was; but his having no Estate, and being run into Debt on this ridiculous account in the Country, made all the Prospect dismal and dreadful, and I knew not what to say, or what to think of my self.

I TOLD him it was very unhappy, that so much Love, and so much Good-nature, as I discovered in him, should be thus precipitated into Misery; that I saw nothing before us but Ruin, for as to me, it was my unhappiness, that what little I had was not able to relieve us a Week, and with that I pull'd out a Bank Bill of 20 *l*, and eleven Guineas, which I told him I had saved out of my little Income; and that by the account that Creature had given me of the way of living in that Country, I expected it would maintain me three or four Year; that if it was taken from me I was left destitute, and he knew what the Condition of a Woman among strangers must be, if she had no Money in her Pocket; however, I told him if he would take it, there it was.

HE told me with a great concern, and I thought I saw Tears stand in his Eyes, that he would not touch it, that he abhorr'd the thoughts of stripping me, and making me miserable; that on the contrary, he had Fifty Guineas left, which was all he had in the World, and he pull'd it out and threw it down on the Table, bidding me take it, tho' he were to starve for want of it.

I RETURN'D, with the same concern for him, that I could not bear to hear him talk so; that on the contrary, if he could propose any probable method of living, I would do any thing that became me on my part, and that I would live as close and as narrow as he cou'd desire.

HE beg'd of me to talk no more at that rate, for it would make him Distracted; he said he was bred a Gentleman, tho' he was reduced to a low Fortune; and that there was but one way left which he cou'd think of, and that would not do, unless I cou'd answer him one Question, which however he said he would not press me to; I told him I would answer it honestly, whether it would be to his Satisfaction or no, that I could not tell.

WHY then, my Dear, tell me plainly, *says he* will the little you have keep us together in any Figure, or in any Station or Place, or will it not?

IT was my happiness hitherto that I had not discovered myself, or my Circumstances at all; no not so much as my Name; and seeing there was nothing to be expected from him, however good Humoured, and however honest he seem'd to be, but to live on what I knew would soon be wasted, I resolv'd to conceal every thing, but the *Bank Bill*, and the Eleven Guineas, which I had own'd; and I would have been very glad to have lost that, and have been set down where he took me up; I had indeed another *Bank Bill* about me of 30 *l.* which was the whole of what I brought with me, as well to Subsist on in the Country, as not knowing what might offer; because this Creature, the *go-between* that had thus betray'd us both, had made me believe strange things of my Marrying to my Advantage in the Country, and I was not willing to be without Money whatever might happen. This Bill I concealed, and that made me the freer of the rest, in Consideration of his Circumstances, for I really pittied him heartily.

BUT to return to his Question, I told him I never willingly Deceiv'd him, and I never would: I was very sorry to tell him that the little I had would not Subsist us; that it was not sufficient to Subsist me alone in the *South* Country; and that this was the Reason that made me put my self into the Hands of that Woman, who call'd him Brother, she having assur'd me that I might Board very handsomely at a Town call'd *Manchester*, where I had not yet been, for about six Pound a Year, and my whole Income not being above 15 *l.* a Year, I thought I might live easie upon it, and wait for better things.

HE shook his Head, and remain'd Silent, and a very melancholly Evening we had; however we Supped together, and lay together that Night, and when we had almost Supp'd he look'd a little better and more chearful, and call'd for a Bottle of Wine; *come* my Dear, *says he*, tho' the Case is bad, it is to no purpose to be dejected, come be as easie as you can, I will endeavour, to find out some way or other to live; if you can but Subsist your self, that is better than nothing, I must try the World again; a Man ought to think like a Man: To be Discourag'd, is to yield to the Misfortune; with this he fill'd a Glass, and Drank to me, holding my Hand, and pressing it hard in his Hand all the while the Wine went down, and Protesting afterward his main concern was for me.

IT was really a truly gallant Spirit he was of, and it was the more Grievous to me: 'Tis something of Relief even to be undone by a Man of Honour, rather than by a Scoundrel; but here the greatest Disappointment was on his side, for he had really spent a great deal of Money, deluded by this Madam the Procuress; and it was very remarkable on what poor Terms she proceeded; first the baseness of the Creature herself is to be observ'd, who for the getting One Hundred Pound herself, could be content to let him spend Three or Four more, tho' perhaps it was all he had in the World, and more than all; when she had not the least Ground, more than a little Tea-Table

Chat, to say that I had any Estate, or was a Fortune, *or the like*: It is true the Design of deluding a Woman of a Fortune, if I had been so, was base enough; the putting the Face of great Things upon poor Circumstances was a Fraud, and bad enough; but the Case a little differ'd too, and that in his Favour, for he was not a Rake that made a Trade to delude Women, and as some have done get six or seven Fortunes after one another, and then riffle[4] and run away from them; but he was really a Gentleman, unfortunate and low, but had liv'd well; and tho' if I had had a Fortune I should have been enrag'd at the Slut for betraying me; yet really for the Man, a Fortune would not have been ill bestow'd on him, for he was a lovely Person indeed; of generous Principles, good Sense, and of abundance of good Humour.

WE had a great deal of close Conversation that Night, for we neither of us Slept much; he was as Penitent, for having put all those Cheats upon me as if it had been Felony, and that he was going to Execution; he offer'd me again every Shilling of the Money he had about him, and said, he would go into the Army and seek the World for more.

I ask'd him, why he would be so unkind to carry me into *Ireland*, when I might suppose he cou'd not have Subsisted me there? He took me in his Arms, my Dear, *said he*, depend upon it, I never design'd to go to *Ireland* at all, much less to have carried you thither; but came hither to be out of the Observation of the People who had heard what I pretended to, and withal, that No Body might ask me for Money before I was furnish'd to supply them.

BUT where then, *said I*, were we to have gone next?

WHY my Dear, *said he*, I'll confess the whole Scheme to you as I had laid it; I purpos'd here to ask you something about your Estate, as you see I did, and when you, as I expected you would had enter'd into some Account with me of the particular, I would have made an excuse to you, to have put off our Voyage to *Ireland* for some time, and to have gone first towards *London*.

THEN my Dear, *said he*, I resolv'd to have confess'd all the Circumstances of my own Affairs to you, and let you know I had indeed made use of these Artifices to obtain your Consent to marry me, but had now nothing to do but to ask you Pardon, and to tell you abundantly, *as I have said above*, I would endeavour to make you forget what was past, by the felicity of the Days to come.

TRULY, *said I to him*, I find you would soon have conquer'd me; and it is my Affliction now, that I am not in a Condition to let you see how easily I should have been reconcil'd to you; and have pass'd by all the Tricks you had put upon me, in Recompence of so much

4. I.e., rifle, plunder, or rob completely by taking everything.

good Humour; but my Dear, *said I*, what can we do now? We are both undone, and what better are we for our being reconcil'd together, seeing we have nothing to live on.

WE propos'd a great many things, but nothing could offer, where there is nothing to begin with: He beg'd me at last to talk no more of it, for *he said*, I would break his Heart; so we talk'd of other things a little, till at last he took a Husbands leave of me, and so we went to Sleep.

HE rise[5] before me in the Morning, and indeed having lain Awake almost all Night, I was very sleepy, and lay till near Eleven a-Clock, in this time he took his Horses, and three Servants, and all his Linnen and Baggage, and away he went, leaving a short, but moving Letter for me on the Table, as follows:

MY DEAR,

I AM a Dog; I have abus'd you; but I have been drawn in to do it by a base Creature, contrary to my Principle, and the general Practice of my Life: Forgive me, my Dear! *I ask you Pardon with the greatest Sincerity; I am the most miserable of Men, in having deluded you: I have been so happy to Possess you, and am now so wretch'd as to be forc'd to fly from you: Forgive me,* my Dear; *once more I say forgive me! I am not able to see you Ruin'd by me, and myself unable to Support you: Our Marriage is nothing, I shall never be able to see you again: I here discharge you from it; if you can Marry to your Advantage do not decline it on my Account; I here swear to you on my Faith, and on the Word of a Man of Honour, I will never disturb your Repose if I should know of it, which however is not likely: On the other Hand, if you should not Marry, and if good Fortune should befall me, it shall be all yours where ever you are.*

I HAVE put some of the Stock of Money I have left, into your Pocket; take Places for your self and your Maid in the Stage-Coach, and go for London; *I hope it will bear your Charges thither, without breaking into your own: Again I sincerely ask your Pardon, and will do so, as often as I shall ever think of you.*

Adieu my Dear for Ever,

I am yours most Affectionatly,

A. E.[6]

NOTHING that ever befel me in my Life, sunk so deep into my Heart as this Farewel: I reproach'd him a Thousand times in my Thoughts for leaving me, for I would have gone with him thro' the World, if I had beg'd my Bread. I felt in my Pocket, and there I found ten Guineas, his Gold Watch, and two little Rings, one a small Diamond Ring, worth only about six Pound, and the other a plain Gold Ring.

5. Acceptable past-tense form in the eighteenth century (cf. "eat" for "ate" below).
6. Changed to "*J. E.*" in the second edition.

I SAT me down and look'd upon these Things two Hours together, and scarce spoke a Word, till my Maid interrupted me, by telling me my Dinner was ready: I eat but little, and after Dinner I fell into a vehement Fit of crying, every now and then, calling him by his Name, which was *James, O Jemy*! said I, *come back, come back*, I'll give you all I have; I'll beg, I'll starve with you, and thus I run Raving about the Room several times, and then sat down between whiles, and then walking about again, call'd upon him to *come back*, and then cry'd again; and thus I pass'd the Afternoon; till about seven a-Clock when it was near Dusk in the Evening, being *August*, when to my unspeakable Surprize he comes back into the Inn, but without a Servant, and comes directly up into my Chamber.

I WAS in the greatest Confusion imaginable, and so was he too: I could not imagine what should be the Occasion of it; and began to be at odds with myself whether to be glad or sorry; but my Affection byass'd all the rest, and it was impossible to conceal my Joy, which was too great for Smiles, for it burst out into Tears. He was no sooner entered the Room, but he run to me and took me in his Arms, holding me fast and almost stopping my Breath with his Kisses, but spoke not a Word; at length I began, my Dear, *said I*, how could you go away from me? To which he gave no Answer, for it was impossible for him to speak.

WHEN our Extasies were a little over, he told me he was gone about 15 Mile, but it was not in his Power to go any farther, without coming back to see me again, and to take his Leave of me once more.

I TOLD him how I had pass'd my time, and how loud I had call'd him to *come back* again; he told me he heard me very plain upon *Delamere Forest*, at a Place about 12 Miles off: *I smil'd; Nay says he*, do not think I am in Jest, for if ever I heard your Voice in my Life, I heard you call me aloud, and sometimes I thought I saw you running after me; why said I, what did I say? for I had not nam'd the Words to him; you call'd aloud, says he, and said, *O Jemy! O Jemy! come back, come back*.

I Laught at him; *my Dear says he*, do not Laugh, for depend upon it, I heard your Voice as plain as you hear mine now; if you please, I'll go before a Magistrate and make Oath of it; I then began to be amaz'd and surpriz'd, and indeed frighted, and told him what I had really done, and how I had call'd after him, as above.

WHEN we had amus'd ourselves a while about this, I said to him, well, you shall go away from me no more, I'll go all over the World with you rather: *He told me*, it would be a very difficult thing for him to leave me, but since it must be, he hoped I would make it as easie to me as I could; but as for him, it would be his Destruction, that he foresaw.

HOWEVER he told me, that he Consider'd he had left me to Travel to *London* alone, which was too long a Journey; and that as he might as well go that way, as any way else, he was resolv'd to see me safe thither, or near it; and if he did go away then without taking his leave, I should not take it ill of him, and this he made me promise.

HE told me how he had dismiss'd his three Servants, sold their Horses, and sent the Fellows away to seek their Fortunes, and all in a little time, at a Town on the Road, I know not where; and *says he*, it cost me some Tears all alone by myself, to think how much happier they were than their Master, for they could go to the next Gentleman's House to see for a Service, whereas, *said he*, I knew not whither to go, or what to do with myself.

I TOLD him, I was so compleatly miserable in parting with him, that I could not be worse; and that now he was come again, I would not go from him, if he would take me with him, let him go whither he would, or do what he would; and in the mean time I agreed that we would go together to *London*; but I could not be brought to Consent he should go away at last, and not take his leave of me, as he propos'd to do; but told him Jesting, that if he did, I would call him back again as loud as I did before; Then I pull'd out his Watch and gave him back, and his two Rings, and his Ten Guineas; but he would not take them, which made me very much suspect that he resolv'd to go off upon the Road,[7] and leave me.

THE truth is, the Circumstances he was in, the passionate Expressions of his Letter, the kind Gentlemanly Treatment I had from him in all the Affair, with the Concern he show'd for me in it, his manner of Parting with that large Share which he gave me of his little Stock left; all these had joyn'd to make such Impressions on me, that I really lov'd him most tenderly, and could not bear the Thoughts of parting with him.

Two Days after this we quitted *Chester*, I in the Stage Coach, and he on Horseback; I dismiss'd my Maid at *Chester*; he was very much against my being without a Maid, but she being a Servant hired in the Country, and I resolving to keep no Servant at *London*, I told him it would have been barbarous to have taken the poor Wench, and have turn'd her away as soon as I came to Town; and it would also have been a needless Charge on the Road, so I satisfy'd him, and he was easie enough on that Score.

HE came with me as far as *Dunstable*, within 30 Miles of *London*, and then he told me Fate and his own Misfortunes oblig'd him to leave me, and that it was not Convenient for him to go to *London* for Reasons, which it was of no value to me to know, and I saw him preparing to go. The Stage Coach we were in, did not usually stop at *Dunstable*, but I desiring it but for a Quarter of an Hour, they

7. Colloquial expression for "to become a highwayman."

were content to stand at an Inn-Door a while, and we went into the House.

BEING in the Inn, I told him I had but one Favour more to ask of him, and that was, that since he could not go any farther, he would give me leave to stay a Week or two in the Town with him, that we might in that time think of something to prevent such a ruinous thing to us both, as a final Separation would be; and that I had something of Moment to offer to him, that I had never said yet, and which perhaps he might find Practicable to our mutual Advantage.

THIS was too reasonable a Proposal to be denied, so he call'd the Landlady of the House *and told her*, his Wife was taken ill, and so ill that she cou'd not think of going any farther in the Stage Coach, which had tyr'd her almost to Death, and ask'd if she cou'd not get us a Lodging for two or three Days in a private House, where I might rest me a little, for the Journey had been too much for me? The Landlady, a good sort of Woman, well bred, and very obliging, came immediately to see me; *told me*, she had two or three very good Rooms in a part of the House quite out of the noise, and if I saw them, she did not doubt but I would like them, and I should have one of her Maids, that should do nothing else but be appointed to wait on me; this was so very kind, that I could not but accept of it and thank her; so I went to look on the Rooms, and lik'd them very well, and indeed they were extraordinarily Furnish'd, and very pleasant Lodgings; so we paid the Stage Coach, took out our Baggage, and resolv'd to stay here a while.

HERE *I told him* I would live with him now till all my Money was spent, but would not let him spend a Shilling of his own: We had some kind squabble about that, but *I told him* it was the last time I was like to enjoy his Company, and I desir'd he would let me be Master in that thing only, and he should govern in every thing else, so he acquiesc'd.

HERE one Evening taking a Walk into the Fields, *I told him* I would now make the Proposal to him I had told him of; accordingly I related to him how I had liv'd in *Virginia*, that I had a Mother, I believ'd, was alive there still, tho' my Husband was dead some Years; *I told him*, that had not my Effects miscarry'd, which by the way I magnify'd pretty much, I might have been Fortune good enough to him to have kept us from being parted in this manner: Then I entered into the manner of Peoples going over to those Countries to settle, how they had a quantity of Land given them by the Constitution of the Place; and if not, that it might be purchased at so easie a Rate that it was not worth naming.

I THEN gave him a full and distinct account of the nature of Planting, how with carrying over but two or three Hundred Pounds value in *English* Goods, with some Servants and Tools, a Man of Application would presently lay a Foundation for a Family, and in a very few Years be certain to raise an Estate.

I LET him into the nature of the Product of the Earth, how the Ground was Cur'd and Prepared, and what the usual encrease of it was; and demonstrated to him, that in a very few Years, with such a beginning, we should be as certain of being Rich, as we were now certain of being Poor.

HE was surpriz'd at my Discourse; for we made it the whole Subject of our Conversation for near a Week together, in which time I laid it down in black and white, *as we say*, that it was morally impossible, with a supposition of any reasonable good Conduct,[8] but that we must thrive there and do very well.

THEN I told him what measures I would take to raise such a Sum as 300 *l*. or thereabouts; and I argued with him how good a Method it would be to put an end to our Misfortunes, and restore our Circumstances in the World, to what we had both expected; and I added, that after seven Years, if we liv'd, we might be in a Posture to leave our Plantation in good Hands, and come over again and receive the Income of it, and live here and enjoy it; and I gave him Examples of some that had done so, and liv'd now in very good Circumstances in *London*.

IN short, I press'd him so to it, that he almost agreed to it, but still something or other broke it off again; till at last he turn'd the Tables, and he began to talk almost to the same purpose of *Ireland*.

HE told me that a Man that could confine himself to a Country Life, and that cou'd but find Stock to enter upon any Land, should have Farms there for 50 *l*. a Year, as good as were here let for 200 *l*. a Year; that the Produce was such, and so Rich the Land, that if much was not laid up, we were sure to live as handsomely upon it as a Gentleman of 3000 *l*. a Year could do in *England*; and that he had laid a Scheme to leave me in *London*, and go over and try; and if he found he could lay a handsome Foundation of living suitable to the Respect he had for me, as he doubted not he should do, he would come over and fetch me.

I WAS dreadfully afraid that upon such a Proposal he would have taken me at my Word, (*viz*.) to sell my little Income, as I call'd it, and turn it into Money, and let him carry it over into *Ireland* and try his Experiment with it; but he was too just to desire it, or to have accepted it if I had offered it; and he anticipated me in that, for he added, that he would go and try his Fortune that way, and if he found he cou'd do any thing at it to live, then, by adding mine to it when I went over, we should live like our selves; but that he would not hazard a Shilling of mine till he had made the Experiment with a

8. Management of business affairs.

little, and he assur'd me that if he found nothing to be done in *Ireland*, he would then come to me and join in my Project for *Virginia*.

HE was so earnest upon his Project being to be try'd first, that I cou'd not withstand him; how ever, he promis'd to let me hear from him in a very little time after his arriving there, to let me know whether his prospect answer'd his Design, that if there was not a probability of Success, I might take the Occasion to prepare for our other Voyage, and then, he assur'd me, he would go with me to *America* with all his Heart.

I COULD bring him to nothing farther than this: However, those Consultations entertain'd us near a Month, during which I enjoy'd his Company, which indeed was the most entertaining that ever I met with in my life before. In this time he let me into the whole Story of his own Life, which was indeed surprizing, and full of an infinite Variety sufficient to fill up a much brighter History for its Adventures and Incidents, than any I ever saw in Print: But I shall have occasion to say more of him hereafter.

WE parted at last, tho' with the utmost reluctance on my side, and indeed he took his leave very unwillingly too, but Necessity oblig'd him, for his Reasons were very good why he would not come to *London*, as I understood more fully some time afterwards.

I GAVE him a Direction how to write to me, tho' still I reserv'd the grand Secret, and never broke my Resolution, which was not to let him ever know my true Name, who I was, or where to be found; he likewise let me know how to write a Letter to him, so that he said he wou'd be sure to receive it.

I CAME to *London* the next Day after we parted, but did not go directly to my old Lodgings; but for another nameless Reason took a private Lodging in *St. John's-street*, or as it is vulgarly call'd St. *Jones's* near *Clarkenwell*; and here being perfectly alone, I had leisure to sit down and reflect seriously upon the last seven Months Ramble I had made, for I had been abroad no less; the pleasant Hours I had with my last Husband I look'd back on with an infinite deal of Pleasure; but that Pleasure was very much lessen'd, when I found some time after that I was really with Child.

THIS was a perplexing thing because of the Difficulty which was before me, where I should get leave to Lye Inn; it being one of the nicest things in the World at that time of Day, for a Woman that was a Stranger, and had no Friends, to be entertain'd in that Circumstance without Security,[9] which by the way I had not, neither could I procure any.

I HAD taken care all this while to preserve a Correspondence with

9. In either of two senses: a person vouching for one's good character, or a pledge or guarantee of financial support, both needed (especially the latter) to assure officers of the parish that Moll can support her unborn child. *Nicest*: Most delicate or difficult.

my honest Friend at the Bank, or rather he took care to Correspond with me, for he wrote to me once a Week; and tho' I had not spent my Money so fast as to want any from him, yet I often wrote also to let him know I was alive; I had left Directions in *Lancashire*, so that I had these Letters, which he sent, convey'd to me; and during my Recess at St. *Jones's* I receiv'd a very obliging Letter from him, assuring me that his Process for a Divorce from his Wife went on with Success, tho' he met with some Difficulties in it that he did not expect.

I WAS not displeas'd with the News, that his Process was more tedious than he expected; for tho' I was in no condition to have had him yet, not being so foolish to marry him when I knew my self to be with Child by another Man, as some I know have ventur'd to do; yet I was not willing to lose him, and in a word, resolv'd to have him if he continu'd in the same mind, as soon as I was up again; for I saw apparently I should hear no more from my other Husband; and as he had all along press'd me to Marry, and had assur'd me he would not be at all disgusted at it, or ever offer to claim me again, so I made no scruple to resolve to do it if I could, and if my other Friend stood to his Bargain; and I had a great deal of Reason to be assur'd that he would stand to it, by the Letters he wrote to me, which were the kindest and most obliging that could be.

I NOW grew Big, and the People where I Lodg'd perceiv'd it, and began to take notice of it to me, and as far as Civility would allow, intimated that I must think of removing, this put me to extreme perplexity, and I grew very melancholy, for indeed I knew not what Course to take, I had Money, but no Friends, and was like now to have a Child upon my Hands to keep, which was a difficulty I had never had upon me yet, as the Particulars of my Story hitherto makes appear.

IN the course of this Affair I fell very ill, and my Melancholy really encreas'd my Distemper; my illness prov'd at length to be only an Ague, but my Apprehensions were really that I should Miscarry; I should not say Apprehensions, for indeed I would have been glad to miscarry, but I cou'd never be brought to entertain so much as a thought of endeavouring to Miscarry, or of taking any thing to make me Miscarry, I abhorr'd, I say so much as the thought of it.

HOWEVER, speaking of it in the House, the Gentlewoman who kept the House propos'd to me to send for a Midwife; I scrupled it at first, but after some time consented to it, but told her I had no particular Acquaintance with any Midwife, and so left it to her.

IT seems the Mistress of the House was not so great a Stranger to such Cases as mine was, as I thought at first she had been, as will appear presently, and she sent for a Midwife of the right sort, that is to say, the right sort for me.

THE Woman appear'd to be an experienc'd Woman in her Business, I mean as a Midwife, but she had another Calling too, in which she was as expert as most Women, if not more: My Landlady had told her I was very Melancholy, and that she believ'd that had done me harm; and once, *before me*, said to her, Mrs. *B—— meaning the Midwife*, I believe this Lady's Trouble is of a kind that is pretty much in your way, and therefore if you can do any thing for her, pray do, for she is a very civil Gentlewoman, and so she went out of the Room.

I REALLY did not understand her, but my Mother Midnight[1] began very seriously to explain what she meant, as soon as she was gone: Madam, *says she*, you seem not to understand what your Landlady means, and when you do understand it, you need not let her know at all that you do so.

SHE means that you are under some Circumstances that may render your Lying-Inn difficult to you, and that you are not willing to be expos'd; I need say no more, but to tell you, that if you think fit to communicate so much of your Case to me, *if it be so*, as is necessary; for I do not desire to pry into those things, I perhaps may be in a Condition to assist you, and to make you perfectly easie, and remove all your dull Thoughts upon that Subject.

EVERY word this Creature said was a Cordial to me, and put new Life and new Spirit into my very Heart; my Blood began to circulate immediately, and I was quite another Body; I eat my Victuals again, and grew better presently after it: She said a great deal more to the same purpose, and then having press'd me to be free with her, and promis'd in the solemnest manner to be secret, she stop'd a little, as if waiting to see what Impression it made on me, and what I would say.

I WAS too sensible of the want I was in of such a Woman, not to accept her offer; *I told her* my Case was partly as she guess'd, and partly not, for I was really married, and had a Husband, tho' he was in such Circumstances, and so remote at that time, as that he cou'd not appear publickly.

SHE took me short, *and told me*, that was none of her Business, all the Ladies that came under her Care were married Women to her; every Woman, *says she*, that is with Child has a Father for it, and whether that Father was a Husband or no Husband, was no Business of hers; her Business was to assist me in my present Circumstances, whether I had a Husband or no; for, *Madam, says she*, to have a Husband that cannot appear, is to have no Husband in the sense of the Case, and therefore whether you are a Wife or a Mistress is all one to me.

1. Contemporary cant term for a midwife, with the strong insinuation of "another Calling" as bawd or procuress.

I FOUND presently, that whether I was a Whore or a Wife, I was to pass for a Whore here, so I let that go; *I told her*, it was true as she said, but that however, if I must tell her my Case, I must tell it her as it was: So I related it to her as short as I could, and I concluded it to her thus, *I trouble you with all this*, Madam, said I, *not that, as you said before, it is much to the purpose* in your Affair, but this is to the purpose, *namely, that I am not in any pain about being seen, or being publick or conceal'd, for 'tis perfectly indifferent to me; but my difficulty is, that I have no* Acquaintance *in this part of the Nation.*

I UNDERSTAND you, Madam, *says she*, you have no Security to bring to prevent the Parish Impertinences usual in such Cases; and perhaps, *says she*, do not know very well how to dispose of the Child when it comes; the last, *says I*, is not so much my concern as the first: Well, Madam, *answers the Midwife*, dare you put your self into my Hands, I live in such a place, tho' I do not enquire after you, you may enquire after me, my Name is *B*—— I live in such a Street, naming the Street, at the Sign of the *Cradle*, my Profession is a Midwife, and I have many Ladies that come to my House to Lye-Inn; I have given Security to the Parish in General Terms to secure them from any Charge, from whatsoever shall come into the World under my Roof; I have but one Question to ask in the whole Affair, Madam, *says she*, and if that be answer'd, you shall be entirely easie for all the rest.

I presently understood what she meant, and told her, Madam, *I believe I understand you*; I thank God, *tho' I want Friends in this Part of the World, I do not want Money, so far as may be Necessary, tho' I do not abound in that neither*: This I added, because I would not make her expect great things; well Madam, *says she*, that is the thing indeed, without which nothing can be done in these Cases; and yet, *says she*, you shall see that I will not impose upon you, or offer any thing that is unkind to you, and if you desire it, you shall know every thing before hand, that you may suit your self to the Occasion, and be either costly or sparing as you see fit.

I told her, she seem'd to be so perfectly sensible of my Condition, that I had nothing to ask of her but this, that as I had told her that I had Money sufficient, but not a great Quantity, she would order it so, that I might be at as little superfluous Charge as possible.

SHE replyed, that she would bring in an Account of the Expences of it, in two or three Shapes, and like a *Bill of Fare* I should chuse as I pleas'd, and I desir'd her to do so.

THE next Day she brought it, and the Copy of her three Bills was as Follow.

	l. s. d.
1. For Three Months Lodging in her House, including my Dyet at 10*s.* a Week	06 00 0
2. For a Nurse for the Month, and Use of Child-bed Linnen	01 10 0
3. For a Minister to Christen the Child, and to the Godfathers and Clark	01 10 0
4. For a Supper at the Christening if I had five Friends at it	01 00 0
For her Fees as a Midwife, and the taking off the Trouble of the Parish	03 03 0
To her Maid-Servant attending.	00 10 0
	13 13 0

THIS was the first Bill, the second was in the same Terms.

	l. s. d.
1. For Three Months Lodging and Diet, &c. at 20*s. per* Week	13 00 0
2. For a Nurse for the Month, and the Use of Linnen and Lace	02 10 0
3. For the Minister to Christen the Child, &c. as above	02 00 0
4. For a Supper, and for Sweetmeats	03 03 0
For her Fees, as above	05 05 0
For a Servant-Maid	01 00 0
	26 18 0

THIS was the second rate Bill, the third, *she said*, was for a degree Higher, and when the Father, or Friends appeared.

	l. s. d..
1. For Three Months Lodging and Diet, having two Rooms and a Garret for a Servant	30 00 0
2. For a Nurse for the Month, and the finest Suit of Child-bed Linnen	04 04 0
3. For the Minister to Christen the Child, &c.	02 10 0
4. For a Supper, the Gentlemen to send in the Wine	06 00 0
For my Fees, &c.	10 10 0
The Maid, besides their own Maid only	00 10 0
	53 14 0

I LOOK'D upon all the three Bills, and smil'd, *and told her* I did not see but that she was very reasonable in her Demands, all things Consider'd, and for that I did not doubt but her Accommodations were good.

SHE told me, I should be Judge of that, when I saw them: *I told her*, I was sorry to tell her that I fear'd I must be her lowest rated Customer, and *perhaps Madam*, said I, *you will make me the less Welcome upon that Account*. No not at all, *said she*, for where I have One of the third Sort, I have Two of the Second, and Four to One of the First, and I get as much by them in Proportion, as by any; but if you doubt my Care of you, I will allow any Friend you have to overlook, and see if you are well waited on, or no.

THEN she explain'd the particulars of her Bill; in the first Place, Madam, *said she*, I would have you Observe, that here is three Months Keeping, you are but 10*s*. a Week, I undertake to say you will not complain of my Table: I suppose, *says she*, you do not live Cheaper where you are now; no indeed, *said I*, nor so Cheap, for I give six Shillings *per* Week for my Chamber, and find my own Diet as well as I can, which costs me a great deal more.

THEN Madam, *says she*, If the Child should not live, or should be dead Born, as you know sometime happens, then there is the Minister's Article saved; and if you have no Friends to come to you, you may save the Expence of a Supper; so that take those Articles out Madam, *says she*, your Lying-In will not cost you above 5*l*. 3*s*. in all, more than your ordinary Charge of Living.

THIS was the most reasonable thing that I ever heard of; so I smil'd, and told her I would come and be her Customer; but *I told her also*, that as I had two Months, and more to go, I might perhaps be oblig'd to stay longer with her than three Months, and desir'd to know if she would not be oblig'd to remove me before it was proper; no, *she said*, her House was large, and besides, she never put any Body to remove, that had lain Inn, till they were willing to go; and if she had more Ladies offer'd, she was not so ill belov'd among her Neighbours, but she could provide Accommodation for Twenty, if there was occasion.

I FOUND she was an eminent Lady in her way, and *in short*, I agreed to put myself into her Hands, and promis'd her: She then talk'd of other things, look'd about into my Accommodations, where was found fault with my wanting Attendance, and Conveniences, and that I should not be us'd so at her House: *I told her*, I was shy of speaking, for the Woman of the House look'd stranger, or at least I thought so since I had been Ill, because I was with Child; and I was afraid she would put some Affront or other upon me, supposing that I had been able to give but a slight Account of myself.

O DEAR, *said she*, her Ladyship is no stranger to these things; she has try'd to entertain Ladies in your Condition several times, but could not secure the Parish;[2] and besides, she is not such a nice Lady as you take her to be; however, since you are agoing you shall not meddle with her, but I'll see you are a little better look'd after while you are here, than I think you are, and it shall not cost you the more neither.

I DID not understand her at all; however I thank'd her, and so we parted; the next Morning she sent me a Chicken roasted and hot, and a pint Bottle of Sherry, and order'd the Maid to tell me that she was to wait on me every Day as long as I stay'd there.

THIS was surprisingly good and kind, and I accepted it very willingly: At Night she sent to me again, to know if I wanted any thing, and how I did, and to order the Maid to come to her in the morning for my Dinner; the Maid had order to make me some Chocolat in the Morning before she came away, and did so, and at Noon she brought me the Sweetbread of a Breast of Veal whole, and a Dish of Soup for my Dinner, and after this manner she Nurs'd me up at a distance, so that I was mightily well pleas'd, and quickly well, for indeed my Dejections before were the principal Part of my Illness.

I expected as usually is the Case among such People, that the Servant she sent me would have been some impudent brazen Wench of *Drury-Lane*[3] Breeding, and I was very uneasie at having her with me, upon that Account, so I would not let her lie in that House, the first Night by any means, but had my Eyes about me as narrowly as if she had been a publick Thief.

MY Gentlewoman guess'd presently what was the matter, and sent her back with a short Note, that I might depend upon the honesty of her Maid; that she would be answerable for her upon all Accounts; and that she took no Servants into her House, without very good Security for their Fidelity: I was then perfectly easie, and indeed the Maids behaviour spoke for its self, for a modester, quieter, soberer Girl never came into any bodies Family, and I found her so afterwards.

As soon as I was well enough to go Abroad, I went with the Maid to see the House, and to see the Apartment I was to have; and every thing was so handsome and so clean and well; that in short, I had nothing to say, but was wonderfully pleas'd, and satisfy'd with what

2. Either give assurances to the parish officers that she has enough money to care for all such "Ladies" in her house, or bribe those officers (usually at the rate of two to five guineas per transaction) to take the children off her hands or to allow her to dispose of them as she sees fit. A shrewd businesswoman, Mother Midnight passes this expense on to her customers; all three of her sample bills include "fees" for "the taking off the Trouble of the Parish."

3. The area surrounding the Drury Lane Theater was infamous for its bawdy houses and other forms of street crime.

I had met with, which considering the melancholy Circumstances I was in, was far beyond what I look'd for.

IT might be expected that I should give some Account of the Nature of the wicked Practice of this Woman, in whose Hands I was now fallen; but it would be but too much Encouragement to the Vice, to let the World see, what easie Measures were here taken to rid the Women's unwelcome Burthen of a Child clandestinely gotten: This grave Matron had several sorts of Practise, and this was one particular, that if a Child was born, tho' not in her House, for she had the occasion to be call'd to many private Labours, she had People at Hand, who for a Peice of Money would take the Child off their Hands, and off from the Hands of the Parish too; and those Children, as she said were honestly provided for, and taken care of: What should become of them all, Considering so many, as by her Account she was concern'd with, I cannot conceive.

I HAD many times Discourses upon that Subject with her; but she was full of this Argument, that she sav'd the Life of many an innocent Lamb, as she call'd them, which would otherwise perhaps have been Murder'd; and of many a Woman, who made Desperate by the Misfortune, would otherwise be tempted to Destroy their Children, and bring themselves to the Gallows: I granted her that this was true, and a very commendable thing, provided the poor Children fell into good Hands afterwards, and were not abus'd, starv'd, and neglected by the Nurses that bred them up; she answer'd, that she always took care of that, and had no Nurses in her Business, but what were very good honest People, and such as might be depended upon.

I COU'D say nothing to the contrary, and so was oblig'd to say, Madam I do not question you do your part honestly, but what those People do afterwards, is the main Question, and she stop'd my Mouth again with saying, that she took the utmost Care about it.

THE only thing I found in all her Conversation on these Subjects, that gave me any distaste, was, that one time in Discoursing about my being so far gone with Child, and the time I expected to come, she said something that look'd as if she could help me off with my Burthen sooner, if I was willing; or in *English*, that she could give me something to make me Miscarry, if I had a desire to put an end to my Troubles that way; but I soon let her see that I abhorr'd the Thoughts of it; and to do her Justice, she put it off so cleverly, that I cou'd not say she really intended it, or whether she only mentioned the practise as a horrible thing; for she couch'd her words so well, and took my meaning so quickly, that she gave her Negative before I could explain my self.

To bring this part into as narrow a Compass as possible, I quitted my Lodging at St. *Jones*'s and went to my new Governess, for so they call'd her in the House, and there I was indeed treated with so much Courtesy, so carefully look'd to, so handsomely provided, and every thing so well, that I was surpris'd at it, and cou'd not at first see what Advantage my Governess made of it; but I found afterwards that she profess'd to make no Profit of the Lodgers Diet, nor indeed cou'd she get much by it, but that her Profit lay in the other Articles of her Management, and she made enough that way, I assure you; for 'tis scarce credible what Practice she had, as well Abroad as at Home, and yet all upon the private Account, or in plain *English*, the whoring Account.

WHILE I was in her House, which was near Four Months, she had no less than Twelve Ladies of Pleasure[4] brought to Bed within Doors, and I think she had Two and Thirty, or thereabouts, under her Conduct without Doors, whereof one, as nice as she was with me, was Lodg'd with my old Landlady at St. *Jones*'s.

THIS was a strange Testimony of the growing Vice of the Age, and such a one, that as bad as I had been my self, it shock'd my very Senses, I began to nauceate[5] the place I was in, and above all, the wicked Practice; and yet I must say that I never saw, or do I believe there was to be seen, the least indecency in the House the whole time I was there.

NOT a Man was ever seen to come up Stairs, except to visit the Lying-Inn Ladies within their Month, nor then without the old Lady with them, who made it a piece of the Honour of her Management, that no Man should touch a Woman, no not his own Wife, within the Month; nor would she permit any Man to lye in the House upon any pretence whatever, no not tho' she was sure it was with his own Wife, and her general saying for it was, that she car'd not how many Children was born in her House, but she would have none got[6] there if she could help it.

IT might perhaps be carried farther than was needful, but it was an Error of the right Hand[7] if it was an Error, for by this she kept up the Reputation, such as it was, of her Business, and obtain'd this Character, that tho' she did take Care of the Women when they were Debauch'd, yet she was not Instrumental to their being Debauch'd at all, and yet it was a wicked Trade she drove too.

WHILE I was here, and before I was brought to Bed, I receiv'd a Letter from my Trustee at the Bank full of kind obliging things, and earnestly pressing me to return to *London*: It was near a Fortnight old when it came to me, because it had been first sent into *Lancashire*, and then return'd to me; he concludes with telling me that he

4. Prostitutes.
5. Find nauseating, loathe.
6. Begotten.
7. On the right or correct side.

had obtain'd a Decree,[8] I think he call'd it, against his Wife, and that he would be ready to make good his Engagement to me, if I would accept of him, adding a great many Protestations of Kindness and Affection, such as he would have been far from offering if he had known the Circumstances I had been in, and which as it was I had been very far from deserving.

I RETURNED an Answer to this Letter, and dated it at *Leverpool*, but sent it by a Messenger, alledging that it came in Cover to a Friend in Town; I gave him Joy of his Deliverance, but rais'd some Scruples at the Lawfulness of his Marrying again, and told him, I suppos'd he would consider very seriously upon that Point before he resolv'd on it, the Consequence being too great for a Man of his Judgment to venture rashly upon a thing of that Nature; so concluded, wishing him very well in whatever he resolv'd, without letting him into any thing of my own Mind, or giving any Answer to his Proposal of my coming to *London* to him, but mention'd at a distance my intention to return the latter end of the Year, this being dated in *April*.

I WAS brought to Bed about the middle of *May*, and had another brave[9] Boy, and my self in as good Condition as usual on such Occasions: My Governess did her part as a Midwife with the greatest Art and Dexterity imaginable, and far beyond all that ever I had had any Experience of before.

HER Care of me in my Travail, and after in my Lying-Inn, was such, that if she had been my own Mother it cou'd not have been better; let none be encourag'd in their loose Practises from this Dexterous Lady's Management, for she is gone to her place, and I dare say has left nothing behind her that can or will come up to it.

I THINK I had been brought to Bed about twenty two Days when I receiv'd another Letter from my Friend at the Bank, with the surprizing News that he had obtain'd a final Sentence of Divorce against his Wife, and had serv'd her with it on such a Day, and that he had such an Answer to give to all my Scruples about his Marrying again, as I could not expect, and as he had no Desire of; for that his Wife, who had been under some Remorse before for her usage of him, as soon as she had the account that he had gain'd his Point, had very unhappily destroy'd her self that same Evening.

HE express'd himself very handsomly as to his being concern'd at her Disaster, but clear'd himself of having any hand in it, and that he had only done himself Justice in a Case in which he was notoriously Injur'd and Abus'd: However, he said that he was extremely afflicted at it, and had no view of any Satisfaction left in this World,

8. Not yet "a final Sentence of Divorce" (see below) but a favorable court ruling issued prior to it.
9. Excellent. According to Samuel Johnson, "an indeterminate word, used to express the superabundance of any valuable quality in men or things."

but only in the hope that I wou'd come and relieve him by my Company; and then he press'd me violently indeed to give him some hopes, that I would at least come up to Town and let him see me, when he would farther enter into Discourse about it.

I WAS exceedingly surpriz'd at the News, and began now seriously to reflect on my present Circumstances, and the inexpressible Misfortune it was to me to have a Child upon my Hands, and what to do in it I knew not; at last I open'd my Case at a distance to my Governess, I appear'd melancholy and uneasie for several Days, and she lay at me continually to know what troubl'd me; I could not for my life tell her that I had an offer of Marriage, after I had so often told her that I had a Husband, so that I really knew not what to say to her: I own'd I had something which very much troubl'd me, but at the same time told her I cou'd not speak of it to any one alive.

SHE continued importuning me several Days, but it was impossible, *I told her*, for me to commit the Secret to any Body; this, instead of being an Answer to her, encreas'd her Importunities; she urg'd her having been trusted with the greatest Secrets of this Nature, that it was her business to Conceal every thing, and that to Discover things of that Nature would be her Ruin; she ask'd me if ever I had found her Tatling to her[1] of other People's Affairs, and how could I suspect her? *she told me* to unfold my self to her, was telling it to no Body; that she was silent as Death; that it must be a very strange Case indeed, that she could not help me out of; but to conceal it, was to deprive myself of all possible Help, or means of Help, and to deprive her of the Opportunity of Serving me. *In short*, she had such a bewitching Eloquence, and so great a power of Perswasion, that there was no concealing any thing from her.

So I resolv'd to unbosome myself to her, I told her the History of my *Lancashire* Marriage, and how both of us had been Disappointed; how we came together, and how we parted: How he absolutely Discharg'd me, as far as lay in him, and gave me free Liberty to Marry again, protesting that if he knew it he would never Claim me, or Disturb, or Expose me; that I thought I was free, but was dreadfully afraid to venture, for the fear of the Consequences that might follow in case of a Discovery.

THEN I told her what a good Offer I had; show'd her my Friends two last Letters, inviting me to come to *London*, and let her see with what Affection and Earnestness they were written, but blotted out the Name, and also the Story about the Dissaster of his Wife, only that she was dead.

SHE fell a Laughing at my scruples about marrying, and told me the other was no Marriage, but a Cheat on both Sides; and that as

1. A likely misprint for "to me." The second edition deletes "to her" and thus offers what is arguably a better reading: "if ever I had found her Tatling of other People's Affairs."

we were parted by mutual Consent, the nature of the Contract was destroy'd, and the Obligation was mutually discharg'd: She had Arguments for this at the tip of her Tongue; and *in short*, reason'd me out of my Reason; not but that it was too by the help of my own Inclination.

BUT then came the great and main Difficulty, and that was the Child; this she told me in so many Words must be remov'd, and that so, as that it should never be possible for any one to discover it: I knew there was no Marrying without entirely concealing that I had had a Child, for he would soon have discover'd by the Age of it, that it was born, nay and gotten too, since my Parly with him, and that would have destroy'd all the Affair.

BUT it touch'd my Heart so forcibly to think of Parting entirely with the Child, and for ought I knew, of having it murther'd, or starv'd by Neglect and Ill-usuage, (which was much the same) that I could not think of it, without Horror; I wish all those Women who consent to the disposing their Children out of the way, *as it is call'd* for Decency sake, would consider that 'tis only a contriv'd Method for Murther; that is to say, a killing their Children with safety.

IT is manifest to all that understand any thing of Children, that we are born into the World helpless and uncapable, either to supply our own Wants, or so much as make them known; and that without help, we must Perish; and this help requires not only an assisting Hand, whether of the Mother, or some Body else; but there are two Things necessary in that assisting Hand, that is, Care and Skill, without both which, half the Children that are born would die; nay, tho' they were not to be deny'd Food; and one half more of those that remain'd would be Cripples or Fools, loose their Limbs, and perhaps their Sense: I Question not, but that these are partly the Reasons why Affection was plac'd by Nature in the Hearts of Mothers to their Children; without which they would never be able to give themselves up, as 'tis necessary they should, to the Care and waking Pains needful to the Support of their Children.

SINCE this Care is needful to the Life of Children, to neglect them is to Murther them; again to give them up to be Manag'd by those People, who have none of that needful Affection, plac'd by Nature in them, is to Neglect them in the highest Degree; nay, in some it goes farther, and is a Neglect in order to their being Lost; so that 'tis even an intentional Murther, whether the Child lives or dies.

ALL those things represented themselves to my View, and that in the blackest and most frightful Form; and as I was very free with my Governness, who I had now learn'd to call Mother; I represented to her all the dark Thoughts which I had upon me about it, and told her what distress I was in: She seem'd graver by much at this Part than at the other; but as she was harden'd in these things beyond all possibility of being touch'd with the Religious part, and the Scruples about the Murther; so she was equally impenetrable in that Part, which related to Affection: She ask'd me if she had not been Careful, and Tender of me in my Lying-Inn, as if I had been her own Child? I told her I own'd she had. Well my Dear, *says she*, and when you are gone, what are you to me? and what would it be to me if you were to be Hang'd? Do you think there are not Women, who as it is their Trade, and they get their Bread by it, value themselves upon their being as careful of Children, as their own Mothers can be, and understand it rather better? Yes, yes, Child, *says she*, fear it not, How were we Nurs'd ourselves? Are you sure, you was Nurs'd up by your own Mother? and yet you look fat, and fair Child, says the old Beldam,[2] and with that she stroak'd me over the Face; never be concern'd Child, *says she*, going on in her drolling way; I have no Murtherers about me, I employ the best, and the honestest Nurses that can be had; and have as few Children miscarry under their Hands, as there would, if they were all Nurs'd by Mothers; we want neither Care nor Skill.

SHE touch'd me to the Quick, when she ask'd if I was sure that I was Nurs'd by my own Mother; on the contrary I was sure I was not; and I trembled, and look'd pale at the very Expression; sure said I, to myself, this Creature cannot be a Witch, or have any Conversation with a Spirit that can inform her what was done with me before I was able to know it myself; and I look'd at her as if I had been frighted; but reflecting that it cou'd not be possible for her to know any thing about me, that Disorder went off, and I began to be easie, but it was not presently.

SHE perceiv'd the Disorder I was in, but did not know the meaning of it; so she run on in her wild Talk upon the weakness of my supposing, that Children were murther'd, because they were not all Nurs'd by the Mother; and to perswade me that the Children she dispos'd of, were as well us'd as if the Mothers had the Nursing of them themselves.

IT may be true Mother, *says I*, for ought I know, but my Doubts are very strongly grounded, indeed; come then, *says she*, lets hear some of them: Why first, *says I*, you give a Piece of Money to these People to take the Child off the Parents Hands, and to take Care of it as long as it lives; now we know Mother, *said I*, that those are poor People, and their Gain consists in being quit of the Charge as soon as they can; how can I doubt but that, as it is best for them to have the Child die, they are not over Solicitous about its Life?

THIS is all Vapours[3] and Fancy, *says the old Woman*, I tell you their

2. Old woman, with the possible connotation of "hag" or "witch."
3. Commonly used in the eighteenth century to refer to depression of spirits, hypochondria,

Credit depends upon the Child's Life, and they are as careful as any Mother of you all.

O Mother, *says I*, if I was but sure my little Baby would be carefully look'd to, and have Justice done it, I should be happy indeed; but it is impossible I can be satisfy'd in that Point, unless I saw it, and to see it, would be Ruin and Destruction to me, as now my Case stands, so what to do I know not.

A FINE Story! *says the Governess*, you would see the Child, and you would not see the Child; you would be Conceal'd and Discover'd both together; these are things impossible my Dear, so you must e'n do as other conscientious Mothers have done before you; and be contented with things as they must be, tho' they are not as you wish them to be.

I understood what she meant by conscientious Mothers, she would have said conscientious Whores; but she was not willing to disoblige me, for really in this Case I was not a Whore, because legally Married, the force of my former Marriage excepted.

HOWEVER let me be what I would, I was not come up to that pitch of Hardness, common to the Profession; I mean to be unnatural, and regardless of the Safety of my Child, and I preserv'd this honest Affection so long, that I was upon the Point of giving up my Friend at the *Bank*, who lay so hard at me to come to him, and Marry him, that *in short*, there was hardly any room to deny him.

AT last my old Governness came to me, with her usual Assurance. Come my Dear, *says she*, I have found out a way how you shall be at a certainty, that your Child shall be used well, and yet the People that take Care of it shall never know you, or who the Mother of the Child is.

O Mother, *says I*, If you can do so, you will engage me to you for ever: Well, *says she*, are you willing to be at some small Annual Expence, more than what we usually give to the People we Contract with? Ay, *says I*, with all my Heart, provided I may be conceal'd; as to that, *says the Governness*, you shall be Secure, for the Nurse shall never so much as dare to Enquire about you, and you shall once or twice a Year go with me and see your Child, and see how 'tis used, and be satisfy'd that it is in good Hands, no Body knowing who you are.

WHY, *said I*, do you think Mother, that when I come to see my Child, I shall be able to conceal my being the Mother of it, do you think that possible?

WELL, well, *says my Governess*, if you discover it, the Nurse shall

hysteria, or other nervous disorder; so called because believed to originate from exhalations or "vapors" occurring within the organs of the body.

be never the wiser; for she shall be forbid to ask any Questions about you, or to take any Notice; if she offers it she shall lose the Money which you are to be suppos'd to give her, and the Child be taken from her too.

I WAS very well pleas'd with this; so the next Week a Country Woman was brought from *Hertford*, or thereabouts, who was to take the Child off our Hands entirely, for 10 *l.* in Money; but if I would allow 5 *l.* a Year more to her, she would be obliged to bring the Child to my Governesses House as often as we desired, or we should come down and look at it, and see how well she us'd it.

THE Woman was a very wholesome look'd likely Woman, a Cottager's Wife, but she had very good Cloaths and Linnen, and every thing well about her, and with a heavy Heart and many a Tear I let her have my Child: I had been down at *Hertford* and look'd at her and at her Dwelling, which I lik'd well enough; and I promis'd her great Things if she would be kind to the Child, so she knew at first word that I was the Child's Mother; but she seem'd to be so much out of the way, and to have no room to enquire after me, that I thought I was safe enough, so in short I consented to let her have the Child, and I gave her Ten Pound, that is to say I gave it to my Governess, who gave it the poor Woman before my Face, she agreeing never to return the Child back to me, or to claim any thing more for its keeping or bringing up; only that I promised, if she took a great deal of Care of it, I would give her something more as often as I came to see it; so that I was not bound to pay the Five Pound, only that I promised my Governess I would do it: And thus my great Care was over, after a manner, which tho' it did not at all satisfie my Mind, yet was the most convenient for me, as my Affairs then stood, of any that cou'd be thought of at that time.

I THEN began to write to my Friend at the Bank in a more kindly Style, and particularly about the beginning of *July* I sent him a Letter, that I purpos'd to be in Town sometime in *August*; he return'd me an Answer in the most Passionate Terms imaginable, and desir'd me to let him have timely Notice, and he would come and meet me two Days Journey: This puzzl'd me scurvily,[4] and I did not know what Answer to make to it; once I was resolv'd to take the Stage Coach to *West-Chester* on purpose only, to have the satisfaction of coming back, that he might see me really come in the same Coach; for I had a jealous[5] thought, though I had no Ground for it at all, least he should think I was not really in the Country, and it was no ill-grounded Thought, as you shall hear presently.

I endeavour'd to Reason my self out of it, but it was in vain, the Impression lay so strong on my Mind, that it was not to be resisted;

4. Sorrily.
5. Apprehensive.

at last it came as an Addition to my new Design of going in the Country, that it would be an excellent Blind to my old Governess, and would cover entirely all my other Affairs, for she did not know in the least whether my new Lover liv'd in *London* or in *Lancashire*; and when I told her my Resolution, she was fully perswaded it was in *Lancashire*.

HAVING taken my Measures for this Journey, I let her know it, and sent the Maid that tended me from the beginning, to take a Place for me in the Coach; she would have had me let the Maid have waited on me down to the last Stage, and come up again in the Waggon,[6] but I convinc'd her it wou'd not be convenient; when I went away she told me, she would enter into no Measures for Correspondence, for she saw evidently that my Affection to my Child would cause me to write to her, and to visit her too when I came to Town again; I assur'd her it would, and so took my leave, well satisfied to have been freed from such a House, however good my Accommodations there had been, as I have related above.

I took the Place in the Coach not to its full Extent, but to a place call'd *Stone*[7] in *Cheshire*, I think it is, where I not only had no manner of Business, but not so much as the least Acquaintance with any Person in the Town or near it: But I knew that with Money in the Pocket one is at home any where, so I Lodg'd there two or three Days, till watching my opportunity, I found room in another Stage Coach, and took Passage back again for *London*, sending a Letter to my Gentleman, that I should be such a certain Day at *Stony-Stratford*, where the Coachman told me he was to Lodge.

IT happen'd to be a Chance Coach that I had taken up, which having been hired on purpose to carry some Gentlemen to *West-Chester* who were going for *Ireland*, was now returning, and did not tye it self up to exact Times or Places as the Stages did, so that having been oblig'd to lye still a *Sunday*,[8] he had time to get himself ready to come out, which otherwise he cou'd not have done.

HOWEVER, his warning was so short, that he could not reach to *Stony-Stratford* time enough to be with me at Night, but he met me at a Place call'd *Brickill* the next Morning, as we were just coming into the Town.

I CONFESS I was very glad to see him, for I had thought my self a little disappointed over Night, seeing I had gone so far to contrive

6. I.e., the maid would accompany Moll to the end of her journey and then return to London on the cheaper, less genteel "waggon," which transported not only passengers but also merchandise.
7. Located in Staffordshire, about twelve miles from Cheshire. As previous editors have noted, Moll's "mistake" is not necessarily Defoe's, given his extensive knowledge of the geography of Great Britain. Stony Stratford and Little Brickhill, both in Buckinghamshire, were stage stops on the London–Chester route.
8. In compliance with the Sunday Observance Act (1677), stage coaches did not run on Sunday.

my coming on purpose: He pleas'd me doubly too by the Figure he came in, for he brought a very handsome (Gentleman's) Coach and four Horses with a Servant to attend him.

HE took me out of the Stage Coach immediately, which stop'd at an Inn in *Brickill*, and putting in to the same Inn he set up his own Coach, and bespoke his Dinner; I ask'd him what he meant by that, for I was for going forward with the Journey; he said no, I had need of a little Rest upon the Road, and that was a very good sort of a House, tho' it was but a little Town; so we would go no farther that Night, whatever came of it.

I DID not press him much, for since he had come so far to meet me, and put himself to so much Expence, it was but reasonable I should oblige him a little too, so I was easy as to that Point.

AFTER Dinner we walk'd to see the Town, to see the Church, and to view the Fields, and the Country as is usual for Strangers to do, and our Landlord was our Guide in going to see the Church; I observ'd my Gentleman enquir'd pretty much about the Parson, and I took the hint immediately, that he certainly would propose to be married; and tho' it was a sudden thought, it follow'd presently, that in short I would not refuse him; for to be plain with my Circumstances, I was in no condition now to say NO, I had no reason now to run any more such hazards.

BUT while these Thoughts run round in my Head, which was the work but of a few Moments, I observ'd my Landlord took him aside and whisper'd to him, tho' not very softly neither, for so much I overheard, *Sir, if you shall have occasion*—the rest I cou'd not hear, but it seems it was to this purpose, *Sir, if you shall have occasion for a Minister, I have a Friend a little way off that will serve you, and be as private as you please*; my Gentleman answer'd loud enough for me to hear, *very well, I believe I shall*.

I WAS no sooner come back to the Inn, but he fell upon me with irresistable Words, that since he had had the good Fortune to meet me, and every thing concurr'd, it wou'd be hastening his Felicity if I would put an end to the matter just there; what do you mean, *says I*, colouring a little, what in an Inn, and upon the Road! Bless us all, *said I*, as if I had been surpriz'd, how can you talk so! O I can talk so very well, *says he*, I came a purpose to talk so, and I'll show you that I did, and with that he pulls out a great Bundle of Papers; you fright me, *said I*, what are all these; don't be frighted, my Dear, *said he*, and kiss'd me, *this was the first time that he had been so free to call me my Dear*; then he repeated it, don't be frighted, you shall see what it is all, then he laid them all abroad; there was first the Deed or Sentence of Divorce from his Wife, and the full Evidence of her playing the Whore; then there was the Certificates of the Minister and Church-wardens of the Parish where she liv'd, proving that she was buried, and intimating the manner of her Death; the Copy of the Coroner's Warrant for a Jury to sit upon her, and the Verdict of the Jury, who brought it in *Non Compos Mentis*;[9] all this was indeed to the purpose, and to give me Satisfaction, tho', by the way, I was not so scrupulous, had he known all, but that I might have taken him without it: However, I look'd them all over as well as I cou'd, and told him; that this was all very clear indeed, but that he need not have given himself the Trouble to have brought them out with him, for it was time enough: Well *he said*, it might be time enough for me, but no time but the present time was time enough for him.

THERE were other Papers roll'd up, and I ask'd him, what they were? Why, Ay, *says he*, that's the Question I wanted to have you ask me; so he unrolls them, and takes out a little Chagreen[1] Case, and gives me out of it a very fine Diamond Ring; I could not refuse it, if I had a mind to do so, for he put it upon my Finger; so I made him a Curtsy, and accepted it; then he takes out another Ring, and this, *says he*, is for another Occasion, so he puts that in his Pocket. Well, but let me see it tho', *says I*, and smil'd, I guess what it is, I think you are Mad: I should have been Mad if I had done less, *says he*, and still he did not show it me, and I had a great mind to see it; so I says, well but let me see it; hold, *says he*, first look here, then he took up the Roll again, and read it, and behold! it was a License for us to be married: Why, *says I*, are you Distracted? why you were fully satisfy'd that I would comply, and yield at first Word, or resolv'd to take no denial; the last is certainly the Case, *said he*; but you may be mistaken, *said I*, no, no, *says he*, how can you think so? I must not be denied, I can't be denied, and with that he fell to Kissing me so violently, I could not get rid of him.

THERE was a Bed in the Room, and we were walking too and again, eager in the Discourse, at last he takes me by surprize in his Arms, and threw me on the Bed and himself with me, and holding me fast in his Arms, but without the least offer of any Undecency, Courted me to Consent with such repeated Entreaties and Arguments; protesting his Affection and vowing he would not let me go, till I had promised him, that at last I said, why you resolve not to be deny'd indeed, I think: No, no, *says he*, I must not be denyed, I won't be deny'd, I can't be deny'd: Well, well, *said I*, and giving him a slight Kiss, then you shan't be deny'd, *said I*, let me get up.

HE was so Transported with my Consent, and the kind manner of it, that I began to think Once, he took it for a Marriage, and would not stay for the Form, but I wrong'd him, for he gave over Kissing me, took me by the Hand, pull'd me up again, and then giving me

9. Not of sound mind. Legally speaking, the banker's wife was not in control of her mental faculties when she killed herself.
1. I.e., shagreen, a kind of untanned leather with a rough surface, frequently dyed green.

two or three Kisses again, thank'd me for my kind yielding to him; and was so overcome with the Satisfaction and Joy of it, that I saw Tears stand in his Eyes.

I TURN'D from him, for it fill'd my Eyes with Tears too; and I ask'd him leave to retire a little to my Chamber: If ever I had a Grain of true Repentance for a vitious and abominable Life for 24 Years past, it was then. O! what a felicity is it to Mankind, *said I*, to myself, that they cannot see into the Hearts of one another! How happy had it been for me, if I had been Wife to a Man of so much honesty, and so much Affection from the Beginning?

THEN it occurr'd to me what an abominable Creature am I! and how is this innocent Gentleman going to be abus'd by me! How little does he think, that having Divorc'd a Whore, he is throwing himself into the Arms of another! that he is going to Marry one that has lain with two Brothers, and has had three Children by her own Brother! one that was born in *Newgate*, whose Mother was a Whore, and is now a transported Thief; one that has lain with thirteen Men, and has had a Child since he saw me! poor Gentleman! *said I*, What is he going to do? After this reproaching my self was over, it followed thus: Well, if I must be his Wife, if it please God to give me Grace, I'll be a true Wife to him, and love him suitably to the strange Excess of his Passion for me; I will make him amends, if possible, by what he shall see, for the Cheats and Abuses I put upon him, which he does not see.

HE was impatient for my coming out of my Chamber, but finding me long, he went down Stairs, and talk'd with my Landlord about the Parson.

MY Landlord, an Officious, tho' well-meaning Fellow, had sent away for the Neighbouring Clergy Man; and when my Gentleman began to speak of it to him, and talk of sending for him, Sir, says he to him, my Friend is in the House; so without any more words he brought them together: When he came to the Minister, he ask'd him if he would venture to marry a couple of Strangers that were both willing? The Parson said that Mr.—— had said something to him of it; that he hop'd it was no Clandestine Business; that he seem'd to be a grave Gentleman, and he suppos'd Madam was not a Girl, so that the consent of Friends should be wanted; to put you out of doubt of that, says my Gentleman, read this Paper, and out he pulls the License; I am satisfied, says the Minister, where is the Lady? you shall see her presently, says my Gentleman.

WHEN he had said thus, he comes up Stairs, and I was by that time come out of my Room, so he tells me the Minister was below, and that he had talk'd with him, and that upon showing him the License, he was free to marry us with all his Heart, but he asks to see you, so he ask'd if I would let him come up.

'Tis time enough, *said I*, in the Morning, is it not? Why, *said he*, my Dear, he seem'd to scruple whether it was not some young Girl stolen from her Parents, and I assur'd him we were both of Age to command our own Consent; and that made him ask to see you; well, *said I*, do as you please; so up they brings the Parson, and a merry good sort of Gentleman he was; he had been told, it seems, that we had met there by accident, that I came in the *Chester* Coach, and my Gentleman in his own Coach to meet me; that we were to have met last Night at *Stony-Stratford*, but that he could not reach so far: Well, Sir, *says the Parson*, every ill turn has some good in it; the Disappointment, Sir, *says he to my Gentleman*, was yours, and the good Turn is mine, for if you had met at *Stony-Stratford* I had not had the Honour to Marry you: LANDLORD *have you a Common-Prayer Book?*

I started as if I had been frighted; Lord, *says I*, what do you mean, what to marry in an Inn, and at Night too: Madam, *says the Minister*, if you will have it be in the Church you shall; but I assure you your Marriage will be as firm here as in the Church; we are not tyed by the Canons to Marry no where but in the Church; and if you will have it in the Church it will be as publick as a Country Fair; and as for the time of Day it does not at all weigh in this Case, our Princes are married in their Chambers, and at Eight or Ten a Clock at Night.[2]

I WAS a great while before I could be perswaded, and pretended not to be willing at all to be married but in the Church; but it was all Grimace;[3] so I seem'd at last to be prevail'd on, and my Landlord, and his Wife, and Daughter, were call'd up: My Landlord was Father and Clark and all together, and we were married, and very Merry we were; tho' I confess the self-reproaches which I had upon me before, lay close to me, and extorted every now and then a deep sigh from me, which my Bridegroom took notice of, and endeavour'd to encourage me, thinking, poor Man, that I had some little hesitations at the Step I had taken so hastily.

WE enjoy'd our selves that Evening compleatly, and yet all was kept so private in the Inn, that not a Servant in the House knew of it, for my Landlady and her Daughter waited on me, and would not let any of the Maids come up Stairs, except while we were at Supper: My Landlady's Daughter I call'd my Bride-maid, and sending for a Shop-keeper the next Morning, I gave the young Woman a good Suit of Knots, as good as the Town would afford, and finding it was a

2. According to the canons of the Church of England, marriage ceremonies could be performed only at specific hours and places, with exceptions being made (as the minister notes) for members of the upper classes. The minister is flattering Moll and her suitor with presumption of gentility. As we learn below, the landlord wants this "Neighbouring Clergy Man," rather than the "Minister of the Parish," to marry the couple, thus keeping all profits within his establishment.

3. Affectation, pretense.

Lace-making Town, I gave her Mother a piece of Bone-lace[4] for a Head.

ONE Reason that my Landlord was so close[5] was, that he was unwilling the Minister of the Parish should hear of it; but for all that somebody heard of it, so as that we had the Bells set a Ringing the next Morning early, and the Musick,[6] such as the Town would afford, under our Window; but my Landlord brazen'd it out, that we were marry'd before we came thither, only that being his former Guests,[7] we would have our Wedding Supper at his House.

WE cou'd not find in our Hearts to stir the next Day; for in short having been disturb'd by the Bells in the Morning, and having perhaps not slept over much Before, we were so sleepy afterwards that we lay in Bed till almost Twelve a Clock.

I BEG'D my Landlady that we might not have any more Musick in the Town, nor Ringing of Bells, and she manag'd it so well that we were very quiet: But an odd Passage interrupted all my Mirth for a good while; the great Room of the House look'd into the Street, and my new Spouse being below Stairs, I had walk'd to the end of the Room, and it being a pleasant warm Day, I had opened the Window, and was standing at it for some Air, when I saw three Gentlemen come by on Horseback and go into an Inn just against[8] us.

IT was not to be conceal'd, nor was it so doubtful as to leave me any room to question it, but the second of the three was my *Lancashire* Husband: I was frighted to Death, I never was in such a Consternation in my Life, I thought I should have sunk into the Ground, my Blood run Chill in my Veins, and I trembl'd as if I had been in a cold Fit of an Ague: I say there was no room to question the Truth of it, I knew his Cloaths, I knew his Horse, and I knew his Face.

THE first sensible Reflection I made was, that my Husband was not by to see my Disorder, and that I was very glad of: The Gentlemen had not been long in the House but they came to the Window of their Room, as is usual; but my Window was shut you may be sure: However, I cou'd not keep from peeping at them, and there I saw him again, heard him call out to one of the Servants of the House for something he wanted, and receiv'd all the terrfying Confirmations of its being the same Person, that were possible to be had.

MY next concern was to know, if possible, what was his Business

4. Lace, usually of linen thread, made by knitting upon a pattern marked by pins, with bobbins originally made of bone. *Knots*: Brightly colored bows made of ribbon to decorate gowns or dresses.
5. Secretive.
6. It was customary for newlyweds to be serenaded in this fashion.
7. In the first and second editions, the text reads "Guess," an apparently correct form according to the *OED*.
8. Across from, opposite.

there; but that was impossible; sometimes my Imagination form'd an Idea of one frightful thing, sometimes of another; sometimes I thought he had discover'd me, and was come to upbraid me with Ingratitude and Breach of Honour; and every Moment I fancied he was coming up the Stairs to Insult me; and innumerable fancies came into my Head of what was never in his Head, nor ever could be, unless the Devil had reveal'd it to him.

I REMAIN'D in this fright near two Hours, and scarce ever kept my Eye from the Window or Door of the Inn, where they were: At last hearing a great clutter in the Passage of their Inn, I run to the Window, and, to my great Satisfaction, see them all three go out again and Travel on Westward; had they gone towards *London*, I should have been still in a fright, least I should meet him on the Road again, and that he should know me; but he went the contrary way, and so I was eas'd of that Disorder.

WE resolv'd to be going the next Day, but about six a Clock at Night we were alarm'd with a great uproar in the Street, and People riding as if they had been out of their Wits, and what was it but a Hue and Cry[9] after three Highway Men, that had rob'd two Coaches, and some other Travellers near *Dunstable* Hill, and notice had, it seems, been given, that they had been seen at *Brickill* at such a House, meaning the House where those Gentlemen had been.

THE House was immediately beset and search'd, but there were witnesses enough that the Gentlemen had been gone above three Hours; the Crowd having gathered about, we had the News presently; and I was heartily concern'd now another way: I presently told the People of the House, that I durst to say those were not the Persons, for that I knew one of the Gentlemen to be a very honest Person, and of a good Estate in *Lancashire*.

THE Constable, who came with the Hue and Cry, was immediately inform'd of this, and came over to me to be satisfy'd from my own Mouth, and I assur'd him that I saw the three Gentlemen as I was at the Window, that I saw them afterwards at the Windows of the Room they din'd in; that I saw them afterwards take Horse, and I could assure him I knew one of them to be such a Man, that he was a Gentleman of a very good Estate, and an undoubted Character in *Lancashire*, from whence I was just now upon my Journey.

THE assurance with which I deliver'd this, gave the Mob Gentry[1] a Check, and gave the Constable such Satisfaction, that he immediately sounded a Retreat, told his People these were not the Men, but that he had an account they were very honest Gentlemen, and

9. An outcry for the pursuit of a felon. Moll is referring to a group of people, led by a constable, raising such an outcry.
1. Moll uses this sarcastic epithet to refer to the unruly lower-class rabble ("mob") involved in the Hue and Cry.

so they went all back again; what the Truth of the matter was I knew not, but certain it was that the Coaches were rob'd at *Dunstable* Hill, and 560 *l.* in Money taken, besides some of the Lace Merchants that always Travel that way had been visited too; as to the three Gentlemen, that remains to be explain'd hereafter.

WELL, this Allarm stop'd us another Day, tho' my Spouse was for Travelling, and told me that it was always safest Travelling after a Robbery, for that the Thieves were sure to be gone far enough off when they had allarm'd the Country; but I was afraid and uneasy, and indeed principally least my old Acquaintance should be upon the Road still, and should chance to see me.

I NEVER liv'd four pleasanter Days together in my life, I was a meer Bride all this while, and my new Spouse strove to make me entirely easie in every thing; O could this State of Life have continued! how had all my past Troubles been forgot, and my future Sorrows been avoided? but I had a past life of a most wretched kind to account for, some of it in this World as well as in another.

WE came away the fifth Day; and my Landlord, because he saw me uneasie, mounted himself, his Son, and three honest Country Fellows with good Fire-Arms, and, without telling us of it, follow'd the Coach, and would see us safe into *Dunstable*; we could do no less than treat them very handsomely at *Dunstable*, which Cost my Spouse about Ten or Twelve Shillings, and something he gave the Men for their Time too, but my Landlord would take nothing for himself.

THIS was the most happy Contrivance for me that could have fallen out, for had I come to *London* unmarried, I must either have come to him for the first Night's Entertainment, or have discovered to him that I had not one Acquaintance in the whole City of *London* that could receive a poor Bride for the first Night's Lodging with her Spouse: But now being an old married Woman, I made no scruple of going directly home with him, and there I took Possession at once of a House well Furnish'd, and a Husband in very good Circumstances, so that I had a prospect of a very happy Life, if I knew how to manage it; and I had leisure to consider of the real Value of the Life I was likely to live; how different it was to be from the loose ungovern'd part I had acted before, and how much happier a Life of Virtue and Sobriety is, than that which we call a Life of Pleasure.

O HAD this particular Scene of Life lasted, or had I learnt from that time I enjoy'd it, to have tasted the true sweetness of it, and had I not fallen into the Poverty which is the sure Bane of Virtue, how happy had I been, not only here, but perhaps for ever? for while I liv'd thus, I was really a Penitent for all my Life pass'd, I look'd back on it with Abhorrence, and might truly be said to hate my self for it; I often reflected how my Lover at the *Bath*, strook by the Hand of

God, repented and abandon'd me, and refus'd to see me any more, tho' he lov'd me to an extreme; but I, prompted by that worst of Devils, Poverty, return'd to the vile Practice, and made the Advantage of what they call a handsome Face, be the Relief to my Necessities, and Beauty be a Pimp to Vice.

NOW I seem'd landed in a safe Harbour, after the Stormy Voyage of Life past was at an end; and I began to be thankful for my Deliverance; I sat many an Hour by my self, and wept over the Remembrance of past Follies, and the dreadful Extravagances of a wicked Life, and sometimes I flatter'd my self that I had sincerely repented.

BUT there are Temptations which it is not in the Power of Human Nature to resist, and few know what would be their Case, if driven to the same Exigences: As Covetousness is the Root of all Evil,[2] so Poverty is, I believe, the worst of all Snares: But I wave that Discourse till I come to the Experiment.

I LIV'D with this Husband in the utmost Tranquility; he was a Quiet, Sensible, Sober Man, Virtuous, Modest, Sincere, and in his Business Diligent and Just: His Business was in a narrow Compass, and his Income sufficient to a plentiful way of Living in the ordinary way; I do not say to keep an Equipage,[3] and make a Figure as the World calls it, nor did I expect it, or desire it; for as I abhorr'd the Levity and Extravagance of my former Life, so I chose now to live retir'd, frugal, and within our selves; I kept no Company, made no Visits; minded my Family, and oblig'd my Husband; and this kind of Life became a Pleasure to me.

WE liv'd in an uninterrupted course of Ease and Content for Five Years, when a sudden Blow from an almost invisible Hand, blasted all my Happiness, and turn'd me out into the World in a Condition the reverse of all that had been before it.

MY Husband having trusted one of his Fellow Clarks with a Sum of Money too much for our Fortunes to bear the Loss of, the Clark fail'd, and the Loss fell very heavy on my Husband, yet it was not so great neither, but that if he had had Spirit and Courage to have look'd his Misfortunes in the Face, his Credit was so good, that as I told him, he would easily recover it; for to sink under Trouble is to double the Weight, and he that will Die in it shall Die in it.

IT was in vain to speak comfortably to him, the Wound had sunk too deep, it was a Stab that touch'd the Vitals, he grew Melancholy and Disconsolate, and from thence Lethargick, and died; I foresaw the Blow, and was extremely oppress'd in my Mind, for I saw evidently that if he died I was undone.

I HAD had two Children by him and no more, for to tell the Truth,

2. 1 Timothy 6:10: "For the love of money is the root of all evil: which while some coveted after, they have erred from the faith, and pierced themselves through with many sorrows."
3. Carriage and horses, with attendant servants.

it began to be time for me to leave bearing Children, for I was now Eight and Forty, and I suppose if he had liv'd I should have had no more.

I WAS now left in a dismal and disconsolate Case indeed, and in several things worse than ever: First it was past the flourishing time with me when I might expect to be courted for a Mistress; that agreeable part had declin'd some time, and the Ruins only appear'd of what had been; and that which was worse than all was this, that I was the most dejected, disconsolate Creature alive; I that had encourag'd my Husband, and endeavour'd to support his Spirits under his Trouble, could not support my own; I wanted that Spirit in Trouble which I told him was so necessary to him for bearing the burthen.

BUT my Case was indeed Deplorable, for I was left perfectly Friendless and Helpless, and the Loss my Husband had sustain'd had reduc'd his Circumstances so low, that tho' indeed I was not in Debt, yet I could easily foresee that what was left would not support me long; that while it wasted daily for Subsistence, I had no way to encrease it one Shilling, so that it would be soon all spent, and then I saw nothing before me but the utmost Distress, and this represented it self so lively to my Thoughts, that it seem'd as if it was come, before it was really very near; also my very Apprehensions doubl'd the Misery, for I fancied every Sixpence that I paid but for a Loaf of Bread, was the last that I had in the World, and that To-morrow I was to fast, and be starv'd to Death.

IN this Distress I had no Assistant, no Friend to comfort or advise me, I sat and cried and tormented my self Night and Day; wringing my Hands, and sometimes raving like a distracted Woman; and indeed I have often wonder'd it had not affected my Reason, for I had the Vapours to such a degree, that my Understanding was sometimes quite lost in Fancies and Imaginations.

I LIV'D Two Years in this dismal Condition wasting that little I had, weeping continually over my dismal Circumstances, and as it were only bleeding to Death, without the least hope or prospect of help from God or Man; and now I had cried so long, and so often, that Tears were, as I might say, exhausted, and I began to be Desperate, for I grew Poor apace.

FOR a little Relief I had put off my House and took Lodgings, and as I was reducing my Living so I sold off most of my Goods, which put a little Money in my Pocket, and I liv'd near a Year upon that, spending very sparingly, and eeking things out to the utmost; but still when I look'd before me, my very Heart would sink within me at the inevitable approach of Misery and Want: O let none read this part without seriously reflecting on the Circumstances of a desolate State, and how they would grapple with meer want of Friends and want of Bread; it will certainly make them think not of sparing what they have only, but of looking up to Heaven for support, and of the wise Man's Prayer, *Give me not Poverty least I Steal.*[4]

LET 'em remember that a time of Distress is a time of dreadful Temptation,[5] and all the Strength to resist is taken away; Poverty presses, the Soul is made Desperate by Distress, and what can be done? It was one Evening, when being brought, as I may say, to the last Gasp, I think I may truly say I was Distracted and Raving, when prompted by I know not what Spirit, and as it were, doing I did not know what, or why; I dress'd me, for I had still pretty good Cloaths, and went out: I am very sure I had no manner of Design in my Head, when I went out, I neither knew or considered where to go, or on what Business; but as the Devil carried me out and laid his Bait for me, so he brought me to be sure to the place, for I knew not whither I was going or what I did.

WANDRING thus about I knew not whither, I pass'd by an Apothecary's Shop in *Leadenhall-street*,[6] where I saw lye on a Stool just before the Counter a little Bundle wrapt in a white Cloth; beyond it, stood a Maid Servant with her Back to it, looking up towards the top of the Shop, where the Apothecary's Apprentice, as I suppose, was standing up on the Counter, with his Back also to the Door, and a Candle in his Hand, looking and reaching up to the upper Shelf for something he wanted, so that both were engag'd mighty earnestly, and no Body else in the Shop.

THIS was the Bait; and the Devil who I said laid the Snare, as readily prompted me, as if he had spoke, for I remember, and shall never forget it, 'twas like a Voice spoken to me over my Shoulder, take the Bundle; be quick; do it this Moment; it was no sooner said but I step'd into the Shop, and with my Back to the Wench, as if I had stood up for a Cart that was going by, I put my Hand behind me and took the Bundle, and went off with it, the Maid or the Fellow not perceiving me, or any one else.

IT is impossible to express the Horror of my Soul all the while I did it: When I went away I had no Heart to run, or scarce to mend my pace; I cross'd the Street indeed, and went down the first turning I came to, and I think it was a Street that went thro' into *Fenchurch-street*, from thence I cross'd and turn'd thro' so many ways and turnings that I could never tell which way it was, nor where I went, for

4. See Proverbs 30:8–9.

5. Cf. *Colonel Jack*: "Necessity is not only the Temptation, but is such a Temptation as human Nature is not empower'd to resist . . . [and] . . . shows us the need we have of the Petition in the Lord's Prayer: *Lead us not into Temptation*; and of *Solomon's* or *Agar's* Prayer: *Give me not Poverty, least I Steal.*"

6. Taking its name from the ancient Leadenhall Market, this was a busy commercial thoroughfare in the City of London, as was Fenchurch Street (running roughly east–west just below it, after diverging at Aldgate).

I felt not the Ground, I stept on, and the farther I was out of Danger, the faster I went, till tyr'd and out of Breath, I was forc'd to sit down on a little Bench at a Door, and then I began to recover, and found I was got into *Thames-street* near *Billinsgate*:[7] I rested me a little and went on, my Blood was all in a Fire, my Heart beat as if I was in a sudden Fright: In short, I was under such a Surprize that I still knew not whither I was a going, or what to do.

AFTER I had tyr'd my self thus with walking a long way about, and so eagerly, I began to consider and make home to my Lodging, where I came about Nine a Clock at Night.

WHAT the Bundle was made up for, or on what Occasion laid where I found it, I knew not, but when I came to open it I found there was a Suit of Child-bed Linnen in it, very good and almost new, the Lace very fine; there was a Silver Porringer[8] of a Pint, a small Silver Mug and Six Spoons, with some other Linnen, a good Smock, and Three Silk Handkerchiefs, and in the Mug wrap'd up in a Paper Eighteen Shillings and Six-pence in Money.

ALL the while I was opening these things I was under such dreadful Impressions of Fear, and in such Terror of Mind, tho' I was perfectly safe, that I cannot express the manner of it; I sat me down and cried most vehemently; Lord, *said I*, what am I now? a Thief! why I shall be taken next time and be carry'd to *Newgate* and be Try'd for my Life! and with that I cry'd again a long time, and I am sure, as poor as I was, if I had durst for fear, I would certainly have carried the things back again; but that went off after a while: Well, I went to Bed for that Night, but slept little, the Horror of the Fact was upon my Mind, and I knew not what I said or did all Night, and all the next Day: Then I was impatient to hear some News of the Loss; and would fain know how it was, whether they were a Poor Bodies Goods, or a Rich; perhaps, *said I*, it may be some poor Widow like me, that had pack'd up these Goods to go and sell them for a little Bread for herself and a poor Child, and are now starving and breaking their Hearts, for want of that little they would have fetch'd, and this Thought tormented me worse than all the rest, for three or four Days time.

BUT my own Distresses silenc'd all these Reflections, and the prospect of my own Starving, which grew every Day more frightful to me, harden'd my Heart by degrees; it was then particularly heavy upon my Mind, that I had been reform'd, and had, as I hop'd, repented of all my pass'd wickednesses; that I had liv'd a sober, grave, retir'd Life for several Years, but now I should be driven by the dreadful Necessity of my Circumstances to the Gates of Destruction, Soul and

7. Site of a well-known fish market, Billingsgate was also legendary for abusive, foul-mouthed language. Moll's labyrinthine wanderings are taking her south, toward the River Thames.
8. A small basin or vessel from which soup, broth, porridge, or children's food is eaten.

Body; and two or three times I fell upon my Knees, praying to God, as well as I could, for Deliverance; but I cannot but say my Prayers had no hope in them; I knew not what to do, it was all Fear without, and Dark within; and I reflected on my pass'd Life as not sincerely repented of, that Heaven was now beginning to punish me on this side the Grave, and would make me as miserable as I had been wicked.

HAD I gone on here I had perhaps been a true Penitent; but I had an evil Counsellor within, and he was continually prompting me to relieve my self by the worst means; so one Evening he tempted me again by the same wicked Impulse that had said, *take that Bundle*, to go out again and seek for what might happen.

I WENT out now by Day-light, and wandred about I knew not whither, and in search of I knew not what, when the Devil put a Snare in my way of a dreadful Nature indeed, and such a one as I have never had before or since; going thro' *Aldersgate-street* there was a pretty little Child had been at a Dancing-School, and was going home, all alone, and my prompter, like a true Devil, set me upon this innocent Creature; I talk'd to it, and it prattl'd to me again, and I took it by the Hand and led it a long till I came to a pav'd Alley that goes into *Batholomew Close*, and I led it in there; the Child said that was not its way home; I said, yes, my Dear it is, I'll show you the way home; the Child had a little Necklace on of Gold Beads, and I had my Eye upon that, and in the dark of the Alley I stoop'd, pretending to mend the Child's Clog that was loose, and took off her Necklace and the Child never felt it, and so led the Child on again: Here, I say, the Devil put me upon killing the Child in the dark Alley, that it might not Cry; but the very thought frighted me so that I was ready to drop down, but I turn'd the Child about and bad it go back again, for that was not its way home; the Child said so she would, and I went thro' into *Bartholomew Close*, and then turn'd round to another Passage that goes into *Long-lane*, so away into *Charterhouse-Yard* and out into *St. John's-street*, then crossing into *Smithfield*, went down *Chick-lane* and into *Field-lane*[9] to *Holbourn-bridge*, when mixing with the Crowd of People, usually passing there, it was not possible to have been found out; and thus I enterpriz'd my second Sally into the World.

THE thoughts of this Booty put out all the thoughts of the first, and the Reflections I had made wore quickly off; Poverty, as I have said, harden'd my Heart, and my own Necessities made me regardless of any thing: The last Affair left no great Concern upon me, for as I did the poor Child no harm, I only said to my self, I had given

9. At this point, Moll is traversing one of the most notorious high-crime sections of Defoe's London. Her "second Sally" takes place in the streets and alleys surrounding Smithfield Market.

the Parents a just Reproof for their Negligence in leaving the poor little Lamb to come home by it self, and it would teach them to take more Care of it another time.

THIS String of Beads was worth about Twelve or Fourteen Pounds, I suppose it might have been formerly the Mother's, for it was too big for the Child's wear, but that, perhaps, the Vanity of the Mother to have her Child look Fine at the Dancing School, had made her let the Child wear it, and no doubt the Child had a Maid sent to take care of it, but she, like a careless Jade, was taken up perhaps with some Fellow that had met her by the way, and so the poor Baby wandred till it fell into my Hands.

HOWEVER, I did the Child no harm, I did not so much as fright it, for I had a great many tender Thoughts about me yet, and did nothing but what, as I may say, meer Necessity drove me to.

I HAD a great many Adventures after this, but I was young in the Business, and did not know how to manage, otherwise than as the Devil put things into my Head; and indeed he was seldom backward to me: One Adventure I had which was very lucky to me; I was going thro' *Lombard-street* in the dusk of the Evening, just by the end of *Three King Court*,[1] when on a sudden comes a Fellow running by me as swift as Lightning, and throws a Bundle that was in his Hand just behind me, as I stood up against the corner of the House at the turning into the Alley; just as he threw it in he said, God bless you Mistress let it lie there a little, and away he runs swift as the Wind: After him comes two more, and immediately a young Fellow without his Hat, crying stop Thief, and after him two or three more, they pursued the two last Fellows so close, that they were forced to drop what they had got, and one of them was taken into the bargain, the other got off free.

I STOOD stock still all this while till they came back, dragging the poor Fellow they had taken, and luging the things they had found, extremely well satisfied that they had recovered the Booty, and taken the Thief; and thus they pass'd by me, for I look'd only like one who stood up while the Crowd was gone.

ONCE or twice I ask'd what was the matter, but the People neglected answering me, and I was not very importunate; but after the Crowd was wholly pass'd, I took my opportunity to turn about and take up what was behind me and walk away: This indeed I did with less Disturbance than I had done formerly, for these things I did not steal, but they were stolen to my Hand: I got safe to my Lodgings with this Cargo, which was a Peice of fine black Lustring Silk, and a Peice of Velvet; the latter was but part of a Peice of about a 11 Yards; the former was a whole Peice of near 50 Yards; it seems

1. Moll is immediately west of the area of her first theft. Running east into Fenchurch Street, Lombard Street was inhabited by bankers, goldsmiths, and other tradesmen.

it was a *Mercer's* Shop that they had rifled, I say rifled, because the Goods were so considerable that they had Lost; for the Goods that they Recover'd were pretty many, and I believe came to about six or seven several[2] Peices of Silk: How they came to get so many I could not tell; but as I had only robb'd the Thief I made no scruple at taking these Goods, and being very glad of them too.

I HAD pretty good Luck thus far, and I made several Adventures more, tho' with but small Purchase,[3] yet with good Success, but I went in daily dread that some mischief would befal me, and that I should certainly come to be hang'd at last: The impression this made on me was too strong to be slighted, and it kept me from making attempts that for ought I know might have been very safely perform'd; but one thing I cannot omit, which was a Bait to me many a Day. I walk'd frequently out into the Villages round the Town to see if nothing would fall in my Way there; and going by a House near *Stepney*, I saw on the Window-board two Rings, one a small Diamond Ring, and the other a plain Gold Ring, to be sure laid there by some thoughtless Lady, that had more Money than Forecast,[4] perhaps only till she wash'd her Hands.

I WALK'D several times by the Window to observe if I could see whether there was any Body in the Room or no, and I could see no Body, but still I was not sure; it came presently into my Thoughts to rap at the Glass, as if I wanted to speak with some Body, and if any Body was there they would be sure to come to the Window, and then I would tell them to remove those Rings, for that I had seen two suspicious Fellows take notice of them: This was a ready Thought, I rapt once or twice and no Body came, when seeing the Coast clear, I thrust hard against the Square of Glass, and broke it with very little Noise, and took out the two Rings, and walk'd away with them very safe, the Diamond Ring was worth about 3*l.* and the other about 9*s.*

I WAS now at a loss for a Market for my Goods, and especially for my two Peices of Silk, I was very loth to dispose of them for a Trifle; as the poor unhappy Theives in general do, who after they have ventured their Lives for, perhaps a thing of Value, are fain to sell it for a Song when they have done; but I was resolv'd I would not do thus whatever shift I made, unless I was driven to the last Extremity; however I did not well know what Course to take: At last I resolv'd to go to my old Governness, and acquaint myself with her again: I had punctually supply'd the 5*l.* a Year to her for my little Boy as long as I was able; but at last was oblig'd to put a stop to it: However I had written a Letter to her, wherein I had told her that my Circumstances were reduc'd very low; that I had lost my Husband, and that

2. Separate.
3. Acquisition, gain.
4. Foresight.

I was not able to do it any longer, and so beg'd that the poor Child might not suffer too much for its Mother's Misfortunes.

I Now made her a Visit, and I found that she drove something of the old Trade still, but that she was not in such flourishing Circumstances as before; for she had been Sued by a certain Gentleman, who had had his Daughter stolen from him; and who it seems she had helped to convey away; and it was very narrowly that she escap'd the Gallows; the Expence also had ravag'd her, and she was become very poor; her House was but meanly Furnished, and she was not in such repute for her Practice as before; however she stood upon her Legs, as they say, and as she was a stirring bustling Woman, and had some Stock left, she was turn'd *Pawn Broker, and liv'd pretty well.*

SHE receiv'd me very civily, and with her usual obliging manner told me, she would not have the less respect for me, for my being reduc'd; that she had taken Care my Boy was very well look'd after, tho' I could not pay for him, and that the Woman that had him was easie,[5] so that I needed not to Trouble myself about him, till I might be better able to do it effectually.

I TOLD her I had not much Money left, but that I had some things that were Monies worth, if she could tell me how I might turn them into Money; she ask'd me what it was I had, I pull'd out the string of gold Beads, and told her it was one of my Husbands Presents to me; then I show'd her the two Parcels of Silk which I told her I had from *Ireland*, and brought up to Town with me; and the little Diamond Ring; as to the small Parcel of Plate and Spoons, I had found means to dispose of them myself before; and as for the Childbed Linnen I had, she offer'd me to take it herself, believing it to have been my own; she told me that she was turn'd *Pawn-Broker*, and that she would sell those things for me as pawn'd to her, and so she sent presently for proper Agents that bought them, being in her Hands, without any scruple, and gave good Prizes[6] too.

I Now began to think this necessary Woman might help me a little in my low Condition to some Business; for I would gladly have turn'd my Hand to any honest Employment if I could have got it; but here she was defficient; honest Business did not come within her reach; if I had been younger, perhaps she might have helped me to a Spark,[7] but my Thoughts were off of that kind of Livelihood, as being quite out of the way after 50, which was my Case, and so I told her.

SHE invited me at last to come, and be at her House till I could find something to do, and it should cost me very little, and this I gladly accepted of, and now living a little easier, I enter'd into some

5. I.e., in easy or good financial circumstances.
6. Sums of money.
7. Beau, lover, or suitor.

Measures to have my little Son by my last Husband taken off;[8] and this she made easie too, reserving a Payment only of 5*l.* a Year, if I could pay it. This was such a help to me, that for a good while I left off the wicked Trade that I had so newly taken up; and gladly I would have got my Bread by the help of my Needle if I cou'd have got Work, but that was very hard to do for one that had no manner of Acquaintance in the World.

HOWEVER at last I got some Quilting-Work for Ladies Beds, Petticoats, and the like; and this I lik'd very well and work'd very hard, and with this I began to live; but the diligent Devil who resolv'd I should continue in his Service, continually prompted me to go out and take a Walk, that is to say, to see if any thing would offer in the old Way.

ONE Evening I blindly obeyed his Summons, and fetch'd a long Circuit thro' the Streets, but met with no purchase and came Home very weary, and empty; but not content with that, I went out the next Evening too, when going by an Alehouse I saw the Door of a little room open, next the very Street, and on the Table a silver Tankard, things much in use in publick Houses at that time; it seems some Company had been drinking there, and the careless Boys had forgot to take it away.

I WENT into the Box frankly,[9] and setting the silver Tankard on the Corner of the Bench, I sat down before it, and knock'd with my Foot, a Boy came presently, and I bad him fetch me a pint of warm Ale, for it was cold Weather; the Boy run, and I heard him go down the Sellar to draw the Ale; while the Boy was gone, another Boy come into the Room, and cried, *d' ye call*, I spoke with a melancholly Air, and said, no Child, the Boy is gone for a Pint of Ale for me.

WHILE I sat here, I heard the Woman in the Bar say are they all gone in the Five, which was the Box I sat in, and the Boy said *yes*; who fetch'd the Tankard away? *says the Woman*, I did, *says another Boy*, that's it, pointing it seems to another Tankard, which he had fetch'd from another Box by Mistake; or else it must be, that the Rogue forgot that he had not brought it in, which certainly he had not.

I HEARD all this, much to my satisfaction, for I found plainly that the Tankard was not mist, and yet they concluded it was fetch'd away; so I drank my Ale, call'd to Pay, and as I went away, *I said*, take care of your Plate Child, meaning a silver pint Mug, which he brought me Drink in; the Boy said, *yes Madam, very welcome*, and away I came.

8. I.e., taken off her hands.
9. Without concealment or disguise, openly. *Box*: A compartment partitioned off in the public room of a coffee-house or tavern.

I CAME Home to my Governness, and now I thought it was a time to try her, that if I might be put to the Necessity of being expos'd, she might offer me some assistance; when I had been at Home some time, and had an opportunity of Talking to her, I told her I had a Secret of the greatest Consequence in the World to commit to her if she had respect enough for me to keep it a Secret: She told me she had kept one of my Secrets faithfully; why should I doubt her keeping another? I told her the strangest thing in the World had befallen me, and that it had made a Thief of me, even without any design; and so told her the whole Story of the Tankard: And have you brought it away with you my Dear, *says she*, to be sure I have, *says I*, and shew'd it her. But what shall I do now, *says I*, must not I carry it again?

CARRY it again! *says she*, Ay, if you are minded to be sent to *Newgate* for stealing it; why, *says I*, they can't be so base to stop me, when I carry it to them again? You don't know those Sort of People Child, *says she*, they'll not only carry you to *Newgate*, but hang you too without any regard to the honesty of returning it; or bring in an Account of all the other Tankards they have lost for you to pay for: What must I do then? *says I*; Nay, *says she*, as you have plaid the cunning part and stole it, you must e'n keep it, there's no going back now; besides Child, *says she*, Don't you want it more than they do? I wish you cou'd light of such a Bargain once a Week.

THIS gave me a new Notion of my *Governess*, and that since she was turn'd *Pawn Broker*, she had a Sort of People about her, that were none of the honest ones that I had met with there before.

I HAD not been long there, but I discover'd it more plainly than before, for every now and then I saw Hilts of Swords, Spoons, Forks, Tankards, and all such kind of Ware brought in, not to be Pawn'd, but to be sold down right; and she bought every thing that came without asking any Questions, but had very good Bargains as I found by her Discourse.

I FOUND also that in the following this Trade, she always melted down the Plate she bought, that it might not be challeng'd; and she came to me and told me one Morning that she was going to Melt, and if I would, she would put my Tankard in, that it might not be seen by any Body; I told her with all my Heart; so she weigh'd it, and allow'd me the full value in Silver again; but I found she did not do the same to the rest of her Customers.

SOMETIME after this, as I was at Work, and very melancholly, she begins to ask me what the Matter was? as she was us'd to do; I told her my Heart was heavy, I had little Work, and nothing to live on, and knew not what Course to take; she Laugh'd and told me I must go out again and try my Fortune; it might be that I might meet with another Peice of Plate. O, Mother! *says I*, that is a Trade I have no skill in, and if I should be taken I am undone at once; *says she*, I cou'd help you to a School-Mistress,[1] that shall make you as dexterous as her self: I trembled at that Proposal for hitherto I had had no Confederates, nor any Acquaintance among that Tribe; but she conquer'd all my Modesty, and all my Fears; and in a little time, by the help of this Confederate I grew as impudent a Thief, and as dexterous as ever *Moll Cut-Purse*[2] was, tho' if Fame does not belie her, not half so Handsome.

THE Comrade she helped me to, dealt in three sorts of Craft, (*viz.*) Shop-lifting, stealing of Shop-Books and Pocket-Books, and taking off Gold Watches from the Ladies Sides, and this last she did so dexteriously that no Woman ever arriv'd to the Perfection of that Art, so as to do it like her: I lik'd the first and the last of these things very well, and I attended her some time in the Practise, just as a Deputy attends a Midwife without any Pay.

AT length she put me to Practise, she had shewn me her Art, and I had several times unhook'd a Watch from her own side with great dexterity; at last she show'd me a Prize, and this was a young Lady big with Child who had a charming Watch, the thing was to be done as she came out of Church; she goes on one side of the Lady, and pretends, just as she came to the Steps, to fall, and fell against the Lady with so much violence as put her into a great fright, and both cry'd out terribly; in the very moment that she jostl'd the Lady, I had hold of the Watch, and holding it the right way, the start she gave drew the Hook out and she never felt it; I made off immediately, and left my School-mistress to come out of her pretended Fright gradually, and the Lady too; and presently the Watch was miss'd; ay, *says my Comrade*, then it was those Rogues that thrust me down, I warrant ye; I wonder the Gentlewoman did not miss her Watch before, then we might have taken them.

SHE humour'd[3] the thing so well that no Body suspected her, and I was got home a full Hour before her: This was my first Adventure in Company; the Watch was indeed a very fine one, and had a great many Trinkets about it, and my Governess allow'd us 20 *l.* for it, of which I had half, and thus I was enter'd a compleat Thief, harden'd to a Pitch above all the Reflections of Conscience or Modesty, and to a Degree which I must acknowledge I never thought possible in me.

1. A teacher or governess, to "school" Moll in the art and craft of thieving.
2. Alias of Mary Frith (1584?–1659), renowned thief and bawd, whose "pranks" were recorded in several contemporary accounts and adapted for the stage by Middleton and Dekker in *The Roaring Girle, Or Moll Cut-Purse* (1611). In *The Life and Death of Mrs. Mary Frith. Commonly Called Mal Cutpurse* (1662), she is labeled an "Epicoene Wonder" because of her masculine dress and complete lack of feminine charms. A "cut-purse" is a pickpocket; the term originally referred to someone who stole a purse by cutting it off its owner's girdle or belt.
3. Devised.

THUS the Devil who began, by the help of an irresistable Poverty, to push me into this Wickedness, brought me on to a height beyond the common Rate, even when my Necessities were not so great, or the prospect of my Misery so terrifying; for I had now got into a little Vein of Work, and as I was not at a loss to handle my Needle, it was very probable, as Acquaintance came in, I might have got my Bread honestly enough.

I must say, that if such a prospect of Work had presented it self at first, when I began to feel the approach of my miserable Circumstances; I say, had such a prospect of getting my Bread by working presented it self then, I had never fallen into this wicked Trade, or into such a wicked Gang as I was now embark'd with; but practise had hardened me, and I grew audacious to the last degree; and the more so, because I had carried it on so long, and had never been taken; for in a word, my new Partner in Wickedness *and I* went on together so long, without being ever detected, that we not only grew Bold, but we grew Rich, and we had at one time One and Twenty Gold Watches in our Hands.

I REMEMBER that one Day being a little more serious than ordinary, and finding I had so good a Stock before-hand as I had, for I had near 200 *l.* in Money for my Share; it came strongly into my Mind, no doubt from some kind Spirit, if such there be; that as at first Poverty excited me, and my Distresses drove me to these dreadful Shifts; so seeing those Distresses were now relieved, and I could also get something towards a Maintenance by working, and had so good a Bank to support me, why should I not now leave off, as they say, while I was well; that I could not expect to go always free; and if I was once surpris'd, and miscarry'd, I was undone.

THIS was doubtless the happy Minute, when if I had hearken'd to the blessed hint from whatsoever hand it came, I had still a cast for an easie Life; but my Fate was otherwise determin'd, the busie Devil that so industriously drew me in, had too fast hold of me to let me go back; but as Poverty brought me into the Mire, so Avarice kept me in, till there was no going back; as to the Arguments which my Reason dictated for perswading me to lay down, Avarice stept in and said, go on, go on; you have had very good luck, go on till you have gotten Four or Five Hundred Pound, and then you shall leave off, and then you may live easie without working at all.

THUS I that was once in the Devil's Clutches, was held fast there as with a Charm, and had no Power to go without the Circle, till I was ingulph'd in Labyrinths of Trouble too great to get out at all.

HOWEVER, these Thoughts left some Impression upon me, and made me act with some more caution than before, and more than my Directors us'd for themselves. My Comerade, as I call'd her, but rather she should have been called my Teacher, with another of her

Scholars, was the first in the Misfortune, for happening to be upon the hunt for Purchase, they made an attempt upon a Linnen-Draper in *Cheapside*, but were snap'd by a Hawks-ey'd Journey-man,[4] and seiz'd with two pieces of Cambrick, which were taken also upon them.

THIS was enough to Lodge them both in *Newgate*, where they had the Misfortune to have some of their former Sins brought to remembrance; two other Indictments being brought against them, and the Facts being prov'd upon them, they were both condemned to Die; they both pleaded their Bellies, and were both voted Quick with Child;[5] tho' my Tutress was no more with Child than I was.

I WENT frequently to see them, and Condole with them, expecting that it would be my turn next; but the place gave me so much Horror, reflecting that it was the place of my unhappy Birth, and of my Mother's Misfortunes, that I could not bear it, so I was forc'd to leave off going to see them.

AND O! cou'd I have but taken warning by their Disasters, I had been happy still, for I was yet free, and had nothing brought against me; but it could not be, my Measure was not yet fill'd up.

MY Comerade having the Brand of an old Offender,[6] was Executed; the young Offender was spar'd, having obtain'd a Reprieve; but lay starving a long while in Prison, till at last she got her Name into what they call a Circuit Pardon,[7] and so came off.

THIS terrible Example of my Comerade frighted me heartily, and for a good while I made no Excursions; but one Night, in the Neighbourhood of my Governesses House, they cryed Fire; my Governess look'd out, for we were all up, and cryed immediately that such a Gentlewoman's House was all of a light Fire a top, and so indeed it was: Here she gives me a jog, now, Child, says she, there is a rare opportunity, the Fire being so near that you may go to it before the Street is block'd up with the Crowd; she presently gave me my Cue, go, Child, *says she*, to the House, and run in and tell the Lady, or any Body you see, that you come to help them, and that you came from such a Gentlewoman (that is one of her Acquaintance farther up the Street); she gave me the like Cue to the next House, naming another Name that was also an Acquaintance of the Gentlewoman of the House.

AWAY I went, and coming to the House I found them all in Con-

4. A hired employee, specifically one who, having completed his apprenticeship, was then qualified to work at his craft or trade for days' wages. *Cheapside*: A grand street in the vicinity of St. Paul's Cathedral and not far from Newgate Prison, it featured the establishments of dealers in cloth and fabrics.
5. Judged to be pregnant (by the vote of members of a jury).
6. See n. 9, p. 71.
7. It is possible, as other editors have speculated, that "Circuit" is a mistaken reading for "Court."

fusion, you may be sure; I run in, and finding one of the Maids, Lord! Sweetheart, *said I*, how came this dismal Accident? Where is your Mistress? And how does she do? Is she safe? And where are the Children? I come from Madam—— to help you; away runs the Maid; Madam, Madam, *says she*, screaming as loud as she cou'd yell, *here is a Gentlewoman come from Madam—— to help us*: The poor Woman half out of her Wits, with a Bundle under her Arm, and two little Children, comes towards me, *Lord, Madam, says I*, let me carry the poor Children to Madam——, she desires you to send them; she'll take care of the poor Lambs, and immediately I takes one of them out of her Hand, and she lifts the tother up into my Arms; *ay, do, for God sake*, says she, *carry them to her; O thank her for her kindness*: Have you *any thing else to secure*, Madam? says I, *she will take care of it*: O dear! ay, says she, *God bless her, and thank her, take this bundle of Plate and carry it to her too; O she is a good Woman; O Lord, we are utterly ruin'd, utterly undone*; and away she runs from me out of her Wits, and the Maids after her, and away comes I with the two Children and the Bundle.

I WAS no sooner got into the Street, but I saw another Woman come to me, O! *says she*, Mistress, in a piteous Tone, you will let fall the Child; come, this is a sad time, let me help you, and immediately lays hold of my Bundle to carry it for me; no, *says I*, if you will help me, take the Child by the Hand, and lead it for me but to the upper end of the Street, I'll go with you and satisfie you for your pains.

SHE cou'd not avoid going, after what I said, but the Creature, in short, was one of the same Business with me, and wanted nothing but the Bundle; however, she went with me to the Door, for she cou'd not help it; when we were come there I whisper'd her, *go Child*, said I, *I understand your Trade*, you may meet with Purchase enough.

SHE understood me and walk'd off; I thundered at the Door with the Children, and as the People were rais'd before by the noise of the Fire, I was soon let in, and I said, *is Madam awake, pray tell her* Mrs.—— *desires the favour of her to take the two Children in*; poor Lady, *she will be undone, their House is all of a Flame*; they took the Children in very civily, pitied the Family in Distress, and away came I with my Bundle; one of the Maids ask'd me, if I was not to leave the Bundle too? I said no, Sweetheart, 'tis to go to another place, it does not belong to them.

I WAS a great way out of the hurry now, and so I went on, clear of any Body's enquiry, and brought the bundle of Plate, which was very considerable, strait home, and gave it to my old Governess; she told me she would not look into it, but bad me go out again to look for more.

SHE gave me the like Cue to the Gentlewoman of the next House to that which was on Fire, and I did my endeavour to go, but by this time the allarm of Fire was so great, and so many Engines playing, and the Street so throng'd with People, that I cou'd not get near the House, whatever I cou'd do; so I came back again to my Governesses, and taking the Bundle up into my Chamber, I began to examine it: It is with Horror that I tell what a Treasure I found there; 'tis enough to say, that besides most of the Family Plate, which was considerable, I found a Gold Chain, an old fashion'd thing, the Locket of which was broken, so that I suppose it had not been us'd some Years, but the Gold was not the worse for that; also a little Box of burying Rings,[8] the Lady's Wedding-Ring, and some broken bits of old Lockets of Gold, a Gold Watch, and a Purse with about 24 *l.* value in old pieces of Gold Coin, and several other things of Value.

THIS was the greatest and the worst Prize that ever I was concern'd in, for indeed, tho' as I have said above, I was harden'd now beyond the Power of all Reflection in other Cases, yet it really touch'd me to the very Soul, when I look'd into this Treasure, to think of the poor disconsolate Gentlewoman who had lost so much by the Fire besides; and who would think to be sure that she had sav'd her Plate and best things; how she wou'd be surpriz'd and afflicted when she should find that she had been deceiv'd, and should find that the Person that took her Children and her Goods, had not come, as was pretended, from the Gentlewoman in the next Street, but that the Children had been put upon her without her own knowledge.

I SAY I confess the inhumanity of this Action mov'd me very much, and made me relent exceedingly, and Tears stood in my Eyes upon that Subject: But with all my Sense of its being cruel and Inhuman, I cou'd never find in my Heart to make any Restitution: The Reflection wore off, and I began quickly to forget the Circumstances that attended the taking them.

NOR was this all, for tho' by this jobb I was become considerably Richer than before, yet the Resolution I had formerly taken of leaving off this horrid Trade, when I had gotten a little more, did not return; but I must still get farther, and more; and the Avarice join'd so with the Success, that I had no more thoughts of coming to a timely Alteration of Life; tho' without it I cou'd expect no Safety, no Tranquility in the Possession of what I had so wickedly gain'd; but a little more, and a little more, was the Case still.

AT length yielding to the Importunities of my Crime, I cast off all Remorse and Repentance; and all the Reflections on that Head, turn'd to no more than this, that I might perhaps come to have one Booty more that might compleat my Desires; but tho' I certainly had

8. It was customary for mourners at funerals to be given rings in memory of the deceased or for wills to include bequests to friends for the purchase of "mourning rings."

that one Booty, yet every hit look'd towards another, and was so encouraging to me to go on with the Trade, that I had no Gust to the Thought of laying it down.

IN this Condition, harden'd by Success, and resolving to go on, I fell into the Snare in which I was appointed to meet with my last Reward for this kind of Life: But even this was not yet, for I met with several successful Adventures more in this way of being undone.

I remain'd still with my Governess, who was for a while really concern'd for the Misfortune of my Comerade that had been hang'd, and who it seems knew enough of my Governess to have sent her the same way, and which made her very uneasy; indeed she was in a very great fright.

IT is true, that when she was gone, and had not open'd her Mouth to tell what she knew; My Governess was easy as to that Point, and perhaps glad she was hang'd; for it was in her power to have obtain'd a Pardon at the Expence of her Friends; But on the other Hand, the loss of her, and the Sense of her Kindness in not making her Market[9] of what she knew, mov'd my Governess to Mourn very sincerely for her: I comforted her as well as I cou'd, and she in return harden'd me to Merit more compleatly the same Fate.

HOWEVER as I have said it made me the more wary, and particularly I was very shie of Shoplifting, especially among the *Mercers*, and *Drapers* who are a Set of Fellows that have their Eyes very much about them: I made a Venture or two among the Lace Folks, and the Mileners, and particularly at one Shop, where I got Notice of two young Women who were newly set up, and had not been bred to the Trade: There, I think I carried off a Peice of Bonelace, worth six or seven pound, and a Paper of Thread; but this was but once, it was a Trick that would not serve again.

IT was always reckon'd a safe Job[1] when we heard of a new Shop, especially when the People were such as were not bred to Shops; such may depend upon it, that they will be visited once or twice at their beginning, and they must be very Sharp indeed if they can prevent it.

I MADE another Adventure or two, but they were but Trifles too, tho' sufficient to live on; after this nothing considerable offering for a good while, I began to think that I must give over the Trade in Earnest; but my Governess, who was not willing to lose me, and expected great Things of me, brought me one Day into Company with a young Woman and a Fellow that went for her Husband, tho' as it appear'd afterwards she was not his Wife, but they were Partners

9. I.e., profiting, by turning in her associates. By providing evidence leading to the conviction of two other thieves or burglars, a felon convicted of theft or burglary was entitled to receive a pardon.

1. Theft or robbery (thieves' slang); the *OED* cites this passage from *Moll Flanders* as illustration.

it seems in the Trade they carried on; and Partners in something else too. *In short*, they robb'd together, lay together, were taken together, and at last were hang'd together.

I CAME into a kind of League with these two, by the help of my Governess, and they carried me out into three or four Adventures, where I rather saw them commit some Course and unhandy Robberies, in which nothing but a great Stock of impudence on their Side, and gross Negligence on the Peoples Side who were robb'd, could have made them Successful; so I resolv'd from that time forward to be very Cautious how I Adventur'd upon any thing with them; and indeed when two or three unlucky Projects were propos'd by them, I declin'd the offer, and perswaded them against it: One time they particularly propos'd Robbing a Watchmaker of 3 Gold Watches, which they had Ey'd in the Day time, and found the Place where he laid them; one of them had so many Keys of all kinds, that he made no Question to open the Place, where the Watchmaker had laid them; and so we made a kind of an Appointment; but when I came to look narrowly into the Thing, I found they propos'd breaking open the House; and this as a thing out of my Way, I would not Embark in; so they went without me: They did get into the House by main Force, and broke up the lock'd Place where the Watches were, but found but one of the Gold Watches, and a Silver one, which they took, and got out of the House again very clear, but the Family being alarm'd cried out Thieves, and the Man was pursued and taken, the young Woman had got off too, but unhappily was stop'd at a Distance, and the Watches found upon her; and thus I had a second Escape, for they were convicted, and both hang'd, being old Offenders, tho' but young People; as I *said before*, that they robbed together, and lay together, so now they hang'd together, and there ended my new Partnership.

I BEGAN now to be very wary, having so narrowly escap'd a Scouring,[2] and having such an Example before me; but I had a new Tempter, who prompted me every Day, I mean my Governess; and now a Prize presented, which as it came by her Management, so she expected a good Share of the Booty; there was a good Quantity of Flanders-Lace Lodg'd in a private House, where she had gotten Intelligence of it; and Flanders-Lace, being then Prohibited,[3] it was a good Booty to any Custom-House Officer that could come at it: I had a full Account from my Governess, as well of the Quantity as of the very Place where it was conceal'd, and I went to a Custom-House Officer, and told him I had such a Discovery to make to him, of such

2. A beating, drubbing, or chastising.
3. Banned by several acts of Parliament since the time of Charles II, the highly prized Flanders lace continued to be widely available to English customers, despite many government seizures such as the one Moll orchestrates here.

a Quantity of Lace, if he would assure me that I should have my due Share of the Reward: This was so just an offer, that nothing could be fairer; so he agreed, and taking a Constable, and me with him, we beset the House; as I told him, I could go directly to the Place, He left it to me, and the Hole being very dark, I squeez'd myself into it with a Candle in my Hand, and so reach'd the Peices out to him, taking care as I gave him some, so to secure as much about myself as I could conveniently Dispose of: There was near 300 *l.* worth of Lace in the whole; and I secur'd about 50 *l.* worth of it to myself: The People of the House were not owners of the Lace, but a Merchant who had entrusted them with it; so that they were not so surpriz'd as I thought they would be.

I LEFT the Officer overjoy'd with his Prize, and fully satisfy'd with what he had got, and appointed to meet him at a House of his own directing, where I came after I had dispos'd of the Cargo I had about me, of which he had not the least Suspicion; when I came to him, he began to Capitulate[4] with me, believing I did not understand the right I had to a Share in the Prize, and would fain have put me off with Twenty Pound, but I let him know that I was not so ignorant as he suppos'd I was; and yet I was glad too, that he offer'd to bring me to a certainty;[5] I ask'd 100 *l.* and he rise up to 30 *l.* I fell to 80 *l.* and he rise again to 40 *l.* in a Word, he offer'd 50 *l.* and I consented, only demanding a Peice of Lace, which I thought came to about 8 or 9 Pound, as if it had been for my own Wear, and he agreed to it, so I got 50 *l.* in Money paid me that same Night, and made an End of the Bargain; nor did he ever know who I was, or where to enquire for me; so that if it had been discover'd, that part of the Goods were embezzel'd; he could have made no Challenge upon me for it.

I VERY punctually divided this Spoil with my Governess, and I pass'd with her from this time for a very dexterous Manager in the nicest Cases; I found that this last was the best, and easiest sort of Work that was in my way, and I made it my business to enquire out prohibited Goods; and after buying some usually betray'd them, but none of these Discoveries amounted to any thing Considerable; not like that I related just now; but I was willing to act safe, and was still Cautious of running the great Risques which I found others did, and in which they Miscarried every Day.

THE next thing of Moment, was an attempt at a Gentlewoman's gold Watch, it happen'd in a Crowd, at a Meeting-House,[6] where I was in very great Danger of being taken; I had full hold of her Watch, but giving a great Jostle, as if some body had thrust me against her, and in the Juncture giving the Watch a fair pull, I found it would

4. Make conditions or stipulations, bargain.
5. Definite account.
6. A nonconformist or dissenting place of worship.

not come, so I let it go that Moment, and cried out as if I had been kill'd, that some body had Trod upon my Foot, and that there was certainly *Pick-pockets* there; for some body or other had given a pull at my Watch, for you are to observe, that on these Adventures we always went very well Dress'd, and I had very good Cloaths on, and a Gold Watch by my Side, as like a Lady as other Folks.

I HAD no sooner said so, but the tother Gentlewoman cried out *a Pick-pocket* too, for some body, *she said*, had try'd to pull her Watch away.

WHEN I touch'd her Watch, I was close to her, but when I cry'd out, I stop'd as it were short, and the Crowd bearing her forward a little, she made a Noise too, but it was at some Distance from me, so that she did not in the least suspect me; but when she cried out *a Pick-pocket*, some body cried Ay, and here has been another, this Gentlewoman has been attempted too.

AT that very instant, a little farther in the Crowd, and very Luckily too, they cried out *a Pick-pocket* again, and really seiz'd a young Fellow in the very Fact. This, tho' unhappy for the Wretch was very opportunely for my Case, tho' I had carried it off handsomely enough before, but now it was out of Doubt, and all the loose part of the Crowd run that way, and the poor Boy was deliver'd up to the Rage of the Street,[7] which is a Cruelty I need not describe, and which however they are always glad of, rather than to be sent to *Newgate*, where they lie often a long time, till they are almost perish'd, and sometimes they are hang'd, and the best they can look for, if they are Convicted, is to be Transported.

THIS was a narrow Escape to me, and I was so frighted, that I ventur'd no more at Gold Watches a great while; there was indeed a great many concurring Circumstances in this Adventure, which assisted to my Escape; but the chief was, that the Woman whose Watch I had pull'd at was a Fool; that is to say, she was Ignorant of the nature of the Attempt, which one would have thought she should not have been, seeing She was wise enough to fasten her Watch, so, that it could not be slipt up; but she was in such a Fright, that she had no thought about her proper for the Discovery; for she, when she felt the pull scream'd out, and push'd herself forward, and put all the People about her into disorder, but said not a Word of her Watch, or of a *Pick-pocket*, for at least two Minutes time; which was time enough for me, and to spare; for as I had cried out behind her, *as I have said*, and bore myself back in the Crowd as she bore forward; there were several People, at least seven or eight, the Throng being

7. Before he understood that he could be hanged for "picking Pockets," the young Colonel Jack believed that "if we were catch'd, we run the Risque of being Duck'd or Pump'd, which we call'd Soaking, and then all was over. . . ." This kind of rough street justice, though sometimes fatal, was preferable (as Moll suggests) to the certainty of execution or transportation.

still moving on, that were got between me and her in that time, and then I crying out *a Pick-pocket*, rather sooner than she, or at least as soon, she might as well be the Person suspected as I, and the People were confus'd in their Enquiry; whereas, had she with a Presence of Mind needful on such an Occasion, as soon as she felt the pull, not skream'd out as she did, but turn'd immediately round, and seiz'd the next Body that was behind her, she had infallibly taken me.

THIS is a Direction not of the kindest Sort to the Fraternity; but 'tis certainly a Key to the Clue[8] of a *Pick-pockets* Motions, and whoever can follow it, will as certainly catch the Thief as he will be sure to miss if he does not.

I HAD another Adventure, which puts this Matter out of doubt, and which may be an Instruction for Posterity in the Case of *a Pick-pocket*, my good old Governess to give a short touch at her History, tho' she had left off the Trade, was as I may say, born *a Pick-pocket*, and as I understood afterward had run thro' all the several Degrees of that Art, and yet had never been taken but once; when she was so grossly detected, that she was convicted and ordered to be Transported; but being a Woman of a rare Tongue, and withal having Money in her Pocket; she found Means, the Ship putting into *Ireland* for Provisions, to get on Shore there, where she liv'd and practis'd her old Trade for some Years; when falling into another sort of bad Company, she turn'd Midwife and Procuress, and play'd a Hundred Pranks there, which she gave me a little History of in Confidence between us as we grew more intimate; and it was to this wicked Creature that I ow'd all the Art and Dexterity I arriv'd to, in which there were few that ever went beyond me, or that practis'd so long without any Misfortune.

IT was after those Adventures in *Ireland*, and when she was pretty well known in that Country, that she left *Dublin*, and came over to *England*, where the time of her Transportation being not expir'd, she left her former Trade, for fear of falling into bad Hands again, for then she was sure to have gone to Wreck: Here she set up the same Trade she had followed in *Ireland*, in which she soon by her admirable Management, and a good Tongue, arriv'd to the Height, which I have already describ'd, and indeed began to be Rich tho' her Trade fell off again afterwards; as I have hinted before.

I mention thus much of the History of this Woman here, the better to account for the concern she had in the wicked Life I was now leading; into all the particulars of which she led me as it were by the Hand, and gave me such Directions, and I so well follow'd them, that I grew the greatest Artist of my time, and work'd myself out of

8. Literally, a ball of yarn or thread, employed to guide or "thread" one's way into or out of a labyrinth or maze.

every Danger with such Dexterity, that when several more of my Comrades run themselves into *Newgate* presently, and by that time they had been Half a Year at the Trade, I had now Practis'd upwards of five Year, and the People at *Newgate*, did not so much as know me; they had heard much of me indeed, and often expected me there; but I always got off, tho' many times in the extreamest Danger.

ONE of the greatest Dangers I was now in, was that I was too well known among the Trade, and some of them whose hatred was owing rather to Envy, than any Injury I had done them began to be Angry, that I should always Escape when they were always catch'd and hurried to *Newgate*. These were they that gave me the Name of *Moll Flanders*: For it was no more of Affinity with my real Name, or with any of the Names I had ever gone by, than black is of Kin to white, except that once, as before I call'd my self Mrs. *Flanders*, when I sheltered myself in the *Mint*; but that these Rogues never knew, nor could I ever learn how they came to give me the Name, or what the Occasion of it was.

I WAS soon inform'd that some of these who were gotten fast into *Newgate*, had vowed to Impeach[9] me; and as I knew that two or three of them were but too able to do it, I was under a great concern about it, and kept within Doors for a good while; but my Governess who I always made Partner in my Success, and who now plaid a sure Game with me, for that she had a Share of the Gain, and no Share in the hazard, *I say*, my Governess was something impatient of my leading such a useless unprofitable Life, as she call'd it ; and she laid a new Contrivance for my going Abroad, and this was to Dress me up in Mens Cloths, and so put me into a new kind of Practise.

I WAS Tall and Personable, but a little too smooth Fac'd for a Man; however as I seldom went Abroad, but in the Night, it did well enough; but it was a long time before I could behave in my new Cloths: I mean, as to my Craft; it was impossible to be so Nimble, so Ready, so Dexterous at these things, in a Dress so contrary to Nature; and as I did every thing Clumsily, so I had neither the success, or the easiness of Escape that I had before, and I resolv'd to leave it off; but that Resolution was confirm'd soon after by the following Accident.

As my Governess had disguis'd me like a Man, so she joyn'd me with a Man, a young Fellow that was Nimble enough at his Business, and for about three Weeks we did very well together. Our principal Trade was watching Shop-Keepers Compters,[1] and Slipping off any kind of Goods we could see carelesly laid any where, and we made several very good Bargains as we call'd them at this Work: And as we kept always together, so we grew very intimate, yet he never knew

9. Give accusatory evidence against.
1. Counters.

that I was not a Man; nay, tho' I several times went home with him to his Lodgings, according as our business directed, and four or five times lay with him all Night: But our Design lay another way, and it was absolutely necessary to me to conceal my Sex from him, as appear'd afterwards: The Circumstances of our Living, coming in late, and having such and such Business to do as requir'd that no Body should be trusted with coming into our Lodgings, were such as made it impossible to me to refuse lying with him, unless I would have own'd my Sex, and as it was I effectually conceal'd my self.

BUT his ill, and my good Fortune, soon put an end to this Life, which I must own I was sick of too, on several other Accounts: We had made several Prizes in this new way of Business, but the last would have been extraordinary; there was a Shop in a certain Street which had a Warehouse behind it that look'd into another Street, the House making the corner of the turning.

THROUGH the Window of the Warehouse we saw lying on the Counter or Show-board which was just before it, Five pieces of Silks, besides other Stuffs; and tho' it was almost dark, yet the People being busie in the fore shop with Customers, had not had time to shut up those Windows, or else had forgot it.

THIS the young Fellow was so overjoy'd with, that he could not restrain himself, it lay all within his reach he said, and he swore violently to me that he would have it, if he broke down the House for it; I disswaded him a little, but saw there was no remedy, so he run rashly upon it, slipt out a Square out of the Sash Window dexterously enough, and without noise, and got out four pieces of the Silks, and came with them towards me, but was immediately pursued with a terrible Clutter and Noise; we were standing together indeed, but I had not taken any of the Goods out of his Hand, when I said to him hastily, you are undone, fly for God sake; he run like Lightning, and I too, but the pursuit was hotter after him because he had the Goods, than after me; he dropt two of the Pieces which stop'd them a little, but the Crowd encreas'd and pursued us both; they took him soon after with the other two pieces upon him, and then the rest followed me; I run for it and got into my Governesses House, whither some quick-eyed People follow'd me so warmly as to fix me there; they did not immediately knock at the Door, by which I got time to throw off my Disguise, and dress me in my own Cloths; besides, when they came there, my Governess, who had her Tale ready, kept her Door shut, and call'd out to them and told there was no Man came in there; the People affirm'd there did a Man come in there, and swore they would break open the Door.

MY Governess, not at all surpriz'd, spoke calmly to them, told them they should very freely come and search her House, if they would bring a Constable, and let in none but such as the Constable would admit, for it was unreasonable to let in a whole Crowd; this they could not refuse, tho' they were a Crowd; so a Constable was fetch'd immediately, and she very freely open'd the Door, the Constable kept the Door, and the Men he appointed search'd the House, my Governess going with them from Room to Room; when she came to my Room she call'd to me, and said aloud; Cousin, pray open the Door, here's some Gentlemen that must come and look into your Room.

I HAD a little Girl with me, which was my Governesses Grand-child, as she call'd her; and I bad her open the Door, and there sat I at work with a great litter of things about me, as if I had been at Work all Day, being my self quite undress'd, with only Night-cloaths on my Head, and a loose Morning Gown wrapt about me: My Governess made a kind of excuse for their disturbing me, telling me partly the occasion of it, and that she had no Remedy but to open the Doors to them, and let them satisfie themselves, for all she could say to them would not satisfie them: I sat still, and bid them search the Room if they pleas'd, for if there was any Body in the House, I was sure they was not in my Room; and as for the rest of the House I had nothing to say to that, I did not understand what they look'd for.

EVERY thing look'd so innocent and so honest about me, that they treated me civiller than I expected, but it was not till they had search'd the Room to a nicety, even under the Bed, in the Bed, and every where else, where it was possible any thing cou'd be hid; when they had done this, and cou'd find nothing, they ask'd my Pardon for troubling me, and went down.

WHEN they had thus searched the House from Bottom to Top, and then from Top to Bottom, and cou'd find nothing, they appeas'd the Mob pretty well; but they carried my Governess before the Justice: Two Men swore that they see the Man, who they pursued, go into her House: My Governess rattled and made a great noise that her House should be insulted, and that she should be used thus for nothing; that if a Man did come in, he might go out again presently for ought she knew, for she was ready to make Oath that no Man had been within her Doors all that Day as she knew of, and that was very true indeed; that it might be indeed that as she was above Stairs, any Fellow in a Fright might find the Door open, and run in for shelter when he was pursued, but that she knew nothing of it; and if it had been so, he certainly went out again, perhaps at the other Door, for she had another Door into an Alley, and so had made his escape and cheated them all.

THIS was indeed probable enough, and the Justice satisfied himself with giving her an Oath, that she had not receiv'd or admitted any

Man into her House to conceal him, or protect or hide him from Justice: This Oath she might justly take, and did so, and so she was dismiss'd.

IT is easie to judge what a fright I was in upon this occasion, and it was impossible for my Governess ever to bring me to Dress in that Disguise again; for, as I told her, I should certainly betray my self.

MY poor Partner in this Mischief was now in a bad Case, for he was carried away before my Lord Mayor, and by his Worship committed to *Newgate*, and the People that took him were so willing, as well as able, to Prosecute him, that they offer'd themselves to enter into Recognisances[2] to appear at the Sessions, and persue the Charge against him.

HOWEVER, he got his Indictment deferr'd, upon promise to discover his Accomplices, and particularly, the Man that was concern'd with him in this Robbery, and he fail'd not to do his endeavour, for he gave in my Name who he call'd *Gabriel Spencer*,[3] which was the Name I went by to him, and here appear'd the Wisdom of my concealing my Name and Sex from him, which if he had ever known I had been undone.

HE did all he cou'd to discover this *Gabriel Spencer*; he describ'd me, he discover'd the place where he said I Lodg'd, and in a word, all the Particulars that he cou'd of my Dwelling; but having conceal'd the main Circumstances of my Sex from him, I had a vast Advantage, and he never cou'd hear of me; he brought two or three Families into Trouble by his endeavouring to find me out, but they knew nothing of me, any more than that I had a Fellow with me[4] that they had seen, but knew nothing of; and as for my Governess, tho' she was the means of his coming to me, yet it was done at second hand, and he knew nothing of her.

THIS turn'd to his Disadvantage, for having promis'd Discoveries, but not being able to make it good, it was look'd upon as a trifling with the Justice of the City, and he was the more fiercely persued by the Shopkeepers who took him.

I WAS however terribly uneasie all this while, and that I might be quite out of the way, I went away from my Governesses for a while; but not knowing whither to wander, I took a Maid Servant with me, and took the Stage Coach to *Dunstable* to my old Landlord and Landlady, where I had liv'd so handsomly with my *Lancashire* Husband: Here I told her a formal Story, that I expected my Husband every

2. A bond or obligation entered into before a court or magistrate, engaging to appear at the trial when called upon; a sum of money pledged as a surety for such performance and rendered forfeit by neglect of it.
3. As previous editors have noted, the celebrated playwright Ben Jonson (1572–1637) had killed a fellow actor by that name in a duel in 1598; it is not clear whether Moll's alias is coincidence or allusion.
4. Changed to "he had a Fellow with him" in the second edition.

Day from *Ireland*, and that I had sent a Letter to him that I would meet him at *Dunstable* at her House, and that he would certainly Land, if the Wind was fair, in a few Days, so that I was come to spend a few Days with them till he should come, for he would either come Post,[5] or in the *West-Chester* Coach, I knew not which, but which soever it was, he would be sure to come to that House to meet me.

My Landlady was mighty glad to see me, and My Landlord made such a stir with me, that if I had been a Princess I cou'd not have been better used, and here I might have been welcome a Month or two if I had thought fit.

But my Business was of another Nature, I was very uneasie (tho' so well Disguis'd that it was scarce possible to Detect me) least this Fellow should some how or other find me out; and tho' he cou'd not charge me with this Robbery, having perswaded him not to venture, and having also done nothing in it my self but run away, yet he might have charg'd me with other things, and have bought his own Life at the Expence of mine.

This fill'd me with horrible Apprehensions: I had no Recourse, no Friend, no Confident but my old Governess, and I knew no Remedy but to put my Life in her Hands, and so I did, for I let her know where to send to me, and had several Letters from her while I stayed here, some of them almost scar'd me out of my Wits; but at last she sent me the joyful News that he was hang'd, which was the best News to me that I had heard a great while.

I Had stay'd here five Weeks, and liv'd very comfortably indeed, (the secret Anxiety of my Mind excepted) but when I receiv'd this Letter I look'd pleasantly again, and told my Landlady that I had receiv'd a Letter from my Spouse in *Ireland*, that I had the good News of his being very well, but had the bad News that his business would not permit him to come away so soon as he expected, and so I was like to go back again without him.

My Landlady complemented[6] me upon the good News however, that I had heard he was well, for I have observ'd, Madam, *says she*, you han't been so pleasant as you us'd to be; you have been over Head and Ears in Care for him, I dare say, *says the good Woman*; 'tis easie to be seen there's an alteration in you for the better, *says she*: Well, I am sorry the Esquire can't come yet, *says my Landlord*, I should have been heartily glad to have seen him, but I hope, when you have certain News of his coming, you'll take a step hither again, Madam; *says he*, you shall be very welcome whenever you please to come.

5. I.e., Ride swiftly on horseback, by the method of hiring horses from men stationed at suitable distances along the post-road.
6. Complimented.

WITH all these fine Complements we parted, and I came merry enough to *London*, and found my Governess as well pleas'd as I was; and now she told me she would never recommend any Partner to me again, for she always found, *she said*, that I had the best luck when I ventur'd by my self; and so indeed I had, for I was seldom in any Danger when I was by my self, or if I was, I got out of it with more Dexterity than when I was entangled with the dull Measures of other People, who had perhaps less forecast, and were more rash and impatient than I; for tho' I had as much Courage to venture as any of them, yet I used more caution before I undertook a thing, and had more Presence of Mind when I was to bring my self off.

I HAVE often wondered even at my own hardiness another way, that when all my Companions were surpriz'd, and fell so suddainly into the Hand of Justice, and that I so narrowly escap'd, yet I could not all that while enter into one serious Resolution to leave off this Trade; and especially Considering that I was now very far from being poor, that the Temptation of Necessity, which is generally the Introduction of all such Wickedness was now remov'd; for I had near 500 *l.* by me in ready Money, on which I might have liv'd very well, if I had thought fit to have retir'd; but *I say*, I had not so much as the least inclination to leave off; no not so much as I had before when I had but 200 *l.* before-hand, and when I had no such frightful Examples before my Eyes as these were; From hence 'tis Evident to me, that when once we are harden'd in Crime, no Fear can affect us, no Example give us any warning.

I HAD indeed one Comrade, whose Fate went very near me for a good while, tho' I wore it off too in time, that Case was indeed very unhappy; I had made a Prize of a Piece of very good Damask in a *Mercers* Shop, and went clear off[7] myself; but had convey'd the Peice to this Companion of mine, when we went out of the Shop; and she went one way, and I went another: We had not been long out of the Shop, but the *Mercer* mist his Peice of Stuff, and sent his Messengers, one, one way, and one another, and they presently seiz'd her that had the Peice, with the Damask upon her, as for me, I had very Luckily step'd into a House where there was a Lace Chamber, up one Pair of Stairs, and had the Satisfaction, or the Terror indeed of looking out of the Window upon the Noise they made, and seeing the poor Creature drag'd away in Triumph to the Justice, who immediately committed her to *Newgate*.

I WAS careful to attempt nothing in the Lace-Chamber, but tumbl'd their Goods pretty much to spend time; then bought a few Yards of Edging, and paid for it, and came away very sad Hearted

7. Got away completely, without carrying the piece of damask on her. *Very near me*: Closely touched or affected me.

indeed; for the poor Woman, who was in Tribulation for what I only had stolen.

HERE again my old Caution stood me in good stead; Namely, that tho' I often robb'd with these People, yet I never let them know who I was, or where I Lodg'd; nor could they ever find out my Lodging, tho' they often endeavour'd to Watch me to it. They all knew me by the Name of *Moll Flanders*, tho' even some of them rather believ'd I was she, than knew me to be so; my Name was publick among them indeed; but how to find me out they knew not, nor so much as how to guess at my Quarters, whether they were at the East-End of the Town, or the West; and this wariness was my safety upon all these Occasions.

I KEPT close a great while upon the Occasion of this Womans disaster; I knew that if I should do any thing that should Miscarry, and should be carried to Prison she would be there, and ready to Witness against me, and perhaps save her Life at my Expence; I consider'd that I began to be very well known by Name at the *Old Baily*, tho' they did not know my Face; and that if I should fall into their Hands, I should be treated as an old Offender; and for this Reason, I was resolv'd to see what this poor Creatures Fate should be before I stirr'd Abroad, tho' several times in her Distress I convey'd Money to her for her Relief.

AT length she came to her Tryal, she pleaded she did not steal the Things; but that one Mrs. *Flanders*, as she heard her call'd, (for she did not know her) gave the Bundle to her after they came out of the Shop, and bad her carry it Home to her Lodging. They ask'd her where this Mrs. *Flanders* was? but she could not produce her, neither could she give the least Account of me; and the *Mercers* Men swearing positively that she was in the Shop when the Goods were stolen; that they immediately miss'd them, and pursu'd her, and found them upon her; Thereupon the Jury brought her in Guilty; but the Court considering that she really was not the Person that stole the Goods, an inferiour Assistant, and that it was very possible she could not find out this Mrs. *Flanders, meaning me*, tho' it would save her Life, which indeed was true; I say considering all this, they allow'd her to be Transported, which was the utmost Favour she could obtain, only that the Court told her, that if she could in the mean time produce the said Mrs. *Flanders*, they would intercede for her Pardon, that is to say, if she could find me out, and hang me, she should not be Transported: This I took care to make impossible to her, and so she was Shipp'd off in pursuance of her Sentence a little while after.

I MUST repeat it again, that the Fate of this poor Woman troubl'd me exceedingly; and I began to be very pensive, knowing that I was really the Instrument of her disaster; but the Preservation of my own

Life, which was so evidently in Danger, took off all my tenderness; and seeing she was not put to Death, I was very easie at her Transportation, because she was then out of the way of doing me any Mischief whatever should happen.

THE Disaster of this Woman was some Months before that of the last recited Story, and was indeed partly the Occasion of my Governess proposing to Dress me up in Mens Cloths, that I might go about unobserv'd, as indeed I did; but I was soon tir'd of that Disguise, as *I have said*, for indeed it expos'd me to too many Difficulties.

I WAS now easie, as to all Fear of Witnesses against me, for all those, that had either been concern'd with me, or that knew me by the Name of *Moll Flanders*, were either hang'd or Transported; and if I should have had the Misfortune to be taken, I might call myself any thing else, as well as *Moll Flanders*, and no old Sins could be plac'd to my Account; so I began to run a Tick[8] again, with the more freedom, and several successful Adventures I made, tho' not such as I had made before.

WE had at that time another Fire happen'd not a great way off from the Place where my Governess liv'd, and I made an attempt there, as before, but as I was not soon enough before the Crowd of People came in, and could not get to the House I aim'd at, instead of a Prize, I got a mischief, which had almost put a Period to my Life, and all my wicked doings together; for the Fire being very furious, and the People in a great Fright in removing their Goods, and throwing them out of Window; a Wench from out of a Window threw a Featherbed just upon me; it is true, the Bed being soft it broke no Bones; but as the weight was great, and made greater by the Fall, it beat me down, and laid me dead for a while; nor did the People concern themselves much to deliver me from it, or to recover me at all; but I lay like one Dead and neglected a good while; till some body going to remove the Bed out of the way, helped me up; it was indeed a wonder the People in the House had not thrown other Goods out after it, and which might have fallen upon it, and then I had been inevitably kill'd; but I was reserved for further Afflictions.

THIS Accident however spoil'd my Market for that time, and I came Home to my Governess very much hurt, and Bruised, and Frighted to the last degree, and it was a good while before she could set me upon my Feet again.

IT was now a Merry time of the Year, and *Bartholomew* Fair[9] was

8. A debit account (i.e., Moll began to run a fresh tab or ledger keeping score of her new crimes).
9. Held annually since the twelfth century at West Smithfield, the oldest and best-known English fair began on August 24 (St. Bartholomew's Day) and ran for two weeks; by Defoe's time, it was widely deplored as a scene of dissipation and debauchery. The "common Part of the Fair" likely refers to the trading of cattle and other "market" activities for which the fair was presumably held.

begun; I had never made any Walks that Way, nor was the common Part of the Fair of much Advantage to me; but I took a turn this Year into the Cloisters, and among the rest, I fell into one of the Raffling Shops:[1] It was a thing of no great Consequence to me, nor did I expect to make much of it; but there came a Gentleman extreamly well Dress'd, and very Rich, and as 'tis frequent to talk to every Body in those Shops he singl'd me out, and was very particular with me; first he told me he would put in for me to Raffle, and did so; and some small matter coming to his Lot, he presented it to me; I think it was a Feather Muff: Then he continu'd to keep talking to me with a more than common Appearance of Respect; but still very civil and much like a Gentleman.

HE held me in talk so long till at last he drew me out of the Raffling Place to the Shop-Door, and then to take a walk in the Cloister, still talking of a Thousand things Cursorily without any thing to the purpose; at last he told me that without Complement he was charm'd with my Company, and ask'd me if I durst trust myself in a Coach with him; he told me he was a Man of Honour, and would not offer any thing to me unbecoming him as such: I seem'd to decline it a while, but suffer'd myself to be importun'd a little, and then yielded.

I WAS at a loss in my Thoughts to conclude at first what this Gentleman design'd; but I found afterward he had had some drink in his Head; and that he was not very unwilling to have some more: He carried me in the Coach to the *Spring-Garden*, at *Knight's-Bridge*,[2] where we walk'd in the Gardens, and he Treated me very handsomely; but I found he drank very freely, he press'd me also to drink, but I declin'd it.

HITHERTO he kept his Word with me, and offer'd me nothing amiss; we came away in the Coach again, and he brought me into the Streets and by this time it was near Ten a-Clock at Night, and he stop'd the Coach at a House, where it seems he was acquainted, and where they made no scruple to show us up Stairs into a Room with a Bed in it; at first I seem'd to be unwilling to go up, but after a few Words, I yielded to that too, being indeed willing to see the End of it, and in Hopes to make something of it at last; as for the Bed, &c. I was not much concern'd about that Part.

HERE he began to be a little freer with me than he had promis'd; and I by little and little yielded to every thing, so that in a Word, he did what he pleas'd with me; I need say no more; all this while he

1. Houses or booths featuring games of chance such as "raffle," a game played with three dice, in which the winner was the player who threw the three all alike or, if no triplet occurred, the highest pair. *Cloisters*: Covered walks or arcades, commonly associated with lewd behavior.
2. Unlike the fashionable, upscale pleasure-gardens in Hyde Park and at Vauxhall, that located in Knightsbridge had an unsavory reputation, especially as a place for hiring prostitutes.

drank freely too, and about One in the Morning we went into the Coach again; the Air, and the shaking of the Coach made the Drink he had get more up in his Head than it was before, and he grew uneasy in the Coach, and was for acting over again, what he had been doing before; but as I thought my Game now secure, I resisted him, and brought him to be a little still, which had not lasted five Minutes, but he fell fast asleep.

I TOOK this opportunity to search him to a Nicety; I took a gold Watch, with a silk Purse of Gold, his fine full bottom Perrewig, and silver fring'd Gloves, his Sword, and fine Snuff-box, and gently opening the Coach-door, stood ready to jump out while the Coach was going on; but the Coach stopping in the narrow Street beyond *Temple-Bar* to let another Coach pass, I got softly out, fasten'd the Door again, and gave my Gentleman and the Coach the slip both together, and never heard more of them.[3]

THIS was an Adventure indeed unlook'd for, and perfectly undesign'd by me; tho' I was not so past the Merry part of Life, as to forget how to behave, when a Fop so blinded by his Appetite should not know an old Woman from a young: I did not indeed look so old as I was by ten or twelve Year; yet I was not a young Wench of Seventeen, and it was easie enough to be distinguish'd: There is nothing so absurd, so surfeiting, so ridiculous as a Man heated by Wine in his Head, and a wicked Gust in his Inclination together; he is in the possession of two Devils at once, and can no more govern himself by his Reason than a Mill can Grind without Water; His Vice tramples upon all that was in him that had any good in it, if any such thing there was; nay, his very Sense is blinded by its own Rage, and he acts Absurdities even in his View; such is Drinking more, when he is Drunk already; picking up a common Woman, without regard to what she is, or who she is; whether Sound or rotten,[4] Clean or Unclean; whether Ugly or Handsome, whether Old or Young, and so blinded, as not really to distinguish; such a Man is worse than Lunatick; prompted by his vicious corrupted Head he no more knows what he is doing, than this Wretch of mine knew when I pick'd his Pocket of his Watch and his Purse of Gold.

THESE are the Men of whom *Solomon says, they go like an Ox to the slaughter, till a Dart strikes through their Liver*;[5] an admirable Description, *by the way*, of the foul Disease, which is a poisonous deadly Contagion mingling with the Blood, whose Center or Fountain is in the Liver; from whence, by the swift Circulation of the

3. This clause was deleted in the second edition, since Moll does indeed hear more of her gentleman in the ensuing narrative. *Temple-Bar*: The name of the barrier or gateway (removed in 1878) closing the entrance into the City of London from the Strand. The gate Moll would have passed had been designed by Sir Christopher Wren.
4. Infected or "rotten" with venereal disease.
5. See Proverbs 7:22–23.

whole Mass, that dreadful nauceous Plague strikes immediately thro' his Liver, and his Spirits are infected, his Vitals stab'd thro' as with a Dart.

IT is true this poor unguarded Wretch was in no Danger from me, tho' I was greatly apprehensive at first, of what Danger I might be in from him; but he was really to be pityed in one respect, that he seem'd to be a good sort of a Man in himself; a Gentleman that had no harm in his Design; a Man of Sense, and of a fine Behaviour; a comely handsome Person, a sober solid Countenance, a charming beautiful Face, and every thing that cou'd be agreeable; only had unhappily had some Drink the Night before, had not been in Bed, as he told me when we were together, was hot, and his Blood fir'd with Wine, and in that Condition his Reason *as it were* asleep, had given him up.

As for me, my Business was his Money, and what I could make of him, and after that if I could have found out any way to have done it, I would have sent him safe home to his House, and to his Family, for 'twas ten to one but he had an honest virtuous Wife, and innocent Children, that were anxious for his Safety, and would have been glad to have gotten him Home, and have taken care of him, till he was restor'd to himself; and then with what Shame and Regret would he look back upon himself? how would he reproach himself with associating himself with a Whore? pick'd up in the worst of all Holes, the Cloister, among the Dirt and Filth of all the Town? how would he be trembling for fear he had got the Pox,[6] for fear a Dart had struck through his Liver, and hate himself every time he look'd back upon the Madness and Brutality of his Debauch? how would he, if he had any Principles of Honour, as I verily believe he had, I say how would he abhor the Thought of giving any ill Distemper, if he had it, as for ought he knew he might, to his Modest and Virtuous Wife, and thereby sowing the Contagion in the Life-blood of his Posterity?

WOULD such Gentlemen but consider the contemptible Thoughts which the very Women they are concern'd with, in such Cases as these, have of them, it wou'd be a surfeit to them: As I said above, they value not the Pleasure, they are rais'd by no Inclination to the Man, the passive Jade thinks of no Pleasure but the Money; and when he is as it were drunk in the Extasies of his wicked Pleasure, her Hands are in his Pockets searching for what she can find there; and of which he can no more be sensible in the Moment of his Folly, than he can fore-think of it when he goes about it.

I KNEW a Woman that was so dexterous with a Fellow, who indeed deserv'd no better usage, that while he was busie with her another

6. Syphilis. This is "the foul Disease" Moll refers to above.

way, convey'd his Purse with twenty Guineas in it out of his Fob Pocket, where he had put it for fear of her, and put another Purse with guilded Counters[7] in it into the room of it: After he had done, he says to her, now han't you pick'd my Pocket? she jested with him, and told him she suppos'd he had not much to loose; he put his Hand to his Fob, and with his Fingers felt that his Purse was there, which fully satisfy'd him, and so she brought off his Money; and this was a Trade with her, she kept a sham Gold Watch, that is a Watch of Silver Guilt, and a purse of Counters in her Pocket to be ready on all such Occasions; and I doubt not practis'd it with Success.

I CAME home with this last Booty to my Governess, and really when I told her the Story it so affected her, that she was hardly able to forbear Tears, to think how such a Gentleman run a daily Risque of being undone, every time a Glass of Wine got into his Head.

BUT as to the Purchase I got, and how entirely I stript him, she told me it pleas'd her wonderfully; nay, Child, *says she*, the usage may, for ought I know, do more to reform him, than all the Sermons that ever he will hear in his Life, and if the remainder of the Story be true, so it did.

I FOUND the next Day she was wonderful inquisitive about this Gentleman; the description I had given her of him, his Dress, his Person, his Face, every thing concur'd to make her think of a Gentleman whose Character she knew, and Family too; she mus'd a while, and I going still on with the Particulars, she starts up, *says she*, I'll lay a Hundred Pound I know the Gentleman.

I AM sorry you do, *says I*, for I would not have him expos'd on any account in the World; he has had Injury enough already by me, and I would not be instrumental to do him any more: No, no *says she*, I will do him no Injury, I assure you, but you may let me satisfie my Curiosity a little, for if it is he, I warrant you I find it out: I was a little startled at that, and told her with an apparent concern in my Face, that by the same Rule he might find me out, and then I was undone: *she return'd warmly*, why, do you think I will betray you, Child? No, no, *says she*, not for all he is worth in the World; I have kept your Counsel in worse things than these, sure you may trust me in this: So I said no more at that time.

SHE laid her Scheme another way, and without acquainting me of it, but she was resolv'd to find it out, if possible; so she goes to a certain Friend of hers who was acquainted in the Family, that *she* guess'd at, and told her Friend she had some extraordinary business with such a Gentleman (who by the way was no less than a Baronet, and of a very good Family) and that she knew not how to come at him without somebody to introduce her: Her Friend promis'd her

7. Imitation coins or tokens. *Fob Pocket*: A small pocket in waistband of trousers to store watches, money, or other valuable items.

very readily to do it, and accordingly goes to the House to see if the Gentleman was in Town.

THE next Day she comes to my Governess and tells her, that Sir—— was at Home, but that he had met with a Disaster and was very ill, and there was no speaking with him; what Disaster, *says my Governess hastily*, as if she was surpriz'd at it? Why, *says her Friend*, he had been at *Hampstead*[8] to Visit a Gentleman of his Acquaintance, and as he came back again he was set upon and Robb'd; and having got a little Drink too, as they suppose, the Rogues abus'd him, and he is very ill: Robb'd, *says my Governess*, and what did they take from him; why, *says her Friend*, they took his Gold Watch, and his Gold Snuff-box, his fine Perriwig, and what Money he had in his Pocket, which was considerable to be sure, for Sir——— never goes without a Purse of Guineas about him.

PSHAW! says my old Governess jeering, I warrant you he has got drunk now and got a Whore, and she has pick'd his Pocket, and so he comes home to his Wife and tells her he has been Robb'd; that's an old sham, a thousand such tricks are put upon the poor Women every Day.

FYE, *says her Friend*, I find you don't know Sir———, why he is as Civil a Gentleman, there is not a finer Man, nor a soberer grave modester Person in the whole City; he abhors such things, there's no Body that knows him will think such a thing of him: Well, well, *says my Governess*, that's none of my Business, if it was, I warrant I should find there was something of that kind in it; your Modest Men in common Opinion are sometimes no better than other People, only they keep a better Character, or if you please, are the better Hypocrites.

NO, no, *says her Friend*, I can assure you Sir——— is no Hypocrite, he is really an honest sober Gentleman, and he has certainly been Robb'd: Nay, *says my Governess*, it may be he has, it is no Business of mine I tell you; I only want to speak with him, my Business is of another Nature; but, *says her Friend*, let your Business be of what nature it will, you cannot see him yet, for he is not fit to be seen, for he is very ill, and bruis'd very much: Ay, *says my Governess*, nay then he has fallen into bad Hands to be sure; and then she ask'd gravely, pray where is he bruised? Why in his Head, *says her Friend*, and one of his Hands, and his Face, for they us'd him barbarously. Poor Gentleman, *says my Governess*, I must wait then till he recovers, and adds, I hope it will not be long, for I want very much to speak with him.

AWAY she comes to me and tells me this Story, I have found out your fine Gentleman, and a fine Gentleman he was, *says she*, but Mercy on him, he is in a sad pickle now, I wonder what the D——l

8. Situated a few miles northwest of the City of London and famous for its wells and walks, Hampstead was at that time a fashionable retreat and resort for well-to-do Londoners.

you have done to him; why you have almost kill'd him: I look'd at her with disorder enough; I kill'd him! *says I*, you must mistake the Person, I am sure I did nothing to him, he was very well when I left him, *said I*, only drunk and fast asleep; I know nothing of that, *says she*, but he is in a sad pickle now, and so she told me all that her Friend had said to her: Well then, *says I*, he fell into bad Hands after I left him, for I am sure I left him safe enough.

ABOUT ten Days after, or a little more, my Governess goes again to her Friend, to introduce her to this Gentleman; she had enquir'd other ways in the mean time, and found that he was about again, if not abroad again, so she got leave to speak with him.

SHE was a Woman of an admirable Address, and wanted no Body to introduce her; she told her Tale much better than I shall be able to tell it for her, for she was a Mistress of her Tongue, as I have said already: She told him that she came, tho' a Stranger, with a single design of doing him a Service, and he should find she had no other End in it; that as she came purely on so Friendly an account, she beg'd a promise from him, that if he did not accept what she should officiously propose, he would not take ill, that she meddl'd with what was not her Business; she assur'd him that as what she had to say was a Secret that belong'd to him only, so whether he accepted her offer or not, it should remain a Secret to all the World, unless he expos'd it himself; nor should his refusing her Service in it, make her so little show her Respect, as to do him the least Injury, so that he should be entirely at liberty to act as he thought fit.

HE look'd very shy at first, and said he knew nothing that related to him that requir'd much secresie; that he had never done any Man any wrong, and car'd not what any Body might say of him; that it was no part of his Character to be unjust to any Body, nor could he imagine in what any Man cou'd render him any Service; but that if it was so disinterested a Service as she said, he could not take it ill from any one that they should endeavour to serve him; and so, as it were, left her at liberty either to tell him, or not to tell him, as she thought fit.

SHE found him so perfectly indifferent, that she was almost afraid to enter into the point with him; but however, after some other Circumlocutions, she told him, that by a strange and unaccountable Accident she came to have a particular knowledge of the late unhappy Adventure he had fallen into; and that in such a manner, that there was no Body in the World but herself and him that were acquainted with it, no not the very Person that was with him.

HE look'd a little angrily at first, what Adventure? *said he*; why, Sir, *said she*, of your being Robb'd coming from *Knightsbr——*, *Hampstead*, Sir, I should say, *says she*; be not surpris'd, Sir, *says she*, that I am able to tell you every step you took that Day from the

Cloyster in *Smithfield*, to the *Spring-Garden* at *Knightsbridge*, and thence to the ——— in the *Strand*, and how you were left asleep in the Coach afterwards; I say let not this surprize you, for Sir I do not come to make a Booty of you, I ask nothing of you, and I assure you the Woman that was with you knows nothing who you are, and never shall; and yet perhaps I may serve you farther still, for I did not come barely to let you know, that I was inform'd, of these things, as if I wanted a Bribe to conceal them; assure your self, Sir, *said she*, that whatever you think fit to do or say to me, it shall be all a secret as it is, as much as if I were in my Grave.

HE was astonish'd at her Discourse, and said gravely to her, Madam, you are a Stranger to me, but it is very unfortunate, that you should be let into the Secret of the worst action of my Life, and a thing that I am so justly asham'd of, that the only satisfaction of it to me was, that I thought it was known only to God and my own Conscience: Pray, Sir, *says she*, do not reckon the Discovery of it to me, to be any part of your Misfortune; it was a thing, I believe, you were surprised into, and perhaps the Woman us'd some Art to prompt you to it; however, you will never find any just Cause, *said she*, to repent that I came to hear of it; nor can your own Mouth be more silent in it than I have been, and ever shall be.

WELL, *says he*, but let me do some Justice to the Woman too, whoever she is, I do assure you she prompted me to nothing, she rather declin'd me, it was my own Folly and Madness that brought me into it all, ay and brought her into it too; I must give her her due so far, as to what she took from me, I cou'd expect no less from her in the condition I was in, and to this Hour I know not whether she Robb'd me or the Coachman; if she did it I forgive her, and I think all Gentlemen that do so, should be us'd in the same manner; but I am more concern'd for some other things than I am for all that she took from me.

MY Governess now began to come into the whole matter, and he open'd himself freely to her; first, she said to him, in answer to what he had said about me, I am glad Sir you are so just to the Person that you were with; I assure you she is a Gentlewoman, and no Woman of the Town; and however you prevail'd with her so far as you did, I am sure 'tis not her Practise; you run a great venture indeed, Sir, but if that be any part of your Care, I am perswaded you may be perfectly easie, for I dare assure you no Man has touch'd her, before you, since her Husband, and he has been dead now almost eight Year.

IT appear'd that this was his Grievance, and that he was in a very great fright about it; however, when my Governess said this to him he appeared very well pleased; and said, well, Madam, to be plain with you, if I was satisfy'd of that, I should not so much value what

I lost; for as to that, the Temptation was great, and perhaps she was poor and wanted it: If she had not been poor Sir———, *says my Governess*, I assure you she would never have yielded to you; and as her Poverty first prevailed with her to let you do as you did, so the same Poverty prevail'd with her to pay her self at last, when she saw you was in such a Condition, that if she had not done it, perhaps the next Coach-man or Chair-man[9] might have done it.

WELL, *says he*, much good may it do her; I say again, all the Gentlemen that do so, ought to be us'd in the same manner, and then they would be cautious of themselves; I have no more concern about it, but on the score which you hinted at before, Madam: Here he entred into some freedoms with her on the Subject of what pass'd between us, which are not so proper for a Woman to write, and the great Terror that was upon his Mind with relation to his Wife, for fear he should have receiv'd any Injury from me, and should communicate it farther; and ask'd her at last if she cou'd not procure him an opportunity to speak with me; my Governess gave him farther assurances of my being a Woman clear from any such thing, and that he was as entirely safe in that respect, as he was with his own Lady; but as for seeing me, she said it might be of dangerous consequence; but however, that she would talk with me, and let him know my Answer; using at the same time some Arguments to perswade him not to desire it, and that it cou'd be of no Service to him; seeing she hop'd he had no desire to renew a Correspondence with me, and that on my account it was a kind of putting my Life in his Hands.

HE told her, he had a great desire to see me, that he would give her any assurances that were in his Power, not to take any Advantages of me, and that in the first place he would give me a general release from all Demands of any kind; she insisted how it might tend to a farther divulging the Secret, and might in the end be injurious to him, entreating him not to press for it, so at length he desisted.

THEY had some Discourse upon the Subject of the things he had lost, and he seem'd to be very desirous of his Gold Watch, and told her if she cou'd procure that for him, he would willingly give as much for it, as it was worth, she told him she would endeavour to procure it for him and leave the valuing it to himself.

ACCORDINGLY the next Day she carried the Watch, and he gave her 30 Guineas for it, which was more than I should have been able to make of it, tho' it seems it cost much more; he spoke something of his Perriwig, which it seems cost him threescore Guineas, and his Snuff-box, and in a few Days more, she carried them too; which oblig'd him very much, and he gave her Thirty more, the next Day I

9. Carrier of a sedan chair, a closed vehicle to seat one person, borne on two poles by two bearers, one in front and one behind.

sent him his fine Sword, and Cane *Gratis*, and demanded nothing of him, but I had no mind to see him, unless it had been so, that he might be satisfy'd I knew who he was, which he was not willing to.

THEN he entered into a long Tale with her of the manner how she came to know all this matter; she form'd a long Talk of that part; how she had it from one, that I had told the whole Story to, and that was to help me dispose of the Goods, and this Confident brought the Things to her, she being by Profession a *Pawn-Broker*; and she hearing of his Worship's dissaster, guess'd at the thing in general; that having gotten the Things into her Hands, she had resolv'd to come and try as she had done: She then gave him repeated Assurances that it should never go out of her Mouth, and tho' she knew the Woman very well, yet she had not let her know, *meaning me*, any thing of it; *that is to say*, who the Person was, which by the way was false; but however it was not to his Damage, for I never open'd my Mouth of it to any Body.

I HAD a great many Thoughts in my Head about my seeing him again, and was often sorry that I had refus'd it; I was perswaded that if I had seen him, and let him know that I knew him, I should have made some Advantage of him, and perhaps have had some Maintenance from him; and tho' it was a Life wicked enough, yet it was not so full of Danger as this I was engag'd in. However those Thoughts wore off, and I declin'd seeing him again, for that time; but my Governess saw him often, and he was very kind to her, giving her something almost every time he saw her; one time in particular she found him very Merry, and as she thought he had some Wine in his Head, and he press'd her again very earnestly to let him see that Woman, that *as he said*, had Bewitch'd him so that Night; my Governess, who was from the beginning for my seeing him, told him, he was so desirous of it, that she could almost yield to it, if she cou'd prevail upon me; adding that if he would please to come to her House in the Evening she would endeavour it, upon his repeated Assurances of forgetting what was pass'd.

ACCORDINGLY she came to me and told me all the Discourse; *in short*, she soon byass'd me to consent, in a Case which I had some regret in my mind for declining before: so I prepar'd to see him: I dress'd me to all the Advantage possible I assure you, and for the first time us'd a little Art; I say for the first time, for I had never yielded to the baseness of Paint before, having always had vanity enough to believe I had no need of it.

AT the Hour appointed he came; and as she observ'd before, so it was plain still, that he had been drinking, tho' very far from what we call being in drink: He appear'd exceeding pleas'd to see me, and enter'd into a long Discourse with me, upon the old Affair, I beg'd his pardon very often, for my share of it; protested I had not any such design when first I met him; that I had not gone out with him, but that I took him for a very civil Gentleman; and that he made me so many promises of offering no uncivility to me.

HE alledg'd the Wine he drank, and that he scarce knew what he did, and that if it had not been so, I should never have let him take the freedom with me that he had done: He protested to me that he never touch'd any Woman but me since he was married to his Wife, and it was a surprise upon him; Complimented me upon being so particularly agreeable to him, and the like, and talk'd so much of that kind, till I found he had talk'd himself almost into a temper to do the same thing over again: But I took him up short, I protested I had never suffer'd any Man to touch me since my Husband died, which was near eight Year; he said he believed it to be so truly; and added that Madam, had intimated as much to him, and that it was his Opinion of that part which made him desire to see me again; and that since he had once broke in upon his Vertue with me, and found no ill Consequences, he cou'd be safe in venturing there again; and so in short it went on to what I expected, and to what will not bear relating.

MY old Governess had foreseen it, as well as I, and therefore led him into a Room which had not a Bed in it, and yet had a Chamber within it, which had a Bed, whither we withdrew for the rest of the Night, and in short, after some time being together; he went to Bed, and lay there all Night, I withdrew, but came again undress'd in the Morning before it was Day, and lay with him the rest of the time.

THUS you see having committed a Crime once, is a sad Handle to the committing of it again; whereas all the Regret, and Reflections wear off when the Temptation renews it self; had I not yielded to see him again, the Corrupt desire in him had worn off, and 'tis very probable he had never fallen into it, with any Body else, as I really believe he had not done before.

WHEN he went away, I told him I hop'd he was satisfy'd he had not been robb'd again; he told me he was satisfy'd in that Point, and cou'd trust me again; and putting his Hand in his Pocket gave me five Guineas, which was the first Money I had gain'd that way for many Years.

I HAD several Visits of the like kind from him, but he never came into a settled way of Maintenance, which was what I would have been best pleas'd with: Once indeed he ask'd me how I did to live, I answer'd him pretty quick, that I assur'd him I had never taken that Course that I took with him; but that indeed I work'd at my Needle, and could just Maintain myself, that sometimes it was as much as I was able to do, and I shifted hard enough.

HE seem'd to reflect upon himself, that he should be the first Person to lead me into that, which he assur'd me he never intended to do himself; and it touch'd him a little, *he said*, that he should be the Cause of his own Sin, and mine too: He would often make just Reflections also upon the Crime itself, and upon the particular Circumstances of it, with respect to himself; how Wine introduc'd the Inclinations, how the Devil led him to the Place, and found out an Object to tempt him, and he made the Moral always himself.

WHEN these thoughts were upon him he would go away, and perhaps not come again in a Months time or longer; but then as the serious part wore off, the lewd Part would wear in, and then he came prepar'd for the wick'd Part; thus we liv'd for sometime; tho' he did not KEEP,[1] as they call it, yet he never fail'd doing things that were Handsome, and sufficient to Maintain me without working, and which was better; without following my old Trade.

BUT this Affair had its End too; for after about a Year, I found that he did not come so often as usual, and at last he left it off altogether without any dislike,[2] or bidding adieu; and so there was an End of that short Scene of Life, which added no great Store to me, only to make more Work for Repentance.

HOWEVER during this interval, I confin'd my self pretty much at Home; at least being thus provided for, I made no Adventures, no not for a Quarter of a Year after he left me; but then finding the Fund fail, and being loth to spend upon the main Stock, I began to think of my old Trade, and to look Abroad into the Street again; and my first Step was lucky enough.

I HAD dress'd myself up in a very mean Habit, for as I had several Shapes[3] to appear in I was now in an ordinary Stuff-Grown, a blue Apron and a Straw-Hat; and I plac'd myself at the Door of the three Cups-Inn in St. *John Street*: There were several Carriers us'd the Inn, and the Stage Coaches for *Barnet*, for *Toteridge*, and other Towns that way, stood always in the Street, in the Evening, when they prepar'd to set out; so that I was ready for any thing that offer'd for either one or other: The meaning was this, People come frequently with Bundles and small Parcels to those Inns, and call for such Carriers, or Coaches as they want; to carry them into the Country; and there generally attends Women, Porters Wives, or Daughters, ready to take in such things for their respective People that employ them.

IT happen'd very odly that I was standing at the Inn-Gate, and a Woman that had stood there before, and which was the Porter's Wife belonging to the *Barnet* Stage Coach, having observ'd me, ask'd if I waited for any of the Coaches; I told her yes, I waited for my Mistress, that was coming to go to *Barnet*; she ask'd me who was my

1. I.e., did not formally keep Moll as a mistress.
2. Disagreement, discord.
3. Disguises.

Mistress, and I told her any Madam's Name that came next me;[4] but as it seem'd I happen'd upon a Name, a Family of which Name liv'd at *Hadly* just beyond *Barnet*.

I SAID no more to her, or she to me a good while, but by and by, some body calling her at a Door a little way off, she desir'd me that if any body call'd for the *Barnet* Coach, I would step and call her at the House, which it seems was an Ale-house; I said yes very readily, and away she went.

SHE was no sooner gone; but comes a Wench and a Child, puffing and sweating, and asks for the *Barnet* Coach, I answer'd presently *Here*, do you belong to the *Barnet* Coach, *says she*? yes Sweetheart, *said I*, what do ye want? I want Room, for two Passengers, *says she*, Where are they Sweetheart, *says I*? Here's this Girl, pray let her go into the Coach, *says she*, and I'll go and fetch my Mistress, make hast then Sweetheart, *says I*, for we may be full else; the Maid had a great Bundle under Arm; so she put the Child into the Coach, and *I said*, you had best put your Bundle into the Coach too; No, *says she*, I am afraid some body should slip it away from the Child, give it me then, *said* I, and I'll take care of it; do then, *says she*, and be sure you take care of it; I'll answer for it, *said I*, if it were for Twenty Pound value. There take it then, *says she*, and away she goes.

As soon as I had got the Bundle, and the Maid was out of Sight, I goes on towards the Ale-house, where the Porter's Wife was, so that if I had met her, I had then only been going to give her the Bundle, and to call her to her Business, as if I was going away, and cou'd stay no longer; but as I did not meet her I walk'd away, and turning into *Charter-house-Lane*, made off thro' *Charter-house-Yard*, into *Long-Lane*, then cross'd into *Bartholomew-Close*, so into *Little-Britain*, and thro' the *Blue-Coat-Hospital*[5] into *Newgate-Street*.

To prevent my being known, I pull'd off my blue Apron, and wrapt the Bundle in it, which before was made up in a Piece of painted Callico, and very Remarkable; I also wrapt up my Straw-Hat in it, and so put the Bundle upon my Head; and it was very well, that I did thus, for coming thro' the *Blue-Coat-Hospital*, who should I meet but the Wench, that had given me the Bundle to hold; it seems she was going with her Mistress, who she had been gone to fetch to the *Barnet* Coaches.

I SAW she was in hast, and I had no Business to stop her; so away she went, and I brought my Bundle safe Home to my Governess; there was no Money, nor Plate, or Jewels in the Bundle; but a very good Suit of *Indian* Damask, a Gown and Petticoat, a lac'd Head

4. First name that popped into my head.
5. Popular name of Christ's Hospital, a charity school, whose uniform was a long dark blue gown.

and Ruffles of very good Flanders-Lace, and some Linnen, and other things, such as I knew very well the value of.

THIS was not indeed my own Invention, but was given me by one that had practis'd it with Success, and my Governess lik'd it extreamly; and indeed I try'd it again several times, tho' never twice near the same Place; for the next time I try'd it in *White-Chappel* just by the Corner of *Petty-Coat-Lane*, where the Coaches stand that go out to *Stratford* and *Bow*, and that Side of the Country, and another time at the *Flying-Horse*, without *Bishops-gate*, where the *Cheston*[6] Coaches then lay, and I had always the good Luck to come off with some Booty.

ANOTHER time I plac'd myself at a Warehouse by the Waterside, where the Coasting Vessels[7] from the *North* come, such as from *New-Castle* upon *Tyne, Sunderland*, and other Places; here the Warehouse, being shut, comes a young Fellow with a Letter; and he wanted a Box, and a Hamper that was come from *New-Castle* upon *Tyne*, I ask'd him if he had the Marks[8] of it, so he shows me the Letter, by Vertue of which he was to ask for it, and which gave an Account of the Contents, the Box being full of Linnen, and the Hamper full of Glass-Ware; I read the Letter, and took care to see the Name, and the Marks, the Name of the Person that sent the Goods, the Name of the Person that they were sent to, then I bad the Messenger come in the Morning, for that the Warehouse Keeper, would not be there any more that Night.

AWAY went I, and getting Materials in a publick House, I wrote a Letter from Mr. *John Richardson* of *New-Castle* to his Dear Cousin *Jemey Cole*, in *London*, with an Account that he had sent by such a Vessel, (for I remember'd all the Particulars to a tittle,) so many pieces of Huckaback Linnen, so many Ells of *Dutch* Holland and the like, in a Box, and a Hamper of Flint Glasses from Mr. *Henzill*'s Glass-house,[9] and that the Box was mark'd I C. No I. and the Hamper was directed by a Label on the Cording.

ABOUT an Hour after I came to the Warehouse, found the Warehouse-keeper, and had the Goods deliver'd me without any scruple; the value of the Linnen being about 22 Pound.

6. Very likely a mistake for "*Chester*," this reading appears in both the first and second editions.
7. Ships trading along the English coast.
8. I.e., identifying marks or labels. *Hamper*: A large wickerwork receptacle, with a cover, generally used as a packing-case.
9. Founded in the reign of Elizabeth I by the Henzell family of Lorraine, this well-known glass works, along with other like establishments, was located next to the River Tyne, in Newcastle. *Huckaback Linnen*: A stout linen fabric, with a rough surface, used for toweling. *Ells*: A measure of length varying in different countries (e.g., the English ell was 45 inches, the Scotch 37.2, and the Flemish 27). *Flint Glasses*: Pure lustrous glasses, originally made with ground flint or pebble.

I COULD fill up this whole Discourse with the variety of such Adventures which daily Invention directed to, and which I manag'd with the utmost Dexterity, and always with Success.

AT length, as when does the Pitcher come safe home that goes so very often to the Well, I fell into some small Broils,[1] which tho' they cou'd not affect me fatally, yet made me known, which was the worst thing next to being found Guilty, that cou'd befall me.

I HAD taken up the Disguise of a Widow's Dress; it was without any real design in view, but only waiting for any thing that might offer, as I often did: It happen'd that while I was going along the Street in *Covent Garden*, there was a great Cry of stop Thief, stop Thief; some Artists had it seems put a trick upon a Shop-keeper, and being pursued, some of them fled one way, and some another; and one of them was, they said, dress'd up in Widow's Weeds, upon which the Mob gathered about me, and some said I was the Person, others said no, immediately came the Mercer's Journe[y]man, and he swore aloud I was the Person, and so seiz'd on me; however, when I was brought back by the Mob to the Mercer's Shop, the Master of the House said freely that I was not the Woman that was in his Shop, and would have let me go immediately; but another Fellow said gravely, pray stay till Mr.———, *meaning the Journeyman* comes back, for he knows her; so they kept me by force near half an Hour; they had call'd a Constable, and he stood in the Shop as my Jayler; and in talking with the Constable I enquir'd where he liv'd, and what Trade[2] he was; the Man not apprehending in the least what happened afterwards, readily told me his Name, and Trade, and where he liv'd; and told me as a Jest, that I might be sure to hear of his Name when I came to the *Old Bayley*.

SOME of the Servants likewise us'd me saucily, and had much ado to keep their Hands off of me, the Master indeed was civiler to me than they; but he would not yet let me go, tho' he owned he could not say I was in his Shop before.

I BEGAN to be a little surly with him, and told him I hop'd he would not take it ill, if I made my self amends upon him in a more legal way another time; and desir'd I might send for Friends to see me have right done me: No, *he said*, he could give no such liberty, I might ask it when I came before the Justice of Peace, and seeing I threaten'd him, he would take care of me in the mean time, and

1. Quarrels, disturbances.
2. Since London did not yet have a professional police force, parish officials selected local citizens every year to serve as constables, without any compensation. Those who chose not to serve would pay a fine, in which case the job would often fall to the sort of presumably ignorant and easily bribed "hir'd Officer" Moll disparages below. The corruption endemic in this largely unregulated system of law enforcement was decried by many, including Defoe.

would lodge me safe in *Newgate*: I told him it was his time now, but it would be mine by and by, and govern'd my Passion as well as I was able; however, I spoke to the Constable to call me a Porter, which he did, and then I call'd for Pen, Ink, and Paper, but they would let me have none; I ask'd the Porter his Name, and where he liv'd, and the poor Man told it me very willingly; I bad him observe and remember how I was treated there; that he saw I was detain'd there by Force; I told him I should want his Evidence in another place, and it should not be the worse for him to speak; the Porter said he would serve me with all his Heart; but, Madam, *says he*, let me hear them refuse to let you go, then I may be able to speak the plainer.

WITH that I spoke aloud to the Master of the Shop, and said, Sir, you know in your own Conscience that I am not the Person you look for, and that I was not in your Shop before, therefore I demand that you detain me here no longer, or tell me the reason of your stopping me; the Fellow grew surlier upon this than before, and said he would do neither till he thought fit; very well, said I to the Constable and to the Porter, you will be pleas'd to remember this, Gentlemen, another time; the Porter said, *yes, Madam*, and the Constable began not to like it, and would have perswaded the Mercer to dismiss him, and let me go, since, as he said, he own'd I was not the Person; Good Sir, *says the Mercer to him Tauntingly*, are you a Justice of Peace, or a Constable? I charg'd you with her, pray do you do your Duty: The Constable told him a little mov'd, but very handsomely, *I know my Duty, and what I am, Sir, I doubt you hardly know what you are doing*; they had some other hard words, and in the mean time the Journey-men, impudent and unmanly to the last degree, used me barbarously, and one of them, the same that first seized upon me, pretended he would search me, and began to lay Hands on me: I spit in his Face, call'd out to the Constable, and bad him take notice of my usage; and pray, Mr. Constable, *said I*, ask that Villain's Name, pointing to the Man; the Constable reprov'd him decently, told him that he did not know what he did, for he knew that his Master acknowledg'd I was not the Person that was in his Shop; and, says the Constable, I am afraid your Master is bringing himself and me too into Trouble, if this Gentlewoman comes to prove who she is, and where she was, and it appears that she is not the Woman you pretend to; Dam her, *says the Fellow again*, with an impudent harden'd Face, she is the Lady, you may depend upon it, I'll swear she is the same Body that was in the Shop, and that I gave the pieces of Satin that is lost into her own hand, you shall hear more of it when Mr. *William* and *Anthony, those were other Journeymen*, come back, they will know her again as well as I.

JUST as the insolent Rogue was talking thus to the Constable, comes back Mr. *William* and Mr. *Anthony*, as he call'd them, and a great Rabble with them, bringing along with them the true Widow that I was pretended to be; and they came sweating and blowing into the Shop, and with a great deal of Triumph dragging the poor Creature in a most butcherly manner up towards their Master, who was in the back Shop, and cryed out aloud, here's the Widow, Sir, we have catch'd her at last; what do ye mean by that, *says the Master*, why we have her already, there she sits, *says he*, and Mr.——— *says he*, can swear this is she: The other Man who they call'd Mr. *Anthony* replyed, Mr.——— may say what he will, and swear what he will, but this is the Woman, and there's the Remnant of Sattin she stole, I took it out of her Cloaths with my own Hand.

I SAT still now, and began to take a better Heart, but smil'd and said nothing; the Master look'd Pale; the Constable turn'd about and look'd at me; *let 'em alone Mr. Constable*, said I, *let 'em go on*; the Case was plain and could not be denied, so the Constable was charg'd with the right Thief, and the Mercer told me very civily he was sorry for the mistake, and hoped I would not take it ill; that they had so many things of this nature put upon them every Day, that they cou'd not be blam'd for being very sharp in doing themselves Justice: Not take it ill, Sir! *said I*, how can I take it well? if you had dismiss'd me when your insolent Fellow seiz'd on me in the Street, and brought me to you; and when you your self acknowledg'd I was not the Person, I would have put it by, and not taken it ill, because of the many ill things I believe you have put upon you daily; but your Treatment of me since has been unsufferable, and especially that of your Servant, I must and will have Reparation for that.

THEN he began to parly with me, said he would make me any reasonable Satisfaction, and would fain have had me told him what it was I expected; I told him I should not be my own Judge, the Law should decide it for me, and as I was to be carried before a Magistrate, I should let him hear there what I had to say; he told me there was no occasion to go before the Justice now, I was at liberty to go where I pleased, and so calling to the Constable told him, he might let me go, for I was discharg'd; the Constable said calmly to him, Sir, you ask'd me just now, if I knew whether I was a Constable or a Justice, and bad me do my Duty, and charg'd me with this Gentlewoman as a Prisoner; now, Sir, I find you do not understand what is my Duty, for you would make me a Justice indeed; but I must tell you it is not in my Power: I may keep a Prisoner when I am charg'd with him, but 'tis the Law and the Magistrate alone that can discharge that Prisoner; therefore 'tis a mistake, Sir, I must carry her before a Justice now, whether you think well of it or not: The Mercer was very high with the Constable at first; but the Constable happening to be not a hir'd Officer, but a good Substantial kind of Man,

I think he was a Corn-chandler,[3] and a Man of good Sense, stood to his Business, would not discharge me without going to a Justice of the Peace; and I insisted upon it too: When the Mercer see that; well, *says he to the Constable*, you may carry her where you please, I have nothing to say to her; but Sir, *says the Constable*, you will go with us, I hope, for 'tis you that charg'd me with her; no not I, *says the Mercer*, I tell you I have nothing to say to her: But pray Sir do, *says the Constable*, I desire it of you for your own sake, for the Justice can do nothing without you: Prithee Fellow, *says the Mercer*, go about your Business, I tell you I have nothing to say to the Gentlewoman, I charge you in the King's Name to dismiss her: Sir, *says the Constable*, I find you don't know what it is to be a Constable, I beg of you don't oblige me to be rude to you; I think I need not, you are rude enough already, *says the Mercer*: No, Sir, *says the Constable*, I am not rude, you have broken the Peace in bringing an honest Woman out of the Street, when she was about her lawful Occasion, confining her in your Shop, and ill using her here by your Servants; and now can you say I am rude to you? I think I am civil to you in not commanding or charging you in the King's Name to go with me, and charging every Man I see, that passes your Door, to aid and assist me in carrying you by Force, this you cannot but know I have power to do, and yet I forbear it, and once more entreat you to go with me: Well, he would not for all this, and gave the Constable ill Language: However, the Constable kept his Temper, and would not be provoked; and then I put in and said, come, Mr. Constable, let him alone, I shall find ways enough to fetch him before a Magistrate, I don't fear that; but there's the Fellow, *says I*, he was the Man that seized on me, as I was innocently going along the Street, and you are a Witness of his Violence with me since, give me leave to charge you with him, and carry him before the Justice; yes, Madam, *says the Constable*; and turning to the Fellow, come young Gentleman, *says he to the Journey-man*, you must go along with us, I hope you are not above the Constable's Power, tho' your Master is.

THE Fellow look'd like a condemn'd Thief, and hung back, then look'd at his Master, as if he cou'd help him; and he, like a Fool, encourag'd the Fellow to be rude, and he truly resisted the Constable, and push'd him back with a good Force when he went to lay hold on him, at which the Constable knock'd him down, and call'd out for help, and immediately the Shop was fill'd with People, and the Constable seiz'd the Master and Man, and all his Servants.

THE first ill Consequence of this Fray was, that the Woman they had taken, who was really the Thief, made off, and got clear away in

3. A retail dealer in grains and allied products.

the Crowd; and two others that they had stop'd also, whether they were really Guilty or not, that I can say nothing to.

BY this time some of his Neighbours having come in, and, upon inquiry, seeing how things went, had endeavour'd to bring the hot-brain'd Mercer to his Senses; and he began to be convinc'd that he was in the wrong; and so at length we went all very quietly before the Justice, with a Mob of about 500 People at our Heels; and all the way I went I could hear the People ask what was the matter? and others reply and say, a Mercer had stop'd a Gentlewoman instead of a Thief, and had afterwards taken the Thief, and now the Gentlewoman had taken the Mercer, and was carrying him before the Justice; this pleas'd the People strangely, and made the Crowd encrease, and they cry'd out as they went, which is the Rogue? which is the Mercer? and especially the Women, then when they saw him they cryed out, *that's he, that's he*; and every now and then came a good dab of Dirt at him; and thus we march'd a good while, till the Mercer thought fit to desire the Constable to call a Coach to protect himself from the Rabble; so we Rode the rest of the way, the Constable and I, and the Mercer and his Man.

WHEN we came to the Justice, which was an ancient Gentleman in *Bloomsbury*, the Constable giving first a summary account of the Matter the Justice bad me speak, and tell what I had to say; and first he asked my Name, which I was very loath to give, but there was no remedy, so I told him my Name was *Mary Flanders*, that I was a Widow, my Husband being a Sea Captain, dyed on a Voyage to *Virginia*; and some other Circumstances I told, which he cou'd never contradict, and that I lodg'd at present in Town with such a Person, naming my Governess; but that I was preparing to go over to *America*, where my Husband's Effects lay, and that I was going that Day to buy some Cloaths to put my self into second Mourning,[4] but had not yet been in any Shop, when that Fellow, pointing to the Mercer's Journeyman came rushing upon me with such fury, as very much frighted me, and carried me back to his Masters Shop; where tho' his Master acknowledg'd I was not the Person; yet he would not dismiss me, but charg'd a Constable with me.

THEN I proceeded to tell how the Journeyman treated me; how they would not suffer me to send for any of my Friends; how afterwards they found the real Thief, and took the very Goods they had Lost upon her, and all the particulars as before.

THEN the Constable related his Case; his Dialogue with the *Mercer* about Discharging me, and at last his Servants refusing to go with him, when he[5] had Charg'd him with him, and his Master encour-

4. A less austere style of dress replacing the unadorned black clothes worn during the first year of mourning.
5. Changed to "I" in the second edition.

aging him to do so; and at last his striking the Constable, and the like, all as I have told it already.

THE Justice then heard, the *Mercer* and his Man; the *Mercer* indeed made a long Harangue of the great loss they have daily by Lifters and Thieves; that it was easy for them to Mistake, and that when he found it, he would have dismiss'd me, *&c.* as above, as to the Journeyman he had very little to say, but that he pretended other of the Servants told him, that I was really the Person.

UPON the whole, the Justice first of all told me very courteously I was Discharg'd; that he was very sorry that the *Mercers* Man should in his eager pursuit have so little Discretion, as to take up an innocent Person for a guilty Person; that if he had not been so unjust as to detain me afterward; he believ'd I would have forgiven the first Affront; that however it was not in his Power to award me any Reparation for any thing, other, than by openly reproving them, which he should do; but he suppos'd I would apply to such Methods as the Law directed; in the mean time he would bind him over.

BUT as to the Breach of the Peace committed by the Journeyman, he told me he should give me some satisfaction for that, for he should commit him to *Newgate* for Assaulting the Constable, and for Assaulting of me also.

ACCORDINGLY he sent the Fellow to *Newgate*, for that Assault, and his Master gave Bail, and so we came away; but I had the satisfaction of seeing the Mob wait upon them both, as they came out Holooing, and throwing Stones and Dirt at the Coaches they rod in, and so I came Home to my Governess.

AFTER this hustle, coming home, and telling my Governess the Story, she falls a Laughing at me; Why are you merry, *says I*? the Story has not so much Laughing room in it, as you imagine; I am sure I have had a great deal of Hurry and Fright too, with a Pack of ugly Rogues. *Laugh*, says my Governess, I laugh Child to see what a lucky Creature you are; why this Jobb will be the best Bargain to you, that ever you made in your Life, if you manage it well: I warrant you, *says she*, you shall make the *Mercer* pay you 500 *l.* for Damages, besides what you shall get of the Journeyman.

I HAD other Thoughts of the Matter than she had; and especially, because I had given in my Name to the Justice of Peace; and I knew that my Name was so well known among the People at *Hick's-Hall*,[6] the *Old Baily*, and such Places, that if this Cause came to be tryed openly, and my Name came to be enquir'd into, no Court would give much Damages; for the Reputation of a Person of such a Character; however, I was oblig'd to begin a Prosecution in Form, and accordingly my Governess found me out a very creditable sort of a Man to

6. The sessions house (a court of justice) for the county of Middlesex.

manage it, being an Attorney of very good Business, and of good Reputation, and she was certainly in the right of this; for had she employ'd a petty Fogging hedge Soliciter,[7] or a Man not known, and not in good Reputation, I should have brought it to but little.

I MET this Attorney, and gave him all the particulars at large, as they are recited above; and he assur'd me, it was a Case, *as he said*, that would very well support itself, and that he did not Question, but that a Jury would give very considerable Damages on such an Occasion; so taking his full Instructions, he begàn the Prosecution, and the *Mercer* being Arrested, gave Bail; a few Days after his giving Bail, he Comes with his Attorney to my Attorney, to let him know, that he desir'd to Accommodate the matter; that it was all carried on in the Heat of an unhappy Passion; that his Client, *meaning me*, had a sharp provoking Tongue, that I us'd them ill, gibbing at them, and jeering them, even while they believed me to be the very Person, and that I had provok'd them, and the like.

MY Attorney manag'd as well on my Side; made them believe I was a Widow of Fortune, that I was able to do myself Justice, and had great Friends to stand by me too, who had all made me promise to Sue to the utmost, and that if it cost me a Thousand Pound, I would be sure to have satisfaction, for that the Affronts I had receiv'd were unsufferable.

HOWEVER they brought my Attorney to this that he promis'd he would not blow the Coals, that if I enclin'd to an Accommodation, he would not hinder me, and that he would rather perswade me to Peace than to War; for which they told him he should be no looser all which he told me very honestly, and told me that if they offer'd him any Bribe, I should certainly know it; but upon the whole he told me very honestly that if I would take his Opinion, he would Advise me to make it up with them; for that as they were in a great Fright, and were desirous above all things to make it up, and knew that let it be what it would, they would be alotted to bear all the Costs of the Suit; he believ'd they would give me freely more than any Jury or Court of Justice would give upon a Trial: I ask'd him what he thought they would be brought to; he told me he could not tell, as to that; but he would tell me more when I saw him again.

SOME time after this, they came again to know if he had talk'd with me: He told them he had, that he found me not so Averse to an Accommodation as some of my Friends were, who resented the Disgrace offer'd me, and set me on; that they blow'd the Coals in secret, prompting me to Revenge, or to do myself Justice, as they call'd it; so that he could not tell what to say to it; he told them he would do his endeavour to persuade me, but he ought to be able to tell me

7. A disreputable lawyer, plying his trade from no settled abode and thus said to set up practice under hedges by the side of the road.

what Proposal they made: They pretended they could not make any Proposal, because it might be made use of against them; and he told them, that by the same Rule he could not make any offers, for that might be pleaded in Abatement of what Damages a Jury might be inclin'd to give: However after some Discourse and mutual Promises that no Advantage should be taken on either Side, by what was transacted then, or at any other of those Meetings, they came to a kind of a Treaty; but so remote, and so wide from one another, that nothing could be expected from it; for my Attorney demanded 500 *l.* and Charges, and they offer'd 50 *l.* without Charges; so they broke off, and the *Mercer* propos'd to have a Meeting with me myself; and my Attorney agreed to that very readily.

MY Attorney gave me Notice to come to this Meeting in good Cloaths, and with some State, that the *Mercer* might see I was something more than I seem'd to be that time they had me: Accordingly I came in a new Suit of second Mourning, according to what I had said at the Justices; I set myself out too, as well as a Widows dress in second Mourning would admit; my Governess, also furnish'd me with a good Pearl Neck-lace, that shut in behind with a Locket of Diamonds, which she had in Pawn; and I had a very good gold Watch by my Side; so that in a Word, I made a very good Figure, and as I stay'd, till I was sure they were come; I came in a Coach to the Door with my Maid with me.

WHEN I came into the Room, the *Mercer* was surpriz'd, he stood up and made his Bow, which I took a little Notice of, and but a little, and went and Sat down, where my own Attorney had pointed to me to sit, for it was his House; after a little while, the *Mercer* said, he did not know me again, and began to make some Compliments his way; I told him, I believe he did not know me at first, and that if he had, I believ'd he would not have treated me as he did.

HE told me was very sorry for what had happen'd, and that it was to testifie the willingness he had to make all possible Reparation, that he had appointed this Meeting; that he hop'd I would not carry things to extremity, which might be not only too great a Loss to him, but might be the ruin of his Business and Shop, in which Case I might have the satisfaction of repaying an Injury with an Injury ten times greater; but that I would then get nothing, whereas he was willing to do me any Justice that was in his Power, without putting himself, or me to the Trouble or Charge of a Suit at Law.

I TOLD him I was glad to hear him talk so much more like a Man of Sense than he did before; that it was true, acknowledgement in most Cases of Affronts was counted Reparation sufficient; but this had gone too far to be made up so; that I was not Revengeful, nor did I seek his Ruin, or any Mans else, but that all my Friends were unanimous not to let me so far neglect my Character as to adjust a thing of this kind without a sufficient Reparation of Honour: That to be taken up for a Thief was such an Indignity as could not be put up, that my Character was above being treated so by any that knew me; but because in my Condition of a Widow, I had been for sometime Careless of myself, and Negligent of myself, I might be taken for such a Creature, but that for the particular usage I had from him afterward; and then I repeated all as before, it was so provoking I had scarce Patience to repeat it.

WELL he acknowledg'd all, and was mighty humble indeed; he made Proposals very handsome; he came up to a Hundred Pounds, and to pay all the Law Charges, and added that he would make a Present of a very good Suit of Cloths; I came down to three Hundred Pounds, and I demanded that I should publish an Advertisement of the particulars in the common News Papers.

THIS was a Clause he never could comply with; however at last he came up by good Management of my Attorney to 150 *l.* and a Suit of black silk Cloaths and there I agreed and as it were at my Attornies request complied with it; he paying my Attornies Bill and Charges, and gave us a good Supper into the Bargain.

WHEN I came to receive the Money, I brought my Governess with me, dress'd like an old Dutchess, and a Gentleman very well dress'd, who we pretended Courted me, but I call'd him Cousin, and the Lawyer was only to hint privately to him, that this Gentleman Courted the Widow.

HE treated us handsomely indeed, and paid the Money chearfully enough; so that it cost him 200 *l.* in all, or rather more: At our last Meeting when all was agreed, the Case of the Journeyman came up, and the *Mercer* beg'd very hard for him, told me he was a Man that had kept a Shop of his own, and been in good Business, had a Wife and several Children, and was very poor that he had nothing to make satisfaction with, but he should come to beg my pardon on his Knees, if I desir'd it as openly as I pleas'd: I had no Spleen at the sawcy Rogue, nor were his Submissions any thing to me, since there was nothing to be got by him; so I thought it was as good to throw that in generously as not, so I told him I did not desire the Ruin of any Man, and therefore at his Request I would forgive the Wretch, it was below me to seek any Revenge.

WHEN we were at Supper he brought the poor Fellow in to make acknowledgement, which he would have done with as much mean Humility, as his Offence was with insulting Haughtiness and Pride, in which he was an Instance of a compleat baseness of Spirit, imperious, cruel, and relentless[8] when Uppermost, and in Prosperity; abject and low Spirited when Down in Affliction: However I abated

8. I am following the second edition here; the first edition reads "impious, cruelter, and relentless."

his Cringes, told him I forgave him, and desir'd he might withdraw, as if I did not care for the sight of him, tho' I had forgiven him.

I WAS now in good Circumstances indeed, if I could have known my time for leaving off, and my Governess often said I was the richest of the Trade in *England*, and so I believe I was; for I had 700 *l.* by me in Money, besides Cloaths, Rings, some Plate, and two gold Watches, and all of them stol'n, for I had innumerable Jobbs, besides these I have mention'd; O! had I even now had the Grace of Repentance, I had still leisure to have look'd back upon my Follies, and have made some Reparation; but the satisfaction I was to make for the publick Mischiefs I had done, was yet left behind; and I could not forbear going Abroad again, *as* I *call'd it now*, than any more I could when my Extremity really drove me out for Bread.

IT was not long after the Affair with the *Mercer* was made up, that I went out in an Equipage[9] quite different from any I had ever appear'd in before; I dress'd myself like a Beggar Woman, in the coursest and most despicable Rags I could get, and I walk'd about peering, and peeping into every Door and Window I came near; and indeed I was in such a Plight now, that I knew as ill how to behave in as ever I did in any; I naturally abhorr'd Dirt and Rags; I had been bred up Tite[1] and Cleanly, and could be no other, whatever Condition I was in; so that this was the most uneasie Disguise to me that ever I put on: I said presently to myself that this would not do, for this was a Dress that every body was shy, and afraid of; and I thought every body look'd at me, as if they were afraid I should come near them, least I should take something from them; or afraid to come near me, least they should get something from me: I wandered about all the Evening the first time I went out, and made nothing of it, but came home again wet, draggl'd and tired; However I went out again, the next Night, and then I met with a little Adventure, which had like to have cost me dear; as I was standing near a Tavern Door, there comes a Gentleman on Horse back, and lights at the Door, and wanting to go into the Tavern, he calls one of the Drawers[2] to hold his Horse; he stay'd pretty long in the Tavern, and the Drawer heard his Master call, and thought he would be angry with him; seeing me stand by him, when he call'd to me, here Woman, *says he*, hold this Horse a while, till I go in, if the Gentleman comes, he'll give you something; *yes says I*, and takes the Horse, and walks off with him very soberly, and carri'd him to my Governess.

THIS had been a Booty to those that had understood it; but never was poor Thief more at a loss to know what to do with any thing that was stolen; for when I came home, my Governess was quite con-

9. Attire.
1. Neat in appearance; neatly and carefully dressed. *Plight*: State of mind or dress.
2. Tapsters, bartenders.

founded, and what to do with the Creature, we neither of us knew; to send him to a Stable was doing nothing, for it was certain that publick Notice would be given in the *Gazette*,[3] and the Horse describ'd, so that we durst not go to fetch it again.

ALL the remedy we had for this unlucky Adventure was to go and set up the Horse at an Inn, and send a Note by a Porter to the Tavern, that the Gentleman's Horse that was lost such a time, was left at such an Inn, and that he might be had there; that the poor Woman that held him, having led him about the Street, not being able to lead him back again, had left him there, we might have waited till the owner had publish'd, and offer'd a Reward, but we did not care to venture the receiving the Reward.

So this was a Robbery and no Robbery, for little was lost by it, and nothing was got by it, and I was quite Sick of going out in a Beggar's dress, it did not answer at all, and besides I thought it was Ominous and Threatning.

WHILE I was in this Disguise, I fell in with a parcel of Folks of a worse kind than any I ever sorted with, and I saw a little into their ways too, these were Coiners[4] of Money, and they made some very good offers to me, as to profit; but the part they would have had me have embark'd in, was the most dangerous Part; I mean that of the very working the Dye,[5] as they call it, which had I been taken, had been certain Death, and that at a Stake, *I say*, to be burnt to Death at a Stake; so that tho' I was to Appearance, but a Beggar; and they promis'd Mountains of Gold and Silver to me, to engage; yet it would not do; it is True if I had been really a Beggar, or had been desperate as when I began, I might perhaps have clos'd with it, for what care they to Die, that can't tell how to Live? But at present this was not my Condition, at least I was for no such terrible Risques as those; besides the very Thoughts of being burnt at a Stake, struck terror into my very Soul, chill'd my Blood, and gave me the Vapours to such a degree as I could not think of it without trembling.

THIS put an End to my Disguise too, for as I did not like the Proposal, so I did not tell them so; but seem'd to relish it, and promis'd to meet again; but I durst see them no more, for if I had seen them, and not complied, tho' I had declin'd it with the greatest assurances of Secresy in the World, they would have gone near to have murther'd me to make sure Work, and make themselves easy,

3. Begun in 1665, *The London Gazette* was an official government journal published twice a week; it contained lists of government appointments and promotions, names of bankrupts, and other public notices.
4. Counterfeiters. Coining was deemed high treason and punishable by burning to death at the stake.
5. An engraved stamp used for impressing a design or figure upon some softer material, as in coining money, striking a medal, etc. Moll puns on the various senses of "die" and "stake."

as they call it; what kind of easiness that is, they may best Judge that understand how easy Men are, that can Murther People to prevent Danger.

THIS and Horse stealing were things quite out of my way, and I might easily resolve I would have no more to say to them; my business seem'd to lye another way, and tho' it had hazard enough in it too, yet it was more suitable to me, and what had more of Art in it, more room to Escape, and more Chances for a coming off, if a Surprize should happen.

I HAD several Proposals made also to me about that time, to come into a Gang of House-Breakers; but that was a thing I had no mind to venture at neither, any more than I had at the Coining Trade; I offer'd to go along with two Men, and a Woman, that made it their Business to get into Houses by Stratagem, and with them I was willing enough to venture; but there was three of them already, and they did not care to part, nor I to have too many in a Gang, so I did not close with them, but declin'd them, and they paid dear for their next Attempt.

BUT at length I met with a Woman that had ofen told me what Adventures she had made, and with Success at the Water-side, and I clos'd with her, and we drove on our Business pretty well: One Day we came among some *Dutch* People at St. *Catherines*,[6] where we went on pretence to buy Goods that were privately got on Shore: I was two or three times in a House, where we saw a good Quantity of prohibited Goods, and my Companion once brought away three Peices of *Dutch* black Silk that turn'd to good Account, and I had my Share of it; but in all the Journeys I made by myself, I could not get an Opportunity to do any thing, so I laid it aside, for I had been so often, that they began to suspect something, and were so shy, that I saw nothing was to be done.

THIS baulk'd me a little, and I resolv'd to push at something or other, for I was not us'd to come back so often without Purchase; so the next Day I dress'd myself up fine, and took a Walk to the other End of the Town, I pass'd thro' the *Exchange*[7] in the *Strand*, but had no Notion of finding any thing to do there, when on a sudden I saw a great Clutter in the Place, and all the People, Shopkeepers as well as others, standing up, and staring, and what should it be? but some great Dutchess come into the *Exchange*; and they said the Queen was coming; I set myself close up to a Shop-side with my back to the Compter, as if to let the Crowd pass by, when keeping my Eye upon a parcel of Lace, which the Shop-keeper was showing to some Ladies

6. East of the Tower of London, this riverfront district had a large Dutch and Flemish population.
7. Not the Royal (or Old) Exchange in the City of London, but the New Exchange, an area of merchants' shops a short walk south of Covent Garden Market.

that stood by me; the Shop-keeper and her Maid were so taken up with looking to see who was a coming, and what Shop they would go to, that I found means to slip a Paper[8] of Lace into my Pocket, and come clear off with it, so the Lady Millener paid dear enough for her gaping after the Queen.

I WENT off from the Shop, as if driven along by the Throng, and mingling myself with the Crowd, went out at the other Door of the *Exchange*, and so got away before they miss'd their Lace; and because I would not be follow'd, I call'd a Coach and shut myself up in it; I had scarse shut the Coach Doors up, but I saw the Milleners Maid, and five or six more come running out into the Street, and crying out as if they were frighted; they did not cry stop Thief, because no body ran away, but I cou'd hear the Word robb'd, and Lace, two or three times, and saw the Wench wringing her Hands, and run staring, too and again, like one scar'd; the Coachman that had taken me up, was getting up into the Box, but was not quite up, so that the Horses had not begun to move, so that I was terrible uneasy; and I took the Packet of Lace and laid it ready to have dropt it out at the Flap of the Coach, which opens before just behind the Coachman; but to my great satisfaction in less than a Minute, the Coach began to move, that is to say, as soon as the Coachman had got up, and spoken to his Horses; so he drove away without any interruption, and I brought off my Purchase, which was worth near twenty Pound.

THE next Day I dress'd me up again, but in quite different Cloths, and walk'd the same way again; but nothing offer'd till I came into *St. James's Park*, where I saw abundance of fine Ladies in the *Park*, walking in the *Mall*,[9] and among the rest, there was a little Miss, a young Lady of about 12 or 13 Years old, and she had a Sister, as I suppose it was, with her, that might be about Nine Year old: I observ'd the biggest had a fine gold Watch on, and a good Necklace of Pearl, and they had a Footman in Livery with them; but as it is not usual for the Footmen to go behind the Ladies in the *Mall*; so I observ'd the Footman stop'd at their going into the *Mall*; and the biggest of the Sisters spoke to him, which I perceiv'd was to bid him be just there when they came back.

WHEN I heard her dismiss the Footman, I step'd up to him, and ask'd him, what little Lady that was? and held a little Chat with him, about what a pretty Child it was with her, and how Genteel, and well Carriag'd the Lady, the eldest would be; how Womanish, and how Grave; and the Fool of a Fellow told me presently who she was, that she was Sir *Thomas———'s* eldest Daughter of *Essex*, and that she

8. Parcel, packet.
9. Tree-lined promenade in St. James's Park; created at the beginning of the reign of Charles II, it was the most fashionable walk in Restoration and eighteenth-century London.

was a great Fortune, that her Mother was not come to Town yet; but she was with Sir *William———'s* Lady of *Suffolk*, at her Lodgings in *Suffolk Street*, and a great deal more; that they had a Maid and a Woman to wait on them, besides, Sir *Thomas*'s Coach, the Coachman and himself and that young Lady was Governess to the whole Family as well here, as at Home too; and in short, told me abundance of things enough for my business.

I WAS very well dress'd, and had my gold Watch, as well as she; so I left the Footman, and I puts myself in a Rank with[1] this young Lady, having stay'd till she had taken one double Turn in the *Mall*, and was going forward again, by and by, I saluted her by her Name, with the Title of Lady *Betty*: I ask'd her when she heard from her Father? when my Lady her Mother would be in Town, and how she did?

I TALK'D so familiarly to her of her whole Family that she cou'd not suspect, but that I knew them all intimately: I ask'd her why she would come Abroad without Mrs. *Chime* with her (that was the Name of her Woman) to take care of Mrs. *Judith* that was her Sister. Then I enter'd into a long Chat with her about her Sister, what a fine little Lady she was, and ask'd her if she had learn'd *French*, and a Thousand such little things to entertain her, when on a sudden we see the Guards come, and the Crowd run to see the King go by to the Parliament-House.

THE Ladies run all to the Side of the *Mall*, and I help'd my Lady to stand upon the edge of the Boards on the side of the *Mall*, that she might be high enough to see; and took the little one and lifted her quite up; during which, I took care to convey the gold Watch so clean away from the Lady *Betty*, that she never felt it, nor miss'd it, till all the Crowd was gone, and she was gotten into the middle of the *Mall* among the other Ladies.

I TOOK my leave of her in the very Crowd, and said to her, as if in haste, dear Lady *Betty* take care of your little Sister, and so the Crowd did, as it were Thrust me away from her, and that I was oblig'd unwillingly to take my leave.

THE hurry in such Cases is immediately over, and the Place clear as soon as the King is gone by; but as there is always a great running and clutter just as the King passes; so having drop'd the two little Ladies, and done my Business with them, without any Miscarriage, I kept hurrying on among the Crowd, as if I run to see the King, and so I got before the Crowd and kept so, till I came to the End of the *Mall*; when the King going on toward the Horse-Guards;[2] I went forward to the Passage, which went then thro' against the lower End

1. Walked next to.
2. Barracks building for the Royal Horse Guards, opposite Whitehall Palace. While the King and his entourage are moving east, Moll is moving north and exiting St. James's Park.

of the *Hay-Market*, and there I bestow'd a Coach upon myself, and made off; and I confess I have not yet been so good as my word (*viz.*) to go and visit my Lady *Betty*.

I WAS once of the mind to venture staying with Lady *Betty*, till she mist the Watch, and so have made a great Out-cry about it with her, and have got her into her Coach, and put myself in the Coach with her, and have gone Home with her; for she appear'd so fond of me, and so perfectly deceiv'd by my so readily talking to her of all her Relations and Family, that I thought it was very easy to push the thing farther, and to have got at least the Neck-lace of Pearl; but when I consider'd that tho' the Child would not perhaps have suspected me, other People might, and that if I was search'd I should be discover'd; I thought it was best to go off with what I had got, and be satisfy'd.

I CAME accidentally afterwards to hear, that when the young Lady miss'd her Watch, she made a great Out-cry in the *Park*, and sent her Footman up and down, to see if he could find me out, she having describ'd me so perfectly, that he knew presently that it was the same Person that had stood and talked so long with him, and ask'd him so many Questions about them; but I was gone far enough out of their reach before she could come at her Footman to tell him the Story.

I MADE another Adventure after this, of a Nature different from all I had been concern'd in yet, and this was at a Gaming-House near *Convent-Garden*.

I SAW several People go in and out; and I stood in the Passage a good while with another Woman with me, and seeing a Gentleman go up that seem'd to be of more than ordinary Fashion, I said to him, Sir, pray don't they give Women leave to go up? *yes Madam, says he*, and to play too if they please; I mean so Sir, *said* I; and with that, he said he would introduce me if I had a mind; so I followed him to the Door, and he looking in, there, Madam, *says he*, are the Gamesters, if you have a mind to venture; I look'd in and said to my Comrade, aloud, here's nothing but Men, I won't venture among them; at which one of the Gentlemen cry'd out, you need not be afraid Madam, here's none but fair Gamesters, you are very welcome to come and Set[3] what you please; so I went a little nearer and look'd on, and some of them brought me a Chair, and I sat down and see the Box and Dice go round a pace; then I said to my Comrade, the Gentlemen play too high for us, come let us go.

THE People were all very civil, and one Gentleman in particular encourag'd me, and said, come Madam, if you please to Venture, if you dare Trust me I'll answer for it; you shall have nothing put upon

3. Stake, wager.

you here; no Sir, *said I*, smiling, I hope the Gentlemen wou'd not Cheat a Woman; but still I declin'd venturing, tho' I pull'd out a Purse with Money in it, that they might see I did not want Money.

AFTER I had sat a while, one Gentleman said to me Jeering, come Madam, I see you are afraid to venture for yourself; I always had good luck with the Ladies, you shall Set for me, if you won't Set for yourself; I told him, Sir I should be very loth to loose your Money, tho' I added, I am pretty lucky too; but the Gentlemen play so high, that I dare not indeed venture my own.

WELL well, *says he*, there's ten Guineas Madam, Set them for me; so I took his Money and set, himself looking on; I run out Nine of the Guineas by One and Two at a Time, and then the Box coming to the next Man to me, my Gentleman gave me Ten Guineas more, and made me Set Five of them at once, and the Gentleman who had at the Box threw out,[4] so there was Five Guineas of his Money again; he was encourag'd at this, and made me take the Box, which was a bold Venture: However, I held the Box so long that I had gain'd him his whole Money, and had a good handful of Guineas in my Lap, and which was the better Luck, when I threw out, I threw but at One or Two of those that had Set me, and so went off easie.

WHEN I was come this length, I offer'd the Gentleman all the Gold, for it was his own; and so would have had him play for himself, pretending I did not understand the Game well enough: He laugh'd, and said if I had but good Luck, it was no matter whether I understood the Game or no; but I should not leave off: However he took out the 15 Guineas that he had put in at first, and bad me play with the rest: I would have told[5] them to see how much I had got, but he said no, no, don't tell them, I believe you are very honest, and 'tis bad Luck to tell them, so I play'd on.

I UNDERSTOOD the Game well enough, tho' I pretended I did not, and play'd cautiously; it was to keep a good Stock in my Lap, out of which I every now and then convey'd some into my Pocket; but in such a manner, and at such convenient times, as I was sure he cou'd not see it.

I PLAY'D a great while, and had very good Luck for him, but the last time I held the Box, they Set me high, and I threw boldly at all; I held the Box till I gain'd near Fourscore Guineas, but lost above half of it back at the last throw; so I got up, for I was afraid I should lose it all back again, and said to him, pray come Sir now and take

4. Made a losing throw. The game being played appears to be Hazard, in which the chances are complicated by a number of arbitrary rules, varying according to place or the choice of the players. In this case, it seems that the players are betting on the outcome of each throw, against the "bank" or person rolling the dice—and thus casting the "main" or chance for the company—until he or she makes a losing throw, at which point another player takes the box.
5. Counted.

it and play for your self, I think I have done pretty well for you; he would have had me play'd on, but it grew late, and I desir'd to be excus'd. When I gave it up to him, I told him I hop'd he would give me leave to tell it now, that I might see what I had gain'd, and how lucky I had been for him; when I told them, there was Threescore, and Three Guineas. Ay *says I*, if it had not been for that unlucky Throw I had got you a Hundred Guineas; so I gave him all the Money, but he would not take it till I had put my Hand into it, and taken some for myself, and bid me please myself; I refus'd it, and was positive I would not take it myself, if he had a mind to any thing of that kind it should be all his own doings.

THE rest of the Gentlemen seeing us striving, cry'd give it her all; but I absolutely refus'd that; then one of them said, D——n ye *Jack*, half it with her, don't you know you should be always upon even Terms with the Ladies; so in short, he divided it with me, and I brought away 30 Guineas, besides about 43, which I had stole privately, which I was sorry for afterwards, because he was so generous.

THUS I brought Home 73 Guineas, and let my old Governess see what good Luck I had at Play: However, it was her Advice that I should not venture again, and I took her Council, for I never went there any more; for I knew as well as she, if the Itch of Play came in, I might soon lose that, and all the rest of what I had got.

FORTUNE had smil'd upon me to that degree, and I had Thriven so much, and my Governess too, for she always had a Share with me, that really the old Gentlewoman began to talk of leaving off while we were well, and being satisfy'd with what we had got; but, I know not what Fate guided me, I was as backward to it now as she was when I propos'd it to her before, and so in an ill Hour we gave over the Thoughts of it for the present, and in a Word, I grew more hardn'd and audacious than ever, and the Success I had, made my Name as famous as any Thief of my sort ever had been at *Newgate*, and in the *Old-Bayly*.

I HAD sometimes taken the liberty to Play the same Game over again, which is not according to Practice, which however succeeded not amiss; but generally I took up new Figures, and contriv'd to appear in new Shapes every time I went abroad.

IT was now a rumbling time of the Year, and the Gentlemen being most of them gone out of Town, *Tunbridge*, and *Epsom*,[6] and such Places were full of People, but the City was Thin, and I thought our Trade felt it a little, as well as others; so that at the latter End of the Year I joyn'd myself with a Gang, who usually go every Year to *Sturbridge* Fair, and from thence to *Bury* Fair,[7] in *Suffolk*: We promis'd

6. Tunbridge Wells and Epsom were fashionable spas within easy reach of London.
7. Famous fairs held in the autumn. In *A Tour Thro' the Whole Island of Great Britain* (1724–26), Defoe praises Sturbridge Fair, outside Cambridge, as "not only the greatest in

our selves great things here, but when I came to see how things were, I was weary of it presently; for except meer Picking of Pockets, there was little worth meddling with; neither if a Booty had been made, was it so easy carrying it off, nor was there such a variety of occasion for Business in our way, as in *London*; all that I made of the whole Journey, was a gold Watch at *Bury* Fair, and a small parcel of Linnen at *Cambridge*, which gave me an occasion to take leave of the Place: It was an old Bite,[8] and I thought might do with a Country Shop keeper, tho' in *London* it would not.

I BOUGHT at a Linnen Draper's Shop, not in the Fair, but in the Town of *Cambridge*, as much fine Holland and other things as came to about seven Pound; when I had done, I bad them be sent to such an Inn, where I had purposely taken up my being the same Morning, as if I was to Lodge there that Night.

I ORDER'D the Draper to send them Home to me, about such an Hour to the Inn where I lay, and I would pay him his Money; at the time appointed the Draper sends the Goods, and I plac'd one of our Gang at the Chamber Door, and when the Innkeeper's Maid brought the Messenger to the Door, who was a young Fellow, an Apprentice, almost a Man; she tells him her Mistress was a sleep, but if he would leave the things, and call in about an Hour, I should be awake, and he might have the Money; he left the Parcel very readily, and goes his way, and in about half an Hour my Maid and I walk'd off, and that very Evening I hired a Horse, and a Man to ride before me, and went to *Newmarket*, and from thence got my Passage in a Coach that was not quite full to St. *Edmund's Bury*; Where as I told you I could make but little of my Trade, only at a little Country *Opera*-House, made a shift to carry off a gold Watch from a Ladies side, who was not only intollerably Merry, but as I thought a little Fuddled,[9] which made my Work much easier.

I MADE off with this little Booty to *Ipswich*, and from thence to *Harwich*; where I went into an Inn, as if I had newly arriv'd from *Holland*, not doubting but I should make some Purchase among the Foreigners that came on shore there; but I found them generally empty of things of value, except what was in their Portmanteuas, and *Dutch* Hampers, which were generally guarded by Footmen; however, I fairly[1] got one of their Portmanteuas one Evening out of the Chamber where the Gentleman lay, the Footman being fast a sleep on the Bed, and I suppose very Drunk.

---

the whole Nation, but in the World." He was considerably less complimentary about the fair at Bury St. Edmunds, likening it to Bartholomew Fair for encouraging frivolous diversions over trade.

8. Swindle or fraud.
9. Intoxicated.
1. Quietly, completely. *Portmanteuas*: Portmanteaus.

THE Room in which I Lodg'd, lay next to the *Dutchman*'s and having dragg'd the heavy thing with much a-do out of the Chamber into mine; I went out into the Street, to see if I could find any possibility of carrying it off; I walk'd about a great while but could see no probability, either of getting out the thing, or of conveying away the Goods that was in it if I had open'd it, the Town being so small, and I a perfect Stranger in it; so I was returning with a resolution to carry it back again, and leave it where I found it: Just in that very Moment I heard a Man make a Noise to some People to make hast, for the Boat was going to put off, and the Tide would be spent; I call'd to the Fellow, What Boat is it Friend, *says I*, that you belong to? the *Ipswich* Wherry, Madam, *says he*: When do you go off, *says I*? this Moment Madam, *says he*, do you want to go thither? yes, *said I*, if you can stay till I fetch my things: Where are your things Madam, *says he*? At such an Inn, *said I*: Well I'll go with you Madam, *says he*, very civilly, and bring them for you: come away then, *says I*, and takes him with me.

THE People of the Inn were in great hurry, the Packet-Boat[2] from *Holland*, being just come in, and two Coaches just come also with Passengers from *London*, for another Packet-Boat that was going off for *Holland*, which Coaches were to go back next Day with the Passengers that were just Landed: In this hurry it was not much minded, that I came to the Bar, and paid my Reckoning, telling my Landlady I had gotten my Passage by Sea in a Wherry.

THESE Wherries are large Vessels, with good Accommodation for carrying Passengers from *Harwich* to *London*; and tho' they are call'd Wherries, which is a word us'd in the *Thames* for a small Boat, Row'd with one or two Men; yet these are Vessels able to carry twenty Passengers, and ten or fifteen Ton of Goods, and fitted to bear the Sea; all this I had found out by enquiring the Night before into the several ways of going to *London*.

MY Landlady was very Courteous, took my Money for my Reckoning, but was call'd away, all the House being in a hurry; so I left her, took the Fellow up to my Chamber, gave him the Trunk, or Portmanteua, for it was like a Trunk, and wrapt it about with an old Apron, and he went directly to his Boat with it, and I after him, no Body asking us the least Question about it; for as the drunken *Dutch* Footman he was still a sleep, and his Master with other Foreign Gentlemen at Supper, and very Merry below; so I went clean off with it to *Ipswich*, and going in the Night, the People of the House knew nothing, but that I was gone to *London*, by the *Harwich* Wherry as I had told my Landlady.

I WAS plagu'd at *Ipswich* with the Custom-House Officers, who

2. A boat or vessel sailing at regular intervals between two ports for the conveyance of mail, goods, and passengers.

stopt my Trunk, *as I call'd it*, and would open, and search it; I was willing I told them, they should search it, but my Husband had the Key, and he was not yet come from *Harwich*; this I said, that if upon searching it, they should find all the things be such, as properly belong'd to a Man rather than a Woman, it should not seem strange to them; however, they being positive to open the Trunk, I consented to have it be broken open, that is to say, to have the Lock taken off, which was not difficult.

THEY found nothing for their turn, for the Trunk had been search'd before, but they discover'd several things very much to my satisfaction, as particularly a parcel of Money in *French* Pistoles, and some *Dutch* Ducatoons, or *Rix* Dollars, and the rest was chiefly two Perriwigs, wearing Linnen, and Razors, Wash-balls,[3] Perfumes and other useful things. Necessaries for a Gentleman; which all pass'd for my Husband's, and so I was quit of them.

IT was now very early in the Morning, and not Light, and I knew not well what Course to take; for I made no doubt but I should be pursued in the Morning, and perhaps be taken with the things about me; so I resolv'd upon taking new Measures; I went publickly to an Inn in the Town with my Trunk, *as I call'd it*, and having taken the Substance out, I did not think the Lumber of it worth my concern; however, I gave it the Landlady of the House with a Charge to take great Care of it, and lay it up safe till I should come again, and away I walk'd into the Street.

WHEN I was got into the Town a great way from the Inn, I met with an antient Woman who had just open'd her Door, and I fell into Chat with her, and ask'd her a great many wild Questions of things all remote to my Purpose and Design, but in my Discourse I found by her how the Town was situated, that I was in a Street which went out towards *Hadly*; but that such a Street went towards the Water-side, such a Street went into the Heart of the Town; and at last such a Street went towards *Colchester*, and so the *London* Road lay there.

I HAD soon my Ends of this old Woman; for I only wanted to know which was *London* Road, and away I walk'd as fast as I could; not that I intended to go on Foot, either to *London* or to *Colchester*, but I wanted to get quietly away from *Ipswich*.

I WALK'D about two or three Mile, and then I met a plain Countryman, who was busy about some Husbandry work I did not know what; and I ask'd him a great many Questions first, not much to the

3. Balls of soap, sometimes perfumed or medicated, used for washing the hands and face, and for shaving. *Pistoles*: Gold coins, each worth about 17 shillings. Later on, Moll receives a gift of Spanish pistoles from her son (see n. 5, p. 262), suggesting that the coin referred to here might be the louis d'or of Louis XIII, issued in 1640. The Dutch ducatoon and the rix dollar were both made of silver; the former was worth about five or six shillings, the latter from about two shillings, three pence, to four shillings, six pence.

purpose; but at last told him I was going for *London*, and the Coach was full, and I cou'd not get a Passage, and ask'd him if he cou'd not tell me where to hire a Horse that would carry double, and an honest Man to ride before me to *Colchester*, that so I might get a Place there in the Coaches; the honest Clown look'd earnestly at me, and said nothing for above half a Minute; when scratching his Pole,[4] a Horse say you, and to *Colchester* to carry double; why yes Mistress, alack-a-day, you may have Horses enough for Money; well Friend, *says I*, that I take for granted, I don't expect it without Money: Why but Mistress, *says he*, how much are you willing to give; nay, says I again, Friend, I don't know what your Rates are in the Country here, for I am a Stranger; but if you can get one for me, get it as Cheap as you can, and I'll give you somewhat for your Pains.

WHY that's honestly said too, says the Countryman; *not so honest neither*, said I, to myself, *if thou knewest all*; why Mistress, *says he*, I have a Horse that will carry Double, and I don't much care if I go my self with you; *and the like*: Will you, *says I*? well I believe you are an honest Man, if you will, I shall be glad of it, I'll pay you in Reason; why look ye Mistress, *says he*, I won't be out of Reason with you then, if I carry you to *Colechester*, it will be worth five Shillings for myself and my Horse, for I shall hardly come back to Night.

IN short, I hir'd the honest Man and his Horse; but when we came to a Town upon the Road, I do not remember the Name of it, but it stands upon a River, I pretended myself very ill, and I could go no farther that Night, but if he would stay there with me, because I was a Stranger I would pay him for himself, and his Horse with all my Heart.

THIS I did because I knew the *Dutch* Gentlemen and their Servants would be upon the Road that Day, either in the Stage Coaches, or riding Post, and I did not know but the drunken Fellow, or some body else that might have seen me at *Harwich*, might see me again, and so I thought that in one Days stop they would be all gone by.

WE lay all that Night there, and the next Morning it was not very early when I set out, so that it was near Ten a-Clock by that time I got to *Colechester*: It was no little Pleasure that I saw the Town, where I had so many pleasant Days, and I made many Enquiries after the good old Friends, I had once had there, but could make little out, they were all dead or remov'd: The young Ladies had been all married or gone to *London*; the old Gentleman and the old Lady, that had been my early Benefactress all dead; and which troubled me most the young Gentleman my first Lover, and afterwards my Brother-in-Law was dead; but two Sons Men grown, were left of him, but they too were Transplanted to *London*.

4. Poll, head. *Clown*: Rustic, farmer.

I DISMISS'D my old Man here, and stay'd incognito for three or four Days in *Colechester*, and then took a Passage in a Waggon, because I would not venture being seen in the *Harwich* Coaches; but I needed not have used so much Caution, for there was no Body in *Harwich* but the Woman of the House, could have known me; nor was it rational to think that she, considering the hurry she was in, and that she never saw me but once, and that by Candle light, should have ever discover'd me.

I WAS now return'd to *London*, and tho' by the Accident of the last Adventure, I got something considerable, yet I was not fond of any more Country rambles, nor should I have ventur'd Abroad again if I had carried the Trade on to the End of my Days; I gave my Governess a History of my Travels, she lik'd the *Harwich* Journey well enough, and in Discoursing of these things between our selves she observ'd, that a Theif being a Creature that Watches the Advantages of other Peoples mistakes, 'tis impossible but that to one that is vigilant and industrious many Opportunities must happen, and therefore she thought that one so exquisitely keen in the Trade as I was, would scarce fail of something extraordinary where ever I went.

ON the other hand, every Branch of my Story, if duly consider'd, may be useful to honest People, and afford a due Caution to People of some sort, or other to Guard against the like Surprizes, and to have their Eyes about them when they have to do with Strangers of any kind, for 'tis very seldom that some Snare or other is not in their way. The Moral indeed of all my History is left to be gather'd by the Senses and Judgment of the Reader; I am not Qualified to preach to them, let the Experience of one Creature compleatly Wicked, and compleatly Miserable be a Storehouse of useful warning to those that read.

I AM drawing now towards a new Variety of the Scenes of Life: Upon my return, being hardened by a long Race of Crime, and Success unparalell'd, at least in the reach of my own Knowledge, I had, as I have said, no thoughts of laying down a Trade, which if I was to judge by the Example of others, must however End at last in Misery and Sorrow.

IT was on the *Christmas-day* following in the Evening, that to finish a long Train of Wickedness, I went Abroad to see what might offer in my way; when going by a Working Silver-Smiths in *Foster-lane*, I saw a tempting Bait indeed, and not to be resisted by one of my Occupation; for the Shop had no Body in it, as I could see, and a great deal of loose Plate lay in the Window, and at the Seat of the Man, who usually as I suppose Work'd at one side of the Shop.

I WENT boldly in and was just going to lay my Hand upon a peice of Plate, and might have done it, and carried it clear off, for any care that the Men who belong'd to the Shop had taken of it; but an officious Fellow in a House, not a Shop, on the other side of the Way, seeing me go in, and observing that there was no Body in the Shop, comes running over the Street, and into the Shop, and without asking me what I was, or who, seizes upon me, and cries out for the People of the House.

I HAD not as I said above, touch'd any thing in the Shop, and seeing a glimpse of some Body running over to the Shop, I had so much presence of Mind, as to knock very hard with my Foot on the Floor of the House, and was just calling out too, when the Fellow laid Hands on me.

HOWEVER as I had always most Courage, when I was in most danger, so when the Fellow laid Hands on me, I stood very high upon it, that I came in, to buy half a Dozen of silver Spoons, and to my good Fortune, it was a Silversmith's that sold Plate, as well as work'd Plate, for other Shops: The Fellow laugh'd at that Part, and put such a value upon the Service that he had done his Neighbour, that he would have it be that I came not to buy, but to steal, and raising a great Crowd, I said to the Master of the Shop, who by this time was fetch'd Home from some Neighbouring Place, that it was in vain to make Noise, and enter into Talk there of the Case; the Fellow had insisted, that I came to steal, and he must prove it, and I desir'd we might go before a Magistrate without any more Words; for I began to see I should be too hard for the Man that had seiz'd me.

THE Master and Mistress of the Shop were really not so violent, as the Man from tother side of the Way, and the Man said, Mistress you might come into the Shop with a good Design for ought I know, but it seem'd a dangerous thing for you to come into such a Shop as mine is, when you see no Body there, and I cannot do Justice to my Neighbour, who was so kind to me, as not to acknowledge he had reason on his Side; tho' upon the whole I do not find you attemp'd to take any thing, and I really know not what to do in it: I press'd him to go before a Magistrate with me, and if any thing cou'd be prov'd on me, that was like a design of Robbery, I should willingly submit, but if not I expected reparation.

JUST while we were in this Debate, and a Crowd of People gather'd about the Door came by Sir *T. B.* an Alderman of the City, and Justice of the Peace, and the Goldsmith hearing of it goes out, and entreated his Worship to come in and decide the Case.

GIVE the Goldsmith his due, he told his Story with a great deal of Justice and Moderation, and the Fellow that had come over, and seiz'd upon me, told his with as much Heat, and foollish Passion, which did me good still, rather than Harm: It came then to my turn to speak, and I told his Worship that I was a Stranger in *London*, being newly come out of the *North*, that I Lodg'd in such a Place, that I was passing this Street, and went into the Goldsmiths Shop to buy half a Dozen of Spoons, by great good Luck I had an old silver Spoon in my Pocket, which I pull'd out, and told him I had carried that Spoon to match it with half a Dozen of new ones, that it might match some I had in the Country.

THAT seeing no Body in the Shop, I knock'd with my Foot very hard to make the People hear, and had also call'd aloud with my Voice: Tis true, there was loose Plate in the Shop, but that no Body cou'd say I had touch'd any of it, or gone near it; that a Fellow came running into the Shop out of the Street, and laid Hands on me in a furious manner, in the very Moments, while I was calling, for the People of the House; that if he had really had a mind to have done his Neighbour any Service, he should have stood at a distance, and silently watch'd to see whether I had touch'd any thing, or no, and then have clap'd in upon me, and taken me in the Fact: That is very true, *says Mr. Alderman*, and turning to the Fellow that stopt me, he ask'd him if it was true that I knock'd with my Foot, he said yes I had knock'd, but that might be because of his coming; Nay, says *the Alderman*, taking him short, now you contradict yourself, for just now you said, she was in the Shop with her back to you, and did not see you till you came upon her; now it was true, that my back was partly to the Street, but yet as my Business was of a kind that requir'd me to have my Eyes every way, so I really had a glance of him running over, as I said before, tho' he did not perceive it.

AFTER a full Hearing, the Alderman gave it as his Opinion, that his Neighbour was under a mistake, and that I was Innocent, and the Goldsmith acquiesc'd in it too, and his Wife, and so I was dismiss'd; but as I was going to depart, Mr. *Alderman* said, but *hold Madam*, if you were designing to buy Spoons I hope you will not let my Friend here lose his Customer by the Mistake: I readily answer'd, no Sir, I'll buy the Spoons still if he can Match my odd Spoon, which I brought for a Pattern, and the Goldsmith shew'd me some of the very same Fashion; so he weigh'd the Spoons, and they came to five and thirty Shillings, so I pulls out my Purse to pay him, in which I had near 20 Guineas, for I never went without such a Sum about me, what ever might happen, and I found it of use at other times as well as now.

WHEN Mr. *Alderman* saw my Money, *he said*, well Madam, now I am satisfy'd you were wrong'd, and it was for this Reason, that I mov'd you should buy the Spoons, and staid till you had bought them, for if you had not had Money to pay for them, I should have suspected that you did not come into the Shop with an intent to buy, for indeed the sort of People who come upon those Designs that you have been Charg'd with, are seldom troubl'd with much Gold in their Pockets, as I see you are.

I SMIL'D, and told his Worship, that then I ow'd something of his

Favour to my Money, but I hop'd he saw reason also in the Justice he had done me before; he said, yes he had, but this had confirm'd his Opinion, and he was fully satisfy'd now of my having been injur'd; so I came off with flying Colours, tho' from an Affair, in which I was at the very brink of Destruction.

IT was but three Days after this, that not at all made Cautious by my former Danger as I us'd to be, and still pursuing the Art which I had so long been employ'd in, I ventur'd into a House where I saw the Doors open, and furnish'd myself as I thought verily without being perceiv'd, with two Peices of flower'd Silks, such as they call Brocaded Silk, very rich; it was not a Mercers Shop, nor a Warehouse of a Mercer, but look'd like a private Dwelling-House, and was it seems Inhabited, by a Man that sold Goods for the Weavers to the Mercers, like a Broker or Factor.

THAT I may make short of this black Part of this Story, I was attack'd by two Wenches that came open Mouth'd at me just as I was going out at the Door, and one of them pull'd me back into the Room, while the other shut the Door upon me; I would have given them good Words, but there was no room for it; two fiery Dragons cou'd not have been more furious than they were; they tore my Cloths, bully'd and roar'd as if they would have murther'd me; the Mistress of the House came next, and then the Master, and all outrageous, for a while especially.

I GAVE the Master very good Words, told him the Door was open, and things were a Temptation to me, that I was poor, and distress'd, and Poverty was what many could not resist, and beg'd him with Tears to have pity on me; the Mistress of the House was mov'd with Compassion, and enclin'd to have let me go, and had almost perswaded her Husband to it also, but the sawcy Wenches were run even before they were sent, and had fetch'd a Constable, and then the Master said, he could not go back, I must go before a Justice, and answer'd his Wife that he might come into Trouble himself if he should let me go.

THE sight of the Constable indeed struck me with terror, and I thought I should have sunk into the Ground; I fell into faintings, and indeed the People themselves thought I would have died, when the Woman argued again for me, and entreated her Husband, seeing they had lost nothing to let me go: I offer'd him to pay for the two Peices whatever the value was, tho' I had not got them, and argued that as he had his Goods, and had really lost nothing, it would be cruel to pursue me to Death, and have my Blood for the bare Attempt of taking them, I put the Constable in mind that I had broke no Doors, nor carried any thing away; and when I came to the Justice, and pleaded there that I had neither broken any thing to get in, nor carried any thing out, the Justice was enclin'd to have releas'd me;

but the first sawcy Jade that stop'd me, affirming that I was going out with the Goods, but that she stop'd me and pull'd me back as I was upon the Threshold, the Justice upon that point committed me, and I was carried to *Newgate*; that horrid Place! my very Blood chills at the mention of its Name; the Place, where so many of my Comrades had been lock'd up, and from whence they went to the fatal Tree;[5] the Place where my Mother suffered so deeply, where I was brought into the World, and from whence I expected no Redemption, but by an infamous Death: To conclude, the Place that had so long expected me, and which with so much Art and Success I had so long avoided.

I WAS now fix'd indeed; 'tis impossible to describe the terror of my mind, when I was first brought in, and when I look'd round upon all the horrors of that dismal Place: I look'd on myself as lost, and that I had nothing to think of, but of going out of the World, and that with the utmost Infamy; the hellish Noise, the Roaring, Swearing and Clamour, the Stench and Nastiness, and all the dreadful croud of Afflicting things that I saw there; joyn'd together to make the Place seem an Emblem of Hell itself, and a kind of an Entrance into it.

Now I reproach'd myself with the many hints I had had, *as I have mentioned above*, from my own Reason, from the Sense of my good Circumstances, and of the many Dangers I had escap'd to leave off while I was well, and how I had withstood them all, and hardened my Thoughts against all Fear; it seem'd to me that I was hurried on by an inevitable and unseen Fate to this Day of Misery, and that now I was to Expiate all my Offences at the Gallows, that I was now to give satisfaction to Justice with my Blood, and that I was come to the last Hour of my Life, and of my Wickedness together: These things pour'd themselves in upon my Thoughts in a confus'd manner, and left me overwhelm'd with Melancholly and Despair.

THEN I repented heartily of all my Life past, but that Repentance yielded me no Satisfaction, no Peace, no not in the least, because, *as I said to myself*, it was repenting after the Power of farther Sinning was taken away: I seem'd not to Mourn that I had committed such Crimes, and for the Fact, as it was an Offence against God and my Neighbour; but I mourn'd that I was to be punish'd for it; I was a Penitent as I thought, not that I had sinn'd, but that I was to suffer, and this took away all the Comfort, and even the hope of my Repentance in my own Thoughts.

I GOT no sleep for several Nights or Days after I came into that wretch'd Place, and glad I wou'd have been for some time to have died there, tho' I did not consider dying as it ought to be consider'd neither, indeed nothing could be fill'd with more horror to my Imag-

5. The gallows; also known as "Tyburn tree," from Tyburn, the place of public execution in Middlesex until 1783.

ination than the very Place, nothing was more odious to me than the Company that was there: O! if I had but been sent to any Place in the World, and not to *Newgate*, I should have thought myself happy.

IN the next Place, how did the harden'd Wretches that were there before me Triumph over me? what! Mrs. *Flanders* come to *Newgate* at last? what Mrs. *Mary*, Mrs. *Molly*, and after that plain *Moll Flanders*? They thought the Devil had help'd me they said, that I had reign'd so long, they expected me there many Years ago, and was I come at last? then they flouted me with my Dejections, welcom'd me to the Place, wish'd me Joy, bid me have a good Heart, not to be cast down, things might not be so bad as I fear'd, and the like; then call'd for Brandy, and drank to me; but put it all up to my Score, for they told me I was but just come to the College,[6] *as they call'd it*, and sure I had Money in my Pocket, tho' they had none.

I ASK'D one of this Crew how long she had been there? she said four Months; I ask'd her, how the Place look'd to her when she first came into it? just as it did now to me, *says she*, dreadful and frightful, that she thought she was in Hell, and I believe so still, *adds she, but it is natural to me now, I don't disturb myself about it*: I suppose says I, you are in no danger of what is to follow: Nay, *says she*, for you are mistaken there I assure you, for I am under Sentence,[7] only I pleaded my Belly, but I am no more with Child, than the Judge that try'd me, and I expect to be call'd down next Sessions; *this* CALLING DOWN, is calling down *to their former Judgment, when a Woman has been respited for her Belly, but proves not to be with Child, or if she has been with Child, and has been brought to Bed*. Well says I, and are you thus easy? ay, *says she*, I can't help myself, what signifyes being sad? If I am hang'd there's an End of me, *says she*, and away she turns Dancing, and Sings as she goes the following Peice of *Newgate* Wit,

*The Bell at St. *Sepulcher's* which Tolls upon Execution Day.

If I swing by the String,
*I shall hear the *Bell ring.*

And then there's an End of poor *Jenny*.

I MENTION this, because it would be worth the Observation of any Prisoner, who shall hereafter fall into the same Misfortune and come to that dreadful Place of *Newgate*; how Time, Necessity, and Conversing with the Wretches that are there Familiarizes the Place to them; how at last they become reconcil'd to that which at first was the greatest Dread upon their Spirits in the World, and are as impu-

6. Contemporary criminal slang for Newgate. *Score*: I.e., put it on Moll's tab. It was customary for new arrivals to treat other prisoners to drinks.
7. Condemned to death.

dently Chearful and Merry in their Misery, as they were when out of it.

I CAN not say, as some do, this Devil is not so black, as he is painted; for indeed no Colours can represent the Place to the Life; nor any Soul conceive aright of it, but those who have been Sufferers there: But how Hell should become by degrees so natural, and not only tollerable, but even agreeable, is a thing Unintelligible, but by those who have Experienc'd it, as I have.

THE same Night that I was sent to *Newgate*, I sent the News of it to my old Governess, who was surpriz'd at it you may be sure, and spent the Night almost as ill out of *Newgate*, as I did in it.

THE next Morning, she came to see me, she did what she cou'd to Comfort me, but she saw that was to no purpose; however, as she said, to sink under the Weight, was but to encrease the Weight, she immediately applied her self to all the proper Methods to prevent the Effects of it, which we fear'd; and first she found out the two fiery Jades that had surpriz'd me; she tamper'd with them, persuad'd them, offer'd them Money, and in a Word, try'd all imaginable ways to prevent a Prosecution; she offer'd one of the Wenches 100 *l.* to go away from her Mistress, and not to appear against me; but she was so resolute, that tho' she was but a Servant-Maid, at 3 *l.* a Year Wages or thereabouts, she refus'd it, and would have refus'd it, as my Governess said she believ'd, if she had offer'd her 500 *l.* Then she attack'd the tother Maid, she was not so hard Hearted in appearance as the other; and sometimes seem'd inclin'd to be merciful; but the first Wench kept her up, and chang'd her Mind, and would not so much as let my Governess talk with her, but threatn'd to have her up for Tampering with the Evidence.

THEN she apply'd to the Master, that is to say, the Man whose Goods had been stol'n, and particularly to his Wife, who as I told you was enclin'd at first to have some Compassion for me; she found the Woman the same still, but the Man alledg'd he was bound by the Justice that committed me, to Prosecute, and that he should forfeit his Recognizance.[8]

MY Governess offer'd to find Friends that should get his Recognizances off of the File, as they call it, and that he should not suffer; but it was not possible to Convince him, that could be done, or that he could be safe any way in the World, but by appearing against me; so I was to have three Witnesses of Fact, against me, the Master and his two Maids, that is to say, I was as certain to be cast for my Life, as I was certain that I was alive, and I had nothing to do, but to think of dying, and prepare for it: I had but a sad foundation to build upon,

8. See n. 2, p. 172.

as I said before, for all my Repentance appear'd to me to be only the Effect of my fear of Death, not a sincere regret for the wicked Life that I had liv'd, and which had brought this Misery upon me, or for the offending my Creator, who was now suddenly to be my Judge.

I LIV'D many Days here under the utmost horror of Soul; I had Death as it were in view, and thought of nothing Night and Day, but of Gibbets and Halters, evil Spirits and Devils; it is not to be express'd by Words how I was harrass'd, between the dreadful Apprehensions of Death, and the Terror of my Conscience reproaching me with my past horrible Life.

THE Ordinary of *Newgate*[9] came to me, and talk'd a little in his way, but all his Divinity run upon Confessing my Crime, as he call'd it, (tho' he knew not what I was in for) making a full Discovery, and the like, without which he told me God would never forgive me; and he said so little to the purpose, that I had no manner of Consolation from him; and then to observe the poor Creature preaching Confession and Repentance to me in the Morning, and find him drunk with Brandy and Spirits by Noon; this had something in it so shocking, that I began to Nauseate the Man more, than his Work, and his Work too by degrees for the sake of the Man; so that I desir'd him to trouble me no more.

I KNOW not how it was, but by the indefatigable Application of my diligent Governess I had no Bill preferr'd against me the first Sessions, I mean to the Grand Jury, at *Guild-Hall*;[1] so I had another Month, or five Weeks before me, and without doubt this ought to have been accepted by me, as so much time given me for Reflection upon what was past, and preparation for what was to come, or in a Word, I ought to have esteem'd it, as a space given me for Repentance, and have employ'd it as such; but it was not in me, I was sorry (*as before*) for being in *Newgate*, but had very few Signs of Repentance about me.

ON the contrary, like the Waters in the Caveties, and Hollows of Mountains, which putrifies[2] and turns into Stone whatever they are suffer'd to drop upon; so the continual Conversing with such a Crew of Hell-Hounds as I was, which had the same common Operation upon me, as upon other People, I degenerated into Stone; I turn'd first Stupid and Senseless, then Brutish and thoughtless, and at last raving Mad as any of them were; and in short, I became as naturally pleas'd and easie with the Place, as if indeed I had been Born there.

9. The chaplain of Newgate prison, whose principal duty was to comfort and advise prisoners sentenced to death, not to extract confessions (as here) from those not yet tried and convicted. As previous editors have noted, this episode might be specifically aimed at Paul Lorrain, long-time Ordinary of Newgate, who had died in October 1719, and whom Defoe had attacked in *A Hymn to the Funeral Sermon* (1703).
1. The council or town hall of the City of London.
2. Changed to "peterifies" in the second edition.

IT is scarce possible to imagine that our Natures should be capable of so much Degeneracy, as to make that pleasant and agreeable that in it self is the most compleat Misery. Here was a Circumstance, that I think it is scarce possible to mention a worse; I was as exquisitely miserable as speaking of common Cases, it was possible for any one to be that had Life and Health, and Money to help them as I had.

I HAD a weight of Guilt upon me enough to sink any Creature who had the least power of Reflection left, and had any Sense upon them of the Happiness of this Life, or the Misery of another then; I had at first remorse indeed, but no Repentance; I had now neither Remorse or Repentance: I had a Crime charg'd on me, the Punishments of which was Death by our Law; the Proof so evident, that there was no room for me so much as to plead not Guilty; I had the Name of old Offender, so that I had nothing to expect but Death in a few Weeks time, neither had I myself any thoughts of Escaping, and yet a certain strange Lethargy of Soul possess'd me, I had no Trouble, no Apprehensions, no Sorrow about me, the first Surprize was gone; I was, I may well say I know not how my Senses, my Reason, nay, my Conscience were all a-sleep; my Course of Life for forty Years had been a horrid Complication of Wickedness, Whoredom, Adultery, Incest, Lying, Theft, and in a Word, every thing but Murther, and Treason had been my Practice from the Age of Eighteen, or thereabouts to Threescore; and now I was ingulph'd in the misery of Punishment, and had an infamous Death just at the Door, and yet I had no Sense of my Condition, no Thought of Heaven or Hell at least, that went any farther than a bare flying Touch, like the Stitch or Pain that gives a Hint and goes off; I neither had a Heart to ask God's Mercy, or indeed to think of it, and in this I think I have given a brief Description of the compleatest Misery on Earth.

ALL my terrifying Thoughts were past the Horrors of the Place, were become Familiar, and I felt no more uneasiness at the Noise and Clamours of the Prison, than they did who made that Noise; in a Word, I was become a meer *Newgate-Bird*, as Wicked and as Outragious as any of them; nay, I scarce retain'd the Habit and Custom of good Breeding, and Manners, which all along till now run thro' my Conversation; so thro' a Degeneracy had possess'd me, that I was no more the same thing that I had been, than if I had never been otherwise than what I was now.

IN the middle of this harden'd Part of my Life, I had another sudden Surprize, which call'd me back a little to that thing call'd Sorrow, which indeed I began to be past the Sense of, before they told me one Night, that there was brought into the Prison late the Night before three Highway-Men, who had committed a Robbery somewhere on the Road to *Windsor, Hounslow-Heath*,[3] I think it was, and were pursu'd to *Uxbridge* by the Country, and were taken there after a gallant Resistance, in which I know not how many of the Country People were wounded, and some kill'd.

IT is not to be wonder'd that we [that] were Prisoners, were all desirous enough to see these brave topping Gentlemen that were talk'd up to be such, as their Fellows had not been known, and especially because it was said they would in the Morning be remov'd into the Press-Yard,[4] having given Money to the Head-Master of the Prison, to be allow'd the liberty of that better Part of the Prison: So we that were Women plac'd ourselves in the way that we would be sure to see them; but nothing cou'd express the Amazement and Surprize I was in, when the very first Man that came out I knew to be my *Lancashire* Husband, the same who liv'd so well at *Dunstable*,[5] and the same who I afterwards saw at *Brickill*, when I was married to my last Husband, as has been related.

I WAS struck Dumb at the Sight, and knew neither what to say, or what to do; he did not know me, and that was all the present Relief I had, I quitted my Company, and retir'd as much as that dreadful Place suffers any Body to retire, and I cry'd vehemently for a great while; dreadful Creature, that I am, *said I*, How many poor People have I made Miserable? How many desperate Wretches have I sent to the Devil; This Gentleman's Misfortunes I plac'd all to my own Account: He had told me at *Chester*, he was ruin'd by that Match, and that his Fortunes were made Desperate on my Account; for that thinking I had been a Fortune he was run into Debt more than he was able to pay, and that he knew not what Course to take; that he would go into the Army, and carry a Musquet, or buy a Horse and take a Tour,[6] as he call'd it; and tho' I never told him that I was a Fortune, and so did not actually Deceive him myself, yet I did encourage the having it thought that I was so, and by that means I was the occasion originally of his Mischief.

THE Surprize of this thing only, struck deeper into my Thoughts, and gave me stronger Reflections than all that had befallen me before; I griev'd Day and Night for him, and the more, for that they told he was the Captain of the Gang, and that he had committed so many Robberies, that *Hind*, or *Whitney*, or the *Golden Farmer* were Fools to him;[7] that he would surely be hang'd if there were no more

3. Notorious haunt of highwaymen in Defoe's time.
4. So called from a "press"—a machine used to wring confessions from prisoners by placing heavy iron weights on their chests—this area of Newgate had apartments affording better treatment to those able to pay for it.
5. Changed to "the same with whom I liv'd so well at *Dunstable*" in the second edition.
6. Become a highwayman. For a variant of this criminal slang, see n. 7, p. 123.
7. I.e., his robberies were so many, that these three legendary seventeenth-century criminals were nothing compared to him. James Hind had been hanged, then drawn and quartered, in 1652; James Whitney, a butcher turned highwayman, was put to death in 1694; and

Men left in the Country he was born in; and that there would abundance of People come in against him.

I WAS overwhelm'd with grief for him; my own Case gave me no disturbance compar'd to this, and I loaded my self with Reproaches on his Account; I bewail'd his Misfortunes, and the ruin he was now come to, at such a Rate, that I relish'd nothing now, as I did before, and the first Reflections I made upon the horrid detestable Life I had liv'd, began to return upon me, and as these things return'd my abhorrance of the Place I was in, and of the way of living in it, return'd also; in a word, I was perfectly chang'd, and become another Body.

WHILE I was under these influences of sorrow for him, came Notice to me that the next Sessions approaching, there would be a Bill preferr'd to the Grand Jury against me, and that I should be certainly try'd for my Life at the *Old-Baily*: My Temper was touch'd before, the harden'd wretch'd boldness of Spirit, which I had acquir'd, abated, and Conscious in the Prison Guilt began to flow in upon my Mind: In short, I began to think, and to think is one real Advance from Hell to Heaven; all that Hellish harden'd state and temper of Soul, which I have said so much of before, is but a deprivation of Thought; he that is restor'd to his Power of thinking, is restor'd to himself.

As soon as I began, I say to Think, the first thing that occurr'd to me broke out thus; Lord! what will become of me, I shall certainly die! I shall be cast[8] to be sure, and there is nothing beyond that but Death! I have no Friends, what shall I do? I shall be certainly cast; Lord, have Mercy upon me, what will become of me? This was a sad Thought, you will say, to be the first after so long time that had started into my Soul of that kind, and yet even this was nothing but fright, at what was to come; there was not a Word of sincere Repentance in it all: However, I was indeed dreadfully dejected, and disconsolate to the last degree; and as I had no Friend in the World to communicate my distress'd Thoughts to, it lay so heavy upon me, that it threw me into Fits, and Swoonings several times a-Day: I sent for my old Governess, and she, *give her her due*, acted the Part of a true Friend, she left me no Stone unturn'd to prevent the Grand Jury[9] finding out one or two of the Jury Men, talk'd with them, and endeavour'd to possess them with favourable Dispositions, on Account that nothing was taken away, and no House broken, *&c.*

William Davis, called "the Golden Farmer" because he paid his debts in gold and kept a farm in Gloucestershire, was executed in 1689.

8. Found guilty, convicted.

9. I.e., keep the Grand Jury from issuing a bill of indictment. Although there is no punctuation at this point in the text, "finding out" begins a new clause explaining how Moll's governess has tried to influence the jurymen.

but all would not do, they were over-ruled by the rest, the two Wenches swore home to the Fact, and the Jury found the Bill against me for Robbery and Housebreaking, that is for Felony and Burglary.

I SUNK down when they brought me News of it, and after I came to myself again, I thought I should have died with the weight of it: My Governess acted a true Mother to me, she pittied me, she cryed with me, and for me; but she cou'd not help me; and to add to the Terror of it, 'twas the Discourse all over the House,[1] that I should die for it; I cou'd hear them talk it among themselves very often; and see them shake their Heads, and say they were sorry for it, and the like, as is usual in the Place; but still no Body came to tell me their Thoughts, till at last one of the Keepers came to me privately, and said with a Sigh, well Mrs. *Flanders*, you will be tried a *Friday*, (this was but a *Wednesday*,) what do you intend to do? I turn'd as white as a Clout,[2] and said, God knows what I shall do, for my part I know not what to do; why, *says he*, I won't flatter you, I would have you prepare for Death, for I doubt you will be Cast, and as they say, you are an old Offender; I doubt you will find but little Mercy; They say, *added he*, your Case is very plain, and that the Witnesses swear so home against you, there will be no standing it.

THIS was a stab into the very Vitals of one under such a Burthen as I was oppress'd with before, and I cou'd not speak to him a Word good or bad, for a great while, but at last I burst out into Tears, and said to him, Lord! Mr.——— What must I do? Do, *says he*, send for the Ordinary send for a Minister, and talk with him, for indeed Mrs. *Flanders*, unless you have very good Friends, you are no Woman for this World.

THIS was plain dealing indeed, but it was very harsh to me, at least I thought it so: He left me in the greatest Confusion imaginable, and all that Night I lay awake; and now I began to say my Prayers, which I had scarce done before since my last Husband's Death, or from a little while after; and truly I may well call it, saying my Prayers; for I was in such a Confusion, and had such horrour upon my Mind, that tho' I cry'd, and repeated several times the Ordinary Expression of, *Lord have Mercy upon me*; I never brought my self to any Sense of my being a miserable Sinner, as indeed I was, and of Confessing my Sins to God, and begging Pardon for the sake of Jesus Christ; I was overwhelm'd with the Sense of my Condition, being try'd for my Life, and being sure to be Condemn'd, and then I was as sure to be Executed, and on this Account, I cry'd out all Night, Lord! what will become of me? Lord! what shall I do? Lord! I shall be hang'd, Lord have mercy upon me, and the like.

1. Newgate.
2. A piece of cloth. Contemporary expression for turning pale; the *OED* cites this passage from *Moll Flanders* as illustration.

MY poor afflicted Governess was now as much concern'd as I, and a great deal more truly Penitent; tho' she had no prospect of being brought to Tryal and Sentence, not but that she deserv'd it as much as I, and so she said herself; but she had not done any thing herself for many Years, other than receiving what I, and others stole, and encouraging us to steal it: But she cry'd and took on, like a distracted Body, wringing her Hands, and crying out that she was undone, that she believ'd there was a Curse from Heaven upon her, that she should be damn'd, that she had been the Destruction of all her Friends, that she had brought such a one, and such a one, and such one to the Gallows; and there she reckon'd up ten or eleven People, some of which I have given an Account of that came to untimely Ends, and that now she was the occasion of my Ruin, for she had persuaded me to go on, when I would have left off: I interrupted her there; no Mother, no, *said I*, don't speak of that, for you would have had me left off when I got the Mercer's Money again, and when I came home from *Harwich*, and I would not hearken to you, therefore you have not been to blame, it is I only have ruin'd myself, I have brought myself to this Misery, and thus we spent many Hours together.

WELL there was no Remedy, the Prosecution went on, and on the *Thursday* I was carried down to the Sessions House, where I was arraign'd, as they call'd it, and the next Day I was appointed to be Try'd. At the Arraignment I pleaded not Guilty, and well I might, for I was indicted for Felony and Burglary; that is for feloniously stealing two Pieces of Brocaded Silk, value 46 *l.* the Goods of *Anthony Johnson*, and for breaking open his Doors; whereas I knew very well they could not pretend to prove I had broken up the Doors, or so much as lifted up a Latch.

ON the *Friday* I was brought to my Tryal, I had exhausted my Spirits with Crying for two or three Days before, that[3] I slept better the *Thursday* Night than I expected, and had more Courage for my Tryal, than indeed I thought possible for me to have.

WHEN the Tryal began, and the Indictment was read, I would have spoke, but they told me the Witnesses must be heard first, and then I should have time to be heard. The Witnesses were the two Wenches, a Couple of hard Mouth'd Jades indeed, for tho' the thing was Truth in the main, yet they aggravated it to the utmost extremity, and swore I had the Goods wholly in my possession, that I had hid them among my Cloaths, that I was going off with them, that I had one Foot over the Threshold when they discovered themselves, and then I put tother over, so that I was quite out of the House in the Street with the Goods before they took hold of me, and then they

3. So that.

seiz'd me, and brought me back again, and they took the Goods upon me: The Fact in general was all true, but I believe, and insisted upon it, that they stop'd me before I had set my Foot clear of the Threshold of the House; but that did not argue much, for certain it was, that I had taken the Goods, and that I was bringing them away, if I had not been taken.

BUT I pleaded that I had stole nothing, they had lost nothing, that the Door was open, and I went in seeing the Goods lye there, and with Design to buy, if seeing no Body in the House, I had taken any of them up in my Hand, it cou'd not be concluded that I intended to steal them, for that I never carried them farther than the Door to look on them with the better Light.

THE Court would not allow that by any means, and made a kind of a Jest of my intending to buy the Goods, that being no Shop for the Selling of any thing, and as to carrying them to the Door to look at them, the Maids made their impudent Mocks upon that, and spent their Wit upon it very much; told the Court I had look'd at them sufficiently, and approv'd them very well, for I had pack'd them up under my Cloaths, and was a going with them.

IN short, I was found Guilty of Felony, but acquited of the Burglary, which was but small Comfort to me, the first bringing me to a Sentence of Death, and the last would have done no more: The next Day, I was carried down to receive the dreadful Sentence, and when they came to ask me what I had to say, why Sentence should not pass, I stood mute a while, but some Body that stood behind me, prompted me aloud to speak to the Judges, for that they cou'd represent things favourably for me: This encourag'd me to speak, and I told them I had nothing to say to stop the Sentence; but that I had much to say, to bespeak the Mercy of the Court, that I hop'd they would allow something in such a Case, for the Circumstances of it, that I had broken no Doors, had carried nothing off, that no Body had lost any thing; that the Person whose Goods they were was pleas'd to say, he desir'd Mercy might be shown, which indeed he very honestly did, that at the worst it was the first Offence, and that I had never been before any Court of Justice before: And in a Word, I spoke with more Courage than I thought I cou'd have done, and in such a moving Tone, and tho' with Tears, yet not so many Tears as to obstruct my Speech, that I cou'd see it mov'd others to Tears that heard me.

THE Judges sat Grave and Mute, gave me an easy Hearing, and time to say all that I would, but saying neither Yes, or No to it, Pronounc'd the Sentence of Death upon me; a Sentence that was to me like Death itself, which after it was read confounded me; I had no more Spirit left in me, I had no Tongue to speak, or Eyes to look up either to God or Man.

MY poor Governess was utterly Disconsolate, and she that was my Comforter before, wanted Comfort now herself, and sometimes Mourning, sometimes Raging, was as much out of herself (as to all outward Appearance) as any mad Woman in *Bedlam*:[4] Nor was she only Disconsolate as to me, but she was struck with Horror at the Sense of her own wicked Life, and began to look back upon it with a Taste quite different from mine; for she was Penitent to the highest Degree for her Sins, as well as Sorrowful for the Misfortune: She sent for a Minister too, a serious pious good Man, and apply'd herself with such earnestness by his assistance to the Work of a sincere Repentance, that I believe, and so did the Minister too, that she was a true Penitent, and which is still more, she was not only so for the Occasion, and at the Juncture, but she continu'd so, as I was inform'd to the Day of her Death.

IT is rather to be thought of, than express'd what was now my Condition; I had nothing before me but present Death; and as I had no Friends to assist me, or to stir for me, I expected nothing but to find my Name in the Dead Warrant, which was to come down for the Execution the *Friday* afterward, of five more and myself.

IN the mean time my poor distress'd Governess sent me a Minister, who at her request first, and at my own afterwards came to visit me: He exhorted me seriously to repent of all my Sins, and to dally no longer with my Soul; not flattering myself with hopes of Life, which he said, he was inform'd there was no room to expect, but unfeignedly to look up to God with my whole Soul, and to cry for Pardon in the Name of Jesus Christ. He back'd his Discourses with proper Quotations of Scripture, encouraging the greatest Sinner to Repent, and turn from their Evil way, and when he had done, he kneel'd down and pray'd with me.

IT was now, that for the first time I felt any real signs of Repentance; I now began to look back upon my past Life with abhorrence, and having a kind of view into the other Side of time, the things of Life, as I believe they do with every Body at such a time, began to look with a different Aspect, and quite another Shape, than they did before; the greatest and best things, the views of felicity, the joy, the griefs of Life were quite other things; and I had nothing in my Thoughts, but what was so infinitely Superior to what I had known in Life, that it appear'd to me to be the greatest stupidity in Nature to lay any weight upon any thing tho' the most valuable in this World.

THE word Eternity represented itself with all its incomprehensible Additions, and I had such extended Notions of it, that I know not how to express them: Among the rest, how vile, how gross, how absurd did every pleasant thing look? I mean, that we had counted

4. Popular name for the Hospital of St. Mary of Bethlehem, an asylum for lunatics.

pleasant before; especially when I reflected that these sordid Trifles were the things for which we forfeited eternal Felicity.

WITH these Reflections came in, of meer Course, severe Reproaches of my own Mind for my wretched Behaviour in my past Life; that I had forfeited all hope of any Happiness in the Eternity that I was just going to enter into, and on the contrary was entitul'd to all that was miserable, or had been conceiv'd of Misery; and all this with the frightful Addition of its being also Eternal.

I AM not capable of reading Lectures of Instruction to any Body, but I relate this in the very manner in which things then appear'd to me, as far as I am able; but infinitely short of the lively impressions which they made on my Soul at that time; indeed those Impressions are not to be explain'd by words, or if they are, I am not Mistress of Words enough to express them; It must be the Work of every sober Reader to make just Reflections on them, as their own Circumstances may direct; and without Question, this is what every one at sometime or other may feel something of; I mean a clearer Sight into things to come, than they had here, and a dark view of their own Concern in them.

BUT I go back to my own Case; the Minister press'd me to tell him, as far as I thought convenient, in what State I found myself as to the Sight, I had of things beyond Life; he told me he did not come as Ordinary of the Place, whose business it is to extort Confessions from Prisoners, for private Ends,[5] or for the farther detecting of other Offenders; that his business was to move me to such freedom of Discourse as might serve to disburthen my own Mind, and furnish him to administer Comfort to me as far as was in his Power; and assur'd me, that whatever I said to him should remain with him, and be as much a Secret as if it was known only to God and myself; and that he desir'd to know nothing of me, but as above, to qualifie him to apply proper Advice and Assistance to me, and to pray to God for me.

THIS honest friendly way of treating me, unlock'd all the Sluces of my Passions: He broke into my very Soul by it; and I unravell'd all the Wickedness of my Life to him: In a word, I gave him an Abridgement of this whole History; I gave him the Picture of my Conduct for 50 Years in Miniature.

I HID nothing from him, and he in return exhorted me to a sincere Repentance, explain'd to me what he meant by Repentance, and then drew out such a Scheme of infinite Mercy, proclaim'd from Heaven to Sinners of the greatest Magnitude, that he left me nothing to say,

5. See n. 9, p. 218. The good minister is insinuating here that the Ordinary of Newgate profits from trading in Newgate biographies, immensely popular accounts of the lives of condemned criminals purporting to record their actual confessions and dying speeches.

that look'd like despair or doubting of being accepted, and in this Condition he left me the first Night.

HE visited me again the next Morning, and went on with his Method of explaining the Terms of Divine Mercy, which according to him consisted of nothing more, or more Difficult than that of being sincerely desirous of it, and willing to accept it; only a sincere Regret for, and hatred of those things I had done, which render'd me so just an Object of divine Vengeance: I am not able to repeat the excellent Discourses of this extraordinary Man; 'tis all that I am able to do to say, that he reviv'd my Heart, and brought me into such a Condition, that I never knew any thing of in my Life before: I was cover'd with Shame and Tears for things past, and yet had at the same time a secret surprizing Joy at the Prospect of being a true Penitent, and obtaining the Comfort of a Penitent, I mean the hope of being forgiven; and so swift did Thoughts circulate, and so high did the impressions they had made upon me run, that I thought I cou'd freely have gone out that Minute to Execution, without any uneasiness at all, casting my Soul entirely into the Arms of infinite Mercy as a Penitent.

THE good Gentleman was so mov'd also in my behalf, with a view of the influence, which he saw these things had on me, that he blessed God he had come to visit me, and resolv'd not to leave me till the last Moment, that is not to leave visiting me.

IT was no less than 12 Days after our receiving Sentence, before any were order'd for Execution, and then upon a *Wednesday* the Dead Warrant, *as they call it*, came down, and I found my Name was among them; a terrible blow this was to my new Resolutions, indeed my Heart sunk within me, and I swoon'd away twice, one after another, but spoke not a word: The good Minister was sorely Afflicted for me, and did what he could to comfort me with the same Arguments, and the same moving Eloquence that he did before, and left me not that Evening so long as the Prison-keepers would suffer him to stay in the Prison, unless he wou'd be lock'd up with me all Night, which he was not willing to be.

I wonder'd much that I did not see him all the next Day, *it being but the Day before the time appointed for Execution*; and I was greatly discouraged, and dejected in my Mind, and indeed almost sunk for want of that Comfort, which he had so often, and with such Success yeilded me on his former Visits; I waited with great impatience, and under the greatest oppressions of Spirits imaginable; till about four a-Clock he came to my Apartment, for I had obtain'd the Favour by the help of Money, nothing being to be done in that Place without it, not to be kept in the Condemn'd Hole, as they call it, among the rest of the Prisoners, who were to die, but to have a little dirty Chamber to my self.

MY Heart leap'd within me for Joy, when I heard his Voice at the Door even before I saw him; but let any one Judge what kind of Motion I found in my Soul, when after having made a short excuse for his not coming, he shew'd me that his time had been employ'd on my Account; that he had obtain'd a favourable Report from the Recorder[6] to the Secretary of State in my particular Case, and in short that he had brought me a Reprieve.

HE us'd all the Caution that he was able in letting me know a thing, which it would have been a double Cruelty to have conceal'd; and yet it was too much for me; for as Grief had overset me before, so did Joy overset now, and I fell into a much more dangerous Swooning than I did at first, and it was not without a great Difficulty that I was recover'd at all.[7]

THE good Man having made a very Christian Exhortation to me, not to let the Joy of my Reprieve, put the Remembrance of my past Sorrow out of my Mind; and having told me that he must leave me, to go and enter the Reprieve in the Books, and show it to the Sheriffs, stood up just before his going away, and in a very earnest manner pray'd to God for me, that my Repentance might be made Unfeign'd and Sincere; and that my coming back as it were into Life again, might not be a returning to the Follies of Life, which I had made such solemn Resolutions to forsake, and to repent of them; I joyn'd heartily in the Petition, and must needs say, I had deeper Impressions upon my Mind all that Night, of the Mercy of God in sparing my Life; and a greater Detestation of my past Sins, from a Sense of the goodness which I had tasted in this Case, than I had in all my Sorrow before.

THIS may be thought inconsistent in it self, and wide from the Business of this Book; Particularly, I reflect that many of those who may be pleas'd and diverted with the Relation of the wild and wicked part of my Story, may not relish this, which is really the best part of my Life, the most Advantageous to myself, and the most instructive to others; such however will I hope allow me the liberty to make my Story compleat: It would be a severe Satyr[8] on such, to say they do not relish the Repentance as much as they do the Crime; and that they had rather the History were a compleat Tragedy, as it was very likely to have been.

BUT I go on with my Relation, the next Morning there was a sad Scene indeed in the Prison; the first thing I was saluted with in the Morning, was the Tolling of the great Bell at St. *Sepulchres*, as they call it, which usher'd in the Day: As soon as it began to Toll, a dismal

6. A magistrate or judge having criminal and civil jurisdiction in a city or borough.
7. It was a commonplace of the period, often exemplified in Defoe's writings, that (as Colonel Jack puts it) "Joy is as Extravagant as Grief."
8. Satire.

groaning and crying was heard from the Condemn'd Hole, where there lay six poor Souls, who were to be Executed that Day, some for one Crime, some for another, and two of them for Murther.

THIS was follow'd by a confus'd Clamour in the House; among the several sorts of Prisoners, expressing their awkward Sorrows for the poor Creatures that were to die, but in a manner extreamly differing one from another; some cried for them; some huzza'd, and wish'd them a good Journey; some damn'd and curst those that had brought them to it, that is meaning the Evidence,[9] or Prosecutors; many pittying them; and some few, but very few praying for them.

THERE was hardly room for so much Composure of Mind, as was requir'd for me to bless the merciful Providence that had as it were snatch'd me out of the Jaws of this Destruction: I remained as it were Dumb and Silent, overcome with the Sense of it, and not able to express what I had in my Heart; for the Passions on such Occasions as these, are certainly so agitated as not to be able presently to regulate their own Motions.

ALL the while the poor condemn'd Creatures were preparing to their Death, and the Ordinary *as they call him*, was busy with them, disposing them to submit to their Sentence: I say all this while I was seiz'd with a fit of trembling, as much as I cou'd have been, if I had been in the same Condition, as to be sure the Day before I expected to be; I was so violently agitated by this Surprising Fit, that I shook as if it had been in the cold Fit of an Ague; so that I could not speak or look, but like one Distracted: As soon as they were all put into the Carts and gone, which however I had not Courage enough to see, *I say*, as soon as they were gone, I fell into a fit of crying involuntarily, and without Design, but as a meer Distemper, and yet so violent, and it held me so long, that I knew not what Course to take, nor could I stop, or put a Checque to it, no not with all the Strength and Courage I had.

THIS fit of crying held me near two Hours and as I believe held me till they were all out of the World, and then a most humble Penitent serious kind of Joy succeeded; a real transport it was, or Passion of Joy, and Thankfulness, but still unable to give vent to it by Words, and in this I continued most part of the Day.

IN the Evening the Good Minister visited me again, and then fell to his usual good Discourses, he Congratulated my having a space yet allow'd me for Repentance, whereas the state of those six poor Creatures was determin'd, and they were now pass'd the offers of Salvation; he earnestly press'd me to retain the same Sentiments of the things of Life, that I had when I had a view of Eternity; and at the End of all, told me I should not conclude that all was over, that

9. Not in the sense of proof to support a conviction, but as a synonym for witness.

a Reprieve was not a Pardon, that he could not yet answer for the Effects of it; however, I had this Mercy, that I had more time given me, and that it was my business to improve that time.

THIS Discourse, tho' very seasonable, left a kind of sadness on my Heart, as if I might expect the Affair would have a tragical Issue still, which however he had no certainty of, and I did not indeed at that time question him about it, he having said that he would do his utmost to bring it to a good End, and that he hoped he might, but he would not have me secure;[1] and the Consequence prov'd that he had Reason for what he said.

IT was about a Fortnight after this, that I had some just Apprehensions that I should be included in the next dead Warrant at the ensuing Sessions; and it was not without great difficulty, and at last an humble Petition for Transportation, that I avoided it, so ill was I beholding to Fame, and so prevailing was the fatal Report of being an old Offender, tho' in that they did not do me strict Justice, for I was not in the Sense of the Law an old Offender, whatever I was in the Eye of the Judge; for I had never been before them in a judicial way before, so the Judges could not Charge me with being an old Offender, but the Recorder was pleas'd to represent my Case as he thought fit.

I HAD now a certainty of Life indeed, but with the hard Conditions of being order'd for Transportation, which indeed was a hard Condition in it self, but not when comparatively considered; and therefore I shall make no Comments upon the Sentence, nor upon the Choice I was put to; we shall all choose any thing rather than Death, especially when 'tis attended with an uncomfortable prospect beyond it, which was my Case.

THE good Minister whose interest, tho' *a Stranger to me*, had obtain'd me the Reprieve, mourn'd sincerely for this part; he was in hopes, *he said*, that I should have ended my Days under the Influence of good Instruction, that I might not have forgot my former Distresses, and that I should not have been turned loose again among such a wretched a Crew as they generally are, who are thus sent Abroad where, *as he said*, I must have more than ordinary secret Assistance from the Grace of God, if I did not turn as wicked again as ever.

I HAVE not for a good while mentioned my Governess, who had during most, if not all of this part been dangerously Sick, and being in as near a view of Death, by her Disease, as I was by my Sentence, was a very great Penitent; I say, I have not mention'd her, nor indeed did I see her in all this time, but being now recovering, and just able to come Abroad, she came to see me.

1. Have certainty that a full pardon will follow the reprieve.

I TOLD her my Condition, and what a different flux and reflux of Fears, and Hopes I had been agitated with; I told her, what I had escap'd, and upon what Terms, and she was present, when the Minister express'd his fears of my relapsing into wickedness upon my falling into the wretch'd Companies, that are generally Transported: Indeed I had a melancholly Reflection upon it in my own Mind, for I knew what a dreadful Gang was always sent away together, and I said to my Governess, that the good Minister's fears were not without Cause: Well, well, *says she*, but I hope you will not be tempted with such a horrid Example as that, and as soon as the Minister was gone, she told me, she would not have me discourag'd, for perhaps ways and means might be found out to dispose of me in a particular way, by my self, of which she would talk farther to me afterward.

I LOOK'D earnestly at her, and I thought she look'd more chearful than she usually had done, and I entertain'd immediately a Thousand Notions of being deliver'd, but could not for my Life imagin the Methods, or think of one that was in the least feizible; but I was too much concerned in it, to let her go from me without explaining herself, which tho' she was very loth to do, yet my importunity prevail'd, and while I was still pressing, she answer'd me in few Words, thus, Why, *you have Money, have you not*? did you ever know one in your Life that was Transported, and had a Hundred Pound in his Pocket, I'll warrant you Child, *says she*.

I UNDERSTOOD her presently, but told her I would leave all that to her, but I saw no room to hope for any thing, but a strict Execution of the order, and as it was a severity that was esteem'd a Mercy, there was no doubt but it would be strictly observ'd; she said no more, but this, *we will try what can be done*, and so we parted for that Night.

I LAY in the Prison near fifteen Weeks after this order for Transportation was sign'd; what the Reason of it was, I know not, but at the end of this time I was put on Board of a Ship in the *Thames*, and with me a Gang of Thirteen, as harden'd vile Creatures as ever *Newgate* produc'd in my time; and it would really well take up a History longer than mine to describe the degree of Impudence, and audacious Villany that those Thirteen were arriv'd to; and the manner of their behaviour in the Voyage; of which I have a very diverting Account by me, which the Captain of the Ship, who carried them over gave me the Minutes of, and which he caus'd his Mate to write down at large.

IT may perhaps be thought Trifling to enter here into a Relation of all the little incidents which attended me in this interval of my Circumstances; I mean between the final order for my Transportation, and the time of my going on board the Ship, and I am too near the End of my Story, to allow room for it, but something relating to me, *and my Lancashire Husband*, I must not omit.

HE had, *as I have observ'd already* been carried from the Master's side[2] of the ordinary prison, into the Press-Yard, with three of his Comrades, for they found another to add to them after some time; here for what Reason I knew not, they were kept in Custody without being brought to Tryal almost three Months, it seems they found means to Bribe or buy off some of those who were expected to come in against them, and they wanted Evidence some time to Convict them: After some puzzle on this Account, at first they made a shift to get proof enough against two of them, to carry them off; but the other two, of which my *Lancashire* Husband was one, lay still in Suspence: They had I think one positive Evidence against each of them; but the Law strictly obliging them to have two Witnesses,[3] they cou'd make nothing of it; yet it seems they were resolv'd not to part with the Men neither, not doubting but a farther Evidence would at last come in; and in order to this, I think Publication was made, that such Prisoners being taken, any one that had been robb'd by them might come to the Prison and see them.

I TOOK this opportunity to satisfy my Curiosity, pretending that I had been robb'd in the *Dunstable* Coach, and that I would go to see the two Highway-Men; but when I came into the Press-Yard, I so disguis'd myself, and muffled my Face up so, that he cou'd see little of me, and consequently knew nothing of who I was; and when I came back, I said publickly that I knew them very well.

IMMEDIATELY it was Rumour'd all over the Prison, that *Moll Flanders* would turn Evidence against one of the Highway Men, and that I was to come off by it from the Sentence of Transportation.

THEY heard of it, and immediately my Husband desir'd to see this Mrs. *Flanders* that knew him so well, and was to be an Evidence against him, and accordingly, I had leave given to go to him. I dress'd myself up as well as the best Cloths that I suffer'd myself ever to appear in there, would allow me, and went to the Press-yard, but had for some time a Hood over my Face; he said little to me at first, but ask'd me if I knew him; I told him, yes, very well; but as I conceal'd my Face, so I Counterfeited my Voice, that he had not the least guess at who I was: He ask'd me where I had seen him, I told him between *Dunstable* and *Brickhill*, but turning to the Keeper that stood by, I ask'd if I might not be admitted to talk with him alone, he said, yes, yes, as much as I pleas'd, and so very civilly withdrew.

As soon as he was gone, and I had shut the Door, I threw off my Hood, and bursting out into Tears, *my Dear*, says I, *do you not know me*? He turn'd pale and stood Speechless, like one Thunder struck,

2. Newgate Prison was divided into three main parts: the Master-side (reputed to be the worst), the Common-side, and the Press-yard.
3. As previous editors have noted, Defoe might be mistaken here since, except for treason, one single "evidence" or witness was sufficient to prosecute and convict.

and not able to conquer the Surprize, said no more but this, *let me sit down*; and sitting down by a Table, he laid his Elbow upon the Table, and leaning his Head on his Hand, fix'd his Eyes on the Ground as one stupid: I cry'd so vehemently on the other Hand, that it was a good while e'er I could speak any more; but after I had given some vent to my Passion by Tears, I repeated the same Words: MY DEAR, *do you not know me*? at which he answer'd YES, and said no more a good while.

AFTER some time continuing in the Surprize, *as above*, he cast up his Eyes towards me and said, *How could you be so cruel*? I did not readily understand what he meant; and I answer'd, How can you call me Cruel? What have I been Cruel to you in? *To come to me*, says he, *in such a Place as this, is it not to insult me? I have not robb'd you? at least not on* the Highway?

I PERCEIV'D by this, that he knew nothing of the miserable Circumstances I was in, and thought that having got some Intelligence of his being there, I had come to upbraid him with his leaving me; but I had too much to say to him to be affronted, and told him in few Words, that I was far from coming to Insult him, but at best I came to Condole mutually, that he would be easily satisfy'd, that I had no such View, when I should tell him that *my Condition was worse than his, and that many ways*: He look'd a little concern'd at the general Expression of my Condition being worse than his; but with a kind of a smile, look'd a little wildly, and said, How can that be? when you see me Feter'd, and in *Newgate*, and two of my Companions Executed already; can you say your Condition is worse than Mine?

COME my Dear, *says I*, we have a long piece of Work to do, if I should be to relate, or you to hear my unfortunate History; but if you are dispos'd to hear it, you will soon conclude with me that my Condition is worse than yours: How is that possible, *says he again*, when I expect to be cast for my Life the very next Sessions? Yes *says I*, 'tis very possible when I shall tell you that I have been cast for my Life three Sessions ago, and am under Sentence of Death, is not my Case worse than yours?

THEN indeed he stood silent again, like one struck Dumb, and after a little while he starts up; unhappy Couple! *says he*, How can this be possible? I took him by the Hand, come MY DEAR, *said I*, sit down, and let us compare our Sorrows: I am a Prisoner in this very House, and in a much worse Circumstance than you, and you will be satisfy'd I do not come to Insult you, when I tell you the particulars; and with this we sat down together, and I told him so much of my Story as I thought was convenient, bringing it at last to my being reduc'd to great Poverty, and representing myself as fallen into some Company that led me to relieve my Distresses by a way that I had been utterly unacquainted with, and that they making an attempt at a Tradesman's House I was seiz'd upon, for having been but just at the Door, the Maid-Servant pulling me in; that I neither had broke any Lock, or taken any thing away, and that notwithstanding that I was brought in Guilty, and Sentenc'd to Die; but that the Judges having been made sensible of the Hardship of my Circumstances, had obtain'd leave to remit the Sentence upon my consenting to be transported.

I TOLD him I far'd the worse for being taken in the Prison for one *Moll Flanders*, who was a famous successful Thief, that all of them had heard of, but none of them had ever seen, but that *as he knew well* was none of my Name; but I plac'd all to the account of my ill Fortune, and that under this Name I was dealt with as an old Offender, tho' this was the first thing they had ever known of me. I gave him a long particular of things that had befallen me, since I saw him; but I told him if I had seen him since, he might think I had, and then gave him an Account how I had seen him at *Brickhill*; how furiously he was pursued, and how by giving an Account that I knew him, and that he was a very honest Gentleman, one Mr.——— the *Heu and Cry* was stopp'd, and the High Constable went back again.

HE listen'd most attentively to all my Story, and smil'd at most of the particulars, being all of them petty Matters, and infinitely below what he had been at the Head of; but when I came to the Story of little *Brickill*, he was surpriz'd, *and was it you my Dear*, said he, *that gave the Check to the Mob that was at our Heels there*, at *Brickill*: Yes *said I*, it was I indeed, and then I told him the particulars which I had observ'd of him there. *Why then*, said he, *it was you that sav'd my Life at that time*, and I am glad I owe my Life to you, for I will pay the Debt to you now, and I'll deliver you from the present Condition you are in, or I will die in the attempt.

I TOLD him by no means; it was a Risque too great, not worth his running the hazard of, and for a Life not worth his saving; 'twas no matter for that he said, it was a Life worth all the World to him; a Life that had given him a new Life; for *says he*, I was never in real Danger of being taken, but that time; till the last Minute when I was taken: Indeed *he told* me his Danger then lay in his believing he had not been pursued that way; for they had gone off from *Hockly* quite another way, and had come over the enclos'd Country into *Brickill*, not by the Road and were sure they had not been seen by any Body.

HERE he gave a long History of his Life, which indeed would make a very strange History, and be infinitely diverting. He told me he took to the Road about twelve Year before he marry'd me; that the Woman which call'd him Brother, was not really his Sister, or any Kin to him; but one that belong'd to their Gang, and who keeping Correspondence with them, liv'd always in Town, having good store of Acquaintance, that she gave them a perfect Intelligence of Persons going out of Town, and that they had made several good Booties by her Correspondence; that she thought she had fix'd a Fortune for him, when she brought me to him, but happen'd to be Disappointed, which he really could not blame her for: That, if it had been his good Luck, that I had had the Estate, which she was inform'd I had, he had resolv'd to leave off the Road, and live a retired sober Life, but never to appear in publick till some general Pardon had been pass'd, or till he could, for Money have got his Name into some particular Pardon, that so he might have been perfectly easy, but that as it had proved otherwise he was oblig'd to put off his Equipage, and take up the old Trade again.

HE gave me a long Account of some of his Adventures, and particularly one, when he robb'd the *West Chester* Coaches, near *Lichfield*, when he got a very great Booty; and after that, how he robb'd five Grasiers,[4] in the *West*, going to *Burford* Fair in *Wiltshire*[5] to buy Sheep; he told me he got so much Money on those two Occasions, that if he had known where to have found me, he would certainly have embrac'd my Proposal of going with me to *Virginia*; or to have settled in a Plantation, on some other Parts of the *English* Colonies in *America*.

HE told me he wrote two or three Letters to me, directed according to my Order, but heard nothing from me: This I indeed knew to be true, but the Letters coming to my Hand in the time of my latter Husband, I could do nothing in it, and therefore chose to give no answer, that so he might rather believe they had miscarried.

BEING thus Disappointed, *he said*, he carried on the old Trade ever since, tho' when he had gotten so much Money, *he said*, he did not run such desperate Risques as he did before; then he gave me some Account of several hard and desperate Encounters which he had with Gentlemen on the Road, who parted too hardly with their Money; and shew'd me some Wounds he had receiv'd, and he had one or two very terrible Wounds indeed, as particularly one by a Pistol Bullet which broke his Arm; and another with a Sword, which ran him quite thro' the Body, but that missing his Vitals he was cur'd again; one of his Comrades having kept with him so faithfully, and so Friendly, as that he assisted him in riding near 80 Miles before his Arm was Set, and then got a Surgeon in a considerable City, remote from that Place where it was done, pretending they were Gentlemen Traveling towards *Carlisle*, and that they had been attack'd on the Road by Highway-Men, and that one of them had shot him into the Arm, and broke the Bone.

4. Graziers, men who graze or feed cattle for the market.
5. Burford is located in Oxfordshire.

THIS *he said*, his Friend manag'd so well, that they were not suspected at all, but lay still till he was perfectly cur'd: He gave me so many distinct Accounts of his Adventures, that it is with great reluctance, that I decline the relating them; but I consider that this is my own Story, not his.

I THEN enquir'd into the Circumstances of his present Case at that time, and what it was he expected when he came to be try'd; he told me that they had no Evidence against him, or but very little; for that of three Robberies, which they were all Charg'd with, it was his good Fortune, that he was but in one of them, and that there was but one Witness to be had for that Fact, which was not sufficient; but that it was expected some others would come in against him; that he thought indeed, when he first see me, that I had been one that came of that Errand; but that if no Body came in against him, he hop'd he should be clear'd; that he had had some intimation, that if he would submit to Transport himself, he might be admitted to it without a Tryal, but that he could not think of it with any Temper,[6] and thought he could much easier submit to be Hang'd.

I BLAM'D him for that, and told him I blam'd him on two Accounts; first because, if he was Transported, there might be an Hundred ways for him that was a Gentleman, and a bold enterprizing Man to find his way back again, and perhaps some Ways and Means to come back before he went. He smil'd at that Part, and said he should like the last the best of the two, for he had a kind of Horror upon his Mind at his being sent over to the Plantations as *Romans* sent condemn'd Slaves to Work in the Mines; that he thought the Passage into another State, let it be what it would, much more tolerable at the Gallows, and that this was the general Notion of all the Gentlemen, who were driven by the Exigence of their Fortunes to take the Road; that at the Place of Execution there was at least an End of all the Miseries of the present State, and as for what was to follow, a Man was in his Opinion, as likely to Repent sincerely in the last Fortnight of his Life under the Pressures and Agonies of a Jayl, and the condemn'd Hole, as he would ever be in the Woods and Wildernesses of *America*; that Servitude and hard Labour were things Gentlemen could never stoop to, that it was but the way to force them to be their own Executioners afterwards, which was much worse, and that therefore he could not have any Patience when he did but think of being Transported.

I USED the utmost of my endeavour to perswade him, and joyn'd that known Womans Rhetorick to it, I mean that of Tears: I told him the infamy of a publick Execution was certainly a greater pressure upon the Spirits of a Gentleman, than any of the Mortifications that

6. Moderation, composure.

he could meet with Abroad could be; that he had at least in the other a Chance for his Life, whereas here he had none at all; that it was the easiest thing in the World for him to manage the Captain of the Ship, who were generally speaking, Men of good Humour, and some Gallantry; and a small matter of Conduct; especially if there was any Money to be had, would make way for him to buy himself off, when he came to *Virginia*.

HE look'd wishfully at me, and I thought I guess'd at what he meant, *that is to say*, that he had no Money, but I was mistaken, his meaning was another way; *you hinted just now*, my Dear said he, that there might be a way of coming back before I went, by which I understood you, that it might *be possible to buy it off here; I had rather give* 200 *l. to prevent going, than* 100 *l. to be set at Liberty when I came there*. That is my Dear, said I, *because you do not know the Place so well as I do*: that may be, said he, *and yet I believe as well as you know it, you would do the same unless it is, because* as you told me, *you have a Mother there*.

I TOLD him, as to my Mother, it was next to impossible, but that she must be dead many Years before; and as for any other Relations that I might have there, I knew them not now: That since the Misfortunes I had been under, had reduc'd me to the Condition I had been in for some Years, I had not kept up any Correspondence with them; and that he would easily believe, I should find but a cold Reception from them, if I should be put to make my first visit in the Condition of a Transported Felon; that therefore if I went thither, I resolv'd not to see them; But that I had many Views in going there, if it should be my Fate, which took off all the uneasy Part of it; and if he found himself oblig'd to go also, I should easily Instruct him how to manage himself, so as never to go a Servant at all, especially since I found he was not destitute of Money, which was the only Friend in such a Condition.

HE smil'd, and said, he did not tell me he had Money; I took him up short, and told him I hop'd he did not understand by my speaking, that I should expect any supply from him if he had Money; that on the other Hand, tho' I had not a great deal, yet I did not want, and while I had any I would rather add to him, than weaken him in that Article, seeing what ever he had, I knew in the Case of Transportation he would have Occasion of it all.

HE express'd himself in a most tender manner upon that Head: he told me what Money he had was not a great deal, but that he would never hide any of it from me if I wanted it; and that he assur'd me he did not speak with any such Apprehensions; that he was only intent upon what I had hinted to him before he went; that here he knew what to do with himself, but there he should be the most ignorant helpless Wretch alive.

I TOLD him he frighted and terify'd himself with that which had no Terror in it; that if he had Money, as I was glad to hear he had, he might not only avoid the Servitude, suppos'd to be the Consequence of Transportation; but begin the World upon a new Foundation, and that such a one as he cou'd not fail of Success in, with but the common Application usual in such Cases; that he could not but call to Mind, that it was what I had recommended to him many Years before, and had propos'd it for our mutual Subsistence, and restoring our Fortunes in the World; and I would tell him now, that to convince him both of the certainty of it, and of my being fully acquainted with the Method, and also fully satisfy'd in the probability of Success, he should first see me deliver myself from the Necessity of going over at all, and then that I would go with him freely, and of my own Choice, and perhaps carry enough with me to satisfy him that I did not offer it, for want of being able to live without Assistance from him; but that I thought our mutual Misfortunes had been such, as were sufficient to Reconcile us both to quitting this part of the World, and living where no Body could upbraid us with what was past, or we be in any dread of a Prison; and without the Agonies of a condemn'd Hole to drive us to it, where we should look back on all our past Disasters with infinite Satisfaction, when we should consider that our Enemies should entirely forget us, and that we should live as new People in a new World, no Body having any thing to say to us, or we to them.

I PRESS'D this Home to him with so many Arguments, and answer'd all his own passionate Objections so effectually, that he embrac'd me, and told me, I treated him with such a Sincerity, and Affection as overcame him; that he would take my Advice, and would strive to submit to his Fate, in hope of having the comfort of my Assistance, and of so faithful a Counsellor, and such a Companion in his Misery; but still he put me in mind of what I had mention'd before, Namely, that there might be some way to get off, before he went, and that it might be possible to avoid going at all, which he said would be much better. I told him he should see, and be fully satisfy'd that I would do my utmost in that Part too, and if it did not succeed, yet that I would make good the rest.

WE parted after this long Conference, with such Testimonies of Kindness and Affection as I thought were Equal, if not Superior to that at our parting at *Dunstable*; and now I saw more plainly than before, the Reason why he declin'd coming at that time any farther with me toward *London* than *Dunstable*; and why when we parted there, he told me it was not convenient for him to come part of the way to *London* to bring me going,[7] as he would otherwise have done:

7. Along.

I have observ'd that the Account of his Life, would have made a much more pleasing History, than this of mine; and indeed nothing in it, was more strange than this Part, (*viz.*) that he had carried on that desperate Trade full five and Twenty Year, and had never been taken, the Success he had met with, had been so very uncommon, and such, that sometimes he had liv'd handsomely and retir'd, in one Place for a Year or two at a time, keeping himself and a Man-Servant to wait on him, and has often sat in the Coffee-Houses, and heard the very People who he had robb'd give Accounts of their being robb'd, and of the Places and Circumstances, so that he cou'd easily remember that it was the same.

IN this manner it seems he liv'd near *Leverpool* at the time, he unluckily married me for a Fortune: Had I been the Fortune he expected, I verily believe, as he said, that he would have taken up and liv'd honestly all his Days.

HE had with the rest of his Misfortunes the good luck not to be actually upon the spot, when the Robbery was done, which he was committed for; and so none of the Persons robb'd cou'd swear to him, or had any thing to Charge upon him; but it seems as he was taken, with the Gang, one hard-mouth'd Countryman swore home to him; and they were like to have others come in according to the Publication they had made, so that they expected more Evidence against him, and for that Reason he was kept in hold.

HOWEVER, the offer which was made to him of admitting him to Transportation was made, as I understood upon the intercession of some great Person who press'd him hard to accept of it before a Tryal; and indeed as he knew there were several that might come in against him, I thought his Friend was in the Right, and I lay at him Night and Day to delay it no longer.

AT last, with much difficulty he gave his consent, and as he was not therefore admitted to Transportation in Court, and on his Petition as I was, so he found himself under a difficulty to avoid embarking himself as I had said he might have done his great Friend, who was his Intercessor for the Favour of that Grant, having given Security for him that he should Transport himself, and not return within the Term.[8]

THIS hardship broke all my Measures, for the steps I took afterwards for my own deliverance, were hereby render'd wholly ineffectual, unless I would abandon him, and leave him to go to *America* by himself; than which he protested he would much rather venture,[9] altho' he were certain to go directly to the Gallows.

I must now return to my own Case, the time of my being Trans-

8. I.e., should he return to England within the term of his transportation (customarily seven years), his friend would forfeit the money he has put up as security.
9. Risk going to trial.

ported according to my Sentence was near at Hand; my Governess who continu'd my fast Friend, had try'd to obtain a Pardon, but it could not be done unless with an Expence too heavy for my Purse, considering that to be left naked and empty, unless I had resolv'd to return to my old Trade again, had been worse than my Transportation, because there I knew I could live, here I could not. The good Minister stood very hard on another Account to prevent my being Transported also; but he was answer'd, that indeed my Life had been given me at his first Solicitations, and therefore he ought to ask no more; he was sensibly griev'd at my going, because, *as he said*, he fear'd I should lose the good impressions, which a prospect of Death had at first made on me, and which were since encreas'd by his Instructions, and the pious Gentleman was exceedingly concern'd about me on that Account.

ON the other Hand, I really was not so sollicitous about it, as I was before, but I industriously conceal'd my Reasons for it from the Minister, and to the last he did not know, but that I went with the utmost reluctance and affliction.

IT was in the Month of *February* that I was with seven other Convicts, *as they call'd us*, deliver'd to a Merchant that Traded to *Virginia*, on board a Ship, riding, as they call'd it, in *Deptford* Reach: The Officer of the Prison deliver'd us on board, and the Master of the Vessel gave a Discharge for us.

WE were for that Night clapt under Hatches, and kept so close, that I thought I should have been suffocated for want of Air, and the next Morning the Ship weigh'd, and fell down the River[1] to a Place they call *Bugby's Hole*, which was done, as they told us by the agreement of the Merchant, that all opportunity of Escape should be taken from us: However when the Ship came thither, and cast Anchor, we were allow'd more Liberty, and particularly were permitted to come upon the Deck, but not upon the Quarter-Deck, that being kept particularly for the Captain, and for Passengers.

WHEN by the Noise of the Men over my Head, and the Motion of the Ship, I perceiv'd that they were under Sail, I was at first greatly surpriz'd, fearing we should go away directly, and that our Friends would not be admitted to see us any more; but I was easy soon after when I found they had come to an Anchor again, and soon after that we had Notice given by some of the Men where we were, that the next Morning we should have the Liberty to come upon Deck, and to have our Friends come and see us if we had any.

ALL that Night I lay upon the hard Boards of the Deck, as the other Prisoners did, but we had afterwards the Liberty of little Cabins for such of us as had any Bedding to lay in them; and room to stow

1. Weighed anchor and sailed down the River Thames. *Hatches*: Placed below deck.

any Box or Trunk for Cloths, and Linnen, if we had it, (which might well be put in) for some of them had neither Shirt or Shift, or a Rag of Linnen or Woollen, but what was on their Backs, or a Farthing of Money to help themselves; and yet I did not find but they far'd well enough in the Ship, especially the Women, who got Money of the Seamen for washing their Cloths sufficient to purchase any common things that they wanted.

WHEN the next Morning we had the liberty to come upon the Deck, I ask'd one of the Officers of the Ship, whether I might not have the liberty to send a Letter on Shore to let my Friends know where the Ship lay, and to get some necessary things sent to me. This was it seems the Boatswain, a very civil courteous sort of Man, who told me I should have that, or any other liberty that I desir'd, that he could allow me with Safety; I told him I desir'd no other; and he answer'd that the Ships Boat would go up to *London* the next Tide, and he would order my Letter to be carried.

ACCORDINGLY when the Boat went off, the Boatswain came to me, and told me the Boat was going off, and that he went in it himself, and ask'd me if my Letter was ready, he would take care of it; I had prepared myself you may be sure, Pen, Ink and Paper beforehand, and I had gotten a Letter ready directed to my Governess, and enclos'd another for my fellow Prisoner, which however I did not let her know was my Husband, not to the last; in that to my Governess, I let her know where the Ship lay, and press'd her earnestly to send me what things I knew she had got ready for me, for my Voyage.

WHEN I gave the Boatswain the Letter, I gave him a Shilling with it, which I told him was for the Charge of a Messenger or Porter, which I entreated him to send with the Letter, as soon as he came on Shore, that if possible I might have an Answer brought back by the same Hand, that I might know what was become of my things, for SIR, *says I*, if the Ship should go away before I have them on Board I am undone.

I TOOK care when I gave him the Shilling, to let him see that I had a little better Furniture[2] about me, than the ordinary Prisoners, for he saw that I had a Purse, and in it a pretty deal of Money, and I found that the very sight of it, immediately furnish'd me with very different Treatment from what I should otherwise have met with in the Ship; for tho' he was very Courteous indeed before, in a kind of natural Compassion to me, as a Woman in distress; yet he was more than ordinarily so, afterwards, and procur'd me to be better treated in the Ship, than, *I say*, I might otherwise have been as shall appear in its Place.

HE very honestly had my Letter deliver'd to my Governess own

2. Provisions, personal effects.

Hands, and brought me back an Answer from her in writing; and when he gave me the Answer, gave me the Shilling again, *there*, says he, there's your Shilling again too, for I deliver'd the Letter my self; I could not tell what to say, I was so surpris'd at the thing; but after some Pause, *I said*, Sir you are too kind, it had been but Reasonable that you had paid yourself Coach hire then.

No, no, *says he*, I am over paid: What is the Gentlewoman your Sister?

No, Sir, *said I*, she is no Relation to me, but she is a dear Friend, and all the Friends I have in the World: well, *says he*, there are few such Friends in the World: why she cryes after you like a Child, Ay, *says I again*, she would give a Hundred Pound, I believe, to deliver me from this dreadful Condition I am in.

Would she so? *says he*, for half the Money I believe, I cou'd put you in a way how to deliver yourself, but this he spoke softly that no Body cou'd hear.

Alas! Sir, *said I*, but then that must be such a Deliverance as if I should be taken again, would cost me my Life; Nay, *said he*, if you were once out of the Ship you must look to yourself afterwards, that I can say nothing to; so we drop'd the Discourse for that time.

In the mean time my Governess faithful to the last Moment, convey'd my Letter to the Prison to my Husband, and got an Answer to it, and the next Day came down herself to the Ship, bringing me in the first Place a *Sea-Bed* as they call it, and all its Furniture, such as was convenient, but not to let the People think it was extraordinary; she brought with her a *Sea-Chest*, that is a Chest, such as are made for Seamen with all the Conveniences in it, and fill'd with every thing almost that I could want; and in one of the corners of the Chest, where there was a Private Drawer was my Bank of Money, *that is to say*, so much of it as I had resolv'd to carry with me; for I order'd a part of my Stock to be left behind me, to be sent afterwards in such Goods as I should want when I came to settle; for Money in that Country is not of much use where all things are bought for Tobacco, much more is it a great loss to carry it from Hence.[3]

But my Case was particular; it was by no Means proper to me to go thither without Money or Goods, and for a poor Convict that was to be sold as soon as I came on Shore, to carry with me a Cargo of Goods would be to have Notice taken of it, and perhaps to have them seiz'd by the Publick; so I took part of my Stock with me thus, and left the other part with my Governess.

My Governess brought me a great many other things, but it was not proper for me to look too well provided in the Ship, at least, till I knew what kind of a Captain we should have. When she came into

3. I.e., England. Tobacco, rather than money, was the standard for trade in Maryland and Virginia.

the Ship, I thought she would have died indeed; her Heart sunk at the sight of me, and at the thoughts of parting with me in that Condition, and she cry'd so intolerably, I cou'd not for a long time have any talk with her.

I TOOK that time to read my fellow Prisoners Letter, which however greatly perplex'd me; he told me he was determin'd to go, but found it would be impossible for him to be Discharg'd time enough for going in the same Ship, and which was more than all, he began to question whether they would give him leave to go in what Ship he pleas'd, tho' he did voluntarily Transport himself; but that they would see him put on Board such a Ship as they should direct, and that he would be charg'd upon the Captain as other convict Prisoners were; so that he began to be in dispair of seeing me till he came to *Virginia*, which made him almost desperate; seeing that on the other Hand, if I should not be there, if any Accident of the Sea, or of Mortality should take me away, he should be the most undone Creature there in the World.

THIS was very perplexing, and I knew not what Course to take; I told my Governess the Story of the Boatswain, and she was mighty eager with me to treat with him; but I had no mind to it, till I heard whether my Husband, or fellow Prisoner, *so she call'd him*, cou'd be at liberty to go with me or no; at last I was forc'd to let her into the whole matter, except only, that of his being my Husband; I told her I had made a positive Bargain or Agreement with him to go, if he could get the liberty of going in the same Ship, and that I found he had Money.[4]

IN this Condition I lay for three Weeks in the Ship, not knowing whether I should have my Husband with me or no; and therefore not resolving how, or in what manner to receive the honest Boatswain's proposal, which indeed he thought a little strange at first.

AT the End of this time, behold my Husband came on Board; he look'd with a dejected angry Countenance, his great Heart was swell'd with Rage and Disdain; to be drag'd along with three Keepers of *Newgate*, and put on Board like a Convict, when he had not so much as been brought to a Tryal; he made loud complaints of it by his Friends, for it seems he had some interest;[5] but his Friends got some Checque in their Application, and were told he had had *Favour enough*, and that they had receiv'd such an Account of him since the last Grant of his Transportation, that he ought to think himself very well treated that he was not prosecuted a new. This answer quieted him at once, for he knew too much what might have happen'd, and

4. In the first edition, the next two paragraphs appear before the paragraph beginning "The Ship began now to fill. . . ." (p. 387). For the two paragraphs appearing at this point in the first edition, and an explanation of this emendation, see pp. 269–72 below.

5. Influence (because of well-connected people working on his behalf to advance his "interest"). *With*: By. *Keepers*: Guardians, wardens.

what he had room to expect; and now he saw the goodness of the Advice to him, which prevail'd with him to accept of the offer of a voluntary Transportation, and after his chagrine at these Hell Hounds, *as he call'd them*, was a little over; he look'd a little compos'd, began to be chearful, and as I was telling him how glad I was to have him once more out of their Hands, took me in his Arms, and acknowledg'd with great Tenderness, that I had given him the best Advice possible, *My Dear*, says he, *Thou hast twice sav'd my Life, from hence forward it shall be all employ'd for you, and I'll always take your Advice*.

OUR first business was to compare our Stock: He was very honest to me, and told me his Stock was pretty good when he came into the Prison, but the living there as he did in a Figure like a Gentleman, *and which was ten times as much*, the making of Friends, and soliciting his Case, had been very Expensive; and in a Word, all his Stock that he had left was an Hundred and Eight Pounds, which he had about him all in Gold.

I GAVE him an Account of my Stock as faithfully, that is to say of what I had taken to carry with me, for I was resolv'd what ever should happen, to keep what I had left with my Governess, in Reserve; that in Case I should die, what I had with me was enough to give him, and that which was left in my Governess Hands would be her own, which she had well deserv'd of me indeed.

MY Stock which I had with me was two Hundred forty six Pounds, some odd Shillings; so that we had three Hundred and fifty four Pound between us, but a worse gotten Estate was scarce ever put together to begin the World with.

OUR greatest Misfortune as to our Stock, was that it was all in Money, which every one knows is an unprofitable Cargoe to be carryed to the Plantations; I believe his was really all he had left in the World, as he told me it was; but I who had between seven and eight Hundred Pounds in Bank when this Disaster befel me, and who had one of the faithfulest Friends in the World to manage it for me, considering she was a Woman of no manner of Religious Principles, had still Three Hundred Pounds left in her Hand, which I reserv'd, as above, besides some very valuable things, as particularly two gold Watches, some small Peices of Plate, and some Rings; all stolen Goods; the Plate, Rings and Watches were put up in my Chest with the Money, and with this Fortune, and in the Sixty first Year of my Age, I launch'd out into a new World, as I may call it, in the Condition (as to what appear'd) only of a poor nak'd Convict, order'd to be Transported in respite from the Gallows, my Cloaths were poor and mean, but not ragged or dirty, and none knew in the whole Ship that I had any thing of value about me.

HOWEVER, as I had a great many very good Cloaths, and Linnen in abundance, which I had order'd to be pack'd up in two great Boxes, I had them Shipp'd on Board, not as my Goods, but as consign'd to my real Name in *Virginia*; and had the Bills of Loading sign'd by a Captain in my Pocket; and in these Boxes was my Plate and Watches, and every thing of value except my Money, which I kept by itself in a private Drawer in my Chest, which cou'd not be found, or open'd if found, without splitting the Chest to peices.

THE Ship began now to fill, several Passengers came on Board, who were embark'd on no Criminal account, and these had Accommodations assign'd them in the great Cabbin, and other Parts of the Ship, whereas we *as Convicts* were thrust down below, I know not where; but when my Husband came on Board, I spoke to the Boatswain, who had so early given me Hints of his Friendship in carrying my Letter; I told him he had befriended me in many things, and I had not made any suitable Return to him, and with that I put a Guinea into his Hands; I told him that my Husband was now come on Board, that tho' we were both under the present Misfortunes, yet we had been Persons of a differing Character from the wretched Crew that we came with, and desir'd to know of him, whether the Captain might not be mov'd, to admit us to some Conveniences in the Ship, for which we would make him what Satisfaction he pleas'd, and that we would gratifie him for his Pains in procuring this for us. He took the Guinea as I cou'd see with great Satisfaction, and assur'd me of his Assistance.

THEN he told us, he did not doubt but that the Captain, who was one of the best humour'd Gentlemen in the World, would be easily brought to Accommodate us, as well as we cou'd desire, and to make me easie, told me he would go up the next Tide on purpose to speak to the Captain about it. The next Morning happening to sleep a little longer than ordinary, when I got up, and began to look Abroad, I saw the Boatswain among the Men in his ordinary Business; I was a little melancholly at seeing him there, and going forwards to speak to him, he saw me, and came towards me, but not giving him time to speak first, I said smiling, *I doubt, Sir, you have forgot us*, for I see you are very busy; he return'd presently,[6] come along with me, and you shall see, so he took me into the great Cabbin, and there sat a good sort of a Gentlemanly Man for a Seaman writing, and with a great many Papers before him.

HERE says the Boatswain to him that was a writing, is the Gentlewoman that the Captain spoke to you of, and turning to me, he said, I have been so far from forgetting your Business, that I have been up at the Captain's House, and have represented faithfully to the Captain what you said, relating to your being furnished with better

6. Answered immediately.

Conveniences for your self, and your Husband; and the Captain has sent this Gentleman, who is Mate of the Ship down with me, on purpose to show you every thing, and to Accommodate you fully to your Content, and bid me assure you that you shall not be treated like what you were at first expected to be, but with the same respect as other Passengers are treated.

THE Mate then spoke to me, and not giving me time to thank the Boatswain for his kindness confirm'd what the Boatswain had said, and added that it was the Captain's delight to show himself Kind, and Charitable, especially, to those that were under any Misfortunes, and with that he shew'd me several Cabbins built up, some in the Great Cabbin, and some partition'd off, out of the Steerage,[7] but opening into the great Cabbin on purpose for the Accommodation of Passengers, and gave me leave to choose where I would; however I chose a Cabbin, which open'd into the Steerage, in which was very good Conveniences to set our Chest, and Boxes, and a Table to eat on.

THE Mate then told me, that the Boatswain had given so good a Character of me, and of my Husband, as to our civil Behaviour, that he had orders to tell me, we should eat with him, if we thought fit, during the whole Voyage on the common Terms of Passengers; that we might lay in some fresh Provisions, if we pleas'd; or if not, he should lay in his usual Store, and we should have Share with him: This was very reviving News to me, after so many Hardships, and Afflictions as I had gone thro' of late; I thank'd him, and told him, the Captain should make his own Terms with us, and ask'd him leave to go and tell my Husband of it who was not very well, and was not yet out of his Cabbin: Accordingly I went, and my Husband whose Spirits were still so much sunk with the Indignity (as he understood it) offered him, that he was scarce yet himself, was so reviv'd with the Account I gave him of the Reception we were like to have in the Ship, that he was quite another Man, and new vigour and Courage appear'd in his very Countenance; so true is it, that the greatest of Spirits, when overwhelm'd by their Afflictions, are subject to the greatest Dejections, and are the most apt to Despair and give themselves up.

AFTER some little Pause to recover himself, my Husband come up with me, and gave the Mate thanks for the kindness, which he had express'd to us, and sent suitable acknowledgement by him to the Captain, offering to pay him by Advance, what ever he demanded for our Passage, and for the Conveniences he had help'd us to; the Mate told him, that the Captain would be on Board in the Afternoon,

7. Not the part of a passenger ship allotted to passengers paying the cheapest rates, but that division of the after part of a ship which is immediately in front of the chief cabin; the second cabin.

and that he would leave all that till he came; accordingly in the Afternoon the Captain came, and we found him the same courteous obliging Man, that the Boatswain had represented him to be; and he was so well pleas'd with my Husband's Conversation, that in short, he would not let us keep the Cabbin we had chosen, but gave us one, that as I said before, open'd into the great Cabbin.

NOR were his Conditions exorbitant, or the Man craving and eager to make a Prey of us, but for fifteen Guineas we had our whole Passage and Provisions, and Cabbin, eat at the Captain's Table, and were very handsomely Entertain'd.

THE Captain lay himself in the other part of the Great Cabbin, having let his round House,[8] *as they call it*, to a rich Planter, who went over, with his Wife, and three Children, who eat by themselves; he had some other ordinary Passengers, who Quarter'd in the Steerage, and as for our old Fraternity, they were kept under the Hatches while the Ship lay there, and came very little on the Deck.

I COULD not refrain acquainting my Governess with what had happen'd, it was but just that she, who was so really concern'd for me, should have part in my good Fortune; besides I wanted her Assistance to supply me with several Necessaries, which before I was shy of letting any Body see me have; that it might not be publick, but now I had a Cabbin and room to set things in; I order'd abundance of good things for our Comfort in the Voyage, as Brandy, Sugar, Lemons, &*c.* to make Punch, and Treat our Benefactor, the Captain; and abundance of things for eating and drinking in the Voyage; also a larger Bed, and Bedding proportion'd to it; so that in a Word, we resolv'd to want for nothing in the Voyage.

ALL this while I had provided nothing for our Assistance, when we should come to the Place, and begin to call ourselves Planters; and I was far from being ignorant of what was needful on that Occasion; particularly all sorts of Tools for the Planters-Work, and for building; and all kinds of Furniture for our Dwelling, which if to be bought in the Country, must necessarily cost double the Price.

SO I discours'd that Point with my Governess, and she went and waited upon the Captain, and told him, that she hop'd ways might be found out, for her two unfortunate Cousins, *as she call'd us*, to obtain our Freedom when we came into the Country, and so enter'd into a Discourse with him about the Means and Terms also, of which I shall say more in its Place; and after thus sounding the Captain, she let him know, tho' we were unhappy in the Circumstance that occasion'd our going, yet that we were not unfurnish'd to set our selves to Work in the Country; and were resolv'd to settle, and live there as Planters, if we might be put in a way how to do it: The

8. Cabin or apartment located on the after part of the quarter-deck.

Captain readily offer'd his Assistance, told her the Method of entering upon such Business, and how easy, nay, how certain it was for industrious People to recover their Fortunes in such a manner: Madam, *says he*, 'tis no Reproach to any Man in that Country to have been sent over in worse Circumstances than I perceive your Cousins are in, provided they do but apply with diligence and good Judgment to the Business of that Place when they come there.

SHE then enquir'd of him what things it was Necessary we should carry over with us, and he like a very honest as well as knowing Man, told her thus: Madam, your Cousins in the first Place must procure some Body to buy them as Servants, in Conformity to the Conditions of their Transportation, and then in the Name of that Person, they may go about what they will; they may either Purchase some Plantations already begun, or they may purchase Land of the Government of the Country, and begin where they please, and both will be done reasonably; she bespoke his Favour in the first Article, which he promis'd to her to take upon himself; and indeed faithfull perform'd it, and as to the rest, he promis'd to recommend us to such as should give us the best Advice, and not to impose upon us, which was as much as could be desir'd.

SHE then ask'd him, if it would not be Necessary to furnish us with a Stock of Tools and Materials for the Business of Planting, and he said, yes, by all means, and then she begg'd his Assistance in it; she told him she would furnish us with every thing that was Convenient whatever it cost her; he accordingly gave her a long particular of things Necessary for a Planter, which by his Account came to about fourscore, or an Hundred Pounds; and in short, she went about as dexterously to buy them, as if she had been an old *Virginia* Merchant; only that she bought by my Direction above twice as much of every thing as he had given her a List of.

THESE she put on Board in her own Name, took his Bills of Loading for them, and Endorst those Bills of Loading to my Husband, Ensuring the Cargo afterwards in her own Name, by our order; so that we were provided for all Events, and for all Disasters.

I SHOULD have told you that my Husband gave her all his whole Stock of 180 *l.*[9] which as I have said, he had about him in Gold, to lay out thus, and I gave her a good Sum besides; so that I did not break into the Stock, which I had left in her Hands at all, but after we had sorted out our whole Cargo, we had yet near 200 *l.* in Money, which was more than enough for our purpose.

IN this Condition very chearful, and indeed joyful at being so happily Accommodated as we were; we set Sail from *Bugby's-Hole* to *Gravesend*, where the Ship lay about ten Days more, and where the

9. Changed to "108 *l.*" (the amount mentioned on p. 244 above) in the second edition.

Captain came on Board for good and all. Here the Captain offer'd us a civility, which indeed we had no Reason to expect. Namely, to let us go on Shore, and refresh ourselves, upon giving our Words in a solemn manner, that we would not go from him, and that we would return peaceably on Board again: This was such an Evidence of his Confidence in us, that it overcome my Husband, who in a meer Principle of Gratitude, told him as he could not be in any Capacity to make a suitable return for such a Favour, so he could not think of accepting of it; nor could he be easy that the Captain should run such a Risque: After some mutual Civilities, I gave my Husband a Purse, in which was 80 Guineas, and he puts it into the Captain's hand: There Captain, *says he*, there's part of a Pledge for our Fidelity, if we deal dishonestly with you on any Account, 'tis your own, and on this we went on Shore.

INDEED the Captain had assurance enough of our Resolutions to go, for that having made such Provision to Settle there; it did not seem Rational that we would chose[1] to remain here at the Expence and Peril of Life, for such it must have been, if we had been taken again. In a Word, we went all on Shore with the Captain, and Supp'd together in *Gravesend*; where we were very Merry, staid all Night, lay at the House where we Supp'd, and came all very honestly on Board again with him in the Morning. Here we bought ten dozen Bottles of good Beer, some Wine, some Fowls, and such things as we thought might be acceptable on Board.

MY Governess was with us all this while, and went with us Round into the *Downs*,[2] as did also the Captain's Wife with whom she went back; I was never so sorrowful at parting with my own Mother as I was at parting with her, and I never saw her more: We had a fair Easterly Wind sprung up the third Day after we came to the *Downs*, and we sail'd from thence the 10th of *April*; nor did we touch any more at any Place, till being driven on the Coast of *Ireland* by a very hard Gale of Wind, the Ship came to an Anchor in a little *Bay*, near the Mouth of a River, whose Name I remember not, but they said the River came down from *Limerick*, and that it was the largest River in *Ireland*.[3]

HERE being detain'd by bad Weather for some time, the Captain who continu'd the same kind good humour'd Man as at first, took us two on Shore with him again: He did it now in kindness to my Husband indeed, who bore the Sea very ill, and was very Sick, especially when it blew so hard: Here we bought in again, store of fresh Provisions, especially Beef, Pork, Mutton and Fowls, and the Captain stay'd to Pickle up five or six Barrels of Beef to lengthen out the

1. Choose.
2. A roadstead or area of water off the Kentish coast.
3. The Shannon.

Ships Store. We were here not above five Days, when the Weather turning mild, and a fair Wind; we set Sail again and in two and Forty Days came safe to the Coast of *Virginia*.

WHEN we drew near to the Shore, the Captain call'd me to him, and told me that he found by my Discourse, I had some Relations in the Place, and that I had been there before, and so he suppos'd I understood the Custom, in their disposing the convict Prisoners when they arriv'd; I told him I did not, and that as to what Relations I had in the Place, he might be sure I would make my self known to none of them while I was in the Circumstances of a Prisoner, and that as to the rest, we left ourselves entirely to him to Assist us, as he was pleas'd to promise us he wou'd do. He told me I must get some Body in the Place to come and buy us as Servants, and who must answer for us to the Governor of the Country, if he demanded us; I told him we should do as he should direct; so he brought a Planter to treat with him, as it were for the Purchase of these two Servants, my Husband and me, and there we were formally sold to him, and went a Shore with him: The Captain went with us, and carried us to a certain House whether it was to be call'd a Tavern or not, I know not, but we had a Bowl of Punch there made of Rum, &c. and were very Merry. After some time the Planter gave us a Certificate of Discharge, and an Acknowledgement of having serv'd him faithfully, and we were free from him the next Morning, to go whither we would.

FOR this Peice of Service the Captain demanded of us 6000 weight of Tobacco, which he said he was Accountable for to his Freighter, and which we immediately bought for him, and made him a present of 20 Guineas, besides, with which he was abundantly satisfy'd.

IT is not proper to Enter here into the particulars of what Part of the Colony of *Virginia* we Settled in, for divers[4] Reasons; it may suffice to mention that we went into the great River of *Potomack*, the Ship being bound thither; and there we intended to have Settled at first, tho' afterwards we altered our Minds.

THE first thing I did of Moment after having gotten all our Goods on Shore, and plac'd them in a Storehouse, or Warehouse, which with a Lodging we hir'd at the small Place or Village, where we Landed; I say the first thing was to enquire after my Mother, and after my Brother, (that fatal Person who I married as a Husband, as I have related at large;) a little enquiry furnish'd me with Information that Mrs.———, that is my Mother was Dead; that my Brother (or Husband) was alive, which I confess I was not very glad to hear; but which was worse, I found he was remov'd from the Plantation where he liv'd formerly, and where I liv'd with him, and liv'd with one of

4. Various, several.

his Sons in a Plantation just by the Place where we Landed, and where we had hir'd a Warehouse.

I WAS a little surpriz'd at first, but as I ventured to satisfy my self, that he could not know me, I was not only perfectly easy, but had a great mind to see him, if it was possible to do so without his seeing me; in order to that I found out by enquiry a Plantation, where he liv'd, and with a Woman of that Place, who I got to help me, like what we call a *Chairwoman*,[5] I rambl'd about towards the Place, as if I had only a mind to see the Country, and look about me; at last I came so near that I saw the Dwelling-house: *I ask'd the Woman* whose Plantation that was, *she said*, it belong'd to such a Man, and looking out a little to our right Hands, there says she, is the Gentleman that owns the Plantation, and his Father with him: What are their Christian Names? said I, I know not *said she*, what the old Gentlemans Name is, but his Sons Name is *Humphry*, and I believe, *says she*, the Fathers is so too; you may guess, if you can, what a confus'd mixture of Joy and Fright possest my Thoughts upon this Occasion, for I immediately knew that this was no Body else, but my own Son, by that Father she shewed me, who was my own Brother: I had no Mask, but I ruffled my Hoods so about my Face, that I depended upon it, that after above 20 Years absence, and withal not expecting any thing of me in that part of the World, he would not be able to know any thing of me; but I need not have us'd all that Caution, for the old Gentleman was grown dim Sighted, by some Distemper, which had fallen upon his Eyes, and could but just see well enough to walk about, and not run against a Tree, or into a Ditch. The Woman that was with me, had told me that, by a meer Accident, knowing nothing of what importance it was to me: As they drew near to us, *I said*, does he know you Mrs. *Owen*? so they call'd the Woman, yes, *said she*, if he hears me speak, he will know me; but he can't see well enough to know me, or any Body else; and so she told me the Story of his Sight, as I have related: This made me secure, and so I threw open my Hoods again, and let them pass by me: It was a wretched thing for a Mother thus to see her own Son, a handsome comely young Gentleman in flourishing Circumstances, and durst not make herself known to him; and durst not take any notice of him; let any Mother of Children that reads this, consider it, and but think with what anguish of Mind I restrain'd myself; what yearnings of Soul I had in me to embrace him, and weep over him; and how I thought all my Entrails turn'd within me, that my very Bowels mov'd,[6] and I knew not what to do; as I now know not how

5. Obsolete form of "charwoman," a woman hired by the day to do odd jobs of household work. *A Plantation, where*: Changed to "the Plantation where" in the second edition.
6. Moll's strong physiological reaction reflects the old belief of the bowels as the seat of the tender and sympathetic emotions.

to express those Agonies: When he went from me I stood gazing and trembling, and looking after him as long as I could see him; then sitting down on the Grass, just at a Place I had mark'd, I made as if I lay down to rest me, but turn'd from her, and lying on my Face wept, and kiss'd the Ground that he had set his Foot on.

I COU'D not conceal my Disorder so much from the Woman, but that she perceiv'd it, and thought I was not well, which I was oblig'd to pretend was true; upon which she press'd me to rise, the Ground being damp and dangerous, which I did accordingly, and walk'd away.

As I was going back again, and still Talking of this Gentleman, and his Son, a new Occasion of melancholy offer'd itself *thus*: The Woman began, as if she would tell me a Story to divert me; there goes, *says she*, a very odd Tale among the Neighbours where this Gentleman formerly liv'd: What was that, *said I*? why, says she, that old Gentleman going to *England*, when he was a young Man, fell in Love with a young Lady there, one of the finest Women that ever was seen, and Married her, and brought her over hither to his Mother, who was then living. He liv'd here several Years with her, *continu'd she*, and had several Children by her, of which the young Gentleman that was with him now, was one, but after some time, the old Gentlewoman his Mother talking to her, of something relating to herself; when she was in *England*, and of her Circumstances in *England*, which were bad enough; the Daughter-in-Law, began to be very much surpriz'd, and uneasy, and in short, examining further into things it appear'd past all Contradiction, that she the old Gentlewoman was her own Mother, and that consequently, that Son was his Wives own Brother, which struck the whole Family with Horror, and put them into such Confusion, that it had almost ruin'd them all; the young Woman would not live with him, the Son, her Brother and Husband, for a time went Distracted, and at last, the young Woman went away for *England*, and has never been heard of since.

IT is easy to believe that I was strangely affected with this Story; but 'tis impossible to describe the Nature of my Disturbance; I seem'd astonish'd at the Story, and ask'd her a Thousand Questions about the particulars, which I found she was thoroughly acquainted with; at last I began to enquire into the Circumstances of the Family, how the old Gentlewoman, *I mean, my Mother* died, and how she left what she had; for my Mother had promis'd me very solemnly, that when she died, she would do something for me, and leave it so, as that, if I was Living, I should one way or other come at it, without its being in the Power of her Son, *my Brother and Husband* to prevent it: She told me she did not know exactly how it was order'd; but she had been told, that *my Mother* had left a Sum of Money, and had tyed[7] her Plantation for the Payment of it, to be made good to the Daughter, if ever she could be heard of, either in *England*, or else where; and that the Trust was left with this Son, who was the Person that we saw with his Father.

THIS was News too good for me to make light of, and you may be sure fill'd my Heart with a Thousand Thoughts, what Course I should take, how, and when, and in what manner I should make myself known, or whether I should ever make myself known, or no.

HERE was a Perplexity that I had not indeed skill to manage myself in, neither knew I what Course to take: It lay heavy upon my mind Night, and Day, I could neither Sleep or Converse, so that my Husband perceiv'd it, and wonder'd what ail'd me, strove to divert me, but it was all to no purpose; he press'd me to tell him what it was troubled me, but I put it off, till at last importuning me continually, I was forc'd to form a Story, which yet had a plain Truth to lay it upon too; I told him I was troubled because I found we must shift our Quarters, and alter our Scheme of Settling, for that I found I should be known, if I stay'd in that part of the Country, for that my Mother being dead, several of my Relations were come into that Part where we then was, and that I must either discover myself to them, which in our present Circumstances was not proper on many Accounts, or remove, and which to do I knew not, and that this it was that made me so Melancholly, and so Thoughtful.

HE joyn'd with me in this, that it was by no means proper for me to make myself known to any Body in the Circumstances, in which we then were; and therefore he told me he would be willing to remove to any other part of the Country, or even to any other Country if I thought fit; but now I had another Difficulty, which was, that if I remov'd to any other Colony, I put myself out of the way of ever making a due Search after those Effects, which my Mother had left: Again, I could never so much as think of breaking the Secret of my former Marriage to my new Husband; It was not a Story, as I thought that would bear telling, nor could I tell what might be the Consequences of it; and it was impossible to search into the bottom of the thing without making it Publick all over the Country, as well who I was, as what I now was also.

IN this perplexity I continu'd a great while, and this made my Spouse very uneasy; for he found me perplex'd, and yet thought I was not open with him, and did not let him into every part of my Grievance; and he would often say, he wondred what he had done, that I would not Trust him with what ever it was, especially if it was Grievous, and Afflicting; the Truth is, he ought to have been trusted

7. Bound, entailed, as a rule or condition of descent settled on the estate.

with every thing; for no Man in the World could deserve better of a Wife; but this was a thing I knew not how to open to him, and yet having no Body to disclose any part of it to, the Burthen was too heavy for my mind; for let them say what they please of our Sex not being able to keep a Secret; my Life is a plain Conviction to me of the contrary; but be it our Sex, or the Man's Sex, a Secret of Moment should always have a Confident, a bosom Friend, to whom we may Communicate the Joy of it, or the Grief of it, be it which it will, or it will be a double weight upon the Spirits, and perhaps become even insupportable in itself; and this I appeal to all human Testimony for the Truth of.

AND this is the Cause why many times Men as well as Women, and Men of the greatest, and best Qualities other ways, yet have found themselves weak in this part, and have not been able to bear the weight of a secret Joy, or of a secret sorrow; but have been oblig'd to disclose it, even for the meer giving vent to themselves, and to unbend the Mind oppress, with the Load and Weights, which attended it; nor was this any Token of Folly, or Thoughtlessness at all, but a natural Consequence of the thing; and such People had they struggl'd longer with the Oppression, would certainly have told it in their Sleep, and disclos'd the Secret, let it have been of what fatal Nature soever, without regard to the Person to whom it might be expos'd: This Necessity of Nature, is a thing which Works sometimes with such vehemence, in the Minds of those who are guilty of any atrocious Villany; such as secret Murther in particular, that they have been oblig'd to Discover it, tho' the Consequence would necessarily be their own Destruction: Now tho' it may be true that the divine Justice ought to have the Glory of all those Discoveries and Confessions, yet 'tis as certain that Providence which ordinarily Works by the Hands of Nature, makes use here of the same natural Causes to produce those extraordinary Effects.

I COULD give several remarkable Instances of this in my long Conversation with Crime, and with Criminals; I knew one Fellow, that while I was a Prisoner in *Newgate*, was one of those they called then *Night-Flyers*, I know not what other Word they may have understood it by since; but he was one, who by Connivance was admitted to go Abroad every Evening, when he play'd his Pranks, and furnish'd those honest People they call Thief-Catchers[8] with business to find

8. For a gratuity, these men or women (e.g., Moll's governess) would reunite victims of theft with their possessions; they could also, when a thief was no longer useful, or to settle a personal score, turn him or her over to the authorities and collect a substantial reward. Three years after *Moll Flanders*, Defoe would write a biography of the most celebrated of these "honest People," Jonathan Wild, who had been hanged at Tyburn on May 24, 1725, despite his defense that, as "Thief-Catcher-General of Great Britain," he had been performing a public service. The attribution of this work to Defoe has recently been questioned. *Connivance*: I.e., with his jailers or "Keepers" (see n. 5 p. 243), with whom he would split the loot.

out next Day, and restore *for a Reward*, what they had stolen the Evening before: This Fellow was as sure to tell in his sleep all that he had done, and every Step he had taken, what he had stole, and where, as sure as if he had engag'd to tell it waking, and that there was no Harm or Danger in it; and therefore he was oblig'd after he had been out to lock himself up, or be lock'd up by some of the Keepers that had him in Fee,[9] that no Body should hear him; but on the other Hand, if he had told all the Particulars, and given a full account of his Rambles and Success to any Comrade, any Brother Thief, or to his Employers, *as I may justly call them*, then all was well with him, and he slept as quietly as other People.

As the publishing this Account of my Life, is for the sake of the just Moral of every part of it, and for Instruction, Caution, Warning and Improvement to every Reader, so this will not pass I hope for an unnecessary Digression concerning some People, being oblig'd to disclose the greatest Secrets either of their own, or other Peoples Affairs.

UNDER the certain Oppression of this weight upon my Mind, I labour'd in the Case I have been Naming; and the only relief I found for it, was to let my Husband into so much of it, as I thought would convince him of the Necessity there was, for us to think of Settling, in some other Part of the World, and the next Consideration before us, was, which part of the *English* settlements we should go to; my Husband was a perfect Stranger to the Country, and had not yet so much as a Geographical knowledge of the Situation of the several Places; and I, that till I wrote this, did not know what the word Geographical signify'd, had only a general Knowledge from long Conversation with People that came from, or went to several Places; but this I knew, that *Maryland*, *Pensilvania*, East and West, *Jersy*, *New York*, and *New England*, lay all North of *Virginia*, and that they were consequently all colder Climates, to which, for that very Reason, I had an Aversion; for that as I naturally lov'd warm Weather, so now I grew into Years, I had a stronger Inclination to shun a cold Climate; I therefore consider'd of going to *Carolina*, which is the only Southern[1] Colony of the *English*, on the Continent of *America*, and hither I propos'd to go; and the rather, because I might with great ease come from thence at any time, when it might be proper to enquire after my Mothers effects, and to make myself known enough to demand them.

WITH this Resolution, I propos'd to my Husband our going away from where we was, and carrying all our Effects with us to *Carolina*, where we resolv'd to Settle, for my Husband readily agreed to the first Part (*viz.*) that it was not at all proper to stay where we was,

9. In their pay or employment.
1. Changed to "most Southern" in the second edition.

since I had assur'd him we should be known there, and the rest I effectually conceal'd from him.

BUT now I found a new Difficulty upon me: The main Affair grew heavy upon my Mind still, and I could not think of going out of the Country, without *some how or other* making enquiry into the grand Affair of what my Mother had done for me; nor cou'd I with any patience bear the thought of going away, and not make myself known to my old Husband, (*Brother*) or to my Child, his Son, only I would fain have had this done without my new Husband having any knowledge of it, or they having any knowledge of him, or that I had such a thing as a Husband.

I CAST about innumerable ways in my Thoughts how this might be done: I would gladly have sent my Husband away to *Carolina*, with all our Goods, and have come after myself; but this was impracticable, he would never stir without me, being himself perfectly unacquainted with the Country, and with the Methods of settling there, or any where else: Then I thought we would both go first with part of our Goods, and that when we were Settled I should come back to *Virginia*, and fetch the remainder; but even then I knew he would never part with me, and be left there to go on alone; the Case was plain, he was bred a Gentleman, and by Consequence was not only unacquainted, but indolent, and when we did Settle, would much rather go out into the Woods with his Gun, which they call there Hunting,[2] and which is the ordinary Work of the *Indians*, and which they do as Servants; I say he would much rather do that, than attend the natural Business of his Plantation.

THESE were therefore difficulties unsurmountable, and such as I knew not what to do in, I had such strong impressions on my Mind about discovering myself to my *Brother*, formerly my *Husband*, that I could not withstand them; and the rather, because it run constantly in my Thoughts, that if I did not do it, while he liv'd, I might in vain endeavour to convince my Son afterward, that I was really the same Person, and that I was his Mother, and so might both lose the assistance and comfort of the Relation, and the benefit of whatever it was my Mother had left me; and yet on the other Hand, I cou'd never think it proper to discover myself to them in the Circumstances I was in; as well relating to the having a Husband with me, as to my being brought over by a legal Transportation, as a Criminal; on both which Accounts it was absolutely necessary to me to remove from the Place where I was, and come again to him, as from another Place, and in another Figure.

UPON those Considerations, I went on with telling my Husband,

2. As an Englishwoman, Moll distinguishes between "shooting" animals with a gun and "hunting" them with dogs. *Unacquainted*: Inexperienced, ignorant, not acquainted with labor.

the absolute necessity there was of our not Settling in *Potomack* River, at least that we should be presently made publick there, whereas if we went to any other Place in the World, we should come in, with as much Reputation, as any Family that came to Plant: That as it was always agreeable to the Inhabitants to have Families come among them to Plant, who brought Substance with them, either to purchase Plantations, or begin New ones, so we should be sure of a kind agreeable Reception, and that without any possibility of a Discovery of our Circumstances.

I TOLD him in general too, that as I had several Relations in the Place where we was, and that I durst not now let myself be known to them, because they would soon come into a knowledge of the Occasion and Reason of my coming over, which would be to expose myself to the last degree; so I had Reason to believe that my Mother who died here had left me something, and perhaps considerable, which it might be very well worth my while to enquire after; but that this too could not be done without exposing us publickly, unless we went from hence; and then where ever we Settled, I might come as it were to visit and to see my Brother and Nephews, make myself known to them, claim and enquire after what was my Due, be receiv'd with Respect, and at the same time have justice done me with chearfulness and good will; whereas if I did it now, I could expect nothing but with trouble, such as exacting it by force, receiving it with Curses and Reluctance, and with all kinds of Affronts; which he would not perhaps bear to see; that in Case of being oblig'd to legal Proofs of being really her Daughter, I might be at loss, be oblig'd to have recourse to *England*, and it may be to fail at last, and so lose it, whatever it might be: With these Arguments, and having thus acquainted my Husband with the whole Secret so far as was needful to him, we resolv'd to go and seek a Settlement in some other Colony, and at first Thoughts, *Carolina* was the Place we pitch'd upon.

IN order to this we began to make enquiry for Vessels going to *Carolina*, and in a very little while got information, that on the other side the *Bay, as they call it*, namely, in *Maryland* there was a Ship, which came from *Carolina*, loaden with Rice, and other Goods, and was going back again thither, and from thence to *Jamaica*, with Provisions: On this News we hir'd a Sloop to take in our Goods, and taking as it were a final farewel of *Potowmack* River, we went with all our Cargo over to *Maryland*.

THIS was a long and unpleasant Voyage, and my Spouse said it was worse to him than all the Voyage from *England*, because the Weather was but indifferent, the Water rough, and the Vessel small and inconvenient; in the next Place we were full a hundred Miles up *Potowmack* River, in a part which they call *Westmorland* County, and as that River is by far the greatest in *Virginia*, and I have heard say, it is the greatest River in the World that falls into another River, and not directly into the Sea; so we had base Weather in it, and were frequently in great Danger; for tho' they call it but a River, 'tis frequently so broad, that when we were in the middle, we could not see Land on either Side for many Leagues together: Then we had the great River, or Bay of *Chesapeake* to cross, which is where the River *Potowmack* falls into it, near thirty Miles broad, and we entered more great vast Waters, whose Names I know not, so that our Voyage was full two hundred Mile, in a poor sorry Sloop with all our Treasure, and if any Accident had happened to us, we might at last have been very miserable; supposing we had lost our Goods and saved our Lives only, and had then been left naked and destitute, and in a wild strange Place, not having one Friend or Acquaintance in all that part of the World? The very thoughts of it gives me some horror, even since the Danger is past.

WELL, we came to the Place in five Days sailing, I think they call it *Philips's Point*,[3] and behold when we came thither, the Ship bound to *Carolina*, was loaded and gone away but three Days before. This was a Disappointment, but however, I that was to be discourag'd with nothing, told my Husband that since we could not get Passage to *Carolina*, and that the Country we was in, was very fertile and good; we would if he lik'd of it, see if we could find out any thing for our Turn where we was, and that if he lik'd things we would Settle here.

WE immediately went on Shore, but found no Conveniences just at that Place, either for our being on Shore, or preserving our Goods on Shore, but was directed by a very honest Quaker, who we found there to go to a Place, about sixty Miles East; that is to say, nearer the Mouth of the *Bay*, where he said he liv'd, and where we should be Accommodated, either to Plant, or to wait for any other Place to Plant in, that might be more Convenient, and he invited us with so much kindness and simple Honesty that we agreed to go, and the Quaker himself went with us.

HERE we bought us two Servants, (*viz.*) an *English* Woman-Servant just come on Shore from a Ship of *Leverpool*, and a *Negro* Man-Servant; things absolutely necessary for all People that pretended to Settle in that Country: This honest Quaker was very helpful to us, and when we came to the Place that he propos'd to us, found us out a convenient Storehouse, for our Goods, and Lodging for ourselves, and our Servants; and about two Months, or thereabout afterwards, by his Direction we took up a large peice of Land from the Governor of that Country, in order to form our Plan-

3. As some critics have surmised, Moll is probably referring to the present-day Clay Island, situated at the mouth of the Nanticoke River in Dorchester County, Maryland.

tation, and so we laid the thoughts of going to *Carolina* wholly aside, having been very well receiv'd here, and Accommodated with a convenient Lodging, till we could prepare things, and have Land enough cur'd, and Timber and Materials provid'd for building us a House, all which we manag'd by the Direction of the Quaker; so that in one Years time, we had near fifty Acres of Land clear'd, part of it enclos'd, and some of it Planted with Tobacco, tho' not much; besides, we had Garden ground, and Corn sufficient to help supply our Servants with Roots, and Herbs, and Bread.

AND now I perswaded my Husband to let me go over the *Bay* again, and enquire after my Friends; he was the willinger to consent to it now, because he had business upon his Hands sufficient to employ him, besides his Gun to divert him, which they call Hunting there, and which he greatly delighted in; and indeed we us'd to look at one another, sometimes with a great deal of Pleasure, reflecting how much better that was, not than *Newgate* only, but than the most prosperous of our Circumstances in the wicked Trade that we had been both carrying on.

OUR Affair was in a very good posture, we purchased of the Proprietors of the Colony, as much Land for 35 Pound, paid in ready Money, as would make a sufficient Plantation to employ between fifty and sixty Servants, and which being well improv'd, would be sufficient to us as long as we could either of us live; and as for Children I was past the prospect of any thing of that kind.

BUT our good Fortune did not End here, I went, *as I have said*, over the *Bay*, to the Place, where my Brother, once a Husband liv'd; but I did not go to the same Village, where I was before, but went up another great River, on the East side of the River *Potowmack*, call'd *Rapahannock* River, and by this means came on the back of his Plantation, which was large, and by the help of a Navigable Creek, or little River, that run into the *Rapahannock*, I came very near it.

I WAS now fully resolv'd to go up *Point-blank*, to my Brother (Husband) and to tell him who I was; but not knowing what Temper I might find him in, or how much out of Temper rather, I might make him by such a rash visit. I resolv'd to write a Letter to him, first to let him know, who I was, and that I was come not to give him any trouble upon the old Relation, which I hop'd was entirely forgot; but that I apply'd to him as a Sister to a Brother, desiring his Assistance in the Case of that Provision, which our Mother at her decease had left for my Support, and which I did not doubt but he would do me Justice in, especially considering that I was come thus far to look after it.

I said some very tender kind things in the Letter about his Son, which I told him he knew to be my own Child, and that as I was guilty of nothing in Marrying him any more than he was in Marrying me, neither of us having then known our being at all related to one another; so I hop'd he would allow me the most Passionate desire of once seeing my one, and only Child, and of showing something of the Infirmities of a Mother in preserving a violent Affection for him, who had never been able to retain any thought of me one way or other.

I did believe that having receiv'd this Letter, he would immediately give it to his Son to Read; I having understood his Eyes being so dim, that he cou'd not see to read it; but it fell out better than so, for as his Sight was dim, so he had allow'd his Son to open all Letters that came to his Hand for him, and the old Gentleman being from Home, or out of the way when my Messenger came, my Letter came directly to my Sons Hand, and he open'd and read it.

HE call'd the Messenger in, after some little stay, and ask'd him where the Person was who gave him the Letter, the Messenger told him the Place, which was about seven Miles off, so he bid him stay, and ordering a Horse to be got ready, and two Servants, away he came to me with the Messenger: Let any one judge the Consternation I was in, when my Messenger came back, and told me the old Gentleman was not at Home, but his Son was come along with him, and was just coming up to me: I was perfectly confounded, for I knew not whether it was Peace or War, nor cou'd I tell how to behave: However, I had but a very few Moments to think, for my Son was at the Heels of the Messenger, and coming up into my Lodgings, ask'd the Fellow at the Door, something, I suppose it was, *for I did not hear it, so as to understand it*, which was the Gentlewoman that sent him, for the Messenger said, *there she is Sir*, at which he comes directly up to me, kisses me, took me in his Arms, and embrac'd me with so much Passion, that he could not speak, but I could feel his Breast heave and throb like a Child that Cries, but Sobs, and cannot cry it out.

I CAN neither express or describe the Joy, that touch'd my very Soul, when I found, *for it was easy to discover that Part*, that he came not as a Stranger, but as a Son to a Mother, and indeed as a Son, who had never before known what a Mother of his own was; in short, we cryed over one another a considerable while, when at last he broke out first, MY DEAR MOTHER, says he, *are you still alive! I never expected to have seen your Face*; as for me, I cou'd say nothing a great while.

AFTER we had both recover'd ourselves a little, and were able to talk, he told me how things stood, as to what I had written to his Father, he told me he had not shewed my Letter to his Father, or told him any thing about it; that what his Grandmother left me, was in his Hands, and that he would do me Justice to my full Satisfaction;

that as to his Father, he was old and infirm both in Body and Mind, that he was very Fretful, and Passionate, almost Blind, and capable of nothing; and he question'd whether he would know how to act in an Affair, which was of so nice a Nature as this, and that therefore he had come himself, as well to satisfy himself in seeing me, which he could not restrain himself from, as also to put it into my Power, to make a Judgement after I had seen how things were, whether I would discover myself to his Father, or no.

THIS was really so prudently, and wisely manag'd, that I found my Son was a Man of Sense, and needed no Direction from me; I told him, I did not wonder that his Father was, as he had describ'd him, for that his Head was a little touch'd before I went away; and principally his Disturbance was, because I could not be perswaded to conceal our Relation, and to live with him as my Husband, after I knew that he was my Brother: That as he knew better than I, what his Fathers present Condition was, I should readily joyn with him in such Measures as he would direct: That I was indifferent, as to seeing his Father, since I had seen him first, and he cou'd not have told me better News, than to tell me that what his Grandmother had left me, was entrusted in his Hands, who I doubted not now he knew who I was, would *as he said*, do me Justice: I enquir'd then how long my Mother had been dead, and where she died, and told so many particulars of the Family, that I left him no room to doubt the Truth of my being really and truly his Mother.

MY Son then enquir'd where I was, and how I had dispos'd myself; I told him I was on the *Maryland* side of the *Bay*, at the Plantation of a particular Friend, who came from *England* in the same Ship with me, that as for that side of the *Bay* where he was, I had no Habitation; he told me I should go Home with him, and live with him, if I pleas'd, as long as I liv'd: That as to his Father he knew no Body, and would never so much as guess at me; I consider'd of that a little, and told him, that tho' it was really no concern to me to live at a distance from him; yet I could not say it would be the comfortablest[4] thing in the World to me to live in the House with him; and to have that unhappy Object always before me, which had been such a blow to my Peace before; that tho' I should be glad to have his Company (my Son) or to be as near him as possible while I stay'd, yet I could not think of being in the House where I should be also under constant Restraint, for fear of betraying myself in my Discourse, nor should I be able to refrain some Expressions in my Conversing with him as my Son, that might discover the whole Affair, which would by no means be Convenient.

HE acknowledged that I was right in all this, but then DEAR

4. The text actually reads "comfortabless," which might be a correct though obsolete form; changed to "most comfortable" in the second edition.

MOTHER, says he, *you shall be as near me as you can*; so he took me with him on Horseback to a Plantation, next to his own, and where I was as well entertain'd as I cou'd have been in his own; having left me there he went away home, telling me we would talk of the main Business the next Day, and having first called me his Aunt, and given a Charge to the People, who it seems were his Tenants, to treat me with all possible Respect; about two Hours after he was gone, he sent me a Maid-Servant, and a *Negro* Boy to wait on me, and Provisions ready dress'd for my Supper; and thus I was as if I had been in a new World, and began secretly now to wish that I had not brought my *Lancashire* Husband from *England* at all.

HOWEVER, that wish was not hearty neither, for I lov'd my *Lancashire* Husband entirely, as indeed I had ever done from the beginning; and he merited from me as much as it was possible for a Man to do, but that by the way.

THE next Morning my Son came to visit me again almost as soon as I was up; after a little Discourse, he first of all pull'd out a Deer skin Bag, and gave it me, with five and fifty *Spanish* Pistoles[5] in it, and told me that was to supply my Expenses from *England*, for tho' it was not his Business to enquire, yet he ought to think I did not bring a great deal of Money out with me; it not being usual to bring much Money into that Country: Then he pull'd out his Grandmother's Will, and read it over to me, whereby it appear'd, that she had left a small Plantation, *as he call'd it*, on *York* River, that is, where my Mother liv'd, to me, with the Stock of Servants and Cattle upon it, and given it in Trust to this Son of mine for my Use, when ever he should hear of my being alive, and to my Heirs, if I had any Children, and in default of Heirs, to whomsoever I should by Will dispose of it; but gave the Income of it, till I should be heard of, or found, to my said Son; and if I should not be living, then it was to him, and his Heirs.

THIS Plantation, tho' remote from him, he said he did not let out, but manag'd it by a head Clerk, Steward, as he did another that was his Fathers, that lay hard by it, and went over himself three or four times a Year to look after it; I ask'd him what he thought the Plantation might be worth, *he said*, if I would let it out, he would give me about sixty Pounds a Year for it; but if I would live on it, then it would be worth much more, and he believ'd would bring me in about 150 *l.* a Year; but seeing I was likely either to Settle on the other side the *Bay*, or might perhaps have a mind to go back to *England* again, if I would let him be my Steward he would manage it for me, as he had done for himself, and that he believ'd he should be able

5. Gold coins, each worth from 16 shillings, 6 pence, to 18 shillings. For French pistoles, see n. 3, p. 209.

to send me as much Tobacco to *England* from it, as would yield me about 100 *l.* a Year, sometimes more.

THIS was all strange News to me, and things I had not been us'd to; and really my Heart began to look up more seriously, than I think it ever did before, and to look with great Thankfulness to the Hand of Providence, which had done such wonders for me, who had been myself the greatest wonder of Wickedness, perhaps that had been suffered to live in the World; and I must again observe, that not on this Occasion only, but even on all other Occasions of Thankfulness, my past wicked and abominable Life never look'd so Monstruous to me, and I never so compleatly abhorr'd it, and reproach'd myself with it, as when I had a Sense upon me of Providence doing good to me, while I had been making those vile Returns on my part.

BUT I leave the Reader to improve these Thoughts, as no doubt they will see Cause, and I go on to the Fact; my Sons tender Carriage, and kind Offers fetch'd Tears from me, almost all the while he talk'd with me; indeed I could scarce Discourse with him, but in the intervals of my Passion; however, at length I began, and expressing myself with wonder at my being so happy to have the Trust of what I had left, put into the Hands of my own Child; I told him, that as to the Inheritance of it, I had no Child but him in the World, and was now past having any, if I should Marry, and therefore would desire him to get a Writing Drawn, which I was ready to execute, by which I would after me give it wholly to him, and to his Heirs; and in the mean time smiling, I ask'd him, what made him continue a Batchelor so long; his answer was kind, and ready, that *Virginia* did not yield any great plenty of Wives, and since I talk'd of going back to *England*, I should send him a Wife from *London*.

THIS was the Substance of our first days Conversation, the pleasantest Day that ever past over my Head in my Life, and which gave me the truest Satisfaction: He came every Day after this, and spent great part of his time with me, and carried me about to several of his Friends Houses, where I was entertain'd with great Respect; also I Dined several times at his own House, when he took care always to see his half dead Father so out of the way, that I never saw him, or he me: I made him one Present, and it was all I had of value, and that was one of the gold Watches, of which I mention'd above, that I had two in my Chest, and this I happen'd to have with me, and I gave it him at his third Visit: I told him, I had nothing of any value to bestow but that, and I desir'd he would now and then kiss it for my sake; *I did not indeed tell him* that I had stole it from a Gentlewomans side, at a Meeting-House in *London*, that's by the way.

HE stood a little while Hesitating, as if doubtful whether to take it or no; but I press'd it on him, and made him accept it, and it was not much less worth than his Leather-pouch full of *Spanish* Gold; no, tho' it were to be reckon'd, as if at *London*, whereas it was worth twice as much there, where I gave it him; at length he took it, kiss'd it, told me the Watch should be a Debt upon him, that he would be paying, as long as I liv'd.

A FEW Days after he brought the Writings of Gift,[6] and the Scrivener with them, and I sign'd them very freely, and deliver'd them to him with a hundr'd Kisses; for sure nothing ever pass'd between a Mother, and a tender dutiful Child, with more Affection: The next Day he brings me an Obligation under his Hand and Seal, whereby he engag'd himself to Manage, and Improve the Plantation for my account, and with his utmost Skill, and to remit the Produce to my order where-ever I should be, and withal, to be oblig'd himself to make up the Produce a hundred Pound a Year to me: When he had done so, he told me, that as I came to demand it before the Crop was off, I had a right to the Produce of the current Year, and so he paid me an hundred Pound in *Spanish* Peices of Eight,[7] and desir'd me to give him a Receipt for it as in full for that Year, ending at *Christmas* following; this being about the latter End of *August*.

I STAY'D here above five Weeks, and indeed had much a do to get away then. Nay, he would have come over the *Bay* with me, but I would by no means allow him to it; however, he would send me over in a Sloop of his own, which was built like a Yatch,[8] and serv'd him as well for Pleasure as Business: This I accepted of, and so after the utmost Expressions both of Duty, and Affection, he let me come away, and I arriv'd safe in two Days at my Friends the Quakers.

I BROUGHT over with me for the use of our Plantation, three Horses with Harness, and Saddles; some Hogs, two Cows, and a thousand other things, the Gift of the kindest and tenderest Child that ever Woman had: I related to my Husband all the particulars of this Voyage, except that I called my Son (my Cousin;) and first I told him, that I had lost my Watch, which he seem'd to take as a Misfortune; but then I told him how kind my Cousin had been, that my Mother had left me such a Plantation, and that he had preserv'd it for me, in hopes some time or other he should hear from me; then I told that I had left it to his Management, that he would render me a faithful Account of its Produce; and then I pull'd him out the hundred Pound in Silver, as the first Years produce, and then pulling out the Deer skin Purse, with the Pistoles, and here my Dear, *says I*, is the gold Watch. My Husband, *so is Heavens goodness sure to work the same Effects, in all sensible Minds, where Mercies touch the Heart*; lifted up both his Hands, and with an extasy of Joy, *What is*

6. Legal documents transferring ownership to Moll. *Scrivener*: A professional penman.
7. Spanish dollars or *pesos*, marked with the figure 8, each worth about 4 shillings, 6 pence.
8. Yacht.

God a doing says he, *for such an ungrateful Dog as I am*! Then I let him know, what I had brought over in the Sloop, besides all this; I mean the Horses Hogs, and Cows, and other Stores for our Plantation; all which added to his surprize, and fill'd his Heart with thankfulness; and from this time forward I believe he was as sincere a Penitent, and as thoroughly a reform'd Man, as ever God's goodness brought back from a Profligate a Highway-man, and a Robber. I could fill a larger History than this, with the Evidences of this Truth, and but that I doubt that part of the Story will not be equally diverting, as the wicked Part I have had thoughts of making a Volume of it by itself.

As for myself, as this is to be my own Story, not my Husbands, I return to that Part which relates to myself; we went on with our Plantation, and manag'd it with the help and diversion of such Friends as we got there, by our obliging Behaviour, and especially the honest Quaker, who prov'd a faithful generous and steady Friend to us; and we had very good Success; for having a flourishing Stock to begin with, as *I have said*; and this being now encreas'd, by the Addition of a Hundred and fifty Pound *Sterling* in Money, we enlarg'd our Number of Servants, built us a very good House, and cur'd every Year a great deal of Land. The second Year I wrote to my old Governess, giving her part with us of the Joy of our Success, and order'd her how to lay out the Money I had left with her, which was 250 *l.* as above, and to send it to us in Goods, which she perform'd, with her usual Kindness and Fidelity, and all this arriv'd safe to us.

HERE we had a supply of all sorts of Cloaths, as well for my Husband, as for myself; and I took especial care to buy for him all those things that I knew he delighted to have; as two good long Wigs, two silver hilted Swords, three or four fine Fowling peices, a fine Saddle with Holsters and Pistoles[9] very handsome with a Scarlet Cloak; and in a Word, every thing I could think of to oblige him; and to make him appear, as he really was, a very fine Gentleman: I order'd a good Quantity of such Househould-stuff, as we yet wanted with Linnen of all sorts for us both, as for my self, I wanted very little of Cloths, or Linnen, being very well furnished before: The rest of my Cargo consisted in Iron-Work, of all sorts, Harness for Horses, Tools, Cloaths for Servants, and Wollen-Cloth, stuffs, Serges, Stockings, Shoes, Hats and the like, such as Servants wear, and whole peices[1] also to make up for Servants, all by direction of the Quaker; and all this Cargo arriv'd safe, and in good Condition, with three Women Servants, lusty Wenches, which my old Governess had pick'd up for me, suitable enough to the Place, and to the Work we had for them

9. Pistols.
1. Lengths (e.g., ells or yards), varying according to the material, in which cloth or other textile fabric is woven.

to do; one of which happen'd to come double, having been got with Child by one of the Seamen in the Ship, as she own'd afterwards, before the Ship got so far as *Gravesend*; so she brought us a stout Boy, about 7 Months after her Landing.

MY Husband you may suppose was a little surpriz'd at the arriving of all this Cargo from *England*, and talking with me after he saw the Account of the particular; my Dear, *says he*, what is the meaning of all this? I fear you will run us too deep in Debt: When shall we be able to make Return for it all? I smil'd, and told him that it was all paid for, and then I told him, that not knowing what might befal us in the Voyage, and considering what our Circumstances might expose us to; I had not taken my whole Stock with me, that I had reserv'd so much in my Friends Hands, which now we were come over safe, and was Settled in a way to live, I had sent for as he might see.

HE was amaz'd, and stood a while telling upon his Fingers, but said nothing, at last he began thus, Hold lets see, *says he, telling upon his Fingers still*; and first on his Thumb, there's 246 *l.* in Money at first, then two gold Watches, Diamond Rings, and Plate, *says he*, upon the fore Finger, then upon the next Finger, here's a Plantation on *York* River, a 100 *l.* a Year, then 150 in Money; then a Sloop load of Horses, Cows, Hogs and Stores, and so on to the Thumb again; and now, *says he*, a Cargo cost 250 *l.* in *England*, and worth here twice the Money, well, *says I*, What do you make of all that? make of it, *says he*, why who says I was deceiv'd, when I married a Wife in *Lancashire*? I think I have married a Fortune, and a very good Fortune too, *says he*.

IN a Word, we were now in very considerable Circumstances, and every Year encreasing; for our new Plantation grew upon our Hands insensibly; and in eight Year which we lived upon it, we brought it to such a pitch, that the Produce was, at least, 300 *l.* Sterling a Year; I mean, worth so much in *England*.

AFTER I had been a Year at Home again, I went over the Bay to see my Son, and to receive another Year's Income of my Plantation; and I was surpriz'd to hear, just at my Landing there, that my old Husband was dead, and had not been bury'd above a Fortnight. This, I confess, was not disagreeable News, because now I could appear as I was in a marry'd Condition; so I told my Son before I came from him, that I believed I should marry a Gentleman who had a Plantation near mine; and tho' I was legally free to marry, as to any Obligation that was on me before, yet that I was shye of it, least the Blot should some time or other be reviv'd, and it might make a Husband uneasy; my Son the same kind dutiful and obligating Creature as ever, treated me now at his own House, paid me my hundred Pound, and sent me Home again loaded with Presents.

SOME time after this, I let my Son know I was marry'd, and invited him over to see us; and my Husband wrote a very obliging Letter to him also, inviting him to come and see him; and he came accordingly some Months after, and happen'd to be there just when my Cargo from *England* came in, which I let him believe belong'd all to my Husband's Estate, not to me.

IT must be observ'd, that when the old Wretch, my Brother (Husband) was dead, I then freely gave my Husband an Account of all that Affair, and of this Cousin, as I had call'd him before, being my own Son by that mistaken unhappy Match: He was perfectly easy in the Account, and told me he should have been as easy if the old Man, as we call'd him, had been alive; for, *said he*, it was no Fault of yours, nor of his; it was a Mistake impossible to be prevented; he only reproach'd him with desiring me to conceal it, and to live with him as a Wife, after I knew that he was my Brother, that, he said, was a vile part: Thus all these little Difficulties were made easy, and we liv'd together with the greatest Kindness and Comfort imaginable; we are now grown Old: I am come back to *England*, being almost seventy Years of Age, my Husband sixty eight, having perform'd much more than the limited Terms of my Transportation: And now notwithstanding all the Fatigues, and all the Miseries we have both gone thro', we are both in good Heart and Health; my Husband remain'd[2] there sometime after me to settle our Affairs, and at first I had intended to go back to him, but at his desire I alter'd that Resolution, and he is come over to *England* also, where we resolve to spend the Remainder of our Years in sincere Penitence, for the wicked Lives we have lived.

Written in the Year 1683.

F I N I S.

2. Second edition reading, changed from "remain" in the first edition. *Heart*: I am following the second edition here; the first edition reads, "we are both of in good Heart. . . ."

A Textual Problem in *Moll Flanders*

This excerpt from the first edition of *Moll Flanders* (pp. 383–87) contains a textual problem, first noted by J. Paul Hunter in his edition of the novel (Crowell, 1970). Briefly, two contradictory passages, of approximately the same length, appear at this point in the narrative. The contradictions are even more pronounced in the second edition, which prints both passages consecutively. In Hunter's view, the printer of the first edition was supposed to replace one passage with the other but, for some reason, ended up printing both. Believing that Defoe had revised his manuscript to make the role of the governess more prominent, Hunter retained the first passage ("Then I read a long Lecture . . . but by Directions") and deleted the second ("In this Condition . . . *always take your Advice*"), relegating it to an appendix. Two years later, Rodney M. Baine argued that, while Hunter was certainly right in suggesting that one passage was meant to replace the other, the second passage is actually the revision because it fits in better with the surrounding context and the ensuing events in the novel. In short, Hunter had canceled the wrong passage in his edition. After examining the evidence and discussing the matter with Hunter, who now agrees with Baine's assessment, I have corrected the text of *Moll Flanders* to eliminate this apparent compositor's error. I reprint the original text here so that both passages may be read as they initially appeared.

* * *

THIS was very perplexing, and I knew not what Course to take; I told my Governess the Story of the Boatswain, and she was mighty eager with me to treat with him; but I had no mind to it, till I heard whether my Husband, or fellow Prisoner, *so she call'd him*, cou'd be at liberty to go with me or no; at last I was forc'd to let her into the whole matter, except only, that of his being my Husband; I told her I had made a positive Bargain or Agreement with him to go, if he could get the liberty of going in the same Ship, and that I found he had Money.

THEN I read a long Lecture to her of what I propos'd to do when we came there, how we could Plant, Settle; and in short, grow Rich without any more Adventures, and as a great Secret, I told her that we were to Marry as soon as he came on Board.

She soon agreed chearfully to my going, when she heard this, and she made it her business from that time to get him out of the Prison in time, so that he might go in the same Ship with me, which at last was brought to pass tho' with great difficulty, and not without all the Forms of a Transported Prisoner *Convict*, which he really was not yet, for he had not been try'd, and which was a great Mortification to him. As our Fate was now determin'd, and we were both on Board, actually bound to *Virginia*, in the despicable Quality of Transported Convicts destin'd to be sold for Slaves, I for five Year, and he under Bonds and Security not to return to *England* any more, as long as he liv'd; he was very much dejected and cast down; the Mortification of being brought on Board, as he was like a Prisoner, piqu'd him very much, since it was first told him he should Transport himself, and so that he might go as a Gentleman at liberty; it is true he was not order'd to be sold when he came there, as we were, and for that Reason he was oblig'd to pay for his Passage to the Captain, which we were not; as to the rest, he was as much at a loss as a Child what to do with himself, or with what he had, but by Directions.

Our first business was to compare our Stock: He was very honest to me, and told me his Stock was pretty good when he came into the Prison, but the living there as he did in a Figure like a Gentleman, *and which was ten times as much*, the making of Friends, and soliciting his Case, had been very Expensive; and in a Word, all his Stock that he had left was an Hundred and Eight Pounds, which he had about him all in Gold.

I Gave him an Account of my Stock as faithfully, that is to say of what I had taken to carry with me, for I was resolv'd what ever should happen, to keep what I had left with my Governess, in Reserve; that in Case I should die, what I had with me was enough to give him, and that which was left in my Governess Hands would be her own, which she had well deserv'd of me indeed.

My Stock which I had with me was two Hundred forty six Pounds, some odd Shillings; so that we had three Hundred and fifty four Pound between us, but a worse gotten Estate was scarce ever put together to begin the World with.

Our greatest Misfortune as to our Stock, was that it was all in Money, which every one knows is an unprofitable Cargoe to be carryed to the Plantations; I believe his was really all he had left in the World, as he told me it was; but I who had between seven and eight Hundred Pounds in Bank when this Disaster befel me, and who had one of the faithfulest Friends in the World to manage it for me, considering she was a Woman of no manner of Religious Principles, had still Three Hundred Pounds left in her Hand, which I reserv'd, as above, besides some very valuable things, as particularly two gold Watches, some small Peices of Plate, and some Rings; all stolen Goods; the Plate, Rings and Watches were put up in my Chest with the Money, and with this Fortune, and in the Sixty first Year of my Age, I launch'd out into a new World, as I may call it in the Condition (as to what appear'd) only of a poor nak'd Convict, order'd to be Transported in respite from the Gallows; my Cloaths were poor and mean, but not ragged or dirty, and none knew in the whole Ship that I had any thing of value about me.

HOWEVER, as I had a great many very good Cloaths, and Linnen in abundance, which I had order'd to be pack'd up in two great Boxes, I had them Shipp'd on Board, not as my Goods, but as consign'd to my real Name in *Virginia*; and had the Bills of Loading sign'd by a Captain in my Pocket; and in these Boxes was my Plate and Watches, and every thing of value except my Money, which I kept by itself in a private Drawer in my Chest, which cou'd not be found, or open'd if found, without splitting the Chest to peices.

IN this Condition I lay for three Weeks in the Ship, not knowing whether I should have my Husband with me or no; and therefore not resolving how, or in what manner to receive the honest Boatswain's proposal, which indeed he thought a little strange at first.

AT the End of this time, behold my Husband came on Board; he look'd with a dejected angry Countenance, his great Heart was swell'd with Rage and Disdain; to be drag'd along with three Keepers of *Newgate*, and put on Board like a Convict, when he had not so much as been brought to a Tryal; he made loud complaints of it by his Friends, for it seems he had some interest; but his Friends got some Checque in their Application, and were told he had had *Favour enough*, and that they had receiv'd such an Account of him since the last Grant of his Transportation, that he ought to think himself very well treated that he was not prosecuted a new. This answer quieted him at once, for he knew too much what might have happen'd, and what he had room to expect; and now he saw the goodness of the Advice to him, which prevail'd with him to accept of the offer of a voluntary Transportation, and after his chagrine at these Hell Hounds, *as he call'd them*, was a little over; he look'd a little compos'd, began to be chearful, and as I was telling him how glad I was to have him once more out of their Hands, took me in his Arms, and acknowledg'd with great Tenderness, that I had given him the best Advice possible, *My Dear*, says he, *Thou hast twice sav'd my Life; from hence forward it shall be all employ'd for you, and I'll always take your Advice*.

THE Ship began now to fill, several Passengers came on Board, who were embark'd on no Criminal account, and these had Accommodations assign'd them in the great Cabbin, and other Parts of the

Ship, whereas we *as Convicts* were thrust down below, I know not where; but when my Husband came on Board, I spoke to the Boatswain, who had so early given me Hints of his Friendship in carrying my Letter; I told him he had befriended me in many things, and I had not made any suitable Return to him, and with that I put a Guinea into his Hands; I told him that my Husband was now come on Board, that tho' we were both under the present Misfortunes, yet we had been Persons of a differing Character from the wretched Crew that we came with, and desir'd to know of him, whether the Captain might not be mov'd, to admit us to some Conveniences in the Ship, for which we would make him what Satisfaction he pleas'd, and that we would gratifie him for his Pains in procuring this for us. He took the Guinea as I cou'd see with great Satisfaction, and assur'd me of his Assistance.

* * *

CONTEXTS

DANIEL DEFOE

[Benefits of Transportation]†

* * *

BUT Heaven and kind Masters, make up all those things to a diligent Servant; and I mention it, because People, who are either Transported, or otherwise Trappan'd into those Places, are generally thought to be rendered miserable, and undone; whereas, on the contrary, I would encourage them upon my own Experience to depend upon it, that if their own Diligence in the time of Service, gains them but a good Character, which it will certainly do, if they can deserve it, there is not the poorest, and most despicable Felon that ever went over, but may after his time is serv'd, begin for himself, and may in time be sure of raising a good Plantation.

FOR Example, I will now take a Man in the meanest Circumstances of a Servant, who has serv'd out his 5 or 7 Years, (suppose a Transported Wretch for 7 Years.) The custom of the Place was then (what it is since I know not) that on his Master's certifying that he had serv'd his time out faithfully he had 50 Acres of Land allotted him, for Planting, and on this Plan he begins.

SOME had a Horse, a Cow, and three Hogs given, or rather lent them as a Stock for the Land, which they made an allowance for, at a certain Time and Rate.

CUSTOM has made it a Trade, to give Credit to such Beginners as these, for Tools, Cloths, Nails, Iron-work, and other things necessary for their Planting; and which the Persons so giving Credit to them, are to be paid for out of the Crop of *Tobacco* which they shall Plant; nor is it in the Debtors power to Defraud the Creditor of Payment in that manner; and as *Tobacco* is their Coin, as well as their Product; so all things are to be Purchas'd at a certain quantity of *Tobacco*, the Price being so Rated.

THUS the naked Planter has Credit at his Beginning, and immediately goes to Work, to cure the Land, and Plant *Tobacco*; and from this little Beginning, have some of the most considerable Planters in *Virginia* and in *Maryland* also, rais'd themselves, namely, from being without a Hat, or a Shoe, to Estates of 40 or 50000 Pound; and in this Method, I may add, no Diligent Man ever Miscarried, if he had Health to Work, and was a good

† From *The History and Remarkable Life of the truly Honourable Col. Jacque, commonly call'd Col. Jack* (London, 1722), pp. 194–96, 221–22.

Husband; for he every Year encreases a little, and every Year adding more Land, and Planting more *Tobacco*, which is real Money, he must Gradually encrease in Substance, till at length he gets enough to Buy *Negroes*, and other Servants, and then never Works himself any more.

IN a Word, every *Newgate* Wretch, every Desperate forlorn Creature; the most Despicable ruin'd Man in the World, has here a fair Opportunity put into his Hands to begin the World again, and that upon a Foot of certain Gain, and in a Method exactly Honest; with a Reputation, that nothing past will have any Effect upon; and innumerable People have thus rais'd themselves from the worst Circumstance in the World; Namely, from the *Condemn'd-Hole* in *Newgate*.

* * *

1. THAT *Virginia*, and a State of Transportation, may be the happiest Place and Condition they were ever in, for this Life, as by a sincere Repentance, and a diligent Application to the Business they are put to; they are effectually deliver'd from a Life of a flagrant Wickedness, and put in a perfectly new Condition, in which they have no Temptation to the Crimes they formerly committed, and have a prospect of Advantage for the future.
2. THAT in *Virginia*, the meanest, and most despicable Creature after his time of Servitude is expir'd, if he will but apply himself with Diligence and Industry to the Business of the Country, is sure (Life and Health suppos'd) both of living Well and growing Rich.

As this is a foundation, which the most unfortunate Wretch alive is entitul'd to; a Transported Felon, is in my Opinion a much happier Man, than the most prosperous untaken Thief in the Nation; nor are those poor young People so much in the wrong, as some imagine them to be, that go voluntarily over to those Countries, and in order to get themselves carried over, and plac'd there, freely bind themselves there; especially if the Persons into whose Hands they fall, do any thing honestly by them; for as it is to be suppos'd that those poor People knew not what Course to take before, or had miscarried in their Conduct before; here they are sure to be immediately provided for, and after the expiration of their time, to be put into a Condition to provide for themselves. * * *

* * *

ANONYMOUS

[Moll's Final Years in Ireland]†

Moll Flanders *having sold her Estate in* Virginia, *comes over with her Husband to* Ireland, *at 70 Years of Age; liv'd at Galway, and became a Widow again. She lives very honest; is a great Penitent; makes her last Will and Testament; dies much lamented by the Poor; and is buried in Saint* Nicholas's *Church; having a Marble Tombstone put over her Grave, with an Epitaph cut on it.*

HAVING by the Consent of my Husband sold our Estate in *Virginia*, and what Goods and Plate we had by us, we made up the Sum of 10000 Pounds, and taking Shipping at Saint *James-Town*, we safely arriv'd at *Kinsale* in *Ireland* and went thence to the City of *Galway*, the Place of my Husband's Birth, whose Name was *Patrick Carrol*; and my right Name *Elizabeth Atkins*.

Here we purchas'd an Estate of 400 Pounds *per annum*, in the seventieth Year of my Age, and liv'd very happy and honestly with my Husband for two Years, when it pleas'd the irreversible Decree of Heaven to take him out of the Land of the Living, and so I became a Widow again. Now also being on the last Stage of my Life, I began seriously to reflect on the past Follies and Wickedness thereof, truly repenting of all my former Sins and Transgressions; praying thrice or four Times a Day in my Closet to God to forgive me, who had been so vile a Sinner, and pouring forth an Abundance of Tears in my private Devotion, to shew an utter Abhorrence of those Vices of which I had been too frequently guilty.

I never miss'd going to Church when well, and tho' I had been a most unworthy Member of the *Protestant* Communion, yet now I

† From *The Life and Actions of Moll Flanders* (London, 1723), pp. 185–90. "Adorn'd with Cuts suitable to each Chapter," this abridgement, we are informed on the title page, was "Printed and Sold by *T. Read*." Below a woodcut frontispiece of Moll Flanders appears the following poem:

> See here the Wonder of the British Land,
> Whose various Life doth just Surprize command;
> From *Tyburn* freed by her indulgent Fate,
> Sh' attain'd a wealthy and a worthy State;
> So just is what's proverbially said,
> *None truly know their Fortune till they're dead*:
> Kindly accept what vertuous doth appear,
> And at what's faulty be not too severe;
> But her last Hours, and pious *Exit* weigh,
> And, like hers, let your Evening crown the Day.

hop'd my endeavouring to be a true Penitent would bring me into Favour again with a long incensed God, who had suffer'd me to run thro' a long Series of Wickedness, but in the midst of many Afflictions, which at last brought me to a due Sense of my manifold Negligences in the Duties of Religion, which till latterly I utterly abhorr'd.

Thus I past my latter Days in a total Resignation of myself to the Will and Pleasure of my heavenly Father, till he was pleas'd to visit me with a *Dropsie* and *Asthma*, or Shortness of Breath, whereby finding Nature daily to decay more and more, and that I was not a Woman for this World long, I began to set my Houshold in Order, and made my last Will and Testament as follows.

I *Elizabeth Atkins*, of the City of *Galway*, in the County of *Galway*, (being at this Time in good and perfect Memory, thro' the Mercy of God, but weak and sickly in Body) do make this my last Will and Testament, in Manner following; that is to say, I give to my deceased Husband's Brother, *Charles Carrol*, all my real Estate, lying about *Athlone*, in the Counties of *Roscommon*, and *West-Meath*, and to his Heirs and Assigns for ever.

Item, I give to my Gardiner, *Henry Kelly*, the Sum of 50 Pounds of current Money of *England*.

Item, To *Jane Burke*, my Chamber-maid, I give the Sum of 40 Pounds.

Item, To *Catherine O-Neal*, my Cook-Maid, I give the Sum of 30 Pounds.

Item, To *Dorothy Macknamarra*, my Housemaid, I give the Sum of 20 Pounds.

Item, To my deceas'd Husband's Brother, *William Carrol*, I give all the rest of my Goods, and Chattels, and personal Estate whatsoever; but out of the same to be decently interr'd, and all Funeral Charges to be paid, by the said *William Carrol*.

Lastly, I make and constitute my abovesaid Brother-in-Law, *Charles Carrol*, Executor of this my last Will and Testament, written with my own Hand this 30th Day of *March*, in the Year of our Lord Christ, according to the *English* Computation, 1722.

Eliz. Atkins

Seal'd, publish'd, and declar'd by the said Elizabeth Atkins, *for and as her last Will and Testament, in the Presence of* Patrick Magey, James Mullens, *and* John Hara.

In the time of her Sickness, which held for about nine Months, she was very penitent, and most zealously fervent in her Devotion, not in the least minding the Affairs of this World, but entirely prepar'd herself for a future State. She was constantly attended by some eminent Divines, but particularly one Mr. *Price*, Master of the Free-School in *Galway*. In this godly Disposition for her latter End she continu'd till the 10th of *April* following the Date of her last Will and Testament, when she departed this mortal Life, in the 75th Year of her Age, to the no small Grief and Sorrow of the Poor, to whom she had been very charitable whilst alive; for she allow'd 25 old Men 40 Shillings a-piece yearly; to 20 old Women she allow'd 30 Shillings a-piece yearly; and forty Pounds a Year for putting out poor Children to be Apprentices.

No sooner was the Death of *Moll Flanders* nois'd over the Kingdom of *Ireland*, but the prime Wits of Trinity College in *Dublin* compos'd on her the following Elegy.

ALas! what News doth now our Ears invade?
What Havock has grim Death among us made?
With the impetuous Fury of his Dart,
Moll Flanders he has wounded thro' the Heart:
Moll Flanders, once the Wonder of the Age,
Whilst the remain'd on this terrestrial Stage,
Is gone to take a Nap for many Years,
For which ye ought to shed as many Tears.
We mean her chiefest Mourners ought to be
The chief Proficients in all Villany,
Such Persons who go on the sneaking Budge,
And will for Mops and Pails thro' *Dublin* trudge;
House-breakers, Doxies who can file a Cly,
And those who out of Shops steal privately.
But you that can't cry, yet would seem to weep,
Your Handkerchiefs in Juice of Onions steep,
Then rail upon the cruel Hand of Fate,
Which wou'd not grant *Moll*'s Reign a longer Date.
A longer Date, said we? Indeed too long
She liv'd to do some honest People wrong;
Such Wrong, that had she her deserved Due,
She had been whipt, and glimm'd, and hanged too;
But all the Paths of Vice so much she trac'd,
That hanging her had any Tree disgrac'd.
Howe'er take care below, among the Dead,
For tho' the mortal Life of *Moll* is fled,
She may perhaps as now ye cannot feel,
Your Shrouds, and Coffins, else your Bodies steal,
As Grave-diggers in *England* do, to be
Mangled to Pieces in Anatomy.

But hold, deceased *Moll* we must not blame
Too much, for tho' she glory'd in her Shame,
Of being dextrous Thief, and arrant Whore,
Yet we some Pity for her must implore,
And give her deathless Memory some Praise,
In that she ended well her latter Days,
For of her num'rous Sins she did repent,
And dy'd a very hearty Penitent.

Death having now clos'd the last Scene of her Life, she lay in State in a very splendid Manner, her House being hung from Top to Bottom with black Baize, a black Velvet Pall covering her Coffin to the Ground, which was rail'd round, the Room being all dark, and illuminated with several wax Tapers put into silver Sconces. Having thus lain three Days, her Corpse was carried to St. *Nicholas*'s Church, being attended thither by all her Husband's Relations, both Men and Women, in deep Mourning, besides above one hundred and twenty other Persons, who had gold Rings given them, with these Words engrav'd in them, *Memento mori. Elizabetha Atkins obiit* 1722; that is, Remember to die. *Elizabeth Atkins* died in 1722.

Four Women went before strewing sweet Herbs and Flowers all the Way; after whom follow'd two Beadles, with their Staves cover'd with Cypress; next them two Ministers and the Clerk; the Pall was supported by the Wives of the Recorder of *Galway*, the two Sheriffs, the Town-Clerk, and two other Gentlewoman, led all by their Husbands. When the Corps was brought into the Church, after the usual Prayers were said, the Rev. Dr. *Shaw* preach'd the Funeral Sermon, which being over, she was decently interr'd in the same Grave with her Husband; and shortly after a fine white Marble Tombstone was put over her, with the following Epitaph cut on it.

BEhold the cruel Hand of Death,
Hath snatch'd away Elizabeth.
Twelve Years she was an arrant Whore;
Was sometimes rich, and sometimes poor;
Which made her, when she'd no Relief,
Be full as many Years a Thief.
In this Carier of Wickedness,
Poor Betty *always had Success;*
Till caught at last, was doom'd to die,
But Rope b'ing not her Destiny,
Eight Years she was transported, where
She Wealth obtain'd by Pains and Care.
Of Husbands five, one was her Brother,
Which was discover'd by her Mother,
Yet tho' she was both Thief and Whore,
She with this Mate wou'd live no more.

When People all, in after Times,
Shall read the Story of her Crimes,
They'll stand amaz'd, but more admire
That one so bad should e'er desire
To live a godly, righteous Life,
And be a loving, faithful Wife.
Of all her Sins she did repent,
And really dy'd a Penitent.

F I N I S.

ANONYMOUS

The Life of James Mac-Faul, Husband to Moll Flanders, &c.†

JAMES MAC-FAUL was born at *Caricfergus*, in the *North* of *Ireland*, in the Time of the *Irish* Massacre, wherein his Father had a great Hand, being forward, upon all Occasions, to plunder and destroy the *Protestants*, where ever he could meet with 'em, and did not care what Mischief he did, so he could but enrich himself; till at last he was taken by a Detachment from the King's Army, and hang'd up on the next Tree as an Example, to deter others from such Cruelties.

His Son *James* was brought up by his Uncle, and put to School under a Popish Priest, who being very unlucky, could never be kept to his Book, but would run away for a Month together, till his Uncle, not knowing what to do with him, determin'd to send him to *England* and let him try his Fortune; being certain, that the Boy had Assurance enough to live in any Part of the World and Impudence enough to stick at nothing: Yet *Jemmy* could not be persuaded to travel, unless his Uncle would equip him with a Sword, a Pair of Dice, and a Pack of Cards, with which he thought he could do well enough.

He made the best of his Way for *London*, but found it absolutely necessary in his Way, to commit some small pilfering Robberies, for his better Support: for one of which he was well flogg'd at *Bristol*, and all his Utensils, Dice, and Cards taken from him; when not knowing what to do, he had some Thoughts of going to Service,

† From *Fortune's Fickle Distribution: In Three Parts Containing, First, The Life and Death of Moll Flanders . . . Part II. The Life of Jane Hackabout, her Governess . . . Part III. The Life of James Mac-Faul, Moll Flanders's Lancashire Husband; who was born in Ireland; came into England; turn'd Gentleman, Gamester, Highwayman; transported to Virginia; his Return to Galway in Ireland, Settlement and Death* (London and Dublin, 1730), pp. 113–24.

which he did for a little while; but Work not agreeing with him at all, he borrow'd a Silver Spoon, and some other odd Trifles, and march'd off one Evening, without taking his Leave, and went directly to one of his Countrymen, who dispos'd of his Things, but was angry with him, for leaving his Place with so little Booty, which *Jemmy* begg'd him not to take Notice of, for another Time he should find he would do better.

In a little after, he got into a Noble Lord's Family, where he behav'd for twelve Months very well, and got the Love of all the Servants, particularly of Mrs. *Betty*, the Chambermaid, who was continually treating him with one good Thing or other, and he, in Return, professing a great deal of Love and Sincerity; which made the Girl grow so fond of him, that he presently work'd her out of all she had, and then look'd as cold on her, as a sinking Tradesman does on a desperate Dunn; which *Betty* perceiving, *try'd* all manner of Ways to endear her self to him, but all to no purpose, for the young Spark was fallen in Love with an Alehouse-man's Daughter, where the Servants were used to drink, and had no more to say to poor *Betty*; who enrag'd at such Usage, could not forbear exposing her Folly, by upbraiding of him, which had no other Effect, but making her self be laugh'd at, and hardening him in his Impudence; who went on without Controul in his Amours with his new Mistress, and left his old one to learn more Wit.

The young Taplash, proud of her Conquest, that she should rival one of my Lord's Maids, easily gave up her self to his Embraces, and denied him nothing that was in her Power to grant, which put *Jemmy* quite upon another's Footing with the rest of his fellow Servants; she keeping the Bar, had the Care of all the Money, so that *Jemmy* had his Watch, and what not, and appeared as great as Master any body, and neglected his Lord's Service, to follow Gaming-Tables and Whores, for which he soon lost his Place, and had nothing to depend on, but what he got from his Sweet-heart; who continually supplying his Extravagancies, reduced her Father to such Necessities, that he was obliged to confess a Judgment to the Brewer, who, a little after, seized upon all he had, and turn'd him out of Doors.

Jemmy had nothing now to depend on, but his own good Fortune, and she proving a Jilt, as she often does to Persons of his Extravagancies, he was soon reduced to very great Wants, when being arrested, and thrown into the *Marshallsea*, he got acquainted with one *Thomas Butler*, a Country-man of his, with whom he agreed to break out of Prison and go upon the *Lay*, which they did very successfully for some time, till *Butler* was taken, and committed to *Newgate*, and hang'd the next Sessions, and *Jemmy* very hardly escap'd by fighting his Way thro' the Mob.

He still kept a Correspondence with his Mistress, and made her to become as wicked as himself; she turning Shoplifter and Pick-pocket, and he robbing on the Highway, by which they had got near a thousand Pounds, and then agreed to part, but upon Condition, of being serviceable to one another, and the Town being too hot for him, he remov'd into *Lancashire*, a Fortune-hunting, and she continu'd in Town, to see what would offer in her Way, where she got acquainted with *Moll Flanders*, who lodging in the same House with her, pass'd for a great Fortune, and persuaded her to go down with her into the Country, where she might live much cheaper, and with more Pleasure at her Brother's House, who was a Gentleman of a very good Estate in *Ireland*, or at her Sister's, who liv'd near *Liverpool*; which *Moll* at length agreed to, not knowing well what else to do with herself; but that was more than the other knew.

Upon the Road, she treated *Moll* with all the Civilities imaginable, and at *Warrington*, her pretended Brother met them in a Gentleman's Coach, and carried them to *Liverpool*, where they were entertain'd in a Merchant's House three or four Days very handsomly, and from thence they went to a Gentleman's House, about forty Miles distance, where was a numerous Family, a noble Seat, and good Company, whom she call'd Cousins: Here they stay'd about six Weeks, and then came back to a Village near *Liverpool*, where her Brother as she call'd him, begun to make Love to *Moll*, setting himself out as a Man of a thousand Pounds a Year, and indeed talk'd as big of his Seats and Parks, as one would have thought he had had such an Estate, but all a Sham: *Moll* was not behind him in putting her self off, although she never plainly told them what she had, yet she did not contradict what her Companion said, who reported her to be a young Widow, worth ten thousand Pounds; which so enflam'd 'Squire *Mac-Faul*, that he was ready to run mad at the Bait, and plung'd in Debt over Head and Ears, for the Expences of his Courtship, and for fear his Estate should be look'd into, he never so much as ask'd about her Fortune; but took upon Trust whatsoever his old Mistress told him, and promis'd his new one such brave things, that she imagin'd she should have been a Lady, when she had got unto her Estate.

They were soon Married, and nothing but Love and Kindness pass'd between them, he every day telling her of the fine Things she was to have when they came to *Ireland*, and she endeavouring to improve his Affection by her Fondness and good Behaviour; till at length he begun to discover his Intentions of going to *West-Chester* in order to embark for *Ireland*, but asked his Wife, if she had no Affairs to settle at *London* before she went off; to which she Answering, *No*; he seem'd much surprized, and said, Madam, What have we been adoing; I thought the Bulk of your Estate, lay in the *Bank*; Indeed, Sir, saith she, I have no Estate, nor did *I* ever tell you I had:

I know what your Sister might say to you, but *I* did never tell her or you any such thing; at which he star'd like a Madman, and swore he had been imposed upon to the last Degree; and then calling his Sister, he asked her, how she could serve him so? *Very well*, saith she, *and not half so much as you deserved; How could you ruin my poor aged Father, debauch me, and bring me into all the Vices of Life; and at last neglect me, and set up for a Fortune in the Country*? But, saith he, what had this Gentlewoman done to you, that you shou'd ruin her? and then looking upon his Wife, he fell down upon his Knees, and said, You would indeed have been cheated, My Dear, but you would not have been undone: for ten thousand Pounds would have maintain'd us both very handsomly in *Ireland*, and *I* resolved to have dedicated it every Groat to you; *I* would not have wronged you of a Shilling, and the Rest *I* would have made up in my Affection to you, and Tenderness of you as long as I lived; which he said with Tears in his Eyes, and offered to give her a Bill of Fifty Pounds, which he swore was all he had in the World; which he assuring him was more than she had, and that she came into the Country only to live Cheap, her whole Income not exceeding Fifteen Pounds a Year; at which he shook his Head, and remain'd silent for some time; and then said, *Come My Dear, tho' the Case is bad it is to no purpose to be dejected; be easy as you can; I will endeavour to find out some way or other to live; if you can but subsist Yourself, that is better than nothing, I must try the World again; A Man ought to think like a Man; To be discourag'd, is to yield to the Misfortune*. And then going to Bed he propos'd a great many Things, but nothing could offer, when there was nothing to begin with, till at last he fell asleep, and rose betimes in the Morning, and took his Horses and three Servants, and all his Linnen and Baggage, and went away, leaving a Letter on the Table, with twenty Guineas in it, advising her with that Money to make the best of her Way to *London*; but a Terror falling upon his Mind, when he had rid about fifteen Miles, he dismiss'd his Servants, sold their Horses, and came back, and told her he would accompany her in her Way to *London*, which she agreed to, and in two Day's Time, they set out from *Chester*, he on Horseback, and she in the Stage-Coach, and came to *Dunstable* together; where he told her, it was convenient to leave her, for Reasons which were improper for her to know.

She desir'd him to stay with her there a Week or two, which he agreed to, in which time, she told him how that she had been in *Virginia*, and that she had now a Mother there and that if her Effects had come safe to hand, she might have had enough to have maintain'd them both very handsomly as long as they liv'd; and that if he had a mind to go there, she believ'd she cou'd raise about Three Hundred Pounds, which was sufficient to establish a Plantation, upon which they might live very well; but he wou'd upon no Account agree to it; but said, such a Sum of Money as that, would stock a Farm in *Ireland* of a Hundred Pounds a Year, of which they might live as handsomly as a Gentleman of Five Hundred here, and that he had laid a Scheme to go over and try; which if it did not succeed, he assur'd her, he would go with her to *America* with all his Heart; and then he let her into the secret part of his Life, and gave her Reasons why he could not accompany her to *London*, and so took his Leave, with a great deal of Tenderness and Affection.

He had not rid far, before he met with the three young Gentlemen who were his Servants, and were newly set up in the same Business, with whom he joyn'd Strength, and they all went in Pursuit of a Prize together: At first, he seem'd a little fearful; but he soon found they were all as great Rogues as himself; and that if they had not had Knowledge what he was, they never would have serv'd him half so long, which they did, only that they might have had an Opportunity to rob him, as soon as he had received his Wife's great Fortune, as was expected; which when they told him, it made him begin to bless himself, that his Wife did not prove a Fortune; for if she had, thought he, in all Probability it would have been the Cause of both our Deaths; certainly, saith he, GOD knows what is better for us, than we our selves; however, I must give these Rogues good Words, or it is twenty to one but that they will either hang or kill me, for I find that they are let into the secret Part of my Life, and to save themselves, what will not such a Parcel of Villains swear against a Man, which was very true; for one of them being in Love with a Widow, that kept an Inn at *Northampton*, had determin'd, as soon as they came there, to have given an Information against him, and have him secur'd, altho' he knew nothing of the Matter, but what he had by Hearsay; which Mr. *Mac-Faul* understanding by one of them, who was more honest than the rest, resolved to leave them in the next convenient Place, which as he was about to do, a Dispute arose, and two were for going one Way and two another; when he found that his old Man *John*, the Groom, took his Part, who was far the stoutest of them all, and so he got away without much Difficulty; only a Volley or two of Curses, swearing they would be reveng'd on him some time or other.

He, with trusty *John*, return'd to *Brickhill*, where the Landlord received them with all the Tokens of Respect imaginable, and after Supper and a Bottle, each went to his Bed, and in the Morning each took Horse and went about their Business; when they had not rid far before they met with the *Chester* Stage-Coach, in which was an old rich Petty-fogger, who was coming to *London* about Law; which they knew was not his right proper Business, and therefore they made bold to borrow of him an hundred Pieces, which they told him they would lay out to better Uses; and so left the Lawyer to patch up his Cause as well as he could, all which *Mac-Faul* gave to *John*, to settle him in some Business, and then made the best of his Way cross the Country, towards *Bristol*, in order to pass over into *Ireland*.

In his Journey, he happen'd to meet the *Bath-Coach*, in which were two Citizens Wives, who were going to drink the Waters, in Hopes to return pregnant home to their Husbands, from whom he took their Gold-Watches, Rings, and above forty Pounds in Money, and then posted to *Bristol*, where a Ship being ready to sail for *Ireland* he went on Board, and in two Days arrived at *Cork*, from whence he went to *Caricfergus*, where he set himself up for a Man of Fortune, and told his Countrymen, that he had been in *England*, and that he had marry'd a great Fortune, and that she was dead, and had left him very rich, and that he was come over there to purchase an Estate to settle amongst them. By my Shoul, that is very good News, saith his Sister *Nanny*, for we heard long ago, that you were turn'd *Rapparee*, and hang'd at *London*. No, you Fool, saith he, there's no such things as hanging of *Irishmen* in that Country: We borrow a little Money of some good natur'd Woman or other as soon as possible, and turn Gentleman, marry half a Score, rather than not be obliging to the Fair Sex, and when we have done, break their Hearts, as soon as we can. I' faith, saith *Nanny*, I'll go over, and see if I can't have as many Husbands; for one may stay here all one's Life-time and never be marry'd; but I will be married and what then, and who has to do with that? So thou shalt, *Nanny*, saith he, but stay till I return, and I'll take thee along with me, which happen'd sooner than he expected; for he having got acquainted with an *English* Gentleman's Family, pretended to great Riches, and that he had a Mind to settle there, was admitted to court his Sister, who had a thousand Pounds to her Fortune, which he manag'd so artfully, by his Assurance and Application, that he soon got the Lady's Consent; and he presented her with one of the Gold-Watches and a Diamond-Ring, that he had taken away from the Citizens Wives in the *Bath-Coach*, which made a mighty Figure in that Part of the Country; with which they were us'd to walk Abroad, as if they had been already marry'd, till all Things were prepared for the Wedding; when an unlucky Accident happen'd, which knock'd all in the Head: For as the Lovers were riding out one Day, he dropt a Letter, which he had lately receiv'd from *Moll Flanders*, wherein she inform'd him, what a *Hue* and *Cry* there was after him, and told him, he would certainly be hang'd, if ever he return'd to *England*, and therefore advis'd him to settle there; for she was marry'd to a Change-Broker at *London*, which being taken up by one of the Servants, and brought to the Gentleman, he grew very uneasy till his Sister came Home, for fear they should be marry'd privately: As soon as she came Home, he call'd her aside, and shew'd her the Letter, advising her to return those Presents she had received from him, and have no more to say to him; which the young Lady was very unwilling to do; but her Brother telling her, *Mac-Faul* was certainly a Rogue, and this *Moll Flanders*, from whom he received this Letter, was one of the greatest Thieves in *London*, I hearing an hundred Stories of her, saith he, when I was last Summer in *England*, and yet no body can take her, altho' she is playing her Pranks in one Disguise or other every Day.

This was very unpleasant News to the young Gentlewoman, who had plac'd her Affections entirely upon *Mac-Faul*, who had a very pretty Way of Address, and in himself was a good personable Man; and what troubled her most of all was, to part with the Gold-Watch and Diamond-Ring, with which he she had made a Figure among the Ladies above a Month; but if it must be so, saith she, and then she fell a Crying, Mac-Faul *can never be a Rogue; so fine a Gentleman as* Mac-Faul *to be a Thief, it can never be; this* Moll Flanders *is some ill Woman, who has contrived this Letter, on purpose to ruin my Happiness; I will never leave him, I will die with him*; and a great deal of such silly Stuff; so that with all the Brother could do, he could scarce prevail with her to forbear marrying him, till he heard from *England*.

The next Time *Mac-Faul* came to the House, the Gentleman shew'd him the Letter, which he stifly deny'd, and protested, that it did not belong to him, and seem'd to wonder, who should put such a Trick upon him, for he swore ten thousand Oaths, that he knew no more of it, than the *Man in the Moon*; but all would not avail, the Gentleman civilly desir'd him to forbear coming to his House, till he could be better satisfy'd from his Friends in *London*, and in the mean time gave his Word, no Man should make Application to his Sister, in the Way of Courtship, till then. *Mac-Faul* begg'd only to see her, that he might take his Leave civilly of her; which upon no Account would be granted, for the young Lady was as disconsolate as he, and narrowly watch'd, so that it was not possible for 'em to have any Intercourse, which so enrag'd *Mac-Faul*, that he sent the Gentleman a Challenge, who accepted it, and the next Morning was to determine the Justice of their Pretensions, when the Gentleman going to a Coffee-House, to look for another to be his Second, happen'd to take up a Gazette, which over Night come from *England*, wherein he found an Advertisement of the Watch and Ring his Sister had, and a Reward of twenty Guineas for taking the Man, who, by the Description, he knew could be no other than *Mac-Faul*, which he shewing to his Friend, and informing him how the whole Matter stood, they resolved to secure him; but *Mac-Faul* having a Second with him, they resisted, so that *Mac-Faul* made his Escape, and left his ill-gotten Goods behind him, and writ a Letter to his Sister, to bring his Money and Cloaths to *London*, where he would meet her.

Mac-Faul made the best of his Way to the Bogs, and there shelter'd himself among a Parcel of Rapparees, till he met with an Opportunity, in Disguise, to ship himself for *England*, which he did in the Habit of a *Highlander*, and got safe to *Brecknock* in *Wales*, where he took a Lodging at a Widow-woman's House, whom he gagg'd, and robb'd of about five and forty Shillings, and brush'd off in the Night; and from thence cross'd the Country, till he came to *Shrewsbury*, where he stole a Nag out of *Kingsland*, and made the best of his Way towards *London*, and about two Hours after, meeting with a Country Farmer, who was going to pay Rent, he told him, he thought he rid uneasy, and would lend him his Horse, for the Sake of his Company, which the Farmer modestly refus'd, and he as impudently insisted on it, till coming to a convenient Place, he knock'd him off his Horse, and swore, if he would not change Horses he must Saddles, for that he could ride no further on a Piece of a Blanket; and so taking his, he found in it fourscore Pounds, which made his Heart full glad, and much more than he expected, he having no other Design but to saddle his Nag, and never dreamt of any Booty, till he came to take it off, and found by the Weight there must be something in it more than Straw, altho' by the outside it did not seem to be worth a Shilling; but he wanted a Saddle, and a Saddle he must have, to prevent his being suspected of stealing the Gelding.

He had no sooner discover'd his Prey, but he rode for Life, and that Day he came to a little House four Miles on this Side *Coventry*, where being benighted, he asked, if he could have any Lodging for a Man and Horse, which the Host told him very readily he might; and introduc'd him into the Kitchen, where he saw the Spit saddled with some Fowls and other Necessaries of Life; he ask'd, who they were for, they told him for a couple of Gentlemen, who they believ'd would be very glad of his Company, which he was very well pleas'd with, and desir'd the Landlord, to enquire, if a Stranger might be admitted, which they readily agreed to, and Mr. *Mac-Faul* was admitted, with as much Ceremony as if he had been a Country Justice of the Peace, who behav'd himself with so much Courtesy, that after a Bottle or two, a Friendship seem'd to be cemented amongst them: The Gentlemen were very frank and open, and *Mac-Faul* as full of his Enquiry as was consistent with his Interest, till at last he perceiv'd they were a couple of Graziers just come from *London*, whom he thought Persons worth his better Acquaintance, and having inform'd himself which Way they were to travel in the Morning, he said, he should be glad of their Company, and accordingly setting out together, they had not rid above two Miles before he told them his Business, and that he must have a little ready Money, which was what they did not care to hear of; however, for Quietness sake they were forced to submit, and give him what they had about them, which amounted to about one hundred Pounds, with which he rode off, and bid them take care what Company they fell into for the future, which they very wisely told him, they would, and wish'd him good Luck with his Bargain; but it seems it was done with a Curse.

In half an Hour after this, a couple of jolly Fellows met him, and gave him the Word, *Stand*; which Language he not being us'd to, immediately drew his Pistol, and let fly; this so surpriz'd the two Thieves, that they presently begun to capitulate, and upon a little further Enquiry, found one another to be all *Cavalier* Collectors on the King's Highway; and although it is said, two of a Trade can never agree, yet they enter'd into so fast a triple Alliance, that it was never broken, till two of them were hang'd, and their Necks broken with a Rope, as you shall hear more of hereafter. And now they frankly communicated to each other the Danger they were in, and judged it safest, to make the best of their Way towards *Dunstable*, near which Place they robbed two Coaches, and some Travellers of Lace, which in all amounted to near five hundred Pounds, but were immediately pursu'd to *Brickhill*, where staying a little too long, they had like to have been taken, had not *Moll Flanders*, who was marry'd to another Husband that Day, in the Town, prevented the *Hue* and *Cry* going after 'em, by assuring the High Constable that she knew the Gentlemen to be very honest Men, and that one of 'em was a Gentleman of a very good Estate in *Lancashire*, from whence she was then upon her Journey.

After this, he robb'd sometimes with his Companions, and sometimes by himself; but having got seven or eight hundred Pounds, he did not run such desperate Risques as formerly, altho' he met with several hard and desperate Encounters on the Road, by which he had received several Wounds, and some very terrible ones indeed, particularly one with a Pistol Bullet, which broke his Arm, and another with a Sword, which run him quite thro' the Body; but it missing his Vitals, he was cur'd again: One of his new Comrades having kept with him so faithfully, that he assisted him in riding fourscore Miles before his Arm was set, and then got a Surgeon in a considerable City, remote from the Place where it was done, pretending they were Gentlemen travelling towards *Carlisle*, and had been attack'd upon the Road by Highwaymen, whom they resisting, one of them had shot him in the Arm.

The Cure being pretty chargeable, and they lying about six Months out of Business, they made the best of their Way towards *Hounslow*, where meeting with a Coach and six, they robb'd it of near two hundred Pounds in Money and Jewels, and two Gold-Watches, but *Mac-Faul* being not quite recover'd of his Lameness, did not ride up to the Coach with the other, but stood upon the Watch, at a Distance, whilst they robb'd the Coach; when some Gentlemen coming on Horseback from *Windsor*, hearing there were Highwaymen in the

Road, pursued them, he not being able to keep Company with the others, on Account of his Wound; who utterly deny'd that he had any Knowledge of the Highwaymen, and swore he had like to have been robb'd himself; but that would not avail, for he was known to be an old Offender, and was carry'd before a Justice of the Peace, who committed him to *Newgate*, where he lay for above half a Year; but no Evidence coming in against him, he was order'd to transport himself, which he did, and an Account of what happen'd to him afterwards, you have before, in *Moll Flanders*'s Life.

FRANCIS KIRKMAN

[The Counterfeit Lady Unveiled]†

Before you proceed in reading this Book, I would have you begin here, and then you are likely to know what you shall find in it; I intend for you a particular account of the Birth, Life, most remarkable actions, and death, of a famous woman called *Mary Carleton*, but better known by the name of the *German Princess*. You have had some account of her by Books already printed, but I think as this is the last, so it is the best. I am sure here is most in this, and most pains hath been taken about this, I have gathered my intelligence from several that knew her, and from all that hath been written of her; and in having this Book you will have all that is, or I think can, or will be said of her; had she given any account her self of her actions she could best have done it, but as she acted them with all privacy, so she desired to conceal them, and she would never answer any particular question, nor would she own any particular action; if any told her they had heard she had twenty husbands and desired to know the truth, she would answer that she had been told she had fifty, but would not answer punctually to any question. You will find her temper by reading the passages of her life, which I in this manner describe to you. I first give you the best and truest account of her Birth, the place where, and time when, and who were her Parents. I acquaint you with the manner of her education and first marriage with one *Stedman*; her supposed second marriage with one *Day*: then some of her rambles, and her travelling to her pretended Countrey *Collen*; where by a mistake she gets the name and title of Lady *Maria Wolway*, and how by the continuation of that mistake she gets a quantity of Jewels, and cheating her Landlady who had been her

† From Francis Kirkman, *The Counterfeit Lady Unveiled. Being a full Account of the Birth, Life, most remarkable Actions, and untimely Death of* MARY CARLETON, *Known by the Name of the German Princess* (London, 1673) "To the Reader," and pp. 168–76, 216–20.

assistant, she leaves that place and comes for *England*. Upon her arrival here, she chances into the house of Mr. *King*, her Husband *Carletons* Brother in law, who supposing her to a be a *Princess* at best, and a Lady at least, contrives how to get her married to his wifes Brother *John Carleton*. I give you a full account of all Passages in the wooing, Wedding, and pretended discovering of this Lady. Her Indictment for having two Husbands, and her being acquitted, and the circumstances how. You then have an account of her Acting at the Theatre, and her leaving that employ at the entreaty of two young *Novices* who she cheats and abuses. Next how a Countrey Gentleman entertains her as his wife, or Mistress rather, till she finding her opportunity cheats him of money and jewels and leaves him. She then cheats a young man of a round Summe of money by a counterfeit Letter, which induces him to entertain her in his Lodgings, where she robs him and leaves him. After that she pretends to bury a Friend, and getting a Pall of Velvet and several pieces of Plate for the Solemnity, she runs away with all, leaving a Coffin with Hay and Brickbats. She then cheats a Mercer, and after him a Weaver and Laceman of several rich Commodities; and causing a Taylor to make her Cloaths, she not only gets off without payment for them, but also robs him of Plate *&c.* She likewise gets gloves, Ribbons, Hoods, Scarfs, *&c.* from an Exchange-Shop without payment. She draws in and trappans a young Lawyer out of a hundred pound. She often changes her Lodging and steals silver Tankards, and as often visits Ale houses and gets silver Bowls and other drinking Cups; for some of these Facts she is caught, Indicted, found guilty, and sent to *Jamaica*. I then relate to you the manner of her Voyage thither, entertainment there, and her return to *London*; where she presently falls to her old Trade of Pilfering and Cheating of several, till she meets with an *Apothecary*, to whom she pretending to be a Rich Citizens Neece, thereby Cheats him of a hundred pound. Lastly her Cheating a Watch-Maker of a round sum of money and several Watches. After all this, she is taken in *Southwark*; I give you a clear account of the manner how, and how she behaved her self in the Prison of the *Marshalsea*, and afterwards in *Newgate*. The manner of her Tryal and Condemnation at the Sessions in the *Old Baily*; and her deportment in prison from the time of her Condemnation till her Execution; her penitence before, and at her Execution, and lastly, her last Speech, death and Burial. This is the Sum of what you shall read in this ensuing Treatise, before which I have placed her true original Picture as it was taken by her own order and appointment in the year 1663, when she was tryed about her marriage with her Husband *Carleton*, and being acquitted, she was so Confident as to write, print, and publish a Book, calling it the Case of *Mary Carleton*, and under her Picture she caused these Lines to be placed,

Behold my Innocence after this disgrace,
Dares shew an honest and a noble face;
Henceforth there needs no mark of me be known,
For the true Counterfeit is hereby shewn.

And underneath was added these words
Ætatis meæ proximo 22. Januar. Stilo novo vicessimo primo 1663. M.C.

So that she began with a lye, for her Age was as I have said, seven or eight years more, only the day was true as she alledged to the last; If you behold her Picture, and did know her, or ever see her, you will conclude it very like; only she was somewhat thinner faced, nine years time had made that alteration; and you will find that the dressing of her Head is different from the present fashion, and from what she now wore, which was *a-la-mode*; a large parcel of frizled hair, which is called a Towr, and her habit now at her Tryal was an *Indian* strip'd Gown, silk Petticoat, white shooes with slaps, laced with green, and in these she was hanged, and I think buried. This was her outside, what her inside was, by reading this Book you will be sufficiently acquainted, for I have related at large all these several passages which you have here read in *Epitomy*. And she may very well serve as a Looking glass, wherein we may see the Vices of this Age Epitomized. And to the end that we may see her vices and thereby amend our own wicked lives, is the intent of

Your Friend,
F. K.

* * *

[B]ut although the best of our Writing is past, the worst of her Adventures are to come, which I shall thus relate to you. She had thus fortunately enough performed all the aforementioned Projects: Success had flush'd her, and she finding with how much ease she gained money, she was as free in spending it; she knew she had the same tools her wits to work with, and so long as they lasted she assured her self of a brave Livelihood, and therefore sought no other way, took no other course to live by; but her money being gone, she attempted to get more, and her ordinary course was this, she pretending to be some Countrey Gentlewoman, would take a Lodging, carry her self very demurely, keep good hours, and although she went abroad about her urgent affairs in the day-time, yet she still returned early at nights. I would hold any discourse with her Landlady or Landlord, and pry into the affairs of the house, and be sure to mind what Plate was stirring, and if there were a silver Tankard, that she would assure her self of, by pretending sickness in her head and stomach, and desiring a Posset, which was commonly brought her in the silver Tankard; some she would eat, and the rest must stand by for her breakfast the next morning. And thus would she become Mistress of the Tankard, which with her self would the next morning be invisible, for she would be sure to be up early and watch her opportunity to give her Landlady the slip, neither did the Tankard alone serve the turn, but if there were any Chest, Trunk, or Box in the Room, she would break it open and rifle it of all that was considerable and worth her carriage. This was her trick for Tankards, this was her usual common way to serve her Landladyes, and this she did so often in so many places that it is admirable she should escape; I can name at least half a score of these Tankard-adventures in several places, and all performed much after one and the same manner, in *Covent-Garden*, *Milford-lane*, *Lothbury*, *New-Market*, and several other places; and for one of these adventures was she at last taken and Indicted, found guilty, Condemned, Reprieved and banished to *Jamaica*, but before I let her pass from *England* I will relate another adventure of hers and a pretty one, wherein she took much pains for little gains, to shew you that she would play at small Game rather than stand out, and that she would not be daunted nor put by her undertaking, she could not endure to be baffled. She came one evening into an Alehouse near *West-Smithfield*, being scarfed and masked, and pretending to be very cold, was admitted to the Kitchin-fire, she calls for a Cup of Ale and her Landlady; one was brought, and the other came, desiring to know her pleasure, only said she to have your company, for I cannot drink; I do not so much value that as your fire, being newly come to Town, just now alighted out of the Coach; from what Countrey I pray said the Landlady? from such a place in *Essex*, naming it, said our Counterfeit. Oh dear said the Landlady, I know the Parson of a Parish close by! naming it; and so do I said our Princess, and he is a brave Preacher, I love to hear him; and much more she and her Landlady enlarged upon this Subject, in all which discourse she was very confident. And now she was not only acquainted with the Landlady, but her daughter coming into the Kitchin, she enters into a Dialogue with her, who being at work upon a Point-Lace, she looks on it and much commends it, telling her that she would come again suddenly and show her work, and thus she invites her self into an acquaintance, and finding there was no good to be done at present, she paid for her drink and departed, but came again the next evening, and calls for more drink, and enters into a familiar discourse with the Landlady; she enlarging and sitting there a great while and being troublesome, the Landlord takes her into examination what she was, she replies a Maiden Gentlewoman, which had a thousand pound to her portion in her own hands, and lived upon the interest-mony of it; who gave you that portion said the Landlord, my Father said she, who allows me to receive the interest-mony of it, and truly what I do not spend I bestow upon the poor, and other Charitable uses; away away said mine Host, I cannot believe any man to be so mad as to leave a thousand pounds to your dispose, neither do I believe you to be such a person as you name your self, if you were, you would not sit tippling here at this time of the night: The Host having given her this Tart discourse left her; and so did she the house in short time after, but was not in the least daunted, but made excuses for his peevishness. One would have thought that this would have beat her off for coming hither any more, but it did not; now she was resolved not to lose her labour, nor to leave things done by the halfs, and it may be she was resolved to be revenged of her Host; for the next morning she comes again early before the mistris or Master was up, calls for a pot of Ale and a Tost, the maid brings it her but pours it out into a pewter pot: Alas said our Counterfeit, what do you do maid, you know I cannot drink in pewter, I hate it above all things, and I know you have Plate enough in the house, therefore fetch some or else I cannot drink one drop; truly said the maid my Master carries all the plate up every night, he is not up yet, but if you please I will go up and fetch a Beaker, do so said she, the wench went up and told her Master and Mistris that the Gentlewoman was there below, and wanted a silver Cup to drink in, she shall have none said the man, why said his wife, she is a Cheat said the man, no said the woman I cannot believe it, but to be more sure I will go down and watch her, and thereupon she leaps out of the bed and with her cloaths half on and half off went down, by this time the Lady had dispatched her drink and was contriving how to secure the Cup, but the Landlady came and prevented her, withall seeing that her drink was off she went to take the Cup out of her hands; she was unwilling to part from her Cup, therefore said, nay Madam, what do you mean, now you are come down I will have the other pot of Ale to drink with you. The Landlady being willing to take mony, was content; her maid was stept out of an errant, and a neighbours maid came for some drink, she therefore her self went into the cellar to draw for her Guest and neighbours maid, leaving them together in the Kitchin; she was but just down in the Cellar and was beginning to draw the Ale when she heard one tread, and being jealous of her guest, ran up immediately to see if all were well, but she found that the bird was flown, she asked the maid where was the Gentlewoman, I know not said the maid, she stept to the door as she said, to see what weather it was and I saw her no more: Good lack my Beaker said the woman, where is it, I saw none said the maid, they both looked for that and for our Counterfeit, but they were both invisible neither to be seen nor heard of. And now her husband being come down, understood the case, and was very angry but to no purpose, it was too late. They were both troubled the more because it was an ancient peece of plate worth about three pound, but more or less, old or new, it was gone and no more to be heard of. And now Reader I have no more projects to relate to you, for it was not long after this that she was taken and secured in *Newgate* for one of her Tankard-adventures, she had used so many of them that was at last caught. She had lived like a Duck hunted by the Spaniell, who had often forced her to dive and hide her self, but at last she must be taken and the sport at an end: She was endicted for stealing a Silver Tankard, was found guilty, and condemned to be hang'd, but had the mercy of Transportation, and was two days before Shrovetide, in the year 1670 sent on board a Ship at *Gravesend* bound for *Jamaica*, so that from her banishment to her late death, was under two years.

* * *

She was now led out of her Lodging into the Common Hall, to have the Halter tyed about her, which was done, and there she met with five young men, who for several Facts were to suffer with her; she was the Eldest of the Six, for the other Five could not make 120 years. They were all much of her temper and humour, and indeed more unconcerned and unsensible of their Condition, for they went into their several Carts as if they had only been going to return again; but she employed all the time of her being in the Cart in meditations and reading in two Popish Books which she had in her hands; one intituled, the Key of Paradice, and the other the Manual of daily Devotion; which books when she came to the Gallows, she delivered to a friend in the Cart; by the way as she went into St. *Gile's-street* the Cart stop'd, and she had a Pint of *Canary*, one glass full of which she drank off, delivering the rest to one in the Cart; soon after her arrival at *Tyburn* she was lifted out of the Cart into an other, where all the rest of the Prisoners were, and there she was tyed up; and then she took her Husbands Picture and put it into her bosome; then the Subordinary coming into the Cart to them, asked them all twice if they had any thing to say before they departed this world? no answer being made he began his Prayers; which being ended, another Person also desired to pray with them, this was granted, and when he had finished his Prayer, *Mary Carleton* desired the liberty to speak to the People, and being permitted so to do, she thus began. You will make me a President for sin, I confess I have been a vain woman, I have had in the world the height of glory, and misery in abundance; and let all people have a care of ill company. I have been condemned by the world, and I have much to answer for; I pray God forgive me and my husband, I beseech God lay nothing to his charge for my fault. A Gentleman hearing her speak of her Husband, asked her if she desired any thing to him, only (said she) my recommendations, and that he will serve God and repent, for I fear he wants sober counsel, and I beseech God lay nothing to his charge upon my account; you are in perfect charity with him said one, yes said she, and with all the world; and thus the Cart being ready to be drawn away she began and continued in pious Ejaculations, saying, *Lord Jesus* receive my Soul. *Lord* have mercy upon me. *Christ* have mercy upon me; and thus she continued till the Cart was gone and she ended her life. After she had hanged about an hour, she was cut down, and her friends having paid all due fees for her body and Clothes, they put her into a Coach which carried her to her Coffin not far off, and being put into that, she was the next day buried in St. *Martins* Church yard. Thus have I brought this unlucky woman from her birth to her burial; as she was born obscurely and lived viciously, so she dyed ignominiously. Such crimes as she was guilty of deserve such end and punishment as was inflicted on her; and without repentance and amendment infallibly find them here and worse hereafter. The only way therefore for Christians to avoid the one and contemn the other, is with sanctified hearts and unpolluted hands still to pray to God for his grace, continually to affect Prayer and incessantly to practise piety in our thoughts, and godliness in our resolutions and actions; the which if we be careful and conscionable to perform, God will then shrowd us under the wings of his favour, and so preserve and protect us with his mercy and providence as we shall have no cause to fear either Hell or Satan. But if we give our selves over to ill Company or our own wicked inclinations, we are infallibly led to the Practice of those Crimes, which although they may be pleasing at the present, yet they have a sting behind, and we shall be sensible thereof when we shall be hurried to an untimely end, as you have seen in the vicious life and untimely death of this our Counterfeit Lady.

ALEXANDER SMITH

[The Golden Farmer, a Murderer and Highway-man]†

THE *Golden-Farmer* was so called from his Occupation, and paying People, if it was any considerable Sum, always in Gold; but his real Name was *William Davis*, born at *Wrexham* in *Denbighshire*, in *North-Wales*; from whence he remov'd, in his younger Years, to *Sudbury* in *Glocestershire*, where he married the Daughter of a wealthy Inn-keeper, by whom he had 18 Children, and follow'd the Farmer's Business to the Day of his Death, to shroud his Robbing on the Highway; which irregular Practice he had follow'd for 42 Years, without any Suspicion among his Neighbours.

He generally robb'd alone, and one Day meeting three or four Stage-Coaches going to *Salisbury*, he stop'd one of them, which was full of Gentlewomen, one of which was a Quaker. All of 'em satisfy'd the *Golden-Farmer*'s Desire, excepting this Precisian, with whom he held a long Argument to no purpose; for, upon her solemn Vow and Asseveration, she told him she had no Money, nor any thing valuable about her; whereupon fearing he should lose the Booty of the other Coaches, he told her he would go and see what they had to afford him, and he would wait on her again. So having robb'd the other three Coaches, he return'd according to his Word, and the Quaker persisting still in her old Tone of having nothing for him; it put the *Golden Farmer* into a Rage, and taking hold of her Shoulder, shaking her as a Mastiff does a Bull, he cried, *You canting B——ch, if you dally with me at this rate, you'll certainly provoke my Spirit to be damnable rude with you: you see these good Women here were so tender-hearted as to be charitable to me, and you, you whining Whore, are so covetous as to lose your Life for the sake of Mammon. Come, come, you hollow B——ch, open your Purse-strings quickly, or else I shall send you out of the Land of the Living.* Now the poor Quaker being frighten'd out of her Wits at these bullying Expressions of the wicked one, she gave him a Purse of Guineas, a Gold Watch, and Diamond Ring, and parted then as good Friends as if they'd never fall'n out at all.

† From Alexander Smith, *A Compleat History of the Lives and Robberies of the most Notorious Highway-men, Foot-Pads, Shop-Lifts, and Cheats, of both Sexes, in and about* London, Westminster, *and all Parts of* Great Britain, *for above an hundred Years past, continu'd to the present Time* (London, 1719), I, pp. 2–12. Originally published in 1714, under a slightly different title, this famous compilation of criminal biographies, revised and expanded, had reached its fifth edition by 1719. "Capt. Alex. Smith," as the author's name appears on the title page, is probably a pseudonym; attempts to attribute the work to Defoe have been unconvincing.

Another time this Desperado meeting with the Dutchess of *Albemarle* in her Coach, as riding over *Salisbury-Plain*, he was put to his Trumps before he could assault her Grace, by reason he had a long engagement with a Postilion, Coachman, and two Footmen, before he could proceed in his Robbery; but having wounded them all, by the discharging several Pistols, he then approach'd to his Prey, whom he found more refractory than his Female Quaker had been, which made him very saucy and more eager, for fear of any Passengers coming by in the mean while. But still Her Grace deny'd parting with any thing, whereupon, by main Violence, he pull'd three Diamond Rings off her Fingers, and snatch'd a rich Gold Watch from her side, crying to her at the same time, because he saw her Face painted, *You B——ch incarnate, you had rather read over your Face in the Glass every Morning, and blot out Pale to put in Red, than give an honest Man, as I am, a small Matter, to support him in his Lawful Occasions on the Road*. And then rid away as fast as he could, without searching Her Grace for any Money; because he perceiv'd another Person of Quality's Coach making towards them, with a good Retinue of Servants belonging to it.

Not long after this Exploit the *Golden-Farmer* meeting with Sir *Thomas Day*, a Justice of Peace living at *Bristol*, on the Road betwixt *Glocester* and *Worcester*, they fell into Discourse together; and, as Riding along, he told Sir *Thomas*, whom he knew, tho' the other did not know him, how he had like to have been robb'd but a little before by a couple of Highway-Men, but, as good luck wou'd have it, his Horse having better Heels than theirs, he got clear of 'em; or else if they had robb'd him of his Money, which was about Forty Pounds, they had certainly undone him for ever. *Truly* (quoth Sir *Thomas Day*) *that had been very hard; but nevertheless, as you had been robb'd betwixt Sun and Sun, the County, upon Suing it, must have been oblig'd to have made your Loss good again*. But not long after their chatting together, coming to a convenient place, the *Golden Farmer* shooting Sir *Thomas*'s Man's Horse under him, and obliging him to retire some distance from it, that he might not make use of the Pistols which were in the Holsters, he presented a Pistol to Sir *Thomas*'s Breast, and demanded his Money of him. Quoth Sir *Thomas, I thought, Sir, that you had been an honest Man*. The *Golden-Farmer* reply'd, *You see your worship's mistaken, and, had you any Guts in your Brains, you might easily have perceiv'd by my Face that my Countenance was the very Picture of mere Necessity; therefore deliver presently, for I'm in haste*. Then Sir *Thomas Day* giving the *Golden Farmer* what Money he had, which was about Sixty Pounds in Gold and Silver, he humbly thank'd His Worship, and told him, that what he had parted with was not lost, because he was robb'd betwixt Sun and Sun, therefore the County (as he told him) must pay it again.

One Mr. *Hart*, a young Gentleman of *Enfield*, who had a good Estate, but not overmuch Wit, and therefore could sooner change a piece of Gold than a piece of Sense, Riding one Day over *Finchley Common*, where the *Golden-Farmer* had been hunting about four or five Hours for a Prey, he rides up to him, and giving the Gentleman a slap with the flat of his drawn Hanger o'er his Shoulders, quoth he, *A plague on you, how slow you are, to make a Man wait on you all this Morning; come, deliver what you have, and be poxt to you, and then go to Hell for Orders*. The Gentleman, who was wont to find a more agreeable Entertainment betwixt his Mistress and his Snush-box, being surpriz'd at this rustical sort of Greeting, he began to make several Excuses, and say he had no Money about him; but his Antagonist not believing him, he made bold to search his Pockets himself, and finding in them above an hundred Guineas, besides a Gold Watch, he gave him two or three good slaps over his Shoulders again, with his Hanger, and at the same time bad him not give his Mind to Lying any more, when an honest Gentleman requir'd a small Boon of him.

Another time this notorious Robber had paid his Landlord about Eighty Pounds for Rent, who going home with it, his goodly Tenant disguising himself, met the Old grave Gentleman and bidding him Stand, quoth he, *Come, Mr. Gravity from Head to Foot, but from neither Head nor Foot to the Heart, deliver what you have in a trice*. The Old Man fetching a deep Sigh, to the hazard of losing several Buttons off his Wastcoat, he told him, that he had not above two Shillings about him, therefore he hop'd he was more a Gentleman than to take such a small matter from a poor Man. Quoth the *Golden-Farmer, I have not the Faith to believe you, for you seem, by your Mein and Habit, to be a Man of better Circumstances than you pretend, therefore open your Budget, or else I shall fall foul about your House. Dear Sir* (reply'd his Landlord) *you can't be so barbarous sure to an Old Man: What have you no Religion, Pity, or Compassion in you? Have you no Conscience? Nor have you no Respect for your own Body and Soul, which must certainly be in a miserable Case, if you follow these unlawful Courses? D——n you* (said his Tenant to him) *don't talk of Age or Barbarity to me, for I shew neither Pity nor Compassion to any. D——n you, what, talk of Conscience to me! I have no more of that dull Commodity than you have; nor do I allow my Soul and Body to be govern'd by Religion, but Interest; therefore deliver what you have, before this Pistol makes you repent your Obstinacy*. So delivering his Money to the *Golden Farmer*, he receiv'd it without giving his Landlord any Receipt for it, as his Landlord had him.

Not long after the committing of his Robbery, overtaking an old Grasier on *Putney-Heath*, in a very ordinary Attire, but yet very Rich, he takes half a score Guineas out of his Pocket, and giving them to the Old Man, he said, *There were three or four Persons behind them, who look'd very suspicious, therefore he desir'd the Favour of him to put that Gold into his Pocket, for in case they were Highway-men, his indifferent Apparel would make them believe he had no such Charge about him.* The Old Grasier, looking upon his Intentions to be honest, quoth he, *I have Fifty Guineas ty'd up in the Fore-lappit of my Shirt, and I'll put it to that for Security.* So riding along both of them Cheek by Jole for above half a Mile, and the Coast being still clear, the *Golden-Farmer* said to the Old Man, *I believe there's no Body will take the pains of robbing you or me to Day, therefore I think I had as good take the trouble upon me of robbing you my self, so, instead of delivering your Purse, pray give me the Lappit of your Shirt.* The old Grasier was horridly startled at these Words, and began to beseech him not to be so cruel in robbing a Poor Old Man. *Prithee* (quoth the *Golden-Farmer*) *don't tell me of Cruelty, for who can be more Cruel than Men of your Age, whose Pride it is to teach their Servants their Duties with as much Cruelty, as some People teach their Dogs to fetch and carry*? So, being obliged to cut off the Lappit of the Old Man's Shirt himself, for he would not, he rid away to seek out for another Booty.

Another time this bold Robber lying at the *Red-Lion*-Inn in *Uxbridge*, he happen'd into Company with one Esquire *Broughton*, a Barrister of the *Middle-Temple*; which he understanding, pretended to him, that he was going up to *London*, to advise with a Lawyer about some Business, wherefore he should be much oblig'd to him if he could recommend him to a good one. Counsellor *Broughton*, thinking he might be a good Client, he bespoke him for himself; then the *Golden-Farmer* telling his Business was about several of his Neighbours Cattle breaking into his Grounds, and doing a great deal of Mischief, the Barrister told him that was very Actionable, as being *Damage fesant. Damage fesant*! said the *Golden-Farmer, what's that, pray Sir*? He told him, that it was an Action brought against Persons, when their Cattle broke through Hedges or other Fences, into Peoples Grounds, and did them Damage. Next Morning, as they were both riding towards *London*, quoth the *Golden-Farmer* to the Barrister, *If I may be so bold as to ask you, pray Sir, what is that you call Trover and Conversion*? He told him, it signified, in our Common Law, an Action which a Man hath against one, that having found any of his Goods, refuses to deliver them upon Demand, and perhaps converts them to his own use also. The *Golden-Farmer*, being now at a Place convenient for his purpose, he reply'd, *Very well, Sir; and so if I should find any Money about you, and convert it to my use, why, then that is but only Actionable I find. That's a Robbery*, said the Barrister, *which requires no less Satisfaction than a Man's Life. A robbery*, reply'd the *Golden-Farmer, why then I must e'en commit one, for once and not use it; therefore deliver your Money, or else behold this Pistol shall presently prevent you from ever Reading* Cook *upon* Littleton *any more*. The Barrister strangely surprized at his Client's rough Behaviour, and asking him if he thought there was neither Heaven nor Hell, that he could be guilty of such wicked Actions? Quoth the *Golden-Farmer, Why, you Son of a Whore, thy Impudence is very great, to talk of Heaven and Hell to me, when you think there's no way to Heaven but thro'* Westminster-Hall. *Come, come, down with your Rino this Moment, for I have other Customers to mind, than to wait on your A——se all Day*. The Barrister being very loath to part with his Money, he was still insisting on the Injustice of the Action, saying that it was against both Law and Conscience to Rob any Man. However the *Golden-Farmer* heeding not his Pleading, he swore that he was not to be guided by Law nor Conscience, any more than them of his Profession, whose Law is always furnished with a Commission to arraign their Conscience; but upon Judgment given, they usually had the knack of setting it at large. So putting a Pistol to the Barrister's Breast, he quietly deliver'd his Money, amounting to about thirty Guineas, and eleven Broad Pieces of Gold, besides some Silver, and a Gold Watch.

One time overtaking a Tinker, on *Black-Heath*, whom he knew to have seven or eight Pounds about him, quoth he, *Well overtook, honest Tinker, methinks you seem very Devout, for your Life is a continual Pilgrimage, and in Humility you go almost barefoot, thereby making Necessity a Vertue*. Ay, Master (reply'd the Tinker) needs must when the Devil drives; and, had you no more than I, you might go without Boots and Shoes too. *That may be*, (quoth the *Golden Farmer*;) *and I suppose you march all over* England *with your Bag and Baggage*. Yes (said the Tinker) I go a great deal of Ground; but not so much as you ride. *Well* (quoth the *Golden Farmer*) *go where you will, it is my Opinion, your Conversation is unreprovable, because thou'rt ever mending*. I wish (reply'd the Tinker) that I could say as much by you. *Why, you Dog of Egypt* (quoth the other,) *you don't think, I hope, that I'm like you, in observing the Statutes, and therefore had rather Steal than Beg, in spite of Whips or Imprisonment*. (Said the Tinker again) I'll have you to know, that I take a great deal of Pains for a Livelyhood. *Yes* (reply'd the *Golden Farmer*) *I know thou'rt such a strong Enemy to Idleness, that in mending one Hole, you make three, rather than want Work*. That's as you say (quoth the Tinker) however I wish that you and I, Sir, were farther asunder, for i'faith I don't like your Company, *Nor I yours* (said the other) *for tho' thou'rt entertain'd in every place, yet you enter no farther than the Door, to avoid Suspicion*. Indeed (reply'd the Tinker) I have a great Suspicion of you. *Have you so?* (quoth the *Golden Farmer*) *why, then it shall not be without a Cause; come, open your Wallet straight, and deliver that Parcel of Money that's in it.* Here their Dialogue being on a Conclusion, the Tinker pray'd heartily that he would not rob him, for if he did, he must be forc'd to Beg his way home, from whence he was above an Hundred Miles. *D——n me* (quoth the *Golden Farmer*) *I don't care if you Beg your way Two hundred Miles, for if a Tinker 'scapes* Tyburn *and* Banbury, *it is his Fate to die a Beggar.* So taking Money and Wallet too, from the Tinker, he left him to his old Custom of conversing still in open Fields and low Cottages.

Thus the *Golden farmer* having run a long Course in Wickedness, he was at last Discover'd in *Salisbury-Court*, but as he was running along, a Butcher endeavouring to stop him, he Shot him Dead with a Pistol; nevertheless being apprehended, he was committed to *Newgate*, and shortly after Executed at the End of *Salisbury-Court*, in *Fleetstreet*, on *Friday* the 20th of *December*, 1689; and afterwards was Hang'd in Chains, in the Sixty-fourth Year of his Age, on *Bagshot-Heath*.

ALEXANDER SMITH

[Whitney, a Highway-man]†

THIS notorious Robber on the Highways, *Whitney* the Butcher, meeting, in the County of *Kent*, with one Mr. *Wawen*, Lecturer of the Church at *Greenwich* for some Years; he and his Gang set upon this Gentleman, and Robb'd him; after which *Whitney* said, That it being a long time since he had heard a Sermon, as having bid adieu to the Church for ever, it was his earnest Desire that the Parson would be pleas'd to oblige him with one there. Mr. *Wawen* perceiving him and his Companions resolute in their Frolick, and fearing a Mischief might be done him, as being in a very by sort of a place, in case he deny'd their Request, he proceeded to gratify them as follows.

Gentlemen, my Text is *T H E F T*; which being not to be divided into Sentences nor Syllables, as being but one Word, which is only a Monosyllable, Necessity therefore obliges me to divide it into Letters, which I find to be these five, *T*, *H*, *E*, *F*, *T*, *Theft*. Now *T*, my beloved, is *Theological*; *H*, is *Historical*; *E*, is *Exegetical*; *F*, is *Figurative*; and *T*, is *Tropological*.

† From Alexander Smith, *A Compleat History of the Lives and Robberies of the most Notorious Highway-men, Foot-Pads, Shop-Lifts, and Cheats, of both Sexes, in and about* London, Westminster, *and all Parts of* Great Britain, *for above an hundred Years past, continu'd to the present Time* (London, 1719), I, pp. 24–40.

Now the *Theological* part of my Text is, according to the Effects that it works, which I find to be of two kinds. *First*, In this World. *Secondly*, In the World to come. In this World, the Effects which it works are, *T*, *Tribulation*; *H*, *Hatred*; *E*, *Envy*; *F*, *Fear*; and *T*, *Torment*. For what greater *Tribulation* can befal a Man than to be debarr'd from sweet Liberty, by a close Confinement in a nasty Prison? which must needs be a perfect Representation of the Iron-Age, since nothing is heard there but the Jingling of Shackles, Bolts, Grates, and Keys, as large as that put up for a Weather-Cock on St. *Peter*'s Steeple in *Cornhil*: However, I must own that you Highway-Men may be a sort of Christians whilst under this Tribulation, because ye are a kind of Martyrs, and suffer really for the Truth. Again, Ye have the *Hatred* of all honest People, as well as the *Envy* of Jaylors, if you go under their Jurisdiction without Money in your Pockets. I'm sure all of your Profession are very sensible, that a Jaylor expects not only to distill Money out of your Irregularities, but also to grow fat by your Curses; wherefore his Ears are stopp'd to the Cries of others, as GOD's are to his; and good Reason, for lay the Life of a Man in one Scale, and his Fees in the other, he would lose the first, to find the second. Next, ye are always in as much *Fear* of being apprehended, as poor Tradesmen in Debt are of a Serjeant, who goes muffled like a Thief too, and always carries the Marks of one, for he steals upon a Man cowardly, plucks him by the Throat, and makes him stand till he fleeces him; but only in this they differ, the Thief is more valiant, and the honester Man of the two. And then when ye are apprehended, nothing but *Torment* ensues; for when once ye are clapt up in Jayl, as I have hinted before, soon after you come under the Hangman's Clutches and he Hangs you up, like so many Dogs, for using those scaring Words, *Stand and Deliver*.

The Effect which *Theft* works in the World to come, being much the same with the other, but only as they were Temporary, these being Eternal; I shall proceed to the *Historical* part of my Text, which will prove, from Humane Histories, that the Art of *Theft* is of some Antiquity, in that *Paris* stole *Helen*, *Theseus* stole *Ariadne*, and *Jason* stole *Medea*. However Antiquity ought to be no Plea for Vice, since Laws both Divine and Humane forbid base Actions, especially *Theft*: For History again informs us, that *Scyron* was thrown headlong into the Sea for thieving; *Cacus* was kill'd by *Hercules*; *Sysiphus* was cut in pieces; *Brunellus* was hanged for stealing *Angelica*'s Ring; and the Emperor *Frederick* the Third condemn'd all Thieves to the Gallies.

The *Exegetical* Part of my Text, is a sort of Commentary on what was last said, when I set forth, that your Transgressions were a Breach of both Divine and Humane Ordinances, which are utterly repugnant to all manner of *Theft*; wherefore if ye are resolv'd to pursue these Courses still, note, my respect is such to you, for all you have robb'd me, that if you can but keep your selves from being ever took, I'll engage to keep you always from being hang'd.

The *Figurative* Part of my Text is to set forth, That tho' I call you Gentlemen, yet, in my heart, I think ye to be all Rogues; but only I mollify my Spleen by a *Charientismus*, which is a Figure or Form of Speech mitigating hard Matters with pleasant Words. Thus a certain Man being Apprehended, and brought before *Alexander* the Great, King of *Macedon*, for railing against him, and being demanded by *Alexander* why he and his Company had so done? he made this Answer. *Had not the Wine failed, we had spoken much worse*. Whereby he signified, that those Words proceeded rather from Wine than Malice; by which free and pleasant Confession, he asswaged *Alexander*'s great Displeasure, and obtained Remission.

But now, coming to the *Tropological* Part of my Text, which is drawing a Word from its proper and genuine Signification, to another Sense, as in calling you most famous Thieves; I desire your most serious Attention, and that you will embrace this Exhortation of St. *Paul* the Apostle, *Let him that stole steal no more*. Or else the Letters of my Text points towards a Tragical Conclusion, for *T, Take care*; *H, Hanging*; *E, Ends not*; *F, Felony*: *T, at Tyburn*.

The Parson having ended his Sermon, which some of *Whitney*'s Gang took down in Shorthand, they were so well pleas'd with what he had Preach'd, that they were contented to pay him Tythes; so telling the Money over, which they had took from him, and finding it to be just Ten Pounds, they gave him Ten Shillings for his pains, and then rid away to seek whom they might next devour.

Another time *Whitney* and his Gang meeting a Gentleman on *Bagshot-Heath*, they commanded him to Stand, whereupon the Gentleman said, *I was just going to say the same to you, Gentlemen*. Why (quoth Whitney) are you a Gentleman-Thief? He reply'd, *Yes, Sir; but I have had very bad luck to Day, for I have been Riding up and down all this Morning, and as yet have not lit on a Prize*. Then *Whitney* and his Comrades wishing the Gentleman good luck, as supposing him to be one of their Profession, they parted; but at Night happening into an Inn, where they overheard this Gentleman telling another, how he had saved an Hundred Pounds from being took from him to day, by a parcel of Highway-men, in pretending to be one of their Robbing Society, they were very mad with themselves to think what a Booty they had lost, by believing the Person, whom they set on, to be one of their Fraternity: And hearing the Gentleman, to whom the Story was told, say he had a pretty considerable Summ of Money about him, therefore if he should be assaulted on the Road before he got home, he would use the like Stratagem, they swore they would narrowly watch his waters. So next Morning *Whitney* and his Gang being out first, they laid an Ambuscade for this other Gentleman, who suddenly falling into it, *Whitney*, commanded him to stand; on which, he cry'd, *I vow Gentlemen, I was just going to say the same to you*. Quoth *Whitney* then, *Are you a Gentleman-Thief, Sir?* Yes (reply'd the Gentleman.) *Why then* (quoth *Whitney*) *as it is an old Saying,* That two of a Trade can never agree, *I must make bold to take what you have, wherefore Deliver what you have presently, or else I must be oblig'd to send a Brace of Balls thro' your Head*. These scaring Words putting the Gentleman into a *Panick Fear*, he gave One hundred and twenty Guineas to *Whitney*, who then taking his leave of the Robb'd Person, he desir'd him to acquaint the other Gentleman, whenever he saw him, that *I was going to say the same to you*, would never save his Bacon again; for he should know him for a Black Sheep another time.

One time *Whitney* and his Gang meeting with one Mr. *Hull*, an Old Usurer, formerly living in the *Strand*, as he was Riding over *Hounsloe-Heath*, he order'd him to Stand and Deliver; hereupon the Old Man was in a great Consternation, trembling as if he had been afflicted with a Palsy, and expostulating with the Highway-men, by pretending he was a poor Man, and should be utterly ruin'd and undone if they should be so hard hearted as to take his Money from him; besides, it was a very wicked thing for 'em to follow such illegal Courses, wherefore he humbly desired them to do as they'd be done by. Quoth *Whitney*, in a great Passion, *You Old Rogue, do you pretend to read Lectures of Morality to honest Men? You Old Suffocated Rascal, I know you to be a miserable Miser and Usurer, that puts out your Money to the unnatural Act of Generation, therefore you seem to be the Son of a Jaylor, for all your Estate is in most heavy and cruel Hands. You Dog in a Doublet, do you presume to Catechize better Christians than yourself? No, no, we know better things than to be Disciplin'd by you, whose Conscience hates looking into the Court of Chancery; and since your Impudence admonishes us to do as we'd be done by, we will deal with you as you deal with other Men, to whom you can be no Friend, since it is your main Study to Undo all Mankind*. After this, taking all Old *Hull*'s Money from him, which was about Eighteen Pounds, he was in such a Rage at his Loss, that he said, he should see them one time or another ride up *Holburn-Hill* backwards. Hereupon *Whitney* pulling Mr. *Hull* off his Horse, and putting him on again with his Face towards the Horse's Tail, he ty'd his Legs under the Horse's Belly, and said, *Now, you Son of a Whore, we'll see what a Figure you'll make, when you ride backwards*. So giving the Horse half a dozen good Licks with his Whip, the Beast ne'er stopt nor staid till he brought his Master into *Hounsloe* Town, where the People set the Old Man at Liberty.

This notorious Robber *Whitney*, going one Morning into the *Red-*

Lyon-Inn in *Doncaster*, in *Yorkshire*, he pulls out of his Portmanteau an Hundred Pound Bag, fill'd with Brass Counters, and taking thereout, in the sight of the Man of the House, a handful of good Money, which was separated from the Counters, by a Piece of Cloth sew'd betwixt one and the other, and then tying the Bag up and locking it in his Portmanteau again, quoth he, *Landlord, be so kind as to lay my Portmanteau safe up for me*. Then, having eaten a good Breakfast, he went out to look about the Fair kept there that day; and about an hour after going back to the Inn, in a sort of a hurry, he told his Landlord, that he had given Earnest for a couple of Horses in the Fair, wherefore having not Money about him to pay for them, he desired him to lend him Twenty Guineas, and to fetch him his Horse, which he design'd to swop away for another. Accordingly the Man of the House lent *Whitney* twenty Guineas, as not doubting he had a Pledge in his Hands sufficient enough for it; but not returning to his Inn that Day nor the next, the Inn-keeper began to be uneasy about the matter, and searching the Portmanteua before Witnesses, he found nothing therein like Money, but a parcel of Brass Counters, which made him swear like a Mad Man, for lending his good Money on a Pig in a Poke.

Not long after this Trick plaid on the Inn-keeper, *Whitney* and one more of his Gang, meeting with one Esq; *Long* on *New Market-Heath*, they rid up to him, and honest Mr. *Whitney*'s first Salutation was, *D——n me, you Son of a Whore, Stand and Deliver*; at which his Comrade, seeming to be displeas'd, cry'd to *Whitney*. *Why can't you Rob a Gentleman civilly, but you must Curse and call Names, like I know not what*? However *Whitney* took out of the Gentleman's Portmanteau about an Hundred Pounds; who having no more Money about him, told the Highway-men his Condition, and that having a great way to go, he hoped they would take his Circumstances so far into their most judicious Consideration, as to give him somewhat to bear his Charges. Whereupon *Whitney* opening the Mouth of the Bag, *Here* (quoth he) *take some*. The Gentleman then putting his Hand into the Bag, he took out as much as he could hold; which making *Whitney* stare at him, he cry'd, *Why, Sir, have you no Conscience at all in you*? Which indeed was a very unconscionable thing in him to abuse the Civility of those Blades who had the Conscience to take all he had from him; but letting the Gentleman keep what he had recover'd of his own again, they rid away with what Speed they could to consume the Remainder in their Riotous and Wicked manner of Living.

When *Whitney* had first an Inclination to take to ill Courses, going into *Essex*, with another loose Butcher, to buy Calves, there was one particular Calf to which he had a great Fancy; but the Owner asking an extraordinary Price for it, quoth *Whitney*, to his Comrade, *Why should we be so much Money out of Pocket, which at present is somewhat short with us, when we may have the Calf for nothing at Night?* The other Butcher approv'd of his Project, and sat Drinking all Day at *Rumford*, till it was time to put their Design in Execution; but a Fellow coming into that Town in the Evening, with a great She Bear, of which he made a Show up and down the Country, he happen'd to put into this Man's House from whom *Whitney* was to steal the Calf, for he kept an Ale-house about a quarter of a Mile in the Road from *Rumford*; where being at a loss for some place to put up his Bear, quoth the Maid, *We have a Calf in the Yard, which I'll carry up to my Room, and then you may put your Bear into his Stall.* Accordingly, the Bear being Muzzled, he was conducted into the Calf's Tenement; and in the middle of the Night, which was very dark, *Whitney* and his Comrade coming for their Prey, he got into the Stall without making the least Disturbance, and groping about for the Calf, at length he got hold of the Bear, which lying after its Sluggish way very heavy, he began to tickle it to make it rise; but being disturb'd, she fell a Booing, and rouzing on her hind Legs, she hugg'd *Whitney* with her two fore feet, very close. Now the other Butcher thinking his Comrade somewhat tedious, he, in a low Voice, cry'd, *What a Pox, will ye be all Night getting the Calf?* A Calf (quoth *Whitney*) I believe I've got the D——l, for he hugs me as close as he did the Witch. *Prithee* (said the Butcher again) *bring it away then if you've found him.* I can't (replied *Whitney.*) *Why then* (said his Comrade) *come away your self.* Why (replied *Whitney*) he won't let me. Hereupon the Butcher going in himself, he releas'd *Whitney* out of his Adversary's Clutches, but for this Trick, he swore he would never go to steal Calves again.

After this Conflict with the Bear, *Whitney* kept the *George Inn* at *Cheston* in *Hertfordshire*, but not thriving by this Occupation, he soon left it, and came up to *London*, to live an irregular Life for good and all. Going now well Dress'd and Apparell'd, much like a Gentleman, and one Morning standing at a Mercer's Door, on *Ludgate-Hill*, waiting for a Friend that was coming to him, a couple of Town Misses very well habited then passing by, and taking *Whitney* to belong to the Shop, she askt whether he had any fine Silks of the newest Fashion; he told them no; but in a Day or two he should have some pieces brought home from his Weavers, and then, if they pleas'd to tell him where he might wait on 'em, he would bring Patterns of such as were very Rich and Fashionable. This stumbled the Harlots a little; but after they had compar'd Notes together, they said, that being Persons newly come out of the Country, and never were in *London* before, they knew not the name of the Street where they lodg'd; but if he would go with 'em, they would shew him the Place of their Habitation. *Whitney* knew this was a Wheedle, yet resolv'd to venture with 'em; thereupon stepping into the Shop to the Prentice, as if he had given him Charge of his Business, but on the contrary he only askt him for a Sham Name, which the Lad knew not, he came out again to Squire the Ladies to their Lodgings. Conducting them to their Door, he would have taken his leave; but they cry'd, *Nay, Sir, but you shall walk in, and take a Glass of Wine, since you have taken this Trouble upon you*: For they now took him for no less than the Master, seeing him, as he came along, bow to some Noblemen in their Coaches, as well as Wealthy Citizens, and they in Civility resaluted him, and shew'd him into a very fine Chamber well furnisht, where sitting down at a Table, he drank very plentifully as to his part, but they only seemingly, as to any purpose; then came in a very fine Collation of Cold Meats, which being over, the Maid came in, and whispering one of the Courtezans, she withdrew, and left *Whitney* with the other, who, after some Discourse, began to talk very amorously, understanding him to be a Batchelor, or leastwise he pretended so, and refrained not to proffer herself as his School-Mistress, to teach him, as she said, a soft Love-Lesson. He was very willing to learn, but fear'd he should pay too dear for it; for he knew she expected as much Silk as would make her a Gown, or Petticoat at least, but how to come by it, he knew not. At last, by her Perswasions, *Whitney* consented to be her faithful Servant, and ruled by her every way. Now being a little Hot-headed, that he might not seem to be less than he had proposed himself, he in a Bravado pull'd out a handful of Money, which Allurement sweeten'd his Mistresses Conceit, who taking him into her Bed Chamber, he there enjoy'd the Favours of Love, which he repeated with such Vigour, that she seem'd mightily pleas'd with his Performance: But, as he thought before, the Burden of the Song was hopes of Gain. After this, she gave him her Hand, and led him into the Dining room again, where after caressing themselves with another Flask or two of Wine on Free cost, he took his leave, promising to send her several rich Presents. Upon this, away he trudg'd to a *Mercer* in *Ludgate-street*, and told him, a certain Lady had sent him to desire him to let his Man carry her some of the richest Silks the Shop afforded: To which he consented, as knowing the Person of Quality whom *Whitney* mention'd, and he gave the Silks in Charge to a Youth, who was but newly come to him, and therefore the easier to be impos'd on. He led the young Apprentice thro' as many bye Streets as he could, to lose his way, and at last fixing his Eyes on a House in *Suffolk-Street*, which had a thorough fare into *Hedge-lane*, in *Whitney* went, desiring the Apprentice at the Door to deliver his Cargo, that he might show it his Lady; but instead of doing that, he made an Excuse to the People, after he had asked for a strange Name, and they had told him no such Person lodged there, that he found himself mistaken, and desiring to go thro' the House into the back Lane, he left his young Merchant in the Lurch, to return to his Master with a lamentable Story of Sharpers. Having thus gotten what he aim'd at, away he went to his Mistresses, who receiv'd him very kindly, and there he revell'd some Days, but at length, being cloy'd with the Enjoyment of these Harlots, on whom he bestow'd the Prize which he cheated the 'Prentice of, he bad them adieu, and sent a Letter to the *Mercer*, wherein he inform'd him where he might find his Goods again. He went straight for a Warrant, then taking a Constable with him to these Strumpets Lodgings, he there, upon strict Search, found his Silks in their Custody; hereupon, notwithstanding all the Excuses they made, they were hurried, after their Examination before a Magistrate, to *Bridewell* in *Tuttle-Fields*; where their Backs, for their supposed Eleemosinary Finery, were curiously whipt by that once famous Lictor Mr. *Redding*; but many a hearty Curse did they generously bestow on *Whitney*, whilst they were under the hard Labour of Beating Hemp for Six Months.

The Speech of Sir *S——l L——l* Knight[1], Recorder of *London*, made to *Whitney*, and other Prisoners, before he pass'd Sentence of Death on 'em.

I Am heartily sorry for this sorrowful Occasion, which obliges me to perform the Office of passing Sentence of Death upon you, for the notorious Crimes which ye have committed, both against the Laws of GOD and Man. But so exorbitant have ye been in all manner of Wickedness, that Justice hath long cry'd out, to cut you out of the Land of the Living, as being a common Nusance to all Mankind. I take no Pride in destroying my Fellow-Creatures; but when your intolerable Enormities are no longer to be born with, it is an Indispensable Duty incumbent upon me to pronounce Judgment against you, after ye have been fairly and justly Cast by your Country. 'Tis true, some of you are greater Offenders than others, and in particular, you, Mr. Whitney; *for considering how many poor Horses you have kill'd on the Road, dost thou not think the Blood of those dumb Creatures will not at the Last Day rise up in Judgment against you? Yes, to be sure will they; and therefore of all the Criminals here, you deserve the least Mercy. Indeed it is a lamentable thing to think on't! that so many poor Horses, who thought no body any harm, should be untimely cut off in the Prime of their Age; therefore, as thou has shed so much Innocent Blood, to maintain thyself in irregular Courses, it is my Advice to instruct you and the rest to prepare yourselves for another World; and so proceed to declare your fatal Doom, which is, that all of you convicted for your*

1. Sir Salathiel Lovell (1619–1713), a well-known judge who served as Recorder of London, 1692–1708.

Lives, return to the Place from whence ye came, and from thence be convey'd to the Place of Execution, where ye shall be hang'd by the Necks till ye are dead: And the Lord have Mercy upon your Souls.

Indeed *Whitney* was a very profligate sort of a Fellow, born at *Stevenage* in *Hertfordshire*: and not long after he had serv'd his Apprenticeship to a Butcher, he took to the Highway, and committed several Robberies; but at length being betray'd by one Madam *Cosens*, who kept a Bawdy-House in *Milford-Lane*, over against St. *Clement*'s Church in the *Strand*, she had him Apprehended in *White-Fryars*, and sent to *Newgate*. Not long after his Confinement, being try'd and condemn'd at the Sessions-House in the *Old-Baily* he went with other Malefactors to be executed at *Tyburn*; but in his Journey thither, a Reprieve overtaking him, he was brought back again; and the Week following was Hang'd at *Porters-Block* by *Smithfield*, on *Wednesday* the 19th of *December*, 1694. When he came thither to die, he was in great Expectation still of another Reprieve, but all hopes being past of having another Respite from Death, he confess'd his Condemnation was just; and after some few Minutes were allow'd him for his more Private Devotion, he was tumbled out of this World into another, when he was about Thirty-four Years of Age.

ALEXANDER SMITH

[Moll Raby, a House-breaker]†

THIS second *German* Princess being one of sweet St. *Giles*'s Breed, which is better to hang than to feed, her Talent originally lay in bilking Lodgings, at which she was as dexterous as ever Mad *Ogle* was in bilking Hackney Coaches. Her first Exploit in this kind, was at a House in *Great-Russel-Street*, by *Bloomsbury Square*; where passing for a great Fortune, who was oblig'd to leave the Country by reason of the importunate troublesomness of a great many Suitors, she was courteously entertain'd with all the Civility imaginable; but this seeming honest Creature, who was a Saint without, but a Devil within, had not been there above a Fortnight, making a very good Appearance as to her Habit, (for to be sure she had a Talley-Man in every quarter of the Town) and understanding that all the Family was to take their Pleasure, as to Morrow, at *Richmond*, when they

† From Alexander Smith, *A Compleat History of the Lives and Robberies of the most Notorious Highway-men, Foot-Pads, Shop-Lifts, and Cheats, of both Sexes, in and about* London, Westminster, *and all Parts of* Great Britain, *for above an hundred Years past, continu'd to the present Time* (London, 1719), I, pp. 125–30.

were all gone, excepting the Maid, she desired her to call a Porter, and gave him a sham Bill drawn on a Banker in *Lombard street* for One hundred and fifty Pounds, which she desir'd might be all in Gold; but fearing such a quantity of Money might be a Temptation to make the Porter dishonest, she privately requested the Maid to go along with him, and she, in the mean time, would take care of the House; the poor Maid, thinking no harm, went with the Porter to *Lombard-Street*, where they were stopt for a couple of Cheats; but they alledging their Innocency, and proving from whence they came, a Messenger was sent home with 'em, who found it to be a Trick put upon the Servant to rob the House, for before she came back, *Moll Rabby* was gone off with above Eighty Pounds in Money, One hundred and sixty Pounds worth of Plate, and several other things of a considerable Value.

At length, being Burnt thrice in the Hand, for acting Quality in Disguise, she Marry'd one *Humphery Jackson*, a Butcher, who not following his Trade, went upon the sweetning Lay of *Luck in a Bag* by Day, and she upon the *Buttock and Twang* by Night; which is picking up a *Cull*, *Cully*, or *Spark*, and pretending not to expose her Face in a Publick House, she takes him into some dark Alley, so whilst the decoy'd Fool is groping her with his Breeches down, she picks his Fob or Pocket, of his Watch or Money, and giving a sort of Hem as a signal she hath succeeded in her Design, then the Fellow with whom she keeps Company, blundering up in the Dark, he knocks down the Gallant, and carries off the Prize.

After the Death of her Husband, *Moll* turn'd arrant Thief, and in the first Exploit she went then upon, she had like to have come scurvily off; for going upon the *Night-Sneak*, she found a Door half open, in *Downing-street* at *Westminster*, where stealing softly up Stairs into a great Bed Chamber, and hiding herself under the Bed, she had not been there above an Hour, before a couple of Footmen brought Candles into the Room, and made a Fire, whilst the Maid, with great Diligence, was laying the Cloth for Supper. The Table being furnisht with two or three Dishes of Meat, five or six Persons sat down, besides the Children that were in the House; which so affrighted *Moll*, that she verily thought, that if their Voices and the Noise of the Children had not hinder'd them, they might have heard her very Joynts smite one against another, and the Teeth chatter in her Head. Moreover there being a little Spaniel running about to gnaw the Bones that fell from the Table, and one of the Children having thrown him a Bone, a Cat that watch'd under the Table, being more nimble, catch'd it, and ran with it under the Bed, where *Moll* lay *incognito*; the Dog snarling and striving to take the Bone from her, the Cat so well us'd her Claws to defend her Prize, that having given the *Buffer*, that is their canting Name for a Dog, two or three

Scratches on the Nose, there began so great a Skirmish betwixt 'em, that, to allay the Hurly-burly, one of the Servants took a Fire-shovel out of the Chimny, and flung it so furiously under the Bed, that it gave *Moll* a Blow on the Nose and Forehead, that stun'd her for near half an Hour; the Cat rush'd out as quick as Lightning, but the Dog stay'd behind, barking and grinning with such Fury, that neither her Fawning nor Threatning could quiet him, till one of the Servants flung a Fire-fork at him, which chas'd him from under the Bed, but gave her another unlucky Blow cross the Jaws. At length, Supper was ended, but the Dog still growling in the Room, the Fear of his betraying her rais'd such a sudden Looseness in her, that she could by no means avoid discharging herself, which made such a great stink that it offended the People, who supposing it to be the Dog, they turn'd him out, and not long after they all withdrew themselves; when *Moll* coming from under the Bed, she wrapt the Sheets up in the Quilt, and sneaking down Stairs, she made off the Ground as fast as she could.

Another time *Moll Raby* being drinking at an Alehouse in *Wapping*, she observ'd the Woman of the House, who was sleeping by the Fire-side, to have a good Pearl Necklace about her Neck, at which her Mouth sadly water'd; so having drunk a Pot of Drink with a Consort which she had also in her Company, she sent the Maid down in the Cellar to fill the Pot again, and in the mean time cut off the Necklace with a pair of Scissars, and taking the Pearls off the String, swallow'd them. But before they had made an end of that Pot of Drink, the Woman awaking, she miss'd her Necklace, for which she made a great Outcry, and charged *Moll* and her Comrade with it; they stood upon their Innocency, and going into a private Room stript themselves, but nothing being found upon 'em, the Woman thought her Accusation might be false, and so was forc'd to lose it.

This *Mary Raby*, alias *Rogers*, alias *Jackson*, alias *Brown*, was Condemn'd for a Burglary committed in the House of the Lady *Cavendish* in *Soho-Square*, the 3d of *March* 1702–3, upon the Information of two Villains, namely, *Arthur Chambers* and *Joseph Hatfield*, who made themselves Evidences against her. At the Place of Execution at *Tyburn*, on *Wednesday* the 3d of *November* 1703, she said she was thirty Years of Age, born in the Parish of St. *Martins in the Fields*, that she was well brought up at first, and knew good Things, but did not practise them, having given up herself to all manner of Wickedness and Vice, namely, Whoredom, Adultery, and unjust Doings. But as for the Fact she stood Condemned for, she only own'd so much, and no more of it, than this, That some part of the Goods stoll'n out of that Lady's House, being brought to hers, in the *Spring Garden*, where she then liv'd, she understood, the next Day after the Robbery was committed, and not before, whose Goods they were.

She farther said, That she had a Husband, she thought, in *Ireland*, if still alive, but she was not certain of it, because it was now six Years since he left her. However she was very sorry she had defiled his Bed, and desired him to forgive her that Injury. She begg'd also Pardon of all the World in general, for the Scandalous, Impious, and Wicked Life she had led. And she pray'd, That all wicked Persons, especially those she had been concern'd with, would take Warning by her, and might have Grace so to reform and amend their Lives betimes, that they might not be overtaken in their Sins. Before she was turn'd off, being again press'd to speak the whole, in relation to the Fact she was now to die for, she persisted in what she had said before about it: But still own'd that she had been a very great Sinner indeed, as being one that was guilty of Sabbath-breaking, Swearing, Drinking, Lewdness, Buying, Receiving, and disposing of stoll'n Goods, and harbouring of ill People.

ALEXANDER SMITH

[Anne Holland, a Pick-pocket]†

THIS was her right Name, tho she went by the Names of *Andrews*, *Charlton*, *Edwards*, *Goddard*, and *Jackson*, which is very usual for Thieves to change them, because falling oftentimes into the Hands of Justice and as often convicted of some Crimes, yet thereby it appears sometimes, that when they are arraign'd at the Bar again, that it is the first Time that they have been taken, and the first Crime whereof they have ever been accus'd: Moreover, if they should happen to be cast, People, by not knowing their right Names, cannot say the Son or Daughter of such a Man or Woman is to be whip'd, burnt, or hang'd on such a Day of the Month, in such a Year; from whence would proceed more Sorrow to them that suffer'd, as well as Disgrace to their Parents. For this Reason, many such Persons are indicted with an *alias* prefix'd to several Names, whose Delight is to be Gentlemen and Gentlewomen without Rents, to have other Folks Goods for their own, and dispose of them at their own Will and Pleasure, without costing them any more than the Pains of stealing them. But as concerning *Anne Holland* her usual Way of thieving, was the *Service-Lay*, which was hiring herself for a Servant in any good Family, and then, as Opportunity serv'd, robb'd them: Thus

† From Alexander Smith, *A Compleat History of the Lives and Robberies of the most Notorious Highway-men, Foot-Pads, Shop-Lifts, and Cheats, of both Sexes, in and about* London, Westminster, *and all Parts of* Great Britain, *for above an hundred Years past, continu'd to the present Time* (London, 1719) I, pp. 163–70.

living once with a Master Taylor, in *York-Buildings* in the *Strand*, her Mistress was but just gone out to a Christening, as her Master came Home booted and spurr'd out of the Country, and going up into his Chamber where she was making his *Bed*, he had a great Mind to try his Manhood with his Maid, and accordingly threw her on her Back; but she made a great Resistance, and would not grant him his Desire, without he pull'd off his Boots; whereupon she first pluck'd one off, and whilst she was pulling off the other, one knocking at the Door, she ran down Stairs, taking a Silver Tankard off the Window, which would hold two Quarts, saying, she must draw some Beer, for she was very dry: However, she returning not presently, poor *Stitch* was swearing, and staring, and bawling for his Maid *Nan*, to pull off his t'other Boot, which was half on and half off, but being extraordinary strait, he could neither get his Leg farther in nor out: And there he might remain 'till Doomsday for *Nan*, for she was gone far enough off with the *Wedge*, that's to say, Plate, which she had converted into another Shape and Fashion in a short Time.

And once *Nan*, having been at a Fair in the Country, and coming up to *London*, she lay at *Uxbridge*, where being a good pair of *Holland* Sheets to the Bed, she was so industrious as to sit up most Part of the Night, to make her a couple of good Smocks out of one of 'em; so in the Morning, putting the other Sheet double towards the Head of the Bed, she came down Stairs to Breakfast. In the Interim, the Mistress sent up her Maid to see if the Sheets were there, who turning the single Sheet a little down as it lay folded, she came and whisper'd in her Mistress's Ear, that the Sheets were both there; so *Nan* discharging her Reckoning, she brought more Shifts to Town than she carry'd out with her; and truly she had a pretty many, or else she could not have liv'd as she did for some Years.

This unfortunate Creature, at her first launching out into the Region of Vice, was a very personable young Woman, being clear-skinn'd, well shap'd, having a sharp piercing Eye, a proportionable Face, and exceeding small Hand; which natural Gifts serv'd rather to make her miserable, than happy; for several lewd Fellows flocking about her, like so many Ravens about a Piece of Carrion, to enter her under *Cupid*'s Banners, and obtaining their Ends, she soon commenc'd and took Degrees in all manner of Debauchery; for if once a Woman passes the Bounds of Modesty, she seldom stops, 'till she hath arriv'd to the very Height of Impudence.

However, it was her Fortune to light on a good Husband; for one Mr. *French*, a Comb-maker, living formerly on *Snow-hill*, taking a Fancy to her in a Coffee-house where she was a Servant, 'till she had an Opportunity to rob her Master; such was his Affection, but not in the least knowing she had been debauch'd, that he marry'd her, and was better satisfy'd with his matching with her who had nothing, than many are with Wives of great Portions. But the *Comb-maker*'s Joys soon vanish'd, for his Spouse being brought to Bed of a Girl within six Months after *Hymen* had join'd them together, it bred such a great Confusion betwixt them, that there was scarce any Thing in the Kitchin, or other Part of the House, which did not continually fly at one another's Heads; Whereupon her Husband confessing a Judgment to a Friend in whom he could confide, all his Goods were presently seiz'd, and she turn'd out of House and Home, to the great Satisfaction of Mr. *French*, who shortly after went to *Ireland*, and there dy'd.

Nan Holland being thus metamorphos'd from a House keeper to a Vagabond, she was oblig'd to shift among the Wicked for a Livelihood; for though but young, yet could she cant tolerably well, wheedle most cunningly, lie confoundedly, swear desperately, pick a Pocket dexterously, dissemble undiscernably, drink and smoak everlastingly, whore insatiately, and brazen out all her Actions impudently. A little after this Disaster, she was marry'd to one *James Wilson*, an eminent Highway-man, very expert in his Occupation, for he was never without false Beards, Vizards, Patches, Wens, or Mufflers, to disguise the natural *Phisiognomy* of his Face. He knew how to give the Watch-word for his Comrades to fall on their Prey; how to direct 'em to make their Boots dirty, as if they had rid many Miles, when they are not far from their private Place of Rendezvous; and how to cut the Girths and Bridles of them whom they rob, and bind 'em fast in a Wood, or some other obscure Place. But these pernicious Actions justly bringing him to be hang'd in a little Time, at *Maidstone* in *Kent*, *Nan* was left a hempen Widow, and forc'd to shift for herself again.

After this Loss of a good Husband, *Nan Holland* being well apparell'd, she in Company with one *Tristram Savage*, who had lain under a Fine for crying the scurrilous Pamphlet, entitl'd *The Black-List*, about Streets, a long Time in *Newgate*, where they became first acquainted, went to Dr. *Trotter* in *Moor-Fields*, to have her Nativity calculated. When they were admitted into the Conjurer's Presence, he took 'em to be both of the Female Sex, because *Savage* was also dress'd in Womens Clothes, and being inform'd by *Nan* what she came about, he presently drew a Scheme of the 12 Houses, and filling them with the insignificant Characters of the Signs, Planets, and Aspects, display'd about the Time and Place of her Birth in the middle of 'em: That the *Sun* being upon the Cusp of the 10th House, and *Saturn* within it, but five Degrees from the Cusp, it denotes a Fit of Sickness, which would shortly afflict her; but then *Mercury* being in the 11th House, just in the Beginning of *Sagittarius*, near *Aldebaran*, and but six Degrees from the Body of *Saturn*, in a Mundane Square to the *Moon* and *Mars*, it signify'd her speedy Recovery from it. Again, *Cancer* being in a Zodiacal Trine to the *Sun*, *Saturn* and *Mercury*, she might depend upon having a good Husband in a short Time; and moreover, it was a sure Sign, that he who marry'd her, should be a very rich thriving Man. Thus having gone through his Astrological Cant, quoth *Tristram Savage* to Dr. *Trotter*, *Can you tell me, Sir, what I think*? The Conjurer reply'd with a surly Countenance, *It is none of my Profession to tell Peoples Thoughts. Why then* (said *Savage*) *I'll shew 'em you*: Whereupon pulling a Pistol out of his Pocket, and clapping it to the Doctor's Breast, he swore he was a dead Man, if he made but the least Outcry; which so surpriz'd him, that trembling like an Aspen Leaf, he submitted to what ever they desir'd. So whilst *Nan* was busy in tying him Neck and Heels, *Savage* stood over him with a Penknife in one Hand, and his *Pop*, that's what they call any Thing of a Gun, in t'other, still swearing, that if he did but whimper, his present Punishment should be either the Blade of his Penknife thrust into his Wind-pipe, or else a Brace of Balls convey'd thro' his Guts. But to be sure of preventing the Conjurer's Cackling, they gagg'd him; and then rifling his Pockets, they found a Gold Watch, 20 Guineas, and a Silver Tobacco-Box, which they carry'd away, besides taking two good Rings off his Finger. After these good Customers were gone, the Conjurer began to make what Noise he could for Relief, by rowling about the Floor like a Porpoise in a great Storm, and kicking on the Boards with such Violence, that the Servants verily thought there was a Combat indeed betwixt their Master and the Devil. But when they went up Stairs, and found him ty'd and gagg'd, they were in no small Astonishment; and quickly unloosing him, he told them how he was robb'd; whereupon they made a quick Pursuit after *Nan Holland* and the other Offender, but to no Purpose, for they were got out of their Reach, and the Knowledge of all the Stars in Heaven.

Altho' she had receiv'd Mercy once before, yet she took no Warning thereby, but when at Liberty, still pursu'd her old Courses, which in 1705 brought her to *Tyburn*; where instead of imploring for Mercy from above, she cry'd out upon the hard Heart of her Judge, and the Rigour of the Laws; also cursing the Hang-man, but forgetting to repent of the Fact which brought her into the Executioner's Hands, and would, unrepented of, deliver her Soul into the far less merciful Hands of another hereafter.

ALEXANDER SMITH

[Capt. James Hind, Murderer and Highway-man]†

CApt. *James Hind* was the Son of a Saddler living in *Chipping-Norton* in *Oxfordshire*, where he inhabited many Years in good Credit and Reputation; and sending this his Son to School to learn to read *English*, and to write, he was, when 15 Years of Age, bound an Apprentice to a Butcher in the same Town; but his Master being a very surly, cross Man, who led *Hind* a weary Life, he ran away from him before he had serv'd two Years of his Time, and getting about three Pounds of his Mother, who intirely lov'd this her only Child, he went for *London*, where getting drunk one Night, he was took up by the Watch, and sent to the *Poultry-Compter*, which he did not like when he came to be sober: but here getting acquainted with one *Thomas Allen*, a noted Highway-man in those Days, when they were at Liberty, they went a robbing together on the Road, and at *Shooters-hill* meeting with a Gentleman and his Servant, *Hind* had the Courage to rob them of fifteen Pounds without the Assistance of his Companion, who stood at a Distance to be aiding as Occasion should require. However, our new Highway man, for Handsale sake, was so generous as to give the Gentleman twenty Shillings of his Money, to bear his Charges on his Journey; which Generosity made *Tom Allen* very Proud, to see his Comrade rob a Person with a good Grace.

Another Time Capt. *Hind* meeting *Hugh Peters* in *Enfield Chace*, he commanded that celebrated Regicide to stand and deliver; whereupon he began to cudgel this bold Robber with some Parcels of Scripture, saying, *The eighth Commandment commands*, That you should not steal; *besides, it is said by* Solomon, Rob not the Poor, because he is poor. Then *Hind* recollecting what he could remember of his reading the *Bible* in his Minority, he began to pay the Presbyterian Parson with his own Weapon, saying, *Friend, if you had obey'd God's Precepts as you ought, you would not have presum'd to have wrested his holy Word to a wrong Sense, when you took this Text*, [Bind their Kings with Chains, and their Nobles with Fetters of Iron] *to aggravate the Misfortunes of your Royal Master, whom your cursed Republican Party unjustly murder'd before his own Palace*. Here *Hugh Peters* began to extenuate that horrid Crime, and farther to alledge, for the Defence of his Money, other Places of Scripture against Theft: To which *Hind* reply'd, *Pray, Sir, make no Reflections on my*

† From Alexander Smith, *A Compleat History of the Lives and Robberies of the most Notorious Highway-men, Foot-Pads, Shop-Lifts, and Cheats, of both Sexes, in and about* London, Westminster, *and all Parts of* Great Britain, *for above an hundred Years past, continu'd to the present Time* (London, 1719) I, pp. 206–13.

Profession, when Solomon *plainly says,* Do not despise a Thief. *Therefore deliver your Money presently, or else I shall send you out of the World in a Moment.* These scaring Words frighting *Hugh Peters* almost out of his Wits, he gave *Hind* thirty broad Pieces of Gold, and then they parted. But *Hind* being not satisfy'd with this Booty, he rode after *Hugh Peters* again, and overtaking him, said, *Sir, now I think on't, this Disaster hath befel you, because you did not observe that Place in the Scripture, which says,* Provide neither Gold, nor Silver, nor Brass, in your Purses, for your Journey. *And truly, Sir, you must now pardon me for taking away your Cloak and Coat too, because the Scripture says in another Place,* And him that taketh away thy Cloak, forbid not to take away thy Coat also. Accordingly *Hind* stript him of both: And the *Sunday* after, *Hugh Peters* designing to preach against the Sin of Theft, he took these Words for his Text, *I have put off my Coat, how shall I put it on?* Cant. Chap. 5, Vers. 3. But an honest Cavalier being just by him then, who knew of his Mischance, he cry'd out aloud, *Upon my Word, Sir, I can't tell, unless Capt.* Hind *was here.* Which ready Answer to *Hugh Peters*'s Scriptural Question, put the Congregation into such an excessive Fit of Laughter, that the Fanatick Parson being asham'd of himself, he quitted his Chattering Box without proceeding any farther in his Sermon.

One time Capt. *Hind* meeting a Gentleman's Coach on the Road betwixt *Petersfield* and *Portsmouth*, fill'd with Gentlewomen, he robb'd the same of about 3000 Pounds in Gold, which was the Portion of one of the young Ladies therein, going to be marry'd; but the Money being lost before she perform'd the Rites of Matrimony, the Sport was all spoil'd, for her Sweet-heart's Love was not so hot, but this News quickly cool'd it, which evidently shews that Money in those Days too was the chiefest Drug to get a young Woman a Husband. And not long after the purchasing of this great Booty, which caus'd several Hue-and-Cries after him, but to no Purpose, he and *Tom Allen* his Comrade setting upon that infamous Usurper *Oliver Cromwell* as coming from *Huntington* to *London*, they were so overpower'd by Number, for there were not less than seven Men along with old *Noll*, that *Hind* had much ado to make his Escape, being oblig'd to leave his Partner behind, who was apprehended, and shortly after hang'd.

Nevertheless, Capt. *Hind* having a great Respect for the Royal Family, who were now all Exiles, he attempted once more to set upon their Enemies, and who should the next Person be, but that celebrated Villain Sergeant *Bradshaw*; so stopping his Coach, as he met him on the Road betwixt *Sherbourn* and *Shaftsbury* in *Dorsetshire*, he demanded his Money. The Sergeant thinking to fright *Hind*, by telling him who he was; quoth Hind, *I fear you not, nor never a King-killing Son of a Whore alive; therefore if you do not give me your*

Money presently, I'll in a Moment send you out of the World without any Benefit of the Clergy at all. The Sergeant's Conscience now flying in his Face, for the horrid Murder of his lawful Sovereign, and dreading his being sent out of the World without Repentance for so horrid a Crime as dooming his King with a *Mene Tekel*, he gave *Hind* about forty Shillings in Silver; but not being satisfy'd with that Sort of Metal, he swore he would shoot him through the Heart, if he did not find other Coin for him: Whereupon, to save his Life, he gave him a Purse full of *Jacobuses*. At the Sight whereof, quoth *Hind, I, marry, Sir, this is the Metal that wins my Heart for ever! Oh! precious Gold, I admire thee as much as* Bradshaw, Pryn *or other such Villains, who would for the sake of it, sell our Redeemer again, were he now upon Earth. Nay, I'm sure this is that incomparable Medicament which (as a Friend of mine tells me) the Republican Physicians call* The Wonder-working Plaister; *truly Catholick in Operation, somewhat of Kin to the Jesuits Powder, but more effectual. The Virtues of it are strange and various, it makes Justice deaf, as well as blind, and takes out Spots of the deepest Treason, more cleverly than Castle-Soap does common Stains. It alters a Man's Constitution in two or three Days, more than the Virtuoso's Transfusion of Blood in Seven Years. 'Tis a great Alexipharmack, and helps, poisonous Principles of Rebellion, and those that use them. It miraculously exalts and purifies the Eye-sight, and makes Traytors behold nothing but Innocency in the blackest Malefactors. 'Tis a mighty Cordial for a declining Cause, it stifles Faction and Schism as certainly as the Itch is destroy'd by Butter and Brimstone. In a Word, it makes Fools wise Men, and wise Men Fools, and both of them Knaves. The Colour of this precious Balm, you see, is bright and dazling; and being apply'd privately to the Fist, in decent Manner, and a competent Dose, infallibly performs all the abovesaid Cures, and many others, too long now to be mention'd.* Then pulling out his Pistols, he farther said, *You and your infernal Crew have hitherto ran on* Jehu-*like, therefore 'tis Time now to stop your Career.* So shooting all the six Horses belonging to *Bradshaw*'s Coach, *Hind* rid off as fast as he could, to seek for another Prey.

Now, this bold Robber having reign'd a long Time in this Course of Life, even nine or ten Years, an intimate Acquaintance of his at last discover'd his Lodging, which was at one Mr. *Denzie*'s, a Barber, living over against St. *Dunstan*'s Church in *Fleet-street*, and where he had Lodg'd about a Month, by the Name of *Brown*. Here being apprehended, and carry'd before the Speaker of the House of Commons living in *Chancery-Lane*, he was, after a long Examination, committed, with Fetters on his Legs, to *Newgate*: where, one Capt. *Compton*, who convey'd him thither, shew'd the Keeper of the Goal a Warrant for his Commitment, and such close Imprisonment, that no Person whatsoever was to have Access to him 'till farther Orders.

On *Friday* the 12th of *December* 1651, Capt. *James Hind* was brought to the Bar at the Sessions-house in the *Old-Baily*, where nothing being prov'd against him to reach his Life, he was convey'd in a Coach from *Newgate* to *Reading* in *Berkshire*, on the 1st of *March* 1651–2. where he was arraign'd before Judge *Warberton*, for killing one *George Sympson* at *Knole*, a small Village in that County, and the Evidence being plain against him, he was found guilty of wilful Murder; but next day an Act of Oblivion being issued out to forgive all former Offences, except Indictments against the State, he was in great Hopes of saving his Life, 'till by an Order of Council he was soon after remov'd by Virtue of a Writ of *Habeas Corpus* to *Worcester* Jayl, where a Bill of High Treason being preferr'd against him, he was there drawn, hang'd, and quarter'd on *Friday* the 24th of *September* 1652, aged 34 Years; and at the Place of Execution, confess'd, that most of the Robberies which he ever committed, were upon the Republican Party, of whose Principles he had such an Abhorrence, that nothing troubled him so much as to die before he saw his Royal Master establish'd in his Throne, from which he was most unjustly and illegally excluded by such a rebellious and disloyal Crew, who deserv'd hanging more than him. After he was executed, his Head was set on the Bridge-Gate, over the River *Severn*, and his Quarters on other Gates of the City, where they remain'd 'till Time and Weather had reduc'd them into nothing, except his Head, which was privately took down and bury'd within a Week after it was set up.

ALEXANDER SMITH

[Moll Cutpurse, a Pick-Pocket and Highwaywoman]†

Mary Frith, otherwise call'd *Moll Cutpurse*, from her Original Profession of cutting Purses, was born in *Barbican*, near *Aldersgate-street*, in the year 1589. Her Father was a Shoe-maker; and though no remarkable Thing happen'd at her Nativity, such as the flattering Soothsayers pretend in Eclipses, and other the like Motions Above, or Tides, and Whales, and great Fires, adjusted and tim'd to the Genitures of Crown'd Heads; yet, for a She Politician, she was not

† From Alexander Smith, *A Compleat History of the Lives and Robberies of the most Notorious Highway-men, Foot-Pads, Shop-Lifts, and Cheats, of both Sexes, in and about* London, Westminster, *and all Parts of* Great Britain, *for above an hundred Years past, continu'd to the present Time* (London, 1719) II, pp. 137–52. This biography does not appear in the 1714 edition.

much inferior to Pope *Joan*; for in her Time, she was the great Cabal and Oracle of the Mystery of diving into Purses and Pockets, and was very well read, and skill'd too, in the Affairs of the Placket among the great ones.

Both the Parents (as having no other Child living) were very tender of this Daughter; but especially the Mother, according to the Tenderness of that Sex, which is naturally more indulgent than the Male; most affectionate she was to her in her Infancy, most careful of her in her Youth, manifested especially in her Education, which was the stricter and diligenter attended, by Reason of her boisterous and masculine Spirit, which then shew'd it self, and soon after became predominant above all Breeding and Instruction. A very *Tomrig* or *Rampscuttle* she was, and delighted and sported only in Boys Play and Pastime, not minding or companying with the Girls; many a Bang and Blow this Hoyting procur'd her, but she was not so to be tam'd, or taken off from her rude Inclinations; she could not endure that sedentary Life of Sewing or Stitching; a Sampler was as grievous to her as a Winding-sheet, and on her Needle, Bodkin, and Thimble, she could not think quietly, wishing them chang'd into Sword and Dagger for a Bout at Cudgels. Her Head-geer and Handkerchief (or what the Fashion of those Times were for Girls to be dress'd in) were alike tedious to her, wearing them as handsomely as a Dog would a Doublet; and so cleanly, that the driven Pot-hooks would have blush'd at the Comparison. This perplex'd her Friends, who had only this Proverb favourable to their Hope, *That an unlucky Girl may make a good Woman*; but they liv'd not to the Length of that Expectation, dying in her Minority, and leaving her to the Swing and Sway of her own unruly Temper and Disposition.

She would fight with Boys, and courageously beat them; Run, Jump, Leap, or Hop, with any of her contrary Sex, or recreate her self with any other Play whatsoever. She had an Uncle, Brother to her Father, who was a Minister, and of him she stood in some Awe, but not so powerfully, as to restrain her in these Courses; so that seeing he could not effectually remedy that inveterate Evil in her Manners, he trepann'd her on Board a Merchant Ship lying at *Gravesend*, and bound for *New-England*, whither he design'd to have sent her; but having learn'd to Swim, she one Night jump'd Overboard, and swimm'd to Shore, and after that escape, would never go near her Uncle again. Farthermore, it is to be observ'd, that *Mercury* was in Conjunction with, or rather in the House of *Venus*, at the Time of her Nativity; the former of which Planets is of a thievish, cheating, deceitful Influence; and the other hath Dominion over all Whores, Bawds, and Pimps; and, join'd with *Mercury*, over all Trepanners and Hectors: She hath a more general Influence, than all the other Six Planets put together; for no Place nor Person is exempted from her, invading alike both Sacred and Prophane; Nunneries and Monasteries, as well as the common Places of Prostitution; *Cheapside* and *Cornhill*, as well as *Bloomsbury*, or *Covent-Garden*. Under these benevolent and kind Stars, she grew up to some Maturity; she was now a lusty and sturdy Wench, and fit to put out to Service, having not a Competency of her own left her by her Friends to maintain her without Working; but as she was a great Libertine, she liv'd too much in common, to be inclos'd in the Limits of a Private Domestick Life. A Quarter-Staff was fitter for her than a Distaff; *Stave* and *Tail*, instead of Spinning and Reeling. She would go to the Ale-house, when she had made Shift for some little Stock, and spend her Penny, and come into any one's Company, and club another 'till she had none left, and then she was fit for any Enterprize. Moreover, she had a natural Abhorrence to the tending of Children, to whom she ever had an Averseness in her Mind, equal to the Sterility and Barrenness in her Womb, never (to our best Information) being made a Mother.

She generally went Dress'd in Man's Apparel; which puts me in Mind how *Hercules*, *Nero*, and *Sardanapalus* are laugh'd at and exploded, for their Effeminacy and degenerated Dissoluteness in this extravagant Debauchery; the first is pourtrayed with a Distaff in his Hand; the other recorded to be marry'd as a Wife, and all the Conjugal and Matrimonial Rites perform'd at the Solemnity of the Marriage; and the other lacks the Luxury of a Pen, as loose as his Female Riots, to describe them. These were all Monsters of Men, and have no Parallels either in Old or Modern Histories, 'till such Time as *Moll Cutpurse* approach'd their Examples; for her heroick Impudence hath quite outdone every Romance; for never was Woman so like her in her Cloaths. No doubt but *Moll*'s Converse with her self, whose Disinviting Eyes and Look sunk inwards to her Breast, inform'd her of her Defects, and that she was not made for the Pleasure or Delight of Man; and therefore since she could not be honour'd with him, she would be honour'd by him in that Garb and Manner of Rayment which he wore; for from the first Entrance into a Competency of Age, she would wear a Man's Habit, and to her dying Day she would not leave it off.

Though she was so ugly in any Dress, as never to be woo'd nor sollicited by any Man, yet she never had the *Green-Sickness*, that epidemical Disease of Maidens, after they have once pass'd their Puberty; she did never eat Lime, Coals, Oatmeal, Tobacco-Pipes, Cinders, or such like Trash; no Sighs, dejected Looks, or Melancholy, clouded her vigorous Spirits, or repress'd her Jollity in the retir'd Thoughts and Despair of a Husband; she was troubled with none of those Longings which poor Maidens are subject to: She had the Power and Strength (if not the Will) to command her own Pleasure of any Person of reasonable Ability of Body; and therefore she needed not whine for it; as she was able to beat a Fellow to a Compliance, without the unnecessary Trouble of Intreaties.

Now *Moll* thinking what Course of Life she should betake her self to, she got acquainted with some Fortune-tellers of the Town, from whom learning some Smatch and Relish of that Cheat, by their insignificant Schemes and Figure-flinging, she got a tolerable good Livelihood; but her Incomes being not equivalent to her Expences, she enter'd her self into the Society of *Divers*, otherwise call'd *File-clyers*, *Cut-purses*, or *Pick-pockets*; which People are a kind of Land-Pyrates, trading altogether in other Mens *Bottoms*, for no other Merchandize than *Bullion*, and ready Coin, and keep most of the great Fairs and Marts in the World. In this unlawful Way she got a vast deal of Money, but having been very often in *Old-Bridewell*, the *Compters*, and *Newgate*, for her irregular Practices, and burnt in the Hand Four Times, she left off this petty Sort of Theft, and went on the *Highway*, committing many great Robberies, but all of 'em on the *Round-Heads*, or Rebels, that fomented the Civil War against King *Charles* the First; against which Villains she had as great an Antipathy, as an unhappy Man, that for counterfeiting a Half Crown in those Rebellious Times, was executed at *Tyburn*, where he said, *That he was adjudg'd to die for but counterfeiting a Half Crown; but those that usurp'd the whole Crown, and stole away its Revenue, and had counterfeited its Seal, were above Justice, and escap'd unpunish'd.*

A long Time had *Moll Cutpurse* robb'd on the Road; but at last robbing General *Fairfax* of 250 Jacobus's on *Hounslow Heath*, whom she shot through the Arm in opposing her, and killing Two Horses, on which a Couple of his Servants rid, a close Pursuit being nevertheless made after her by some Parliamentarian Officers quartering in the Town of *Hounslow*, to whom *Fairfax* had told his Misfortune, her Horse failing her at *Turnham-Green*, they there apprehended her, and carry'd her to *Newgate*, after which she was condemn'd; but procur'd her Pardon, by giving her Adversary 2000 Pounds. Now *Moll* being frighten'd by this Disaster, she left off going on the Highway any more, and took a House within Two Doors of the *Globe-Tavern* in *Fleet-street*, over against the Conduit, almost facing *Shoe-Lane* and *Salisbury Court*, where she dispens'd Justice among the wrangling Tankard-Bearers, by often exchanging their Burden of Water for a Burden of Beer, as far the lighter Carriage, though not so well portable, and for which Kindness she had the Command of those Water-works, being Admiraless of the Vessels that sail on Folks Backs, (as they have Ships in *China* which sail over dry Land) and unlade themselves in Kitchens.

In her Time Tobacco being grown a great Mode, she was mightily taken with the Pastime of Smoaking, because of its Singularity, and that no Woman ever smoak'd before her, though a great many of her Sex since have follow'd her Example. But now (as I hinted before) *Moll* being quite scar'd from Thieving herself, she turn'd *Fence*, that is to say, a Buyer of stollen Goods, by which Occupation she got a great deal of Money. In her House she set up a kind of Brokery, or a distinct Factory for Jewels, Rings and Watches, which had been pinch'd or stollen any manner of way, at never so great Distances from any Person. It might properly enough be call'd the *Insurance-Office* for such Merchandize; for the Losers were sure, upon Composition, to recover their Goods again, and the Pyrates were sure to have a good Ransom, and she so much in the Gross for Brokerage, without any more Danger; the *Hue-and-Cry* being always directed to her for the Discovery of the Goods, not the Takers. Once a Gentleman that had lost his Watch by the busy Fingers of a Pick-pocket, came very anxiously to *Moll*, enquiring if she could help him to it again; she demanded of him the Marks and Signs thereof, with the Time when and where he lost it, or by what Crowd or other Accident. He replied, *That coming thro'* Shoe-Lane, *there was a Quarrel betwixt two Men; one of which he afterwards heard, was a* Grasier, *whom they had set in* Smithfield, *having seen him receive the Sum of 200 Pounds, or thereabouts, in Gold; and it being a hazardous and great Purchase, the choicest and most excellent of the Art were assembled to do this Master-piece. There was one* Bat Rud, *as he was since inform'd, who was the Bulk; and observing the Man held his Hand in his Pocket where his Gold was, just in the middle of the Lane whither they dogged him, overthrew a Barrel trimming at an Ale-house Door, while one behind the Grasier push'd him over, who withal threw down* Bat, *who was ready for the Fall. Betwixt these two, presently arose a Quarrel; the Pick-pocket demanding Satisfaction, while his Comrades interposing, after two or three Blows in Favour of the Countryman, who had drawn his Hands out of his Pocket to defend himself, soon drew out his Treasure; and while he was looking on the Scuffle, some of them had lent him a Hand too, and finger'd out his Watch. Moll* smil'd at the Adventure, and told him, *He should hear farther of it within a Day or two at the farthest*. When the Gentleman coming again, and understanding by his Discourse, that he would not lose it for twice its Value, because it was given him by a particular Friend, she squeez'd 20 Guineas out of him before he could obtain his Watch.

Moll, who was always accounted by her Neighbours to be a *Hermaphrodite*, but at her Death was found otherwise, had not lived long in *Fleestreet*, before she became acquainted with a new sort of Thieves, call'd *Heavers*, whose Employment was stealing Shop-Books from *Drapers* or *Mercers*, or other rich Traders; which bringing to her, she, for some considerable Profit for herself, got them a *Quantum meruit* for restoring them again to the Losers. While she thus reign'd free from the Danger of the Common Law, an Apparator, set on by an Adversary of hers, cited her to appear in the Court of *Arches*, where was an Accusation exhibited against her for wearing indecent and manly Apparel. She was advised by her Proctor to demur to the Jurisdiction of the Court, as for a Crime, if such, not cognizable there or elsewhere; but he did it to spin out the Cause, and get her Money; for in the End, she was there sentenc'd to stand and do Penance in a White Sheet at St. *Paul's-Cross* during Morning-Sermon on a *Sunday*. They might as soon have sham'd a Black Dog as *Moll*, with any kind of such Punishment; for a Halfpenny she would have travell'd through all the Market-Towns in *England* with her penitential Habit, and been as proud of it as that Citizen who rode to his Friends in the Country in his Livery-Gown and Hood. Besides, many of the Spectators had little Cause to sport themselves then at the Sight; for some of her Emissaries, without any Regard to the Sacredness of the Place, spoil'd a good many Cloaths, by cutting part of their Cloaks and Gowns, and sending them Home as naked behind as *Æsop*'s Crow, when every Bird took its own Feather from her.

However, this Penance did not reclaim her, for she still went in Mens Apparel, very decently dress'd; nor were the Ornaments of her House less curious and pleasing in Pictures, than in the Delight of Looking-Glasses, so that she could see her sweet self all over in any Part of her Rooms. This gave Occasion to Folks to say, that she used magical Glasses, wherein she could shew the Querists who resorted to her for Information, them that stole their Goods; as likewise to others, curious to know the Shapes and Features of their Husbands that should be, the very true and perfect Idea of them, as is very credibly reported of your *African* Sorcerers; and we have a Tradition of it in the Story of *Jane Shore*'s Husband, who, by one of the like Glasses, saw the unchast Embraces of his Wife and *Edward* IV. One Night late, *Moll* going home almost drunk from the *Devil* Tavern, she tumbled over a great Black Sow that was rousting on a Dunghill near the Kennel; but getting up again in a sad dirty Pickle, she drove her to her House, where finding her full of Pigs, she made her a Drench to hasten her Farrowing, and the next Morning she brought her 11 curious Pigs, which *Moll* and her Companions made shift to eat; and then she turn'd the Sow out of Doors, who presently repair'd to her old Master, a Bumpkin at *Islington*, who with Wonder received her again; and having given her some Grains, turn'd her out of his Gates, watching what Course she would take, and intending to have Satisfaction for his Pigs wheresoever he should find her to have laid them. The Sow naturally mindful of her squeaking Brood, went directly to *Moll*'s Door, and there kept a lamentable Noise to be admitted. This was Evidence enough for the Fellow, that there his Sow had laid her Belly; when knocking, and having Entrance, he tells *Moll* a Tale of a Sow and her Litter. She replied, he's mad; he swore he knows his Sow's Meaning by her grunting, and that he would give her Sawce to her Pigs. *Goodman Coxcomb*, quoth *Moll*, *come in, and see if this House looks like a Hogs-stye*; when going into all her Rooms, and seeing how neat and clean they were kept, he was convinc'd that the Litter was not laid there, and went home cursing his Sow.

To get Money, *Moll* would not stick out too to bawd for either Men or Women, insomuch that her House became a double Temple for *Priapus* and *Venus*, frequented by Votaries of both Sorts, who being generous to her Labour, their Desires were favourably accommodated with Expedition; whilst she linger'd with others, delaying their Impatience, by laying before them the difficult, but certain Attainment of their Wishes, which serv'd as a Spur to the Dulness of their Purses; for the Lady *Pecunia* and she kept the same Pace, but still in the End she did the Feat. *Moll* having a great Antipathy against the Rump-Parliament, she lit on a Fellow very dextrous for imitating Peoples Hands, with him she communicated her Thoughts, and they concurr'd to forge and counterfeit their Commissioners and Treasurers Hands to the respective Receivers and Collectors, to pay the Sums of Money they had in their Hands without Delay, to such as he in his counterfeited Orders appointed: So that wheresoever he had Intelligence of any great Sum in the Country, they were sure to forestal the Market. This Cheat lasted for half a Year, till it was found out at *Guildhall*, and such a politick Course taken, that no Warrants would pass among themselves to avoid Cozenage. But when the Government was seiz'd and usurp'd by that Arch-Traitor *Oliver Cromwell*, they began this Trade afresh, it being very easy to imitate his single Sign Manual, as that ambitious Usurper would have it stil'd; by which Means her Man also drew good Sums of Money out of the Customs and Excise; nay, out of the *Exchequer* it self, till *Oliver* was forced to use a private Mark, to make his Credit authentick among his own Villains.

After 74 Years of Age, *Moll* being grown crazy in her Body, and discontented in Mind, she yielded to the next Distemper that approach'd her, which was the *Dropsy*, a Disease which had such strange and terrible Symptoms, that she thought she was possess'd, and that the Devil was got within her Doublet. Her Belly, from a wither'd, dry'd, wrinkled Piece of Skin, was grown to the titest, roundest Globe of Flesh, that ever any beauteous young Lady strutted with, to the Ostentation of her Fertility, and the Generosity of her Nature. However, there was no Blood that was generative in her Womb, but only that destructive of the Grape, which by her Excesses was now turn'd into Water, so that the tympany'd Skin thereof sounded like a Conduit-Door. If we anatomize her any farther, we must say her Legs represented a couple of Mill-posts; and her Head was so wrapt with Cloaths, that she look'd like Mother *Shipton*.

It may well be expected, that considering what a deal of Money she got by her wicked Practices, she might make a Will; but yet of 5000 Pounds which she had once by her in Gold, she had not above 100 Pounds left her latterly, which she thought too little to give to the charitable Uses of building Hospitals and Alms-houses. The Money that might have been design'd that Way, as it came from the Devil, so it return'd to the Devil again in the *Rump*'s Exchequer and Treasury at *Haberdashers* and *Goldsmiths-Hall*. Yet, to preserve something of her Memory, and not leave it to the Courtesy of an Executor, she anticipated her Funeral Expences; for it being the Fashion of those Times to give Rings, to the undoing of the *Confectioners*, who liv'd altogether by the Dead and the New-born, she distributed some that she had by her, (but of far greater Value than your pitiful hollow Ware of 6 or 7 Shillings a piece, that a Juggler would scorn to shew Tricks with) among her chief Companions and Friends.

These Rings (like Princes Jewels) were notable ones, and had their particular Names likewise, as the *Bartholomew*, the *Ludgate*, the *Exchange*, and so forth, deriving their Appellations from the Places whence they were stollen. They needed no Admonition of a Deaths Head, nor the Motto, *Memento mori*, for they were the Wages and Monuments of their thieving Masters and Mistresses who were interr'd at *Tyburn*, and she hoped her Friends would wear them both for her sake and theirs. In short, she made no Will at all, because she had had it so long before to no better Purpose; and that if she had had her Desert, she should have had an Executioner instead of an Executor. Out of the 100 Pounds which she had by her, she dispos'd of 30 Pounds to her three Maids which she kept, and charg'd them to occupy it the best way they could; for that and some of her Arts in which they had had Time to be expert, would be beyond the Advantage of their Spinning and Reeling, and would be able to keep them in Repair, and promote them to *Weavers*, *Shoemakers* and *Taylors*. The rest of her Personal Estate in Money, Moveables, and Houshold-Goods, she bequeath'd to her Kinsman *Frith*, a Master of a Ship, dwelling at *Redriff*, whom she advised not to make any Ventures therewith, but stay at Home and be drunk, rather than go to Sea and be drown'd with them. And now the Time of her Dissolution drawing near, she desired to be bury'd with her Breech upwards, that she might be as preposterous in her Death, as she had been all along in her infamous Life. When she was dead, she was interr'd in St. *Bridget*'s Church-yard, having a fair Marble-stone put over her

Grave, on which was cut the following Epitaph, compos'd by the ingenious Mr. *Milton*, but destroy'd in the great Conflagration of *London*:

Here lies under this same Marble,
Dust, for Time's last Sieve to garble;
Dust, to perplex a Sadducee,
Whether it rise a He or She,
Or two in one, a single Pair,
Nature's Sport, and now her Care:
For how she'll cloath it at last Day,
Unless she sighs it all away;
Or where she'll place it, none can tell,
Some middle Place 'twixt Heav'n and Hell;
And well 'tis Purgatory's *found,*
Else she must hide her under Ground.
These Reliques do deserve the Doom,
That Cheat of Mahomet's *fine Tomb;*
For no Communion she had,
Nor sorted with the Good or Bad;
That when the World shall be calcin'd,
And the mix'd Mass of human Kind
Shall sep'rate by that melting Fire,
She'll stand alone, and none come nigh her.
Reader, here she lies till then,
When truly you'll see her agen.

[Virginia Laws on Servants]†

I. All Servants hereafter coming into this Country without Indenture, shall serve 5 years if above 16 years of Age, and all under that Age shall serve till they be 24 Years old.

II. All Servants at the expiration of their time, shall enter their Freedom by their Masters Certificate, at the County Court, and take a Certificate thereof from the Clerk of the said Court, which shall be a sufficient Warrant for any Person to entertain him or them.

III. In case such Servant be hired a second time, his new Master shall take his Certificate and keep it, till his second Service be expired.

† From *An Abridgement of the Laws in Force and Use in Her Majesty's Plantations; (Viz.) Of Virginia, Jamaica, Barbadoes, Maryland, New-England, New-York, Carolina, &c.* (London, 1704).

IV. Whosoever shall entertain any hired Servant, running away, without a Certificate as aforesaid, shall forfeit to the Master of such Servant 30 *l.* of Tobacco, for every Day and Night they shall harbour him.

V. In case the Servant forges a Certificate, or Steals the true one from his Master, he shall stand in the Pillory 2 Hours in open Court.

VI. If any comes free into the Country and Contracts a Service, and departs before the time agreed for be accomplisht, he shall perform his Service, and also pay such Damages as shall arise by the Breach of his Contract.

VII. Servants absenting themselves from their Masters Service, shall make satisfaction by serving after the time by Custom, or Indenture, is expired, double the time of service so neglected, or longer if the Court shall see fit so to adjudge.

VIII. If an English Servant run away in Company of any Negroes who being Slaves, cannot make satisfaction by addition of time, the English after their own time of Service to their own Master shall be expired, shall serve the Masters of said Negroes so long as the Negroes should have done if they had not been Slaves, &c.

IX. Every Master shall provide for his Servants competent dyet, Cloathing and Lodging, and shall not exceed the Bounds of moderation in correcting them; And any Servant having just cause of Complaint, may complain to the next Commissioner, who finding just cause, shall give order for warning the Master to the next County Court, where the Servant may have Remedy for his grievance.

X. The Servant that shall lay violent Hands on his or her Master, Mistress, or Overseer, and be convicted thereof before any Court in this Country, the same Court shall order such Servant to serve his or her Master, &c. one Year longer than the Expiration of his time.

XI. No Person whatsoever, for any offence committed, shall be adjudged to serve the Country as Colony Servants.

XII. Whoever shall Buy, Sell, Trade, or Truck with any Servant for any Goods, without Licence or Consent of the Master, shall suffer one Months Imprisonment, give Bond for his Good Behaviour, and forfeit to the Servants Master, 4 times the value of the things so bought, sold, &c.

XIII. All Servants bringing Goods into this Country with them, not being their own Wearing Apparel, or having them consigned to them during the time of their Service, shall have the property in such Goods, and by permission of their Masters dispose of the same to their own Advantage.

XIV. A Woman Servant got with Child by her Master, shall, after her time by Indenture, or Custom, is expired, be, by the Church wardens of the Parish where she lived when brought to Bed of such Bastard, sold for 2 Years, and the Tobacco imploy'd for the use of the Parish.

XV. Where any Bastard Child is gotten by a Servant, the Parish shall take care to keep the Child during the time the reputed Father hath to serve by Indenture or Custom, and after the said reputed Father is free he shall make satisfaction to the Parish.

XVI. Every Master buying or bringing in a Servant without Indentures shall carry him to the Court within 4 Months after, when the best Judgment may be given of his Age, or else the Servant shall not serve any longer than those of 16 are to serve by Custom of the Country.

XVII. All Women Servants who are commonly imploy'd to work in the Ground, shall be reputed Tythable and Levy's paid for them accordingly.

XVIII. Every Servant who comes in presumable without Indenture, and so sold for the Custom, shall by his Master be brought before some Justice of Peace, and if upon demand the Servant saith that he hath an Indenture but cannot then produce it, the said Justice shall assign him one Months time, in which time if he fail to produce it, he shall be barr'd from his Claim, by reason of any pretended Indenture whatsoever.

XIX. No Masters shall make any Agreement or Bargain with their Servants before the time of their Service be expired, unless it be made in the presence and with the approbation of some Justice of the Peace of the County where the Parties reside, upon the penalty of forfeiting to such Servant all the time of Service that is due at the Bargain making, besides the avoiding of such Bargain.

XX. Servants coming in without Indentures shall serve, only to the Age of 24, if 19 or under.

[Maryland Laws on Servants, Slaves, and Runaways]†

I. No Servant or Slave shall travel above 10 mile from his Masters House, without a Note under the Hand of his Master or Overseer, under the Penalty of being taken up for a Runaway.

II. Any such Servant absenting from his or her Master or Mistress, shall serve 10 days for every one days absence.

III. Any Person that shall wittingly and willingly detain any Servant unlawfully absenting himself, shall be fined 5 *l.* of Tobacco for every night that such Person shall entertain such Servant, half to the King, half to the Informer.

IV. Any person travelling out of the County where he or she lives or resides, without a Pass under the County Seal (for which is to be paid 10 *l.* of Tobacco, or 1 *s.* in Money) such person, not being sufficiently known, or able to give a good account of himself if apprehended, shall be deemed and taken as a Runaway.

V. Whoever takes up a Runaway travelling without a Pass, and not able to give a good Account of himself, shall have 200 *l.* of Tobacco, to be paid by the Owner of such Runaway, or such other satisfaction as the Justices shall think fit.

VI. And if one of our Neighbouring *Indians* takes up or seizes a Runaway Servant, and brings him before some Magistrate, he shall have a Reward of a Matchcoat paid him, or the Value thereof.

VII. When any person apprehends or seizes a Runaway, he shall bring, or cause him to be brought before the next Magistrate, who shall take him into his Custody, or otherwise secure him, until such Person so seized shall give sufficient Security to answer the Premisses at the next Court for the County, and make satisfaction to him that seized him; and that notice may be given to the Master or Mistress of such Runaway, the Justices of that County shall cause a Note of the Runaways Name to be set up at the next adjacent County Courts, at the Provincial

† From *An Abridgement of the Laws In Force and Use in Her Majesty's Plantations; (Viz.) Of Virginia, Jamaica, Barbadoes, Maryland, New-England, New-York, Carolina, &c.* (London, 1704).

Court, and at the Secretaries Office, that all persons may view the same, and see where such their Servants are.

VIII. Every Man Servant shall have given him at the time of the expiration of his Service, one new Hat, a good Cloath Suit, a new Shift of White Linnen, a pair of new *French* full Shooes and Stockings, two Hoes, and one Axe, and one Gun of 20 *s.* price, not above 4 foot Barrel, nor less than 3 and a half. And every Woman Servant shall have given her at the expiration of her Servitude, the like Provision of Cloaths, and 3 Barrels of *Indian* Corn.

IX. Whoever shall transport, or cause to be transported or convey'd away out of this Province, any Inhabitant indebted here, and not having a sufficient Licence, or Pass, shall be liable to pay all such Debts, Engagements, or Damages, which the person conveyed away was liable to satisfie to any person in this Province, unless the same be otherwise satisfied in some convenient time, or that in short time he procure the person so convey'd away to return again. And whoever shall entice, or privately carry away any Apprentice, Servant or Slave, shall for every such Offence forfeit and pay to the Imployer of such Apprentice, Servant, or Slave, treble Damages and Costs.

X. No person shall trade, barter, or any ways deal with any Servant or Slave belonging to any Inhabitant within this Province, without leave first had of the Master, Mistress or Overseer, under the Penalty of 2000 *l.* of Tobacco, one half to the King, the other to the Master, &c.

XI. If the Goods so traded or bartered as aforesaid shall exceed the sum of 1000 *l.* of Tobacco, the Party whose Goods shall be imbezled or barter'd away as aforesaid, shall have his Action at Law for the Damage sustain'd, against the person so dealing and bartering for the same. And in case the person so offending shall not be able to satisfie the same, then he shall be bound over by some one Justice of the Peace, to appear at the Provincial or County Court, where upon Conviction he shall be punished, by whipping on the bare Back with 30 stripes.

XII. A Servant Imported into this Province, without Indentures, if above the age of 22 years, shall be obliged to serve 5 years, if between 18 and 22, 6 years; if between 15 and 18, 7 years; if under 15, he shall serve till he attains the Age of 22 years.

XIII. Servants transported hither from *Virginia*, shall compleat their time of Service here, which they should have performed there, and no more.

XIV. All Owners or keepers of any such Servant as aforesaid, shall within 6 months after the receiving such Servant into their custody (if they claim more than 5 years service of such Servant) bring him or her into the County Court, where the age of such Servant shall be judged and entred upon record, under the Penalty of 1000 *l.* of Tobacco, to the King for support of the Government, &c.

XV. All Servants transported into this Province, shall have their time of Service commence from the first Anchoring of the Vessel within this Province, any Law or Custom to the contrary notwithstanding.

XVI. No Indenture made by any Servant during the time of his Service, shall any ways oblige such Servant for longer time, than by his first Indenture, or determination of the Court, shall be limited. Provided this Act shall not give any benefit to any Negro or Slave.

XVII. For all Runaway Servants or Slaves that shall be taken up in *Pensilvania* or *Virginia*, and from thence brought into this Province, and deliver'd to a Magistrate, the person who brings them shall have paid him by the Owner of such Runaway 400 *l.* of Tobacco and Cask, or 40 *s.* in Money; except Servants or Runaways brought from *Accomack* into *Somerset* County, or from the side of *Virginia* next the River *Potomack*; and for such, only 200 *l.* of Tobacco, or 20 *s.* And such Runaway, when free, shall make satisfaction by Service or otherwise, more than 10 days for one, as the Court shall adjudge, &c.

XVIII. If any Master, Mistress, or Overseer of any Servant, shall deny sufficient Meat and Drink, Lodging and Cloathing, or unreasonably labour them beyond their Strength, or debar them of necessary Rest and Sleep, the same being sufficiently proved in the County Court, the Justices may fine such Offender for the first and second Offence as they please, not exceeding 1000 *l.* of Tobacco to the King; and for the third offence, set such Servant so wrong'd at Liberty, and free from Servitude.

XIX. All Negroes and other Slaves imported into this Province, and their Children, shall be Slaves during their Natural Lives.

XX. Any White Woman, free or Servant, that suffers herself to be begot with Child, by a Negro, or other Slave, or Free Negro; such Woman, if free, shall become a Servant for 7 years; if a Servant, shall serve 7 years longer than her first term of Service. If the Negro that begot the Child be free, he shall serve 7 years, to be adjudged by the Justices of the County Court, and the Issue of such Copulations shall be Servants till they arrive at the Age of 31 years. And any White Man that shall get a Negro Woman with Child (whether free or Servant) shall undergo the same Penalties as White Women. All which Servitudes by this Act imposed shall be disposed of or employ'd as the Justices of the respective County shall think fit, the Produce to be appropriated towards the relief of the Poor.

XXI. Every Woman Servant, having a Bastard Child, and not able to prove the Father, shall only be liable to satisfie the Damages sustain'd, by her Servitude, or otherwise as the Court shall see convenient. If such Mother do prove the charge by sufficient testimony of Witnesses, Confession of the Party, or pregnant Circumstances agreeing with her declaration in her extremity of Pains, and her Oath before a Magistrate, then the Party charged, if a Servant, shall satisfy half the damage, if a Freeman, then the whole damage by Servitude or otherwise. And if the Mother can prove by Testimony, or Confession of the Party, that the Father, being a single Person and a Freeman, did before her getting with Child promise her Marriage, it shall be at his choice to perform his Promise, or recompence her abuse according as the Court shall adjudge.

XXII. The Provincial and County Courts may hear and determine any complaints between Masters and Servants by way of Petition, give Judgment, and award Execution upon the same. And upon Appeal no such Judgment shall be reverst for any matter of Form, &c. Provided it appears by Record, that the Defendant was legally summoned, and not condemn'd unheard, &c.

CRITICISM

JULIET McMASTER

The Equation of Love and Money in *Moll Flanders*†

"AND IF A YOUNG WOMAN HAS BEAUTY, birth, breeding, wit, sense, manners, modesty, and all to an extream, yet if she has not money, she's no body."[1] So speaks the sister of Moll's first lover and first husband, in the Colchester household where she makes her sexual and then her matrimonial debut. It is of course a thematically central passage, quoted frequently by the critics of *Moll Flanders*, and its significance is clear enough in a novel about how a woman has to make her way in the world. But what I find as interesting as its explicit meaning is the implication of its rhythm: if one reads it again, doesn't it raise an echo, a memory that that sentence structure and that cadence are more familiar with different words?

> And though I have the gift of prophecy, and understand all mysteries, and all knowledge; and though I have all faith, so that I could remove mountains, and have not charity, I am nothing.

I suspect that the familiar passage from 1 Corinthians 13:2 was at the back of Defoe's mind when he wrote this economic version of the Christian order of virtues, and that he substituted "money" for "charity," or Christian love, deliberately, and with satiric intent. In Moll's world survival rather than salvation is the chief end and object of existence; and though as a tradesman, journalist and man of the world Defoe could sympathize with her ethic and to a marvellous extent identify with her, as a Christian and also as an artist he was not unaware of the inglorious displacement of love by money as man's operative standard.

It is of course evident enough that Moll's standards are economic ones. Ian Watt has persuasively interpreted *Robinson Crusoe* and *Moll Flanders* as illustrations of economic individualism;[2] Denis Donoghue, who also takes Moll to be practising Defoe's own principles, finds a tradesman's ethic in all Defoe's work;[3] and Dorothy Van Ghent has vividly shown how in Moll's narrative "the life of the flesh is faded completely by the glare of the life of the pocketbook."[4] But I would like to examine in some detail the persistence with which

† From *Studies in the Novel* 2 (1970): 131–44. Copyright 1970 by North Texas State University. Reprinted by permission of the publisher. Page numbers in square brackets refer to this Norton Critical Edition. Notes have been edited.

1. *Moll Flanders*, edited by James Sutherland (Boston, 1959), the Riverside edition, p. 20 [20].
2. *The Rise of the Novel* (London, 1957), Chapters 3 and 4.
3. "The Values of *Moll Flanders*," *Sewanee Review*, LXXI (1963): 287–303.
4. *The English Novel, Form and Function* (New York, 1953), p. 36.

Defoe pursues his theme of the confusion between love, in its various forms, and money, in the language and imagery as well as the incident of the novel. It seems to me that this is a consciously developed thematic pattern, so that in the prolonged debate on the issue of whether or not Defoe was being deliberately ironic at Moll's or society's expense my own argument is on the side of Koonce, Novak, and Donovan, who claim Defoe is detached from Moll and definitely judging her,[5] rather than of Watt, Donoghue, and Schorer,[6] who take Defoe's own values to be essentially identical with Moll's, and the effect of irony to be one rather contributed by the reader than deliberately created by the artist.[7] The full extent of Defoe's consciousness is impossible to determine, and of course it is true that in his other writings he does express principles of expediency which are the same as *some* of Moll's; I shall only try to demonstrate that his values are by no means the same as *all* of Moll's; that Defoe is not just exemplifying, but exposing, a world view where financial considerations have taken the place of sexual, moral and spiritual ones; and that he is using some subtle artistic means in doing so.

From the significant initial episode where the child Moll announces her intention to be "a gentlewoman," Defoe shows how she learns to associate approbation, hope of success, and all things enjoyable with money. The Mayoress gushes over the little girl: "Then she look'd upon one of my hands. Nay, she may come to be a gentle-woman, says she, for ought I know; she has a lady's hand, I assure you. This pleased me mightily; but Mrs. Mayoress did not stop there, but put her hand in her pocket, gave me a shilling" (p. 14) [14]. Although Moll is often notoriously vague about such matters as how she disposes of her children, she characteristically gives us vivid detail of gesture and quantity in any transaction that involves putting the hand in the pocket.[8]

Maximillian Novak, in his study of Moll's love affair with the elder brother, has pointed out how "much of the humor in this first part of *Moll Flanders* results from the heroine's inability to separate her

5. See Robert Alan Donovan, "The Two Heroines of *Moll Flanders*" in *The Shaping Vision* (Ithaca, 1966), pp. 21–46; Howard L. Koonce, "Moll's Muddle: Defoe's Use of Irony in *Moll Flanders*," *English Literary History*, XXX (1965): 377–394; and Maximillian E. Novak, "Conscious Irony in *Moll Flanders*: Facts and Problems," *College English*, XXVI (1964): 198–204.
6. Watt and Donoghue as above; Mark Schorer contends "[Defoe] is not telling us *about* Moll Flanders, he *is* Moll Flanders." *"Moll Flanders,"* in *The World We Imagine* (New York, 1968), p. 55.
7. See Ian Watt in his reassessment of the whole debate, "The Recent Critical Fortunes of *Moll Flanders*," *Eighteenth-Century Studies*, I (1967): 125: "By now, perhaps, some readers have been sufficiently exasperated by the present discussion to . . . locate the chief irony not in *Moll Flanders* at all, but in the partial and contradictory solemnities of the critics (not, of course, excluding your humble servant) who have written about it."
8. Robert R. Columbus notes this specificity as part of Defoe's artistry in his article on "Conscious Artistry in *Moll Flanders*," *Studies in English Literature*, III (1963): 424.

desire for wealth from her love for the heir."[9] Defoe has used a good deal of ingenuity in the verbal texture of his narrative to show how love and avarice amalgamate in Moll's mind. At the lovers' first encounter after the elder brother's declaration we hear how he first "threw me down upon the bed, and kissed me there most violently," and then "with that put five guineas into my hand." Moll goes on candidly, "I was more confounded with the money than I was before with the love" (p. 23) [22]. This is at a stage in Moll's career when she does not have the excuse of what she calls "necessity" for her affair: she has in this house a relatively secure position, and indeed the money is more likely to compromise her than benefit her, and she is unable to make any immediate use of it (p. 29) [28].

Throughout this first affair Moll's genuine love is always inextricably associated with money. The older brother confirms his "thousand protestations of his passion for me" with "almost a handful of gold," and Moll "thought of nothing but the fine words and the gold" (p. 24) [23]. The affair progresses consistently in these terms: "he was very kind to me, and kiss'd me a thousand times and more, I believe, and gave me money too" (p. 33) [31]. Absorbed in her romance, Moll tells us she "was taken up only with the pride of my beauty, and of being belov'd by such a gentleman: as for the gold, I spent whole hours in looking upon it; I told the guineas over a thousand times a day" (p. 25) [24]. As the affair progresses she reflects, "as he did not seem in the least to lessen his affection to me, so neither did he lessen his bounty" (p. 29) [28]. Such consistent association of love with money is not a matter of accidental juxtaposition. Defoe is not only making the point that Moll is covetous, but through her narrative is showing just how she becomes so, and how her mind is being trained to work.

By the time the affair is consummated, money has become not so much the proof of love as the thing itself. Their lovemaking is virtually an act of purchase: "Says he, here's an earnest for you; and with that he pulls out a silk purse with an hundred guineas in it, and gave it me." The silk purse itself seems to stir Moll to sexual excitement:

> My colour came and went at the sight of the purse, and with the fire of his proposal together, so that I could not say a word, and he easily perceiv'd it; so putting the purse into my bosom, I made no more resistance to him, but let him do just what he pleas'd, and as often as he pleas'd (p. 27) [26].

The imagery suggests Moll's nineteenth-century descendent, described in *My Secret Life*, who has her vagina filled with shilling

9. "Moll Flanders' First Love," *Papers of the Michigan Academy of Science, Arts and Letters*, XLVI (1961): 640.

pieces.[1] This sexual-financial symbolism is to become more explicit later in Moll's narrative.

Robin, the younger brother, occupies a significant position in the moral pattern of the novel. Although for Moll he is entirely eclipsed by the elder brother, the heir of the family, for Defoe and for the reader, it seems to me, Robin is the norm of goodness, the positive alternative that the misguided narrator does not choose, like Fielding's Heartfree in *Jonathan Wild*. He has a sense of humour, he is open and honest to the point of indiscretion, and generous enough to accept Moll's youth and beauty as assets that can equitably be balanced against his own rank and fortune. Moreover, he is ready to work for his own living as a lawyer, unlike the "gentlemen" in Moll's career—the elder brother, her second husband, and Jemmy—who all despise work as an indignity.[2] Moll's training, however, has not prepared her to appreciate such qualities. Robin woos her not with secret gifts of money and vague promises, but with outright declarations of love, before witnesses; and to prove his is "in earnest" he produces no silk purse, but an offer of immediate marriage (p. 41) [39]. When his sister objects to Moll's want of fortune, he replies, "I love the girl; and I will never please my pocket in marrying, and not please my fancy" (p. 34) [32]. Trained as she is by one who "knows the world better" (p. 42) [40], no wonder Moll despises him, however his generosity makes for her advantage. She follows him to the altar "like a bear to the stake" (p. 51) [48], and while she is his wife "I never was in bed with my husband but I wish'd my self in the arms of his brother" (p. 53) [49]. Apparently he never thought of any such expedient as lining her nightdress with banknotes.

When she has dismissed her married life with Robin in a brief couple of pages, Moll tells us how, as a widow in comfortable circumstances, she has acquired some principles from her experience. She dismisses various gallants, because "the case was alter'd with me, I had money in my pocket, and had nothing to say to them: I had been trick'd once by that cheat call'd love, but the game was over, I was resolv'd now to be married or nothing, and to be well married or not at all" (p. 53) [50]. This is a passage that shows quite clearly how, as Donoghue points out, in Moll's mind "Money, marriage and virtue were . . . linked in a chain of analogies."[3] But Donoghue asserts that this is equally true of Defoe himself, whereas Defoe is quite explicit against the mercenary marriage motive in a work that incorporates most of his late views on marriage, *Conjugal Lewdness*:

1. See Steven Marcus, *The Other Victorians* (New York, 1964), p. 159.
2. Novak, in "Conscious Irony in *Moll Flanders*," cites the exposure of parasitic "gentlemen" as one of the deliberate ironies of the novel.
3. Donoghue, p. 295.

> Ask the Ladies why they marry, they tell you 'tis for a good Settlement; tho' they had their own Fortunes to settle on themselves before. Ask the Men why they marry, it is for the Money. . . . How little is regarded of that one essential and absolutely necessary Part of the Composition, called Love, without which the matrimonial State is, I think, hardly lawful, I am sure it is not rational, and, I think, can never be happy.[4]

And he goes on to declare that those who marry without love "are to me little more than legal Prostitutes."[5] He could hardly be condoning Moll's contempt for "that cheat call'd love."

For all her determination, however, Moll makes another mistake. She holds out for the money and the apparently gentlemanly status that she had admired in the elder brother, but neglects to make sure of their lasting qualities. She and her "gentleman tradesman" husband squander their combined capital on high living in less than a year, and when by mutual consent they part, her estate has dwindled from twelve hundred to five hundred pounds.

Now indeed Moll has completed her apprenticeship, and her experience qualifies her not only to manage her own affairs better but to set up as an instructress in the business of acquiring suitable suitors, securing straying lovers, and bringing them to the point of marriage. She acts as the advisor rather than the principal in getting her friend securely married, and learns in the process the technique of spreading gossip, especially of the kind concerning who has how large a fortune.

It is by this means that she captures her next husband, her "brother husband," as she later succinctly describes him. Moll herself has learned that though in practice money is the one essential in the marriage market, it is not done to admit it, and suitors, for form's sake, profess to a noble indifference to "the dross." Moll, who never appreciated Robin's honesty, is a master of the language that says one thing while it means another. She traps her third husband by exacting his matter-of-course declaration that "virtue alone is an estate" so often that he is finally obliged to take her with what little she has. She describes her tactics at this stage with the confident tone of a smooth operator:

> I pick'd out my man without difficulty by the judgement I made of his way of courting me. I had let him run on with his protestations that he lov'd me above all the world; that if I would make him happy, that was enough; all which I knew was upon supposition that I was very rich, tho' I never told him a word of it myself (p. 69)[64].

4. *Conjugal Lewdness; or, Matrimonial Whoredom* (Gainesville, 1967), a facsimile reproduction of Defoe's 1727 text, introduced by Maximillian E. Novak, pp. 27–28.
5. *Ibid.*, pp. 102–103.

The romantic episode of their poetic exchange may be somewhat out of key with the rest of Moll's practical narrative, but their debate on the claims of love and money in marriage, written with a diamond ring on a windowpane, is both literally and symbolically appropriate to Moll's strategy. Mrs. Bardell might well have wished she had the same lasting and conclusive proof of Pickwick's proposal. Moll may well congratulate herself that, rich or poor, "I had him fast both ways" (p. 71)[66].

As Moll gets older, however, her strategy and her language have to change. After the collapse of her incestuous marriage to her brother she is again in uneasy circumstances, since much of her property has been lost on the voyage back from Virginia. Robin had both preached it, and practiced disinterested love; her brother husband had preached it, and Moll had tricked him into the practice; by the time she arrives at her Bath lover not only is she reduced to bargaining for a maintenance rather than a marriage, but the nature of the courting has changed. Money is not just the implicit enticement, it becomes as well the explicit means of communication. The whole affair, with all its preliminaries, is a courtship conducted not with kisses and rings, but with pounds, shillings, and pence. He woos her first not with a declaration of love, but with an offer of money, and she keeps up his interest not by playing hard to get but by delaying her acceptance of it: "the first time we were together alone, . . . he began to enquire a little into my circumstances, as how I had subsisted my self since I came on shore, and whether I did not want money? I stood off very boldly" (p. 96) [88]. The physical consummation of this affair is long delayed—they even share a bed for two years before "the government of our virtue was broken" (p. 102) [93]—but this abstinence is possible because the real consummation has happened long before, when he first summoned her to his bed:

> He ask'd me to come into his chamber; he was in bed when I came in, and he made me come and sit down on his bed side, for he said he had something to say to me. . . . His request was, he said, to let him see my purse; I immediately put my hand into my pocket, and laughing at him, pull'd it out, and there was in it three guineas and a half. Then he ask'd me, if there was all the money I had. I told him, no, laughing again, not by a great deal.
>
> Well, then, he said, he would have me promise to go and fetch him all the money I had, every farthing. I told him I would, and I went into my chamber, and fetch'd him a little private drawer, where I had about six guineas more, and some silver, and threw it all down upon the bed, and told him there was all my wealth, honestly to a shilling. He look'd a little at it, but did not tell it,

> and huddled it all into the drawer again, and then reaching his pocket, pull'd out a key, and bad me open a little walnut-tree box he had upon the table, and bring him such a drawer, which I did: in this drawer, there was a great deal of money in gold, I believe near 200 guineas, but I knew not how much. He took the drawer, and taking me by the hand, made me put it in, and take a whole handful; I was backward at that, but he held my hand hard in his hand, and put it into the drawer, and made me take out as many guineas almost as I could well take up at once.
>
> When I had done so, he made me put them into my lap, and took my little drawer, and pour'd out all my own money among his (pp. 97–98) [90].

This is surely an ingenious translation into financial terms of a sexual encounter. One recognizes the same sequence in the frank pornography of *Fanny Hill*. This is Fanny's account of her first lover:

> He not only directed his hands there, but . . . placed me favourably for his wanton purpose of inspection. . . . By this time his machine, stiffly risen at me, gave me to see it in its highest bravery. He feels it himself, seems pleas'd at its condition, and, smiling loves and graces, seizes one of my hands, and carries it, with a gentle compulsion, to his pride of nature, and its richest masterpiece.
>
> I, struggling faintly, could not help feeling. . . . [6]

There would be no doubt of the sexual innuendo of Defoe's description if Sterne had written it. But Defoe too, I think, has made his implication sufficiently clear: the couple carry on their transaction in bed, they are mutually excited about seeing and touching the contents of each other's "drawers," and, as a climax to their encounter, in mingling their money they "spend" together. This, for Moll, is the consummation most devoutly to be wished. This explains why, in spite of the sensational title page to the novel, we hear very little explicit talk of sex: we hear of Moll's "fortunes and misfortunes," and Moll understands "fortune" almost exclusively in its financial sense.

A passage like this, I think, refutes those historical critics who assert that Defoe was writing in such haste that he had no time for narrative strategy or the subtleties of irony. It is not only a spirited piece of bawdy double entendre worthy of Sterne, but a fine example

6. John Cleland's *Memoirs of a Woman of Pleasure*, with an introduction by Peter Quennell (New York, 1963), p. 95. Donovan makes the point that "though *Moll Flanders* and *Fanny Hill* both offer accounts of a long series of sexual encounters, they have virtually nothing else in common," *The Shaping Vision*, p. 23. What I am interested in is the nature of the difference: a successful financial transaction is for Moll what a satisfactory tumble in bed is for Fanny.

of how Defoe can, if he chooses, use image and symbol deliberately to reinforce theme.

Moll's next suitor and last husband (whom in fact she does not marry until after her next marriage) is appropriately in the banking business. Again, there is a marked regression in her economic viability as her age advances, and she makes herself attractive not by seeming to refuse money as she did with her Bath lover, but by frankly laying out her own money as bait. The courtship is again a prolonged financial transaction. This is his initial proposal: "At last, says he, Why do you not get a head steward, madam, that may take you and your money together?" (p. 115) [106]. And this, essentially, is Moll's equally cautious acceptance: "Then, as to executors, I assur'd him I had no heirs, nor any relations in England, and I would have neither heirs or executors but himself . . . [The money] should be all his own, and he would deserve it by being so faithful to me, as I was satisfied he would be" (p. 117) [107]. There is even a parallel developed between Moll's financial and his marital situation. She has money, but doesn't know how to lay it out; he has a wife, who knows all too well how to lay herself out. Since neither Moll's money nor his wife are yielding the dividends their owners expect, he may well assure her, "my case is as distracted as yours can be, and I stand in as much need of advice as you do" (p. 119) [109]. A wife and an estate become virtually the same thing.

Moll's banker husband is never much more than a credit statement to her, and it is appropriate that he should die as the result of a broken bank balance. The loss of a sum of money is for him a "wound [that] had sunk too deep, it was a stab that touch'd the vitals" (p. 164) [149], Moll tells us with the vividness that characterizes her narration when she is talking of money matters. As usual, her grief at his death is for the loss rather of his financial support than of his love and companionship.

Jemmy, we are to believe, is Moll's favourite husband, the one she most loves. Indeed with him she regains the ability to combine love with financial concerns, as she had with the elder brother, rather than merely substituting money for love. In her career she has been outsmarted by the elder brother, but has herself had the advantage of Robin, the Bath lover and the banker. But Jemmy and Moll have met their match in each other: they deceive each other in precisely the same way, by pretending to fortunes that neither possesses. Hence their mutual attachment. Moll puts all the blame for the deceit on "this creature, the go-between," the woman who had promoted the match, and assures us that as for Jemmy himself, "it was really a true gallant spirit he was of" (p. 130) [119]. The two speak each other's language, and know how to talk tenderly and devotedly while being in material matters quite unscrupulous:

> You would indeed have been cheated, my dear, says he, but you would not have been undone, for fifteen thousand pounds [the dowry he had expected] would have maintain'd us both very handsomely in this country; and I had resolv'd to have dedicated every groat of it to you; I would not have wrong'd you of a shilling, and the rest I would have made up in my affection to you, and tenderness of you as long as I liv'd (p. 128) [117–18].

"This was very honest indeed," Moll comments on this cool excuse for fraud, almost with a catch in her throat. And of her own behaviour she tells us, "I never willingly deceiv'd him" (p. 130) [119], when she has maintained a correspondence throughout their courtship with her second string, the banker, and has kept her very name from him. But the two of them share a zest for touching emotional displays, and while they calmly go about the business of dissolving the bankrupt firm of Jemmy & Moll, they indulge in sentimental reminiscences and swear they will never part. This counterpoint plays delightfully through Moll's description of her behaviour after Jemmy leaves:

> Nothing that ever befel me in my life sunk so deep into my heart as this farewel. I reproach'd him a thousand times in my thoughts for leaving me, for I would have gone with him thro' the world, if I had beg'd my bread. [And what does she do next?] I felt in my pocket, and there I found ten guineas, his gold watch, and two little rings, one a small diamond ring, worth only about six pound, and the other a plain gold ring (p. 133) [121].

And she proceeds in the same vein, alternating between violent emotional gestures and cool observations about her lunch break and knocking-off time. Defoe gives no stage directions to let us know, for instance, that there must be a change in tone between Moll's romantic avowal that she would beg for her bread with him and her down-to-earth catalogue of the contents of her pocket. But he has sufficiently developed his theme of Moll's confusion of love with money, I think, as well as the point that she is deludedly admiring a bounder, for a fully ironic interpretation of the passage to be justifiable.

Moll earnestly proposes they should go to seek their fortune in Virginia; Jemmy as earnestly urges they should try their luck in Ireland; they both lavish tenderness on each other in the form of gifts of money and rings, and have amiable lovers' tiffs about who should pay for the lodging. Moll has declared early in life that she wanted to be a "gentlewoman"; Jemmy is so committed to his role as gentleman that he envies his own servants because they can find positions in service, whereas he is condemned by his birth to ride off and rob on the highway, as befits a gentleman in reduced circumstances. No wonder they feel they are made for each other. As Moll had found sexual satisfaction in putting silk purses in her bosom and mingling handfuls of cash in her lap, so now she achieves emotional fulfillment in exchanging tender dishonesties with this romantic freeloader. At their reunion years later in Newgate, they still do their courting by offering each other money (pp. 263–64) [237].

After the end of Moll's calculatedly secure marriage with the banker, the career in which she has been able to identify love with money is over. Prostitution is a kind of livelihood she considers "quite out of the way after 50" (p. 172) [156]. So she is obliged to go for the money without the love, and take up her thieving career. Her sense of guilt of course arises from the fact that she is now getting goods without returning any, but at the same time her evident gusto and professional pleasure in her career as a thief seem to be partly the result of her satisfaction that she does not have to render returns any longer. She stops trying to disguise her avarice (p. 176) [160]. Her inclination for sex has been slowly atrophying since her affair with the elder brother. When married to Robin she "never was in bed with my husband but I wish'd my self in the arms of his brother" (p. 53) [49], and she lives with her brother husband some years during which she "loathed the thoughts of bedding with him" (p. 79) [74], and "could almost as willingly have embrac'd a dog" (p. 86) [80]. She does in fact seduce her Bath lover, but their relationship had been sexually cool enough (at the literal level, that is), and she tells us that she beds with men "from necessity," not for "the meer vice of it" (p. 94) [86]. After her brief renewal of enthusiasm with Jemmy and then the petering out of her sexual vitality with the banker, we have the logical culmination of the process in her thieving career when she beds with her male accomplice in her disguise as a man:

> As we kept always together, so we grew very intimate, yet he never knew that I was not a man; nay, tho' I several times went home with him to his lodgings according as our business directed, and four or five times lay with him all night. But our design lay another way . . . (p. 187) [169–70].

This seems to be a situation that suits Moll rather well. One sees why several critics have found her unfeminine, curiously neutral in sex.[7] Her usual indifference to her various bedfellows, apart from their financial contributions, is culminated in her satisfaction at the news that this one has been hanged (p. 191) [173].

In her one sexual adventure of this part of her career, with the baronet lover whom she turns to good account, she tells us, "As for the bed &c., I was not much concern'd about that part," and predictably she robs him when he tries to make love: "I took this oppor-

7. See, for instance, Ian Watt: "as to her being a woman, it merely seems to endow her with a marketable physiological asset." "Recent Critical Fortunes of *Moll Flanders*," p. 14.

tunity to search him to a nicety; I took a gold watch, with a silk purse of gold . . ." etc. (p. 196) [178].

Moll's final relationship with a man is with her son, for whom, after years of neglect, she conceives an instant affection when she sees him "a handsome comely young gentleman in flourishing circumstances" (p. 279) [251]. He, like Jemmy, though apparently without Jemmy's calculation, knows the way to Moll's heart, and the two as usual manifest their affection by gifts of money and gold watches: "My son, the same kind dutiful and obliging creature as ever, treated me now at his own house, paid me my hundred pound, and sent me home again loaded with presents" (p. 296) [266].

Defoe's theme that mercenary values have replaced moral and spiritual ones is most clearly developed in his delineation of Moll's sexual and filial relations, but he touches on other facets of the subject. Moll's readiness to convert to Roman Catholicism in order to placate her hosts in Lancashire smacks of religious prostitution, and is described in the familiar financial terminology: "I was so complaisant that I made no scruple to be present at their mass, and to conform to all their gestures as they shew'd me the pattern, but I would not come too cheap . . ." (pp. 123–24) [113]. It is notable, too, that the one marriage ceremony she describes, of all the many she participated in, is conducted not in a church but an inn.

Moll herself is aware of—and turns to good account—the respectable world's tendency to take money as itself an index of goodness. As a thief, she tells us, she "always went very well dress'd, and I had very good cloths on, and a gold watch by my side, as like a lady as other folks" (p. 184) [167], and so avoids suspicion. And when she is almost caught robbing a goldsmith's shop, the alderman who examines her is satisfied of her innocence when he sees she has the money to pay for the merchandise. "I smil'd, and told his worship that then I ow'd something of his favour to my money" (p. 237) [213–14], she says shrewdly. And later with the boatswain she finds that a display of her property immediately procures her the respect of a gentlewoman, though she is being deported as a condemned criminal: "I took care . . . to let him see . . . that I had a purse, and in it a pretty deal of money, and I found that the very sight of it immediately furnish'd me with very different treatment" (p. 268) [241]. Moll knows that money talks, and not only to avaricious rogues, but to well-meaning citizens. No one, she notes, seems much to consider where the money comes from. [8] The fact that she herself is sardon-

8. When Moll and Jemmy compare their stock she comments drily, "a worse gotten estate was never put together to begin the world with" (p. 271) [244]; and she sardonically tells us of her touching gift of the gold watch to her son: "I told him, I had nothing of any value to bestow but that, and I desir'd he would now and then kiss it for my sake; I did not indeed tell him that I stole it from a gentlewoman's side, at a meeting house in London; that's by the way" (p. 293) [263].

ically explicit about it suggests that Defoe was not himself among the morally deluded Puritans who confused good with goods, and took wealth as the outward and visible sign of an inward and spiritual grace.

Defoe has given us a marvelous picture of a consistent psychology. From the initial affair with the elder brother, where he makes it clear how avarice and lechery become fused in her mind, her history is one where mercenary motives not only supersede emotional, sexual and moral ones, but actually comprehend them. He organizes imagery and incident to dramatize Moll's confusion. Ageing and experience for Moll are matters of dealing more shrewdly with dwindling assets; friendship is a profitable business partnership; religion a property to be traded in when the market is right. Courtship becomes a prolonged negotiation over settlements, lovemaking an exchange of coins and purses; tenderness manifests itself in the payment of a reckoning, and an emotional crisis prompts the automatic gesture of clutching at the contents of the pocket.

I have explored, I realize, only one aspect of the complicated question of how far Defoe is being ironic at Moll's expense, or at the expense of the whole threadbare Puritan morality. I have not examined his attitude to Moll's conversion and her moralizing, nor the question of how we are to take the preface. But I have tried to indicate how exhaustively he pursues this single theme of mercenary values as engulfing all others, and to suggest that such a consistent pattern must be a consciously developed one, involving clear judgment on a woman who is by vocation rather than necessity a prostitute and a thief. The judgment on Moll expands to a judgment on the society which in part trains her to be what she is. Defoe was no doubt himself a Puritan and a tradesman, and can embody the commercially corrupted outlook on life; but he can none the less see that it *is* corrupted, and offer us a Robin as a moral positive, "an exception to your rule" (p. 20) [20], to counterbalance a Moll who lives by and on a society governed by cupidity.

EVERETT ZIMMERMAN

Moll Flanders: Parodies of Respectability†

Robinson Crusoe and *Captain Singleton* have double perspectives, those of the narrator and of the person he once was. In these books, Defoe simulates a character's attempts to organize his own past. But because Defoe's narrators are enmeshed in their own history, their accounts of the past must inevitably be limited or implausible. In *Moll Flanders*, Defoe attempts to measure the impercipience of his narrator. He tries to show the full moral of his fable by developing a third perspective, intermittent but discernible

Defoe's preface is not merely a justification for a salacious book but also a guide to the reader. While insisting on the authenticity of Moll's memoirs, the preface calls attention to editorial interventions. Although the story is Moll's, the language and moralizing are in part the editor's: "In a Word, as the whole Relation is carefully garbl'd of all the Levity, and Looseness that was in it: So it is all applied, and with the utmost care to vertuous and religious Uses." Furthermore, the preface implicitly warns the reader against accepting Moll's perspective:

> The Pen employ'd in finishing her Story, and making it what you now see it to be, has had no little difficulty to put it into a Dress fit to be seen, and to make it speak Language fit to be read: When a Woman debauch'd from her Youth, nay, even being the Off-spring of Debauchery and Vice, comes to give an Account of all her vicious Practises, and even to descend to the particular Occasions and Circumstances, by which she first became wicked; and of all the progression of Crime which she run through in threescore Year, an Authur must be hard put to it to wrap it up so clean, as not to give room, especially for vitious Readers to turn it to his Disadvantage (pp. 3–4).

Defoe prepares the reader to understand more than Moll does: her view is the partially debased one that resulted from her life. She is repentant, but the effects of her wicked life have not mysteriously disappeared by the time that she writes the book.

* * *

The opening passages of *Moll Flanders* specifically identify her as a criminal whose crimes have gone unpunished. She could not give

† From *Defoe and the Novel* (Berkeley and Los Angeles: U of California P, 1975), pp. 75–106. Reprinted by permission of the author. Page numbers in parentheses refer to this Norton Critical Edition. Notes have been edited.

her real name even if a general pardon were issued (p. 9). In substance, there is nothing in this that is different from *Captain Singleton*: it is clear from the title pages of both books that they are about criminals. But Singleton comments on his early life without explicitly identifying himself as a criminal. In contrast, Moll Flanders emphasizes her mature identity even as she describes her early innocent life. Defoe's concern for establishing a limited point of view is shown also by numerous clumsy explanations of Moll's sources of information: * * * "as I heard afterwards" (p. 105) is a recurrent afterthought.

The early episodes show the forming of Moll's consciousness.[1] As a little girl, she needs money to stay with her "Nurse," her surrogate mother. Later, people who are charmed by her give her coins. When her first lover offers guineas for sex, her erotic pleasures confirm the association of gold with love. But when her lover offers her money to abandon him, the symbolism must be revised. She rejects love, and determines to find her pleasure in money.

By the end of the opening segment of *Moll Flanders*, the Colchester episode, Moll's values have undergone the transformation that both protects and corrupts her. Her new attitudes resemble those of the coarse but practical narrator: "The Case was alter'd with me, I had Money in my Pocket, and had nothing to say to them: I had been trick'd once by *that Cheat call'd* LOVE, but the Game was over; I was resolv'd now to be Married, or Nothing, and to be well Married, or not at all" (p. 50). The narrator sees this as a downward step without recognizing its residual force in her present consciousness. The young Moll's deliberate choice is now a part of the narrator's sensibility.

Subtly and precisely, Defoe commingles the hard voice of the old Moll and her passionate younger self:

> In short, if he had known me, and how easy the Trifle he aim'd at, was to be had, he would have troubled his Head no farther, but have given me four or five Guineas, and have lain with me the next time he had come at me; and if I had known his Thoughts, and how hard he thought I would be to be gain'd, I might have made my own Terms with him; and if I had not Capitulated for an immediate Marriage, I might for a Maintenance till Marriage, and might have had what I would; for he was already Rich to Excess, besides what he had in Expectation; but I seem'd wholly to have abandoned all such Thoughts as these, and was taken up Onely with Pride of my Beauty, and of

1. Many studies concentrate heavily, if not exclusively, on this opening section. Two important ones are these: Robert R. Columbus, "Conscious Artistry in *Moll Flanders*," *SEL* 3 (1963): 415–432; Juliet McMaster, "The Equation of Love and Money in *Moll Flanders*," *Studies in the Novel* 2 (1970): 131–144.

> being belov'd by such a gentleman; as for the Gold I spent whole Hours in looking upon it; I told the Guineas over and over a thousand times a Day: Never poor vain Creature was so wrapt up with every part of the Story, as I was, not Considering what was before me, and how near my Ruin was at the Door; indeed I think, I rather wish'd for that Ruin, than studyed to avoid it. (p. 24)

The young girl is ruining herself, as the narrator suggests, but it is to her credit that she "seem'd wholly to have abandoned all such Thoughts" as those that the narrator is thinking. The narrator sees and continues to share her former infatuation with money, but the complexities of her former sexual nature escape her. The young Moll is sexually excited by the money; the narrator's avarice is aroused by the sex.

The young girl's feelings are suppressed with difficulty. She becomes distraught and ill when abandoned by her lover, and she retains her sexual feelings for him, even after marrying his brother: ". . . I committed Adultery and Incest with him every Day in my Desires" (p. 49). As the narrator tells of these events, she communicates the interest that the lurid aspects of her past still hold for her, but she is impatient with the nuances of her past feelings. Indeed, those feelings that are unsubordinated to a utilitarian purpose are precisely what the narrator finds most contemptible about her younger self.

The entire Colchester episode has an emphasis differing from the narrator's. Of the moment that she loses her virginity, the narrator comments: ". . . thus I finish'd my own Destruction at once, for from this Day, being forsaken of my Vertue, and my Modesty, I had nothing of Value left to recommend me, either to God's Blessing, or Man's Assistance" (p. 26). She ignores all the complexities of her story in order to emphasize this conventional judgment. But the more crucial moral event for the young girl is a later one—her marriage to Robin. The account of Moll's relationship to the elder brother suggests that she is not willfully evil but naïve and sexually excited. She believes that she is as effectually married to the elder brother "as if we had been publickly Wedded by the Parson of the Parish" (p. 34). This private betrothal does not excuse her sexual misbehavior, but it does make her subsequent marriage to Robin a greater evil than sex with his elder brother.

Both the young girl's interpretation of the story and the narrator's are distorted. The young girl concludes that she has been cheated by love: the narrator believes that she has managed everything wrong. The moral conception embodied in the episode is a combination of the perceptions of the narrator and of her younger self: practical wisdom and moral insight must not be severed; one must manage shrewdly in order to deliver oneself from evil. When Moll chooses to deny love for the sake of expedience, she severs her practical from her moral and emotional energies. She never fully recovers. The woman who tells the story sees her tactical errors, but she has little conception of what she might have been had she not made them. She thinks vaguely that she might have been better or richer, but she has no comprehension of the impoverishment of her sensibilities.

Conjugal Lewdness; or, Matrimonial Whoredom, Defoe's somewhat overheated and underlit "Treatise concerning the Use and Abuse of the Marriage Bed," discusses at length some of the domestic problems that are the substance of much of *Moll Flanders*.[2] To apply any expository work by Defoe to his fiction is risky. Defoe wrote with a well-developed sense of audience, and he argued to win; consequently his ideas are easily distorted when extracted from their context. And given that *Conjugal Lewdness* was published in 1727, five years after *Moll Flanders*, one must be cautious about using the treatise as if it were a plan for the novel. But the works are closely related in subject, and writing *Moll Flanders* was one of the experiences that shaped the author of *Conjugal Lewdness*.

In *Conjugal Lewdness*, Defoe describes marriage as potentially the best or worst condition in life: it is either the "Center to which all the lesser Delights of life tend, as a Point in the Circle" or a "kind of Hell in miniature" (*C. L.*, pp. 96, 103). Love is "that one essential and absolutely necessary part of the Composition . . . without which the matrimonial State is, I think, hardly lawful, I am sure is not rational, and, I think, can never be happy" (*C. L.*, p. 28). Defoe returns to this theme throughout the treatise; the perversions of marriage are all related to the absence of love. Defoe particularly condemns marriages that are made primarily for economic or sexual reasons.

Defoe's heaviest emphasis in *Conjugal Lewdness* is on abuses of matrimony which are either sexually motivated or manifested. Presumably he is not attacking all sexual activity, but only sex divorced from its legitimating accompaniments—love, marriage, and childbearing (contraception is a conjugal lewdness). Marriage for primarily sexual reasons is "sheltering our Wickedness under the Letter of the Law" (*C. L.*, p. 267).

The treatise is aptly introduced by the couplets of the title page:

> Loose Thoughts, at first, like subterranean Fires,
> Burn inward, smothering, with unchaste Desires;
> But getting Vent, to Rage and Fury turn,

2. References are to the facsimile reproduction introduced by Maximillian E. Novak (Gainesville, Fla.: Scholar's Facsimiles and Reprints, 1967).

Burst in Volcanoes, and like Aetna burn;
The Heat increases as the Flames aspire,
And turns the solid Hills to liquid Fire.
So, sensual Flames, when raging in the Soul,
First vitiate all the Parts, then fire the Whole;
Burn up the Bright, the Beauteous, the Sublime,
And turn our lawful Pleasures into Crime.

Defoe's effort is to discover and suppress hidden lewdness where others may not even look for it—in marriage or in the motives for marrying. Anything that will lend itself to a sexual interpretation is assumed by Defoe to be sexual, if not exclusively, then primarily. Why do widows and widowers remarry precipitately? Why do people marry after the age of childbearing? The answer is almost invariable: ". . . the Effect of a raging, ungoverned Appetite, a furious immodest Gust of Sensuality, a Flame of immoderate Desires" (*C. L.*, pp. 341–342).

Defoe's Freudianism is almost orthodox, although hardly subtle. Sex is everywhere, and the fundamental moral imperative is that it somehow be controlled. Indulged, it is debilitating; repressed, it is disrupting. In pursuit of the sexual, Defoe interprets a dream impeccably. A widow who wishes to marry a much younger man is chided by a relative. The widow answers: "I can't live thus . . . I am frighted to Death . . . ever since Sir *William* died almost, I have been disturbed in my Sleep, either with Apparitions or Dreams" (*C. L.*, p. 234). Sir William appears to her on some nights, but at other times she sees "Another Shape; 'tis Sir *William*, I think, in another Dress" (*C. L.*, p. 234). Sir William does not speak, "but the other Appearance spoke to me, and frighted me to Death: Why, he asked me, to let him come to bed to me; And, I thought, he offered to open the Bed, which waked me, and I was e'en dead with the Fright" (*C. L.*, p. 234). The lady's relative understands that the problem is not with the supernatural: "Upon the whole, her Cousin found what Devil it was haunted her Ladyship; so she confessed, at last, that the Lady had good reasons for marrying; but then she argued warmly against her taking the young Fellow" (*C. L.*, p. 235). But only a young man will do for this Lady, and she subsequently suffers for her self-indulgence.

To Defoe, sex is a constant dangerous pressure, and anything that does not oppose it is in its service. In *Conjugal Lewdness*, Defoe sanctifies the more repressive, even if trivial, social conventions; he finds that deviations from the norm are almost invariably sexually motivated. Some "Customs" are in themselves indecent and must be resisted, and it is always criminal to violate any custom in the direction of greater sexual freedom, even if the freedom is legal (*C. L.*, p. 339). The mere appearance of evil is a real evil: "Though every

Indecency is not equally criminal, yet every Thing scandalous and offensive is really Criminal" (*C. L.*, p. 338).

The intemperate sexualistic morality of *Conjugal Lewdness* in some respects resembles that of the old Moll Flanders, who often condemns her sexual deviations without making any reasonable discriminations; like Defoe, she has enormous respect for convention. But Moll often indulges also in pleasant memories of the past, sometimes excusing obvious evil (although not usually sexual evil). In Defoe's terms, she is "committing the Crime again in the Mind, by thinking it over with Delight" (*C. L.*, p. 334).

The rigoristic tone of *Conjugal Lewdness* contrasts with that of *Moll Flanders*; the novel implies at least a small margin for human error. In *Conjugal Lewdness*, Defoe is defining evil that he believes often goes unrecognized. For this reason, he makes little attempt to establish gradations of evil, or to provide excuses for it. Nevertheless, it is possible to derive from the treatise a set of moral assumptions broad enough to apply to the larger world of *Moll Flanders*. Defoe does occasionally write with unusual sympathy of woman's restricted position in society. When a man's mistreatment of his wife causes her to loathe him, "she must have an uncommon Stock of Virtue, and be more a Christian than he ought to expect of her, if she does not single out some other Object of her Affection" (*C. L.*, p. 19).

Conjugal Lewdness deals directly with the issue of sexual experience after a betrothal but before marriage. As might be expected, all restrictions apply: the promise of marriage is binding and sex forbidden. A wife is a property, and any breach of civil restrictions is a moral fault: ". . . the Form [ceremony] gives the legal possession" (*C. L.*, p. 278). Premarital sex is also forbidden because of what it evidences: ". . . a wicked filthy ungovernable Inclination, that could not contain your self from a woman for a few Days" (*C. L.*, p. 281). But in such cases, Defoe places more blame on the man than on a woman who has not been forewarned: ". . . many (till then) innocent women, have been imposed upon by them [men] and ruined" (*C. L.*, p. 288). In *Conjugal Lewdness*, as in *Moll Flanders*, it is a greater evil than simple fornication for a woman to "marry one man and be in love with another . . . a Matrimonial Whoredom . . . one of the worst kinds of it too" (*C. L.*, p. 181).

The code of conduct that Defoe recommends in *Conjugal Lewdness* is higher than nature or law—it conforms, he feels, to Christian virtue. Nature is not by itself sufficient for the Christian: nature teaches the "Propagation of the Kind . . . but does it without regard to the limitations imposed by Heaven" (*C. L.*, p. 60). Anything sexual that is unnatural or illegal is obviously wrong, but Defoe reiterates his hope that he need not deal extensively with these grosser evils. Custom, however, sometimes betrays men into "such Liberties which the Savages and undirected Part of Mankind, do not take" (*C. L.*, p. 306). But there is no excuse for such violations of nature: "To be ignorant of a thing that Nature dictates, is shutting the Eyes against natural Light . . . so that the Ignorance is really as criminal as the Action" (*C. L.*, p. 313).

Moll Flanders deals with these grosser moral issues that Defoe does not wish to emphasize in *Conjugal Lewdness*. Moll retains a crude sense of the natural throughout her career: she avoids incest, and prefers not to wear men's clothes. But she loses the moral inhibitions that would raise her above mere nature, and eventually she is not even moved by the simple social ties that one would expect of "Savages." She does at first have a limited sense of what is right, although she is not motivated by religion. She has no "great Scruples of Conscience," but she "could not think of being a whore to one Brother, and a Wife to the other" (p. 28). She sacrifices this instinctive sense of rightness to expedience, and afterward increasingly suppresses her natural responses. In Newgate she uses religion as a structure for her regeneration, but before she can achieve the social standards of a Christian she must achieve the more primitive ones of nature. After her repentance, Moll would still be subject to some harsh strictures in the context of *Conjugal Lewdness*—but that the more rigorous parts of this treatise might even be appropriately applied to her is in itself evidence of her moral improvement.

The episodes of *Moll Flanders* are carefully, even rigidly, organized to illustrate the loosening of Moll's moral inhibitions and social ties. She first loves a man, although unmarried to him. She then reluctantly marries his brother, although pained at being separated from her lover. She next marries a tradesman for his gentlemanly appearance; she has a pleasant time with him, but parts from him with little feeling except annoyance at his poor management of money. Her developing hostility toward men then motivates her to trick an arrogant man into marriage with her friend. She then chooses a husband for herself because he has money and is good-tempered; he will not abuse her when he discovers that he has been tricked (p. 119). But he turns out to be her brother, and she loathes him: ". . . I could almost as willingly have embrac'd a Dog, as have let him offer any thing of that kind to me, for which Reason I could not bear the thoughts of coming between the Sheets with him" (p. 80).

Her next liaison is at Bath. She is now neither married nor planning to be faithful: ". . . knowing the World as I had done, and that such kind of things do not often last long, I took care to lay up as much Money as I could for a wet Day, as I call'd it" (p. 95). But Moll miscalculates in thinking that her sexuality is completely subordinated to material ends: ". . . the Inclination was not to be resisted . . . I was oblig'd to yield up all even before he ask'd it" (p. 96). Moll feels that sex for pleasure is more shameful than sex for money, but Defoe's structure modifies her evaluation. Her still having "inclination" reveals that she has not yet suppressed every instinct of nature. She has fallen far in Defoe's terms, but she has further to go.

Her next relationships are intertwined. She keeps the bank clerk in ignorant abeyance while she marries Jemy the highwayman. When Jemy proves to be impoverished, she deserts him. Her narrowing conception of prudence is no longer subverted by untrustworthy feelings, even though Jemy is the first man that she has loved since the elder brother: ". . . I really lov'd him most tenderly" (p. 123), but "never broke my Resolution, which was not to let him ever know my true Name" (p. 126). She makes it impossible for him to interfere in her future life, and keeps him from using her money. After having Jemy's child, she marries the bank clerk.

Her marriage to the clerk is described as the only extended tranquility that she has experienced since her youth. But the calmly economic terms that she uses to explain her happiness (p. 149) suggest that this man satisfies her only because she has deliberately restricted her feelings. Moll believes that her rejection of Jemy was wise; nevertheless, her feelings for him survive. Although Moll never again responds to anyone without having her feelings compromised by greed, she later experiences a resurgence of love for Jemy.

Each episode marks how far Moll has fallen, and in addition, further erodes some remaining scruple. Having repressed her feelings for Jemy in order to achieve a secure life, she is prepared to steal when the clerk dies. Moll's first theft is one of the most intense experiences of her life, comparable to her loss of the elder brother. She passes into another circle of her hell, which has Newgate at its bottom: ". . . I was under such dreadful Impressions of Fear, and in such Terror of Mind, tho' I was perfectly safe, that I cannot express the manner of it" (p. 152).

But Moll cannot even be part of the community of thieves; her fellow criminals soon become her gravest danger. Repeatedly she is saved because others are not. She gets the "joyful News" that an accomplice is hanged (p. 173). She is "easie" because all witnesses against her are hanged or transported (p. 176). She is hated by other criminals because she always escapes when they are "catch'd and hurried to Newgate" (p. 169). The "Court" too separates Moll from other criminals: it will pardon anyone who gives the testimony that will hang Moll (p. 175).

As Moll's morality disintegrates, she clutches more desperately at respectability. She adapts her surface to moral conventions, no matter what her deeper feelings may be. The morning-after behavior of Moll and her Bath lover is precisely what would be expected of newly fallen innocents—which they are not: "In the Morning we were both at our Penitentials, I cried very heartily, he express'd himself very sorry" (pp. 93–94). That Moll had long intended to have sexual relations with this man, and that she plans to continue them, is no impediment to her assuming the conventions of penitence. Moll's pretenses of respectability eventually achieve a palpable reality. When importuned to marry the bank clerk, she responds with almost incontrovertible evidence of innocent confusion: ". . . what do you mean, *says I*, colouring a little, what in an Inn, and upon the Road!" (p. 142). She pretends that she wants to be married in a church (where else!). Although Moll is aware of her hypocrisy, the blush is real. She simulates proper responses so devotedly that they acquire a reality of their own.

As her life becomes more openly corrupt, Moll's attempts to hide her evil lead to inner chaos. In her "Terror of Mind" at her first theft, she cries, "Lord . . . what am I now? a Thief" (p. 152)! She calls her "evil Counsellor" the Devil, but she knows that he is "within" (p. 153). To continue to deny her increasingly apparent evil requires enormous effort. Her disguises multiply, and she loses her sense of her own coherence. She takes risks beyond reason, stealing anything, even a horse that she cannot use or sell. Having suppressed those structures provided by the human community, she retains only an inchoate self.

Newgate is the emblem of what Moll has become. Many of Moll's experiences shortly before her imprisonment suggest metaphorically her literal condition at Newgate. One of her last disguises is the beggar's rags that she finds "Ominous and Threatning" (p. 200): "I naturally abhorr'd Dirt and Rags; I had been bred up Tite and Cleanly, and could be no other, whatever Condition I was in" (p. 199). But in prison "I was become a meer *Newgate-Bird*, as Wicked and as Outragious as any of them; nay, I scarce retain'd the Habit and Custom of good Breeding, and Manners, which all along till now run thro' my Conversation; so thoro' a Degeneracy had possess'd me, that I was no more the same thing that I had been, than if I had never been otherwise that what I was now" (p. 219). She is astonished at her irrational adaptation to the place "that had so long expected me" (p. 215): "It is scarce possible to imagine that our Natures should be capable of so much Degeneracy, as to make that pleasant and agreeable that in itself is the most compleat Misery" (p. 219).

Moll feels her impotence in Newgate, where she has "no Friends to assist" (p. 225). One is reminded of a former claustrophobic image, the featherbed that is thrown upon Moll while she is trying to steal goods from a burning house: ". . . nor did the People concern themselves much to deliver me from it, or to recover me at all; but I lay like one Dead and neglected a good while" (p. 176). Moll has in fact lost control of her life well before her capture. She steals what she does not need, even while she is terrorized by the possible consequences of her theft. She almost recognizes her own compulsiveness after the gambling episode: she wins, but will not continue for fear of the "Itch of Play." Immediately she thinks too of ceasing to steal, but, instead, she "grew more hardn'd and audacious than ever" (p. 206).

Moll's repentance is the most detailed one in Defoe's novels.[3] She must not only be brought to reject her evil past but also be made human again: "I degenerated into Stone; I turn'd first Stupid and Senseless, then Brutish and thoughtless, and at last raving Mad" (p. 218). The focus is on Moll's emotions, not on religious abstractions: "the terror of my mind"; "I look'd on myself as lost"; "overwhelm'd with melancholy and Despair"; "horror to my Imagination"; "how did the harden'd Wretches . . . Triumph over me"; "flouted me with my Dejections." (pp. 215–16).

Moll repents immediately, "but that Repentance yielded me no Satisfaction, no Peace, no not in the least" (p. 215). Moll's past has created a difficult epistemological problem for her. Knowing how she has manipulated her own feelings she cannot trust them now. What confirmation of her repentance can there be? She is confined to her solipsistic prison. Her search for the "satisfaction" and "comfort" of repentance is successful only after she is sentenced to death (p. 225): she finally believes in her repentance when it can no longer serve an earthly purpose.

Moll's repentance partially restores the integrity of her feelings: they are no longer always subordinate to her narrow conception of the utilitarian. Essential to Moll's repentance is the reappearance of Jemy, her Lancashire husband, in jail. After her first horror at Newgate, she had become "insensible." Her pain was so deep that all feeling had to be suppressed—a condition that she calls "the compleatest Misery on Earth" (p. 219). But when she sees Jemy, she is "call'd . . . back a little to that thing call'd Sorrow," (p. 221). As she thinks of her responsibility for Jemy's destruction, "the first Reflection I made upon the horrid detestable Life I had liv'd, began to return upon me, and as these things return'd my abhorrance of the Place I was in, and of the way of living in it, return'd also" (p. 221).

Newgate brings Moll to herself—but what is she? Before Newgate she was at least her pretenses. Now she must generate a new identity. She acknowledges, even emphasizes, past wickedness in order to

3. See George A. Starr, *Defoe and Spiritual Autobiography* (Princeton: Princeton UP, 1965), for discussion of the traditional process of repentance.
It seems likely to me that Defoe rewrote and expanded this section. First, Defoe seems to have intended to end the repentance in America. There, Moll's "Heart began to look up more seriously, than I think it ever did before" (p. 263), a statement not compatible with the long section on repentance in Newgate.

separate the present from the past. The new structure for her life is that of *repentant* criminal. Those transported with her are no longer her fellows: ". . . a Gang of Thirteen, as harden'd vile Creatures as ever Newgate produc'd in my time; and it would really well take up a History longer than mine to describe the degrees of Impudence, and audacious Villany that those Thirteen were arriv'd to" (p. 231).

But repentance in the face of death does not solve the problem of living. Moll must learn again to deal with her world; having no principles, she again parodies respectability. After she leaves Newgate, she begins to transform her past, even as she acknowledges it. She comments of her money, "a worse gotten Estate was scarce ever put together" (p. 244), but then says immediately, "Our greatest Misfortune as to our Stock, was that it was all in Money" (p. 244). She is now a prudent planter, not a thief. In Virginia, she presents a gold watch to her son, but "*did not indeed tell him* that I had stole it from a Gentlewoman's side" (p. 263). A stolen watch is now a token of her properly tender affections for her child.

Moll's ludicrous responses to this child are a significant part of the novel's pattern:

> It was a wretched thing for a Mother thus to see her own Son, a handsome comely young Gentleman in flourishing Circumstances, and durst not make herself known to him; and durst not take any notice of him; let any Mother of Children that reads this, consider it, and but think with what anguish of Mind I restrain'd myself; what yearnings of Soul I had in me to embrace, him, and weep over him; and how I thought all my Entrails turn'd within me, that my very Bowels mov'd, and I knew not what to do; as I now know not how to express those Agonies: When he went from me I stood gazing and trembling, and looking after him as long as I could see him; then sitting down on the Grass, just at a Place I had mark'd, I made as if I lay down to rest me . . . and lying on my Face wept, and kiss'd the Ground that he had set his Foot on (pp. 251–52).

This passage appeals to purely conventional assumptions about mothers and children. But convention is no longer something that Moll uses to hide herself but to create herself. Her meeting with this son is genuinely "the pleasantest Day" of her life (p. 263).

Moll achieves the benefits of the maternal relationships that she had forfeited; she is now a good mother with a dutiful son. Her numerous children had been a nagging difficulty because they asserted continuities that she wished to deny. (However, there is no evidence that Moll ever abused her children. She makes substantial efforts to place each in the care of a relative.) Moll's suppressed feelings are sordidly parodied in her criminal career: she repeatedly simulates maternal relationships in order to steal (pp. 153, 161–62, 202–3), and once to avoid capture, she pretends to be sitting with her daughter (p. 203). Having given up any legitimate maternal function of her own, Moll appropriately enough addresses the "Governess" as "Mother" (p. 137). But when Moll finally reconstructs her version of the proper life, she includes a maternal role for herself.

In Virginia, Moll reintegrates two important fragments of her past into her present—Jemy and her brother. They represent two possible conclusions to romantic pretense. Moll's relation with her brother turns into loathing; with Jemy, into good fortune and true love. In both cases, Moll's object is a fortune, her method sentimental cliché.

The emotional climax of Moll's courtship by her brother is the scene that he begins by writing with a diamond upon glass, "*You I Love, and you alone*" (p. 65). The scene then proceeds through a series of banalities. Moll, character and narrator, clearly enjoys this occasion: she is pleased by the semblance of feeling and by the feeble wit, both of which she uses to make a good bargain. She never comments on the irony that this romantic lover turns out to be her brother. She is willing to see herself as wicked but not as a comic fool. Nevertheless, when she returns to Virginia, she wishes to come to terms with this part of her past, for reasons not purely economic. This sordid relationship with her brother is eventually transformed by her joy in her son: the legacy of the beastly brother is a beautiful son.

Moll's relation to Jemy also begins with romantic trappings: both pretend true love and good fortune. But soon they learn that they have duped each other. In this case, however, love does not vanish. It is marked by many kisses, many tears, and possibly a supernatural omen (miles away, Jemy hears Moll call after him). But, unromantically, they separate. Many years later, when Moll sees the swashbuckling highwayman in prison, the romance is revived. He recognizes her immediately, and later gives her "such Testimony of Kindness and Affection as I thought were Equal, if not Superior to that at our parting at *Dunstable*" (p. 238). Out of such gestures Moll can construct a grand illusion. She comfortably evades her past—"I TOLD him I far'd the worse for being taken in the Prison for one *Moll Flanders*" (p. 234)—and they go to the New World. There, after some difficulties, he is re-created in the image that Moll has chosen:

> I took especial care to buy for him all those things that I knew he delighted to have; as two good long Wigs, two silver hilted Swords, three or four fine Fowling pieces, a fine Saddle with Holsters and Pistoles very handsome with a Scarlet Cloak; and in a Word, every thing I could think of to oblige him; and to make him appear, as he really was, a very fine Gentleman. (p. 265)

On Moll's second visit, Virginia truly becomes a new world. It is an odd name for her habitation, but she is able to construct almost anything out of the pieces of her past. Her past gives her little resistance. The Colchester brothers are dead, and her good clerk is too. The governess knows much, but not everything. Even when Moll is being transported, she still does not tell the governess that Jemy is her husband of years ago (p. 243). Somewhere, perhaps, there are still that husband who deserted her and that repentant Bath lover. But she has little to fear from them. When Moll returns to England, she knows that her reputation is finally safe. Now she and Jemy "resolve to spend the Remainder of our Years in sincere Penitence, for the wicked Lives we have lived" (p. 267). Moll can now begin an ideal repentance unencumbered by the embarrassing demands of a past reality.

One final task remains for Moll—writing *Moll Flanders*. The book serves many of Moll's needs. Confession purges her of guilt. Also, she can savor her past as she severs herself from it: her obvious pleasure in her criminal triumphs is excused by the morals that she now draws. And she can explain her past in ways that will suppress what still frightens her. Now that she need no longer accommodate herself to her past or to financial exigencies, she can organize her life in any way that she chooses to. She can derive from her past whatever stability she needs.

Moll is eloquent about the need to confess. One of her constant complaints is that she has no confidant (although she always seems to be telling people about herself, she knowingly limits and distorts what she tells). The first time that she pieces together her life for anyone is when in Newgate she confesses to the minister. Only then does she obtain "the Comfort of a Penitent": "This honest friendly way of treating me, unlock'd all the Sluces of my Passions: He broke into my very Soul by it; and I unravell'd all the Wickedness of my Life to him; In a word, I gave him an Abridgement of this whole History; I gave him the Picture of my Conduct for 50 Years in Miniature" (p. 226). But this confession does not relieve Moll's by now chronic anxiety. In the future, her terrors linger even when their causes end: ". . . if any Accident had happened to us, we might at last have been very miserable . . . The very thoughts of it gives me some horror, even since the Danger is past" (p. 258).

In Virginia, she is especially disturbed because she cannot communicate her secrets even to Jemy: ". . . this was a thing I knew not how to open to him, and yet having no Body to disclose any part of it to, the Burthen was too heavy for my mind . . ." (p. 254). She speaks feelingly of the "Necessity" of confessing criminal actions:

> This Necessity of Nature, is a thing which Works sometimes with such vehemence, in the Minds of those who are guilty of any atrocious Villany; such as secret Murther in particular, that they have been oblig'd to Discover it . . . tho' it may be true that the divine Justice ought to have the Glory of all those Discoveries and Confessions, yet 'tis as certain that Providence which ordinarily Works by the Hands of Nature, makes use here of the same natural Causes to produce those extraordinary Effects (p. 254).

Without denying the possibility of a final and divine cause, she recognizes the desire for confession as human.

Moll cannot of course fully accept the implication that she is writing her story for her own gratification; that would link her too positively to her criminal past. When her pondering on confession brings her too close to this truth, she wrenches the story back to its "purpose":

> As the publishing this Account of my Life, is for the sake of the just Moral of every part of it, and for Instruction, Caution, Warning and Improvement to every Reader, so this will not pass I hope for an unnecessary Digression concerning some People, being oblig'd to disclose the greatest Secrets either of their own, or other Peoples Affairs (p. 255).

Moll insists that she is the reader's instructor, not his parishioner—or patient.

Moll's instructions to us often serve to insulate her from painful episodes of the past. She tells us how she escaped because a "poor Boy was deliver'd up to the Rage of the Street" (p. 167), but immediately gives a practical turn to the account. She explains the art of capturing pickpockets, "a Direction not of the kindest Sort to the Fraternity" (p. 168). In dealing with this event, she suppresses her feelings of guilt, provides a justification for her confession, and reiterates her separation from her old companions.

Her confession requires a book because she will not entrust her life to anyone. Not even the reader knows her real name. "O! what a felicity is it to Mankind . . . that they cannot see into the Hearts of one another!" she once says to herself (p. 144). Moll avoids psychological explanations for fear that they may destroy her precarious mental equilibrium. Nevertheless, pressures that she cannot explain are apparent in much that she says. Her first theft is prompted by "a Voice spoken to me over my Shoulder, take the Bundle; be quick; do it this Moment" (p. 151). Although Moll asserts that this voice is the Devil's, Defoe's focus is on Moll. Her subsequent references to the Devil reveal her loss of rational control of herself: "my Prompter, like a true Devil" (p. 153); "the Devil put me upon killing the Child"

(p. 153); "the Devil put things into my Head" (p. 154); "the diligent Devil . . . continually prompted me" (p. 157); "I blindly obeyed his Summons" (p. 157).

Moll's earlier experience among the debtors in the Mint was unbearable to her. There she saw the compulsions, the irrationality bordering madness, that haunts her ever after:

> [Men] labouring to forget former things, which now it was the proper time to remember . . . Sinning on, as a Remedy for Sin past . . . they did not only act against Conscience, but against Nature; they put a Rape upon their Temper . . . when he has Thought and Por'd on it [his condition] till he is almost Mad, having no Principles to Support him, nothing within him, or above him, to Comfort him; but finding it all Darkness on every Side . . . he repeats the Crime, and thus he goes every Day one Step onward of his way to Destruction (p. 54).

These comments are an acute analysis of the condition to which Moll is inexorably reduced. She is "fill'd with horror" in the Mint, but she cannot leave the condition behind with the place. Newgate itself is another version of the Mint: it too is an emblem of an inner state that Moll is perpetually fleeing.

Moll persistently attempts to give rational explanations for her behavior, glossing over the collapse into irrationality that she senses:

> I have often wondered even at my own hardiness another way, that when all my Companions were surpriz'd, and fell so suddainly into the Hand of Justice, and that I so narrowly escap'd, yet I could not all that while enter into one serious Resolution to leave off this Trade; and especially Considering that I was now very far from being poor, that the Temptation of Necessity, which is generally the Introduction of all such wickedness, was now remov'd; for I had near 500 *l.* by me in ready money, on which I might have liv'd very well, if I had thought fit to have retir'd; but *I say*, I had not so much as the least inclination to leave off; no not so much as I had before when I had but 200 *l.* before-hand, and when I had no such frightful Examples before my Eyes as these were; From hence 'tis Evident to me, that when once we are harden'd in Crime, no Fear can affect us, no Example give us any warning (p. 174).

The concluding statement is question-begging, but its moral ring and its reduction of the incomprehensible to cliché are precisely what Moll needs to soothe her terrors. She must reduce the past to the cosier dimensions of her present.

In telling her story, Moll persists in using the economic and religious explanations that have already failed to explain her behavior (now of course she has the economic, and is constructing the religious, stability that she once lacked). Her experience among the debtors in the Mint impels her to find money; but what terrified her about the debtors was their psychological, not their financial condition. Her later marriage to the bank clerk is motivated by her respect for his money and his good character. But what really satisfies her is the stability—the stodginess—of the relationship; it is the antithesis of her experience in the Mint. Despite all her attempted explanations, the language that she uses to describe the end of her "utmost Tranquility" with the clerk suggests that she was, and still is, uncomprehending: ". . . a sudden Blow from an almost invisible Hand, blasted all my Happiness" (p. 149). She explains her subsequent stealing as necessity, but her "distress" begins while the necessity is still internal: ". . . I saw nothing before me but the utmost Distress, and this represented it self so lively to my Thoughts, that it seem'd as if it was come, before it was really very near; also my very Apprehensions doubl'd the Misery, for I fancied every Sixpence that I paid but for a Loaf of Bread, was the last that I had in the World, and that To-morrow I was to fast, and be starv'd to Death." (p. 150). She needs the "Devil" to explain to herself as well as to us her abrupt movement from outward respectability to crime.

Moll clings desperately to the metaphor that she uses to articulate her private needs—money. It is her metonym for love, sanity, and life itself. After the death of the clerk, her money "wasted daily for Subsistence" (p. 150) and as it is not being replenished, she is "bleeding to Death, without the least hope or prospect of help from God or Man" (p. 150). This equation of her body with money is implicit in the description of her declining beauty: ". . . it was past the flourishing time with me when I might expect to be courted for a Mistress; that agreeable part had declin'd some time, and the Ruins only appear'd of what had been" (p. 150). She is now reduced to taking money and goods alone, without even a semblance of love. For a time, stealing itself provides a new stability: the excitement distracts her from herself. But money has gradually been divested of its meanings, and when she has more than enough for subsistence the irrationality of her actions is again forced upon her consciousness. After her repentance, money and love are again joined: she is reunited with Jemy, and becomes a wealthy planter. She has then returned to her earlier condition—but with a difference. She now has the shrewdness that she then lacked.

Moll's life is too complicated for her to understand. She tries to begin anew—again and again. But when the past impinges too insistently on the present, she loses control. She lives so many lives that she does not know which is hers. At the end of her criminal career, her whirlwind of disguises is both a cause and a symbol of her mental state. Madness lurks on the peripheries of her life. Repeatedly Moll uses the phrase "Reason'd me out of my Reason" (pp. 47, 137). The illness consequent on her desertion by the elder Colchester brother leaves her "Weak," "Alter'd," "Melancholly" (p. 36). Later, in Virginia, her brother threatens to put her into a madhouse (p. 75). At the clerk's death, Moll "sat and cried and tormented my self Night and Day; wringing my Hands, and sometimes raving like a distracted woman; and indeed I have often wonder'd it had not affected my Reason, for I had the Vapours to such a degree, that my Understanding was sometimes quite lost in Fancies and Imaginations" (p. 150). And many who surround her share her instability. Her brother is distracted and attempts suicide. Her clerk's dissolute wife commits suicide. The clerk himself "grew Melancholy and Disconsolate, and from thence Lethargick, and died" (p. 149). Moll's story is designed to banish these threats and provide an understandable order for her life.

In many respects, Moll is an incompetent. Beneath the bustle and boasting lie indecisiveness and misunderstanding. She is repeatedly an easy victim of psychological coercion. The elder brother at Colchester refrains at first from what "they call the last Favour," but "he made that self denyal of his a plea for all his Freedoms with me upon other Occasions" (p. 23). When a variation of the same technique is used on Moll much later, she remains uncomprehending. Her Bath lover lies in bed with her but leaves her "innocent" (p. 93). Although Moll believes that this is a "noble Principle" (p. 93), she subsequently entices him into a sexual relationship. From this time on, Moll bears the responsibility for an affair that he controls. Moll tries desperately to please him, but after having enjoyed her fully he repents. Moll never notices that she is being abused. She met this lover just after her disastrous marriage to her brother. She enticed her brother into marriage by pretending to be uninterested and making him sue; as a consequence, he does not inquire so closely into her finances as he might otherwise have done; nor can he blame Moll for cheating him when he discovers the truth about her fortune (p. 66). At Bath, Moll is trapped by this same method that she has used on her brother. And the episode at Bath is linked to her relationship with her first lover by those guineas that her Bath lover pours into her lap (p. 90). She repeatedly plays a debased Danae to some depraved Jove.

Hardheaded practicality is what Moll admires and tries to simulate, but the "Governess," not Moll, is the embodiment of this quality. In a spasm of enthusiasm for figures and accounts, Moll lists all the prices that the governess charges for maternity care, even those that have nothing to do with the story. Moll simulates the respectable economic virtues without understanding them. In the subsequent discussion, the governess sees through Moll's mealymouthed evasions; the more Moll equivocates about her social status, the more clearly the governess understands her (p. 129). Moll is relieved to have someone care for her, and the name that Moll chooses for this woman describes their relationship. The governess is always what Moll needs: a midwife when Moll is with child, a fence when Moll steals, a penitent when Moll repents. Looked at another way, the governess is whatever can profit from Moll. But Moll is not cheated. She is allowed the comfort of emotional dependence.

From her childhood, Moll looks to the external world to provide a structure for her life. In contrast to Singleton, she easily becomes part of families, groups, and societies. But she always discovers that these structures provide only a pseudo-order. They give her a role to play, but the only moral imperative implied by them is that she have a respectable appearance.

The institution that Moll knows best is the law. Her experiences with it reflect and reinforce her sense that everything is a manipulable surface. Her first arrest occurs because a thief is dressed like a widow and so is she. A mercer swears falsely that Moll is guilty, but later the real thief is caught. Although there is a certain justice in Moll's being taken, she plays the partially justified part of aggrieved innocence with such aplomb that she manages to extract 200 *l.* from the mercer for her false arrest. She hires a respectable lawyer, who lies for her; had the lawyer been a "petty Fogging hedge Soliciter, or a Man not known, and not in good Reputation, I should have brought it to but little" (p. 196). Before the meeting for settlement, the lawyer gives her instructions to appear in "good Cloaths, and with some State, that the *Mercer* might see I was something more than I seem'd to be that time they had me." (p. 197).

Newgate is the rotten core of the legal system. Thieves are set free at night to steal for their jailers (p. 254). Even the smallest comfort has a price; Moll has enough money for a "little dirty Chamber," so that she does not have to be kept in the common cell for condemned prisoners (p. 227). The "ordinary" only tries to collect evidence: ". . . all his Divinity run upon Confessing my Crime" (p. 218). The good minister who visits her warns her to give up hope of life unless she has "very good Friends" (p. 222). After her sentence has been commuted to transportation, she can buy her pardon: ". . . but it could not be done unless with an Expense too heavy for my Purse" (p. 240).

Justice is done at Moll's trial—but *despite* the legal system, witnesses, and judges. The man whose goods were stolen relents but will not withdraw his charge for fear of losing his bond (p. 217). The witnesses lie; they hate Moll, and will say anything to convict her (p. 223). The judges treat her as an old offender, although she is not one "in the sense of the Law" (p. 230). Moll knows that she is guilty, and an old offender too, but she also knows that such matters have little to do with what happens to her. The law is at best a technicality, at worst a means for legal extortion or private vengeance.

Moll finally makes the best of this difficult world. She repents and becomes respectable; however, there are no regenerative miracles. This book embodies a view of events that is not entirely the narrator's. In fact, Defoe seems deliberately to be avoiding some of the limitations of his earlier novels, especially of *Captain Singleton*. Instead of making Moll the sole repository of the wisdom of the book, Defoe allows us to escape her point of view even as she tells the story.

Nevertheless, Defoe's role in the book is not simply that of ironic historian of Moll's consciousness. The ironies of Moll's decline suggest a set of values by which to judge her: love, community, even respectability. But Moll loses her moral bearings—and her story does too. The writing that describes Moll's life between her first theft and her imprisonment is unusually untidy, even for Defoe. There are repetitions, incidents introduced too early, events without any clear point. In one sense, the confusions in Moll's narration are imitative of her moral and psychological condition at the described period of her life. But early in the book, Defoe clearly took a position outside the narrator. Where is the ironic distance here? Defoe seems to have reverted to the technique of *Robinson Crusoe* and *Captain Singleton*, reducing himself to the limits of his narrator.

On one occasion, Moll robs a drunken gentleman with whom she has just had a sexual encounter—the only whoring, in the narrow sense of the word, that she ever does. The account is given with a series of evaluations of the characters, all confused and contradictory. Moll's first response is contempt for a man who would lust for her: "There is nothing so absurd, so surfeiting, so ridiculous as a Man heated by Wine in his Head, and a wicked Gust in his Inclination together" (p. 178). Swayed by vanity, she decides that he is "a Man of Sense, and of a fine Behaviour; a comely handsome Person, a sober solid Countenance, a charming beautiful Face, and everything that cou'd be agreeable" (p. 179). Next, she imagines the possible consequences of his action:

> . . . 'twas ten to one but he had an honest virtuous Wife, and innocent Children, that were anxious for his Safety . . . how would he reproach himself with associating himself with a Whore? pick'd up in the worst of all Holes, the Cloister, among the Dirt and Filth of all the Town? how would he be trembling for fear he had got the Pox, for fear a Dart had struck him through his Liver, and hate himself every time he look'd back upon the Madness and Brutality of his Debauch? (p. 179)

She seems almost to have forgotten that she is the woman with whom the man has coupled.

The governess knows the man, and decides to visit him. Blackmail is the only possible motive, but she merely entices the man into a visit with Moll. There is no plausible explanation for the governess's actions. Moll at first wants nothing further to do with him, but changes her mind:

> I had a great many Thoughts in my Head about my seeing him again, and was often sorry that I had refus'd it; I was perswaded that if I had seen him, and let him know that I knew him, I should have made some Advantage of him, and perhaps have had some Maintenance from him; and tho' it was a Life wicked enough, yet it was not so full of Danger as this I was engag'd in (p. 185).

When the man is assured that Moll does not suffer from venereal disease, he visits her regularly and reproves himself conscientiously for debauching her: "He would often make just Reflections also upon the crime itself, and upon the particular Circumstances of it, with respect to himself; how Wine introduc'd the Inclinations, how the Devil led him to the Place and found out an Object to tempt him, and he made the Moral always himself" (p. 187).

There are many possible views of this incident, none of them consistent. Moll and the governess indiscriminately draw morals and prey on the man. Moll censures the relationship, but her comments remain generalized and abstract; she betrays little personal involvement. The man's own moralizing is cynical. One can see the incident as an example of Moll's deterioration—her contradictions verge on the schizophrenic. But there is no sense of a perspective imposed from outside Moll's diseased mind.

Defoe's failure in this incident may be without purpose, but it is not without meaning. Although one can argue that Defoe was careless, the unresolved contradictions in the episode are so egregious that he could hardly have been entirely unaware of them. And this episode is one part of a larger section in which Defoe lost the control that characterizes much of *Moll Flanders*: a carefully defined ironic perspective succumbs to the formlessness of Moll's mind. One must suspect that in some sense Defoe shared Moll's confusion.

Moll lacks any sense of a value that is more than appearance. Her early parodies of respectability collapse in Newgate. She begins again, this time excluding from her life the openly criminal behavior that brought about the previous collapse. She then counterfeits—or conjures, perhaps—the values of love and community which are suggested in the earlier parts of the book. Defoe's reliance on parody reveals his difficulty in imagining any authentic values. When Moll disintegrates, Defoe fails to define any moral world that exists outside her consciousness. Like Moll, he presumably accepts a Christian view of repentance and redemption, but one suspects that his theology is at least in part a device for controlling his fears of those energies that he castigates in *Conjugal Lewdness*. Inner chaos must be suppressed by some order, however arbitrary. Defoe is driven to assert out of fear, not out of belief. In this too, he resembles his creature.

MAXIMILLIAN E. NOVAK

"Unweary'd Traveller" and "Indifferent Monitor": Openness and Complexity in *Moll Flanders*†

Newgate thy dwelling was, thy beauty made thee
A goddess seem, and that alone betray'd thee.
Twelve years a whore, a wife unto thy brother,
And such a thief there scarce could be another.
Unweary'd traveller, whither dost thou roam?
Lo! in this place remote to find a tomb
Transported hence, to heaven, 'tis hop'd thou'rt sent
Who wicked liv'd, but dy'd a penitent.

(POEM APPENDED TO A CHAPBOOK VERSION OF *Moll Flanders*.)[1]

In *Lavengro*, George Borrow tells of his encounter with an old woman who kept a fruit stall on a London Bridge. He notices that she is reading a book "intently" and then finds himself grasped by her as he leans over the edge to see a boat caught in the swift-moving waters. She has been watching him and concluded that he was a pickpocket down on his luck who decided to put an end to his life. He enters into conversation with her and discovers that she has a son at Botany Bay as a transported felon and that she sees no harm in stealing. In fact, she offers to act as a fence for any handkerchiefs he might have taken that day. Her views on theft are conditioned by her continued love for her thieving son who certainly would not do anything wrong and by her admiration for the heroine of the book she reads so eagerly—Moll Flanders. To the author's question about the "harm" in theft, she responds:

† From *Realism, Myth, and History in Defoe's Fiction* (Lincoln: U of Nebraska P, 1983), pp. 71–98. Copyright 1983 by the University of Nebraska Press. Reprinted by permission of the publisher and the author. Page numbers in parentheses refer to this Norton Critical Edition. Notes have been edited.

1. Daniel Defoe, *The Fortunes and Misfortunes of Moll Flanders* (London: A. Swindells, n.d. [ca. 1750]), p. 24.

> 'No harm in the world, dear! Do you think my own child would have been transported, if there had been any harm in it? and what's more, would the blessed woman in the book here have written her life as she has done, and given it to the world, if there had been any harm in faking? She, too, was what they call a thief and a cutpurse; ay, and was transported for it, like my dear son; and do you think she would have told the world so, if there had been any harm in the thing? Oh, it is a comfort to me that the blessed woman was transported, and came back—for come back she did, and rich too—for it is an assurance to me that my dear son, who was transported too, will come back like her.'
>
> 'What was her name?'
>
> 'Her name, blessed Mary Flanders.'[2]

Borrow, who has told his readers how he learned to read by his fascination with *Robinson Crusoe*, offers to buy the book from her as soon as he discovers in it "the air, the style, the spirit" of Defoe, but she refuses to sell it. "Without my book," she tells him, "I should mope and pine, and perhaps fling myself into the river." Instead, for six pence, she allows him to read it whenever he comes by. After some "wicked boys" try to steal the book from her, the old fruit seller loses some of her enthusiasm for the work, but the one time that Borrow, or his autobiographical hero, takes advantage of the chance to read, he finds himself so engrossed in it that hours pass by without his taking his eyes off the pages before him.

Now Borrow is engaging in some mythmaking of his own in creating the old fruit seller, who lives courageously on her slender earnings. Not surprisingly, it is the mythical Moll Flanders who is perceived by the old woman. She knows nothing about the warnings against stealing that Borrow points out to her. She reads it as a fairy tale, noticing only the "funny parts" and reaping from it a fund of hope that keeps her optimistic in spite of the grim facts of her life. Only when she begins to lose hope, which occurs after the attempted theft of the book, does she turn from it and agree to the author's offer to buy her a Bible in its place.[3]

From some standpoints the old fruit woman is a bad reader, but what she perceives in *Moll Flanders* is certainly present in Defoe's work. This is the Moll who will not allow her difficulties to plunge her into despair, who rises above her situation to become a success—a successful servant, mistress, wife, thief, whore, plantation owner,

2. George Borrow, *Works*, ed. Clement Shorter, 16 vols. (London: Constable, 1923), 3: 324.
3. For this view of fairy tales, see Bruno Bettelheim, *The Uses of Enchantment* (New York: Vintage Books, 1976), pp. 132–36. Arguments against Bettelheim's varied readings of individual tales do not generally challenge this part of his thesis. See Eugen Weber, "The Reality of Folktales," *JHI* 42 (1981): 93–113.

and mother. Whatever warnings he wanted to give to thieves, he was more intent on telling them that they could find new lives in a New World. And Defoe knew that his audience tended to find a kind of subversive heroism in the new breed of thief and pirate that emerged at the start of the eighteenth century.[4] Defoe excused many of Moll's acts on the grounds of poverty and necessity and, up to a point, gave the audience what they wanted.

I

Borrow does not tell us what edition of *Moll Flanders* it is that the old woman reads over and over again. If it was long enough to occupy Borrow for a number of hours, it was not one of the brief chapbook versions produced toward the end of the eighteenth century, but it may not have been Defoe's original work for all of that. Yet *Moll Flanders* received even briefer treatment in the ballad versions. The one that follows even deletes part of Defoe's title:

The Misfortunes of Moll Flanders

MOLL Flanders born in Newgate by man it is said.
Her tricks & fine manners I mean for to display
Seventeen times she was a lewd woman 5 times she was a wife,
And a slave to Virginia she was condemned for life.

For fam'd Shoplifting she surely bore the belle
For beauty & for artfulness none could her excell
To her own brother once was marry'd, dreadful tale to tell,
At Hounslow, and at Finchley, did often cut a swell.

The pitcher so often to the well it came home, broke at last.
Moll Flanders famous husband at length was try'd and cast,
The facts against him were so plain and awful did appear.
He at Tyburn suffer'd death for this crime as we hear.

A slave at Virginia she handled the Hoe,
Amongst West Indian Negroes she suffered many a blow,
An Eye witness to the cruelties that was inflicted there
She wish'd herself at home again upon her native shore.

But Providence that reigns above on her cast an eye,
Her mistress shewed her favour shed many a bitter sigh,

4. John Sheppard was visited in his cell by admirers from all classes. See Daniel Defoe, *The History of the Remarkable Life of John Sheppard*, in *Romances and Narratives* by Daniel Defoe, ed. George Aitken, 16 vols. (London: Dent, 1895) 16: 204–5.

Though her misfortunes they were great she proved fortunate at last
Lived honest and dy'd penitent lament her follies past.

Such an extraordinary character you never heard before.
And so you will say I know full well when this book you do read o'er,
No one would scarcely credit what she did undergo.
Be warn'd by her you young and gay & honestly pursue.[5]

Defoe obviously had nothing to do with this piece of doggerel, but it was useful to see what remains of his novel. She is still the child born in Newgate, still the great beauty as well as the great sinner, and still the success in the end. But except for her sex and the incestuous marriage to her brother, most of the events fit the life of Colonel Jack better than they do Moll's. Defoe's Moll is different. Moll's husband is not hanged, she never handles a hoe or has to labor in America, and she is not rescued from life among the slaves by her "mistress." One might well wonder if this was the ballad that inspired Hogarth's Idle Apprentice to commit his crimes.

Defoe's *Moll Flanders* has a brief but open ending in which she tells of her return to England and the penitence for her wicked life that the preface puts in doubt. Like most of the abridgments and chapbook versions, the ballad tries to give it more of an ending with a report of her death and a moral on her life. Borrow's old fruit seller focuses on Moll's return to England at the end as an indication that her son will return from Australia to live rich and happy in England, though most of the abridgments, if they do not have her die after a long and happy life in Virginia, bring her back to her husband's lands in Ireland where she is supposed to die after her husband and be buried in the same grave with him. The longest of the abridgments, *The History of Laetitia Atkins*, published in 1776 and ascribed to Defoe on the title page actually prints her will with its generous gifts to the servants and its assignment of most of her property to her husband's brother, William Carrol, along with an account of her pious death surrounded by "eminent divines."[6]

All of this suggests that *Moll Flanders* has a mythic life of its own. Like Betteredge, who consults *Robinson Crusoe* as a holy book that will provide him with all the answers to the problems of life, Borrow's fruit woman treats her copy of *Moll Flanders* as a magical text.[7] If Moll Flanders could steal, there could be nothing wrong with theft. When Borrow brings the old woman a Bible to replace *Moll Flanders*

5. (London: J. Pitts, n.d., [ca. 1810]). I quote from a copy in the New York Historical Society, Undated Ballads, "M." It was brought to my attention by Dr. Diane Dugaw.
6. Daniel Defoe, *The History of Laetitia Atkins* (London, 1776), pp. 277–78.
7. Betteredge is a character in Wilkie Collins's *The Moonstone*.

as the book by which the woman will guide her life, he replaces one magical text with another. The Bible, however, begins to function for her only after she recalls a dim commandment from her youth: "Thou shalt not steal." Only after she begins to worry about her life and values does she begin to tire of the subversive text by which she has been living.

Of course, Borrow's insistence that she has been misreading Defoe's work has its point too. She transforms Moll into a patron saint of criminals—"blessed Mary Flanders." She sees humor in it, but she is incapable of following the subtleties of Defoe's language, and she simply ignores Moll's direct moralizing on crime. In her own way, she edits as she reads and transforms Defoe's novel into her private rendition of the short, chapbook versions that provided little more than the myth of the clever and successful criminal. That is hardly what *Moll Flanders* is really about. I want to turn now to examine what an ideal reader might discover beyond the myth.

II

Behold the cruel Hand of death,
Hath snatch'd away Elizabeth.
Twelve Years she was an arant Whore;
Was sometimes rich, and sometimes poor;
Which made her, when she'd no Relief,
Be full as many Years a Thief.
In this Carier of Wickedness,
Poor Betty *always had success;*

(FROM A CHAPBOOK VERSION OF *Moll Flanders*)[8]

I leave the Readers of these things to their own just Reflections, which they will be more able to make effectual than I, who so soon forgot my self, and am therefore but a very indifferent Monitor.

DEFOE, *The Fortunes and Misfortunes of the Famous Moll Flanders.* [101]

Among the many contemporary attacks on Daniel Defoe, one of more than usual interest, entitled *The Republican Bullies* (1705), pretended to report a dialogue between Defoe (Mr. Review) and John Tutchin, author of a journal called *The Observator*. After stating that he wants no part of sword fights, Defoe explains that he is more adept at destroying his enemies with irony:

Rev. No man would dispute the Prize with you, if downright Billingsgate was the Weapon to gain by it. He's the Champion for a Modern Readers Mony, that can cut a Throat with a Feather, that

8. Daniel Defoe, *Fortune's Fickle Distribution*, in a chapbook edition of *Moll Flanders* (London: n.p., 1730), p. 91.

can wound the sacred Order by way of Expostulations and fling Dirt upon them by Dint of Irony as I have done.

Obs. The only Figure in Rhetorick that you are Master of! More thanks to Nature than Art, who has given it to you, without so much as letting you know that it is One.[9]

That his contemporaries recognized that his "peculiar Talent" lay in presenting effective arguments through the use of irony, satire, and fiction is obvious enough to anyone who has studied the numerous, grudging compliments given him by his enemies. His reputation as a poet and a pamphleteer declined only when his work for the government forced him into such dull repetition and absurd contradiction that even his amazing wit and intelligence had to fail him.

But whatever his contemporaries may have thought of him, two facts have become apparent from the recent critical debates over *Moll Flanders*: (1) that he may have been ironic in some of his pamphlets is no guarantee that he was being ironic in *Moll Flanders*; (2) that his contemporaries regarded his manner as ironic does not mean that what he did satisfied some modern critics' concepts of irony. Until some universally acceptable definition of irony can be established, critics will continue to disagree, and I have no intention in this essay to revive a discussion that has proved so inconclusive.[1] Instead, I want to examine in detail some of the complexities of language and narrative in *Moll Flanders* that have led me and some other critics to doubt that they are dealing with a fiction involving a straightforward fictional confession and imagine that Moll's was the kind of ironic narrative Defoe might have inherited from picaresque fiction directly or through the influence of the picaresque on criminal biography.[2]

Some useful information about the genesis of Defoe's novel was provided in 1968 by Gerald Howson, whose article in *TLS*, "Who Was Moll Flanders?" tells us a great deal about the criminals who formed the basis for Defoe's narrator.[3] Moll Flanders, we learn, was imaginatively constructed from several women criminals of the time, particularly two known by the names Moll King and Callico Sarah. Since Defoe was visiting his friend, the publisher Mist, in Newgate

9. *The Republican Bullies*, p. 6.
1. For my case for Defoe's irony, see "Conscious Irony in Moll Flanders," *College English* 26 (1964): 198–204.
2. Most picaresque fiction was, in its very nature, a secular version of spiritual autobiography, and the picaresque was the mode to which Defoe was most directly indebted. For my objections to approaching *Moll Flanders* through spiritual autobiography, see my reviews of G. A. Starr's books, *Defoe and Spiritual Autobiography* (Princeton: Princeton UP, 1965), in *JEGP* 66 (1967): 153–155, and *Defoe and Casuistry* (Princeton: Princeton UP, 1971), in *Modern Language Quarterly* 33 (1972): 456–59. For the ingenious interpretation that Moll *thinks* she is writing a spiritual biography while actually writing a picaresque novel, see Richard Bjornson, *The Picaresque Hero* (Madison: U of Wisconsin P; 1977), pp. 193–96.
3. Gerald Howson, "Who Was Moll Flanders?," *TLS* (18 January 1968): 63–64.

at the same time these two ladies were there, he would have had numerous opportunities to converse with them. Moll King managed to survive from five to eight sentences of transportation without being hanged, and if some critics have discovered in Moll Flanders' life a mythic, symbolic sense of human endurance, they might well feel justified.

Defoe may even have taken his heroine's name from an indirect combination of the names of these two women, since *Flanders* was the name for a Flemish lace, a contraband article figuring in one of Moll Flanders' thefts. Howson allows that the contemporary advertisement for *The History of Flanders with Moll's Map*, a reference to the work of the cartographer Herman Moll, may have given Defoe his initial idea, but he advances his suggestion concerning the relation between callico and lace as being more relevant, and I agree. Now the genesis of Defoe's title may seem completely unimportant, but I want to argue that this suggestive use of language is one of the most important elements in *Moll Flanders* and a key to its complexity.

Though Defoe's lapses from consistency have often caused his artistic integrity to be called into question, he was a writer deeply concerned with language and the meaning of words—the way an understanding of subtle shifts in meaning distinguishes the good writer from the bad. Let us suppose for the moment that Defoe set out to present a character who passes over certain points of her life with evasive remarks and comes close to lying about others. How would it be possible to handle the language of narrative in such a way that something resembling a true view of the events would be apparent to the reader? Wayne Booth has pointed out the difficulties with proving ironic intent in a novel written in the first person, and Defoe was not above solving this problem in pamphlets employing a persona by ending them with a direct confession of what he called "Irony."[4] But realistic fiction would prevent a device of this kind. What Defoe needed was a method of making meaning transparent without sacrificing the integrity of his point of view.

One way out was through a complex use of language and what Defoe called "Inuendo," by which he meant all indirect methods of communication from irony to meiosis. If we turn to the point in Defoe's novel when Moll has been abandoned by the lover she picked up at Bath, some of the complications involved will be clear. After receiving a note from him cutting off the affair, Moll writes a letter telling him that she would never be able to recover from the blow of parting from him, that she not only approved of his repentance but

4. See Wayne Booth, *The Rhetoric of Fiction* (Chicago: U of Chicago P, 1961), pp. 320–23. The best example of Defoe's sudden abandonment of an ironic posture at the very end of a work is *King William's Affection to the Church of England Examin'd* (London, 1703), p. 25.

wished "to Repent as sincerely as he had done" (p. 100). All she needs is fifty pounds to return to Virginia. Moll confesses at once that what she said "was indeed all a Cheat," and that "the business was to get this last Fifty Pounds of him," but she does moralize on the situation:

> And here I cannot but reflect upon the unhappy Consequence of too great Freedoms between Persons started as we were, upon the pretence of innocent intentions, Love of Friendship, *and the like*; for the Flesh has generally so great a share in those Friendships, that it is great odds but inclination prevails at last over the most solemn Resolutions and that Vice breaks in at the breaches of Decency, which really innocent Friendship ought to preserve with the greatest strictness; but I leave the Readers of these things to their own just Reflections, which they will be more able to make effectual than I, who so soon forgot my self, and am therefore but a very indifferent Monitor. [p. 101]

Moll's willingness to confess that any admonitions coming from her about manners and morals might well be regarded sceptically should put the reader on guard at once. Would we want to hear morality preached by Moll King or Callico Sarah? And after all, Moll has just testified to her dishonesty. Surely at this point simple solutions (e.g., it is Defoe with his somewhat questionable puritan moral standards speaking) will not work.

There are also disturbing stylistic elements in the passage that might prevent the reader from regarding it as a straightforward confession. Take the phrase, "Love of Friendship, *and the like*." One might also think that Moll was being witty, that "*and the like*" was intended to imply by ironic understatement all the possible kinds of discourses leading ultimately to seduction. Although Professor Watt has warned us against reading into Defoe what is not there, this is an important element in Moll's narrative.[5] She is always qualifying words in order to clarify the distinction between the apparent meaning of a word and the reality behind it. The brother she lived with in incest is "my Brother, *as I now call him*," (p. 101), the first woman who takes care of her is "my Mistress Nurse, *as I call'd her*," (p. 14), the trunk she steals from a Dutchman is "my Trunk, *as I call'd it*" (p. 209). Whether or not Defoe actually added the italics to these phrases (as he did occasionally in the one extensive manuscript of his that we have),[6] they were obviously intended to suggest the dis-

5. See Ian Watt, "The Recent Critical Fortunes of *Moll Flanders*," ECS 1 (1967): 109–26.
6. That containing *The Compleat English Gentleman* and *Of Royall Educacion*, British Library Additional MSS 32, 555.

parity between what something is called and what it is, and to call attention to the narrator's own awareness of this.[7]

Similar to these kinds of phrases is her simple remark, "I WAV'D the Discourse" when her Bank Manager sums up the character of his wife with the remark, "she that will be *a Whore* will be a *Whore*," or her summation of her reaction to the entire tale of this sad cuckold, "Well, I pitied him, and wish'd him well rid of her, and still would have talk'd of my Business" (p. 108). The tone of impatience (the Bank Manager is married and therefore unavailable at this point) is clear enough. Defoe *is* conveying a great deal, then, through tone and language.

In fact Moll is extraordinarily playful in her use of language. When she tries to avoid joining a gang of counterfeiters, she remarks, "tho' I had declin'd it with the greatest assurances of Secresy in the World, they would have gone near to have murther'd me to make sure Work, and make themselves easy, *as they call it*; what kind of easiness that is, they may best Judge that understand how easy Men are, that can murther People to prevent Danger" (pp. 200–1). And the section in which she enters the home for unwed mothers is full of such implications. After the Governess has assured her that she need not worry about the care of her child if she puts it out to a nurse recommended by the house and that she must behave as "other conscientious Mothers," (p. 139) Moll, who is careful to separate herself from "all those Women who consent to the disposing their Children out of the way, *as it is call'd*" (p. 137), comments on her Governess's language: "I understood what she meant by conscientious Mothers, she would have said conscientious Whores; but she was not willing to disoblige me" (p. 139). Moll tells herself that, at least technically, she was married, but then merely contents herself with distinguishing herself from other prostitutes ("the Profession") by her still tender heart. Even the affectionate use of the term *Mother* for her Governess is suspect. Though she might have a right to that title by her affectionate treatment of Moll, or by being Moll's "Mother Midnight" (p. 128), that is, her midwife, the name was usually given to the madam of a brothel. In fact their dialogues resemble nothing so much as those between Mother Cresswell and Dorothea, bawd and neophyte, in *The Whore's Rhetorick* (1683). They, too, refer to each other as mother and daughter, and Moll's Mother-Governess is not above being a bawd as well as an abortionist and a fence.

Perhaps the way in which Moll describes the suggestion of an

7. The tendency of a narrator to suggest moral positions in brief and often oversimplified phrases is part of the tradition of the picaresque from Alemán to Céline. Because I had previously approached Defoe's fiction more from the standpoint of content than technique, like Professor Ian Watt, I sometimes underestimated the very strong influence of picaresque fiction on Defoe's style.

abortion and her rejection of it gives the best clues to the complex use of language in Defoe's novel:

> The only thing I found in all her Conversation on these Subjects, that gave me any distaste, was, that one time in Discoursing about my being so far gone with Child, and the time I expected to come, she said something that look'd as if she could help me off with my Burthen sooner, if I was willing; or in *English*, that she could give me something to make me Miscarry, if I had a desire to put an end to my Troubles that way; but I soon let her see that I abhorr'd the Thoughts of it; and to do her Justice, she put it off so cleverly, that I could not say she really intended it, or whether she only mentioned the practice as a horrible thing; for she couch'd her words so well, and took my meaning so quickly, that she gave her Negative before I could explain myself [p. 133].

Moll used the same pun a few pages before (p. 127); if the reader failed to catch it the first time, he might be at least as clever as Moll's Governess and pick it up the second time around. One can assume, then, that, at times, Moll converses in double-entendres and expects her listeners and readers to understand them.[8]

Such word play is not uncommon in Defoe's narrative. As I have indicated elsewhere,[9] Moll points to her misunderstanding of the use of the word *Miss* by the wife of the mayor who comes to visit her when she is a child in Colchester: "The Word Miss was a Language that had hardly been heard of in our School, and I wondered what sad Name it was she call'd me" (p. 14). It is a sad word because it says something about her future quest after gentility and her future life as a prostitute. In much the same way, thinking of the friend who has passed her off as a woman of fortune, Moll tells of how she decides to take a trip to Bath. "I took the Diversion of going to the *Bath*," she remarks, "for as I was still far from being old, so my Humour, which was always Gay, continu'd so to an *Extream*; and being now, *as it were*, a Woman of Fortune, tho' I was a Woman without a Fortune, I expected something, or other might happen in my way, that might mend my Circumstances, as had been my Case before" (pp. 85–86). Another instance of this type of word play comes in the section on the counterfeiters. Speaking of her refusal to join the gang, Moll remarks that

> the part they would have had me have embark'd in, was the most dangerous Part; I mean that of the very working the Dye, as they

8. A more obvious example of this type of dialogue through hints and suggestions may be found in the courtship scene with her Brother-Husband.
9. See my "Moll Flanders' First Love," *Papers of the Michigan Academy of Science, Arts, and Letters* 46 (1961): 635–43.

> call it, which had I been taken, had been certain Death, and that at a Stake, *I say*, to be burnt to Death at a Stake; so that tho' I was to Appearance, but a Beggar; and they promis'd Mountains of Gold and Silver to me, to engage; yet it would not do; it is True, if I had been really a Beggar, or had been desperate as when I began, I might perhaps have clos'd with it, for what care they to Die, that can't tell how to Live? [p. 200]

The phrase, "working the Dye," which James Sutherland calls a "grim pun" in his edition of *Moll Flanders*, meant to stamp the coin.[1] A terrible death awaits those who would gamble or stake their lives on such an occupation, and in the midst of her punning, Moll is careful to remark that "they" use the term "working the Dye," not she. This is her way of separating herself from such awful people.

It is passages like these that lead the reader to suspect other double meanings. When Moll is made pregnant by her Bath Lover, he assumes the name of Sir Walter Cleave, and Moll says that she was made as comfortable as she would have been had she "really been my Lady *Cleave*" (p. 94). In addition to whatever sexual significance might be attached to this word by a wary reader, a "cleave" is defined as "a forward or wanton woman" in Francis Grose's *A Classical Dictionary of the Vulgar Tongue*. And significantly enough, in the rather pious chapbook versions of Moll Flanders, the name was changed to Clare.[2]

At other times the issue is doubtful. Is Moll aware of any sexual significance in a phrase like that already quoted in Moll's reflections on her Bath Lover, that "Vice breaks in at the breaches of Decency" (p. 000)? If we regard Moll as being, at least in part, a comic figure, we would have to say that Defoe makes her use this phrase with some ambiguity. Is she supposed to understand certain implications in such language? Did Defoe? Having no definite solution, I will follow Moll and waive the discourse. But of Defoe's use of puns and word play as a method to convey subtle meanings playing underneath Moll's narrative there cannot be the slightest doubt.

III

If some passages raise doubts in the reader's mind, there is good reason for it: Moll, herself, is often undecided or uncertain about the way she should interpret the events of her life, and her language often reflects these doubts. She begins the story of her Bath lover's control over his sexual desires with a remark that reveals her unde-

1. Daniel Defoe, *Moll Flanders*, ed. James Sutherland (Boston: Houghton Mifflin, 1959), p. 222.
2. See *The Fortunes and Misfortunes of Moll Flanders* (Birmingham: Joseph Russell, n.d.), p. 3. Some use *Clare* as a partial disguise of Defoe's original meaning, and others omit the name entirely.

cided state. He has spent the night in bed with her entirely naked and without offering any advances that might be regarded as completely sexual in nature. Moll comments, "I OWN it was a noble Principle, but as it was what I never understood before, so it was to me perfectly amazing" (p. 93). Even if one understands by "noble Principle" something that cannot work in practice, we cannot come to such a decision until Moll's final condemnation of the entire relationship several pages later.

Such passages are complex not so much because of the language alone but because Defoe asks us to suspend our judgment on the meaning of certain words and phrases until the events themselves or Moll's last commentary clarifies the situation. Many of Moll's comments on her Governess are rich in this kind of momentary ambiguity. When the woman chosen by the Governess to tutor Moll in the art of thievery has been taken and sentenced to death, the emotions of the Governess have to be ambiguous, since the tutoress has enough information to save her own life by impeaching the Governess. Moll King saved her life several times in this manner. Moll Flanders does not render such a mixture of regret for the loss of a friend and apprehension for personal safety in anything resembling straight description:

> It is true, that when she was gone, and had not open'd her Mouth to tell what she knew; my Governess was easy as to that Point, and perhaps glad she was hang'd; for it was in her power to have obtain'd a Pardon at the Expence of her Friends; But on the other Hand, the loss of her, and the Sense of her Kindness, in not making her Market of what she knew, mov'd my Governess to Mourn very sincerely for her: I comforted her as well as I cou'd, and she in return harden'd me to Merit more compleatly the same Fate [p. 164].

Moll's bitterness is apparent enough, but the language is sometimes pointed, sometimes neutral in a situation that is inherently ambiguous. The Governess, whose life has been spared at this point and later threatened in the same way by Moll's capture, is sincere in her sorrow, but she does not undergo any change of heart. And Moll may be speaking of one point in the past, but she has her mind set on another point—her future sufferings in Newgate.

I will speak more fully of the problems of time in Moll's narrative later in this essay, but it should be noted here that in passages such as these, Moll's narrative may be viewed ironically (by anyone's definition) on the present level of the told narrative, while functioning realistically as a record of the action as it is occurring. Many of the contradictions that appear in the novel are caused by the simple fact that even criminals and fences have to have a morality to live by.

Polls among jail inmates revealing strong moral disapproval of crime are commonplace. As we shall see, such moral judgments need not indicate a permanent change of heart.

When Moll commits her "second Sally into the World" (p. 153), she tells of her experience in a manner that is even more demanding of complex understanding. Having led the little girl out of her way, Moll is confronted by the child's protests. She quiets these objections with the sinister remark, "I'll show you the way home" (p. 153). This piece of direct dialogue is given in a narrative scene to underscore its ironic implication—the possibility that to quiet the child while she was stealing the necklace she might have to murder her. After describing her horror at the impulse to murder, Moll tells of her psychological state after this robbery. "The last Affair," she says, "left no great Concern upon me" (p. 153), explaining that after all she did not harm the child and may have helped improve the care that the parents of the child would show in the future. And after estimating the value of the string of beads, Moll begins to extrapolate about the entire incident. The girl was wearing the necklace because the mother was proud; the child was being neglected by the mother, who had put her in the care of a maid; the maid was doubtless negligent and meeting her lover. And while all these palliations for her crime are being offered—and they sound peculiarly like crimes Moll might have been guilty of at other stages of her career—the "pretty little Child" has gradually become the "poor Child," "poor Lamb," and "poor Baby." In blaming everyone else but herself, Moll is revealing that her psychological involvement is far greater than she is willing to admit, and the energy that she exerts to deny her involvement is undercut verbally by the increasing sympathy she tries to arouse for the child.

As for blaming such moralizing on Defoe's simplemindedness, it should be pointed out that a later incident shows a similar unwillingness to accept guilt mingled with a more obvious callousness toward crime. When Moll seduces a Gentleman in a coach, she moralizes on the possibility that the man might have been seduced by a diseased prostitute. Her moralizing, it should be noted, is a blend of past and present reactions:

> As for me, my Business was his Money, and what I could make of him, and after that if I could have found out any way to have done it, I would have sent him safe home to his House, and to his Family, for 'twas ten to one but he had an honest virtuous Wife, and innocent Children, that were anxious for his Safety, and would have been glad to have gotten him Home, and have taken care of him, till he was restor'd to himself; and then with what Shame and Regret would he look back upon himself? how would he reproach himself with associating him-

> self with a Whore? pick'd up in the worst of all Holes, the Cloister, among the Dirt and Filth of the Town? how would he be trembling for fear he had got the Pox, for fear a Dart had struck through his Liver, and hate himself every time he look'd back upon the Madness and Brutality of his Debauch? how would he, if he had any Principles of Honour, as I verily believe he had, I say how would he abhor the Thought of giving any ill Distemper, if he had it, as for ought he knew he might, to his Modest and Virtuous Wife, and thereby sowing the Contagion in the Life-Blood of his Posterity? [p. 179]

What is curious about this is that Moll is substantially creating a fiction as she goes along in much the same manner as she did with the child she robbed. The fiction about the gentleman led astray by the prostitute is highly moral and has little or none of the word play that, as I have shown, is a customary part of Moll's narrative manner. But it is a fiction for all that, a story woven to cheer herself up in the past and present, and the more graphic it is, the more real it is for her.

And then Moll does something that we ought to expect. She betrays herself by telling a somewhat off-color story of how, by replacing his purse with one filled with tokens during sexual intercourse, a prostitute once managed to pick the pocket of a customer, even though he was on his guard. Doubtless she tells the sad story of the gentleman who might have picked up a diseased prostitute to her Governess in as moving terms as she tells it to the reader, for she described how that good lady "was hardly able to forbear Tears, to think how such a Gentleman run a daily Risque of being undone, every Time a Glass of Wine got into his Head." But the Governess is entirely pleased by the booty Moll has brought her from the gentleman, and after assuring Moll that the incident might "do more to reform him, than all the Sermons that ever he will hear in his life" (p. 180), she proceeds to arrange a liaison between Moll and the gentleman. It is impossible to think that Defoe was napping here. Moll and her Governess possess a great deal of morality, but they are criminals nevertheless, and Defoe never lets us forget it. Moll remains throughout the novel an "indifferent Monitor."

IV

During this discussion of the complexities of language and style in *Moll Flanders*, I have touched on the intricate temporal relationships in individual passages; now I want to turn to the larger issue of time in Defoe's narrative as a further example of Defoe's considerable skill. Most modern discussions of narrative technique in *Moll Flanders* begin with a version of the concept of the "double focus" suggested by Mendilow in his *Time and the Novel*. Mendilow suggested that both *Moll Flanders* and *Roxana* belonged to that type of novel in which, because the narrator is speaking of her youth, "one often senses the gap between the action and its record." Mendilow then remarked that "two characters are superimposed one upon the other, and the impression of the one who acts is coloured and distorted by the interpretations of the one who narrates," and that the "diaries" of Moll and Roxana as they would have been written in their youth would have been far different from these retrospective narratives. Some critics have disagreed with Mendilow's conclusions, but that is probably because they failed to remark that he adds later on that novels often "contain different degrees of pastness."[3]

Certainly *Moll Flanders* is extraordinarily varied in treating levels of time, and a good example of the way we experience Moll's movement between such levels may be seen in the passages preceding the death of her Bank Manager husband. The basic technique is that of summary, but as she carries us breathlessly through the five years of happiness she had with him, she also supplies us with a vivid picture of her psychological state:

> I LIV'D with this Husband in the utmost Tranquility; he was a Quiet, Sensible, Sober Man, Virtuous, Modest, Sincere, and in his Business Diligent and Just: His Business was in a narrow Compass, and his Income sufficient to a plentiful way of Living in the ordinary way; I do not say to keep an Equipage, and make a Figure as the World calls it, nor did I expect it, or desire it; for as I abhorr'd the Levity and Extravagance of my former Life, so I chose now to live retir'd, frugal, and within our selves; I kept no Company, made no Visits; minded my Family, and oblig'd my Husband; and this kind of Life became a Pleasure to me [p. 149].

Such a passage is intended to show Moll's temporary conversion to the ideals of a middle-class marriage. But it also dips vividly into past experience. Unlike Moll's first lover, who carried her off in the coach of Sir W——H——, her Gentleman Tradesman husband, who insisted in travelling in a *"Coach and Six,"* and her Lancashire Husband, Jemmy, who calls for her with his "Chariot . . . , with two Footmen in a good Livery" (p. 113), this husband offers her only the kind of comfort that she had always rejected. In this marriage she has rejected the "World" of fashion, which had been her envy from child-

3. A. A. Mendilow, *Time and the Novel* (New York: Humanities P, 1965; reprint of 1952 ed.), pp. 91–94. For a reading of Moll Flanders in terms of the split time perspective, see Everett Zimmerman, *Defoe and the Novel* (Berkeley: U of California P, 1975), pp. 75–106; and for a somewhat differnt focus on time in this novel, see Paul Alkon, *Defoe and Fictional Time* (Athens: U of Georgia P, 1979), pp. 110–32.

hood, to find pleasure in what was Defoe's ideal—the private life of a contented family.[4]

Defoe had stated such an ideal before, but nowhere so thoroughly as in his *Condoling Letter to the Tatler* (1710), in which he portrayed human happiness as a means illustrated by a thermometer of the human condition:

Madness,
Poverty,
Extravagance,
Excess or Profusion,
Waste,
Generous Liberality,
Plenty
FAMILY
Frugality,
Parsimony,
Niggardliness,
Covetousness,
Sordidly Covetous,
Wretchedness or Rich Poverty
Madness

> Here is the Word FAMILY in the Centre, which signifies the Man, let his Circumstances be what it will, for every Man is a Family to himself. He is plac'd between *Plenty* and *Frugality*; a Blessed, Happy Medium, which makes Men beloved of all, respected of the Rich, blessed by the Poor, useful to themselves, to their Country, and to their Posterity.[5]

In Defoe's thermometer of well-being, madness through wealth or poverty stands at both the bottom and the top. Moll has truly achieved a state that she comes to recognize as ideal, even if it is not what she would want if she had her choice. She is soon close to a state of desperate poverty.

Those who have seen this as the psychological and structural middle of the novel can find justification both in Moll's moral career from this point on and in the narrative. For after this summary of her present condition, which is in itself so full of echoes of the past, Moll tells of her husband's bankruptcy in terms that move forward from the way the event "turn'd . . . [her] out into the World in a Condition the reverse of all that had been before it" (p. 149), goes

4. I agree with Everett Zimmerman's suggestion that "this man satisfies her only because she has deliberately restricted her feelings" (*Defoe and the Novel*, p. 87).
5. Daniel Defoe, *Condoling Letter to the Tatler* (London, 1710), pp. 13–14. For a numerological treatment of this passage, see Douglas Brooks, *Number and Pattern in the Eighteenth-Century Novel* (London: Routledge and Kegan Paul, 1973), pp. 47–48.

back in time to narrate the cause of his troubles, and tells the reader the advice she gave him. One paragraph tells of his death in a manner that skillfully reverses the event and her forebodings: "It was in vain to speak comfortably to him, the Wound had sunk too deep, it was a Stab that touch'd the Vitals, he grew Melancholy and from thence Lethargick, and died; I foresaw the Blow, and was extremely oppress'd in my Mind, for I saw evidently that if he died I was undone" (p. 149). One of the remarkable things about Defoe's style in such passages is the way he can be both concise and repetitious at the same time, a technique that Lévi-Strauss has found to be the essential narrative quality of myth.[6] Thus, when she recognizes her Lancashire Husband riding into the Inn where she is staying with her new husband, the Bank Manager, she says, "I knew his Cloaths, I knew his Horse, and I knew his Face" (p. 146). Nothing could be more dramatic and, without dwelling on her psychological state, tell us how she feels by what appears to be an external description. A similar process is at work in her account of the death of the Bank Manager. Moll is not merely telling the reader about the progress of his disease, she is explaining how she watched his decline with terror.

Much of this may be viewed as a question of style, but the important point is that Defoe was continually manipulating style to achieve narrative effects. He even changes tenses or makes use of contemporary grammatical forms that could stand for either present or past to attain a sense of immediacy in scenes of action. When a fire breaks out in the neighborhood of her Governess, Moll rushes to the scene to pick up what booty she can find:

> Away I went, and coming to the House I found them all in Confusion, you may be sure; I run in, and finding one of the Maids, Lord! Sweetheart, *said I*, how came this dismal Accident? Where is your Mistress? And how does she do? Is she safe? And where are the Children? I come from Madam——— to help you; away runs the Maid, Madam, madam, *says she*, screaming as loud as she cou'd yell, *here is a Gentlewoman come from Madam———to help us*: The poor Woman half out of her Wits, with a Bundle under her Arm, and two little Children, comes towards me, *Lord Madam*, says I, let me carry the poor Children to Madam———, she desires you to send them; she'll take care of the poor Lambs, and immediately I takes one of them out of her Hand, and she lifts the other up into my arms; *ay, do for God sake*, says she . . . and away she runs from out of her Wits, and the Maids after her, and away comes I with the two Children and the Bundle [pp. 161–62].

6. See Claude Lévi-Strauss, *Structural Anthropology*, trans. Claire Jacobson and Brooke Schoepf (New York: Doubleday, 1967), pp. 209–27.

Some curiosities in Defoe's grammar have led older critics to comment on his homely style, but here Defoe is taking advantage either of what would be Moll's ungrammatical manner or simply sacrificing grammar to achieve a sense of hurry and excitement. Both seem to be present in the "away she runs . . . and away comes I" section so typical of Moll in her lighter moments.

In such a passage, of course, the use of dialogue is equally important for giving the feeling of action recreated in the present. If Defoe did not succeed in getting the kind of immediacy achieved by Richardson's technique of "writing to the present," he nevertheless attempted various methods of attaining a similar effect when he needed it. *Moll Flanders* differs from Defoe's two historical novels, *Memoirs of a Cavalier* and *A Journal of the Plague Year*. * * * [B]oth of these function in a specific historical time, although that time is made so dramatically cogent for the present as to make it serve a purpose similar to that of fulfilled vision or prophecy. And *Moll Flanders* is also different from *Roxana*, which * * * completely distorts historical time. Yet the seeming error in having Roxana's career function in both the era of the Restoration and the eighteenth century is certainly understandable, for Defoe wanted to contrast the dissolute court of Charles II with the luxury of his own time. If his transition from one period to the other would have to be achieved by a process that is opposed to any concept of realistic chronology, it was, nevertheless, an experiment that might have been worth trying.[7]

Mendilow's formula, then, is good as far as it goes, but Defoe's world is always synchronic rather than diachronic. The past is imported into the present as a psychologically recreatable state. Hence Moll's reactions are indeed confused and ambiguous. Crusoe does not have the same difficulty separating his past from his present, and Roxana may vary between irony and passion in commenting on her past, but she is seldom without some kind of commentary. Moll's reaction to her past is somewhat reminiscent of the first person narrative of a shaman among the Kwakiutls that Franz Boas recorded. The Narrator, QāsElīd, begins as a skeptic. "Then it occurred to me," he states, "that I was the principal one who does not believe in all the ways of the shamans, for I had said so aloud to them. Now I had an opportunity by what they said that I should really learn whether they were real or whether they only pretended to be shamans."[8] Eventually, after becoming a shaman himself, he

7. For a further discussion of this point, see Chapter 5 of Novak, *Realism, Myth, and History in Defoe's Fiction*.

8. Franz Boas, *The Religion of the Kwakiutl Indians*, Columbia University Contributions to Anthropology, vol. 10 (New York: Columbia University P, 1930), pt. 2, p. 5. Lévi-Strauss uses this story to illustrate the complex psychology of the shaman—his ability to believe even when he knows that much of his "fabulations of a reality" is "just a lie." See *Structural Anthropology*, p. 173.

finds that the cures he works are superior to those of other shamans and comes to believe that somehow he does have curative powers. The narrative reveals a development, yet were he to begin again, he would unquestionably start with his initial scepticism and the lying and fakery among shamans. Like QāsElīd, Moll responds dynamically and ambiguously to her own narrative, reliving her past life for the reader as she recreates it for herself in the present.

This is why her conversion to Christianity, which most students find questionable, is without much of the wit and complexity to be found in most sections of the novel. If we find that her life after conversion is not what we would expect of a good Christian, we share a feeling that the "editor" informs us may have considerable basis in fact. Perhaps Moll's concern and the reader's are too strong at these moments to allow for a definition of *Moll Flanders* as an ironic novel. Certainly it does not deserve such a name if that genre is to be limited to works like Fielding's *Jonathan Wild* or Ford's *The Good Soldier*. But Defoe has Moll relive her life, responding to the emotions of the moment as they reflect her previous emotions and experiences. And if she can be both the ideal convert and the wayward servant-whore-thief at the same time, she shares with the Kwakiutl shaman the natural ability to exist in a number of states simultaneously.

My comparison of QāsElīd and Moll might lead one to the conclusion that the actual thrust of Defoe's fiction was toward a simple mirroring of reality and real personality, though, as I have tried to demonstrate throughout, fictional reality is never simple. In fact, such an argument has been advanced by Ralph Rader, who discusses Moll and her narrative as a story of the "pseudofactual type," one in which Defoe, as author, has disappeared to the extent that any judgment about the moral meaning of the work must remain ambiguous, because we accept Moll as a real person and her narrative as the product of her own pen. Since great fiction, by Rader's definition, must announce itself as artifact, *Moll Flanders* is the last of a tradition of "true stories" rather than the forerunner of the novel.[9]

Such a view represents a misunderstanding of Defoe's art as well as of the tradition of literary history which, until the last half of the nineteenth century, always accorded picaresque fiction a secure, if low, position. It also constitutes a misunderstanding of the nature of Defoe's realism. His fictional rhetoric in *Moll Flanders* includes a central character who assumes not merely the particularity of an individual character but also the generality that makes for the prototype of the eternal female. Her endurance in chapbook form, her

9. "Defoe, Richardson, Joyce, and the Concept of Form in the Novel," in *Autobiography, Biography and the Novel*, by William Matthews and Ralph Rader (Los Angeles: William Andrews Clark Memorial Library, 1973), pp. 45–47.

echo in James Joyce's Molly Bloom and Joyce Cary's Sara Monday of *Herself Surprised* is evidence of this. Moll's language conveys its meanings to the reader through the complexity of word play, innuendo, and ironic asides. And her contradictions, her presentation of various moral views of her actions in a manner that G. S. Starr has properly called "casuistry,"[1] provides a clearer view of the ethical significance of her actions and the ways they are to be judged by the reader than may be found in all but the most didactic novels.

V

I want to conclude this essay by examining a passage that draws together some of the main ideas I have been discussing. Moll, whose tendency to work alone and whose cautious approach to her "Trade" has enabled her to survive and prosper as the greatest "Artist" of her time, tells how she almost went into a partnership that would have proven disastrous:

> I began to think that I must give over the Trade in Earnest; but my Governess, who was not willing to lose me, and expected great Things of me, brought me one Day into Company with a young Woman and a Fellow that went for her Husband, tho' as it appear'd afterwards she was not his Wife, but they were Partners it seems in the Trade they carried on; and Partners in something else too. *In short*, they robb'd together, lay together, were taken together, and at last were hang'd together.
>
> I Came into a kind of League with these two, by the help of my Governess, and they carried me out into three or four Adventures, where I rather saw them commit some Coarse and unhandy Robberies, in which nothing but a great Stock of impudence on their Side, and gross Negligence on the Peoples Side who were robb'd, could have made them Successful; so I resolv'd from that time forward to be very Cautious how I Adventur'd upon any thing with them; and indeed when two or three unlucky Projects were propos'd by them, I declin'd the offer, and perswaded them against it: One time they particularly propos'd Robbing a Watchmaker of 3 Gold Watches, which they had Ey'd in the Day time, and found the Place where he laid them; one of them had so many Keys of all kinds, that he made

1. G. A. Starr, *Defoe and Casuistry* (Princeton: Princeton UP, 1971). Starr's able demonstration that the ethical arguments in Defoe's fiction could be linked to the interest in the application of various approaches to moral problems as it was fostered by Samuel Annesley during the Restoration has a number of implications for the study of Defoe's writings, not the least of which is to point up the relative sophistication of Defoe's background in dealing with speculative matters in ethics. My only major objection to Starr's treatment of casuistry is his implication that it involved a particular ideology rather than a method.

> no Question to open the Place, where the Watchmaker had laid them; and so we made a kind of an Appointment; but when I came to look narrowly into the Thing, I found they propos'd breaking open the house; and this as a thing out of my Way, I would not Embark in; so they went without me: They did get into the House by main Force, and broke up the lock'd Place where the Watches were, but found but one of the Gold Watches, and a Silver one, which they took, and got out of the House again very clear, but the Family being alarm'd cried out Thieves, and the Man was pursued and taken, the young Woman had got off too, but unhappily was stop'd at a Distance, and the Watches found upon her; and thus I had a second Escape, for they were convicted, and both hang'd, being old Offenders, tho' but young People; as *I said before*, that they robbed together, and lay together, so now they hang'd together, and there ended my new Partnership [pp. 164–65].

Such a passage would have amused Borrow's old fruit seller. She would have observed the mythic Moll Flanders in the clever thief who is contemptuous of her potential partners' incompetence as well as of the "gross Negligence on the Peoples Side who were robbed." Moll, who usually makes a distinction between herself and those whom she regards as common thieves, demonstrates her superior understanding of her profession and, at least temporarily, emerges superior to the demands of her social environment. She herself seems to be uncertain whether to pity the young couple or to be scornful about their entire way of life. She identifies more with the "Wife," whose capture she views as unfortunate, but on the whole she rises above the situation of her potential "Partnership." That her Governess, still expecting "great Things" of Moll, urged her to join with them suggests that uneasiness in their relationship that gives a certain edge to the genuine affection they feel for each other.

On a somewhat more complex level, the passage moves to a more general type of judgment. With this couple, partnership in crime is also a sexual partnership. Moll's Jemmy never suggests that she join him in such a life. When he has to return to being a highwayman, he parts from Moll affectionately and leaves her behind. But these "Partners" share in everything, including the violent crime of "breaking open the House." It was this kind of crime that brought so much disapprobation on John Sheppard a few years later, for if the locks on a house were to be broken with such ease, who could be safe? The folly of the crime is a reflection of the levity of the couple, and if sad, their punishment is hardly surprising. And given Defoe's continuous metaphor of crime as a form of trade or business, this self-contained little narrative has larger significance as an illustration of all foolish partnerships in mad "Projects."

In speaking of the couple, Moll selects her words carefully, as if she wonders how much she should tell and how to tell it. Just as the "young Woman and a Fellow" do not add up to husband and wife but rather to "Partners," so they are not actually skilled thieves, and the vague partnership in unreal matters ends in their real hanging. Sensing their insubstantiality, Moll is tentative. For all the "help" of her Governess in this arrangement, she only agrees to a "kind of League," and she does not so much join with them in their crimes as allow herself to be "carried" into what she aptly calls "Adventures." The crime that leads to their capture is real in its circumstantial enumeration of the "3 Gold Watches," but the danger is so obvious that Moll merely arranges "a kind of an Appointment." She reports the failure of the scheme with some satisfaction and returns to her clever line on the relationship of the couple in sex, robbery, and hanging. Her final statement on the end of her "Partnership" has to be read as ironic, since she was never truly in anything resembling a relationship of mutual cooperation and trust. And the finality of her last statement has some of the quality of her farewell to the Colchester family with whom she left her children: "and that by the way was all they got by Mrs. Betty" (p. 49). Unfortunately for Moll, she is unable to say good-bye to her Governess so effectively.

How many writers can lay claim to greater skill in narrative? Defoe carries his plot forward in time, develops Moll's character in her environment, gives us a vivid sense of the kinds of robberies that were occurring at the time, teaches the reader to worry about house-breaking while warning thieves and businessmen against foolish adventures and especially foolish partnerships. And all of this is accomplished while Defoe is both amusing us and giving us a slight chill of horror at the dismal end of the couple. Critics may talk of Defoe's "unconscious artistry," but of what use such a term may be in speaking of a combination of genius and a lifetime of experience in writing is difficult to comprehend.

HENRY KNIGHT MILLER

Some Reflections on Defoe's *Moll Flanders* and the Romance Tradition†

* * *

1

To speak of Defoe and the romance tradition may seem at first a bit odd; for Defoe, like most Puritans and Dissenters, had seldom a good word to say for "meer Romances." The general attitude of his age, in fact, toward such prose fiction was that which spawned the adjective "romantick," meaning extravagant, fantastical, and chimerical. The old chivalric romances had long since been reduced to penny chapbooks and were likely to be thought of as reading for boys or for the cits of the middling ranks, like Defoe himself; and the female-oriented, aristocratic French romances of the seventeenth century had become (if the playwrights and essayists are correct) matter for serving maids and overimaginative young girls. So that the term *romance* was scarcely in good critical odor. But if it had such specific associations, *romance* was also, along with *history*, the most often used generic term for long prose fiction as a literary form. Thus, the Brother in *A New Family Instructor* (1727) argues with his sister about "the Reading or not Reading Romances, or fictitious Stories" (and goes on to contrast "a Fiction, or what they call'd a Romance" with a true history).[1] The terms *history* and *romance* overlap in actual use, of course; and I take *romance* as inclusive of histories and tales of any length, for I am less interested here in seeking to make generic distinctions that perhaps cannot be made than I am in the assumptions that lay behind most long prose fiction of Defoe's era and of earlier periods. And also in the challenges to those assumptions that came to a focus in the eighteenth century. The romance tradition in the Christian world had for centuries reflected the ideals of a feudal and then a merely aristocratic hierarchy; but its Christian vision long continued to shape modes of prose fiction even as the social and political hierarchies crumbled.

† From "Some Reflections on Defoe's *Moll Flanders* and the Romance Tradition," *Greene Centennial Studies*, ed. Paul J. Korshin and Robert R. Allen (Charlottesville: U of Virginia P, 1984), pp. 72–92. Reprinted with permission of the University of Virginia Press. Page numbers in parentheses refer to this Norton Critical Edition. Notes have been edited.

1. London, 1727, pp. 51–52.

* * *

The first and most important fact for the historical scholar to absorb is that Defoe, in what was still very much a functioning Christian environment, is himself a serious and a practising Christian. True, he is a Puritan; and, for the modern world, including many historical scholars, that has been condemnation enough. * * * But informed modern students of Puritanism have * * * pointed out the vast differences between seventeenth-century Puritanism and the targets of modern attack: for, far from being anti-intellectual, Puritanism (especially the dominant Presbyterian version) held Reason in the highest regard and had a vested interest in a learned clergy—a fact to which the seminaries of Harvard, Yale, and Princeton owe their existence. And, far from being * * * primly self-righteous, * * * Puritans held to a tough-minded, independent and various, morally searching faith, centered in the Word of God.[2]

If Defoe's Christian commitment is not taken into account, one can scarcely be said to speak historically of the whole man.[3] * * * Now, of course that personal commitment takes on different shades as one views Defoe the merchant, Defoe the political pamphleteer, Defoe the composer of prose fiction, and Defoe in his multitudinous other guises: but it remains a full commitment throughout, and it remains central to any historical reading of Defoe's fictional and nonfictional work. The works need not, obviously, be read as religious tracts (unless they *are* religious tracts); but they are all rooted in a Christian scheme of values and assumptions that affords them far profounder depth and reverberation than the old-fashioned realistic criticism could fathom. The many other intellectual currents to which Defoe's wide-ranging mind was open must necessarily be referred to the Christian consciousness that received them.

For my purposes, the peculiarities of seventeenth-century Puritanism[4] (and Defoe, of course, became a Puritan, or better, Dis-

2. Among other important studies may be cited William Haller, *The Rise of Puritanism* (New York, 1938); Perry Miller, *The New England Mind*: "The Seventeenth Century" and "From Colony to Province" (Cambridge, Mass., 1939–53); and Owen C. Watkins, *The Puritan Experience: Studies in Spiritual Autobiography* (New York, 1972).
3. Maximillian Novak, although emphasizing the influence of the tradition of natural law, rightly observes, "We must never underestimate Defoe's religious beliefs" (*Defoe and the Nature of Man* [Oxford, 1963], p. 153).
4. Among these peculiarities were its Bible-centered and preacher-centered nature; its emphasis upon the notion that every man is (in a sense) his own priest and need only look into his own heart to find the law of God written there; its conservative emphasis upon the calling, or fixed station in life; its fascination with Particular Providences in the everyday world and its demand that natural events be accorded a spiritual application; its insistence upon the necessity of bearing witness to operations of Grace in the heart; its concern with Old Testament rather than classical heroes, and with Christ the Warrior more than the infant Christ or Christ crucified (which are just the aspects that would be stressed by the Evangelicals of the later eighteenth century); and, finally, in England particularly, its general Arminian softening of Calvinistic doctrine. The diary (or the spiritual autobiography), it has been suggested, took the place of the confessional in the Roman church.

senter, only by virtue of the fact that his parents' Anglican clergyman was a victim of the Act of Uniformity),[5] and, indeed, of Protestantism in general are less important than certain assumptions common to Western Christendom. One of these, for instance, was that the world of human activity, pressing though it unquestionably was, represented merely a limited part of the cosmos; and that human beings were not only surrounded by multitudes of invisible spirits, good and evil,[6] but were spiritually located in a larger moral universe, ultimately hierarchical, orderly, and rational—a universe which the fallen world of man mirrored most imperfectly but from which ideals and images could be drawn that brought some degree of significance and order to the disorderly, passion-driven, meaningless earthly stew. Defoe's characters may sometimes lose sight of the Angelic Vision when most embroiled in vice and sin (which no one, Defoe least of all, would have denied to be *interesting* activities), * * * but this, of course, does not mean that the vision ceases to exist. Even the Lady Roxana is fully aware at the end of her story that she is damned—and why.

Hence, Christian emblems like that old rhythmical triad of the enemies of man, the World, the Flesh, and the Devil * * * had for Defoe a genuine and vibrant resonance that must be recreated imaginatively in reading his fiction. He knew very well the abiding attractions of the world and the flesh, and he assuredly believed in the existence of the devil—even if not in the tricked-up form of popular superstition.[7] For Defoe the omnipresent devil worked rather more subtly, through dreams and hints and suggestions (or, less traditionally, through poverty and want) that appealed to the imagination and the passions of a corrupt and fallen human nature, providing "an evil Counsellor within" (p. 153). It is important to observe * * * that the prompting role of the devil is *not* viewed deterministically: even fallen man has free will and moral choice, and the devil, who operates with God's permission, to test the human soul, cannot compel the will. All that he can do as the motivating agent to crime is work upon the weakness of the human soul itself.

The structure of *Moll Flanders*, as has long since been observed, follows in essence the moral history of mankind as Calvinist (indeed, Anglican) theology would have viewed it: birth in sin—the heritage of post-Adamic man—but in possession still of a primal innocence

5. John Robert Moore, *Daniel Defoe, Citizen of the Modern World* (Chicago, 1958), pp. 13 ff. "Defoe was always more Christian than Presbyterian, more lover of the Church of Christ than Dissenter" (p. 19). This is surely true, although Defoe does follow many of the patterns associated with seventeenth-century Puritanism; and he is looked upon as a typical enough Dissenter by many of his contemporaries.
6. This general topic has been thoroughly canvassed by Rodney M. Baine, *Daniel Defoe and the Supernatural* (Athens, Ga., 1968), one of the few modern studies to treat historically and seriously of Defoe's most serious belief in the Devil.
7. See Baine, p. 41.

toward the world that can be lost through the temptations of the world and the devil, recapitulating the fall of Adam (often in a paradisical setting); the testing of the human soul on this earth; and the soul's ultimate coming to awareness of its sin and seeking reconciliation with God. A simpler and more obvious structural pattern for Moll's checkered career, however, would be merely: the World, the Flesh, and the Devil.[8] It is the devil who prompts Moll in her original fall into the fleshly life, as she observes after her "Vanity prevails over [her] Vertue": "But as the Devil is an unwearied Tempter, so he never fails to find opportunity for that Wickedness he invites to" (p. 24); and the large first section of the narrative, after the opening that brings her to Colchester orphan school, concerns itself with the temptations of the flesh—not only lust, although that has always served as the most obvious emblem of submission to the flesh, but the appeal of vanity and the servile dependence upon those goods that nurture fleshly needs (a dependence that places one firmly within the orbit of mere fortune and subject to her whims, as the complete soul never is). For Defoe, Moll's "thorough Aversion to going to Service" (p. 12) is truly ironic: she is on the way toward creating for herself a servitude more total and profound.

Again, after Moll has run through five husbands and several lovers and subsisted by a life of whoredom, she is thrown upon the world, reduced to poverty and dire need; and the devil, finding this a likely situation, speaks once more: "This was the Bait; and the Devil who I said laid the Snare, as readily prompted me, as if he had spoke, for I remember, and shall never forget it, 'twas like a Voice spoken to me over my Shoulder, take the Bundle; be quick; do it this Moment" (p. 151). And thus Moll is led into her life of thievery, proceeding from a mere chance theft that fills her soul with horror, through a spiritual "hardening of heart,"[9] until, even when she has found through the old midwife some honest work, "the diligent Devil who resolv'd I should continue in his Service, continually prompted me to go out and take a Walk, that is to say, to see if any thing would offer in the old Way" (p. 157). Blindly obeying his summons, she comes off with a tankard that the old "Governess" melts down, with the pointed observation "there's no going back now" (p. 158) The governess becomes, in fact, an agent of Satan, the "new Tempter

8. Most critics have shown some consciousness of the structural division of Moll's criminal career into a sexual pattern and a thieving pattern, despite overlapping elements, such as also attend the distinction between the Flesh and the World. Moll does say, after her second act of theft, "Thus I enterpriz'd my second Sally into the World" (p. 153), which by itself might seem odd, for she has actually been in the world for some time. See also William Bowman Piper, "*Moll Flanders* as a Structure of Topics," *Studies in English Literature* 9 (1969): 485–502.

9. See G. A. Starr, *Defoe and Spiritual Autobiography* (Princeton, 1965), pp. 141 ff. et passim. Starr points out that hardening of heart "is in fact a spiritual state, not merely a psychological one" (p. 141).

who prompted me every Day" (p. 165); and Moll is "enter'd a compleat Thief, harden'd to a Pitch above all the Reflections of Conscience or Modesty" (p. 159).

Entirely in the hands of fortune or fate (cf. p. 206), with no vision of Providence either to sustain or prohibit, Moll eventually comes to the emblematic end for those who have served the World, the Flesh, and the Devil: capture, judgment, and immurement in that "Emblem of Hell itself" (p. 215), Newgate Prison, "whence I expected no Redemption, but by an infamous Death" (p. 215).[1] This brings Defoe to the climactic third part of his narrative, Moll's conversion and true repentance in Newgate, detailed with scrupulous care for authenticity in terms of the tradition of conversion experiences (which shows how significant and central Defoe felt it to be to his narrative);[2] followed by Moll's providential pardon and the departure for Virginia with Jemmy, "as new People in a new World" (p. 238)—the return to paradise or to the *locus amoenus*[3] that so often marked the concludings of the old heroic romances.

2

The overall macrostructure, then, is orderly and logical enough. Criticism has usually, however, been prompted by the microstructure, the episodic manner in which Moll's criminal careers of the flesh and of the world are presented by Defoe. And, although some ingenious (and often even reasonable) orderings of the events within these frames have been suggested,[4] the narrative stubbornly remains episodic in comparison to the more tightly woven "figure in the carpet" of the later art-novel. Of this, one can perhaps say little in modern critical terms—except to say that they are irrelevant to Defoe.

The kind of structure that we properly enough admire in the later novel was in large measure, perhaps, a response to crucial loss—namely, the loss of an external ordering principle that guaranteed, as it were, the ultimate structural significance of narrative. As has been often observed of the Romantic poets, deprived of a Providence that had ensured the meaningfulness of the natural world, they turned to a projection of meaningfulness from within themselves. So, too, as novelists found no longer accessible the certainty of ultimate order in the providential frame, they made a virtue of necessity

1. "Redemption," like "deliverance" in *Robinson Crusoe*, becomes, of course, a term with a double sense.
2. See Starr, *Autobiography*, and Hunter, *Reluctant Pilgrim*.
3. As my former student Albert Rivero reminds me, the typological analogue would be with the Israelites' departure from the fleshpots of Egypt to seek the Promised Land.
4. For example, Terence Martin, "The Unity of *Moll Flanders*," *Modern Language Quarterly*, 22 (1961): 115–24; Piper; and J. A. Michie, "The Unity of *Moll Flanders*," in *Knaves and Swindlers: Essays on the Picaresque Novel in Europe*, ed. Christine J. Whitbourn (Oxford, 1974), pp. 75–92, which has the virtue of emphasizing Moll's personal moral responsibility.

and framed their own order within the narrative—not now as a mirror of the ordered cosmos but as a projection of the artist's ordering mind. Clearly enough, such an ordering could not be simply assumed or taken for granted, as the external providential order had been by readers of romances; hence, much more scrupulous and thoughtful attention had to be devoted to the *internal* ordering principles of narrative than had ever been required before. For, as long as writers of prose fiction could *assume* beyond the frame of their own narrative an external and unquestionable order that gave any narrative significance by reference to that paradigmatic realm of eternal values and certain judgments, the purely internal narrative ordering of the fiction was free to reflect the interestingly disordered and disjointed nature of the world of fortune, the world of man, marked precisely by its episodic, unstructured, ever-changing, and necessarily finite qualities, in implicit contrast to the realm of significance, the rational, immutable, and eternal cosmos of Providence. Presumably this is one reason that the episodic narrative was commonly not felt to be in itself inartistic (even after the rediscovery of Aristotle's *Poetics*), although there was, in any case, a long tradition of praise for the episodic, because it offered the sine qua non of narrative—variety, which, in most cultures, has been honored above other artistic demands. Hence, in the end, there is small need to apologize for Defoe's episodic narratives. The only need is to educate readers in artistic principles not their own.[5]

So, too, with the treatment of character. The conception of a complex or rounded character has been shaped by new secular interests and concerns. The emphasis upon a gradual temporal progress in human affairs in the later eighteenth century, which would ultimately make possible a theory of evolution in the nineteenth, contrasts sharply with earlier conceptions that saw time more often in terms of definite stages (the seven ages of the world or the climacterics of human life) that were ritually demarcated. Ultimate value resided, not in a gradual progress through finite time, but in a vertical reference to the abiding higher paradigms above man's temporal and temporary lot. Not surprisingly, therefore, earlier fiction, from classic times through the early eighteenth century, displays small interest in character development—for, after all, why should it? That was not where significance or value lay. Particular *stages* of man's existence did, however, vibrate with moral and ritual overtones; and, for the Puritan writer (as indeed, for all writers in the Christian tradition),

5. As A. D. McKillop observed, in what is still one of the soundest essays on Defoe, "He does not share our interest in the isolation and exact analysis of narrative intent. His way is to cite detail in support of an argument or moral, and it is hard to say when the detail becomes feigned narrative" (*The Early Masters of English Fiction* [Lawrence, Kan., 1956], p. 8); so also: "We may derive Defoe's fiction from the fact, circumstance, or episode, interesting in its own right and connected with a larger end" (p. 12).

that astonishing leap into a new life called conversion was among the most exciting and complex phenomena with which literature could concern itself. * * *

All fiction, all literature, needs a paradigm of ultimate explanations. Our paradigms tend to be scientific and deterministic: if something can be referred to a scientific (meaning sociological, economic, psychological, as well as physicochemical) root or determination, then it has been explained finally and satisfactorily—there is small need to go further. Thus the modern novelist (and reader) could scarcely do without psychology, for it is our court of final appeal on the nature and behavior of the human animal. If we are to talk about character, we cannot really think of doing so without implying psychology, because for us they are one. But it has not been always so: many ages of the earth have been able to discuss human nature most effectively without any reference to psychology at all. To be sure, they had their equivalents for our psychology; but, when we employ the term *psychology* in speaking of the literature of the past, we are necessarily assimilating *their* equivalents to *our* measure. Earlier writers (Shakespeare, for one) knew not the word *psychology* and did not see human character in the terms that this modern, secular, and deterministic discipline implies.

What Christian literature *was* concerned with, always, was the state of the rational human soul, since it was this that made man human, gave him superiority to the beasts, represented his tie to a realm of value beyond the material and the sensate, and, as the immortal principle within a merely temporal case of flesh, offered him a life beyond death. Small wonder, then, that literature should have focused upon the human soul as the most interesting, the most crucial, the most complex subject it could know.

In Defoe's time, psychology (or as the great Willis spelled it, "psyche-ology")[6] still meant the *logos* of the *psyche*, the state of the soul (although Willis himself would be instrumental in reshaping the term to mean the *logos* of that physical network we call mind);[7] and, although Defoe had his own equivalents for what we denominate psychology—shrewd observation from experience, conceptions of human nature framed from a multitude of written sources (including natural law and economics, moral treatises, criminal biographies, voyage literature, etc.), he was also, very obviously, concerned with the intricate problematics of the soul. * * *

6. Thomas Willis (1621–75), the father of modern neurology. See Richard Hunter and Ida Macalpine, *Three Hundred Years of Psychiatry, 1535–1860* (London, 1963), p. 187 et passim.
7. See the important essay by G. S. Rousseau, "Nerves, Spirits, and Fibres: Towards Defining the Origins of Sensibility," in *Studies in the Eighteenth Century III*, ed. R. F. Brissenden and J. C. Eade (Canberra, 1976), pp. 137–57.

3

The testing of Moll's soul is carried out, of course, in *this* world, as in all the romances and as in actual life, for, even when the romance narrative was allegorized or removed to some exotic and unknown latitude, it always carried an implicit reference (like beast fables, for that matter) to the world of the actual, the world of men, the stage upon which the soul conducted its battles and won or lost its struggle. * * * But, if the narrative action inevitably was located in the world of fortune, the *significance* of that action lay elsewhere. The values by which human action was judged were not presumed to be of merely human creation, as is the case today; rather, they lay in the great realms of divine and natural law, eternal, universal, and abiding. (Even the despised deists normally agreed with this proposition, made it in fact the basis of their own argument for universal religion.)

If the narrative behind the narrative is, then, the adventure of a human soul, Defoe's constant reflections upon evil and sin and the moral life are not at all * * * excrescences: * * * they are, in fact, the central matter of the central story, just as Defoe always insisted they were. Moll's reflections, like her actions, offer Defoe's reader cues to the state of her soul and of her spiritual existence (a truly compelling question for readers who were concerned for the state of their own souls), and this was not a matter of pious moralizing or conventional platitudes, but a life-and-death struggle, with the crucial addendum that it represented a struggle for *eternal* life or death. It concerned forever. * * *

I shall not here trace at large the history of Moll's soul, which is the implicit narrative focus; but to trace it in detail would be to recover most nearly, I think, the book that Defoe's contemporaries read (which is not at all to say that even the most orthodox among them found no enjoyment in her worldly adventures; of course they did). If one tried the experiment of leafing through the various critical studies of *Moll Flanders* in this century, replacing all reference to psychology with "psyche-ology" or "the state of the Soul," and then added to this all the passages that have been dismissed as "mere conventional moralizing," one would have a pretty fair beginning for such a history. Born in sin, Moll displays very early her vanity and her refusal to accept her place in society (both of which we are likely to find admirable, but our opinion means nothing to the integrity of *Defoe's* tale). As usual in the romances, childhood is given only the briefest sketch, primarily to establish traits that belong to the essence of a character; for, once again, the romances were not interested in character development—and neither was Defoe. What should have led him to be? He was not a nineteenth-or early twentieth-century novelist. The narrative proper begins, of course, with the snares of the older brother, which Moll is willing enough to wander into. Though somewhat innocent of the world, she has a "Head full of Pride" (p. 21), which was, after all, sufficient to the original loss of paradise: "But as the Devil is an unwearied Tempter, so he never fails to find opportunity for that Wickedness he invites to: It was one Evening that I was in the Garden. . . ." (p. 24). After her fall, Moll repents only when the younger brother proposes honorable marriage (p. 28); but, of course, the repentance is not genuine and is "dissipated in worldly schemings." For Moll is *in love with* her sin; and even after marriage she commits "Adultery and Incest" in her heart by continuing to yearn after the older brother (p. 49). Actual incest and adultery will follow this prophetic heart-sin in the course of Moll's career. Through her string of husbands, whenever Moll is left to her own devices, she displays some new weakness of soul—from vanity and luxury through greed and near-despair.

Approaching the structural center of Moll's criminal career, just before the death of her last husband, we find her looking back and observing: "I had a past life of a most wretched kind to account for, some of it in this World as well as in another" (p. 148). But as her funds decrease, following the husband's death, the busy Devil appears again; and Moll responds like a sleepwalker: "But as the Devil carried me out and laid his Bait for me, so he brought me to be sure to the place, for I knew not whither I was going or what I did" (p. 151). So, earlier, on occasions when an advisor is serving as agent of the devil, Moll finds herself "Reason'd out of her Reason," which is to say, out of the faculty that can identify and distinguish sin. So, as "the diligent Devil" prompts, "I blindly obeyed his Summons" (p. 157): "Thus I that was once in the Devil's Clutches, was held fast there as with a Charm, and had no power to go without the Circle, till I was ingulph'd in Labyrinths of Trouble too great to get out at all" (p. 160). It is probable that Moll's observation on her lack of power to deny the devil's summons has less to do with a narrator's attempt to palliate her sins than it has with a striking exemplum of the moral impotence that follows upon slavery to Satan: "Ye are of your father the devil, and the lusts of your father ye will do" (John 8:44). By degrees her heart becomes hardened to reflection and she ceases to be a free moral agent: " 'Tis evident to me, that when once we are harden'd in Crime, no Fear can affect us, no Example give us any warning" (p. 174). Hopelessly a slave, genuinely "in service" now, Moll finds that "I could not forbear going Abroad again, *as I call'd it now*, any more than I could when my Extremity really drove me out for Bread" (p. 199). The final stage of degradation comes when Moll actually begins to take *pride* in her capacities as a thief: "I could fill up this whole Discourse with the variety of such Adventures which daily Invention directed to, and which I manag'd with the utmost Dexterity, and always with Success" (p. 190). If Moll, the narrator, is personating the soul's estate of young Moll the thief, we have here a recognizable voice: the mortal sin of presumption, which rises from despair of God's grace; and Moll the thief is at this point no different from the impudently merry inhabitants of Newgate: "But how Hell should become by degrees so natural, and not only tollerable, but even agreeable, is a thing Unintelligible, but by those who have Experienc'd it, as I have" (p. 217). And, in Newgate, Moll will explicitly despair of Grace: "I neither had a Heart to ask God's Mercy, or indeed to think of it, and in this I think I have given a brief Description of the compleatest Misery on Earth" (p. 219).

The stages of her final repentance in Newgate have been soundly outlined by Starr and need not here be recapitulated.[8] One may observe, however, that this phenomenon of repentance is not a psychological phenomenon, as we conceive psychology. It is, rather, "psyche-ological"—a working in the soul. And, since a character's essence—which is what the romance tradition was interested in—resides in the soul, not in the various inessential accidents that for a later tradition would create individuality and realism, a potent change in the soul is quite literally a change in the person's essence, a change in essential character. So that Moll is entirely correct when she declares, as she is awakened to true reflection: "In a word, I was perfectly chang'd, and become another Body" (p. 221). She will take on a new being with her conversion, a new character, reborn and "restor'd" to herself (p. 221):

> I am not capable of reading Lectures of Instruction to any Body, but I relate this in the very manner in which things then appear'd to me, as far as I am able; but infinitely short of the lively Impressions which they made on my Soul at that time. . . . It must be the Work of every sober Reader to make just Reflections on them, as their own Circumstances may direct; and without Question, this is what every one at sometime or other may feel something of; I mean a clearer Sight into things to come, than they had here, and a dark view of their own Concern in them [p. 226].

There are, of course, complexities that follow upon repentance and conversion. John Bunyan's *Grace Abounding to the Chief of Sinners*, which records a soul-wrestling rather more strenuous than Moll's, confronted honestly the problem of backsliding and weakening of resolve; and Christian, in the moral romance of *Pilgrim's Progress*, found that his severest difficulties and the real test of his

8. Starr, *Autobiography*, pp. 155–60.

faith only *began with* his conversion. For God's grace is continually required (as the good minister in Newgate observes to Moll after the sentence of transportation, "*He said*, I must have more than ordinary secret Assistance from the Grace of God, if I did not turn as wicked again as ever" p. 000). And Defoe, as "editor," notes in the Preface that Moll upon her return to England "was not so extraordinary a Penitent, as she was at first" (p. 7). The point * * * is that conversion offers no automatic guarantee of continued Grace (nor does it lift man above the condition of the human, as some modern critics seem to expect; he remains a fallen creature). Thus Bunyan's Christian, at the last stage of his pilgrimage, observes Ignorance being thrust into a door in the side of the Hill: "Then I saw that there was a way to Hell even from the Gates of Heaven, as well as from the City of Destruction."

4

The microcosmic narrative of the pilgrimage or testing of the human soul took place necessarily in the world of man, the world of the actual, which is where the race was run. But throughout the Christian era it was taken for granted (and not only by platonists) that another world, more perfect and more *real*, intersected the world of man precisely through the rational soul. Access to that higher reality was possible only by means of the instructed moral reason and God's good grace; but of its existence no one was in doubt. Even skeptics of the Renaissance and well through Defoe's time seldom doubted the *existence* of such a realm: their "error" lay in trying to reduce its definition to the terms of a different and alien mode of rationality, the mathematical, critical, and scientific. In the heyday of the chivalric romance, this higher world of ultimate value, by which were judged the actions of men in actual life (or those in fictive representations), was often simply assumed; and the romances had no great need to stress the matter, any more than the modern novelist need stress the assumed fact that each of his characters is possessed of an unconscious mind. But, by Defoe's time, the various challenges to religious assumptions of the past century, though still scattered and unfocused, had at least created an atmosphere in which the sure existence of a providential realm was felt in need of emphasis. (Such a feeling lay behind the defenses of poetic justice like that of John Dennis.)[9] Hence, whereas earlier audiences for the romance might

9. For instance, this, in the *Remarks upon Cato* (1713): " 'Tis certainly the Duty of every Tragick Poet, by an exact Distribution of a Poetical Justice, to imitate the Divine Dispensation, and to inculcate a particular Providence. 'Tis true indeed upon the Stage of the World the Wicked sometimes prosper, and the Guiltless suffer. But that is permitted by the Governour of the World, to shew from the Attribute of his infinite Justice that there is a Compensation in Futurity" (*The Critical Works of John Dennis*, ed. Edward N. Hooker [Baltimore, 1943] II, 49).

take for granted the fact that characters of a fiction, though acting in a simulacrum of the actual world, were operating morally and spiritually under the sure-judging eye of Providence (and it was this certainty * * * that provided the ultimate macrocosmic structure for romance narrative), Defoe seems to feel that he must make this still-believed principle explicit: "Really [says Moll] my Heart began to look up more seriously, than I think it ever did before, and to look with great Thankfulness to the Hand of Providence, which had done such wonders for me, who had been myself the greatest wonder of Wickedness, perhaps that had been suffered to live in the World" (pp. 263). And then she can return to "the fact" of her narrative, the microcosmic discourse.

That Defoe was still presuming the structural and judgmental function of Providence in his narrative and expecting that his readers would feel it as an external ordering principle that made scrupulous and minute internal ordering unnecessary, seems to me likely. Narratives had been doing just this for hundreds of years and obviously their audiences had responded properly; there was little reason for Defoe to doubt that they would continue to do so; but he had, in any case, taken care explicitly to point out the providential frame—perhaps for those who might be uninstructed, but also perhaps because the Puritan tradition (like the Anglican, for that matter) simply took pleasure in recognizing the providential hand in the mere natural world.

The major assumption that lies behind my argument, as should be clear by now, is that we have too much tended in our portraits of the early eighteenth century to stress those elements that we should like to see there because they are comfortable (or exciting) to us. But this emphasis on relevance seems to me ultimately a very narrow box, one that does not ask the reader to stretch his imagination and enter into worlds of thought that do *not* provoke mere knee-jerk reactions of recognition and satisfaction. Certainly the historical scholar should not be concerned with what *we* find central, but with what the era under consideration found central. We have much overblown the skeptical currents, deism, secularism, and the impact of science (actually still under a form that has very properly been called by E. A. Burtt "metaphysical"), in the age, and ignored, for a variety of reasons, none of which serves the historical enterprise, the solidly Christian frame in which the greater part of the era's literature was produced.

Nevertheless, if this is admitted one can then agree that there *was* a difference from earlier Christian ages and that within the ruling Christian frame a multitude of tiny divagations was present—directions that before the century was out would be shaping a thoroughly different intellectual and spiritual world. If it is anachronistic to project the values of that brave new world back upon an earlier time when only its seeds were germinating, it is nevertheless not wrong to see that the seeds were there. Daniel Defoe's restless, inquiring mind led him to rake over many of those seeds (as modern scholarship has admirably documented), often without any prevision of what might burgeon forth from them. But it is my conviction that in his fictive narrations, as in his life, the microcosmic world of the insistent actual was brought within the judgmental and ordering macrocosmic configuration of Divine Providence.

IAN A. BELL

Moll Flanders, Crime and Comfort†

In recent years, historians such as Christopher Hill, Keith Thomas, E. P. Thompson and Robert W. Malcolmson have explored the various sub-cultures of late-seventeenth-century life, and so have partially laid open the habits of thought of the prospective contemporary audience for Defoe's fiction. The importance of their work has not only been to lessen the hold of the patrician view of the eighteenth century as an age of exclusive elegance, but also to allow new ways of talking about the low life of the period. In much earlier scholarship, there was a tacit (and sometimes an announced) assumption that low life was only interesting as a kind of background, against which the most interesting figures reacted. Low life was often taken to be synonymous with criminal and vagabond cultures, and the literature of low life was often held to be the literature of various kinds of delinquency. What the recent historians have achieved is the destruction of such an assumption, and the re-creation of the view that low life was diverse and manifold, as capable of variety and complexity as high life, and as multifarious in its views and opinions as any other culture.

The rediscovery of the richness and variety of eighteenth-century low life has very important consequences for the reading of its fiction. Firstly, it is necessary, when dealing with the area of crime fiction, to try to imagine the various possible attitudes towards crime, from which the fiction would draw its resources. The criminal would have been as he (or she) has always been, capable of arousing fear, envy, horror, self-righteousness or pity. His (or her) life story could be presented as a warning, as a pattern of divine intervention, or as

† From *Defoe's Fiction* (Totowa, NJ: Barnes & Noble, 1985), pp. 115–52. Reprinted by permission of Taylor & Francis Books, Ltd., and the author. Page numbers in parentheses refer to this Norton Critical Edition. Notes have been edited.

an economic homily. The fictional modes employed might be comedy, irony, or tragedy. The numerous possibilities were clearly conventionalised into those which overtly tried to warn their readers against criminals (understood as a different, threatening class), and those which offered a prurient, even racy account of how criminals lived. Of course, some books which seemingly offered themselves in the first category would more properly be read in the second, but the two species of presentation are discernible. The Elizabethan cony-catching pamphlets are perhaps the purest members of the first class. For example, Robert Greene's *A Notable Discovery of Cozenage* (1591) was addressed to "Young Gentlemen, Marchants, Apprentices, Farmers, and plain Countrymen", and offered to help and advise them:

> my younger yeeres had uncertaine thoughtes, but now my ripe daies cals on to repentant deedes . . . The odde mad-caps I have been mate too, not as a companion, but as a spie to have an insight into their knaveries, that seeing their traines I might eschew their snares: those mad fellowes I learned at last to loath, by their owne graceless villenies, and what I saw in them to their confusion, I can forewarne in others to my countreis commodity.[1]

Greene was then addressing himself to working people, to prevent others taking advantage of their honesty and simplicity. The audience as conceived here was simple, fair and honest, and rather naive. The subjects of the tale were presented as evil, cruel and avaricious, and were seen as a threat.

When the audience was not conceived of as unfailingly honest, the criminal could be given a more sympathetic treatment, as in *Volpone*. An important strategy in the fostering of criminal fiction, was for the audience to be conceived of as impressionable, and for criminals to be thought of as in some degree the victims of circumstance. If the collapse into a life of crime could be seen as hapless and involuntary, then the audience could simultaneously enjoy the fact that their lives were honest, but that the criminal was a recognisably similar figure to themselves. Criminal fiction gains its meaning from its place within a range of similar fiction, such as voyage fiction or scandalous tales, but also from the way it can draw upon the audience's sense of what crime is.[2] Thus, the criminal life could

1. Robert Greene, *A Notable Discovery of Coosnage* (1591), G.B. Harrison (ed.) (London, 1923), pp. 7–8.
2. Some suggestive comparisons between the criminal in fiction and the criminal as presented at Tyburn and elsewhere are offered by Lennard J. Davis, 'Wicked Actions and Feigned Words: Criminals, Criminality, and the Early English Novel', in *Rethinking History: Time, Myth, and Writing* (Yale French Studies, 59), pp. 106–18. For a broader analysis of eighteenth-century thinking about crime, see Douglas Hay, Peter Linebaugh, John G. Rule, E. P. Thompson and Cal Winslow, *Albion's Fatal Tree: Crime and Society in*

offer itself as a double example—as showing the kind of life to be avoided at all costs, yet as showing also some commendable self-examination and even repentance. This second possibility relies greatly on first-person narration, and is much more obviously a feature of early-eighteenth-century criminal fiction than of earlier works. Even Bunyan's *The Life and Death of Mr Badman* (1680) keeps the central figure at bay, by presenting its narrative in the form of a dialogue between Mr Wiseman and Mr Attentive. Bunyan recognises the danger of the evil criminal becoming sympathetic, and strives to prevent him from taking over the reader's attention as anything other than a moral example. The inevitable ambivalence which arises when an evil, dynamic figure is at the centre of a narrative is nullified by Bunyan's procedures of distancing.

* * * In *Moll Flanders*, Defoe's combination of the criminal tale, the female adventure and the repentance story, all presented in the first person, raises different sorts of narrative problems. By involving the reader, as he always did, Defoe was immediately offering a prurient tale rather than an admonitory one. Moll was to be perceived as a character not remarkably different from the reader, or those of the reader's acquaintance, and the book is clearly not designed to warn us against the likes of Moll. * * * [T]he ambivalence which arises with the criminal as heroine is a persistent feature of the narrative.

Any articulation of *Moll Flanders* must begin with the reader's relationship with the narrator, and it is this issue which has dominated critical discussion of the book. * * * In *The Rise of the Novel*, Ian Watt offered a subtle distinction which seems to rule out the reading of the book in the ironic mode—'*Moll Flanders* is undoubtedly an ironic object, but it is not a work of irony' (p. 135).[3] Against this view of the book's haphazardness, it is possible to put Dorothy Van Ghent's remark that the book is 'a coherent and significant work of art' in the way it presents 'a complex system of ironies or counterstresses'.[4] The way of expressing the issue offered by Van Ghent seems to remove *Moll* from popular literature, and to offer her a place at the high table. Were there to be such persistent irony, then it would be possible to do this, but it would make *Moll* a remarkably uncharacteristic Defoe text. The controversy as stated in these two views does seem to raise rather unanswerable questions about the degree of control Defoe exercised over his material. Do the 'ironies'

Eighteenth Century England (London, 1975). The best collection of the crime fiction of the period is Spiro Peterson (ed.), *The Counterfeit Lady Unveiled and Other Criminal Fiction of Seventeenth Century England* (New York, 1961).

3. See also Watt's 'The Recent Critical Fortunes of *Moll Flanders*', *Eighteenth-Century Studies*, I (1967): pp .109–26.
4. Dorothy Van Ghent, *The English Novel: Form and Function* (New York, 1953) 36.

simply represent inconsistencies and a rather unfeeling temperament? Or are they a deliberately laid strategy, which no eighteenth-century reader seemed able to detect? Again, the terms of debate seem far too polarised, and the whole question seems to demand too much decisiveness and consistency of Defoe. Such decisiveness is not a feature of popular literature, which feels free to be as inconsistent and diffuse as it wants, and would not be a full articulation of the complex feelings raised by the twin issues of crime and femininity. * * * The book is never simply ironic or mimetic, but flits between these two modes, depending on the specific generic supervision in given episodes.

The title page of *Moll* again offers a rich variety of generic references. Moll's life will offer a "continu'd Variety," including the saleable adventures of prostitution, incest, theft, transportation, wealth and penitence. The bizarre conglomeration of adventures is a fairly accurate summary of the book's contents, and indicates just how cluttered are its pages. More importantly, it also indicates the varied categories of reading required, and * * * these do not always seem compatible. How is the scurrilous whoring to be made compatible with the penitence? And how is incest to be made comfortable in the same book as honesty? These questions are perhaps the product of a reading which is trained to seek unity and consistency above variety, to find some partly concealed plan. In Defoe's fiction, the principle of accumulation or compendiousness overrules the aesthetic niceties of unity, and his narrative invites reading as sequence rather than as a purposive development. Variety is not only the most immediate feature of Moll's life, it is also the first principle of Defoe's fiction. The fact that these varied events happen within a chronology, to the same character, should not blind us to their phenomenological status, as sporadic or separate adventures.

Moll Flanders first engages its readers in a Preface, wherein the "Editor" offers a summary of the book, and tries to make it seem educative and grave. * * * [T]he Preface is best seen as a series of instructions in how to read the ensuing narrative, partly misleading, and it should not be taken as a proper description of that narrative. In the Preface, the book is presented *as though* it were consistently moral or pious, when in fact it is no such thing. By presenting it in this way, the editor can invite the reader to participate in judgements, even when the narrative does not fully support these judgements. Defoe seems closest to admitting the tactical role of the prefaces in *Colonel Jack*, where he says:

> this Work needs a *Preface* less than any that ever went before it; the pleasant and delightful Part speaks for itself; the useful and instructive Part is so large, and capable of so many Improve-

> ments, that it would imploy a Book, large as it self, to make Improvements suitable to the vast Variety of the Subject. (*CJ*, p. 1)

Defoe is suggesting that the extant text of *Colonel Jack* has a great deal of potential improvements in it, but that it is largely up to the reader to draw these inferences. In the text as it stands, the emphasis is on variety, rather than on coherence, and the aim is to be 'pleasant and delightful'. So too in *Moll*, the Preface serves to get the necessary moral flummery out of the way, by allowing it much importance, but leaving it in the hands of the reader. The reader is being alerted to the moralising potential of the text, but simultaneously being offered a text with little actual moral content.

Defoe's prefaces regularly perform this tactical function, and only very rarely offer a convincing description of the work in hand. In *Memoirs of a Cavalier*, he offers a catalogue of the various delights to follow, speculates about the identity of the author (who is, of course, Defoe himself), and hints heavily about the possibilities of a sequel:

> for how do we know but that this Author might carry it on, and have another Part finished which might not fall into the same Hands, or may still remain with some of his Family . . . Nor is it very improbable, but that if any such farther part is in being, the publishing these Two Parts may occasion the Proprietors of the Third to let the World see it . . .[5]

In other words, an elaborate game of bluff and entreaty is going on between reader and author, where the various proprieties are going on, and the diplomatic exchanges are taking place. The subdued meaning is that the editor is not fully in control of his material, but is at the mercy not only of his narrators (after all, he cannot alter what they say very much), but also of manuscript owners and eventually readers. This is much more than a device of authentication, and has to be seen as one of Defoe's ways of partially disclaiming responsibility for his work. He confers upon the reader the role of properly categorising the latent text, and invites the reader to draw the proper conclusions.

In other prefaces, he tried to emphasise the separate, irredeemable state of his books. In the Preface to *The True Born Englishman*, he talked of his poem as though it were some event over which he had only vestigial control:

> I may venture to foretell, That I shall be Cavil'd at about my *Mean Stile, Rough Verse*, and *Incorrect Language*; Things I

5. Daniel Defoe, *Memoirs of a Cavalier* (1720), James T. Boulton (ed.) (Oxford, 1978), p. 4.

> might indeed have taken more care in. But the Book is Printed; and tho I see some Faults, 'tis too late to mend them.[6]

The book had rapidly been swallowed up by events, and like his narrators, Defoe had little time for self-recrimination about the past. The pressure of time and the urgency of events bring about error, and there was little Defoe could do to alter things. Elsewhere, on the other hand, he used the prefaces to indulge in some kind of revisionism. In the preface to the *Serious Reflections*, he referred back to *Crusoe*, and tried to alter the category of its reading. He makes the strange claim that "the story, though allegorical, is also historical," and boasts that "there is a man alive, and well known too, the actions of whose life, are the just subject of these volumes." But even this implausible assertion is best seen as a way of disclaiming responsibility for the events of the narrative. Defoe was not responsible for them, as they had to follow the contours of someone else's life, he argued. In all these cases, we are being asked to take the text as an autonomous entity, which Defoe offers as a product. His role is not that of fabricator (in any sense of that word), but that of manager or purveyor. Even this alone would lead us away from seeing the text as some kind of repository in which Defoe as author inscribed meaning. Whether he knew it or not, Defoe's prefaces present a theory of reader-centred meaning which is much more relevant to the understanding of popular fiction than any author-centered theory.

The Preface to *Moll* does offer a number of instructions in how we should understand the narrator. The editor makes the conventionally required distinction between novels and genuine histories, placing *Moll* forcefully in the latter category. Similarly to the avowals of authenticity in *Crusoe*, this is to be taken as an instruction that we should read the book *as though* it were genuine. However, the editor then goes further to suggest his own limitations when he talks of the alterations he has been required to make to his original manuscript. He has had to alter the style of several passages, since his source is rather too bouncy for 'one grown Penitent and Humble' (*MF*, p. 3). To make the book less prurient, certain very vicious parts have been omitted. The editor quietly admits that 'there cannot be the same Life, the same Brightness and Beauty, in relating the penitent Part, as is in the criminal Part' (*MF*, p. 4), which serves to place the book in the category of criminal *exposé* rather than that of repentance tale. As a further tactic of disavowal, the editor puts the blame for his relocation of the narrative not on himself, or even on Moll, but on 'the Gust and Palate of the Reader' (*MF*, p. 4). The book has, then, been refined in the process of publication, but the editor is at

6. See Boulton, p. 53.

the mercy of his readers' whims. Defoe is striving to present himself as a pure, hard-working editor, rather than as the reprehensible vendor of filth. He himself feels his product to be wholesome, but his readers may find crude uses for it.

He even goes so far as to announce that the book has an organising principle, and states it flatly:

> THROUGHOUT the infinite Variety of this Book, this Fundamental is most strictly adhered to; there is not a wicked Action in any Part of it, but is first or last rendered Unhappy and Unfortunate: There is not a superlative Villain brought upon the Stage, but either he is brought to an unhappy End, or brought to be a Penitent: There is not an ill Thing mention'd, but it is condemn'd, even in the Relation, nor a vertuous just Thing, but it carries its Praise along with it . . . (*MF*, p. 5)

Any reading of the book, however cursory, must find this statement to be grossly inaccurate and misleading. Moll's wickedness does not, it is true, lead to complete calmness, but she does succeed in living off the spoils of incest and crime with as little qualm as Captain Singleton. The editor himself offers the possibility of doubt, when he admits that Moll's penitence was temporary:

> where she liv'd it seems, to be very old; but was not so extraordinary a Penitent, as she was at first; it seems only that she always spoke with Abhorrence of her former Life, and of every Part of it (*MF*, p. 7).

Again, this allows the possibilities of doubt to creep in, but it is very misleading. When Moll recounts her past life, she does not evince shame; she reveals glee, gusto and verve.

The Preface, taken as a whole, sets the book adrift from its presenter. The material seems to be beyond control, and there is little he seems to feel he can do to ensure that readers adopt the proper attitudes to what happens in the narrative. The central conflict of the book makes any general statement about it, even by its author, very difficult. That conflict is Moll's combination of 'a zest for criminal ingenuity and a taste for moral preachment'.[7] Such a conflict seems to be a feature of Moll's psychology, but it might be better seen as a feature of the audience's reading procedures. *Moll* seems to seek categorisation in the zestful criminal genre as well as in the penitence tale genre, and such conflicting appeals leave little pos-

7. Howard L. Koonce, 'Moll's Muddle: Defoe's Use of Irony in *Moll Flanders*', *ELH*, XXX (1963): p. 379. Koonce puts forward a very interesting view of the conflicts within the narrative, but sensible and proper doubts have been raised by Pat Rogers, 'Moll's Memory', *English*, XXIV (1975): pp. 67–72. There is some interesting consideration of this issue in M. E. Novak, 'Defoe's "Indifferent Monitor": The Complexity of *Moll Flanders*', *Eighteenth-Century Studies*, III (1969): 351–65.

sibility of cohesion and unity. The narrative reaches beyond the limits of its narrator, into a wider categorisation, and that invites problems when talking about the book as the product of its narrator. Any reading which fully personalises Moll, and tries to make her a consistent character, will fall into difficulties or distortions. Moll has to be seen as a conventional device for the stringing together of various kinds of adventures, though Defoe does make some very interesting gestures in the way of individuation.

The Preface thus offers a religious categorisation of the narrative, which the narrative does not accept. When Moll herself introduces the narrative, she sees herself in an economic and social environment, but not in a religious one. She begins by reminding us of her criminal origins, and gives us only a criminal's alias for her name:

> MY True Name is so well known in the Records, or Registers at *Newgate*, and in the *Old-Baily*, and there are some Things of such Consequence still depending there, relating to my particular Conduct, that it is not to be expected I should set my Name, or the Account of my Family to this Work . . . (*MF*, p. 9)

The device of concealed identity is a necessary tactic in the genre of criminal fiction, as a procedure of authentication, and as a provisional guarantee of plausibility. The criminal is still so heavily entangled in his or her world, that it would be dangerous to reveal all, and so the tale itself becomes a covert, furtive act, thus validating its criminality. In Moll's case, the pseudonym serves to emphasise how violent and estranging her background is. Her social world is seen to be very volatile and wholly material, despite the rhetorical flourishes about Providence or the Devil. Obviously, her world is even more dangerous than Crusoe's, whether in the comfort of York or on the island. Crusoe is rarely faced with the variety of threats with which Moll has to cope. At the opening of the narrative, Moll is already isolated, and so whereas Crusoe had the luxury of being able to act on impulse or inclination, Moll is immediately forced into ensuring her own survival.

Moll opens her account by telling us how sordid her background was. However, as is so typical of the book, she quickly moves on to discuss a rather more hygienic state of affairs.[8] After the age of three, she was raised by a kindly nurse, who instilled in her some rudimentary religious sense. Moll remembers being taught three things, and the order in which she recites them is reminiscent of the order of priority in Crusoe's daily calendar:

8. * * * One of the most idiosyncratic things about *Moll* is the way it hastens over both criminal and sexual misdeeds. Compared with *The English Rogue* or *Fanny Hill*, Moll's tale is remarkably inexplicit and oblique.

> BUT that which was worth all the rest, she bred them up very Religiously, being herself a very sober pious Woman. (2.) Very Housewifly and Clean, and, (3.) Very Mannerly, and with good Behaviour . . . (*MF*, p. 11)

The religious education is mentioned, but it is seen as a useful social accomplishment, rather than as any private spiritual boon. Moll herself sees this early training in purely social terms—'we were brought up as Mannerly and Genteely, as if we had been at the Dancing School' (*MF*, p. 11). The role of religion in the book, then, seems to be as something which genteel people have leisure to accomplish. Moll's persistent desire to be genteel is expressed overtly, and in the rather spurious gentility of her account, and her references to religion are best seen as part of her later, retrospective achievement of mannerly social position.

At the beginning of the book, however, Moll's vestigial sense of gentility leads her only to misery. When she discovers she is most likely to be put into service, she is horrified and deeply distressed. Her distress is shared by her 'good Motherly Nurse' (*MF*, p. 12), and disrupts the very brief domestic stability they have enjoyed. Moll's horror at the idea of being a servant is never fully explained in the novel, and it is presented for a variety of procedural reasons. First of all, it shows early on the abrupt emotional reactions which she presents throughout, and which are used to effect the violent transitions in the narrative. Secondly, it shows the impediments which surround Moll's search for social mobility. Her very naive belief that she can move rapidly through the social ranks by working as a spinner is first seen as comic, but soon makes everyone weep at its folly. The introduction of an episode where Moll mistakes a prostitute for just the kind of 'Gentlewoman' she herself wishes to become is used as dramatic irony, and as an indication that in her world, appearances are never to be trusted.

* * * In *Moll*, society is turbulent and violent throughout. Moll's early days are actually spent in a relatively cloistered environment, since she lives in Colchester, which Defoe thought of as more enlightened and humane than some other places.[9] However, the spectre of Newgate has already been established, as the place of her birth, and as her most likely destiny. So the career we watch is seen as a recurrent series of scrapes, which increase the danger of her return to Newgate, and from which she seems always to escape. The characteristic procedure of the adventure tale, whether it be the voyage or criminal kind, is to place its central figure in danger, and to

9. In his *Tour*, Defoe remarks that Colchester has 'two CHARITY SCHOOLS set up . . . and carried on by a generous subscription, with very good success' (p. 33).

make his or her escape as unlikely as possible. Moll's references to Newgate offer the danger, and her early education offers the means of escape. If there is a principle of organisation uniting Moll's very diffuse adventures, it is the way her desire to be a gentlewoman reappears persistently. Sometimes it leads her to avoid telling us things which a more haphazard narrative would be pleased to include—there are many popular tales which are much more sexually explicit than *Moll*, for instance—and at other times this concern leads to Moll's rather over-eager attempt to make her behaviour seem respectable.

Defoe used such a concern with gentility in a similar way in *Colonel Jack*. In Jack's tale, the narrator is typically unsure of his origins, but relies on local legend to confirm his belief that he is the offspring of a 'Man of Quality' and a 'Gentlewoman', put out to a nurse to remove his (unmarried?) parents from 'the Importunities that usually attend the Misfortune of having a Child to keep that should not be seen or heard of' (*CJ*, p. 3). Jack goes on to recount how his father is thought to have laid down only one stipulation concerning his child's education:

> if I liv'd to come to any bigness, capable to understand the meaning of it, she should always take care to bid me *remember, that I was a Gentleman*, and this was all the Education he would desire of her for me, for he did not doubt, he said, but that sometime or other the very hint would inspire me with Thoughts suitable to my Birth, and that I would certainly act like a Gentleman, if I believed myself to be so (*CJ*, p. 3).

Jack's belief that he is a gentleman does in fact serve as a moral restraint upon him, by ruling out certain crimes as beneath his dignity. He feels impelled, for example, to make restitution when he finds he has robbed some one worse off than himself. Moll's sense of being genteel does not act in such a moral way, as it does not actually prevent her from doing anything. It does, however, prevent her narrative from incorporating everything she claims to have done, out of a sense of modesty and decorum. So whereas gentility in *Colonel Jack* is used as a moral property, to make the hero's actions coherent, it features in Moll as a barrier to full revelation, and so acts as a rhetorical restraint. In each case, it serves as the traditional single motive found in so much popular fiction. Character is reduced to a single notion of what it ought to be, and the main impulse of the book is towards the deferred gratification of that wish. In *Moll*, readers are presented with two schematised possibilities—Newgate and gentility. We know that Moll is likely to end up either in one or having achieved the other, and the process of the narrative is the oscillation between them, in the search for a comic resolution.

In the early part of the narrative, Moll's desire for gentility is seen as eccentric, and it makes her something of a celebrity. She is taken up, for a while, by the Mayor of Colchester and his daughters, largely as a novel plaything. During this period, Moll defines what she means by gentility, which is 'to be able to get my Bread by my own Work' (*MF*, p. 14). When she offers an example of what she means by this, we are forced to see the ironic innocence of her desire. She mentions someone who fulfills her requirements, and though this person is a lacemender (a menial enough activity), she is also a bawd of some kind. The interesting part is when Moll says, 'I insisted she was a Gentlewoman, and I would be such a Gentlewoman as that' (*MF*, p. 15). This is one of the very few overt ironic statements in Defoe's fiction, and its ironies are varied and fairly complex. First of all, there is the unwitting revelation of the paucity of Moll's conception of security, when her paragon is seen to be a lacemender. Secondly, there is the further irony in that this person is actually not a gentlewoman, but someone involved in prostitution. And thirdly, there is the irony that Moll does indeed turn out to be just such a gentlewoman, though she cannot at that time realise the accuracy of her prediction.[1]

The complexity of the irony makes it seem a deliberate part of the narrative, designed to alert us to Moll's possibilities. However, though it seems vivid and obvious to readers, the retrospective Moll offers to comment on its appropriateness. This is very different from, and perhaps more subtle than, the episodes in the other narratives when just such an ironic prediction is heavily underlined by the narrator. In *Colonel Jack*, the fates of Jack's two 'brothers' provide him with the opportunity to make rather weighty and solemn moral comments about himself. In *Crusoe*, the narrator makes an exact prediction of his eventual fate:

> In this manner I used to look upon my Condition with the utmost Regret. I had no body to converse with but now and then this Neighbour; no Work to be done, but by the Labour of my Hands; and I used to say, I liv'd just like a man cast away upon some desolate Island, that had no body there but himself. (*RC*, p. 35)

Had Crusoe said nothing further, then this episode would have been a direct parallel to Moll's unwitting prediction. But Crusoe goes on

1. There has been a great deal of debate about Defoe's use of irony, most of it unilluminating, and stuck in the rigid categories of irony used by Henry James and subsequent writers. The best contributions are two papers by M. E. Novak, 'Defoe's Use of Irony', in *The Uses of Irony: Papers on Defoe and Swift Read at a Clark Library Seminar, 2 April, 1966* (Los Angeles, 1966) and 'Conscious Irony in *Moll Flanders*: Facts and Problems', *College English*, XXVI (1964): pp. 198–204.

to reflect, and in doing so brings out the essential difference in genre between the two books:

> But how just has it been, and how should all Men reflect, that when they compare their present Conditions with others that are worse, Heaven may oblige them to make the Exchange, and be convinc'd of their former Felicity by their Experience. (*RC*, p. 35)

Crusoe's narrative is inviting a reading within the category of the cautionary tale, and this is one of the episodes where a meaning is drawn out of the action, and dangled before the reader.

In a narrative which has fewer pretentions to admonition, no such moralising is appropriate. In *Captain Singleton*, there is a similar piece of prolepsis when the narrator's likely fate is pictured for him by a companion:

> he came to me, takes me by the Hand, and looking into the Palm of my Hand, and into my Face too, very gravely, My Lad, *says he*, thou art born to do a World of Mischief: thou hast commenced Pyrate very young, but have a Care for the Gallows, young Man; have a Care I say, for thou wilt be an eminent Thief. (*CS*, p. 25)[2]

Singleton's response is merely laughter, and he does not dwell upon either the accuracy or the portentousness of the prediction. His narrative is quite clearly an adventure tale, wherein the connection between events is chronological only. He makes no effort to discern any pattern within his life, and the narrative, thus, does not require the presence of irony. His adventures are of such a hectic, diffuse kind, that there is neither the need nor the desirability of reflection.

So too in *Moll*, the narrative does not seek to present itself as a retrospective revelation of the workings of Providence. The irony presented here is dramatic, but has little significance for the overall categorisation of the tale. It is simply another piece of rhetorical opportunism on Defoe's part, cheerfully adding irony to the various zestful delights of the criminal tale. Only very rarely are readers invited to distance themselves from the narrator in any ironic way. The implied procedure of reading is once again unmediated involvement, and even a reader who seeks to be remote from the text finds himself or herself being dragged along by it—as G. A. Starr puts it, 'sympathy keeps breaking in, and our ironic detachment—along with Defoe's—is tempered by imaginative identification'.[3] One method of supporting this sympathy is Defoe's use of Moll's partial (and rather

2. Crusoe also receives a very similar warning, which he too ignores. He does, however, retrospectively recognise its accuracy in a way that Singleton never tries to. See *RC*, 15.
3. *Defoe and Casuistry*, p. 114.

selective) innocence. When the narrative reveals more than the narrator does, our sense of detachment is reinforced, but only rarely does Defoe allow that to be obvious. The more frequent tactic is to force Moll to relate her events in the most immediate, least reflective of ways. Her retrospective stance is rarely made effective, and much of the book could just as well be presented in the present tense.

The main process of the narrative is Moll's convoluted and twisting search for comfort and security. She originally, and innocently, sees the path to stability lying in her own honest efforts as a worker, but, as one critic puts it, 'what Moll will have to learn to do in the course of her narrative is to relinquish this middle-class dream of honest and self-sufficient survival'.[4] It is very interesting that, whereas *Crusoe* showed the possibilities of self-sufficiency, *Moll* shows the impossibilities. Moll lives in a social world, and her attempts to secure stability are disrupted as much by her relationships with other people as by accident or chance. Of course, it may be tempting to see her presentation of this as an attempt at excusing herself, but her character is never as fully motivated and understood as that would require. Whatever the case, the agency of her disillusionment is her romantic life, and the book balances the tale of Moll the criminal adventuress with the Moll who presents herself as the helpless victim of uncontrollable desires. In the later half of the book, these two tales seem rather at odds with one another, but there is little conflict in the earlier part.

Moll's first romantic encounter is with the elder brother of the family she is living with, and it is described in such a way as to allocate the tale to the group of romances about rakes and innocent serving wenches. Moll has already been established as a simple, rather gullible girl, and the seducer is introduced characteristically and conventionally as a rake:

> a gay Gentleman that knew the Town, as well as the Country, and tho' he had Levity enough to do an ill natur'd thing, yet had too much Judgment of things to pay too dear for his pleasures; he began with that unhappy Snare to all Women, (*viz.*) taking Notice upon all Occasions how pretty I was . . . (*MF*, p. 19).

The endangering feature here, presented as familiar to all readers of this sort of fiction, is Moll's innocent vanity. The whole episode is presented without dramatic impetus, as though it is recognised by readers as inevitable, and it is understood in purely conventional terms. Moll affirms 'my Vanity was the Cause of it' (*MF*, p. 19), and the whole episode has a rather stylised, impersonal appearance to it. The most important thing about it is not the loss of Moll's virginity,

4. John J. Richetti, *Defoe's Narratives* (Oxford, 1975), p. 99.

which she is characteristically coy about, but the awakening of insight that it produces. At one point, Moll overhears a conversation between her future seducer and his sister, in which he praises Moll's merits. The sister replies in a very worldly and disdainful way:

> I wonder at you Brother, *says the Sister; Betty* wants but one Thing, but she had as good want every Thing, for the Market is against our Sex just now; and if a young Woman have Beauty, Birth, Breeding, Wit, Sense, Manners, Modesty, and all these to an Extream; yet if she have not Money, she's no Body, she had as good want them all, for nothing but Money now recommends a Woman . . . (*MF*, pp. 19–20).

The sister's sense of the supremacy of money, anticipating Roxana, is largely confirmed by the events of the tale, but Moll never comes fully to this cynical view. Readers are being alerted to the cynicism of the tale's world, but, very interestingly, the narrator does not participate in this all but universal sourness of view. Moll's innocence is damaged by her encounter with the rakish elder brother, but it is never fully dispersed. Defoe uses it to keep the book out of the category of pornography, where the heroine is as cynical as everyone else, and yet he is able to incorporate crime and promiscuity into a largely blithe narrative.

In fact, the issue of love and money was a recurrent theme throughout Defoe's non fiction, as well as appearing in *Colonel Jack, Captain Singleton* and, dominantly, in *Roxana*. It figures prominently in *Religious Courtship* and *The Complete English Gentleman*, and some critics have suggested that Defoe himself was heavily involved in discussing such matters when haggling over the dowry of his daughter Sophia.[5] It would be possible to present the conflict between love and money in any fictional mode, and in non fiction, it appears often as tragedy—brief tales are given of foolish lovers, whose impecunity drives them to grief. However, in *Moll* it is kept in the comic mode by Moll's undying innocence. One critic claims that the book shows Moll's education in the ways of the world—'she learns that charm, wit, grace, and beauty are insufficient assets to the gentle world, but that diamonds are a girl's best friend'.[6] No doubt this view accurately represents the social world of the narrative, but Moll herself never becomes fully hardened to it as so many writers suggest. In the early part of the novel, she seems uncertain about her role, and makes very few recriminations of herself or others. She seems to accept the seducer's behaviour as being the way of the world, and her own innocence as being equally involuntary.

5. See G. A. Starr's edition of *Moll*, p. 363.
6. R. R. Columbus, 'Conscious Artistry in *Moll Flanders*', *SEL*, III (1963): p. 420. There must be some doubt about how many of these qualities Moll displays in the first place. What evidence is there for her grace?

The behaviour of the younger brother, who falls in love with her, at least maintains the possibility of conduct motivated by something other than money, and it helps to maintain Moll's naivety for a surprisingly long time.

Though Moll does recognise the power of economic necessity, it is by no means the only force which motivates her conduct or impedes her progress towards comfort. As her first seduction is completed, and the seducer gives her more and more money, Moll paradoxically announces her own culpability in the affair. She does not see the opportunity for her own self-advancement, and becomes in effect a willing, self-castigating accomplice to his scheme. Eventually, when he gives her a hundred guineas, she says, 'I made no more Resistance to him, but let him do just what he pleas'd; and as often as he pleas'd'.[7] The money she receives is not understood by Moll as a bribe, but as an earnest of his sincerity, and as a confirmation of his good faith. Despite the financial reward, she does not seem to realise, even retrospectively, that her body and charms are marketable assets, though she is tacitly engaged in selling them. She sees the loss of virginity as closing down her economic options, rather than as opening them up, as it were— . . . for from this Day, being forsaken of my Vertue, and my Modesty, I had nothing of Value left to recommend me, either to God's Blessing, or Man's Assistance' (*MF*, p. 26). It is clear that Moll is not scheming to entrap the elder brother, and that she still clings to the foolish notion that virtue is more saleable than vice. Even in retrospect, she does not qualify her view that love is a source of jeopardy rather than comfort, and that it enfeebles her pursuit of stability.

It is at this point that the narrative is complicated by the younger brother Robin's announcement of his love for Moll. Obviously, this serves to involve her in a grim dilemma, in which her emotional security is at odds with her financial stability. Is she to accept the love of Robin, which may entail his being cut off from his family, and rendered destitute? Or is she to stay secretly with the elder brother, and enjoy a covert but profitable affair? For a ruthless narrator, like the narrators of the Spanish picaresque novels, there would be no dilemma. The affair with the elder brother could continue while the marriage to Robin was contracted and carried out. Moll's situation is rendered complex, not by moral qualms, but by her irrational sense of attachment. Her individuality, which is made much greater than Crusoe's, is expressed by her emotional idiosyn-

7. Moll's discussion of sex is always couched in such coy, evasive locutions, which are very different from the way sex is treated in popular pornographic fiction, or in the analogous picaresque novel. The issue is discussed by Robert Alter, *Rogue's Progress: Studies in the Picaresque Novel*. (Cambridge, Mass., 1964), p. 38. The pornographic fiction of the later seventeenth century is well documented in Roger Thompson, *Unfit For Modest Ears* (London, 1979).

cracies, and this aligns her to the romance heroines of Aphra Behn rather than to the criminal narrators. She even goes so far as to say to the elder brother, 'I had much rather, since it is come to that unhappy Length, be your Whore than your Brother's Wife' (*MF*, p. 34). Her distresses cause her to fall ill, and she is diagnosed by the physicians to be 'IN LOVE' (*MF*, p. 36). She still seems to maintain a romantic conception of her affair, though the reader is surely invited to see it as a purely carnal and financial matter on the part of the seducer, who is clearly prepared to pay to get her off his hands. Eventually, she accepts his ending of the affair, and marries Robin. Since this alliance is neither romantic nor criminal, it does not appear in the narrative. * * * We are told only that for five years they 'liv'd very agreeably together', until Robin dies, leaving Moll 'a Widow with about 1200*l.* in my Pocket' (*MF*, p. 49).

All in all, this whole episode serves to bring into the novel the powerful force which Moll later refers to as '*that Cheat call'd* LOVE' (*MF*, p. 50). Moll's view of romantic attachment is initially very unusual in context, and only gradually becomes sour. Defoe's professed views were rather different, and they too can be seen as idiosyncratic. In the context of contemporary debate, Defoe's arguments about romantic love, and its relation to matrimony, can be seen as fairly liberal. However, he still saw that the danger of romantic attachment was that it was often merely a screen for sexual desire, and that marriage based on sexual attraction 'brings madness, desperation, ruin of families, disgrace, self-murders, killings of bastards, etc'.[8] Moll herself never develops any coherent attitude or policy towards her dilemma, and that is one of the ways she is rendered individual, distinct from conventional heroines and from Defoe himself. When describing her early sexual conduct, the retrospective Moll makes very few reflections, as though some of her illusions remain intact. In the Preface, the 'Editor' excuses this part of the book by claiming that it 'has so many happy Turns given to expose the Crime, and warn all whose Circumstances are adapted to it, of the ruinous End of such Things, and the foolish Thoughtless and abhorr'd Conduct of both the Parties' (*MF*, p. 4). Though the editor points out the moral lesson to be drawn, Moll does not, and the narrative does not seem to invite any such solemn reading. Moll's comments are very limited and never seem as strict as the editor would have us believe. Though she may recognise the shoddiness of the elder brother's behaviour in 'shifting off his Whore into his Brothers Arms for a Wife' (*MF*, p. 48), she retains her blinding affec-

8. The quotation comes from a long debate on this topic, in which Defoe's contributions are summarised. See Lawrence Stone, *The Family, Sex and Marriage in England 1500–1800* (Abridged and revised edn, Harmondsworth, 1979), pp. 149–216.

tion for him. She may retrospectively acknowledge that love is a cheat, but she seems helpless to prevent it, and her condemnation affects her behaviour negligibly.

Significantly, Moll does not interpret her treatment as a cruelty, and she does not become hardened against the world as the *pícaro* does. Love is understood as the area of Moll's life most subject to hazard, and it has the narrative function that the weather has in *Crusoe*. The tempests which disrupt the narrative in *Crusoe* are actual; in *Moll*, they are metaphorical, but nonetheless effective as agents of disruption. Moll may fall in love at anytime, though she does become much more self-assured as the book progresses, and there are the attendant hazards of children and illness. Yet though this area of her life is the most subject to chance, it is the area where Moll's moral scruples are most active. If the book presents itself as divided into criminal adventures on the one hand, and romantic interludes on the other, Moll saves her piety for the latter, and even there it actually does very little.[9] In her criminal adventures, her self-reproach is infrequent and perfunctory, though there may be some signs of the pattern of overreaching apparent to the reader. Only in her romantic adventures does she offer any descriptions of evil, or show genuine repugnance or abhorrence, although in that area of her life she seems least responsible for her own behaviour. It may be suggested that what emerges in the narrative is a picture of what Lawrence Stone calls 'the growth of affective individualism', placed within the context of a society which is hostile to such individualism, and within a narrative which relies more heavily on conventions and types.

Moll's self-assurance and calculation increase rapidly after the first marriage, and become the motivating forces for her second wedding. As she puts it, 'I was resolv'd now to be Married, or Nothing, and to be well Married, or not at all' (*MF*, p. 50). However, even within the self-imposed limits of caution and prudence, Moll is characteristically impulsive and excessive in the way she treats her husband's money, and in the way she thinks of love. She learns that life in London is very different from life in the relatively rural Colchester, a fact which was already apparent to the reader in the fast behaviour of the elder brother:

> I was not to expect at *London*, what I had found in the Country; that Marriages were here the Consequences of politick

9. William Bowman Piper, in his '*Moll Flanders* as a Structure of Topics', *SEL*, IX (1969): pp. 489–502, suggests a tripartite division of the book into sexual adventures, adventures in theft, and Virginia adventures. For the purposes of the present generic approach, the Virginia sections can be further subdivided into sexual (like the incest episode), or criminal (like the transportation).

> Schemes, for forming Interests and carrying on Business, and that LOVE had no Share, or but very little in the Matter . . . (*MF*, pp. 55–56).

Though Moll does come to accept the general truth that 'Money only made a Woman agreeable' (*MF*, p. 56), and that good looks and wit were good properties in a mistress, not in a wife, she still thinks of herself as an exception. Certainly, none of her marriages really deserves to be called a 'politick Scheme'. They all may start from that idea, but they are soon changed by foolishness or affection. She is persistently impolitic in spending money so easily, and especially so in paying attention to her feelings for her Lancashire husband, the fellow criminal, Jemmy. The extent to which her dealings are dominated by calculation may be surprisingly less than she herself believes. One critic claims that 'Moll has to set aside many feelings and attitudes which she cannot afford . . . Moll lives a life crowded with event and absolutely bare of feeling'.[1] While it is clearly the case that Moll's life is congested, it is surely a mistake to think of her as devoid of feeling. There are even a number of occasions when feeling wins out over prudence, such as the incest and abortion episodes, and these typify her affairs more than does cynical calculation.

The very important episode concerning her unwitting incest is one of those instances of rediscovered family that appear throughout Defoe's fiction. The reunion between Friday and his father, Jack's rediscovery of his wife in Virginia, and Roxana's furtive reunion with her daughter are all used as central plotting devices in their respective tales. There are a number of these events in *Moll*, notably the meeting of Moll and her highwayman husband in Newgate, but the most important one is her discovery that she has inadvertently married her own brother. The event is her third marriage, and before entering it, Moll has satisfied herself that her spouse is after more than just her cash. Moll then briskly arranges the financial matters, and on this occasion, talks very little about romance. After they have settled in the husband's plantation in Virginia, Moll spends some time with his mother, whom she realises with horror to be her own mother. Moll's first reactions are very dramatic and powerful:

> I WAS now the most unhappy of all Women in the World: O had the Story never been told me, all had been well; it had been no Crime to have lain with my Husband, since as to his being my Relation, I had known nothing of it . . . (*MF*, p. 72).

Were she *only* to be concerned with financial security or comfort, she could accept this accident reasonably calmly, and could tolerate

1. Denis Donoghue, 'The Values of *Moll Flanders*', *Sewanee Review*, LXXI (1963): pp. 287–303.

the living arrangements. But Moll repeatedly asserts that her position is somehow deeply repugnant to 'Nature'. Though she cannot be held in any way responsible for this state, which is the result of pure chance (and, on a narrative level, rather implausibly abrupt chance), she still suffers extreme guilt and shame. This alone would indicate that her life is not 'bare of feeling', though the feelings may seem to be histrionically expressed.

Moll's secrecy about her incestuous marriage lasts a startling three years, a period of time more suitable to the fairy tale than to the realistic report. The truth eventually slips out in a quarrel, and her brother / husband is shocked into serious illness. One critic sees in this illness a parallel to Moll's own sickness before her partly incestuous marriage to Robin.[2] Indeed, the two episodes can be presented as closely related—Moll's illness is interpreted as a kind of punishment for her deceptive marriage to Robin. Certainly, Moll herself has thought of the earlier marriage as incestuous, since she thought of Robin's brother while lying with Robin. There is a long casuistical tradition in which lustful thoughts are no less evil than lustful deeds.[3] Of course, Moll herself makes no mention of any parallel between the two episodes, but that alone does not rule out its validity. Defoe could be said to be surreptitiously unifying his narrative by giving the reader a more coherent view of events than the narrator has, and so turning the narrator into an ironically myopic figure. Such a procedure would be wholly outside the realm of popular fiction, but it is still a possibility. However, the basis for such an analysis of the book's hidden structure is rather unconvincing.

The episode with Robin and the later marriage are only very loosely and chronologically related. Moll's three years of reticence has no parallel with her earlier, brisk behaviour, and generally the incest episode stands on its own, obtruding from rather than cohering with the rest of the tale. *Moll* is, of course, not the only eighteenth-century narrative to encompass incest—it appears, fleetingly, in *Tom Jones* and elsewhere—and Stone's book makes it clear that the whole subject was obviously under widespread discussion. Given the congested accommodation in which most people lived, and the lack of social mobility, acts of incest must have been frequent, though almost always covert. However, the idiosyncratic thing about the episode in *Moll* is the extent to which the narrator's revulsion is developed. Moll describes her feelings acutely and at some length:

> I was really alienated from him in the Consequence of these Things; indeed I mortally hated him as a Husband, and it was

2. Douglas Brooks, '*Moll Flanders*: An Interpretation', *EC*, XIX (1969): pp. 46–59. See also the more fulsome treatment in his *Number and Pattern in the Eighteenth-Century Novel* (London, 1973).
3. See G. A. Starr, *Defoe and Casuistry*, pp. 123, 134–35.

> impossible to remove that riveted Aversion I had to him; *at the same time* it being an unlawful incestuous living added to that Aversion; and tho' I had no great concern about it in point of Conscience, yet every thing added to make Cohabiting with him the most nauseous thing to me in the World; and I think verily it was come to such a height, that I could almost as willingly have embrac'd a Dog, as have let him offer any thing of that kind to me, for which Reason I could not bear the thoughts of coming between the Sheets with him . . . (*MF*, p. 80)

It is made clear here that the revulsion is not simply a kind of moral condemnation (' . . . I had no great concern about it in point of Conscience'), but a kind of irrational, personal revulsion. The very graphic image of the dog enhances the power of Moll's remarks, which do not seem to fit easily into her otherwise rather blithe personality.

The horror which incest holds for Moll is reinforced by her lover's reaction to the discovery. He is so disturbed that he makes two attempts at suicide, and eventually falls into a consumption. This would indicate that Moll is not the only one to feel such powerful reactions, and gives the episode an eerie, frighteningly sombre effect. Yet the reaction is certainly given great dramatic force, by being so much greater than the audience might be likely to expect. M. E. Novak has shown that the condemnation of incest here is much stricter than would be likely from any of the theorists of Natural Law, from whom Defoe drew so much.[4] The theorist Pufendorf, for instance, accepted that some countries might sanction incest, and that any European revulsion at it might only be the result of ingrained custom. Even the customs of the time were much less severe than Moll's reaction might lead us to believe. Lawrence Stone describes the legal position:

> [T]he punishments meted out by Church courts in cases of incest in Elizabethan England were surprisingly lenient, and there is no reason to think that sodomy and bestiality were more repugnant to popular standards of morality than breaking of the laws of incest, which must have been common in those overcrowded houses where adolescent children were still at home . . .[5]

If this was known to be true of Elizabethan courts, it is likely to have been the case in the 1650s, when, by the chronology of the tale, Moll's actions are alleged to have occurred. Bearing all these facts in mind, Moll's reaction to the incestuous marriage is highly dra-

4. *Defoe and the Nature of Man*, pp. 108–10.
5. Stone, *The Family, Sex and Marriage*, p. 309.

matic, and unrepresentative of the way incest was treated in other popular discourses.

The episode serves in the tale to introduce a more thorough delineation of a character's responses to hardship. In *Crusoe*, the narrator's responses to privation were stylised and conventional. In *Moll*, much more of the narrative is taken up in presenting how things felt, and in rendering them immediate. To some extent, this makes *Moll* much more a book about character and development, though the development it portrays is fairly rudimentary. But Moll herself certainly has more than a conventionally unifying function. She is provided with qualities of individuality which keep the book's generic categorisation at bay. Because Moll is somewhat volatile and unpredictable, readers are unable to assimilate the full process of the narrative in advance, and so Defoe is able to move from the criminal tale, to the confessional or romantic tale, without having to change the conventional attributes to his narrator.

Another example of Moll's individuality can be seen in the way she responds to children. Much has previously been made of her rather casual attitude to them, though Stone has shown how common her type of 'fostering-out' was, and though they are understood best as mere narrative props.[6] After all, the narrators of *Moll, Colonel Jack* and *Captain Singleton* are all originally children discarded by their parents. However, it is worthy of note that Moll has curiously strict views about abortion. At one point, she is likely to bear a rather inconvenient child:

> my Apprehensions were really that I should Miscarry; I should not say Apprehensions, for indeed I would have been glad to miscarry, but I cou'd never be brought to entertain so much as a thought of endeavouring to Miscarry, or of taking anything to make me *Miscarry*, I abhorr'd, I say so much as the thought of it (*MF*, p. 127).[7]

Seen in terms exclusively of self-interest and policy, Moll would be well advised to seek abortion. Her rejection of that recourse seems both irrational and fundamental, but not the result of deliberate thought. She rejects both abortion and incest on emotional, instinctive feelings of repugnance, not on the basis of some ethical code.

So far, then, Moll has been given a sporadically individuated characterisation, with eccentricities and idiosyncracies of viewpoint which cannot simply be explained as forgetfulness on the part of the

6. Ibid., pp. 267–99.
7. Moll's plight must have been very common, when contraception was so rudimentary. Examples of the kinds of potion which are available to those less squeamish than Moll are given by Stone, *The Family, Sex and Marriage*, p. 266.

author. Her motivation stems episodically from her sense of gentility, from her desire for economic self-sufficiency and from love. As such, it is much more varied than Crusoe's repeated 'wandering Inclination', and his fears of death. Moll's behaviour is not made coherent (or even presented *as* coherent) by any series of references to the shaping hand of Providence. Nor does her criminal career fit into any obvious pattern of punishment or reward. The intensity of her emotional reactions makes Moll a much more complex character than Crusoe, and allows the narrative a greater flexibility than the more schematic presentation of the earlier tale. Crusoe's emotions were often presented, but only on occasions of guilt or loneliness, which could always potentially correspond to a providential reading.[8] Moll's emotions are much more extensive and varied than those of her generic predecessors * * * and they certainly rely a lot less on the alleged promptings of supernatural intrusion. Even her conscience does not seem to be a very important factor (despite the attention drawn to it by the Preface), and her emotions are largely spontaneous and unpredictable.

In her criminal adventures, Moll fits more readily into the acknowledged fictional patterns of her predecessors. The narrative occasionally takes on the pattern of the confessional tale, with the apparently penitent Moll expressing conventional disapproval of the former conduct with which her narrative is actually trying to entertain us. She sees most of her thieving as voluntary, and so has to see herself as culpable, though throughout the presentation of this part of her life there is a great deal of elision and equivocation. She believes that her earliest crimes arose from necessity, and, therefore, that they are conventionally acceptable. They serve to warn the reader that anyone can be driven to such extremes, and to remove the taint of prurience from reading by fitting the thefts into an admonitory pattern. She is aware that theft can sometimes be acceptable as an alternative to starvation, but even this rudimentary moral point is presented imperceptively and sporadically.

Necessity is offered as an exculpatory plea on a number of occasions. Moll deceives most of her suitors about her true financial position, for instance, and offers the excuse that such deviousness is necessary for an unprotected woman in a hostile world. The degree to which Moll is genuinely in jeopardy, and the degree to which she is a predator in her own right, are kept uncertain throughout the narrative. However, Moll's view is that such crookedness is necessary, and if it is necessary, then it is morally excusable. Such a view is consonant with Natural Law theory, and appears throughout

8. See Benjamin Boyce, 'The Question of Emotion in Defoe', *SP*, L (1953): pp. 44–58.

Defoe's fiction.[9] Her reliance on necessity as a plea of justification is most prominent when she is in difficulties, and when she is discussing her affairs with a banker:

> I was now a loose unguided Creature, and had no Help, no Assistance, no Guide for my Conduct: I knew what I aim'd at, and what I wanted, but knew nothing to pursue the End by direct Means; I wanted to be plac'd in a settled State of Living, and had I happen'd to meet with a good sober Husband, I should have been as faithful and true a Wife as Virtue it self cou'd have form'd: If I had been otherwise, the Vice came in always at the Door of Necessity, not at the Door of Inclination . . . (*MF*, p. 103)

If this position were plausible, then Moll would always be in the clear, and the fact that it sounds so much like arrant self-justification may turn the narrative more towards irony when Moll is being reflective. Moll's attempts to excuse her lapses are never fully convincing. Her greatest criminal excesses arise much more from the fear of eventual or impending poverty than from immediate or imminent poverty. She steals in advance of necessity, in case necessity comes along, which is as morally incoherent as retaliating before provocation.

Though we need not fall for Moll's interpretation of her own life, we are still invited to follow the events avidly, in an involved way. In the narrative, as opposed to Moll's moral interjections, the theme of exculpatory necessity recurs. The banker describes his estranged wife as 'a Whore not by Necessity, which is the common Bait of your Sex, but by Inclination, and for the Sake of Vice' (*MF*, p. 108). Moll's acceptance of this tale helps her justify her own behaviour, and she does consistently approach other people's behaviour in very simple graphic terms—acting from necessity is excusable, but acting viciously from inclination is reprehensible and intolerable. * * * However, even this very simple moral view within the tale, which is the kind of graphic morality necessary for the functioning of popular fiction, is disrupted whenever emotional attachment intrudes. She never applies her standards to the elder brother in Colchester, to her mother, or to Jemmy, and so the narrative, it seems, takes only a fitful and crude interest in the moral status of its events.

Moll's first criminal acts occur after her banker husband has died, leaving her very poor. She is led to quote a remark which becomes familiar in this book, as well as in *Colonel Jack* and *Roxana*, *'Give*

9. See 'The Problem of Necessity in Defoe's Fiction', in *Defoe and the Nature of Man*, Chapter III.

me not Poverty least I Steal' (*MF*, p. 151).[1] Another familiar tactic is her attribution of her criminal inclinations to the Devil's promptings.[2] Certainly, this is the first time in the narrative that Moll offers a supernatural intervention, and it does seem to happen at a disquietingly convenient time:

> THIS was the Bait, and the Devil who I said laid the Snare, as readily prompted me, as if he had spoke, for I remember, and shall never forget it, 'twas like a Voice spoken to me over my Shoulder, take the Bundle; be quick; do it this Moment . . . (*MF*, p. 151)

Moll's dramatic presentation of her own state is less conventional than Crusoe's and more aware of itself as a piece of imaginative reconstruction. The use of a sly 'as if' renders the account dramatic, and yet makes it also appear as though Moll is the victim rather than the aggressor here. As a presentation of the supernatural, it should not be taken seriously. Even in *Crusoe*, the talk of predictions, dreams, 'secret hints' and so on, was never fully sustained or coherent, but it was persistent enough to become an integral part of the narrative, and to assist in its generic categorisation as sporadically a spiritual autobiography. In *Moll*, the reference is too isolated for this, and serves to concentrate attention on the drama of the moment, rather than on any overall plan.

Moll's life of crime is by now established, and in this respect the narrative becomes somewhat uneasy. The mode of presentation is never simple or single, and many passages offer ironic possibilities, as well as admonitory ones. In the famous episode where Moll justifies, or attempts to justify, the theft of a child's necklace, the variety of modes is obvious. If we accept the Natural Law background to the tale, then stealing from someone worse off than yourself is clearly wicked.[3] However, Moll retrospectively tries to make the theft into an act of rough charity and benevolence, in a charmingly flagrant piece of rationalisation:

> Poverty, as I have said, harden'd my Heart, and my own Necessities made me regardless of any thing: The last Affair left no great Concern upon me, for as I did the poor Child no harm, I only said to my self, I had given the Parents a just Reproof for their Negligence in leaving the poor little Lamb to come home

1. G. A. Starr refers to five other allusions to this proverb in other works by Defoe. See *Defoe and Spiritual Autobiography*, p. 78n.
2. Starr refers to Defoe's *Political History of the Devil* for a parallel passage (*MF*, p. 191n), and the whole episode can be compared with the benign supernatural interventions in *Crusoe* and *Singleton*.
3. An episode of this kind occurs in *Colonel Jack*, and it is Jack's realisation that it is a despicable crime that serves to bring him to his senses.

> by it self, and it would teach them to take more Care of it another time . . . (*MF*, pp. 153–54)

Once she has cast herself in the role of protector of innocent children, Moll is captivated by the notion. The child's mother obviously suffers from 'Vanity', and the maid whom Moll supposes to have been looking after the child becomes 'a careless Jade . . . taken up perhaps with some Fellow that had met her by the way' (*MF*, p. 154). This kind of expansive opportunism is typical of Moll's presentation of her criminal life. The quickness of thought, and recognisable consistency of character, is very much more pronounced than it ever was with Crusoe. Defoe makes use of the opportunities of the criminal narrative to incorporate comic capers, and to establish a consistently self-seeking character for his narrator.

So both Moll's career as a thief, and as an autobiographer are best characterised by spontaneity and opportunism. Rather than being carefully planned and organised by Moll, both careers are erratic, wayward and skilful in the exploitation of opportunity. It is possible to think of Moll psychologically, unlike Crusoe, and to see her as consistently impulsive, cunning and volatile. Consequently, Moll's narration is much less stable than Crusoe's, and she seeks to encompass even more forms and modes than he did. The various conflicts and discrepancies in *Crusoe* could not be explained by the character of the narrator, but they can be more readily explained that way in *Moll*. Moll consistently offers us *her* view of the world, rather than simply being used to present a generically competent view of the world.

Such an argument comes close to claiming that the book is consistently ironic, and that reading it depends on the reader's sceptical aloofness from the narrator. However, there is no need to make the book quite as consistent in viewpoint as that. When discussing the episode of the child's necklace, and a later outrage where Moll takes advantage of a drunken gentleman (for his own good, as she says), Dorothy Van Ghent came to this conclusion:

> We are left with two possibilities. Either *Moll Flanders* is a collection of scandal-sheet anecdotes naively patched together with the platitudes that form the morality of an impoverished soul (Defoe's), a 'sincere' soul but a confused and degraded one; or *Moll Flanders* is a great novel, coherent in structure, unified and given shape by a complex system of ironies.[4]

What Van Ghent might mean by a 'complex system of ironies' is not clear, and the alternative views she suggests are surely not the only

4. *The English Novel: Form and Function*, p. 42.

possibilities of articulating the text. It seems fairer to suggest that the book is a collection of anecdotes, some of which would find a home in scandal-sheets (why not?), but that the characteristics of its narrator give it the kind of shape it has. At times, too, an ironic reading is made possible by the tension between what Moll tells us, and what we can deduce from her omissions and distortions. However, the book is too eclectic to be understood as consistently ironic or consistently mimetic. Its modes are various, as are its genres, and the sole consistency lies in the emergent character of the narrator.

The self-serving nature of Moll's narration can be seen by looking at the way she refers to the supernatural. In *Crusoe*, the narrator had nothing to gain by invoking Providence, only an increase in guilt, and yet another threat, so his references to it were not self-serving. However, Moll's use of the plea of necessity, and her supernatural motives, becomes much less convincing as the tale progresses:

> THUS the Devil who began, by the help of an irresistable Poverty, to push me into this Wickedness, brought me on to a height beyond the common Rate, even when my Necessities were not so great, or the prospect of my Misery so terrifying; for I had now got into a little Vein of Work, and as I was not at a loss to handle my Needle, it was very probable, as my Acquaintance came in, I might have got my Bread honestly enough . . . (*MF*, p. 160)

The return of the ideal of working diligently at a small skill is only cursory, and Moll returns to grand acts of theft. There is some sense here of the limits of excusable behaviour, as there is in the incest and abortion episodes, and, in a much more dramatic way, in *Roxana*. However, the most important thing about the passage is the way it signals to the reader that Moll is now exactly the kind of gentlewoman she wished to be at the very beginning. Moll herself does not draw any parallels, and this may indicate a larger organisation of irony than is often apparent. The references to the Devil as the force which prevents her from attaining this sought-after quiet life seem highly unconvincing and conventional, but show Moll herself trying to fit her criminal behaviour into a recognised generic pattern. She wants to present herself as the paradigm of the good person locked in combat with the Devil, losing temporarily, but winning finally. Our recognition that her behaviour does not fully accord with this pattern is strengthened if we are familiar with the popular genres in which it is apparent, such as the confessional tale, and the spiritual autobiography.

The book is entering into a kind of ironic parody of these popular genres, by laying great emphasis on Moll's reticence, and her partial disclosures. In the overt, stated interpretation of her life, Moll moves from childish innocence, into poverty, justifiable theft and unjustifiable theft, before finally being rewarded for her penitence. Clearly, if it is possible to have doubts about any stage in this process, it is possible to doubt the probity of her penitence. Like the early storm repentances of Crusoe, it seems very much in the penitent's interests, and to be motivated entirely by fear. It occurs after Moll has returned to Newgate, and is haunted by her fate.[5] She has been caught red-handed in the act of theft, and has been condemned to death. Her tutor in crime, too, has been condemned to die in prison, and the combination of shocks and frights brings Moll round to a kind of temporary penitence. She had been provided with further admonitory examples—like the arrest of two colleagues (*MF*, p. 165), or the sight of a thief being given over to 'the Rage of the Street' (*MF*, p. 167). Even in court, when she was seeking damages for her wrongful arrest, her earlier bravado prevailed. The significant date of Christmas Day, on which she was arrested, passed without comment. After all these warnings, more apparent to the trained reader of confessional tales than to the narrator, she finds herself in Newgate. In M. E. Novak's view, these episodes are most properly seen as unnoticed examples of stealthy Providence. In discussing Moll's behaviour after her first casual attempt at repentance, at the fire, he says, 'it is suggestive of divine Providence that the next time Moll attempts to steal at a fire, she is struck and almost killed by a mattress which is thrown from a window'.[6] However, the possible providential pattern before her capture is not mentioned by Moll herself, and seems only fortuitous.

Moll's subsequent 'conversion' is made to seem easy and brief, and it has no effect at all on her behaviour. In the oppressive atmosphere of the prison, she feels what she takes to be stirrings of remorse and abhorrence for her past life. The sight of Jemmy, also imprisoned, makes her feel irrationally responsible for his fate. There is no need for this, and it seems like emotional indulgence. Jemmy was, after all, a confirmed and notorious highwayman before meeting Moll, and he had simply returned to his old occupation. Once again, we are not obliged to accept Moll's understanding of events, and the brief possibility of irony is again present. She is still under sentence of death, and the language she uses to express her contrition makes it all seem very self-interested:

> He visited me again the next Morning, and went on with his Method of explaining the Terms of Divine Mercy, which accord-

5. It is possible to make too much of the symbolic nature of Newgate, and to forget that it serves as a genuine, rather than as a symbolic, threat to Moll. Arnold Kettle's claim that it is 'an eighteenth-century *huis clos*' seems strained, if we remember the actual jeopardy Moll is under in Newgate. See Kettle, 'In Defence of *Moll Flanders*', *Of Books and Humankind*, John Butt (ed.) (London, 1964).
6. *Defoe and the Nature of Man*, p. 79.

> ing to him consisted of nothing more than that of being sincerely desirous of it, and willing to accept it; only a sincere Regret for, and hatred of those things I had done which render'd me so just an Object of divine Vengeance . . . I was cover'd with Shame and Tears for things past, and yet had at the same time a secret surprizing Joy at the Prospect of being a true Penitent, and obtaining the Comfort of a Penitent, I mean the hope of being forgiven . . . (*MF*, p. 227)

The paradoxical simultaneous occurrence of shame and joy is typical of the moment of conversion, as represented in Defoe.[7] However, Moll seems to get the shame out of the way fairly quickly, and to get on with the joy as soon as possible. She seems struck by 'Divine Mercy' as a kind of bargain, and her references to its 'Terms' makes the idea of a transaction more apparent. This stress on the convenience of penitence, and on its cheapness, must make it seem like just another violent transition in the narrative, rather than the ultimate, important one.

Moll's conversion seems as naive and impulsive as all her earlier behaviour. Its self-interest is much more apparent to readers than to her. When she tells it, she is not trying to deceive us into thinking it to be more serious than it really was. Rather, she is consistently expressing her eagerness and whimsicality, which she thinks of as earnestness and conviction. This curious kind of persistent innocence is one of the book's most interesting features, and one which moves it out of the adventure category into the character study, at least in parts. The innocence is apparent not only in the conversion scenes, but also in the passages of self-justification, such as the theft of the child's necklace. Moll is emphatically not trying to put one over on us, or to get away with things she believes to be wrong—she simply believes anything that strikes her at any moment. Her most idiosyncratic feature as a criminal narrator is her lack of guile, and her credulity, which is a kind of unworldliness very much at odds with her aggressive criminality. Rather as some people may be tone deaf or colour blind, Moll seems to be morally insensitive to her own behaviour, and to remain somehow remote from its implications. This allows her to change with great speed and agility, and yet also to avoid cynicism and hypocrisy. She understands events spontaneously and irrationally, as in the abortion scene, and never finds an overall view of herself. Though it would be very wrong to think of her as an *ingenue*, she does seem to lack any wholehearted calculation, and retains a freshness and spontaneity to the end.

Such openness to change can be seen in the way Moll eventually

7. See G. A. Starr, *MF*, p. 289n.

does get out of Newgate. Her more worldly fellow prisoners advise her that bribery is the way to secure freedom, and Moll is convinced. It takes little argument to get her to see that lining pockets is a more reliable and immediate way of having her sentence commuted than prayer. As her tutor says, 'did you ever know one in your Life that was Transported, and had a Hundred Pound in his Pocket' (*MF*, p. 231). Moll's ready acceptance of this advice shows the degree to which her conversion is simultaneously genuine and self-seeking. It is adopted as the best way to escape hardship, and as such, it is seen to be a full, if not a profound, emotional experience. It cannot be seen as a moral experience, since it is dispersed as soon as an easier, or quicker, avenue to escape is revealed.

It seems, then, as though Moll's conversion might be wholly genuine as long as it lasts, for Moll is entirely convinced by it. The fact that she does not retrospectively assess its impermanence is very interesting, and shows us something about the conventionality of the narrative posture. At this point in the tale, Moll has not only bribed her way to a reprieve from the gallows, she has also gained a kind of conditional pardon. Though she takes no direct part in the bribery herself, she is certainly prepared to accept the intercessions of others on her behalf, and does not inquire at all closely into their methods. It would be inappropriate to see this as hypocrisy, because of Moll's suddenness of emotion. It may appear inconsistent at first, but once Moll is seen to be volatile and persistently changeable, it seems an appropriate thing for her to do. We are not being invited to respond to this shift morally, but to accept it dramatically as one of the urgent transitions on which popular narrative is organised. These transitions are not deeply laid within the text, but arise suddenly, without premeditation.

Moll's penitence soon passes, and no memory of it lingers. The advantage of her abruptness is that it renders the past null and void, and Moll only exercises her memory as narrator, not as character. Once she has secured her release from Newgate, there are no vestiges of penitence left. When she sets up home in Virginia, she is perfectly prepared to live from the earnings of her criminal life, and even when she is reminded of her bigamous and incestuous state, she does not feel the need to do anything about it. Her money ensures a good trip to Virginia, and by bribing the ship's captain, Moll and Jemmy are allowed their freedom very readily. At this point, stable and secure, Moll reminds us of her alleged purpose in writing her autobiography:

> As the publishing this Account of my Life, is for the sake of the just Moral of every part of it, and for Instruction, Caution, Warning and Improvement to every Reader . . . (*MF*, p. 255)

But would every reader be instructed, cautioned, warned and improved by the narrative? The demands seem very great, and do not seem to accord with the narrative as it stands. The reader is likely to have been enthralled and entertained, as readers of popular fiction are entitled to be, but no other major endeavour has been noticeable. Popular narrative has the dual function of reminding you what the world is actually like, while allowing it not to be effective for a while. In *Moll*, the world is seen to be wholly mercenary and fairly vicious, as it is in *Crusoe*, but the pontentially disastrous consequences of that violence are kept at bay by the conventional structure. *Moll* becomes a comic narrative, because of the self-preserving romantic innocence of the protagonist, and because that innocence is allowed to triumph.

Most critics who have tried to see the book as unified or cohesive have seen it as a consistent search, organised by the characteristics of the heroine. Terence Martin, for instance, sees Moll's desire to be a gentlewoman as the central feature of the text. Moll first tries to secure her status by marriage. When this fails, she turns to crime, and when crime fails she turns to penitence.[8] Martin's case depends on the number of references to be found in the narrative to gentility and to a kind of speculation about a hidden structure which depends on Moll's own character. If his argument is acceptable, the main part of the narrative becomes an ironic examination of the meaning of gentility in a material society. Moll achieves what she desires, and in the process, readers come to see the shabby reality of gentility. However, Martin's argument becomes rather distorted when he overemphasises the degree of singleness of purpose to be found in the book. The ironies of Moll's quest are granted, and her character gives the book its consistency, but it never becomes fully unified or cohesive. Martin pays very little attention to the incest episode, which obtrudes from his scheme, and he deals only sketchily with her penitence. The penitence could certainly be accommodated to an ironic reading of the text, but the incest episode does not seem to fit. Again, as in *Crusoe*, Defoe is adopting the popular standard of compendiousness, rather than the polite standard of single-mindedness. The book simply does not present itself as a linear process of any kind—'Moll's progress is not simply from fear to moral stupidity to repentance. Such a bald moral summary neglects the actual strategies of the narrative . . . '[9] In *Crusoe, Colonel Jack, Captain Singleton* and *A Journal of the Plague Year*, the redemptive process is only one of

8. Terence Martin, 'The Unity of *Moll Flanders*', *MLQ*, XXII (1961): pp. 115–24. For similar arguments, see Koonce, 'Moll's Muddle', and J. A. Michie, 'The Unity of *Moll Flanders*', in *Knaves and Swindlers: Essays on the Picaresque Novel in Europe*, C. J. Whitbourn (ed.) (London, 1974), pp. 75–93.
9. John J. Richetti, *Defoe's Narratives*, p. 139.

several dramatic threads, and is not necessarily superior to the others. In *Moll*, it is offered by the editor as dominant, but the narrative itself is capable of various interpretations, diffuse and lacking in singleness of purpose.

What really prevents a full ironic rendering of the narrative is certainly the odd incest episode. Indeed, it seems as though that episode thwarts *any* reading of the book as a single, linear enterprise. Even Novak's persuasive view of the book as a dramatised presentation of the ideas of Natural Law has to be emended to encompass Moll's inappropriate horror. Similarly, few of the other writers who see the narrative as unified (Van Ghent, Martin, Koonce, Michie) offer much analysis of that topic; and Brook's view that it is the most important episode in the book is surely incompatible with a full reading of the variousness of the narrative. The most plausible view of the event is that it shows the opportunism of Defoe's procedure. Having by accident or design (it does not really matter which) come to present the character of Moll, Defoe offers her adventures in as wide a range of circumstances as his genres will allow. Just as in *The English Rogue*, where Meriton Latroon is allowed to have all manner of adventures, so Defoe's heroine is only restricted by the peculiarities of her situation. By giving her this strange series of irrational scruples, Defoe allows her to be unpredictable, and so incorporates another interesting uncertainty into his drama. Meriton Latroon, like Crusoe to some extent, is only a convenient foil for adventures, and is given only the most rudimentary characterisation. So too with the heroes and heroines of criminal tales, jest books and the like. The central figure of *Long Meg of Westminster*, for instance, is only individuated by her physique and the nature of her adventures. Defoe promises comic adventures in the title, with its references to 'Fortunes and Misfortunes', but he complicates and enhances these by making his heroine capable of idiosyncratic reactions. By making Moll capable of sentimentality, as when she kisses the ground her son has travelled over, Defoe effects a kind of compromise between the criminal tale and the romance. The predominantly comic mode (announced immediately by the breezy first person narration) allows the adventures to continue indeterminately, with the category of ending being comfortably assured. So no abrupt penitence is required to effect the ending, only a kind of accommodation and assimilation of Moll into a family group.

By stressing the popular genres in which *Moll* partly participates, and by stressing the incorporation into her character of coyness, a certain prudishness and some sentimentality, the book becomes both comic and partly heroic. It celebrates the way its heroine survives intact throughout hardship, and offers her adventures as a source of comfort and satisfaction. By trying to wrest the book into the sensitive, even rather desiccated world of polite literature, critics can transform its robustness into a kind of hard insensitivity, and so distort the book's vitality. As Denis Donoghue argues:

> What Defoe says about life, in *Moll Flanders*, is true, as far as it goes, but the book is based upon a set of terms which ignores two-thirds of human existence; these terms cancel all aspects of human consciousness to which the analogies of trade are irrelevant . . . As a result, the book cannot conceive of human action as genial, charitable, or selfless; hence it cannot survive comparison with a novel like *Portrait of a Lady* in which the enabling vision of life is wide, generous, answerable to human possibility.

Donoghue's case seems to be based entirely on a strange view of literature, and on a category mistake in treating Defoe. If you believe, as he seems to, that worthwhile literature has to say something about 'life', and that it has to have a vision which is to be 'wide, generous, answerable to human possibility', then only very few books should be allowable reading or considered seriously. All popular fiction, all journalism and a great deal of ineffective polite literature has to be discarded, in favour of a select canon of great books. The purpose of studying these books becomes one of minute but perceptible moral improvement in the reader. This is clearly not a workable view for a literary historian, interested in the kinds of book which people have read, and why they have found them worth their attention. And only the literary historian of that kind will be able to make any sense of Defoe. Comparing *Moll Flanders* to *Portrait of a Lady* is a worthless and foolish exercise. What is it meant to reveal? The books are obviously different, and offer wholly different kinds of satisfaction. They presume utterly different kinds of reader, and utterly different kinds of reading. *Moll* can easily be made to appear mercenary and squalid by the comparison, but it is unfair.

As well as these reservations about Donoghue's whole procedure, there are two obvious points of disagreement between his position and mine. First of all, it is mistaken to amalgamate Defoe's views and Moll's, since there are obvious attempts at irony, and obvious attempts to make Moll an autonomous character. Secondly by stressing Moll's proneness to 'that Cheat call'd LOVE', and its importance in the narrative, it is possible to see something present other than the mercenary. However, the interest of the book does not lie in avoiding the mercenary. There is, after all, no reason why stories should not be wholly mercenary. But the main interest in the story is the way it exists within a system of genres, and the way it offers variants of these genres, some innovative, some not. The genres which foresee any reading of *Moll* would be the criminal tale, the confessional, the romantic adventure and perhaps the extended jest book. The narrative is unique, however, in the way it begins to establish a character for its narrator, and to base all its events on the cumulative revelation of that character.

As yet, Defoe's fiction is still very monist in its presentation of character. Secondary characters have only a fleeting existence, and the narrative goes beyond egoism to the point of solipsism. In *Crusoe*, the characters of his father, Xury, Friday and the others were presented in a stylised and casual way. In *Moll*, the narrator's various lovers are only lightly sketched (indeed, some are not even mentioned as anything other than components of a total), and only Jemmy and the criminal tutor are given any extensive role. Important characters such as Moll's mother and brother, and Robin, are only very briefly in existence within the tale. So both books have formally presented the adventures of one character, to whom all others are subordinate. The world in which they move has had little room or time for emotional ties of any kind, except with Moll's more serious alliances. In Defoe's final fiction, he went on to dramatise the conflicts which arise from such egoism, and managed to incorporate other people into his narrative. The problem of how to treat others in a hostile world does not arise within the confines of *Crusoe* or *Moll*, but it is fundamental to *Roxana*. The genre of the voyage tale, to which *Crusoe* largely belonged, had no opportunities to deal with matrimony or children. The urgency of the criminal tale in *Moll* meant that such events were of little narrative interest, and could be jettisoned. In *Roxana*, Defoe went on to treat the various social problems of matrimony and courtship, and showed the extent to which the narrator could subdue all ties in favour of self-assertion.

In *Crusoe*, Defoe exploited the possibilities of the adventure tale to present a linear, digressive narrative, based on a simple sense of the protagonist's motivating psychology. In *Moll*, the handling of a supposed internal world is firmer, and the narrator's individual personality becomes more prominent. In neither fiction are public events discussed. Crusoe shows us no interest in affairs of state. Despite being away from England for most of his adult life, he asks no questions about public affairs. Moll, too, seems remarkably remote from the affairs of the day. If we take seriously her offered date of composition, 1683, she must have lived through the Civil War, the Restoration, the Plague and the Great Fire, yet none of these events enters her tale. The supervisory genre of the criminal tale does not demand such omission, and Defoe's concentration on Moll's domestic and amatory life is one of the ways that his fiction begins to emerge from its generic classification. By situating the tale at the intersection of romance and crime, drawing on notions of femininity and money, Defoe is able to concentrate on the idiosyncratic nature of his heroine. The public issues concerned with private lives, such as the need for money or the dangers of imprisonment, are clearly handled. In *Roxana*, the private side of the narrator and her public life are put most interestingly in tension, and that allows Defoe greater room to explore her psychology.

It is in his handling of psychological notions like guilt and misery that Defoe moves beyond contemporary generic classification. That process is fleetingly present in Crusoe's terror, or in his yearnings. It is more conspicuous in Moll's capacity to fall in love. In the first case, Defoe keeps within the limits of the castaway story, and in the second, he puts the whole issue in doubt by putting Moll's protestations of emotional softness alongside her financial cunning. In *Roxana*, however, the examination of public and private life is much more purposeful, and takes the tale beyond the limits of the scandalous disclosure. The move towards a more thorough handling of character, less reliant on typology or convention, makes Roxana more congenial to modern readers, but we should not overlook the vestigial traces of older forms which Defoe retained.

Moll Flanders, then, can be fitted into Defoe's career by showing its further move away from public issues. Remarkably, Defoe dealt with crime and legislation in that fiction from the point of view of its effects. Unlike his earlier treatments of these issues, the political implications are largely ignored, and Defoe can be seen to be increasing his attention to states of mind and personal involvement. The vicariousness of Moll's experiences is offered to readers without the usual sense of mission—there are no concealed projects in *Moll Flanders*, no hidden purpose. By showing us the conflicts of an upwardly mobile woman in a competitive world, Defoe involves us in his social vision, but he asks us to concentrate on Moll, not on anyone else. Moll is less typical than Defoe's earlier characters, and less polemically employed. In the move to *Roxana*, Defoe found a way to consolidate both his private and his public concerns, and that makes it the most complex of his fictions. However widely read *Crusoe* might have been, and however popular *Moll* has subsequently become, it is *Roxana* which shows Defoe's fiction at its most exciting.

CAROL KAY

Moll Flanders: Political Woman†

Born to a condemned criminal and taken up by a gypsy band, Moll Flanders starts her life almost as detached from settled society as Robinson Crusoe on his island. Throughout *Moll Flanders*, as in *Robinson Crusoe*, the lack of an economically secure, legally defined position in society is a terrible threat and yet also a powerful incentive, an opportunity for creativity. Yet Moll's most unattached position is her point of maximum weakness at the outset of her tale, whereas Crusoe's distressing island solitude is also sovereignty. In choosing a female protagonist, Defoe did not abandon his investigation of restless power seeking. His narrative shows nothing like the ideal of feminine debility that Mary Wollstonecraft complained of at the end of the century. Nevertheless, in *Moll Flanders* the inventive resourcefulness that Defoe loved is confined within structures of subordination, deference, and dependency.

Even Locke's theoretical escape hatch of emigration fails to provide Moll with anything like Crusoe's island autonomy. America twice offers Moll the opportunity for enlarged power, but it also proves the site of conflicting authoritative claims that gather about her with threatening force. In the culminating achievement of her career, Moll furnishes a considerable estate in the colonies and so joins the class of landed proprietors, the fundamental base of political power in a nation as most eighteenth-century people conceived it. But Moll will never be lord of the manor; she remains a wife whose authority is delegated, dependent on her husband's lazy trustfulness. Her story, like Crusoe's, is said to amaze people, but she cannot tell it in her real name, much less begin with the history of her name, as Crusoe does. Defoe's "editorial" preface insists on the dependency of Moll's authorial efforts on his own literary and moral values. In a way different from Robinson Crusoe, Moll needs a sponsor and censor.

At no point in her story is Moll pictured entirely without power, but she must exercise power in relation to higher authorities. Money is a crucial tool of her advances toward security, though the reputation of wealth without the substance will sometimes do. But without a clear, honorable legal status, wealth is often insecure and sometimes unusable. Moll is like Defoe: her most important skill is

† From *Political Constructions: Defoe, Richardson, and Sterne in Relation to Hobbes, Hume, and Burke* (Ithaca and London: Cornell UP, 1988), pp. 92–119. Page numbers in parentheses refer to this Norton Critical Edition. Notes have been edited.

the artful management of the opinions of other people. The talent of impersonation and persuasion that Crusoe showed briefly in managing the mutineers are greatly expanded in Moll's story as the authority to rule is commensurately reduced. In *Moll Flanders* Defoe explores the Hobbesian situation of counsel rather than the situation of command. Even Moll's opportunities for contracting are rhetorically and strategically molded by the considerations of subordination that characterize counsel.

The account of counsel in *Leviathan* is strangely relevant to the investigation of the power of women in their households. Because of his hostility to Parliament and the trials of political controversy, Hobbes recommends that a sovereign take counsel in private. He extends the conventional analogy between the sovereign and the head of a household to recommend this containment of political dialogue: "Who is there that so far approves the taking of Counsell from a great Assembly of Counsellours, that wished for, or would accept of their pains, when there is a question of marrying his Children, disposing of his Lands, governing his Household, or managing his private Estate, especially if there be amongst them such as wish not his prosperity?" (II, 25). Hobbes's scene of political counsel has several resemblances to counsel in a gentleman's household. It is "secret" rather than public, and it has an emotional ambience of trust rather than of suspicion and agonistic debate. The good counselor speaks in the interest of the authority he advises—or rather, he "pretendeth only (whatever he intendeth) the good of him, to whom he giveth it" (II, 25); for this reason the counselor should avoid all signs of passionate personal interest, especially figures of eloquence. Unlike those who deliberate in a democratic assembly, the counselor has no right to give counsel but must wait to be asked for it. This view of political counsel limits all members of society, even men who aid in the important processes of governance, to the deferential manners of women and servants, and this transformation is in keeping with Hobbes's persistent effort to debunk classical ideals of masculine virtue.

Yet this crucial chapter of *Leviathan* does acknowledge the necessity of continuing dialogue between governors and subjects in a society, and the ground rules that specify subordination also offer some protection to the inferior parties in the discussion. Since the person in authority has authorized the counselor's speech by requesting advice, he should not punish anyone for it, no matter what they advise. And though the counselor should be brief and not hold forth like a public orator, the "frequent interruptions" that Hobbes thinks will be made by the person in authority suggest a process of give and take that facilitates committed involvement while it allays suspicion.

Moll, like Defoe, exploits the large territory opened up by counsel and the latitude of its rules.

The story opens with Moll's concern to find a minimally secure social position, a parish settlement. She dimly remembers herself as a small child taking the initiative in leaving the gypsies, and though the authorities of Colchester have no legal responsibility to provide for her, somehow her case comes to be widely known, and the compassion of the magistrates moves them to settle her with a parish nurse. The first dramatized scene shows Moll not quite eight years old persuading her nurse not to send her out to service, as the magistrates had ordered. At the end of the conversation Moll comments, "I had no Policy in all this" (p. 13), but her term underlines the singular effectiveness of such a young child.

From the beginning Moll relies on the ability to create in another person a strong belief in her loyal affection. The child has more latitude than the adult would have to show her affection and her fears about the commandments of the authorities, but her impulsive tears effect the opening move typical of Moll's later successful negotiations. She leads the other, stronger, party to inquire about her desires and so authorize the scene of counsel. Moll's response to her nurse's questioning is a vivid account of her (all too realistic) fears about life at the bottom of the domestic hierarchy. First Moll explains that she is crying because she does not know how to do housework and because the maids will beat her, even though she is too young to do much. When the nurse promises that she will not be sent out to service until she is older, Moll goes on crying because she has to go at any time. Finally the nurse asks, "why, what? . . . is the Girl mad? what, would you be a Gentlewoman?" Moll answers yes and goes on crying. First she provokes laughter by her improbable answer and then tears by her childish promise to pay her own way by her needlework and by going without food if only the nurse will let her stay. This piquant exchange, related to the mayor, becomes a "story" that makes him and his family laugh. After they come to prattle with the child about being a gentlewoman, the story becomes even more delightful when the nurse learns that Moll thinks a certain "Madam," who does not go out to service but mends lace is a "gentlewoman." We begin to see that telling a story about oneself and becoming a story that others enjoy can be a substitute for the allusiveness and figures of rhetoric that Hobbes stripped from the language of counsel when he made it private. And telling a story about yourself, when it has been requested, meets Hobbes's most substantial recommendation about counsel: that it be based on relevant experience. Even women and children can meet this standard.

Moll's mistake about what she wants to be seems ominous, given her eventual life of crime, and more than a hint of pride comes into her account of being made a pet by the leading families of Colchester. But her mistake is poignant, since she wants to earn an honest, independent living and does not realize how small is the chance of supporting herself by needlework. Nevertheless, the leaders of the town patronize her. They teach her special skills and give her business, and they supply her with clothes and money enough to support her when she goes off the public maintenance. But as in so many situations of Moll's later life, her independent efforts can be made only in a structure of dependency. When the old nurse dies, Moll is destitute until a genteel family that she had visited takes her in at the top of the servant hierarchy. Along with the daughter of the house, she begins to acquire the education of a gentlewoman.

Critics disagree about Defoe's judgment of Moll's desire to change her status.[1] Even if we decide that Defoe did not view her ambition as immoral, we needn't necessarily conclude that he favored this sort of effort for every servant. The problem of uppity servants brought out the conservative in everyone, including Defoe. But Moll rises first through patronage. Eighteenth-century England was a place in which personal patronage was a kind of wild card in the game, a rule that could suspend other rules. Patronage gained pardons for criminals, educated members of the lower orders, granted government jobs, officerships, clerical livings, and even seats in Parliament. Rising in the social hierarchy by patronage confirms, rather than challenges, the authority of the higher orders who do the patronizing. It is hard to believe that Defoe, who worked so many years with ministerial patrons, should disapprove of this sort of encouragement, yet his relation with Harley demonstrated the difficulties of actually attaining and maintaining the benefits that patronage seemed to open up. Moll's comfortable home and workplace are suddenly swept away with the death of the nurse, so that Moll is in danger of losing both the earnings her attractiveness and skill had won her and also the setting in which she could earn more. This is one of Moll's problems: she must gain the credit of trusting others and the power that comes from patronage yet still develop enough independent resources to protect herself.

Welcomed into the home of genteel people, her natural talents enable Moll to learn gentlewomanly skills more quickly than the daughters of the house, and in ways that further equip her to appeal to them. But this sort of attractiveness in a young woman has an effect on people different from the appealing quickness of a child. The story of Moll's seduction by the elder brother of the house and its consequences is one of the most extended and effectively dram-

1. George A. Starr, for instance, sees it as the spiritual sin of vanity in *Defoe and Spiritual Autobiography* (Princeton: Princeton UP, 1965), p. 127.

atized episodes in the novel. It is important for initiating the spiritual story of sin and redemption: the initial vanity, the lack of serious reflection, the opportunities to repent, the hardening in sin, the final repentance. The seduction also initiates, or rather prefigures, Moll's strong attraction to money, which leads to her grand career in crime, to the threat of the gallows, and yet also to the prudent management of a substantial estate in Virginia. But the special poignancy of the episode is Moll's failure to understand what is at stake—not only her immortal soul but also her public status. The charming mistake of the child about the meaning of being a gentlewoman has serious consequences for the woman.

The elder brother first appeals to Moll's vanity by praising her when he is speaking to his brother and sisters. In this household she is only "Mrs. Betty," a name for any serving girl, so the praise of the elder brother, the heir to the estate, is especially thrilling, and his strategy of appearing to speak behind her back is even more flattering. Yet because he speaks as if she were not there, the elder brother's praise does not have the effect of granting her any kind of formal recognition, the necessary prelude to an honorable address. Moll does not understand the implication of the elder brother's continuing secrecy in declaring his love: his private declaration simply makes her blush with pleasure. The gold he gives her profoundly moves her, but not because she has any economic use for it. She shows no need or wish to spend it, but it "elevated" her. For Moll the first money functions in this episode purely as a symbol of the elder brother's esteem. She is completely ignorant of the possibility or wisdom of making any sort of special bargain with him, after he has promised to marry her when he comes into the estate:

> I seem'd wholly to have abandoned all such Thoughts as these, and was taken up Onely with the Pride of my Beauty, and of being belov'd by such a Gentleman; as for the Gold. I spent whole Hours in looking upon it; I told the Guineas over and over a thousand times a Day: Never poor vain Creature was so wrapt up with every part of the Story, as I was, not Considering what was before me, and how near my Ruin was at the Door; indeed, I think I rather wish'd for that Ruin, than studyed to avoid it (p. 24).

Moll is wrapped up in the story, but she does not have the power to tell it. She listens in rapture to the older brother and gazes at his gold; she shows some "cunning" when they are among the family by scarcely looking at him or speaking to him. But he tells the elaborate tale that gets her away from home, and when he proposes terms for their affair, she "could not say a word." When the younger brother, Robin, "begins a story of the same kind," it is not the same kind of thing at all, since he proposes "fairly and honorably to marry." Oddly enough, this "fair" proposal draws out her argumentative powers for the first time, as Moll tries to discourage him. His "plain" speaking to the family makes her reflect for the first time on the elder brother's secrecy.

Admirable as Robin's behavior is, it alerts the family to the danger of a marriage across status lines and therefore more seriously threatens Moll's position in the household than the elder brother's seduction. Degrees of "free" speech sensitively register differences of authority within the family. Robin, the youngest son, known by his first name in contrast to the "elder brother," whose identity is inseparable from his status, is freer in speech and behavior than his older brother, since his marriage has fewer serious implications for the status of the family. He is free to joke about loving a servant and after some family debate, free to marry her, since he has been brought up to make his own living. But the closer Robin's banter comes to an open declaration of his love, the more pressure on Moll, since the family has a right to know her reasons for refusal. Under this pressure, Moll's private conversations with the elder brother exploit most remarkably the paradoxical value of secrecy. An increasingly self-conscious, feminine reserve aids Moll's argumentative attempts to win public status.

Now Moll must be more indirect than with her nurse. Her troubled silence and signs of her tears provoke the elder brother to beg to question her about the nature of her trouble, and making him beg her to speak sets a tone of loving concern. Her mode of opening the discussion reveals her subjection. She is as good as Defoe at persuading and arguing, but as a woman and a servant she does not have a customary right to speak about her wishes, though others have a right to insist on her explaining herself. Neither her speech nor her silence are altogether a matter of her own choice. There is a reasonable expectation that the inferior will have opportunity to advise the superior, but she cannot claim a right to give advice, because that would be to command her master. Such a situation necessitates a degree of management and courteous pretense. Moll continues to put the responsibility for the conversation on the elder brother by pretending to think that the new antagonism of the family toward her comes from its discovery of their affair. The strategy also keeps subtly before him their commitment to each other. Her pretended anger at his smiles of relief and superior knowledge gives her an opportunity to reproach him with damaging her reputation. The reproach is substantial, even though her pretended ignorance of Robin's interest in her takes the sting out of it at first, since he believes that he can easily dispel her fears. The elder brother cheerfully offers her the explanation that Robin has been making the family suspicious by talking about her (he thinks it's only banter), and he argues that the family's worry about this will prevent suspicion of them.

The family's response to Robin's interest is in fact the story Moll wished to tell, and she prefixes it with tears. She asks for advice because she wants to give advice. She argues that the younger brother's public addresses will jeopardize their position, because people will seek some reason for her refusing the younger brother. She adds cleverly that they will assume "that I am Marry'd already to somebody else, or that I would never refuse a Match so much above me as this was" (p. 30). Only when the elder brother suggests that she avoid a decisive reply does she begin to pull on the bond between them: she argues that she and the elder brother are already married, "he having all along persuaded me to call my self his Wife." Moll tries to give the private name public status, but the elder brother only promises to be "as good as a Husband." He is already withdrawing from the role by avoiding sex with her.

In their next conversation Moll again suggests the cheerful solution of publicly announcing their marriage, but with a great deal of confidence and no hinted doubt of his loyalty, so that she "pleasantly" agrees to keep the secret back (p. 32). Her trust and reliance on his advice lead him to risk advising her to marry his brother, which provokes her to a fainting fit. Moll and the elder brother then become more explicit about what they want from each other and more willing to risk an argument. When the elder brother recommends that Moll marry Robin, Moll accuses him of breaking his promise to marry her. Her appeal seems to be grounded solely on the natural obligation to keep promises,[2] but in *Serious Reflections of Robinson Crusoe* Defoe celebrated the English law that makes a promise to marry enforceable in court. Could Moll expect such a law ever to be enforced to benefit a servant at the expense of the honor of genteel people? The threat of any sort of legal compulsion would only disrupt the impression of trusting affection that Moll has so patiently designed in the previous discussions. Signs of trust are essential in her dependent position: "To believe, to trust, to rely on another, is to Honour him; signe of opinion of his vertue and power. To distrust, or not believe, is to Dishonour" (*Leviathan*, I, 10).

Again and again in eighteenth-century fiction the moral authority of women in situations of familial conflict seems to require the refusal to appeal to the political institutions of the society at large. Their legal position as wards of fathers, husbands, or masters insured that women had little access to political institutions and great depen-

2. Starr cites passages that show Defoe also considered promises of marriage morally binding, even without legal ceremony. See *Defoe and Casuistry* (Princeton: Princeton UP, 1971), pp. 118–19.

dence on customary rules of behavior and on individual relations with men. Since the history of the novel developed a generic commitment to stories about women (a commitment for which Richardson is more responsible than Defoe) it should not be surprising that we expect the form to be set at a distance from political concerns. But the social orientation of the novel, like the social orientation of women, exists within a detectable legal framework. Defoe will not let us forget that feminine manners are only strategies appropriate to particular arrangements of power.

In the debate between Moll and the elder brother, each speaker appeals only to common principles of morality rather than to legal obligations. The elder brother claims that he has adhered to the terms of the promise: to provide for her, but not to marry until he comes into the estate. Moll uses his answer to reconfirm their bond of affection and mutual gratitude: "But why then, *says I*, can you perswade me to such a horrid step, as leaving you, since you have not left me? Will you allow no Affection, no Love on my Side, where there has been so much on your Side? Have I made you no Returns?" (p. 33). The scene is quite passionate: both characters speak convincingly and show strong emotion, and yet the sincerity of each is questionable. Moll has told the reader that she had sex out of vanity, not love, and she has suggested that the elder brother never intended to marry her; since he used money as an inducement, perhaps he never believed in her love. Each could bring forward these accusations, but neither does. Even in such privacy, the character of each in the eyes of the other is extremely important. The elder brother does not want to be seen as someone who would tell a downright lie, and Moll does not want to be seen as someone who would have sex without love. Each grants the other the fair name. But in a particularly daring move of the conversation, when the brother urges marriage to Robin, Moll gives herself the name that her lover is unwilling to pronounce:

> . . . you shall be my Dear Sister, as you are now my Dear—and there he stop'd.
>
> YOUR Dear whore, *says I*, you would have said, if you had gone on; and you might as well have said it; but I understand you (p. 34).

Her attempt to wring his heart reminds him of his responsibility to her and attributes honor to their relation by transforming the title of shame to a title of honor: "I had much rather, since it is come that unhappy Length, be your Whore than your Brothers Wife" (p. 34). Though her bold expression of value moves him, neither master nor servant has the power to transform social opinion by making the legal status of their relation unimportant. The special tender meaning of "Whore" is only a meaning for their privacy, so they continue to seek a better name for Moll.

In their next conversation, Moll appeals to the horror of incest as the ground of her obstinacy, and the elder brother uses her excuse against her, as a reason to avoid living with her, though he recognizes the responsibility to support her. He now attributes formal significance to his avoidance of lovemaking. He argues that there will no longer be any physical symbol of their marriage, so Robin will be no more than minimally injured and his marriage to Moll will be free of any taint of incest. The mounting tension throws Moll into a fever, and at this point in the narrative, Moll assures the reader for the first time, "I Lov'd to Distraction," and "he Lov'd me most passionately" (p. 36). To her horror, Moll's long resistance to Robin finally wins the respect of his mother and sister and wipes out her last legitimate reason for refusing him. The elder brother decisively informs her that, whatever she decides about Robin, their sexual relation, the substantive token of their affection, will not continue. Though he promises to support her clandestinely, she begins to fear expulsion from the family and the helpless isolation of her situation at the opening of the book.

Is the reader supposed to accept Moll's assertions of love as true, or mere excuse, or as expressions of a corrupted sense of love, sincere but misguided? The special insight, the authenticity that the autobiographical memoir might seem to offer, is also hard to assess. How important is the reader's decision about Moll's sincerity for the interpretation of the novel? However genuine the emotions, whether hypocrisy or pathetic suffering, the evident variety of feeling is the mark of the uncertain social status. Whatever their inner opinions, the lovers are committed to the expression of love when they are close, but the elder brother's refusal of a public union drives them apart. To an extraordinary degree, *Moll Flanders* is a book that confines us to the realm of opinion and authority rather than of truth. Since in this book social situation, including legal status, determines meaning, the changing complications the characters face do not make them seem complex. At first the elder brother practices calculating lust and arouses Moll's deluded vanity; then each feels affection appropriate to the bond of a natural, if not legal, marriage that has been cemented by the elder brother's promise; finally, the brother ends the natural sexual marriage and "reasons" Moll into marrying his brother to secure prosperity and reputation. Rejected by the older brother, Moll's feeling eventually turns to jealousy of the woman he marries. Love seems to have no stable, universal meaning in this sequence. We may elucidate this situation through Hobbes's deflating list of "the Interior Beginnings of Voluntary motions; commonly called the PASSIONS. And the speeches by which they are expressed" (*Leviathan*, I, 6):

> *Love* of persons for society, KINDNESS.
> *Love* of Persons for pleasing the sense onely, NATURAL LUST.
> *Love* of the same, acquired from Rumination, that is, Imagination of Pleasure past, LUXURY.
> *Love* of one singularly, with desire to be singularly beloved, THE PASSION OF LOVE. The same, with fear that the love is not mutuall, JEALOUSIE. (*Leviathan*, I, 6)

On the model of Hobbes's definition of religion in the same chapter, we might add, "*Love*, publicly allowed, MARRIAGE; not allowed, LUST; and when truly such as we imagine, TRUE LOVE." True love for Defoe, like true religion for Hobbes, seems to be either an empty category or a belief so absolutely private and individual that it cannot win public credit except by public authority.

The first long episode has the elevated quality of a tragedy of imprudence, punished by painful inner suffering. Moll's belief that she is committing incest by her marriage to Robin has no external support in law. It is as if there were some odd economy of guilt: by failing to suffer for a commonly recognized offense (sex prior to marriage) she suffers for a personally conceived sin (incest in her thoughts). Later in the narrative, when she unintentionally marries her brother, incest is more dangerous, since public knowledge of it would dissolve her marriage and ruin her children. The repetition of the topic may be another example of Defoe's discovery of material, but it can also function thematically. The more extreme punishment follows the gradual process of spiritual hardening. But the topic is further relevant for pursuing questions of power and authority. In both cases Moll's horror of incest seems to be detached from obvious concerns about self-preservation. Few people have access to the information; those who know about it have strong motives of interest not to reveal it. In Virginia, for a long time Moll is the only one who knows about the incest, and she need not have revealed it. Instead of fearing that she'll reveal it inadvertently, she fears that she may never be able to reveal it or may never be believed.

This kind of suffering may seem to expose an ineluctable moral core of personality, truths of character and morals that are not a matter of social opinion or convenience. Yet in *Moll Flanders*, as in his essay on honesty in the *Serious Reflections of Robinson Crusoe*, Defoe shows little interest in the philosophical question: is this moral imperative the product of nature or of education? Rather, he is interested in the drama of a powerful emotion that a person feels impelled to act on that must nevertheless be hidden from the world. Even more than the conversion experiences of Crusoe or Moll, which follow patterns recognized and respected in their world and the world of their readers, Moll's incest opens up the material of the hidden world of personality and private life with which the artistic "development" of individual character has so long been associated. Secrets of sexual behavior are especially associated with the private view of character that novels are supposed to reveal, but this association holds only when sex is seen as a mark of the peculiar, individual life. Prostitution, like marriage, is presented in *Moll Flanders* typically without special detail; both appear as familiar institutions that are tools ready-made for Moll's use.

Twentieth-century readers find the lack of emotional detail puzzling. Defoe opens up the topics of sex and marriage that we recognize as novelistic subjects and then fails to sustain the interest in intimacy that we expect. Defoe does not deprive Moll of intense feelings; he merely puts them in places that surprise us, and the shock can tell us something about the political structures implicit in habits of novel reading. True revelations of the inner life, the visionary promise associated with fiction, is not the presumed goal of this novel; such information has instead a number of explicit functions. In this case, Moll's horror of incest serves to assure the reader that she has moral feelings more deeply rooted than the desire for respectability, feelings with which we can sympathize and which we can believe will be a foundation for her later experience of conversion. These episodes serve the relation of character to reader more than they do any relations within the novel.[3] Moll never finds it difficult to convince other characters of her morality; she inspires trust even as a condemned criminal. But the private suffering caused by her incest is revealed only to the reader.

The reader's belief in the truth of Moll's account of her feelings is especially important if the book is to work as a story of conversion. In the editor's preface, Defoe casts a little doubt on Moll's repentance, but he does not show anyone in the novel seriously questioning her conversion; nevertheless, it surely would occur to any reader, as it has to modern critics, that the conversion is in her interest and could be insincere. The lack of strenuous questioning does not call into doubt the validity of the representation. All of those involved have good reason to accept her claims: her conversion enlarges the credit of the clergyman and provides the colonies with her labor, which is more in the interest of the government than her execution

3. John Preston discusses the importance of this section of the book, concluding that "Moll does in fact stand in closer relationship to any one of her readers than to the characters in the novel." See *The Created Self: The Reader's Role in Eighteenth-Century English Fiction* (New York: Barnes and Noble, 1970), p. 33. Starr has written that Moll's guilt about her unintended incest "matches even the most scrupulous reader in the rigor of his ethical standards" and so amounts to an assertion of moral equality with readers as well as an appeal to their fellow feeling. See *Defoe and Casuistry*, p. 123.

would be. As so often in *Robinson Crusoe*, self-interest and social interest are harmonized, so that there is no need for the protagonist's character to be dissected. The lack of questioning, the lack of evidence for her truthfulness, does jeopardize her credibility with the reader, who has so often seen her persuade people of falsehoods. The conventionality of her account of conversion makes it recognizable, but it also could raise doubts, especially in modern readers. The act of writing her history could itself be one more attempt to win public esteem for the rehabilitated criminal. The story of incest, however, gives the whole narrative a special status as an intimate, and therefore trustworthy, revelation. The effect on the reader's loyalty to the character and the book is the more pervasive because the intimate revelation marks a crisis in counsel and command: no authority is adequate to the peculiar needs of Moll's situation. Readers feel a sense of urgency about deliberating the facts of Moll's case, as if we were asked to supply the deficiency of counsel and command. When fiction in its intimacy veers away from representing itself as advice, it does not escape these forms so much as it seems to invest us with the authority to advise and judge at the most flattering point, where it is the most difficult. And the sense of implication in the book is increased by the numerous difficulties thrown in the way of judgment.

In earlier episodes, before her conversion, judging Moll's behavior may be difficult because she acts under the direction of a male authority. After the death of Robin, Moll understands the value of a legal marriage, and her accumulated wealth allows her to choose a mate according to her taste for a gentleman of wit and virtue. Moll's life with her second husband was a less sinful but more ruinous life of pretense. The gentleman-tradesman is not for Defoe a figure of presumption so much as a fool: he leads a way of life that he can't sustain. The literal masquerade during the comical trip to Oxford, in which they gull poor scholars by pretending to be aristocratic patrons, leads to the more criminal ruse of eluding their creditors. As she sees his fortune decline, Moll steals first from her husband, and then (at her husband's advice) from his creditors. When she goes into hiding in the Mint, she takes on the surname by which we know her, "Mrs. Flanders," so this first theft marks her identity for us in important ways.

Moll's theft from the creditors to preserve something from her husband's ruin is surely the most excusable crime in the book. The reduction of a bankrupt to starvation was something Defoe wrote against in other works and of which his readers could not entirely approve. It is an example of a legal remedy socially frowned upon. Moll's uncertain social status continues. Is she a criminal or not? The laws on debt, like many laws, were very unevenly executed, partly because prosecution was at the individual discretion of the creditor. The very existence of the Mint, a place free from arrest, and of Sunday immunity, suggests a general social leniency.[4] Moll leaves the Mint because her creditors show no intention of prosecuting her.

Many of Moll's crimes occupy areas of socially tolerated criminality. The practice of victims buying back stolen goods instead of seeking to prosecute offenders had the effect of continuously decriminalizing criminals. Moll actually makes friends with the gentleman who buys back his wig, sword, and watch. Her theft from thieves or her theft of smuggled goods especially have the quality of excusable crimes. These acts are clearly morally wrong, part of the spiritual story of hardening, and they give Moll the incentive to go on to her undoubted crimes, but they are typical of her life to the very end of the story. The frequent pardoning or transportation of criminals must have made many crimes seem less criminal, even though, or perhaps in part because, the penalties on the books were so severe. Very often in Moll's story the participation of social authorities—husbands, masters, excise officers—in her crime adds special force to the conflict in opinions about justice that we feel as readers.

Moll's abandonment by two husbands (the tradesman and the highwayman) and the dissolution of her Virginia marriage relegate her to a sort of legal twilight. Is she practicing bigamy? Over time, desertion would become legally recognized as divorce, and besides, a private marriage by a priest may not have been legal, and marriage to a brother certainly is not binding. Defoe makes situations that are morally and legally unclear into creative opportunities. They bind the reader to the book in repeated efforts of judgment, and they open areas of adventurous activity to the characters. Moll learns to use her indeterminate status, the lack of a secure position as a well-known member of a community, to create identities and mold opinion at will. In this positive transformation of uncertainty, Moll usually requires at least one ally to meet threats posed by other people who seek to exploit relatively unregulated situations.

An alliance with another husband-hunting woman prompts Moll's efforts to change the bias of social conventions. Their goal is to acquire husbands of good fortune and good character, and to do this they must inquire into the situation and past of the suitor without his finding out too much about them. The low level of record keeping in their world has the advantage of enabling them to keep their fortunes a secret, but it also makes it hard to detect a suitor's fraudulence. Defoe's picture of marriage partners assumes no special intimacy, no deep knowledge of each other; their negotiation must

4. Starr collects evidence of complicated social attitudes toward debt: acceptance of the immunity of the Mint, reprobation of stealing from creditors, sympathy with the self-preservation of the debtor. See *Defoe and Casuistry*, p. 125.

establish the terms of trust. The Hobbesian problem of knowing character is not only complicated by the lack of a stable social setting, but also made more difficult by the conventions of courtship. Declarations of love imply that a favorable decision on the lover's character has already been made. Suspicious inquiries, requests for evidence, then become contradictory, rude offenses. For this reason, in decorous genteel society, the "friends" (that is, the family connections) of the lovers investigated the credit of the two parties. But men are usually in a better position to make these conventions work in their favor. Moll says they are more valued and more in demand and therefore can ask rude questions without answering similar ones. So Moll offers herself as an adviser when her friend (apparently not under the protection of a family) is rejected by a suitor, a captain who feels himself insulted by inquiries about him.

Moll's solution to her friend's problem is somewhat reminiscent of one of Defoe's fantasies in the *Consolidator*: in order to secure a better hearing, Dissenters take over royally chartered trading companies by dumping their shares, driving down the value further by rumor, and then buying up a majority of the shares at reduced cost and the rest when the price rises again. Moll drives down the market value of the suitor by using a network of gossiping women to circulate damaging rumors about his financial position and his reputation of morals. His material wealth cannot dictate his value in the market of opinion: "The *Value*, or WORTH of a Man, is as of all other things, his Price; that is to say, so much as would be given for the use of his Power: and therefore is not absolute; but a thing dependent on the need and judgement of another" (*Leviathan*, I, 10).[5] Unable to make other matches, the suitor returns crestfallen to try again with Moll's friend. She now has the excuse of his bad reputation to question him, and she is almost taken in by the reality of the fiction she helped create. When she sees how confounded he is by the rumors, "she almost began to believe that all was true, by his disorder, tho' she knew that she had been the raiser of all those Reports herself" (p. 59). The lover, now on the defensive, offers the necessary evidence of his good character and learns to feel grateful to his wife-to-be. But his protestations of love have closed him off from the chance to inquire about her fortune, so she is able to tie up part of it with trustees out of his reach and without his knowledge. In

5. C. B. Macpherson cites this passage in evidence that Hobbes's system reflects a bourgeois market society; but one could reverse his argument. Hobbes and Defoe place economic operations within a larger political context of opinion making, to which economic markets are subject. What is at stake is the status of Macpherson's claims about Hobbes's individualism, the idea of each person's power limiting every other person's power. Hobbes is more interested in (and worried about) group power than Macpherson acknowledges. In our example from Defoe we should note that Moll is trying to make a marriage with the help of a woman friend. See C. B. Macpherson, *The Political Theory of Possessive Individualism* (London: Oxford University Press, 1962), p. 37.

material and moral ways the wife enters her marriage less dependent than she would otherwise be. Taking a woman and equal as a counselor strengthens the position of a woman as a counselor to men, even if it cannot abolish subordination altogether.

Moll's advice to her friend proceeds to an exhortation to the women of her nation to stand their ground during courtship in order to gain what they need from marriage, not only security but also respect. The elaborate strategy, however, shows that the woman needs a pretext for questioning her suitors. Her position does not give her a right to inquire. As in Defoe's *Consolidator* fantasy, Moll's strategy uses the social power of rumor and boycott to make the binding constraints of the law serve the interests of a politically subordinated class. Defoe's practices suggest that he tried to use his journalism to create the context of opinion that would get his counsel a hearing in Parliament and in secret relations with ministers of state. But Defoe's fictional analogue conveniently suppresses the ways that custom and laws could be used by the dominant group to strike back, to reinstate the abusive inequality. Slander laws that were used against Defoe's journalism have been left out of his fictional projects. Advising women to show courage and to stand their ground cannot really make men of them. When her friend uses the rumor machine to help Moll trap a husband, we see how small is the power of women and how carefully it must be concealed.

Moll's own marriage negotiation (her third) with a Virginia plantation owner is more complicated than her friend's, since she has so little money to soothe a husband after pressuring him during courtship. Deceit before marriage would risk bad treatment after marriage, when the husband could exercise the right of corporal punishment. As a result, the friend takes Moll to the country and presents her as a relative whose good circumstances are well known. Since the lie is circulated as the mistake of another person, the husband will have less reason for anger. But so crucial is the credit of a woman for her safety in marriage that Moll carries on a further negotiation to insure her future. She lures her suitor on to protestations of love and draws him into writing a rhyming love dialogue on the window with a diamond. In this context of conventional, playful male hyperbole and modest female skepticism, Moll confesses her poverty in a way that will not be believed. The suitor writes, "*I scorn your Gold, and yet I Love*" (p. 65). Her humor conceals a confession by its very bluntness: "*I'm Poor: Let's see how kind you'll prove*." So he is forced to reiterate his disinterestedness: "*Be mine, with all your Poverty*." This gives Moll the opportunity to probe his good faith almost dangerously deep: "*Yet secretly you hope I lie*."[6] She cannot be later

6. Ignoring such scenes of negotiation as this one, Robert Alter has argued that Moll thinks in capitalist, money-fixated, bookkeeping terms and "expects words to be used with neat,

charged with having deceived him about her wealth. Her air of "indifferency" would hardly make him suspect her of being a woman pressed hard for necessities, yet she manages to get him talking about his fortune. Her apparent reluctance to settle in Virginia makes her seem hard to win and provides her with something to grant him after his initial disappointment over her fortune.

The management of social credit helps Moll enter the marriage, but the maintenance of a good reputation within the family is necessary for Moll to hold on to a share of power. After marriage, Moll first frightens her husband by suggesting that she is utterly destitute, then pleases him by presenting her small holdings: the sum that before marriage would have looked contemptible now gives pleasure, and his gratitude is reinforced by her offer to settle in Virginia. Moll has managed to avoid any positive lies and has even managed to appear as someone eager to explain herself. Moll's strategies, which lead to a happy marriage, bring to mind Defoe's recommendation to Harley of public-spirited dissimulation: it cannot be called lying, because it is in the interest of the people fooled. But also it is not real deceit, because other people are practicing the dissimulation game and are to some extent willing to be fooled as well as willing to fool others. Writing on the window, Moll calls the bluff of hypocrisy in courtship, but like Defoe calling the bluff of high-flying Tories, she counts on the force of conviction behind the conventional pretense of disinterestedness and unity. Moll relies on her Virginian's good humor as well as on her strategies.

All of Moll's cleverness about insuring a stable marriage turns against her when she tries to find a way of separating from her husband after she learns that the marriage is incestuous. The "careful, diligent" husband finds no sense in her appeal to his promise that she could return to England if Virginia proved unsatisfactory. The ability to make a new social identity by changing place has trapped her: to her horror, she discovers that her mother-in-law, who has also come to Virginia to make a new life, is her mother. Her goal must now be to separate without so alienating her husband as to leave herself or her children penniless. She is extremely fearful of revealing her secret and, as her conflict with her husband increases, fearful that he will put her away as a madwoman and that her secret could then never be explained. In a particularly savage argument the husband threatens to use violence to "reduce" Moll to duty to hus-

very definite denotations unobfuscated by any suggestion of multiple meaning or contradiction." See *Rogue's Progress* (Cambridge, Mass.: Harvard University Press, 1965), p. 45. Earlier Dorothy Van Ghent also emphasized Moll's drive to abstract all experience "into numbers, measurements, cash value." See *The English Novel: Form and Function* (1953; New York: Harper, 1961), p. 39. A more interesting treatment of economic topics in Defoe's fiction which could connect meaningfully to his politics would explore the social complexities of credit rather than the illusory simplicities of commodity fetishism.

band and children, and Moll frightens him by hinting at the truth. But she makes a particularly long and careful approach to the final revelation, holding back while both mother and son beg to know her secret. Once again, the emotional preparation for negotiation involves creating a larger context of opinion by bringing the mother over to her side, and then binding the husband by written promises, made this time with solemnity, not as a joke. The result of her carefully prepared revelation does indeed protect her from injury, but it has the unforeseen and dangerous result of leading him to try to kill himself. Moll speculates rather brutally about whether she should leave before their fortunes decline, or whether she should marry again in Virginia if her husband succeeds in killing himself. Rather than rely on an unstable husband, Moll chooses self-reliance and decides to emigrate, but damage to her goods in the crossing reduces her again to necessity and dependence.

The comparison of a family to a state was a moral commonplace; indeed, the bond between governor and governed was compared to the bond between father and family even by those who, like Defoe, were not patriarchalists. But Defoe's political analogy of the family in *Moll Flanders* teaches the mutability and artificiality of the political creations. Moll's first love choices were giddy affairs of impulse, but the Virginia marriage was a carefully planned arrangement, solidly based in wealth, good character, and mutual trust. Moll's skill in negotiation shows that consent to obedience is not a single gesture of submission, but a dialogue conducted under the constraints of respect to authority. There was a well-calculated slight chance of Moll's gentleman-tradesman husband turning up to cause legal complications. But prudent foresight, based on hard-earned experience, is not enough. Incalculable accidents (like the discovery of incest) upset the order and change the terms of legality and morality, feeling and discourse. Moll, her husband, and their mother slowly arrive at their now very private agreement. Though there are natural principles of morality such as keeping promises, there is no natural, inevitable social order. This is surely one meaning of Moll's abandoning her many children to the care of others. *Moll Flanders* is pervaded by an insistent concern about coming out on the right side of the law and using it to further the interests of the characters, but never in a novel has the law seemed so arbitrary, without seeming wicked or absurd. Hobbesian moral philosophy and struggles over political opinion taught Defoe the importance of coordinating human energies by shared law. But the Hobbesian teaching underlines the artificiality of every political order and the inadequacy of any narrowly legalistic code to address the variation of human needs.

The pains of uncertain status afflict Moll's next dependency, her relation with the gentleman at Bath. Their ardent friendship slips over the border into sex very readily, and the more readily because Moll thinks it is the way to secure the relation; but a sickbed repentance undoes it again.[7] The sum of money Moll gains by signing another private agreement with dubious legal status, a general release, is substantial, but not enough for a life income. Money without the knowledge of legal opportunities to invest it cannot provide the security she seeks, and this is why she so often seeks a husband.

At this point in the narrative Defoe and Moll are repeating themselves. The problem of the unhappily married clerk (who serves as her banker) resembles the situation of the gentleman at Bath, and the rumor of her fortune which tricks the Lancashire man resembles the strategy for entrapping the Virginia husband. Compared to her earlier ventures, Moll in some ways shows more prudence won from her experience, but in other ways she is more daring, ready for bold risks, including two concurrent marriage negotiations. Moll has found a reliable and agreeable banker through an attempt to learn how to invest her savings. Though she encourages his advances, Moll declines any sort of unmarried cohabitation with the clerk, as well as any other sort of binding engagement. His respect is greater security than the unlicensed bond of the flesh, and she confirms his respect by showing her trust in him, while leaving herself free to try her luck in the north. Moll's marriage to the Lancashire man was a great gamble for what each party believed was a great prize. Moll has the excuse of having her fortune misrepresented by others, this time by a confederate of the husband's, so she does not take the precautions that preceded the marriage to the Virginia husband.

The negotiation to ensure trust, so typical of Moll's engagements, occurs after the marriage to the Lancashire gentleman. The apparent willingness of each to forgive the other and treat the other with generosity creates a bond that was lacking in their original agreement. Their affection makes them consider daring schemes for making their fortunes, but since they cannot agree on which risk to take, they separate. This incident occasions the first use of Christian names in this episode, as Moll cries out to herself, "O Jemy, come back!" (p. 122), and by a sort of second sight he comes back for a brief stay while they consider and reject both her plan of emigration to Virginia and his answering plan of emigration to Ireland. The episode has an odd, intrusive effect in a narrative that has dealt so much in names that identify social position, family status, or relationship to Moll. The Lancashire husband figures in a special way in Moll's search for power. The intimate affection that grows

7. John Richetti's enthusiasm for Moll's mythic resilience has led him to exaggerate the impression the book gives of her powers. Of the affair with the man at Bath, Richetti writes, "in dominating marriage itself, Moll exercises power over society." See *Defoe's Narratives: Situations and Structures* (Oxford: Clarendon P, 1975), p. 114.

between them is an unexpected luxury in the story, much related to Jemy's dashing, gentlemanly ways. Although she cannot afford this luxury for a while yet, Moll is at least able to play the heroine and save him from a mob. Moll's later decision to continue the relation when she sees him in Newgate is a risk incurred more out of affection than out of need for his power, but the relation is a pleasure that it turns out she can well afford once they are transported to Virginia.

So uncertain is the creation of an entirely new estate that even this resourceful couple won't undertake it until, much later in the book, they are presented with a much worse alternative, the gallows. After they have separated, Moll finds herself with child, and she is presented with a new difficulty of her uncertain status. She has no parish settlement and no husband to protect her. Sex between consenting adults is not an entirely private matter in this society. Social pressures make her unwelcome in her lodgings, and the magistrates are entitled to inquire into the paternity of infants and to compel the father's support. Public exposure could not help her, and it would damage the engagement that she continues to rely on with the clerk.

Her solution is a private maternity hospital, an institution as elaborately detailed in the novel as any of Defoe's projects in his pamphlets. The excitement of these pages is not the bare fascination with money, but an identification with social ingenuity: * * * the public provision of lying-in facilities for unwed mothers was a project that Defoe had seriously proposed to reduce abortions and maintain the population. Partly to overcome the impression of any apparent sympathy with vice, partly to insure credit for his originality of creation, Defoe assures his novel readers that the death of the governess who founded the lying-in facility has "left nothing behind her that can or will come up to it" (p. 135). The sentence lingers in the mind a little sadly, as if the favorite project for a lying-in hospital, preserved rather oddly in a criminal biography, stood for many of Defoe's projects that "have left nothing behind it that can or will come up to it." Like the House of Orphans that Moll wished for at the beginning of the narrative, the lying-in hospital wistfully models large-scale political solutions to the worst effects of poverty and crime. But we learn later that the governess of the hospital was forced by a prosecution to turn away from this useful kind of work, and that she became a pawnbroker and fence.[8]

Marriage to the clerk satisfies Moll, since her restlessness was motivated more by fear than by greed. For five years she lived "retir'd, frugal and within our selves; I kept no Company, made no Visits, minded my Family, and oblig'd my Husband; and this kind of Life

8. Once again John Richetti finds more power in these passages than I do: "These are institutions within institutions, illegal operations which mimic and thereby undercut the legitimate operations of society" (*Defoe's Narratives*, p. 120).

became a Pleasure to me" (p. 149). But if the clerk avoids the faults of luxury that she suffered in the gentleman-tradesman, he is also subject to the distress of a modest livelihood, the lack of surplus. Another clerk's failure brings on his own bankruptcy, and he lacks the "courage" to begin again but instead declines and dies. Moll's advice about looking his misfortune in the face and recovering his credit can only be used by an adventurous spirit like her own. She needs a husband who will take her advice.

After her husband's death, Moll begins her life of crime. Necessity, and what is stronger, the fear of necessity, drive Moll on. The inability to distinguish avarice from a crime justified in conscience, if not in law, by self-preservation makes it difficult to find the point of culpability as Moll becomes hardened to her occupation. For a short while, after going to live at very cheap rent with her governess, Moll supports herself through sewing, though she makes clear how much work it takes her to earn her subsistence, how difficult in this job, as in any other, it is to get on without "acquaintance," without the patronage of friends (p. 157). As in her very first job in Colchester, nearly free rent seems a necessary condition for this way of being self-supporting, and work so near the subsistence line easily slips beneath it. We might remember that the "gentlewoman" whom Moll admired as a child took in sewing but actually supported herself as a prostitute.

Stealing becomes the skilled, lucrative trade that Moll has always needed and never had. The governess who has been a "mother" to her in the lying-in hospital now sees to her education in crime, offers a safe and secret home, and makes the protection of a husband unnecessary. Her success depends on her characteristic quick-witted, imaginative responses to opportunity, the ability to feign gentility as well as other disguises, readiness of tongue, level-headed courage under threat, and most of all the manipulation of her anonymity—her greatest burden and her greatest resource throughout the book.[9] The other thieves refer to her as "Moll Flanders," but they do not know who she is.[1]

For the reader, this part of the book reads like a negative conduct book, what to avoid if you want to protect your property from thieves. Because the scenes function as practical warnings, the curiosity about society's underside, the nooks and crannies in social architecture, can be indulged without the fear of undermining respect for

9. For an admirable Marxist-feminist account of Moll which stresses her anonymity and her relations with women, see Lois A. Chaber, "Matriarchal Mirror: Women and Capitalism in *Moll Flanders*," *PMLA* 97 (1982): 212–26.

1. Paul Alkon notes that the vagueness about the acquisition of this name and the use of the name in the title give the reader a strong impression of consistent criminality, even though these episodes occupy a limited portion of Moll's story. See *Defoe and Fictional Time* (Athens: U of Georgia P, 1979), p. 141.

law and morality; Moll appears in this part as a guide to prudence and morality. Some episodes provide opportunities to attack social abuses: luxury, smuggling, drunkenness, gambling, and prostitution. Defoe teaches the lesson of the interconnection of vices and crimes. The reader's interest in Moll's criminal ingenuity is very different from the interest taken in her marriage episodes, which provoke more reflection and debate about the laws of nature, convention, and government. Moll's career of theft is wrong in law, wrong in convention, and—in spite of initial necessity—even against Defoe's understanding of the laws of nature. Her temptation to murder a child early in the life of crime brands theft with the stigma of unnatural feeling. Once Moll becomes rich, she is driven to more theft by avarice, a sin and an obsession, the clutches of the Devil. Yet the character traits that make Moll a success in crime can be converted, under the right political arrangement, to respectability. Like Crusoe's overproduction, his fortifications, his hoarded money and gunpowder, Moll's avariciously accumulated wealth becomes personally and socially useful under the right legal circumstances.

The book moves inexorably to clear and public condemnation of Moll. The public disgrace and the fear of execution prepare for her conversion and then her public rehabilitation in America, where she can finally take on a name, a husband, a son, and legitimate property management. The moral degeneration, or "hardening," of the protagonist and the reader's increasing moral clarity about her prepare for the public sentence and its transmutation. Yet the sense of accident and the many opportunities for negotiation remind us of the contrast between the fluidity of life and the arbitrariness of justice. Moll has been seized with stolen goods by two women shop assistants. As Moll pleads poverty and then offers to pay for the merchandise, the master of the house hesitates, and his wife argues in Moll's favor. The most obstinate "wench" has already called a constable, but the justice of the peace is persuaded by Moll's arguments until the "Sawcy Jade" swears that Moll was caught leaving the shop. Moll's governess almost succeeds in persuading one maid and the master to drop the prosecution. Moll provokes tears when she addresses the court before sentencing, but the judge pronounces death. Facing death turns Moll toward religion. The minister who gives Moll spiritual guidance promises not to reveal any of her confession to the courts, but on the other hand his testimony to her conversion succeeds in obtaining for Moll a transmuted sentence. The public institutions of law have been essential in the process of Moll's rehabilitation, yet they are not aligned very clearly with the moral action of the story.

What is Defoe's attitude toward the extremely harsh judgment against a woman who is, in strict legal terms, a first offender? The readers, who know her history, can see an appropriate irony that for once Moll suffers worse than the expected consequences, but is Defoe therefore recommending the severity of the judgment? The transmutation of the judgment to transportation without more inquiry into Moll's criminal history might also raise questions about the administration of justice, though even transportation is a severe sentence for those who cannot afford to buy their freedom. Christianity teaches that the secrets of all hearts will only be known in the general resurrection, and the judicial system does not expect either Moll or her minister to reveal those secrets, but the reader is allowed to see that the fit between judicial judgment and the judgment of God is not very good.

Moll's story effects for the reader a rough correspondence between secret truth and social decisions: her unprosecuted crimes are punished by an excessively harsh judgment licensed by excessively harsh laws and biased by rumors and the personal malice of the witnesses. Moll's true repentance is rewarded by the transmutation of execution to transportation and by not having to return the booty, so that the punishment is as light as the complete pardon available only to criminals richer or more socially prominent than Moll. Defoe does not explicitly attack or defend either Moll's unpunished criminality or the abuses of criminal justice; instead he retreats to the impression of factuality and the adversarial structure of the court system. Defoe constructs an account in which he does not assume responsibility for guiding the reader's judgment.

To measure the extent of Defoe's authorial abnegation, we should consider the importance of courts throughout the later history of novelistic fiction. Often, as in Richardson's *Clarissa* or in Hardy's *Tess of the D'Urbervilles*, there is an implicit rivalry between novel and court as sources of judgment about character. The later novelist usually hints that the novel has enabled the reader to know more about the motives and the true worth of the persons in a case than a court procedure could ever reveal. But Defoe connects the moral status of his fiction to the uncertain moral status of his narrator-protagonists, and so he does not seem to offer fiction as a better alternative to any other sort of social authority. In spite of telling secrets to the reader and raising our vanity about our privileged position of judgment, Defoe does not try to create the impression of complete intimacy between reader and character. Lies, faulty memory, editor's revisions—all are invoked by Defoe to excuse inconsistencies and roughness in the narrative. They all affect the reader's respect for the authority of the novel, because Defoe has not tried very hard to win it. But if, as a result, the novel in Defoe's hands fails to "rise," it may be even more important to find that political institutions do not suffer the usual corresponding fall. The interests of novelistic fiction have not yet been set at odds with the fictions of state. The arbitrary, makeshift impression Defoe gives of all kinds of fictions does not prevent him from demonstrating their power.

Along with other happy transmutations in the ending of *Moll Flanders*, we find that Moll's persuasive storytelling, which could not save her from the legal sentence, attains new efficacy as she plans to carry her sentence out. Moll's Lancashire highwayman husband finally takes her advice about accepting transportation to America, and when he learns more about the risk he has escaped in avoiding court trial, he pledges, "*My Dear . . . Thou hast twice sav'd my Life, from hence forward it shall be all employ'd for you, and I'll always take your Advice*" (p. 244). If, as this essay has suggested, Moll's search for a more authoritative position as counselor bears some relation to Defoe's political self-image, it is especially interesting to see how many traditional supports he assembled in the narrative to strengthen the force of her advice.

The husband's conviction that his marriage is his salvation is backed by Moll's consolidation of a large landed estate. Part of Moll's capital derives from the earnings of her criminal career, which remains a secret from her husband, but the most dramatic scenes involve Moll's successful attempts to secure the Virginia estate left by her mother and held in trust for her by her son. Moll's only reunion with a child is celebrated and motivated by a loving exchange of legal documents, by which she wills her son her mother's estate and he contracts to manage it for her. When Moll's husband sees the first installment from this inherited estate, he lifts up his hands to heaven and becomes a true penitent. Moll has been converted into an heiress. Her "bourgeois" features are absorbed into a favorite image of the eighteenth-century elite, the proprietor who is also a good business manager.

But this is not a fable of the bourgeoisie buying into land and hence political power (an impractical model for England until the late nineteenth century).[2] Traditional power, including sex dominance, is not overturned. Even if the gentlemanly husband is kept out of the way by aristocratic toys, Moll's relations with other women, once alliances symbolic of dependents organized against a dominant class, have dwindled. The governess, once a partner in crime, is now a purchasing agent who sends female servants along with other stock for the estate. And for all of her accumulated power, Moll's return to England with her husband is penitent. Like Defoe, she still lacks

2. For a recent synthetic account of the successful preservation of political power by the small, fairly closed landed elite of England, see Lawrence Stone and Jeanne C. Fawtier Stone, *An Open Elite? England, 1540–1800*, abridged ed. (Oxford: Oxford UP, 1986).

the security and authority to write under her real name and tell all her secrets.[3] By giving 1683 as the fictional date of composition, Defoe has in this novel clearly located his beloved Glorious Revolution in the world that is to come after Moll's story ends; and in the book's fiction, Moll is nearly the age in 1683 that Defoe was in 1722 when the book was published, an emblem for persistent ingenuity in the long, frustrating wait for political transformation.[4] The inconclusive feeling that attends Moll's return to England suggests a hopeful as well as fearful insight: when we consider the "final" authority of the institutions of law, we may remember that their pronouncements are final, but not for ever.

PAULA R. BACKSCHEIDER

The Crime Wave and *Moll Flanders*†

Late in his life, Defoe explained that he wrote to be useful. His writing was, he said, "a Testimony of my good Will to my Fellow Creatures."[1] *Moll Flanders* was one of those books, and Defoe's mind and commitments are everywhere in the book. He took up a pressing, immediate problem, and his social, economic, and psychological theories drove the book and assured its profundity. Not only did he contribute to an understanding of crime and criminal individuals, but he wrote powerful propaganda for an increasingly common "solution," the transportation of criminals to the North American colonies.

Defoe and his contemporaries believed that crime had never been so common. Periodicals which Defoe read and for which he wrote carried innumerable reports of crimes and trials. The 22 January 1719 *Whitehall Evening Post*, for instance, included a letter in which a Reading gentleman complained that it was impossible to go to or

3. Not all critics read Moll's pseudonym as pessimistically as I have. Nancy K. Miller follows Leo Braudy in seeing Moll's continuing adherence to a pseudonym as an assertion of autonomy, but Miller stresses the specifically female, family-connected aspect of Moll's fictional creation of identity, and she notes the fantasy of a son endowing his mother with her heritage. See Miller, *The Heroine's Text: Readings in the French and English Novel, 1722–1782* (New York: Columbia UP, 1980), p. 20; and Leo Braudy, "Daniel Defoe and the Anxieties of Autobiography," *Genre* 6, no. 1 (1973): 76–97.
4. Paul Alkon considers a different effect of the double time in *Moll Flanders*: the eighteenth-century reader followed Moll's energetic career as if the story were contemporaneous and then reached the final date 1683, which removed Moll from the reader's condemnation to death and divine judgment. See *Defoe and Fictional Time*, pp. 50–52.

† Based on material originally appearing in *Daniel Defoe: His Life* (Baltimore and London: Johns Hopkins UP, 1989). Reprinted with permission of the Johns Hopkins University Press. Page numbers in parentheses refer to this Norton Critical Edition. Notes have been edited.

1. Defoe, *Augusta Triumphans* (London, 1728), p. 4.

from the town, morning or evening, without being robbed by footpads (highwaymen without horses). He described the county gaol as "pretty well throng'd." The next month, the same paper described the sight of "Above 100 Convicts" being taken from Newgate to Blackfriars for transportation. The *Daily Post* was equally full of the news of crime; its 24 October 1719 paper reported another large number of Newgate convicts taken to a ship for transportation and nearly every paper listed housebreakings, muggings, and highway robberies. The so-called Black Act (1723), the most extensive increase in the number of offenses classified as capital instituted in that century, passed because Walpole and its supporters introduced it with a description of the rising incidence of crime in "clearly lurid and alarmist terms."[2] Americans who read that, in any year, three of every one hundred of them will be the victims of a violent crime,[3] who dare not walk alone at night in any city in the nation, and who turn comparisons of dead-bolt locks and burglar alarms into dinner party conversation would have felt at home in Defoe's London.

Crime had increased in frightening ways. One journalist remarked about its encroachment into previously safe neighborhoods: "So many . . . robberies happen daily that 'tis almost incredible." A modern historian has concluded that "some areas were virtually 'lawless zones.' "[4] The troubled economy drove some people to theft, and, although seldom noticed, *Moll Flanders* shows men as well as women in need. One of Moll's husbands goes broke, another loses a sum of money he loaned and dies in despair, and another, like so many of his countrymen, is forced to emigrate. Urbanization and the return of military men gave a new character to crime in England. The movement of the population into the cities as the rural economy faltered meant that waves of unskilled, naïve men and women became the victims and then the perpetrators of yet more crime. In Defoe's youth, almost every person in a parish or even a ward was known by everyone else. Now the criminal could fade into the amorphous crowd, as Moll Flanders was so adept at doing. A man or woman could be assaulted and robbed in daylight on a London street and the thief never identified. Strangers moving through the crowded streets attracted no attention. Many of Defoe's contemporaries

2. Leon Radzinowicz characterizes the Black Act as an "emergency law," *History of English Criminal Law and Its Administration* (London: Stevens, 1948–56), 3:15–16. E. P. Thompson, who has done the most thorough study of the legislation, points out the confusion exhibited by modern scholars, however, and concludes that a general feeling of fear played a substantial part in the passing of the act "under colour of emergency" by a "compliant and partially corrupted House of Commons," *Whigs and Hunters* (London: Allen Lane, 1975), pp. 23–24, 190–97.
3. *Statistical Abstracts of the United States, 1986* (Washington, D.C.: Bureau of the Census, 1987).
4. Quoted in J. M. Beattie, *Crime and the Courts in England, 1660–1800* (Princeton: Princeton UP, 1986), 217; John Brewer and John Styles, eds., *An Ungovernable People* (New Brunswick: Rutgers UP, 1980), p. 13.

blamed the increase in crime on the return of these men, many of whom were on half pay or less and unable to find jobs. An eighteenth-century ballad has seamen sing, "I have no trade. . . . I will take to the road . . . and every one that comes by, I'll cry, 'Damn you, deliver your purse.' "[5] These men were accustomed to violence, comfortable with swords and guns, and unafraid of civilians. Some of them joined together in gangs or became pirates, but, even when they acted alone, people believed that they added to the number of personal injuries inflicted during robberies.

Between 1718 and 1721, Defoe became increasingly concerned and analytical about crime. *Moll Flanders* is but one of his many books and reports on the subject. His own house had numerous, expensive locks;[6] he remarked in the September 1716 *Mercurius Politicus* on the unusual number of robberies and housebreakings and said, "no House seem'd sufficiently Fortified."[7] In one of the most feared maneuvers, members of gangs disguised themselves as servants and opened the door for their pillaging comrades. In *The Great Law of Subordination*, Defoe said that Jonathan Wild, the famous thief-taker, had a "List of 7000 *Newgate*-Birds, now in Services in this City, and Parts adjacent, all with the Intent to rob the Houses they are in."[8] *Applebee's Journal*, for which he wrote, specialized in the lives and trials of pirates and felons.[9]

With the growing concern about crime came greater interest in criminals. The weekly journals increased the number of items and joined the sessions papers, broadsides, the Newgate Ordinary's *Account*, pamphlet lives, and collections such as Alexander Smith's *A Compleat History of the Lives and Robberies of the Most Notorious Highway-Men, Footpads, Shop-Lifts, and Cheats of Both Sexes*. Always alert to what his contemporaries were interested in and would buy and always eager to analyze, explain, and point out the implications of social change, Defoe began to publish extensively on crime and criminals. The connection between Defoe's journalistic subjects and his publications in the 1720s, including *Moll Flanders*, is very close.[1] Many of the reports in his papers became grist for his novels.

5. To some extent, Beattie's statistics support this opinion; see especially figure 5.4, 215, and 213–28. C. H. Firth, *Naval Songs and Ballads*, Publications of the Navy Records Society 33 (1908), 229, 230. On highwaymen, see Joan Parkes, *Travel in England in the Seventeenth Century* (London: Oxford UP, 1925), pp. 152, 160–84.
6. A. J. Shirren, *Daniel Defoe in Stoke Newington* (Stoke Newington: Public Libraries Committee, 1960), p. 19.
7. *Mercurius Politicus* September (1716): 242.
8. Defoe, *The Great Law of Subordination Consider'd* (London, 1724), p. 210.
9. *White-Hall Evening Post* 5 February 1719; Michael Harris says John Applebee was the leading publisher of criminal lives for twenty-five years; he did both the *Original Weekly Journal* and the Ordinary's *Accounts*, "Trials and Criminal Biographies: A Case Study in Distribution," in *Sale and Distribution of Books from 1700*, eds. Robin Myers and Michael Harris (Oxford: Oxford Polytechnic P, 1982), p. 5.
1. This point has been made by Maximillian Novak and others; see, for example, Novak, "Defoe's Theory of Fiction," *Studies in Philology* 61 (1964): pp. 650–68.

For instance, on 8 October 1719, the *Daily Post* reported the death of Paul Lorrain, Ordinary of Newgate and one model for the greedy Ordinary who cannot save Moll Flanders's soul. Moll describes Jemy as having the reputation of "Hind, Whitney, or the Golden Farmer" (p. 220), all contemporary criminals whose exploits had reached near-mythical proportions.[2] His *Commentator* for 1 August 1720 published a short poem that prefigures passages in *Moll Flanders*:

What makes a homely Woman fair?
About Five Hundred Pounds a Year.
What makes a Virgin of a Whore?
Much about Five Hundred more.
'Tis Money guides the World and Fate,
Makes Virtue Vice, makes Crooked Strait.

Convinced that novelty drew the most readers, Defoe found it in three intriguing groups of criminals: women, gangs, and pirates.

At first, most of his serious attention went to pirates, for they discouraged trade and colonization. Pirates were on everyone's mind. In 1718, Captain Woodes Rogers had defeated a huge pirate colony in the Bahamas and, in the aftermath, some 2000 surrendered and received the royal pardon. The center of pirate operations became Madagascar, and, by 1721, the English dispatched Navy squadrons to protect the East India Company ships. Reports of the capture and subsequent trials of pirates appeared almost daily in the papers. Defoe's *Col. Jack* records the booty taken by a French privateer and comments in the words of many of his creator's contemporaries, "This was a Terrible Loss among the *English* Merchants." The State Papers include numerous petitions from merchants, ship masters, traders, and planters.[3] In September 1717, Addison responded to a report on West Indies trade made by the Lord Commissioners of Trade and Plantations, "His Majesty being sensible that the British Trade in those parts is thereby in great danger." In December 1718, a Royal Proclamation set rewards for the discovery and capture of the pirates.[4]

"Land pirates," highwaymen and gangs, became Defoe's next subject. Particularly frightening because they outnumbered their prey and often encouraged each other in reckless and violent acts, the gangs seemed alarmingly numerous around 1720. One Englishman

2. Lorrain was the Ordinary from 1698–1719. See Robert R. Singleton, "Defoe, Moll Flanders, and the Ordinary of Newgate," *Harvard Library Bulletin* 24 (1976): 407–13, and Lincoln Faller, "In Contrast to Defoe: The Rev. Paul Lorrain, Historian of Crime," *Huntington Library Quarterly* (1976): 59–78. On Hind, Whitney and the Golden Farmer and their place in the literature of crime, see Faller, *Turned to Account: The Forms and Functions of Criminal Biography* (Cambridge: Cambridge UP, 1987), pp. 6–20, 136–44, et passim.
3. Cf. PRO SP 44 / 119, May and July 1717.
4. PRO SP 44 / 119 3 Sept. 1717; PRO T 27 / 24, 21 Dec. 1718.

spoke for many when he said that they threatened "life and safety, as well as property: and . . . render the condition of society wretched, by a sense of personal insecurity."[5] Among the most famous gangs operating around the time that Defoe was completing *Moll Flanders* were the Hawkins, Lemon, Spiggott, Field, Shaw, and Carrick gangs. Carrick was said to have fifteen members in his group and to have loose alliances with four other gangs.[6] By 1718 charity schools for "blackguard boys," the common term for homeless boys believed to join or form adult gangs, existed. The reformist Henry Newman had noted that many of them were the children of military men and, therefore, "are strictly of no parish" and not eligible for parish charity. The nation, he believed, should take care of the children left because their "parents have been knocked in the head in the service" of their sovereign.[7] Other prominent people deplored the way "the distressed children called the Blackguard" "are vagrants and exposed to a multitude of temptations."[8] As children, they, like Moll Flanders, were at risk. As a former parish officer, member of the Society for the Reformation of Manners, and an interested observer of the S.P.C.K., Defoe was undoubtedly aware of Newman's efforts. He understood the preconceptions and fears people had of such children. Random crimes, their youth and lack of principles, and the number of people in the population like them made them especially frightening. By 1720, the gangs threatened inland trade as the pirates did foreign.

Women criminals always fascinated people, and, in 1720, they were appearing in court more frequently than ever before. Without good employment opportunities and displaced from jobs by the returning military men and by the depressed state of the woolen trade, women turned to prostitution and robbery to support themselves. Social change hit women hard. Bad times had sent men to sea and to the colonies; the natural dangers of ocean travel and the wars had contributed to the imbalance of numbers of men and of women, and spinsters, widows, and deserted wives found their fathers and brothers unable to maintain them. With the end of the self-supporting family and the cottage industry, they could contribute little or nothing to the family.

5. Quoted in Beattie, *Crime and the Courts*, p. 148.
6. Gerald Howson, *Thief-Taker General: Jonathan Wild and the Emergence of Crime and Corruption as a Way of Life in Eighteenth-Century England* (New Brunswick: Transaction Books, 1970), pp. 106–7, 171–86, 190 (see especially "Appendix III: Principal Gangs," pp. 312–14); Beattie, pp. 252–63. Beattie describes the same loose associations without fixed members found in *Colonel Jack* (London, 1723), pp. 256–58.
7. Newman's first effort had been in 1713. Leonard Cowie, *Henry Newman, An American in London* (London: SPCK, 1956), pp. 75–76.
8. Quoted in Cowie, 101; the quoted speech by Robert Nelson was published in 1715. See Paul J. deGategno, "Daniel Defoe's Newgate Biographies: An Economic Crisis," *CLIO* 13 (1984): 157–60.

In the seventeenth century, communities tended to handle female offenders privately, but the urban courts had begun to see sizeable numbers of them. In rural Surrey, for instance, only 19% of the women arrested for property crimes were actually prosecuted while 81% were in London. In the city, women were more likely to be on their own, subject to economic hardship, and with the opportunity to commit a crime.[9] The village woman would have been deterred from risking apprehension as a shoplifter by the fact that the shop keeper would know her, that she would probably be handed over to her disgraced family, and that she would be shamed in front of her neighbors and family.

Although scarcely new, even a female petty thief was more intriguing than an ordinary male footpad, and some of them received as much attention from the press as notorious male murderers. More unusual criminals like Moll King, Sally Salisbury, and Betsy Careless captured London's imagination, and convicted females on the scaffold and in the carts headed for ships to the colonies were familiar sights. Moll Flanders resembles the common thieves. How close Defoe's novels could be to popular ephemera can be seen by comparing the plot of *Moll Flanders* to the title of an eight-page criminal life:

> An Account of the Birth and Education, Life and Conversation of Mary Raby; Who was Executed at *Tyburn* on *Wednesday* the 3d of November 1703 . . . Particularly the manner of her several pretended Marriages . . . her many *Cheats*, *Robberies*, *Shop-liftings*, *Clipping*, *Coyning*, *Receiving Stolen goods*, and other strange and astonishing Actions of her Life. . . .

Defoe, however, uses his representation of such women to raise enduring questions.[1] Moll's initiation into society is an initiation into the importance of money, and she rapidly learns how predatory human beings can be and how poverty and desperation feel. Defoe forces readers to confront the extent to which society is to blame for Moll's depraved sensibility and crimes. Over and over, the novel raises the question of the nature of evil. What is its source? Of what are we capable? We cannot ignore her rising series of questions to the unfeeling older brother or the arresting, dreadful moment when Moll says, "the Devil put me upon killing the Child in the dark Alley" (p. 153). At first, the reader wonders what Moll will do next, but soon what kind of person she is becomes the question and with it: What is evil? Is it part of human nature, as basic as hunger or thirst? Is it a misperception of the world—for instance, a focus on self

9. Beattie, *Crime and the Courts*, pp. 237–43, 436–39.
1. This paragraph is adapted from the final chapter of my *Moll Flanders: The Making of a Criminal Mind* (Boston: Twayne Publishers, 1990), pp. 93–99.

instead of God? Is it a person's twisted response to overpowering forces? How does evil grow within the human heart? Why do the "evils" in society, such as ignorance and want, result in moral evil for the ignorant and wanting? Defoe makes judgment difficult and teases the reader into engaging yet again questions that each of us must finally take responsibility for answering for ourselves.

In the aftermath of the South Sea Bubble,[2] Defoe became fascinated by avarice, and he builds this vice and his growing interest in addictive personalities into *Moll Flanders*. In *The Case of Mr. Law* (1721) written the year before the publication of *Moll Flanders*, he called avarice "an unwearied and impatient Vice" (21–22). At the height of the South Sea investment frenzy, he remarked,

> Avarice has a Kind of natural Assurance with it, that steels the Countenance against Blushes, and repels all the Objections rais'd from Modesty, from Reason, from Justice, and even from the Laws of the Land. So true it is, that the Love of Money increases with the Money.
>
> There's a strange Charm in this Sort of Trade of getting Money; they never surfeit of the Quantity, never weary with the Labour.[3]

It is avarice, of course, that takes over Moll and from which she must wean herself. From the time Moll is "more confounded with the money than . . . with the love" (p. 22) of the elder brother to the day she is caught robbing a silk factor, she never tires of money. She insists that poverty makes her what she is and several times resolves "to leave it quite off, if I could but come to lay up money enough to maintain me" (p. 96). She sets amounts of money as targets for retirement but always raises the sum when she reaches her goal. On the day she commits her last robbery, she has more than £1000, and a middle class *family* could live on £100 a year. She has become so addicted to her crime that she takes whatever opportunity puts before her—including a horse which she must abandon at an inn. "Avarice kept me in, till there was no going back; as to arguments which my reason dictated for perswading me to lay down, avarice stept in and said, Go on . . . go on . . ." (160) she says.

As numerous critics have noted, Moll becomes hardened and loses awareness of the effects of social immorality. In an earlier text, Defoe had reflected on what he sees as part of human personality: "how easily, and by what insensible Degree they are drawn to a general

2. The South Sea Company was a trading company founded in 1711; it took over part of the national debt in exchange for extensive trade monopolies in Spanish America. Wild speculative investment and unsound, even corrupt management practices led to the collapse of the stock. A share went from a value of £1000 in July 1720 to £190 in October. The highest number of bankruptcies in British history resulted, and insurance companies, schools, and institutional trustees for estates as well as individuals were seriously affected.
3. *Commentator* 10 June 1720.

Defection of Virtue, and to follow a Practice, which in time will be the Ruin . . . of Religion it self. . . ."[4] Moll Flanders laments that she became "harden'd to a pitch above all the reflections of conscience or modesty" (p. 159). So powerful is this addiction that only some powerful, external force can wean the characters from their ways of life. In *Moll Flanders*, Defoe recommends a controversial solution open to the state and to individuals: transportation.

The Transportation Act of 1718 allowed courts to sentence even clergied felons[5] to transportation to America. On a very limited scale, transportation had been used before the Restoration as an alternative to capital punishment, and, by 1700, had become a fairly common form of conditional pardon. The judge could pronounce it, or the criminal could petition as Moll Flanders did for transportation. A typical text written by a justice of the peace read,

> I reprieved them because it did not appear to me that either of them had committed any such offense before, or were ingaged in any society of offenders . . . But they are lewd idle fellows, and it is fitting the country should be clear'd of them. they are strong able body'd men and may do good service either in her Majestys Plantations or army.[6]

The Secretary of State would then endorse the pardon, conditional upon the prisoner joining the army or accepting transportation. Until 1718, merchants or the prisoners themselves paid the passage to the New World. Because the infirm and female had little or no market value there, the indigent were hanged or simply released.[7] Defoe himself had transported people to Maryland in 1688. He paid £1:7:6 for the transportation of each, and another £1:7:0 for shoes and a coat for them.[8] His expenses are typical. Transportation and board never cost more than five or six pounds, and Defoe, then a partner

4. Defoe, *The Fears of the Pretender Turn'd into the Fears of Debauchery* (London, 1715), pp. 25–26.
5. Some lesser felonies (such as damaging trees or poaching) allowed the offender to claim the ancient "benefit of clergy" for the first conviction only. Before the Restoration, *male* criminals who could read "the neck verse," Psalm 51, were turned over to the representative of the Church for punishment. By the eighteenth century, they were almost invariably simply released.
6. BL Loan 29 / 369, letters from justices of the peace, for 27 and 28 Feb. 1704 / 5.
7. Beattie, *Crime and the Courts*, 470–73, 479–83; Abbot Emerson Smith, *Colonists in Bondage* (Chapel Hill: University of North Carolina P, 1947), 62–63; BL Loan 29 / 369, letters from justices of the peace, 27 and 28 Feb. 1704 / 5; Proceedings of the King's Commission of the Peace collected in Guildhall show that after 1718 transportation became the "order of the day." The State Papers include numerous references to problems before the act; in 1706 merchants had to bring women prisoners back to England at their own expense because none of the women could pay their fare and the plantations would not receive them (PRO SP 44 / 105, for 6 Feb. 1706); here and elsewhere the Secretary of State tried to get the City to accept them in the workhouses, see also PRO SP 44 / 117, Dec. 1714. Information on transportation comes from these sources.
8. PRO 5 / 84 / 9 and C 7 / 122 / 36.

for the ship's voyage, probably was paying the actual cost rather than cost plus the profit expected by the captain or ship owner. The trade was profitable; for instance, Defoe made an £8:5 profit on one of the men he sold. Some courts paid up to £8 per person to merchants willing to take women, but so sure were profits from the sale of the prisoners that most required the merchant pay jail fees and even the clerk's charge for drawing up a pardon.[9]

The 1718 Act gave merchants contracts granting them £3 for each convict transported. In addition, the merchants could sell the prisoners' services at auction in the colonies where men brought an average of £10, healthy, young women £8 to 9, and craftsmen as much as £25. By 1722, the year *Moll Flanders* was published, about 60% of the convicted male, clergyable felons and 46% of the women were transported. In fact, about 70% of all the felons convicted at the Old Bailey were deported and only about 7.5% executed. Although the contract-holder protested, prisoners could still arrange their own passage to the colonies.[1] The experience of Moll Flanders is authentically rendered.

Defoe's depiction of her life included powerful propaganda for the recent Act. Because convicted felons had often been released with a punishment as mild as being branded on the thumb, large numbers of criminals were quickly and repeatedly released. Because there were no satisfactory penalties between branding and whipping at one extreme and hanging at the other, judges and juries often felt the inappropriateness of either, and the lighter sentences were imposed.[2] Moll's case was designed to show the appropriateness of transportation.[3] Moll, although an old offender, is tried only once and for theft of goods valued at £46. To have hanged a person who was technically a first offender for that crime would have seemed cruel indeed.

Defoe presents transportation as both opportunity and the means to break an addictive pattern. Transportation gives both Moll and Jack, and other characters in both books, a new chance. Had Moll's husband not been her brother, she might have lived as peaceful and productive a life as her mother, a transported felon, had. Defoe is careful to show the colonies in a favorable light, and he is informed

9. Beattie, *Crime and the Courts*, pp. 479, 483; Smith, *Colonists in Bondage*, pp. 35–36, 99–100, 103, 105–6; David W. Galenson, *White Servitude in Colonial America: An Economic Analysis* (Cambridge: Cambridge UP, 1981), p. 100; Richard S. Dunn, "Servants and Slaves: The Recruitment and Employment of Labor," in *Colonial British America: Essays in the New History of the Early Modern Era*, ed. Jack P. Greene and J. R. Pole (Baltimore: Johns Hopkins UP, 1984), pp. 159–61, 171.
1. Beattie, pp. 504–5; PRO C 5 / 84 / 9 and C 7 / 122 / 36; Smith, pp. 110–19, 125; Dunn, p. 170.
2. Beattie, pp. 454–55, 469–70 et passim; Smith, pp. 91–2, 128–29.
3. Defoe's novel *The History of Col. Jack* also portrays the advantages of transportation. Although Jack has been kidnapped and sold, his crimes were just the kind committed by most of the felons sent over, and his treatment in American typical.

enough to set his novels in the colonies where land was most easily obtained. Although without amenities, the characters live almost as they might in England. Defoe includes no threatening Indians and gives no sense of the wilderness or, compared to England, the extremes of climate. In *A Plan for the English Commerce* (1728), Defoe described the North American colonies as "wild," "barren," and "inhospitable" and the Indians as fierce, treacherous, "bloody and merciless."[4] *Atlas Maritimus* adds that the Indians were "gigantick," carried seven-to-eight-foot-long bows, and resisted all overtures.[5] Although Maryland and Virginia planters routinely allowed a three-hour midday break in summer and thousands died of the heat anyway,[6] Defoe's characters never mention the heat and humidity of the summer or the damp, cold of winter. Notably, half of Defoe's first six novels show their characters' prosperity based upon New World plantations.

After *Moll Flanders* came the lives of some of the most famous criminals of the 1720's, those of Sheppard and Wild, and a series of pamphlets proposing ways to control street crime. John Sheppard achieved his greatest fame by escaping repeatedly from prisons, and Defoe's *History of the Remarkable Life of Sheppard* and *A Narrative of all the Robberies, Escapes, etc. of John Sheppard* (both 1724) portray Sheppard as a clever jester who exchanges jokes with those who come to gawk at him and tells his own story with: "[I] made the door my humble servant," he says as he describes how he broke a lock.[7] Sheppard, however, was rather easily captured and, like most of the subjects of eighteenth-century criminal lives, went to the gallows penitent.

Jonathan Wild was another kind of subject and part of the inspiration for John Gay's *Beggar's Opera*. He had come to the public's attention first as the proprietor of his "Office for the Recovery of Lost and Stolen Property" and then as the thief-taker chiefly responsible for the destruction of London's four largest gangs. Two years later, Wild was exposed as the monstrous lord of criminals who directed them, received their plunder and sold it back to their victims, and who decided which of them would live and die by turning some over to the authorities and providing witnesses against them. Moreover, he recruited thieves, hired specialists for big robberies, divided the city into districts and deployed gangs to each, and made enormous profits.[8] Convicted in May of 1725, Wild went to the gal-

4. Defoe, *A Plan for the English Commerce*, Shakespeare Head edition (Oxford: Blackwell, 1974), pp. 228–29.
5. Defoe, *Atlas Maritimus* (London, 1728), p. 294.
6. Smith, pp. 254–57, 303–5.
7. Defoe, *A Narrative of all the Robberies, Escapes, &c. of John Sheppard* in *Romances and Narratives by Daniel Defoe*, ed. George A. Aitken (London: Dent, 1905), 16:226.
8. Howson notes that not one conviction of a highwayman is recorded between 1723 and Wild's death in 1725, *Thief-Taker General*, 5. Information about Wild is from this book.

lows disheveled and stupefied from the effects of laudanum taken in an unsuccessful suicide attempt.

Defoe called Wild a "wretched subject" and saw his deceptive art for what it was more clearly than any of his other biographers. Wild's criminal activities were strikingly similar to those of Mother Midnight in *Moll Flanders*. Both of them recruited and trained thieves, encouraged them to continue, received stolen goods, and brokered them back to their original owners. Mother Midnight allows some of her associates to hang and makes serious efforts to save others, as she does Moll. In Wild, Defoe saw the validation of many of his considered opinions about crime. Wild had learned his trade as an imprisoned debtor and could say with Moll's mother that prison made thieves. Defoe concluded bluntly, "Jonathan's avarice hanged him."[9] Defoe always relished a good trick, and some of Wild's crimes, particularly his early ones when he used his double hip joint, delighted him. Rather than suggesting that Defoe was onto Wild two years before anyone else, the similarity to incidents in his novels shows that Wild had improved existing criminal practices. In fact, one of the satiric targets of Defoe's *Reformation of Manners* (1702), Sir Salathiel Lovell, had practiced Wild's game of hanging one thief in order to protect another who happened to be in his employment.

Defoe genuinely believed that all "Members of the Community" were struggling with street violence, and he wrote several pamphlets proposing ways to control crime. Using one of his most characteristic metaphors, he summarized his habitual method of analysis, and that analysis always considered both contexts and individuals:

> The first reasonable Step towards the Cure of a distemper'd Body, is to find out the Nature and Original of the Disorder; whence it proceeds, and what Progress it has made in its Attacks upon the Health of the Patient. . . . [1]

In *Some Considerations upon Street-Walkers* [1726], *Second Thoughts are Best: or a Further Improvement on a late Scheme to Prevent Street Robberies*, *Street Robberies Consider'd*, *Augusta Triumphans* [all 1728], and *An Effectual Scheme for the Immediate Preventing of Street Robberies* (1731), Defoe made inquiries into causes and described kinds of crimes just as his method outlined and then proposed cures.

9. Defoe, *The True and Genuine Account of the Life and Actions of the Late Jonathan Wild* in *Romances and Narratives by Daniel Defoe*, ed. George A. Aitken (London: Dent, 1905), 16:263.
1. Defoe, *An Effectual Scheme for the Immediate Preventing of Street Robberies* (London, 1731), p. 15.

As much as he deplored the fact that "the streets swarmed with rogues" and that "the Armies of Hell" possessed the streets after 10 p.m.,[2] he never loses sight of the part poverty and lack of a trade played in making criminals. His suggestions are as characteristic of him as these pamphlets: they begin with bed-rock practicality and become elaborate baroque creations. For example, he begins by suggesting better lighting for the streets, younger watchmen—for now they have "one Foot in the Grave, and t'other ready to follow"—and robbers prosecuted at the public's, not the witnesses', charge. Soon, however, he wants the city divided in tiny squares with an impossible number of watchmen and a national reformation of manners. Ridiculous as a few of his individual suggestions are, his pamphlets are full of shrewd observations, common sense, and unmistakable public spirit. His "chequer-work" life had left intact the spirit of the young man who wrote *An Essay upon Projects* for the benefit of his country, and, in his sixty-eighth year, Defoe subtitled *Augusta Triumphans*, "The Way to Make London The most flourishing City in the Universe."

Moll Flanders, as did *Col. Jack*, required three editions by 1724 and was serialized between 14 May 1722 and 20 March 1723. In 1724, *A Narrative of all the Robberies . . . of Sheppard* went through eight editions and *The History of the . . . Life of Sheppard* three, and *The Life of Wild* two in 1725. Before he died, Defoe had come to compete with the Newgate Ordinary as the most productive and popular crime writer in Great Britain and to write the "effectual schemes" for the reduction of street robberies. These texts and their sympathy for victims and criminals helped establish the reputation his obituaries would celebrate, a man who understood and cared about the best interests of his country.

2. Quotations are from Defoe, *Brief Historical Account of the Lives of the Six Notorious Street-Robbers, Executed at Kingston* in *Romances and Narratives by Daniel Defoe*, ed. George A. Aitken (London: Dent, 1905), 16:371–72, and *Effectual Scheme*, p. 64.

JOHN RIETZ

Criminal Ms-Representation: *Moll Flanders* and Female Criminal Biography†

I

Femininity and criminality clash in *Moll Flanders*, a fact that may not be immediately evident to the modern reader because Defoe is not thinking of femininity and criminality in quite the same way we do. The best—perhaps only—access to his conception of the relationship between these two qualities is by way of contemporary texts that shed further light on how that relationship was perceived by others at the time. And a close look at some of those texts strongly suggests that the roles of woman and criminal were perceived as mutually exclusive, and that a figure who straddled these two categories gave rise to considerable confusion. Like other biographers of female criminals before him who also struggled to conceive a model of female criminality, Defoe seems to have been unable to reconcile satisfactorily the contradictions of an unfamiliar social hybrid.

But to suggest that certain writers in the seventeenth and eighteenth centuries were unable to grasp a concept that we entertain with little or no difficulty need not be the historical condescension it may appear to be. John J. Richetti, in discussing Defoe's Roxana, offers an explanation of her social status as a criminal that could just as appropriately be applied to Moll Flanders: "As a woman suddenly stripped of her domestic identity, Roxana is an open field, a deserted psycho-social space in which anything can be enacted and in which a newly thorough self-consciousness is possible. The cultural implications of Defoe's book are that female identity in a normal social order is so limited and fragile that once ordinary conditions are altered, a woman is turned into a pure opportunity for free-floating selfhood."[1] His observation is a shrewd one. If a female criminal is unthinkable, then a woman who found her way into such a role could be as uncertain of her identity as anyone. If Richetti is correct, then these women, ungoverned by convention or even a sense of consistent selfhood, could in fact behave in ways that are wildly incongruous, unthinkable, and a return to a more conventional role would involve the return of more comprehensible and consistent behavior

† From "Criminal Ms-Representation: *Moll Flanders* and Female Criminal Biography," *Studies in the Novel* 23 (1991): 183–95. Copyright 1991 by the University of North Texas. Reprinted by permission of the publisher. Page numbers in parentheses refer to this Norton Critical Edition. Notes have been edited.

1. John J. Richetti, "The Family, Sex, and Marriage in Defoe's *Moll Flanders* and *Roxana*," *Studies in the Literary Imagination* 15.2 (1982): 33.

as social scripts would once again exert their usual influence. This is the pattern we see not only in *Moll Flanders* but also in two of its most important predecessors in this subgenre.

Prior to the publication of *Moll Flanders*, there were only two book-length biographies of female criminals in English, Francis Kirkman's *The Counterfeit Lady Unveiled* (1673), concerning Mary Carleton, the so-called German Princess, and the anonymously published *Life and Death of Mrs. Mary Frith* (1662), alias Mal Cutpurse.[2] In these texts, as in *Moll Flanders*, femininity and criminality clash, and when they do, the result is that the crimes of women are portrayed as a perversion of their sexuality. And not only does this leave them at odds with male society and authority, but ultimately, because of the competing claims of their femininity and criminality, they resist categorization and are placed even farther outside the larger social order.

II

In part, the representation of female criminals in these biographies is somewhat predictable, relying on conventional means of portray-

2. It is preferable for our purpose to look at examples of female criminals in sustained narratives such as these since their more detailed and extended portraiture more nearly approximates that of the novel. But there are other reasons why these two texts ought to serve as our standards of what Defoe may have been influenced by or reacting to. Perhaps most obviously, the heroines of *Mary Frith* and *The Counterfeit Lady Unveiled* are mentioned in *Moll Flanders* and *Roxana*, respectively, and in both cases Defoe's women compare themselves directly to their predecessors. Moll claims that she "grew as impudent a Thief, and as dexterous as ever *Moll Cut-Purse* was" (*Moll Flanders*, p. 159); and Roxana says, "I might as well have been the German Princess" (*Roxana* [London: Oxford UP, 1964], p. 271). Moreover, the sheer popularity of these narratives urges their consideration in such a study. Not only is it possible that such texts actively shaped popular conceptions of female criminality, but also the fact that they were so widely read would suggest that their portrayals were in some way congruent with such conceptions to begin with.

It might be objected that the character Defoe created, being fictional, is not really comparable in manner of construction to those found in biographies of actual women. In fact, they are surprisingly close. Ernest Bernbaum (*The Mary Carleton Narratives: 1663–1673* [Cambridge: Harvard UP, 1914]) has convincingly demonstrated that, although based on a core of actual information, *The Counterfeit Lady Unveiled* is largely fictitious, and he points out that one of Kirkman's primary concerns in extrapolating from and fabricating around these facts was, as Kirkman himself says in his introduction, to offer the reader a view of her psychology. Robert Singleton, in his catalogue of "English Criminal Biography, 1651–1722" (*Harvard Library Bulletin* 18 [1970]: 63–83), places *Mary Frith* in his list of those books "known to be fictitious" (p. 79). The fact that *The Counterfeit Lady Unveiled*, factual only in broad outline, is in his list of legitimate biographies indicates how much more thoroughly fictional *Mary Frith* is, even though it does include a handful of substantiated facts. Defoe's impulse and even his methods in writing *Moll Flanders* seem to have been fairly similar to those of Kirkman and Mal Cutpurse's biographer. Literary historians have long suspected that Defoe probably used some—perhaps a significant amount—of factual detail in writing about Moll's career. Gerald Howson, for example, has argued that Moll may have been modelled on one Mary Godson (alias Moll King), a woman Defoe could very possibly have met in Newgate just prior to writing *Moll Flanders* ("Who Was Moll Flanders?" *Times Literary Supplement* [13 January 1968]: 63–64). Like the criminal biographers that preceded him, then, Defoe seems to have built his heroine at least partly on a loose collection of factual materials, his concern, like theirs, being the construction of a compelling character, not the chronicling of an actual life.

ing women. The constellation of basic traits that these women bring to their criminal activities are very much traits of traditional womanhood: wit, passivity, beauty. The hermaphroditic personality of Mal Cutpurse, ironically enough, is helpful in separating what seem to be two distinct sets of characteristics—female and male—that give rise to two distinct approaches to crime. She, of course, embodies both: she was "not to be guided either by the reservedness and modesty of her own Sex, or the more imperious command of the other; she resolved to set up a neutral or Hermaphrodite way of Profession . . . like the *Colossus of Female* subtlety in the wily Arts & *ruses* of that Sex; and of manly resolution in the bold and regardless Rudenesses of the other, so blended and mixed together, that it was hard to say whether she were more cunning, or more impudent."[3] The crimes of these women are aggressive, but physical aggression is clearly set up here as a male domain, whereas a more subtle passive-aggressive style is appropriate for women, a style that involves the use of "cunning" and "ruses." Women are thieves, not robbers. Thus, throughout his narrative, Kirkman refers to Mary Carleton's "old tools, her wits" in explaining the methods of "this subtle female thief."[4] Likewise, Moll Flanders' favorite words to describe her skills are "dexterous" and "art," and although she chooses to focus on physical skill in the former term, hers are the subtle skills of a thief, not the forceful ones of a robber. She is not as insistent on the matter as Kirkman is, but Moll clearly thrives on her wits and cunning. Her most profitable ventures are her confidence scams, not her shoplifting or pocket picking, and even in these her wits must rescue her from occasional lapses in dexterity.

Even in the seemingly aggressive crimes of pocket picking, shoplifting, and confidence games, however, female criminals are figured, as much as they can be, as passive agents, demonstrating the "reservedness and modesty" of which Mal Cutpurse speaks. Kirkman claims that criminal opportunity came to Mary Carleton unbidden: "commonly she did not seek for any because it fell out readily to her hand; the bird usually came into the net of its own accord" (p. 75). Similarly, Moll a number of times describes herself as merely being vigilant for opportunities, not creating them: "The next day I . . . walk'd the same way again; but nothing offer'd" (p. 202). At times her activity seems almost aimless: "I had taken up the Disguise of a Widow's Dress; it was without any real design in view, but only waiting for any thing that might offer, as I often did: It happened that

3. *The Life and Death of Mrs. Mary Frith* (London: W. Gilbertson, 1662), p. 26. Subsequent references will be to this edition and will be noted parenthetically in the text.
4. Francis Kirkman, *The Counterfeit Lady Unveiled*, in *The Counterfeit Lady Unveiled and Other Criminal Fiction of Seventeenth-Century England*, ed. Spiro Peterson (Garden City, NJ: Doubleday, 1961), pp. 86, 93. Subsequent references will be to this edition and will be noted parenthetically in the text.

while I . . ." (p. 190). These situations "happen" to her as much as they happen to her victims.

It is curious, though, that these women, especially Moll and Mary Carleton, who are depicted as attractive, avaricious, and passively waiting for the occasion to sin, should not often—if ever—resort to prostitution, the classic female crime. Kirkman acknowledges that this runs counter to expectation when he points out that "this crime she was not so guilty of, as the world supposes" (p. 55). We see Moll take payment for sex from only one man, and in that case she becomes more of a kept mistress than an indiscriminate whore; at least that is how she views the arrangement.[5] As Lois Chaber points out, Moll carefully disassociates herself from the profession in her defense of it, speaking of the "passive Jade" in the third person.[6]

This is not to say, of course, that female criminals don't make capital use of their most marketable asset, but their use of their female sexuality is presented as a perversion of it. In the accounts of male criminals, such as *Don Tomazo* or *Will Morrell*, for example, a romantic involvement is usually pursued for its own sake and can even be so enthralling that it may temporarily distract them from their criminal pursuits.[7] By contrast, their female counterparts usually pursue such involvements only so far as they are profitable. Both Moll and Mary Carleton parlay the admiration of amorous men into financial support, gifts, or an opportunity to steal. Even Mal Cutpurse is "obeyed from the two great Principles of Subjection, *Love* [female] and *Fear* [male]" (p. 101). But her exploitation of sex is generally more parasitic. As a bawd, she knows how to pique her customers' desires (and thereby maximize her profit) with what she calls her "amorous tricks and pranks," either delaying or suddenly and unexpectedly bringing about their tryst. One young woman, "a very curious Piece" who has drawn many admirers, is "as free for [Mal's] turn as for any bodies" (p. 123). Mal's lust, however, is not for the woman's flesh but for the money that can be gained by pimping for her: "I accosted her, using such Caresses, promises and invitations as I knew the Market would bear, so that I made her entirely mine, and gratified a friend with her" (p. 124). The language of love and trade are used interchangeably here, as once again Mal's position at the outer limits of sexuality allows us to see what are normally subtle traits exaggerated.

5. Shirlene Mason offers a clear analysis of Moll's status as a mistress rather than a prostitute (*Daniel Defoe and the Status of Women* [St. Albans, VT: Eden P, 1978], p. 98).
6. Lois A. Chaber, "Matriarchal Mirror: Women and Capital in *Moll Flanders*," *PMLA* 97 (1982): 214.
7. See *Don Tomazo, or the Juvenile Rambles of Thomas Dangerfield* and Elkanah Settle. *The Complete Memoirs of the Life of that Notorious Impostor Will. Morrell*, both in *The Counterfeit Lady Unveiled and Other Criminal Fiction of Seventeenth-Century England* (pp. 177–289, 291–372).

Clearly, her sexual desire has been perverted into cupidity, and we see a similar pattern in Mary Carleton and Moll, whose relationships with men are more often pursued for financial gain than for love, either by baiting their traps with the promise of sex or by the more legitimate (but still predatory) practice of gold digging. But once the woman's beauty fades, so does the possibility of capitalizing on it. When Moll reaches this stage in her life, she turns to outright thievery—a sort of career change, and one that lays bare the motivation behind her romantic involvements. "I would gladly have turn'd my Hand to any honest Employment if I could have got it," she explains. "If I had been younger, perhaps [my Governess] might have helped me to a Spark, but my Thoughts were off of that kind of Livelihood, as being quite out of the way after 50, which was my Case" (p. 156). Mal Cutpurse's criminal career begins when she comes to a similar conclusion: "*Mals* converse with her self (whose disinviting eyes and look sank inwards to her breast, when they could have no regard abroad,) informed her of her defects; and that she was not made for the pleasure or delight of Man; and therefore since she could not be honoured with him she would be honoured by him in that garb and manner of rayment He wore . . . she resolved to usurp and invade the Doublet, and vye and brave manhood, which she could not tempt nor allure" (pp. 17–18). Believing herself too unattractive to marry, then, and having been cheated out of money by the shoemaker of whom she is enamored—these "took her off from the consideration or thought of Wedlock, but reduced her to some advisement which way she might maintaine her self single," and she settles on "living by the quick" (p. 22). These women turn to crime when legitimate attachments to men seem unlikely—or simply unprofitable. Again, female criminality is portrayed as a perversion of—or, in more extreme cases, a substitute for—female sexuality. Their crimes seem specifically tied to a breach in the social order as they break ties with men, either preying on them or establishing independence from them.

III

The idea that crime involves a breach in the social order, of course, amounts to little more than a tautology, nor does it seem especially enlightening, at first glance, to point out that female criminals disrupt a patriarchal system. The same can be said of male criminals as well. But in the case of women, their crimes are not represented as the violation of a social order that simply happens to be patriarchal. Attention is clearly drawn to the patriarchal nature of the system they renounce, and this is accompanied by the establishment of female authority separate from and hostile to its counterpart. Moreover, just as it is this renunciation that signals the start of a criminal career, so it is a reaffirmation of male authority that signals its end.

Once again, Mal Cutpurse is the exception that proves the rule—and proves it rather convincingly. She is said to have had an especially solicitous mother, and her father is symbolically rejected in the figure of her shoemaker boyfriend who takes advantage of her affection and who is explicitly set up as a parallel to her father. In fact, this incident quite directly precipitates her choosing a life of crime. From this point on, the author seems to be setting up a contrapuntal structure in which the assertion of female power is deliberately counterbalanced by the assertion of its opposite, reflecting not only Mal's uncertain sexual status but also the uncertain status of her fencing operations as legitimate business or crime. As the female organizer of a gang of male thieves—referred to by her with the diminutive appellation "the Boyes"—Mal has inverted the normal social hierarchy and placed herself in a position of authority over a group of men. But at the same time, she is an ardent royalist who has such affection for the king that she shakes his hand and personally welcomes him home during a parade to celebrate his successfully putting down a rebellion among the Scots and reasserting English sovereignty, the same sovereignty her gang of thieves work to undermine. Later in life, she finds herself in financial straits because, ever the royalist, she had been giving too generously to the cavaliers during the Civil War. What money she does have left at her death, however, she bequeaths to her maids—"that and some of my Arts which they have had time to be expert in" (p. 172)—setting them up as financially independent women (and potential criminals, as well). Perhaps the most eloquent expression of Mal's position in regard to male authority is in her alias, "Cutpurse," with its suggestions of castration. Mal says that she "could by no means endure" (p. 84) the name, claiming, "I never Actually or Instrumentally cut any Mans Purse; though I have often restored it" (p. 168). But her henchmen do cut purses and strip men of their economic power, and so she is both the agent of their emasculation and, in selling their stolen goods back to them again, the agent of their restoration.[8]

While Mal Cutpurse lends support to our theory, however, *The Counterfeit Lady Unveiled* provides a pattern that more closely

8. See Capt. Alexander Smith, *A Complete History of the Lives and Robberies of the Most Notorious Highwaymen, Footpads, Shoplifts, and Cheats of Both Sexes*, ed. Arthur L. Hayward (London: George Routledge and Sons, 1926). Smith's account of Simon Fletcher demonstrates that purse cutting was in fact seen as a metaphorical castration by at least one other writer. Fletcher, mistaking the scrotum of one of his victims for a purse as it dangles out of its codpiece, applies his knife and makes his escape. The unfortunate man's response, when he comes to realize what has happened, continues the metaphor: "Oh! I am ruined, I am ruined, & quite undone" he says. "I have lost a good pair of b______ks, for which I shall have more noise with my wife than if I had lost a hundred pounds" (p. 306).

approximates that of *Moll Flanders*. Mary Carleton's criminal career is launched with the creation of her fictitious German parentage with which she "denied her earthly parents, and particularly her father in her words, and in her actions denied or practiced against the laws of God, her Heavenly Father" (p. 14). Throughout her subsequent career, too, her gestures are often anti-patriarchal, as she steals items that are inherited family pieces and often bases her "chouses" on a promised but nonexistent paternal inheritance. When finally apprehended and convicted, she continues to deny her guilt and defies the authority of the court by pleading her belly, which necessitates a second trial presided over by "a jury of women [who] brought in this verdict, 'that she was not quick with child' " (p. 96). She might have effectively circumvented the verdict of the male courtroom with this ruse and did in fact transfer her fate into the hands of the jury of women, but their judgment passes her back to the men who sentence her to death. Her career thus ended, "she was quite altered" (p. 96). She is suddenly penitent and en route to Tyburn puts a picture of John Carleton to her bosom and asks that it be buried with her, suddenly acknowledging him to be her husband once again. In her final speech, she reaffirms both the earthly and the heavenly male authority she had earlier renounced: "I pray God forgive me and my husband. I beseech God lay nothing to his charge for my fault" (p. 101).

This same general pattern is present in *Moll Flanders*, the structure of which centers around Moll's search for a mother, a figure of female authority. Born to an unwed mother in Newgate, it is no accident that the woman whom she comes to call "Mother" is another criminal. Having been abandoned by her husband Jemy, Moll returns to London, pregnant by him. Under the Governess's care, Moll gives birth to a son, which she is then counselled to put out for adoption, thus stripping herself of this final vestige of her relationship with Jemy—and men in general. Their discussion of this plan is framed in the hypothetical third person as the Governess persuades her that affection and "nursing up" are more important for children than biological motherhood—and all the while the two address each other as "Mother" and "Child." In this central passage, Moll finds the mother she has been seeking.

Having thus accepted this woman's authority, she subsequently turns criminal with her; it is about the time that the Governess begins to fence stolen goods that Moll begins to hear the voice that prompts her to steal. And the incident that forces the Governess to curtail her house for lying in and turn to crime images her anti-patriarchal stance and also suggests Moll's current status: the Governess "had been Sued by a certain Gentleman, who had had his Daughter stolen from him; and who it seems that she had helped to convey away" (p. 156). This direct confrontation with the familial and legal authorities over a suspected threat to their sovereignty precipitates the Governess's final break with them as she and her "stolen" daughter Moll begin to operate outside the law.

Like Mary Carleton, Moll's reaffirmation of patriarchal rule comes when she is apprehended and her career is thus brought to an end. In prison, she is reunited with her husband Jemy and is born a second time in Newgate, this time to a life of legitimacy and under a figure of masculine authority. She is socializing with the other female inmates, eagerly awaiting the arrival of a group of freshly captured male criminals, "brave topping Gentlemen" (p. 220), when she discovers that Jemy is one of them. Immediately, she says, "I quitted my Company, and retir'd as much as that dreadful Place suffers any Body to retire" (p. 220) and repents the misery her sins have caused. Not only is the renunciation of her criminal life symbolically enacted here, but the meaning of this gesture is underscored by the mercantile language Moll habitually uses when discussing her "trade": she quitted her company and retired. Tallying up the books one final time, she finds herself indebted to Jemy. "This Gentleman's Misfortune I plac'd all to my own Account" (p. 220), she says, echoing Mary Carleton in assuming the blame for the misery of the husband she has reclaimed. The suddenness of her transformation is striking, and it is precipitated by the reappearance of masculine authority. Finally, it is only after this state of legitimacy is made complete by the death of her husband-brother and the shadow of that marriage is removed from her relationship with Jemy that Moll is able to claim the legacy of her biological (I hesitate to say "natural") family.

IV

Female criminals, then, are figured as being outside the social order, and their behavior is figured as somehow incompatible with their sexuality, crime being either a perversion of or a substitute for it. These two factors complicate the representation of characters like Moll Flanders. How does a writer effectively portray a character with the incompatible traits of femininity and criminality? One way is to render her neuter, or even masculine—or even, in the case of Mal Cutpurse, simultaneously masculine and feminine. But even Mal is predominantly masculine in behavior, if genetically feminine. Except for her housekeeping (in which she is proudly nonpareil), Mal is defeminized in her aversion to all of the traditional female arts and to female sexuality in general, but "above all she had a natural abhorrence to the tending of Children, to whom she ever had an aversness in her mind, equall to the sterility of her womb" (p. 13). Mary Carleton likewise dies without issue and is never cast in a maternal role of any type, and, although her femininity is not as problematic as Mal's, it is perhaps not an accident that Kirkman has rechristened her the counterfeit lady. Critics have long been uneasy with Moll Flanders' sexuality, sensing that she was somehow more male than female. Ian Watt calls her "essentially masculine" in character and action; Richetti calls her a female impersonator; and Frederick R. Karl calls her "virtually interchangeable with a man."[9] But Marsha Bordner is more discriminating and limits Moll's masculinity to her criminal years only, a more telling observation for our purposes.[1] Very commonly Moll is criticized for abandoning her children so easily, and her preying on unescorted children in her pocket picking has been offered as proof of her lack of maternal feeling.

Thus, one solution to the problem of embodying conflicting traits in a single believable character is to focus on one at the expense of the other, but there is a second solution: to mask the incompatibility by having the heroine adopt a role that is foreign to her "true" self. Hence the popularity in female criminal biography of the motif of imposture and disguise—and especially cross-dressing, a practice taken up by both Mal Cutpurse and Moll Flanders. There are, of course, obvious practical reasons for disguise and imposture in crime, and we find these tactics almost as popular with male as with female criminals, but they seem clearly to have a more profound significance in the portrayal of the latter.

Perhaps the popular appeal of a book like *The Counterfeit Lady Unveiled* lies partly in the fact that it allows for the satisfying recuperation of a social anomaly. Kirkman repeatedly compares Mary Carleton to an actress playing a part, a metaphor that becomes literal truth when she plays herself on stage, reenacting her own imposture. In much the same way, Moll Flanders' disguises ease the cognitive dissonance that may go along with imagining a woman committing a crime in that a disguise gives the image a cast of artificiality, and her cross-dressing is particularly effective in this, since it not only is more patently artificial but also obscures her problematic sex. Lincoln Faller has pointed out that such artificiality is a common feature of criminal biographies,[2] but in the case of women, the veneer of unreality often overlays their sexuality—something that we don't see

9. Ian Watt, *The Rise of the Novel* (Berkeley: U of California P, 1964), p. 113; John J. Richetti, "The Portrayal of Women in Restoration and Eighteenth-Century English Literature," in *What Manner of Woman: Essays on English and American Life and Literature*, ed. Marlene Springer (New York: New York UP, 1977), p. 88; and Frederick Karl, "Moll's Many-Colored Coat: Veil and Disguise in the Fiction of Defoe," *Studies in the Novel* 5 (1973): 94.
1. Marsha Bordner, "Defoe's Androgynous Vision in *Moll Flanders* and *Roxana*," *Gypsy Scholar* 2 (1974): 81.
2. Lincoln B. Faller, *Turned to Account: The Forms and Functions of Criminal Biography in Late Seventeenth- and Early Eighteenth-Century England* (Cambridge: Cambridge UP, 1987), p. 169.

happening to their male counterparts. Disguise and imposture are not the tricks of women alone, but cross-dressing does seem to be, and for good reason, I think. If the aggression that crime involves is seen as a masculine trait, it is not unexpected that a woman might adopt a male persona to steal, but for a man to disguise himself as a woman would create the very contradictions that a woman's cross-dressing serves to alleviate.

A third means of representing the paradox of a female criminal is to forego any attempt at recuperation and simply present her with all of her perceived incongruities intact, as did Mal Cutpurse's biographer. In fact, that aspect of her is emphasized. As "the Living Discription and Portraiture of a Schism and Separation" (p. A3), she is the most explicit evidence of the problem of satisfactorily placing female criminals. In the preface, her biographer asks that we "Excuse the Abruptnesse and Discontinuance of the Matter, and the severall independencies thereof; for that it was impossible to make one piece of so Various a Subject, as she was both to her self and others, being forced to take her as we found her though at disadvantage" (p. A6). Such disclaimers are standard fare in criminal biographies and bespeak the fact that, operating outside the social structure, such characters tend to resist categorization. The biographies of male criminals may depict their lives and personalities as motley and irregular also, but this is not tied directly and insistently to their sexuality as it is with women.

Mal Cutpurse's biographer can't seem to go to lengths extreme enough to express the profundity of her sexual contradictions. Her clothes—the man's doublet and the woman's petticoat—are said to be "the chief remarque of her life" (p. 18). Indeed, the sexual confusion to which they point is the book's primary leitmotif, and certain incidents seem to be chosen specifically for the purpose of deepening this confusion beyond its more comprehensible bipolar nature. For instance, on a bet she is induced to ride through the streets one day dressed entirely in men's clothing, but when mocked by onlookers, her response is to fantasize that she is a woman, first the "Squieresse to *Dulcinea* of *Tobosso*, the most incomparably beloved Lady of *Don Quixot*" (p. 77) and then the martyr Jane Shore. Thus, a gesture that could have served to make her less of an enigma by at least bringing her outward appearance more in line with her essentially masculine personality is instead made problematic by her sinking into an uncharacteristically feminine self-image involving romance, grace, and helplessness. Obviously the text is working against our recuperating Mal's character, and that is part of the author's explicit project. She fits into no category; there is "nothing appertaining to her, being to be matcht throughout the whole Course of History or Romance; so unlike her selfe, and of so difficult a mixture, that it is no wonder she was like no body, nor could not be *Sorted* by any *Comparison*, or *Suited* with any Antick *Companion*" (p. A3). She cannot even be comfortably classified as a social outsider since her criminality is ambiguous. The legality of her fencing stolen goods is uncertain, and, when arrested for her strange clothing, her proctor reassures her that her "Crime, if such, [is] not cognizable there or elsewhere" (p. 69). The social space she occupies is without a name. But for all his efforts at delineating Mal's contradictions and "unplaceability," the author betrays his discomfort with them. She may be amusing, but she finally *must* be given a position in the cosmic order. In an epitaph, he imagines her body at the last judgment:

> Dust, to perplex a *Sadducee*,
> Whither it rise a He or She
> Or two in one, a single pair,
> Natures sport and now her care;
> For how she'l cloath it at last day,
> (Unlesse she Sigh it all away)
> Or where she'l place it none can tell,
> Some middle place 'twixt *Heaven* and *Hell* (p. 175).

Not even her maker can figure out what she is or where she belongs—and is anxious about it, too.

A good deal of critical attention has been paid to the contradictions in Moll Flanders' personality, most of it centering around the question of whether these "ironies" are hers or Defoe's—or whether they were altogether unintentional, evidence of primitive or mishandled techniques of characterization. Probably the most often discussed of these contradictions is in her supposed repentance and her apparent lack of moral compunction. Most of her other contradictions, however, stem rather directly from the competing claims of her femininity and criminality. Her femininity urges her portrayal as a passive creature, but as a criminal she must be aggressive. She is both, sometimes simultaneously. Her femininity urges her portrayal as maternal and solicitous towards children, but as a criminal she must be self-serving and predatory. She is both. Not only does she steal from children, but when reunited with Humphrey, one of the sons she has abandoned (with no apparent difficulty) along the way to financial security, she falls weeping to her knees to kiss the ground on which he walks. Her femininity urges her portrayal as submissive in her relationships with men, but as a criminal she must be independent and, again, predatory. At various times, she is both. Is Defoe's narrative getting away from him here? Perhaps we can better understand the genesis of her ironies if we view *Moll Flanders* within the tradition of criminal biographies, a tradition in which disjunction is excused as a feature of the subject and not just the text. Moreover, if we narrow our focus to the tradition of female criminals in particular, we may begin to understand why her contradictions are tied to her sexuality.

Like Mal Cutpurse, although less dramatically, Moll Flanders is a figure whose sexuality heightens her "unplaceability." In a society which defines women by their relationships to men, Moll is hard to fix until the very end of her story. Born without a father, she cannot fall back on a relationship that normally gives a woman her identity when other means fail. She enjoys a brief legitimate marriage with the Younger Brother, but the series of marriages she makes after his death leave her in a shadowy borderland between marital categories. After her separation from the linen draper without legal divorce, Moll says, "My Condition was very odd, for . . . I was a Widow bewitch'd, I had a Husband, and no Husband" (p. 53). Her status is further compromised, as George A. Starr points out, when she "more than once [becomes] involved with men who have 'a wife and no wife,' so that the ambiguities of her own situation will be compounded by those of the people she moves among."[3] One of the men whom she can number among her "husband and no husband" relationships is her own brother, a marriage so problematic that it makes her other entanglements look simple by comparison.

She is gradually placing herself farther and farther outside the law and outside of accepted categories, and once that movement is made complete by her rejection of male authority and the onset of her life of thievery, her contradictions deepen. This process reaches its peak in the episode in which she cross-dresses; at that point she is an outsider even among outsiders. Not only are some of the thieves threatening to turn her in out of jealousy, but one woman who was arrested while acting as Moll's accomplice is being offered a pardon if she can produce Moll. This danger, says Moll, "took off all my tenderness" (p. 176), and so she is psychologically defeminized prior to her outward defeminization. Indeed, once dressed as a man, her impersonation is convincing enough to fool her partner, even though they "grew very intimate" (p. 169). Their relationship is given a sexual cast, set up as something of a marriage—"She [the Governess] joyn'd me with a Man . . . And as we kept always together, so we grew very intimate . . . and four or five times [I] lay with him all Night" (pp. 169–70)—but it is strictly sexless and sterile in actuality, underscoring the completeness of her transformation. But at a moment's notice, after about three weeks in drag, she is able to doff this disguise, don her women's attire, and fool a mob of pursuers. Her ability to straddle categories, her protean nature, allows her to escape detection in both legitimate and illegitimate society. Her

3. George A. Starr, "*Moll Flanders*," in *Twentieth Century Interpretations of "Moll Flanders,"* ed. Robert C. Elliott (Englewood Cliffs, NJ: Prentice-Hall, 1970), p. 89.

status at this point is perhaps best suggested in that she says her partner "never knew that I was not a Man" (p. 170), rather than saying he "never knew that I was a Woman." She defines herself negatively, not as belonging inside categories but outside them. And at this period when she is most thoroughly the outsider, Defoe uses her sexuality as the metaphor for her contradictions.

V

I have argued that Defoe's conception of Moll Flanders is shaped by the conventions of female criminal biography, suggesting that many of the patterns and problems in her characterization are common to that genre. And apparently those patterns and problems have sprung from a difficulty in recuperating a social anomaly, a creature that straddles categories. But what we might take to be evidence of a problem in characterization and an unsuccessful effort at resolving incongruities may actually result in a certain psychological realism if we keep in mind Richetti's image of Roxana as "a deserted psychosocial space." That is not to say that these writers aren't working to resolve incongruities in one way or another; the evidence indicates that they are. But as the record of a mind engaged in this enterprise, such a biography may bring us close to how that mind perceives its subject—or even how the subject may perceive herself. In this way, *Moll Flanders* may be an even more realistic portrait of a female criminal than we have recognized.

ANN LOUISE KIBBIE

[The Birth of Capital in Defoe's *Moll Flanders*]†

While fleeing England to avoid imprisonment for debt, Moll Flanders's second husband (and the last of her "husbands" with a legal right to that title) manages to convey to the Mint—a debtors' sanctuary in Southwark—the little property not yet seized by his creditors. Moll takes his parting advice to conceal herself there as well: "the first thing I did, was to go quite out of my Knowledge, and go by another Name: This I did effectually, for I went into the *Mint* too, took Lodgings in a very private Place, drest me up in the Habit of a Widow, and call'd myself Mrs. *Flanders*" (p. 53). Moll's disguise in

† From "Monstrous Generation: The Birth of Capital in Defoe's *Moll Flanders* and *Roxana*," *PMLA* 110 (1995): 1024–28. Reprinted by permission of the Modern Language Association of America Page numbers in parentheses refer to this Norton Critical Edition. Notes have been edited.

the Mint begins the series of metamorphoses that structures the rest of her narrative. As a term for a place where money is coined, *mint* suggests Moll's identification with currency, while as "any place of invention" (Johnson's *Dictionary*), "a source of invention or fabrication" (*OED*), it hints at the enterprise of fiction.

In the episode of Moll's life immediately following this minting of her character, she marries a man who will turn out to be her brother. Is this horrifying coincidence an ironic coda to Moll's efforts to recast herself, a warning about the dangers of believing that one can ever fully escape from earlier versions of oneself? If so, Moll's incest is curiously without negative consequences for her. Indeed, in the final section of the novel Defoe rehabilitates this potentially tragic accident, as Moll returns to Virginia for a loving and, of course, profitable reunion with Humphry, one of the offspring of the marriage.

Ellen Pollak places the episode of incest in opposition to the narrative of exchange provided by the rest of Defoe's novel: "In the context of this dominant thematic preoccupation [with exchange], Moll's incest acquires emblematic meaning as an extension of her desire to short-circuit or withdraw from 'normal' bourgeois relations in which women are circulated as objects among men."[1] For Pollak, Moll's incest potentially subverts two analogous systems of exchange: the exchange of women in patriarchy and the exchange of goods in a capitalist economy. Moll's violation of the taboo against incest, albeit unwittingly, represents "the ultimate threat to patriarchal authority—a refusal, to borrow Luce Irigaray's phrase, of the goods to go to the market" (16). However, this collapse of patriarchy and capitalism into a monolithic system is not justified by the economic debates of the sixteenth and seventeenth centuries, which cast capitalism as a threat to the traditional system of value and linked this threat to the uncontrollable figure of the woman. While I agree that Moll's incest is the crux of her narrative—"the ideological and structural fulcrum of the text" (Pollak 9)—the event must be understood within a protocapitalist discourse rather than as an exception or alternative to it.

"It is a maxim in commerce," Defoe writes in *The Complete English Tradesman*, "that money gets money" (263). The triteness of this dictum might obscure just how controversial an image it presents of money's increase. The pun on the central word "gets," signifying "obtaining" and "begetting," summons up a tradition of anticapitalist rhetoric. From the Middle Ages on, those who sought to prohibit usury saw in money's potential fecundity a threat not only

1. Ellen Pollak, "*Moll Flanders*, Incest, and the Structure of Exchange,' *The Eighteenth Century: Theory and Interpretation* 30 (1989): 7.

to moral laws but to natural laws as well. Taking as their authority a passage from Aristotle's *Politics*, the antiusury writers asserted that usury is a crime against nature because money is inherently sterile.

Phillipus Caesar's *A General Discourse against the Damnable Sect of Usurers* (translated into English from the Latin by Thomas Rogers in 1578) provides a summary of the form that the argument against the unnaturalness of monetary increase took at the height of the usury debates in England:

> Now consider how greate is the blindnesse, or rather the madnesse of men . . . that to a thyng fruitlesse, barren, without seede, without life, will ascribe generation: and contrary to nature and common sense, will make that to engender, whiche beeyng without life by no way can encrease (5).

Later Caesar warns, "A thing by nature barren is not to be used as if it were fruitful" (14). In a turn characteristic of antiusury literature, Caesar moves in these passages from describing money's barrenness to prescribing it in the face of the knowledge that money can and will increase. Throughout antiusury literature, the forceful assertion of the sterility of money coexists with a contradictory but equally powerful sense of money's infinite capacity for self-generation.

Anxieties about capital generation inevitably lead the antiusury writers to the figure of the woman, first as a normative model of natural increase. Thomas Wilson's *Discourse upon Usury* (1572) exemplifies this position:

> [W]hat is more against nature, than that money should beget or bring forth money, which was ordeined to be a pledge betwixt man and man, in contracts and bargayning, . . . and not to increase it selfe, as a woman dothe, that bringethe foorthe a childe . . . [S]uch money which bringeth forth money is a swelling monster, waxing everye moneth bigger one than another. (286–87)

Woman represents production limited by biology, capital a monstrous increase freed of natural limits. "Living creatures, when they see the fruit of their fruit, as a mother the daughter of her daughter, commonly cease bearing," writes Richard Turnbull in *An Exposition upon the XV Psalm* (1591), "but the Usurer, seeth the monie of his monies monie, to many generations, yet never leaveth. What monster in nature then may be compared unto the usurer?" (44).

While the figure of the woman represents a natural, self-limiting, "moral" economy at some moments, at others it symbolizes the destructive energies of capitalism. Thus, usury is said to spring from covetousness, "as daughter and heire to so fylthy a mother." Usury is "the daughter of covetousness, the mother of mischiefe, and the very hel of evil" (Wilson 222, 366). "Covetousness, desire of money, [and] unsatiable greediness" are called "the nurses and breeders of usury."[2] One writer even describes the purpose of his work as "anatomizing the engendring wombe" of the usurer.[3] In a particularly suggestive passage, Wilson compares the would-be capitalist to a whore in answering the argument that men have the right to use their property as they see fit: "Neyther oughte men to make the most of theire owne that they can . . . for soe, the evill woman maye saye, that, because her body is her own, shee may doe with it what shee list, and company with whome she pleaseth for her best profit and avayle" (268). The criticism of capital turns to a criticism of female nature, as a powerful representation of the insatiability that both creates and feeds on capital. "Merciful God," cries Wilson, alluding to charges that women are acting as usurers, "who would have thought that the devill could have had such power in a woman?" Immediately he answers, "Nay, who would not have thought it, considering their myserable and gredie desires to get" (297).

Although the antiusury writers enlist the figure of the woman to exemplify a natural economy of reproduction that is the antithesis of the perverse generation of capital, the introduction of the feminine into the discourse of capitalism creates a subversive alliance between the two. J.G.A. Pocock's analysis of the feminization of the capitalist after the financial revolution of the 1690s is relevant to an earlier stage of capitalism as well. When the "stability" of the present becomes "linked to the self-perpetuation of the speculation concerning a future," Pocock writes, virtue would seem "to have been placed at the mercy of passion, fantasy and appetite, and these forces were known to feed on themselves and to be without moral limit."[4] The notion of a speculative, insatiable, even self-consuming personality is, he explains, linked to femininity; economic man in the eighteenth century is "a feminised, even an effeminate being, still wrestling with his own passions and hysterias and with interior and exterior forces let loose by his fantasies and appetites" (114). While a number of critics have related this feminization to "the problem of commodification, the association of the female figure with accumulation, consumption, and the products of trade,"[5] in my reading of *Moll Flanders* * * * I interpret the figure of the woman as the embodiment of a "purer," or more purely imaginative, version of cap-

2. John Jewel, *The Works of John Jewel* (Cambridge: Cambridge UP, 1845–50), II, p. 852.
3. John Benbrigge, *Epistle. Usura Accomodata; or, A Ready Way to Rectifie Usury* (London, 1646), n.p.
4. J.G.A. Pocock *Virtue, Commerce, and History: Essays on Political Thought and History, Chiefly in the Eighteenth Century* (Cambridge: Cambridge UP, 1985), p. 112.
5. Laura Brown, *Ends of Empire: Women and Ideology in Early Eighteenth-Century English Literature* (Ithaca: Cornell UP, 1993), p. 14.

italism: the seemingly magical ability of money to increase itself from itself that begins with the eroticization of the coin.

When Moll Flanders's first lover, the elder son of her employers, gives her presents of gold, he initiates an association between money and sexual desire that continues throughout her narrative. Moll is seduced not so much by the man as by the coins he gives her. "I was more confounded," she confesses as she recounts the progress of his advances, "with the Money than I was before with the Love" (p. 22), and it is the money that receives pride of place in Moll's account of her eventual capitulation to his desires. When her lover presents her with a "silk Purse, with an Hundred Guineas in it" as "an Earnest" of his good intentions, "[m]y Colour came, and went, at the Sight of the Purse, and with the fire of his Proposal together; . . . so putting the Purse into my Bosom, I made no more Resistance to him" (p. 26).

If Moll seems to engage in a fairly straightforward act of exchange in this first affair, the quid pro quo is not so baldly asserted in a later episode, between Moll and the gentleman who befriends her in a lodging house in Bath. One morning, as the gentleman lies in bed, he calls for Moll and asks her "to let him see [her] Purse." Moll's response is flirtatious: "I immediately put my Hand into my Pocket, and Laughing at him, pull'd [the purse] out" (p. 90). After she has shown him the contents of her purse, he asks her to get the rest of her money from her room. "I went into my Chamber," Moll recounts,

> and fetch'd him a little private Drawer, where I had about six Guineas more, and some Silver, and threw it all down upon the Bed, and told him there was all my Wealth. . . . He look'd a little at it, but did not tell it, and Huddled it all into the Drawer again, and then reaching into his Pocket, pull'd out a Key, and bad me open a little Walnuttree box . . . in which Drawer, there was a great deal of Money in gold. . . . He took the Drawer, and taking my Hand, made me put it in and take a whole handful; I was backward at that, but he held my Hand hard in his Hand, and put it into the Drawer (p. 90).

As critics have noted, Moll's coyness, the gentleman's forcefulness, and the imagery of purses, private drawers, and keys create a scene of seduction that reaches its culmination in the mingling of money. Moll reports that when she has taken her handful of gold, the gentleman "made me up [his coins] into my Lap, and took my little Drawer, and pour'd out all my own Money among his" (p. 90). Later, when Defoe describes Moll's first act of sexual commerce with this man, the flatness of language indicates that this earlier scene rendered sex redundant, an anticlimax: "there was no resisting him; neither indeed had I any mind to resist him any more, let what would come of it" (p. 93).

These two episodes, central to readings of *Moll Flanders* that emphasize the heroine's (or the author's) confusion of love and money, are used as proof of Moll's growing cynicism about love and of her increasingly mercenary or predatory nature. In my reading, the two scenes achieve significance only in relation to a third, in which Moll visits a gambling house and places a strange man's bets for him at the gaming table. The essentially autoerotic desire enacted by Moll in her transactions with her lovers—the desire of money for itself—becomes most explicit in this third episode. "I Understood the Game well enough," Moll confides; "it was to keep a good Stock in my Lap, out of which I every now and then convey'd some into my Pocket." At the end of the game, she offers the gentleman all the money in her lap, "but he would not take it till I had put my Hand into it, and taken some for myself, and bid me please myself" (pp. 205–6). The description of the coins in Moll's lap and of the gentleman's forcing her to put her hand into the money and take some echoes the scene in Bath, and the association lends Moll's pilfering in the gambling house a similarly erotic quality. Unbeknownst to the gambler, she has been pleasing herself. The erotics of the gaming table is the erotics of capital.

With the increasing irrelevance of her partner in exchange, Moll moves closer to embodying capital. The picture that the gambling scene provides of the self-generation of money (as money multiplies itself suggestively in the heroine's lap) hints at the merging of monetary and biological generation that is both the power and the threat of capitalism for Moll. * * * That money's self-generation could seductively turn into self-consumption is implied by Moll's governess, who warns her against the "Itch of Play," which might consume not only Moll's winnings but also, the heroine says, "all the rest of what I had got" (p. 206).

Despite issuing this warning, the governess herself points toward the collapse of sexual and monetary generation. When Moll first meets her, the governess is a midwife, referred to only as Mother Midnight, whose business depends for its profit entirely on "the private Account, or in plain English, the whoring Account" (p. 134). Mother Midnight makes the generation of children the generation of money. * * * Her reappearance later in the book as a fence for stolen goods ties together Moll's careers as whore and as thief. Moll's description of her feelings after her first theft strengthens the connection: "my Blood was all in a Fire" (p. 152). Although meant to express Moll's terror, this phrase echoes the words she uses to describe her first seduction: "His words I must confess fir'd my Blood" (p. 21). Sexual generation and theft are also joined in Moll's apprenticeship to a pickpocket and shoplifter, arranged by Mother Midnight. "I attended her some time in the Practise," Moll says of her training, "just as a Deputy attends a Midwife without any Pay." The connection is further established in Moll's characterization of her first "Prize": "a young Lady big with Child who had a charming Watch" (p. 159). The significance of the link between monetary and biological generation will become explicit in Moll's reunion with her son Humphry in Virginia.

The greatest material misfortune of Moll's transportation to the colonies with her final "husband," Jemy, is that their stock is "all in Money, which every one knows is an unprofitable Cargoe to be carryed to the Plantations"; "Money in that Country," she explains, "is not of much use where all things are bought for Tobacco" (pp. 244, 242). This emphasis on the uselessness of money in the New World seems to be contradicted during Moll's first visit to Humphry. On the morning after she discovered herself to him, Humphry brings Moll a gift: a "Deer skin Bag . . . with five and fifty Spanish Pistoles in it" (p. 262). In exchange for this purse and as a token of her affection, Moll gives her son a gold watch: "I told him, I had nothing of any Value to bestow but that"—this statement is a lie, like most of Moll's declarations during moments of apparent disarming candor—"and desir'd he would now and then kiss it for my sake" (p. 263). When she returns to Jemy, Moll explains that she no longer has her watch, and she waits for him to express his disappointment. Then, "pulling out the Deer skin Purse," she announces gleefully, "here my Dear . . . is the gold Watch" (p. 264). With the help of her son, Moll has transformed the watch into money.

By offering the coin-filled bag, Humphry comically proves that he is, indeed, his mother's son. This last episode in the series that includes Moll's seduction by the elder son, her flirtatious mingling of money with the Bath gentleman, and her success at the gaming table also signals the final stage in the heroine's progress toward the closed circuit of capital generation, for which incest is an apt figure.

Although the antiusury writers claim to derive from Aristotle their contention that money is sterile, the argument against usury in the *Politics* revolves not around the natural sterility of money but rather around its threatening capacity to reproduce itself from itself. The Greek term for usury (*tokos*) is also the word for offspring. Aristotle explains that in an economic context *tokos* "means the birth of money from money" and that it "is applied to the breeding of money because the offspring resembles the parent. Wherefore of all modes of making money this is the most unnatural" (1258b.1–8). The model that Aristotle presents for money's generation is a natural model of increase. But since he compares money's likeness to itself to the natural likeness between child and parent, why should usury be the most unnatural form of increase? One way of describing the unnaturalness of money's self-generation is to say that the increase is incestuous, the reproduction of kind from kind—a connection implied by Miles Mosse, in *The Arraignment and Conviction of Usurie*(1595):

> I see no reason why the lawes concerning usurie should not be reputed and taken for morall, as well as those which concerne Incest, of which no divine (to my knowledge) ever doubted, but that they ought to abide perpetuall and inviolable, as preceptes of the morall law. (118)

While Mosse does not make explicit any essential similarity between usury and incest, Thomas Dekker's *Worke for Armorours* (1609) identifies them metaphorically: "Usurie was the first that ever taught Money to commit incest" (132–33).

It is true not simply that Moll Flanders "literally 'capitalizes' the incest taboo,"[6] turning the episode with Humphry to account, but also that Moll's incest becomes the model for capitalist increase. The happy ending of the novel redeems the incest. The woman whose life was shattered by the discovery that she was an "unnatural mother" reclaims her son and her peace. But since incest has been a trope for another nightmare of generation—the unnatural increase of capital—the romance ending of Moll's story redeems capital as well. In Moll's reunion with Humphry, biological generation and the generation of wealth become the same in a fantasy of the naturalization of capital.

JOHN RICHETTI

[Freedom and Necessity, Improvisation and Fate in *Moll Flanders*]†

Moll Flanders (1722) is more unified in its rendering of an implicit social coherence [than *Colonel Jack*]. Like Jack, she derives her identity from an avoidance of the inevitability of her circumstances. Looking back and evoking her distinctive subjectivity, Moll renders her introspective self-consciousness as a means of separation from actuality. From her early days at Colchester, Moll resembles Jack in her self-defining apartness, but she is more quickly absorbed as an upper servant and mistress and then as a wife into the middle-class family that adopts her. Moll acquires a greater ease than Jack and learns rather quickly the tricks of self-preservation and plausible self-

6. Michael Seidel, *Exile and the Narrative Imagination* (New Haven: Yale UP, 1986), p. 28.

† From *The English Novel in History 1700–1780* (London and New York: Routledge, 1999), pp. 59–64. Reprinted by permission of Taylor & Francis Books, Ltd., and the author. Page numbers in parentheses refer to this Norton Critical Edition. Notes have been edited.

invention, defining herself as someone who learns quickly to analyze social possibility in generalized terms and to situate herself accordingly. Moll surveys the sexual field after her second husband leaves her: "They, I observe insult us mightily, with telling us of the Number of Women; that the Wars and the Sea, and Trade, and other Incidents have carried the Men so much away, that there is no Proportion between the Numbers of the Sexes; and therefore the Women have the Disadvantage; but I am far from Granting that the Number of the Women is so great, or the Number of the Men so small" (p. 61).[1] The problem, says Moll, lies rather in the limited number of men "fit for a Woman to venture upon." Moll thus begins her career with a cynical sense of the fluidity or indeed the irrelevance of society's categories.

As a female con artist and pickpocket-shoplifter, Moll's *modus operandi* is social impersonation. However, Moll makes crucial errors of social judgment: not only does her (second) tradesman husband prove feckless, but the Irish gentleman she marries later turns out to be a fortune-hunter and the Virginia planter she marries is none other than her brother. Of course, this last is hardly an error of judgment; Moll seems trapped by an inscrutable, unavoidable pattern of enclosing coincidence. Right next to her exuberant chronicle of self-improvisation within the unpredictable, linear sequentiality of her life is a circular pattern of fatality and necessity, exemplified by her inadvertent return to her biological family in Virginia, just when she thought she was getting as far away as possible from her origins. So, too, her career as the most successful thief of her day (the "greatest Artist of my time" [p. 168]) leads inevitably back to her Newgate origins. Yet Moll hardly prepares us for that development. In narrating the relationships that make up her varied life, she ruthlessly renders them in economic terms and shows how she managed them by shrewd sexual liaisons and opportunistic crime. The book has its stabilizing center in just that economic analysis, which reduces and particularizes, tracking (in a proto-cinematic sense) from crowded social possibility and generality to focus on individual motives and solutions within that larger and constantly shifting scene. The force of the individualized narrative perspective is such that the camera looks outward from itself, as it were, at an external scene that appears increasingly fragmentary and foreign next to the emerging wholeness and familiarity of the protagonist.

Moll locates herself within a system of causes, variously social, economic, psychological, and even providential, that point to some-

1. G. A. Starr notes that in *The Great Law of Subordination Consider'd* (1724) Defoe makes the point about the depletion of males that Moll questions here, but that in *Applebee's Journal* for April 10, 1725, he suggests that those numbers are matched by the emigration of women to the plantations in America.

thing like a controlling totality. But the parts do not quite add up to that whole, since these moments of destiny are at one and the same time opportunities for escape and expansion in which experience promotes a more liberating mode whereby necessity becomes redefined as imperfectly confining and serves to release hitherto unexplored resources in the self. Yet Defoe dramatizes a coherence larger than the sum of Moll's individual transactions, and that underlying unity is present in part through the pattern of coincidences that appears as the narrative unfolds. So there is in the narrative a final turn to the screw that evokes something like a social totality. *Moll Flanders* rehearses the contradiction that the free, intensely unique individual is somehow the result of an exactly rendered and accumulating necessity, a social totality partly obscured by the energy and inconsistency of Moll's autobiographical retrospection. Consider Moll's seduction by the elder brother in the family at Colchester. Innocent and inexperienced, she is surprised by the desires he arouses in her but even more flustered by the discovery of the eroticized force of more money than she has ever seen. Young Moll, interloper in the upper middle-class house in Colchester, speaks instinctively in these scenes with her body as the elder brother fires her blood with ardent kisses and declarations: "my heart spoke as plain as a voice, that I liked it; nay, whenever he said, I am in Love with you, my Blushes plainly reply'd, 'would you were, Sir' " (p. 21). After her lover tumbles her on the bed, he gives her five guineas: "I was more confounded with the money than I was before with the love, and began to be so elevated that I scarce knew the ground I stood on" (p. 22). Moll can only look back and wonder at her own inability then to "think," for she "thought of nothing, but the fine Words, and the Gold" (p. 23). The elder brother's person *and* his gold ("I spent whole hours in looking upon it; I told the Guineas over and over a thousand times a Day" [p. 24]) intertwine sexual and social necessity, so that in Moll's rendering sexual and social movement are reciprocally engulfing, one cooperating with the other. Moll, of course, rushes by these implications, translating this unifying cooperation of socioeconomic and sexual desire into a missed and misunderstood opportunity. But she understands as she looks back that she and her seducer were both in their own way unaware of the other's true position, unable to read accurately the motives that Moll retrospectively sees as given so obviously by a supervising network of socioeconomic relationships: "Nothing was ever so stupid on both Sides, had I acted as became me, and resisted as Vertue and Honour requir'd, this Gentleman had either Desisted his Attacks, finding no room to expect the Accomplishment of his Design, or had made fair, and honourable Proposals of Marriage; in which Case, whoever had blam'd him, no Body could have blam'd me" (pp. 23–24).

Such moments are usually admired for their psychological acuity; the heroine speaks of her innocent youth in just the way we would expect from a cynical old veteran of the sexual wars. One can also say that such moments extend the psychological by giving it a social context and by endowing old Moll with a retrospective wisdom that encompasses social as well as personal knowledge. Moll recounts both her immersion in complex circumstances and her acquired sense of how to manage a tactical apartness from them. In her formal capacity as narrator, Moll is forced to balance her character's instinctive tactical awareness against an inescapable fate that she knows looms constantly and is only delayed rather than avoided by such maneuvers. Indeed, by their variety and inventiveness these moves point to a supervising totality, a fate merely postponed. Retrospective narration like hers produces a knowledge of experience by treating it as both freely chosen or at least freely adaptive behavior and fatefully circumscribed and fully determined.

Such contradiction is richly enacted in the climax of the narrative in Newgate. In her rendering, the prison is exactly what she has hitherto evaded: the massive, inexorable force of psychosocial determinants. Newgate implicitly resolves the paradox of Moll's free but fated movement, forcing her to change her conception of her career from clever improvisation to inevitable fate: "It seem'd to me that I was hurried on by an inevitable and unseen Fate to this Day of Misery . . . that I was come to the last hour of my life and of my wickedness together. These things pour'd themselves in upon my Thoughts, in a confus'd manner, and left me overwhelm'd with Melancholy and Despair" (p. 215). Moll's recourse to intensely figurative language is unique here. For once, the scene controls her discourse and resists the mapping of contours that has been her signature, as in the rendering of the London streets, for example, in her days as a thief. Defoe's peculiar strength as a narrator fits Moll's personality: he renders the relationships of persons and objects rather than their integrity and depth as individual substances. For Defoe the political analyst, personal identity is equivalent to position and relationship. But all this changes, at least temporarily, in Newgate, where shifting surfaces yield to stasis and the experience of depth. Moll renders the prison in graphic terms: "the hellish Noise, the Roaring, Swearing and Clamour, the Stench and Nastiness, and all the dreadful croud of Afflicting things that I saw there" (p. 215). Newgate's effects on Moll provoke the novel's single most metaphorical passage:

> Like the Waters in the Caveties, and Hollows of Mountains, which petrifies and turns into Stone whatever they are suffer'd to drop upon; so the continual Conversing with such a crew of Hell-Hounds as I was with had the same common Operation

> upon me, as upon other People, I degenerated into Stone; I turn'd first Stupid and Senseless, then Brutish and thoughtless, and at last raving Mad as any of them were; and in short, I became as naturally pleas'd and easie with the Place, as if indeed I had been Born there (p. 218).

At least for the moment, Moll is completely absorbed by environment, the hitherto self-defining distance between herself and her social relationships canceled by a natural (that is, a social) force. If we think back to Moll's sexual initiation by the elder brother at Colchester, there is an inevitability in this equation of the force of a social institution like Newgate and the transforming power of nature. In the earlier scene, socioeconomic determinants (summed up in the thrilling guineas) are absorbed by the natural, compulsive inevitability of sexual desire. Invoking the natural as an ultimate explanatory frame of reference is an ideological strategy for neutralizing the threatening, alienated objectivity of social institutions by shifting their origins to a universalized interiority. But Newgate can hardly be rendered as just an intense interior experience. Moll insists that she is literally transformed by the place. She becomes just like her brutish fellow prisoners, "a meer *Newgate-Bird*, as Wicked and as Outragious as any of them," but she also becomes someone else, "no more the same thing that I had been, than if I had never been otherwise than what I was now" (p. 219). Newgate as a concrete instance of social totality effectively replaces Moll, and that obliteration leads in due course to a newly distinct self, defined now by *opposition* rather than marginalized or subversive participation.

Paradoxically, Moll becomes pure object here but also at last an even more powerful and coherently self-conscious subject. Up to now, we may say, what Moll's narrative patches together is a fitful local necessity, the intermittent difficulties of survival and the varied obstacles to prosperity. Both as locale and as narrative climax, Newgate offers a pre-existent and self-sufficient system that functions independently and to whose laws she must inevitably conform. But she evades the prison's monumental necessity by slowly turning it into a means of narrative coherence, transforming it from the embodiment of social inevitability for born thieves like her to a locale where her personality acquires a desperate coherence and sharp self-definition in opposition to the now visible determining force of state regulation. In place of the scattered, improvised resistance to a diffuse and inefficient social necessity, Newgate forces her by its totalizing transformation to muster a countervailing transformation.

Moll begins to recover when she sees her Lancashire husband, now a famous highwayman captured at last. As she observes him enter the prison, her sense of her ultimate responsibility for his fate restores her abhorrence of Newgate and something like her old identity. She is restored within an appropriated version of totality, as she constructs a coherence modeled on the fateful ordering that Newgate enforces. She sees Jemy and suddenly perceives a coherent network of guilt and responsibility in her past. Within the totalizing precincts of Newgate, where scattered self-inventiveness has been forced to give way to external social determination, Moll is moved to discover a new and coherent approach to self-understanding. Newgate's confinement brings the experience of the inescapable connection between social circumstances and personality and points implicitly as the resolution of Moll's career to a larger and indeed comprehensive social inevitability.

Moll's repentance, the "freedom of discourse" to which the minister leads her, enables her for the first time in her life to tell her story, indeed to have a coherent story to tell. "In a word, I gave him an abridgement of this whole History; I gave him the Picture of my Conduct for 50 Years in Miniature" (p. 226). Having experienced Newgate, having in fact become indistinguishable from it, Moll can now experience a subjectivity conscious of its relationship to the necessity that Newgate embodies. She is, as she herself says, restored to thinking: "My Temper was touch'd before, the harden'd, wretch'd boldness of Spirit which I had acquir'd in the Prison abated, and conscious Guilt began to flow in upon my Mind. In short, I began to think, and to think is one real advance from Hell to Heaven. All that Hellish, harden'd state and temper of soul . . . is but a deprivation of Thought; he that is restored to his Power of thinking, is restored to himself" (p. 221).

But what possible restoration does Moll have in mind? Moll's redeemed state is, in effect, a new identity, defined and crystallized within Newgate's complex of determining relationships. Moll constructs a moralized individuality that is dialectically related to the impersonality that she has so profoundly experienced. In response to Newgate's alienated objectivity and impersonal subordination of individuals to the pattern of judicial retribution, Moll discovers in her past a personal connection with other subjects like Jemy and replaces secular conviction and impersonal punishment with personal guilt and responsibility as she shifts the defining acts of her narrative from the violation of external statutes to private offenses against God and particular men. In the Newgate episode of *Moll Flanders*, Defoe coherently dramatizes as nowhere else in his fiction, I think, a sense of a determining social totality and something of a solution to the problem that it poses for self-understanding. Moll's new mode of self-apprehension accomplishes what is logically impossible but historically both necessary and inevitable in the emergence of the novel; it constructs a free subject wholly implicated in a determining objectivity but deriving its freedom from an intense apprehension of that surrounding objective world. Next to the improbably resilient Moll who enters the prison, this character has a self-conscious psychological density and coherence that are produced or at least provoked by the experience of social totality. This sequence in *Moll Flanders* thus predicts the main direction that the novel will take in the nineteenth century. As society is increasingly experienced as mysteriously all-encompassing in its determinations, novelistic representation will seek to imagine a compensating richness of subjectivity whereby individuals can extract a version of freedom precisely from the novel's rendering of a nearly suffocating social and historical necessity. Inevitably, such freedom will take place in various sorts of richly imagined guilty subjectivities (like Moll's) that operate as antidotes to a world that seems to lack such meaning.

* * *

ELLEN POLLAK

Moll Flanders, Incest, and the Structure of Exchange†

> Any gift or debt alienates the individual into the circuit of exchanges, compromises one's integrity and autonomy. But assertion of one's uncontaminated selfhood is no practical way out of the circuit.
>
> Jane Gallop, *The Daughter's Seduction*

> The need to think the limit of culture as a problem of the enunciation of cultural difference is disavowed.
>
> Homi K. Bhabha, *The Location of Culture*

In many ways, Defoe's Moll Flanders moves impressively and resiliently outside the constraints of familial, and especially maternal, obligation.[1] Her story, however, reminds us that there are dangers

† From *Incest and the English Novel, 1684–1814* (Baltimore and London: Johns Hopkins UP, 2003), Chapter 5, pp. 110–28 (notes pp. 221–25). Reprinted with permission of The Johns Hopkins University Press. An earlier, slightly shorter version of this chapter appeared in *The Eighteenth Century: Theory and Interpretation* 30 (1989): 3–21; that original material is reprinted by permission of Texas Tech University Press. Page numbers in parentheses refer to this Norton Critical Edition. Notes have been edited.

1. On this aspect of Moll's character, see John J. Richetti, "The Family, Sex, and Marriage in Defoe's *Moll Flanders* and *Roxana*," *Studies in the Literary Imagination* 15 (1982): 19–35; and *Defoe's Narratives: Situations and Structures* (Oxford: Clarendon P, 1975), Ch. 4; James H. Maddox, "On Defoe's *Roxana*," *ELH* 51 (1984): 669–91; Miriam Lerenbaum, "Moll Flanders: 'A Woman on her own Account' " in *The Authority of Experience: Essays*

attendant upon being or believing oneself outside the family. Like the story of Sophocles' Oedipus, another memorable literary figure whom circumstance early removes from the place and knowledge of familial origins, it demonstrates that families are biologically determining and that incest is a possibility always present in not knowing where one belongs. For Moll, who discovers midway through her quest for economic independence that she has unwittingly become the wife of her own brother, the coincidental return of family follows a dual and paradoxical narrative logic: it at once emblematizes an endogamous dissolution of family structure and testifies to kinship's persistent force.

Both *Oedipus the King* and *Moll Flanders* presuppose the existence of certain social necessities or rules governing the distribution of intrafamilial power. As René Girard observes, Oedipus violates a system of family distinctions that limit the son's access to his father's wife.[2] What the rules of familial differentiation are in Moll's case—and how far Defoe's text goes in endorsing them as a cultural, or even a natural, necessity is, to a large extent, the subject of this essay. Suffice it to say here that for Moll the problem of incest is inextricably intertwined with the problem of sexual difference, as it is figured by Defoe, both inside and outside the family.

There is, to be sure, a salient code of sexual differentiation at work in Sophocles' play as well, since—as Girard notes—Jocasta, "the father's wife and son's mother," is casually assumed to be "an object solemnly consecrated as belonging to the father and formally forbidden the son" (74). But a son may incestuously challenge paternal authority without bringing into question (or even into consciousness) the fact that that authority involves the social domination of a woman. In Defoe's text, in which the mythical subject of incest—and thus the transgressor against those systems of difference that organize social relations—is a woman, such relative indifference to the category of gender is difficult, if not impossible, to sustain. Here, a system of social relations that posits the female as a passive form of masculine property at least *appears* to be exposed or put in doubt.

Moll's marriage to her brother violates not one but two interlocking codes of difference: it violates the rules that prohibit sexual union between the offspring of a common parent; and, by virtue of the fact that it is transacted at the point in Moll's career when she attempts to take the reins of sexual power into her own hands, it also violates those rules that constitute her socially as a woman. Moll, nonethe-

in Feminist Criticism, ed. Arlyn Diamond and Lee R. Edwards (Amherst: U of Massachusetts P, 1977), pp. 101–17; and Michael Shinagel, "The Maternal Theme in *Moll Flanders*: Craft and Character," *Cornell Library Journal* 7 (1969): 3–23.

2. René Girard, *Violence and the Sacred*, trans. Patrick Gregory (Baltimore: Johns Hopkins UP, 1977), p. 74.

less, seems to thrive as a result of this dual transgression. Though initially she is horrified by the discovery of her familial circumstance, by the end of her narrative she has managed to turn her disaster into a source of economic gain. The psychic costs of her brush with incest, furthermore, prove minimal. As several critics have noted, while for Roxana the reemergence of family means the utter dissolution of the self, for Moll it means the dissolution of family. Moll's brother-husband gradually succumbs to both physical and mental disintegration, but Moll both physically and mentally distances herself from demoralizing family ties. Recouping the financial losses that she sustains on an unlucky voyage back to Europe, she will at last return to America to capitalize on her maternal inheritance. That she also thereby acquires the filial offices of a loyal and forgiving son with a good head for business and plantation management simply amplifies the material benefits she is able to reap as a result of her incestuous history.[3]

But if, as Michael Seidel aptly observes, Moll Flanders " 'capitalizes' the incest taboo," her repugnance at the discovery of her consanguineous relation to her husband leaves certain lingering questions unresolved.[4] The specific terms of Seidel's remark require pause: what Moll turns to profit is not the crime of incest itself, but its prohibition. Why? As intent as Moll is on material gain in every other circumstance in her life, why is it that Defoe chooses to portray her as so irresistibly moved to repudiate her incestuous liaison?[5] She might much more profitably capitalize on the incest by staying put. Although Moll proves magisterially duplicitous in many another circumstance and has already manipulated her third husband into marriage under fraudulent pretenses, Defoe denies her recourse to bold deception in this case.

It is clear that Moll considers remaining married to Humphrey technically criminal once she has knowledge of their consanguinity: "O had the Story never been told me," she writes, "all had been well; it had been no Crime to have lain with my Husband, since as to his being my Relation, I had known nothing of it" (p. 72). But it is equally clear that, for Defoe, Moll's remaining in her marriage under false appearances is a perfectly imaginable possibility. Although Moll acknowledges that she has been living in "open avowed Incest and Whoredom," she declares that she "was not much touched with the

3. For a comparison of Moll Flanders and Roxana with respect to the question of kinship, see Richetti, "Family, Sex, and Marriage." Maddox develops a parallel argument about the differences between the two heroines, with a particularly interesting analysis of Moll's brother-husband's function as a scapegoat onto whom Moll's negative feelings about her incest are displaced ("On Defoe's *Roxana*," pp. 686–88).
4. Michael Seidel, *Exile and the Narrative Imagination* (New Haven: Yale UP, 1986), p. 28.
5. Even child-murder gets justified in the interest of the survival of the (female) self. On Moll's indirect involvement in child-murder, see Maddox, "On Defoe's *Roxana*," pp. 683–86.

Crime of it" (p. 73). In fact, at first she seems to place her own self-interest as fully as ever in front of any other consideration. She continues "under the appearance of an honest Wife" for more than three years, during which time, she tells us, she was capable of giving "the most sedate Consideration" (p. 73) to the losses she might incur upon sharing her knowledge with another living soul. It is, moreover, only when the risks of secrecy begin to outweigh its benefits—when Moll's "riveted Aversion" (p. 80) to Humphrey so strains relations with him that he threatens to commit her to a madhouse—that Moll decides to reveal her true identity to her mother. Moll, it appears, has come by her knack for lying honestly. Her mother advises continued secrecy on precisely the grounds that have moved the daughter to take her into confidence: Humphrey might respond irrationally and, among other possibilities, take advantage of the law to justify himself in putting Moll away.

Ultimately, however, Moll is driven to abandon strategy. She resolves to tell her story to her husband. The decision is not made on moral grounds, for—as Moll tells us—she "had no great concern about [the incest] in point of Conscience" (p. 80). Nor, since she has already trusted her mother with the truth, can her disclosure be accounted for as the effect of the intolerable pressure of unconfided secrecy.[6] Moll tells Humphrey, rather, because she is compelled to do so by an overpowering and implacable inner necessity to avoid cohabitation with her brother. She "could not bear the thoughts of coming between the Sheets with him," she writes, regardless of whether she "was right in point of Policy" (p. 80).[7] Policy, or reserve, is Moll's characteristic mode of survival throughout her career; but while she will later allow Mother Midnight to assist her in concealing both a pregnancy and a child, the incest is a fact of life that she will not even conspire with her own mother to cover up.

Read literally, this narrative sequence unfolds according to a logic of progression. At the time of her incest, Moll has not yet reached that pitch of hardness and reserve that would enable her to carry off as formidable or sustained a feat of secrecy as concealment of her incest would require. Having undertaken to "Deceive the Deceiver"—man—in the courtship of her third husband (p. 63), she now finds

6. Moll refers to the oppressive weight of secrets on pages 72 and 254; and in a note on page 396 of his edition of the novel (London: Oxford UP, 1971), G. A. Starr points to several other instances in which Defoe discusses the irresistible force of conscience.

7. See W. Daniel Wilson's argument that Moll's response to her incest operates not "on the level of morality, but of impulse and gut feeling" in "Science, Natural Law, and Unwitting Sibling Incest in Eighteenth-Century Literature" in *Studies in Eighteenth-Century Culture* 13 (1984): 257. For earlier comments on the incest in Defoe's text, and other interpretations, see Maximillian E. Novak, *Defoe and the Nature of Man* (London: Oxford UP, 1963), pp. 108–110 and "Conscious Irony in *Moll Flanders*: Facts and Problems," *College English* 26 (1964): 201; G. A. Starr, *Defoe and Casuistry* (Princeton: Princeton UP, 1971), pp. 134–35; and J. Paul Hunter, ed., *Moll Flanders* (New York: Thomas Y. Crowell Co., 1970), p. 74n.

not only that she has been deceived herself but also that she is more unconditionally subject to the imperatives of self-disclosure than at any other time in her career. Only later, when Moll more fully understands prevailing sexual practices and codes, will she be able to work oppressive systems to her own ends. As John Richetti notes, Moll's "fully developed reserve . . . resists even her extravagant desire for Jemy," from whom she withholds her true identity to the very end.[8]

The sheer extraordinariness of what is rendered as the mere coincidence of Moll's incest, however, also encourages an emblematic reading that reveals another narrative logic at work as well. On this reading, Moll's response to her incest functions not simply as a narrative prelude or a logical antithesis to her eventual mastery of reserve as a hardened criminal (or, for that matter, as a dubious penitent) but also as the positive ideological ground on which her triumph as a cheat erects itself. Moll's self-disclosure, that is, is not simply chronologically but also logically prior to her self-concealment. For as I shall argue, in figuring incest as at once the most basic of all prohibitions and the one limit that Moll refuses to cross over willingly, the Virginia episode has the effect of both organizing and ultimately neutralizing the subversive force of Moll's subsequent transgressions against institutional authority. It is surely important to recognize the instrumentality of the incest in advancing Moll to the point where she is able at last to effect what Richetti has called "a synthesis of sexuality and profit" in her relationship with her Lancashire husband, Jemy; but it is also essential to remain clear about the limiting ideological conditions of that imaginative synthesis. Ultimately, it is only within the terms established by Moll's rejection of incest that her life of crime becomes (in both the material and spiritual sense) "redeemable." What is rewarded at the end of *Moll Flanders* is not simply a subversive female criminality but a criminality already constituted within a patriarchal ordering of feminine desire.

Although a number of critics have read Defoe's novel as a critique of bourgeois social relations that objectify women as property, the narrative figuring of individual freedom in the character of Moll Flanders does not necessarily preclude an essentializing view of women as objects of exchange in the formation of culture.[9] Marxist and feminist commentaries on Lévi-Strauss's account of kinship structures demonstrate clearly that it is entirely possible for an incisive analysis of social relations based on the exchange of women to

8. Richetti, *Defoe's Narratives*, p. 118.
9. For readings that emphasize the novel's status as a critique of bourgeois values and institutions, see Richetti, "Family, Sex, and Marriage," esp. 24–25; Maddox, "On Defoe's *Roxana*," p. 688; Juliet McMaster, "The Equation of Love and Money in *Moll Flanders*," *Studies in the Novel* 2 (1970): esp. 142; and Lois Chaber, "Matriarchal Mirror: Women and Capital in *Moll Flanders*," *PMLA* 97 (1982): esp. 213 and 223.

stop short of a thoroughgoing critique of the underlying construction of sexuality that inscribes that gender-coded structure of exchange as a cultural necessity.[1] In *Moll Flanders*, Defoe offers precisely such an attenuated analysis. At one level, the account of Moll's triumphs challenges cultural codes that deny women agency in the realms of economic and symbolic exchange; at another it reinscribes women's status as a fundamental form of sexual currency whose circulation is a necessary condition of social order. Being both "speaker" and "spoken," Moll draws much of her appeal as a character from exactly the cultural tension that Lévi-Strauss identifies as the root of women's sexual mystique. Constructed by Defoe as the narrator of her own text, she is in Lévi-Strauss's terms "at once a sign and a value," both a self-made woman and the product of a discourse whose origins are external to her self.[2] Even "Flanders"—the one alias Moll privileges as the semiotic equivalent of herself—is simultaneously an identity that she dons independently (p. 53) and one that she is *given* by her competitors in crime (p. 9). The story of a woman's self-creation as "the greatest Artist of [her] time" (p. 168), Moll's memoir is also the narrative of a woman's initiation into a specific cultural construction of womanhood.

The ideological significance of the tension between Moll's progressive mastery of social reserve on the one hand and her eventual surrender to an intense internal aversion to her incest on the other is best illuminated by considering Defoe's narrative as a text about exchange.[3] The narrative displays a pervasive preoccupation with

1. See for example Gayle Rubin, "The Traffic in Women: Notes on the 'Political Economy' of Sex" in *Toward an Anthropology of Women*, ed. Rayna R. Reiter (New York: Monthly Review P, 1975), pp. 157–210; Sebastiano Timpanaro, *On Materialism*, trans. Lawrence Garner (London: Verso, 1980), Ch. 4; Teresa de Lauretis, *Alice Doesn't: Feminism, Semiotics, Cinema* (Bloomington: Indiana UP, 1984), esp. Ch.5; and Judith Butler, *Gender Trouble* (New York: Routledge, 1990), Ch. 2.
2. On women's dual nature as sign and generator of signs, see Claude Lévi-Strauss, *The Elementary Structures of Kinship*, trans. James Harle Bell and John Richard von Sturmer (Boston: Beacon Press, 1969), p. 496. See also Rubin, "Traffic," p. 201.
3. Reading the novel as a narrative about exchange eliminates the dichotomy between the subjective and the social that Douglas Brooks finds it necessary to insist upon in his "*Moll Flanders*: An Interpretation," *Essays in Criticism* 19 (1969): 46–59. Brooks attempted to refute the popular belief that Defoe's novel lacks formal unity by analyzing the incest motif as the key to the structural logic of the text. By privileging an economic reading, he argued, previous criticism had minimized or obscured the importance of the psychological drama surrounding Moll's incest. To him, the novel is not so much about "money, poverty, aspirations to gentility" as about personal pathology (46). That a critical tradition that rigidly insisted on reading Defoe in socioeconomic terms had remained blind to the text's more subjective meaning is testimony, Brooks suggests, to the danger of assuming " 'too close an identification of literature with society' " (57). In many ways, I consider Brooks's analysis groundbreaking; he was the first to subject the incest episode in the novel to sustained scrutiny, and many of the details of his reading are highly suggestive. I differ, however, with the underlying theoretical assumptions of his article. Brooks argues the centrality of the incest episode in order to foreground the personal dimension of Defoe's text, those aspects of the narrative that he sees as eluding socioeconomic analysis. By contrast, I treat the subjective and the social as ideologically continuous. My aim is to explore how Moll's incest functions narratologically at once to organize her desire and to elaborate the social implications of her text.

Moll's position in relations of exchange.[4] In the context of this dominant thematic preoccupation, Moll's incest acquires emblematic meaning as an extension of her desire to short-circuit or withdraw from "normal" bourgeois relations in which women are circulated as objects among men. (What, after all, is Moll's mastery of reserve but a refusal to circulate in a male economy?) The inadvertence of the incest and Moll's appalled reaction to it, however, serve at the same time to inscribe Moll's desire for freedom from circulation negatively, or at least to inscribe it as a desire inherently divided from itself. For even as the incest concretizes Moll's impulses toward self-determination, it also figuratively equates that desire for autonomy with a forbidden form of sexuality. Circulation or incest: these are the narrative choices the text allows.

Three dominant forms of exchange are represented in the novel. The most visible, of course, is economic exchange: the exchange of money and commodities. It is something of a critical commonplace to say that *Moll Flanders* is a novel about money, that it represents with astonishing vividness and accuracy the workings of a culture in which goods are sovereign and social power (or class) a function not exclusively of heritage but also of the ability to acquire capital. The economic impulse of Moll's career—which is effectually fulfilled within the course of the narrative—is to master those processes of commercial exchange that will give her the status of gentility.[5]

Two other systems of exchange, however, become essential to Moll's quest. One of these is linguistic or symbolic exchange. Moll's relation to language (broadly conceived as the entire system of semiological exchange—made up of utterances, behavior, and physical appearances—by which social meanings are communicated and understood) is crucial at the level of plot; Defoe's heroine manifests an extraordinary gift for manipulating linguistic and social codes and for carrying off various forms of social masquerade. But language plays a critical role at the generic or narrative level, too, where as pseudo-autobiographer, Moll speaks in her own voice, sometimes in alignment and sometimes in tension with the moral subscript of Defoe's text. Indeed, one of the distinctive features of Defoe's narrative ventriloquism is its ability to produce within a single framed autobiographical utterance a colloquy of voices that ideologically complement even as they contest and demystify one another.

Subtly related to the economic and linguistic systems of exchange

4. Nancy K. Miller touches on the importance of this thematic preoccupation in *The Heroine's Text: Readings in the French and English Novel, 1722–1782* (New York: Columbia UP, 1980), p. 20.

5. For studies that especially emphasize this aspect of the narrative, see Ian Watt, *The Rise of the Novel: Studies in Defoe, Richardson, and Fielding* (Berkeley: U of California P, 1957), Ch. 4; Michael Shinagel, *Daniel Defoe and Middle-Class Gentility* (Cambridge: Harvard UP, 1968), esp. Ch. 7; and McMaster, "Equation."

in which Moll is inextricably implicated is a third form of exchange: kinship or sexual exchange. Sexual exchange in England had traditionally worked to preserve a relatively fixed social hierarchy or kinship system in which power was a function more of lineage than of cash, but in the eighteenth century its role in the acquisition and transmission of property sustained it as an integral part of a social context characterized by class mobility as well. Women in commercial society not only continued to play a crucial role as reproducers in the orderly transmission of both real and personal property but, as Douglas Hay has noted, "the marriage settlement [now also became] . . . the sacrament by which land allied itself with trade."[6]

Positioned at the site where an emergent individualism articulated with the residual operation of feudal structures within the family, women thus occupied a contradictory cultural place within early modern capitalism. To recapitulate Juliet Mitchell's argument: * * * while capitalism rendered kinship structures archaic, it also preserved them in a residual way in the ideology of the biological family, which posits the nuclear family with its oedipal structure as a natural rather than a culturally created phenomenon. The ideology of the biological family comes into its own against the background of the remoteness of a kinship system, but masks the persistence—in altered forms—of precisely those archaic patterns of kinship organization. "[M]en enter into the class-dominated structures of history," Mitchell writes, "while women (as women, whatever their actual work in production) remain defined by the kinship patterns of organization . . . harnessed into the family."[7]

By virtue of the way it organizes the relations among the categories of economic, linguistic and sexual exchange, *Moll Flanders* works at once to articulate and to naturalize this contradiction. Written at the beginning of England's transition both to a market economy and to the conditions under which the visible presence of kinship structures would gradually recede, the novel contains dramas of class and kinship at the same time that it specifically elaborates the contradictory status of women in early capitalist society. Like the recessed but residually operative kinship structures that Juliet Mitchell alludes to in her account of economically advanced societies, moreover, the kinship drama staged in *Moll Flanders*—the heroine's incest—seems on the surface utterly incidental, while in fact it functions as the ideological and structural fulcrum of the text. The class drama in which Moll Flanders thrives as a woman, by means of her femaleness, is a more sustained focus of narrative interest than the drama

6. Douglas Hay, "Property, Authority and the Criminal Law," in *Albion's Fatal Tree: Crime and Society in Eighteenth-Century England*, ed. Hay, et al. (New York: Pantheon Books, 1975), p. 22.
7. Juliet Mitchell, *Psychoanalysis and Feminism* (New York: Vintage Books, 1975), p. 406.

of her incestuous coupling, but structurally and ideologically it is enclosed within and contingent on that less manifest sociosexual narrative. At one level, Moll's incest functions as a figure for the freedom of individual desire from the social imperatives of class; at another, it constitutes a narrative occasion for establishing sexual difference as the site of hierarchical structures of social organization. In *Moll Flanders*, that is to say, the heroine's inadvertently committed and ultimately repudiated incest operates as a necessary condition of possibility for Defoe's narrative of desiring womanhood.

The relationship among the three systems of exchange represented in Defoe's text is embodied in the figure of the heroine; it is her relation to each system that constitutes the locus of their narrative intersection. In exploring this complex intersection, I propose to examine Moll's relation to each type of exchange system—the economic, the linguistic, and the sexual—separately. My point of entry—to which I will repeatedly return—is the heroine's name, a feature of the text that gains metaphoric resonance by condensing into a single figure the interrelated narratives of Moll's relation to all three systems.

Moll Flanders is named for a species of forbidden merchandise, "Flanders" being the shorthand term for usually contraband Flemish lace.[8] The alias seems peculiarly apt for a fictional heroine who inherits a maternal legacy of cloth-stealing, her mother having been convicted of a felony for the theft of three pieces of fine Holland. ("Holland"—or Dutch linen—was also commonly contraband.) Moll's own first theft is of "a little Bundle wrapt in a white Cloth" containing, among other miscellanies, "a Suit of Child-bed Linnen . . . , very good and almost new, the Lace very fine" (p. 152); her last (for which she is apprehended on the spot and returned to Newgate, where she was born) is of "two Pieces of . . . Brocaded Silk, very rich" from the home of a man who acts as a broker between weavers and mercers in the sale of woven goods (p. 214). At a certain point in her career, Moll's preferred mode of criminal dealing consists of clandestinely informing customs officials of the location of illegally imported Flanders lace.

Moll's names tie her to the actual criminal underworld of Defoe's day. As Gerald Howson has pointed out, she is the namesake of the famous pickpocket, Mary Godson (alias Moll King); and she clearly

8. On the smuggling of Flemish lace in the seventeenth century, and on lace's fascination as a forbidden object, see Santina M. Levey, *Lace: A History* (London: Victoria and Albert, 1983), pp. 40, 44. According to Levey, Flanders was the prime offender when, in 1697, the English Parliament passed an act to tighten controls on the importation of foreign lace (44). Defoe's novel is, of course, set in the seventeenth century; Moll claims to have written it in 1683 at the age of almost seventy (p. 267). Useful, too, is Starr's note on "the thriving trade in smuggled lace" (380).

resembles such well-known female criminals as "Calico Sarah" and "Susan Holland," who were also nicknamed after commonly prohibited textiles.[9] But the logic of Defoe's choice in naming his heroine for illegally imported lace goes beyond the demands of historical verisimilitude. It follows from the ideological structure of his text.

In telling a story of a woman who cannot earn an honest livelihood as a seamstress and so becomes a prostitute and then a thief, *Moll Flanders* narratively addresses the problem of women's relation to a capitalist economy.[1] Moll's childhood desire is to support herself by honest needlework. It becomes clear very early, however, that the products of Moll's labor are not her own and that what she can earn for her handiwork (largely in economic transactions with other women) will hardly go far enough to maintain her at the level of subsistence. By setting aside the money that Moll earns, her nurse tries to honor Moll's innocent wish for self-sufficiency. But even at this early stage in her career, that wish can not be "purely" realized, Moll's earnings being adequate to her needs only when they are supplemented by gifts from genteel ladies who patronize her out of amusement at her social innocence. An object of charity, the honest seamstress cannot clothe herself. As Lois Chaber notes, Moll's first guardian—"a fallen gentlewoman who nevertheless maintains a precarious independence as a teacher and weaver"—is tied to a mode of home-centered industry no longer viable in the London that Moll inhabits. Finally, neither she nor Moll's naive hope for *honest* self-sufficiency will survive.[2]

Forced by the death of her guardian into the very servitude she had so vehemently eschewed, Moll soon learns that in the economy in which she moves the value of a woman's sexuality exceeds that of her industrial productivity. As the "Madam" who "mend[s] Lace, and wash[es] . . . Ladies Lac'd-heads" (p. 14) as a front for prostitution demonstrates, material production by women is not as lucrative as the exchange of sexual favors in the world Defoe portrays. The gift of a single shilling from the Mayor's wife, who condescendingly bids Moll "mind [her] Work" (p. 14), may put money in her pocket; but

9. Gerald Howson, "Who Was Moll Flanders?" *The Times Literary Supplement*, no. 3438 (January 18, 1968): 63–64; rpt. in *Moll Flanders: An Authoritative Text, Backgrounds and Sources, Criticism*, ed. Edward Kelly (New York: W. W. Norton and Company, 1973), pp. 312–19.

1. I refer here, of course, to early capitalism and not to the large-scale industrialization of the later part of the eighteenth century. For relevant discussions of the effects of commercialization on the economic position of women in the late seventeenth and early eighteenth centuries, see Ellen Pollak, *The Poetics of Sexual Myth: Gender and Ideology in the Verse of Swift and Pope* (Chicago: U of Chicago P, 1985), 22–39; Alice Clark, *Working Life of Women in the Seventeenth Century* (London: Routledge, 1919); and Susan Cahn, *Industry of Devotion: The Transformation of Women's Work in England, 1500–1660* (New York: Columbia UP, 1987).

2. Chaber, "Matriarchal Mirror," p. 219.

however often that philanthropic gesture is repeated, it creates for Moll far less accumulated capital than the five guineas from the elder brother who interrupts Moll's sewing for another "kind of Work" (p. 22). (It is this same man from whom Moll eventually acquires a plenitude of gold [p. 23].) Moll's consciousness of her relation as a woman to capital will deepen over the course of her career. Schooled in the ways of marriage, she will come to understand the role of female sexuality in men's profit as well as pleasure, to recognize that a woman has social value not just as an object of male libidinal desire but also, in the higher classes, as a medium of exchange in the accumulation and transmission of property.

In the context of this education in the dynamics of exchange, Moll's turn to crime at forty-eight makes perfect sense both as an instance of Defoe's narrative realism and as an emblematic gesture on Moll's part. Occurring at the point when Moll's sexual appeal and reproductive capacity are in decline, it affirms woman's status as a sexual object not only by associating menopause with the loss of sexuality but also by depicting that loss as a desperate economic circumstance. (Moll describes her dismal condition at this point in her narrative as a sort of "bleeding to Death" (p. 150).[3] At the same time, however, Moll's turn to crime functions at a figurative level as an extension, or renewal, of her quest for economic solvency. In theft, and particularly in the theft of woven goods, she achieves unauthorized but nonetheless remunerative possession of the very goods she could not profit from by producing. Having turned her manual skills another way, Moll appropriates what, as a child, she ingenuously assumed belonged to her: the power to dress herself by her own means. By the time Moll reaches sixty, that power has

3. Although, as Hay has pointed out, it was conventional in the eighteenth century to liken the circulation of gold to the circulation of the blood ("Property," 19), it is interesting that Defoe should choose to have Moll use the image of bleeding to death at this particular point in her career, since gold and blood are also conventionally tied to women, childbirth, and taboo. Consider, for example, the lyrics to Air V of Gay's *Beggar's Opera* [*The Beggar's Opera and Companion Pieces*, ed. C. F. Burgess (Arlington Heights, Ill.: AHM Publishing Corp., 1966)]:

> A maid is like the golden ore
> . . . A wife's like a guinea in gold,
> Stampt with the name of her spouse;
> Now here, now there; is bought, or is sold;
> And is current in every house. (act 1, sc. 5)

If Moll's education during the novel is in "reserve," which is ordinarily a male prerogative, it is somehow fitting that her criminal career should begin at this moment of her "death" as a woman. For what is criminal about Moll's thievery is precisely that it enables her to accumulate wealth without reinvesting it (she keeps it in reserve)—without, that is, participating in normal relations of exchange. The one other time in the narrative when Moll describes her poverty as "*bleeding to Death*" is when she spends the "Season" at Bath, just after fleeing her incestuous marriage. Bath, she points out, is the wrong place for a woman to turn her sexuality to profit, for men sometimes find mistresses there, but "very rarely look for a Wife" (p. 86).

accrued a complex layering of meanings, for she has moved beyond the mere ability to support herself to become not only wealthy but an artist in the practice of disguise.

Thus, on one level, Moll's name contains in coded form the narrative of her relation to "material" production. Her quest for gentility is a quest both for economic self-sufficiency and for control over the products of her own labor. Lace is what Moll mends and what she steals, but it is a commodity to which she bears a consistently intermediate relation. In one sense, it is a fitting site for that conjunction of high and low for which Moll's career, indeed for which Moll herself, will come to stand. Lace, said Dr. Johnson, is like Greek; " 'every man gets as much of it as he can.' "[4] Its associations work upwards as well as downwards in the social order; as Santina M. Levey notes, lace "was both one of the most expensive of all fashionable textiles and one of the cheapest of home-made trimmings."[5] At the same time that it suggests a certain indeterminacy of social class, however, lace functions in Defoe as a reminder of a particular set of economic power relations based on gender. Produced exclusively by women, it was purchased (no matter who did the actual buying or wearing) mainly by men. In another anecdote from Boswell, Dr. Johnson again gives an illustrative example: "when a gentleman told him he had bought a suit of laces for his lady, he said, 'Well, Sir, you have done a good thing and a wise thing!' 'I have done a good thing, (said the gentleman,) but I do not know that I have done a wise thing.' JOHNSON. 'Yes, Sir; no money is better spent than what is laid out for domestick satisfaction. A man is pleased that his wife is drest as well as other people; and a wife is pleased that she is drest.' "[6] Like Greek, and like gold, lace serves as a symbolic medium of value. For men it is a sign of social status, for women a symptom of dependency.

If Moll's name suggests the material conditions of her quest, however, it also suggests the means—those elaborate strategies of disclosure and concealment—by which she seeks to realize her desire. Moll's association with lace, that is, tells the story of her evolving relation to language. Covering and revealing at the same time, lace aptly objectifies the discursive logic of a narrative as intent as Moll's on self-exposure and anonymity. The product of a long education in the management of disguise, her memoir is at once confession and disavowal, a narrative space in which she both lays bare her vices and keeps herself covered in a certain artful obscurity. Linguistically, it achieves for Moll what she is eager to achieve in other ways

4. *Boswell's Life of Johnson*, ed. George Birkbeck Hill, rev. L. F. Powell, 6 vols. (Oxford, 1934–64), 4:23.
5. Levey, *Lace*, 1.
6. *Boswell's Life of Johnson*, 2:352. I am grateful to David B. Morris for helping me to make the connections here among lace, gender, and social class.

throughout her life, the condition of being "Conceal'd and Discover'd both together" (p. 139).

Beginning life as a naive interpreter both of experience and of discourse, Moll early becomes a victim of her own inability either to read or to exploit appearances. Her childish tendency to oversimplify the relationship of signifier to signified, first manifest in her excessively literal interpretation of the honorific "Madam," becomes socially catastrophic in her failure to read the "earnestness" of her seducer, the elder brother, as a cover-up for insincerity (pp. 14, 26). At the same time, Moll meets his dissembling with artless transparency (p. 26). Even after the lesson of the elder brother has been learned and Moll assesses love a "*Cheat*" (p. 50), resolving for the future to exercise greater physical and emotional reserve, she continues to be seduced by surfaces, guilelessly "selling herself," as she puts it, to a tradesman who is acceptable to her because he has the "look" of quality (p. 50). Moll's gentleman-draper squanders her money and leaves her "to Rob [his] Creditors for something to Subsist on" (p. 52).

At this point, Moll first adopts the name of "Flanders" and retires to the Mint in an episode that marks a critical transition in her life. It is here that she first undertakes the art of fraud. The hard-won knowledge she has acquired in the affair of the two brothers is a knowledge of the cultural codes that define her social value as a woman. By these, she has discovered, she is reduced—as all women are—at once to nothingness and to a form of currency, a mere means to insure the patrilineal succession of property. As Moll's Colchester sister implied when she observed that on the marriage market a woman without money is "no Body" (p. 20), a woman's fortune merely substitutes for her intrinsic worthlessness. As Moll's experience with the elder brother has made clear, a poor woman is assumed to be a "Ware" that can be transferred rather casually among men (p. 40).

Moll, however, refuses to be reduced to a mere sign. By undertaking to manipulate signs herself, she begins to resist her victimization by cultural codes that define her as a piece of merchandise whose worth is measurable only in relation to male desire. She learns not only how to read those codes correctly but also how to use them to control the way others construe her. Matrimony, she has perceived, is a game of chance—a mere "Lottery"—unless it is played with proper skill (p. 62). That proper skill is entrepreneurial, a canny knowledge of how to market oneself profitably. Like winning in that other man's game of hazard that Moll will play much later on (p. 205), or like maximizing one's profits as a shopkeeper by placing one's finger on the scale, winning here requires the ability to cheat.

The rumors Moll fabricates about the sea-faring suitor of her friend from Redriff demonstrate that Moll's skill at deception is, at least at this stage, fundamentally linguistic. Her poetic courtship of her third husband makes the verbal dimension of her quest for social power clearer still. Having figured in social relations mainly as an object to be exchanged, Moll now resolves to establish herself as an exchanging subject by taking control of a romantic dialogue. Defoe's imagery is, characteristically, at once historically apt and rich in metaphoric implication. Writing on windows with jewelry or diamond-pointed pencils was customary in the eighteenth century.[7] As the site of a written dialogue, however, the pane of inscribed glass also functions emblematically as part of this episode's thematic preoccupation with the ambiguity and impermanence of meaning.

The surface on which Moll and her lover write is transparent, the instrument of inscription a diamond—an emblem of permanence that will etch a physically ineradicable text. Transparency and permanence, however, are belied not simply by the inherent fragility of glass but also by the exquisitely elusive nature of what Moll writes. Having acquired unpleasant knowledge of the instability of lovers' vows, Moll now shatters her lover's professions with disbelief. Indeed, she so challenges his sincerity (the transparency of his text), makes it so difficult for him to give his language force, that he is driven at last to physical violence—literally to holding her "fast" (p. 65). The sexual passion involved in the lover's impatience makes his desire to switch at this point from ring to pen seem a desperate wish to assert masculine, phallic authority over Moll's teasing but impenetrable female elusiveness. But Moll continues to overturn his meanings while cunningly obfuscating all her own, until at last her man lays down his pen. By likening the pen to a cudgel, Moll reveals that, to her, his textual silence marks defeat, that this is a battle being fought on verbal grounds. It is now Moll who has her lover "fast"—not in her arms, but (yet more literally) *"in a word."* Pinning him to his own text, she has "fore-closed all manner of objection" to her poverty on his part; feigning total openness, she has made a proper evaluation of her sincerity or her worth impossible (p. 66). Language has become for Moll a weapon and a veil.

The image of the Mint is similarly situated both in and between realist and emblematic modes. At one level, it lends veracity to the fiction of a woman in debt; at another, it functions as a complex metaphor for Moll's behavior at this point in her career. An area in Southwark that provided legal sanctuary to debtors (so called because Henry VIII kept a Mint there), the Mint figures a place at once where money is manufactured and where Moll (like other debt-

7. See Defoe, *Moll Flanders*, ed. Starr, 361n.1, accompanying text on page 79; and Kelly, *Moll Flanders: An Authoritative Text*, 63n.

ors) is temporarily "freed" from the process of exchange.[8] Moll's hiding there thus neatly emblematizes her strategies of resistance as she emerges from its midst, a counterfeiter who hides behind her status as currency (impersonating a rich widow, she passes herself off as "a fortune") precisely in order to extricate herself from the debt nexus in which, as a woman, she seems doomed to circulate.

Moll's emergence from the Mint thus marks the point of her most centered and intense period of self-creation before her turn to crime. Having become the center of her own authority, she has learned to use resourceful lying to engineer a marriage that brings her what she has most aspired to obtain: a good husband and economic security. She is happily reunited with her mother. The same narrative sequence that figures this self-birth and Moll's return to her own blood, however, also figures the taint of blood in what Moll refers to at the end of her narrative as "the Blot" (p. 266) of her incestuous coupling and reproduction with her brother. The moment in Defoe's narrative that signals Moll's fullest realization of the efficacy of her own desire as a female subject is also the point at which she is most contaminated and "undone."

Social theorists since St. Augustine have routinely ascribed to the incest taboo the positive social function of establishing relations of reciprocity between men; the very survival of the biological family has been understood to depend on such extended alliances.[9] "The prohibition of incest," writes Lévi-Strauss, "is less a rule prohibiting marriage with the mother, sister or daughter, than a rule obliging the mother, sister or daughter to be given to others."[1] Or as Talcott Parsons observes, "it is not so much the prohibition of incest in its negative aspect which is important as the positive obligation to perform functions for the subunit and the larger society by marrying out. Incest is a withdrawal from this obligation to contribute to the formation and maintenance of supra-familial bonds on which major economic, political and religious functions of the society are dependent."[2] Coming as it does at the pinnacle of her efforts to insert herself as a subject into a masculine economy, Moll's incest is constituted as a refusal of just the sort of cultural obligation such theorists describe. Like her assumption of linguistic mastery or her later appropriation of material goods, it emerges in the text as a narrative

8. On the Mint, see *Moll Flanders*, ed. J. Paul Hunter, 52n., and E. P. Thompson, *Whigs and Hunters: The Origin of the Black Act* (New York: Pantheon Books, 1975), pp. 248–49.
9. Augustine, *The City of God*, trans. Marcus Dods (New York: Modern Library, 1950), 4: 509. See also Lévi-Strauss's statement of the "very simple fact" that "the biological family . . . must ally itself with other families in order to endure" (*Kinship*, 485).
1. Lévi-Strauss, *Kinship*, p. 481.
2. Talcott Parsons, "The Incest Taboo in Relation to Social Structure," in *The Family: Its Structures and Functions*, ed. Rose Laub Coser (New York: St. Martin's P, 1964), p. 56.

manifestation of her will to power. It even functions as an emblem (and a fulfillment) of Moll's desire for lucrative exchange with other women, the heroine's brother (by a different father) being nothing less than the conduit of a transaction with her own mother (in, of course, a reversal of the normal kinship pattern by which women become conduits for relations between men). Understood in terms of the positive function that socio-anthropological writing assigns to the incest prohibition, in other words, Moll's incest might be said to represent the ultimate threat to patriarchal authority—a refusal, to borrow Luce Irigaray's phrase, of the goods to go to market.[3] It is important, therefore (though probably not surprising), that Defoe should harness—or even cancel—the subversive force of Moll's desire for economic and symbolic agency by representing it as an inadvertent violation of a deeply internalized aversion that will make Moll not only hate herself but loathe the thought of sleeping with her husband.

There seems to be a kind of contradiction here. On the one hand, Moll's incest emerges in the plot as an extension (almost an allegorical emblem) of her quest for female power in the realms of economic and linguistic exchange. On the other hand, by virtue of its inadvertence and Moll's ultimate repudiation of it, the incest testifies to her lack of desire to extend that quest for female power beyond the limits of economic and linguistic exchange into the realm of sexual exchange where, as Rubin and others have shown, the hierarchies of sexual difference originate. Moll's incest is, in this sense, both a manifestation of her transgressiveness and its limit. Through it, Defoe establishes that however determined Moll may be to acquire agency in the domains of material and symbolic production, she is even more forcefully driven *not* to challenge the basic kinship patterns on which the social order and, more importantly, the hierarchies of gender difference rest. It is thus all the more significant from a structural point of view that Moll does not actually enter into prostitution or hardened crime until *after* her incestuous liaison has been renounced. However transgressive those subsequent violations of social law may seem to be, the prior renunciation of her incest (as Defoe's narrative codes it symbolically) ensures that those transgressions are already inscribed within the limiting conditions of heteropatriarchal sexual exchange.

Moll's loathing of the fruits of her own desire thus triggers a countermovement or neutralizing subtext to the progress of her trans-

3. "*But what if the 'goods' refused to go to market?*" writes Irigaray. "What if they maintained among themselves 'another' kind of trade?" [Luce Irigaray, "When the Goods Get Together," trans. Claudia Reeder, in *New French Feminisms*, ed. Elaine Marks and Isabelle de Courtivron (Amherst: U of Massachusetts P, 1980), 110]. For a slightly different translation, see also *This Sex Which Is Not One*, trans. Catherine Porter with Carolyn Burke (Ithaca: Cornell UP, 1985), p. 196.

gressive womanhood, propelling her back from America and its possibilities for self-generation to the social hierarchies of the Old World. Moll will be able to return to America and economic security only after she has taken her place within those hierarchies and, through her marriage to Jemy and the settlement of her estate upon her son, she is in a position to reenter the system of exchange in the "proper" role of wife and loving mother. As Jemy jests at the end of the book, Moll *has* become his "Fortune" after all—the very currency she has worked so hard throughout her life *not* to be (p. 266). It is true that she has become that fortune largely through maternal inheritance, but even that inheritance carries with it vestigial reminders of patriarchal relations of dominance, having originally been the estate of her mother's master (p. 72).

Moll confesses to a transient dream of endogamous bliss on her return to America; having been treated lavishly by her son, "as if," she writes, "I had been in a new World, [I] began secretly now to wish that I had not brought my *Lancashire* Husband from *England* at all" (p. 262). But she dismisses that wish as "not hearty," as she had rejected her actual incest as not wholesome earlier. At the end of her text, we find Moll using her money to purchase clothes for her fallen gentleman—"two good long Wigs, two silver hilted Swords" (p. 265), the semi-feudal trappings of a male-centered system of gentility. This, it seems, is the fabric her text preserves, the social and symbolic order into which she is woven but which at last she does not make.

The name Moll Flanders thus tells the story of the heroine's relation to the production of gender as well as to the production of language and of goods. As a woman in this text, Moll is herself the essential form of foreign merchandise whose export is required in order to create the supra-familial bonds that make other forms of trade or communication possible. Defoe's narrative represents her as spending her life attempting to work those other systems of exchange and as succeeding to a limited extent: she becomes wealthy; she writes an autobiographical memoir. At the same time, however, Moll can never escape the necessity of always having to circulate outside the circuit of her own authority in order for those very systems of economic and symbolic exchange to operate. Even Moll's own narrative is represented as needing to be "garbl'd," or purified for market, by a masculine editorial violence (p. 5). As he represents it in the Preface to his book, Defoe's task as editor is to "dress" the body of Moll's text in language fit for public consumption (p. 3); "redressing" her act of authorship, he reauthorizes it for a social audience. When Moll does attempt to undo the categories of gender, when she tries to control her own circulation—to make *herself* contraband by expropriating herself out of the necessary condition of being an always dislocated entity—the result is incest, a violation of what Defoe represents as the most basic prohibition of them all. Why Defoe must figure the alternative to female circulation as incest, or female self-sufficiency as an aberrant variety of heterosexual relations, is an ideological secret that his narrative only mutely articulates.

If, as Juliet Mitchell has suggested, Defoe's *Moll Flanders* presents "a society without a father," we would do well at the same time to recall Lacan's insistence that the father's "effective presence is not always necessary for him not to be missing."[4] Moll Flanders' female quest for economic and symbolic agency leads her into the apparent lawlessnes of incest but it also returns her to the very heteropatriarchal economic and symbolic order that is the original aim of her quest to either elude or undermine. This return is effected not by the intervention of a threatening father figure or by some other externally repressive juridical force (the patriarch Humphrey, for instance, goes blind and mad and eventually dies) but rather through the institution of an internal division or split within the heroine herself. The scene of Moll's sibling incest—interestingly also figured as the heroine's return to a maternal plenitude of "Tenderness and Affection" (p. 70)—occupies the empty yet constitutive place of that divided desire, the narrative site where in a double movement the heroine simultaneously *turns away from* and *returns to* the law of masculine privilege. Troped as a series of contradictions or logical impossibilities, that incest marks at once a scene of uncommon filial "Felicity" (p. 70) and of utter abjection; the revisiting of a place of origin and a new beginning in a new world; a foray to Virginia, geographic repository of corruption inhabited and governed by convicted criminals, whose place-name nevertheless evokes an image of unadulterated law. As such, it figures the logical impossibility of the division within which, as female subject, Moll herself is constituted as both outside the law and a product of it.

At the same time, subtending the overlapping and sometimes conflicting systems of sexual, symbolic, and commercial exchange that Moll traverses in the course of her narrative, and within which she is positioned as a female subject, is another economy of exchange. Like the figure of the father (whose immanent force, as I have argued, asserts itself in Moll's relation to the imperatives of sexual exchange), this economy is more implicit than manifest in the narrative, but it has its own immanent, constitutive force. I am referring

4. Juliet Mitchell, introduction to *The Fortunes and Misfortunes of the Famous Moll Flanders*, by Daniel Defoe, ed. Juliet Mitchell (Harmondsworth: Penguin, 1978), 12. The passage from Lacan is quoted by Jacqueline Rose in Juliet Mitchell and Jacqueline Rose, eds. *Feminine Sexuality: Jacques Lacan and the ecole freudienne*, trans. Jacqueline Rose (New York: W. W. Norton & Company; London: Pantheon Books, 1985), p. 39.

to the colonial or slave economy on which Moll's independence as the owner of a profitable tobacco plantation in America itself depends and through whose largely occluded presence her production as a gendered bourgeois subject is implicitly racialized.[5] Race is not an express concern in this novel as it is in *Robinson Crusoe*—or in *Colonel Jack*, where the racial structure of American plantation culture is more overtly specified.[6] It would, nevertheless, be possible to argue that, in its representation of the female subject of early modern capitalism, and despite (if not because of) its virtual silence about race, *Moll Flanders* is engaged in the elaboration of a nationalist myth—just as engaged indeed as *Robinson Crusoe*, of which the later novel might be said to offer a female variant or counterpart.

The narrative's subtle articulation of gender and racial discourses informs the very passage in which Moll fantasizes an incestuous idyll with her son, a passage that in turn exposes the assumption of colonial sovereignty implicit in Defoe's representation of female sexuality. For it is not just being pampered by her son that makes Moll wish that she had left her Lancashire husband behind in England; it is also the specific terms of the pleasures that Humphrey provides—namely, his designation of his mother as the recipient of "all possible Respect" from his tenants and his gift, along with provisions for her supper, of "a Maid-Servant and a *Negro* boy to wait on [her]" (p. 262). These are the constituents of those "new World" pleasures that prompt Moll's secret wish—her desire not to share the services of her "boy" (either her son or her slave) with a surrogate patriarch, whose existence threatens to return her to a merely intermediary position in a male homosocial economy. The fulfillment of that wish would mark the realization of her childhood determination to avoid the dependency of service by obviating her role as Jemy's caretaker and fortune, the prop to shore up his waning aristocratic superiority.[7]

The internal division of Moll's incestuous desire in this passage through her prompt rejection of that desire as only half-hearted both subtly replays the larger drama of her incestuous relation to her brother-husband and reveals the ambivalence and contradictions

5. For relevant theoretical discussion of the "implicit racial grammar [that] underwrote the sexual regimes of bourgeois culture" identified by Michel Foucault, see Ann Laura Stoler, *Race and the Education of Desire: Foucault's* History of Sexuality *and the Colonial Order of Things* (Durham: Duke UP, 1995), p. 12.
6. Daniel Defoe, *Colonel Jack* (London, 1722).
7. It is fitting that the wish for endogamy here should emerge as a counterpoint to marriage with Jemy, whose Irishness significantly designates him as a colonized subject with whom marriage would constitute a form of figurative miscegenation. At the same time, however, Jemy's aristocratic origins guarantee that such a crossing of national boundaries is counterbalanced by its simultaneous figuration of a form of class allegiance associated with the British imperial project. In this connection, see Aparna Dharwadker, "Nation, Race, and the Ideology of Commerce in Defoe," *The Eighteenth Century: Theory and Interpretation* 39 (1998): 63, who quotes Richard Helgerson's observation (in *Forms of Nationhood: The Elizabethan Writing of England* [Chicago: U of Chicago P, 1992]) that British imperial expansion brought merchant and gentry classes into a common enterprise.

inherent in the position of the European colonial female subject as simultaneously the renderer and the recipient of service. This ambivalence is both enabled and resolved when Moll trades the dream of uncompromised female agency in the domestic realm for colonial supremacy abroad. Evading such a compromise would be impossible within the terms of intelligibility of the cultural bargain entailed in the constitution of white European female subjectivity as Defoe conceives it, where the privileges of colonial supremacy accrue only in exchange for the political concessions required by normative heterosexuality. This is the trade—and the trade-off—through which Moll finally acquires a certain paradoxical agency in the reproduction of patriarchal and colonial economies of exchange when, at the end of her narrative, she promises to send her son a white, European wife from London with her next cargo of indentured servants and material goods.

If *Moll Flanders* is a narrative of the production of gender, language, and goods, then, it is also a story of that particular moment of cultural change when England moved from a domestic to a colonial, world economy. By the end of her narrative, the honest seamstress who cannot clothe herself is plentifully stocked with the material resources to attire not just herself but also her husband and a multitude of servants (p. 265).[8] As the dream of honest self-sufficiency yields to the realities of a global colonial order, so too does Moll's quest to overcome the liabilities of sexual difference surrender to another priority: the need within that expanded global network to establish and secure her own sense of European cultural identity.

In a way, that need has been present from the very beginning of Moll's retrospective account of her origins, for which—significantly—she can produce only hearsay evidence. Because England, unlike other European nations, made no public provision for the orphaned children of condemned or transported criminals, Moll is left desolate, with "no Parish to have Recourse to" (p. 10) as an infant and with no certain knowledge as an adult about how she managed to survive. The first account she reports being able to "Recollect, or could ever learn" of herself is that she "had wandred among a Crew of those People they call *Gypsies*, or *Egyptians*" (pp. 10–11). Here Moll is quick to observe that she must have lived with the gypsies "but a very little while . . . , for I had not had my Skin discolour'd or blacken'd, as they do very young to all the Children they carry about with them" (p. 11). Typically viewed as a vaguely crimi-

8. On the relative condition of servants and slaves in colonial Virginia, and the use of the term "servant" to designate both categories, see Defoe, *Moll Flanders*, ed. Starr, 361–62 n.2, accompanying text on page 86. See also Edmund S. Morgan, *American Slavery, American Freedom: The Ordeal of Colonial Virginia* (New York: W. W. Norton and Company, 1975: rpt. New York: W. W. Norton & Company, 1995).

nal, vagabond, Oriental "race" who wandered the European countryside and were wont to kidnap European children—whose faces were then blackened to prevent their being recognized as white, gypsies frequently populated eighteenth- and nineteenth-century stories of displaced and orphaned children in search of origins.[9] But here again, as in other episodes, Moll's narrative functions in both literal and symbolic registers. In this instance, the narrator's anxious desire to assert a cultural identity clearly differentiated from that of the gypsies through the figure of her unblackened face (or recognizable whiteness) takes on a certain overdetermined meaning in relation to the novel's colonial subtext. Ultimately, one might say, Defoe's novel both addresses and satisfies a cultural desire for the reaffirmation of systems of sexual and racial difference in a society where incest and miscegenation emerge as linked emblems of the dangers of increasing cultural dislocation and social mobility. That incest is inscribed in *Moll Flanders* as the inextricable accompaniment to Moll's ultimate fixing of her biological origin through reconnection with her mother simply points to another trade-off, or contingency, inherent in the novel's discursive articulation of sexuality and race; Moll's rejection of her incest works symbolically to normalize her relation to gender imperatives while, at the same time, that very incest—by returning her to biology—secures the symbolic purity of her racial identity. Endogamy is to be avoided, except when required for the preservation of patriarchy or when it sustains empire by preserving the boundaries of cultural difference.

9. See in this connection Deborah Epstein Nord, " 'Marks of Race': Gypsy Figures and Eccentric Femininity in Nineteenth-Century Women's Writing," *Victorian Studies* 41 (1998): 189–210. On the role of Asia in Defoe and Defoe's "Orientalism," see Dharwadker, pp. 78–82.

Daniel Defoe: A Chronology†

1660	Born Daniel Foe in London. Son of James, a tallow chandler, and Alice Foe.
1662	Act of Uniformity forces the family of James Foe and their pastor, Dr. Samuel Annesley, out of the Church of England to become Presbyterians, a dissenting sect.
1665–66	The Great Plague and the Great Fire of London.
c. 1668	Death of Alice Foe.
c. 1671–79	First educated at the Reverend James Fisher's school at Dorking, Surrey; then attended the academy for dissenters of the Reverend Charles Morton at Newington Green in preparation for a ministerial career.
1683	An established merchant living in Cornhill, near the Royal Exchange.
1684	Marries Mary Tuffley, who brings him a dowry of £3,700; together they would have seven children.
c. 1685–92	Prospering in business as a trader in hosiery, importer of wine and tobacco, and insurer of ships. Travels in England and Europe. Publishes political tracts.
1688–1702	Supports and serves in assorted offices William III.
1690–91	Contributor to the *Athenian Mercury* and member of the Athenian Society.
1692	Declared bankrupt for £17,000 and imprisoned for debt.
1695	Adds the prefix "De" to his name publicly for the first time as manager-trustee of royal lotteries; henceforth calls himself "De Foe."
1697	Publishes *An Essay on Projects*, which brings him to the attention of influential men.
1701	*The True-Born Englishman*, a poetic defense of King William and his Dutch ancestry; it outsells any previously published poem in the language.
1702	Death of William III and accession of Anne ends his hopes of preferment. Publishes *The Shortest Way with*

† From Daniel Defoe, *Robinson Crusoe*, ed. Michael Shinagel, 2nd ed. (New York: W. W. Norton & Company, 1994). Reprinted by permission of Michael Shinagel and W. W. Norton & Company, Inc.

the Dissenters, a satiric attack on High Church extremists.

1703 Arrested for writing *The Shortest Way*, charged with seditious libel by the Tory ministry, committed to Newgate, tried, convicted, and sentenced to stand in the pillory (July 29–31). Publishes *Hymn to the Pillory* and an authorized collected edition of his writings. The failure of his brick and tile works near Tilbury while in prison precipitates another bankruptcy.

1703–30 Secures his release from Newgate at the intercession of Robert Harley, who employs his services on behalf of the Tory ministry. Defoe serves successive administrations, Tory and Whig, as political journalist, adviser, and secret agent.

1704–13 Wrote and edited *The Review*, an influential journal appearing three times a week.

1707 Union of England and Scotland, which Defoe worked to promote.

1713–14 Arrested several times for debt and for political writings.

1715 *The Family Instructor*, a popular conduct manual.

1718 Second volume of *The Family Instructor*.

1719 *Robinson Crusoe; The Farther Adventures of Robinson Crusoe*.

1720 *Memoirs of a Cavalier; Captain Singleton; Serious Reflections . . . of Robinson Crusoe*.

1722 *Moll Flanders; Religious Courtship; A Journal of the Plague Year; Colonel Jack*.

1724 *The Fortunate Mistress (Roxana); A General History of the Pyrates; A Tour Thro' the Whole Island of Great Britain* (3 vols., 1724–26).

1725 *The Complete English Tradesman*; also pirate and criminal "lives."

1726 *The Political History of the Devil*.

1727 *Conjugal Lewdness (A Treatise Concerning the Use and Abuse of the Marriage Bed); An Essay on the History and Reality of Apparitions; A New Family Instructor*; second volume of *The Complete English Tradesman*.

1728 *Augusta Triumphans; A Plan of the English Commerce*.

1731 Dies "of a lethargy" (April 24) in Ropemaker's Alley, London; buried (April 26) in Bunhill Fields among Puritan Worthies like John Bunyan.

At the time of his death Defoe left incomplete manuscripts of two works that were published posthumously, *The Compleat English Gentleman* (1890) and *Of Royall Educacion* (1895). Defoe was one of the most prolific and versatile of English authors, whose publications in poetry and prose numbered in the hundreds and treated subjects as varied as economics, politics, religion, education, travel, and literature. As a journalist he was associated with more than two dozen periodicals.

Selected Bibliography

•indicates works included, excerpted, or adapted in this volume.

BIBLIOGRAPHICAL WORKS

Moore, John Robert. *A Checklist of the Writings of Daniel Defoe*. Bloomington: Indiana UP, 1960.

Novak, Maximillian E. "Daniel Defoe." *The New Cambridge Bibliography of English Literature: 1660–1800*. Ed. George Watson. Rev. ed., New York: Cambridge UP, 1971. 882–918.

Peterson, Spiro. *Daniel Defoe: A Reference Guide, 1731–1924*. Boston: G. K. Hall, 1987.

Stoler, John A. *Daniel Defoe: An Annotated Bibliography of Modern Criticism, 1900–1980*. New York: Garland, 1984.

BIOGRAPHICAL WORKS

•Backscheider, Paula R. *Daniel Defoe: His Life*. Baltimore: Johns Hopkins UP, 1989.

Bastian, Frank. *Defoe's Early Life*. Totowa, NJ: Barnes & Noble, 1981.

Chalmers, George. *The Life of Daniel De Foe*. London, 1790.

Healy, George H., ed. *The Letters of Daniel Defoe*. Oxford: Clarendon P, 1955.

Lee, William. *Daniel Defoe: His Life and Recently Discovered Writings 1716–1729*. 3 vols. London: Hotten, 1869.

Moore, John Robert. *Daniel Defoe: Citizen of the Modern World*. Chicago: U of Chicago P, 1958.

Novak, Maximillian E. *Daniel Defoe : Master of Fictions : His Life and Ideas*. New York: Oxford UP, 2001.

Sutherland, James. *Defoe*. London: Methuen, 1937; 2nd ed., 1950.

Trent, W. P. *Daniel Defoe: How to Know Him*. Indianapolis: Bobbs-Merrill, 1916.

Wilson, Walter. *Memoirs of the Life and Times of Daniel De Foe*. 3 vols. London: Hurst, Chance, 1830.

CRITICAL STUDIES

Alkon, Paul K. *Defoe and Fictional Time*. Athens: U of Georgia P, 1979.

Alter, Robert. *Rogue's Progress: Studies in the Picaresque Novel*. Cambridge: Harvard UP, 1964.

Backscheider, Paula R. *Moll Flanders: The Making of a Criminal Mind*. Boston: G. K. Hall, 1990.

Baine, Rodney M. "The Cancelled Passage in *Moll Flanders*." *The Papers of the Bibliographical Society of America* 76 (1972): 55–58.

———. *Daniel Defoe and the Supernatural*. Athens: U of Georgia P, 1968.

•Bell, Ian A. *Defoe's Fiction*. Totowa, NJ: Barnes & Noble, 1985.

———. "Narrators and Narrative in Defoe." *Novel* 18 (1985): 154–72.

Blewett, David. "Changing Attitudes Toward Marriage in the Time of Defoe: The Case of *Moll Flanders*." *Huntington Library Quarterly* 44 (1981): 77–88.

———. *Defoe's Art of Fiction*. Toronto: U of Toronto P, 1979.

Brooks, Douglas. "*Moll Flanders*: An Interpretation." *Essays in Criticism* 19 (1969): 46–59.

Byrd, Max, ed. *Daniel Defoe: A Collection of Critical Essays*. Englewood Cliffs, NJ: Prentice-Hall, 1976.

Chaber, Lois A. "Matriarchal Mirror: Women and Capital in *Moll Flanders*." *PMLA* 97 (1982): 212–26.

Columbus, Robert R. "Conscious Artistry in *Moll Flanders.*" ***Studies in English Literature*** 3 (1963): 415–32.

Donoghue, Denis. "The Values of *Moll Flanders.*" *Sewanee Review* 71 (1963): 287–303.

Donovan, Robert Alan. "The Two Heroines of *Moll Flanders.*" *The Shaping Vision: Imagination in the English Novel from Defoe to Dickens*. Ithaca: Cornell UP, 1966. 21–46.

Earle, Peter. *The World of Defoe*. London: Weidenfeld & Nicolson, 1976.

Elliott, Robert C., ed. *Twentieth Century Interpretations of Moll Flanders: A Collection of Critical Essays*. Englewood Cliffs, NJ: Prentice-Hall, 1970.

Erickson, Robert A. *Mother Midnight: Birth, Sex, and Fate in Eighteenth-Century Fiction (Defoe, Richardson, and Sterne)*. New York: AMS, 1986.

Faller, Lincoln B. *Crime and Defoe: A New Kind of Writing*. Cambridge: Cambridge UP, 1993.

Forster, E. M. *Aspects of the Novel*. New York: Harcourt, Brace, 1927.

Furbank, P. N., and W. R. Owens. *The Canonisation of Daniel Defoe*. New Haven: Yale UP, 1988.

Gifford, George E. "Daniel Defoe and Maryland." *Maryland Historical Magazine* 52 (1957): 307–15.

Hammond, Brean S. "Repentance: Solution to the Clash of Moralities in *Moll Flanders.*" *English Studies* 61 (1980): 329–37.

Howson, Gerald. "Who Was Moll Flanders?" *The Times Literary Supplement* (January 18, 1968): 63–64.

Hunter, J. Paul. "Novels and 'the Novel': The Poetics of Embarrassment." *Modern Philology* 85 (1988): 480–98.

•Kay, Carol. *Political Constructions: Defoe, Richardson, and Sterne in Relation to Hobbes, Hume, and Burke*. Ithaca: Cornell UP, 1988.

Kettle, Arnold. "In Defence of *Moll Flanders.*" *Of Books and Humankind: Essays and Poems Presented to Bonamy Dobrée*. Ed. John Butt. London: Routledge & Kegan Paul, 1964. 55–67.

•Kibbie, Ann Louise. "Monstrous Generation: The Birth of Capital in Defoe's *Moll Flanders* and *Roxana*. *PMLA* 110 (1995): 1023–34.

Koonce, Howard L. "Moll's Muddle: Defoe's Use of Irony in *Moll Flanders.*" *English Literary History* 30 (1963): 377–94.

Lovitt, Carl R. "Defoe's 'Almost Invisible Hand': Narrative Logic as a Structuring Principle in *Moll Flanders*. *Eighteenth-Century Fiction* 6 (1993): 1–28.

Lund, Roger D., ed. *Critical Essays on Daniel Defoe*. New York: G. K. Hall, 1997.

Martin, Terence. "The Unity of *Moll Flanders.*" *Modern Language Quarterly* 22 (1961): 115–24.

McKillop, Alan Dugald. *The Early Masters of English Fiction*. Lawrence: U of Kansas P, 1956.

•McMaster, Juliet. "The Equation of Love and Money in *Moll Flanders.*" *Studies in the Novel* 2 (1970): 131–44.

•Miller, Henry K. "Some Reflections on Defoe's *Moll Flanders* and the Romance Tradition." *Greene Centennial Studies*. Ed. Paul J. Korshin and Robert R. Allen. Charlottesville: UP of Virginia, 1984. 72–92.

Miller, Nancy K. *The Heroine's Text: Readings in the French and English Novel, 1722–1782*. New York: Columbia UP, 1980.

Novak, Maximillian E. *Defoe and the Nature of Man*. Oxford: Oxford UP, 1963.

———. *Economics and the Fiction of Daniel Defoe*. Berkeley: U of California P, 1962.

•———. *Realism, Myth, and History in Defoe's Fiction*. Lincoln: U of Nebraska P, 1983.

Olsen, Thomas Grant. "Reading and Righting *Moll Flanders.*" *Studies in English Literature* 41 (2001): 467–81.

•Pollak, Ellen. "*Moll Flanders*, Incest, and the Structure of Exchange." *The Eighteenth Century: Theory and Interpretation* 30 (1989): 3–21. Revised in Pollak, *Incest and the English Novel, 1684–1814*. Baltimore: Johns Hopkins UP, 2003. 110–28.

Richetti, John. *Daniel Defoe*. Boston: G. K. Hall, 1987.

———. *Defoe's Narratives: Situations and Structures*. Oxford: Clarendon P, 1975.

•———. *The English Novel in History 1700–1780*. New York: Routledge, 1999.

———. "The Family, Sex, and Marriage in Defoe's *Moll Flanders* and *Roxana.*" *Studies in the Literary Imagination* 15 (1982): 19–35.

•Rietz, John. "Criminal Ms-Representation: *Moll Flanders* and Female Criminal Biography." *Studies in the Novel* 23 (1991): 183–95.

Scheuermann, Mona. "An Income of One's Own: Women and Money in *Moll Flanders* and *Roxana.*" *Durham University Journal* 80 (1988): 225–39.

———. "Women and Money in Eighteenth-Century Fiction." *Studies in the Novel* 19 (1987): 311–22.

Sherman, Sandra. *Finance and Fictionality in the Early Eighteenth Century: Accounting for Defoe*. Cambridge: Cambridge UP, 1996.
Shinagel, Michael. *Daniel Defoe and Middle-Class Gentility*. Cambridge: Harvard UP, 1968.
Sill, Geoffrey M. *Defoe and the Idea of Fiction*. Newark: U of Delaware P, 1983.
Starr, George A. *Defoe and Casuistry*. Princeton: Princeton UP, 1971.
———. *Defoe and Spiritual Autobiography*. Princeton: Princeton UP, 1965.
Suarez, Michael F. "The Shortest Way to Heaven? Moll Flanders' Repentance Reconsidered." *1650–1850: Ideas, Aesthetics, and Inquiries in the Early Modern Era* 3 (1997): 3–28.
Sutherland, James. *Daniel Defoe: A Critical Study*. Cambridge: Harvard UP, 1971.
Swan, Beth. "*Moll Flanders*: The Felon as Lawyer." *Eighteenth-Century Fiction* 11 (1998): 33–48.
Van Ghent, Dorothy. *The English Novel: Form and Function*. New York: Rinehart, 1953.
Watt, Ian. "The Recent Critical Fortunes of *Moll Flanders*." *Eighteenth-Century Studies* 1 (1967): 109–26.
———. *The Rise of the Novel: Studies in Defoe, Richardson and Fielding*. Berkeley: U of California P, 1957.
Woolf, Virginia. "Defoe." *The Common Reader*. First Series. New York: Harcourt, Brace & World, Inc., 1925. 89–97.
•Zimmerman, Everett. *Defoe and the Novel*. Berkeley: U of California P, 1975.
Zomchick, John P. " 'A Penetration Which Nothing Can Deceive': Gender and Juridical Discourse in Some Eighteenth-Century Narratives." *Studies in English Literature* 29 (1989): 535–61.